Bridge from Nowhere

Bena Averbukh
Lynne Sinton

HARA
PUBLISHING GROUP

Published by Hara Publishing
P.O. Box 19732, Seattle, WA 98109

Library of Congress Catalog Card Number: 2002116822

Manufactured in the United States
10 9 8 7 6 5 4 3 2 1

Averbukh, Bena.

Bridge from nowhere / by Bena Averbukh and Lynne Sinton.--
Seattle, WA : Hara Publishing, 2003.

      p. ; cm.

      ISBN: 0-9710724-8-5

      1. Russian Americans--Fiction. 2. Russians--United States--
Fiction. 3. Assimilation (Sociology)--Fiction. 4. Interpersonal
relations--Fiction.. 5. Russia--Fiction. 6. Soviet Union--Fiction. I.
Sinton, Lynne. II. Title.

PS3601.V473 B75 2003   2002116822
813.6--dc21   0306

Editor: Vicki McCown
Cover Design: Greg Burns/Lonny Stevens
Book Design & Production: Scott and Shirley Fisher

"It was never a question of escape. It was also a question of transformation."

Michael Chabon
The Amazing Adventures of Kavalier and Clay

"The Things that you cannot reclaim remain an obsession forever."

David Denby
"Good-bye to All That," *New York Magazine*

A narrow bridge, a narrow bridge
But every step across
Might lead you home.

The world in which we live
Can be a narrow bridge
The most important thing
Is not to fear.

Words from Laura Wetzler's song, "Narrow Bridge"

НАМШИФ
АНВОВЛАННА

**ROYAL NETHERLANDS EMBASSY
AT MOSCOW IN CHARGE OF ISRAEL
INTERESTS IN THE U.S.S.R.**

No. 26453

VISA

Name: A Fishman
        Tatyana (70)

Valid for: I S R A E L

Issued on: 09 APR 1976

This visa is valid for: 12 (twelve) months

from: 09 APR 1976

for a single journey.

Signature and stamp
For the Ambassador.

L. V. M. van GORP.

REPUBLIK ÖSTERREICH
ische Botschaft   Kons. Geb.
Moskau   gestundet
                                   BV. Nr:
        Einreise - Sichtvermerk
haber und den im Paß mitein getragenen
        A FISHMAN
        Tatjana (20)
einmalige Einreise nach Österreich
iterreise nach Israel gestattet.

vermerk ist gültig 3 Monate ab Ausstellungsdatum.

                        8. April 1976
Moskau, am

For foreign words, phrases, and names, see the glossary at the back of the book.

one

The envelope had three Soviet stamps on it. One was printed directly on the envelope; the other two, attached to the right edge, were smeared by the thick black ink of a Kiev postal stamp. The return address said "Y. P. Parchomenko." Parchomenko, a common Ukrainian name, meant nothing to me.

Odd, I always thought if I received a letter from the Soviet Union I would cry for joy. But here I am, staring at this envelope, feeling absolutely nothing. Lonya was right, I have no basic human feelings.

It couldn't have been delivered by mistake. It has my last name followed by my first, Fishman Anna, printed directly under USA. Funny, it bears the same initials as Fima's—Yefim Petrovich.

I glanced through the rest of the mail on my way to our little office. Tanya and I are proud of the office we created in the spare bedroom. Bright, abstract pictures hang over the filing cabinets and both desks. A bearskin rug lies on the floor in front of two easy chairs. The rug is one of the few things we splurged on when we vacationed in Canada last year. The antique phone on Tanya's desk was Jack's present to her when we moved into the house last summer.

I haven't seen a Soviet envelope in years. Friends circulate letters they receive, but not in envelopes. This is my first real letter (I don't count the ones from Auntie Olya) in the almost ten years we've been in the United States. When we first arrived, I wrote to Auntie Olya, my old neighbor, begging her for news. She answered a few times, then stopped. I suspected she died—it was too painful to think she didn't want to respond. Asya never answered. I must have sent a dozen letters. Myron and her mother-in-law were always adamantly against any communication abroad. Auntie Olya reported, among the local news and building gossip, that Asya came to read my letters and reminisce. She asked Auntie Olya to tell me she was trying to arrange everything. I supposed that meant our correspondence.

When she had last written, Auntie Olya said Fima had practically moved to his parents' apartment, but came back twice a week to spend the night, so no one could claim the room. The "no one" referred to the Berezovskys who still lived in one room, including both sons, married and drinking. They had more square meters, I mean feet, per person than the law required to make them eligible for the apartment waiting list. They would have immediately reported any long absences to city hall. By Soviet standards, Fima's parents had more than enough room for him, but one just doesn't give up one's room to the government.

Tanya looks so much like Fima. She has his red hair and hard, dark-gray eyes, and his strange, charming smile. From what Lonya told me, I look like my mother. I have only his memories to define my past—no pictures, no relatives, few mementos, no personal connection at all, save my internal dialogues with Sasha. Even after all these years, I still weigh my every action against what I think his reaction would be. He knows my every move, my every thought. Fima always nagged, "What are you thinking about? Tell me, I'm not a stranger. You're supposed to share your thoughts with me. I'm your husband."

Tanya used to ask about her father, and I tried to encourage her. She doesn't ask anymore. So many of the children around her come from divorced families. They talk about the gifts they get or the trips they take on their court-controlled visits. They never mention the parent they were with.

When I was growing up, most of the children I knew had only mothers and grandmothers. Their fathers and grandfathers had been killed in the war. I was the only one who didn't have parents or grandparents and wasn't in an orphanage. Lonya constantly threatened to send me to one, but it was only a ruse. Tanya often demands to hear my how-it-was-in-Russia stories. Her eyes swell with tears as she tries to put herself in my place.

I keep looking out the window every few minutes for Tanya. I want to share opening the Soviet letter with her before Jack comes for me at seven. It's so dark outside. I don't like this time of the year when the days are short and getting shorter.

I don't remember anyone by the name Parchomenko. I had a math teacher named Parchomov, but he turned sixty when I was in the tenth grade.

A cup of tea would be nice while I'm waiting.

Oh, there's a note on the refrigerator. "Mom, I'm sleeping over at Alice's. We've got a test tomorrow. Love, Daughter."

She always signs her notes "Daughter." Fima always addressed her as "Daughter." Until she was two, she thought that was her name.

The dishes aren't washed, of course.

I turned on every light as I walked back through the house. It brought life. I passed the oval hall mirror. It didn't reveal anything I particularly liked.

Jack says I'm sexy. Sasha, when I asked him, laughed, gave me a light smack on the rump and said that all young women are attractive. Asya said I was striking. Natasha's theory is that I'm borderline ugly, just a touch to the beautiful side. She says this makes me uniquely charming and I should use it to my advantage with men. I can't see how broad shoulders, a short neck and short, thick, jet-black hair could produce any of these effects.

Fima proudly called me beautiful and he meant it. Genuinely devoted to me, he never took our divorce seriously. To him, my infatuation with the idea of emigration constituted temporary insanity and he was willing to wait until I regained my senses. What a relief the divorce was!

After my divorce, Sasha called me on the evenings he was on duty at the hospital and we saw each other more often than the usual few times a year. He could still only spare a half-hour and he kept glancing at his watch. The anticipation meant almost as much as his visit. He'd call, "Hi, Anya? Everything all right? I'll be over soon." Occasionally he had more time, like when his wife, Lilya, was away with their daughters. Oh, luxury!

Against reality, against better judgment, against common sense, I still wait for his call. It doesn't matter how much I scold myself, how busy I am, or how much I love my new life—I still wait.

Annoyed with myself, I returned to the kitchen and to the brownies Tanya and her new girlfriend, Vera, had made.

I put the envelope in the middle of the table and retreated to the bedroom. The new bed doesn't feel familiar yet. It is so quiet. Quieter than usual.

The tea kettle began whistling.

I don't remember putting it on the stove, but I usually boil a full kettle when I'm in the kitchen. It's a habit I can't break. Lonya always demanded there be freshly boiled water.

I silenced the kettle. The envelope stared at me disapprovingly. Sealed with long-forgotten, dirty-colored glue, the letter caught on the glue as I removed it from the envelope.

The handwriting, unmistakably Fima's, was signed "Your Fima." So, who is Parchomenko?

My mind and body responded to memories of Fima with annoyance and resignation. My goodness, a page from a school notebook, with blurry, bluish squares, the same kind I had in school! I caught myself folding the letter and only opened it again with effort.

24 October 1985

Dear Anya,

I found your address through distant relatives living in Chicago. You know, of course, about the changes in the life of our country and I assume you've been trying to contact me.

First of all, let me tell you about my life. I have been married for almost seven years. My wife's name is Zhanna, she has a Ph.D. in chemistry and works for a research lab. We have a four-year-old son, Petya. Zhanna uses the last name of her first husband and I took this name to make my life easier. At least the name is not Jewish, even if I am. This hasn't changed.

I was able to exchange my parents' apartment and the room where you and I lived for a three-room apartment in the Pechersk area. My mother died in her sleep soon after you left. My father had a stroke two years later. He was bedridden for seven months and died in my arms. So now we have the apartment to ourselves. Zhanna's son from her first marriage, Igor, lives with us. He's Tanya's age.

I am writing to let you know that I am ready to forget everything and help you come back to the Soviet Union with Tanya, and your husband, if you are married. We could easily spare a room. If, for some reason, you cannot return right away, send Tanya. Tanya Parchomenko now. Our country is changing in front of our eyes, and it is my responsibility to see that my daughter contributes her part to these historic changes. Write me about your plans, so we can prepare for your arrival.

I wish you all the best. Please be open with me, as we are not strangers. It would make me very happy to receive Tanya's picture and a letter from her. Regards from my family.

Your Fima

I sat down, shaking my head in disbelief. What changes is he talking about? Certainly not glasnost. And, Tanya has a half-brother! Like Lonya and me.

When Tanya was ten she told me if I ever remarried she would not let my new husband adopt her. She thought if she changed her name her father would be upset and insulted and he would never be able to find her. Now, after all these years, he reappears—with a new name. I wonder if she'll feel insulted.

If this letter had been written to someone else I'd laugh. But it's written to me, and I don't find it funny.

Tanya is at that age when logic doesn't seem to work. When I was fifteen Lonya probably had a hard time with me, too. My teenage years came during the short period of awakening after Stalin's death, along with new slogans like "Our generation of Soviet people will live in communism" and "We will catch up with and surpass the United States in per capita meat, milk, and butter production." The discovery that we, the most modern and caring country in the world, had to catch up with a rotting capitalistic country like the United States was shocking.

In the short thaw after Stalin's death, new poets, new writers, courageous, frighteningly defying, intoxicating ideas emerged. The thaw gave
way to a freeze, less brutal than Stalin's, but my world was changed irrevocably. Lonya lamented that without Stalin there now would be no order and only due to Stalin had he been able to survive with a baby. He
said I was ungrateful and easily influenced by cheap talk. The older I get
the more difficult it is to think of Lonya—of his miserable, angry,
distrusting existence.

Tanya's teenage years, the choices she has, the problems she has—
no money for a sports camp or for the "right" brand of clothes—don't
compare. Tanya's a good kid, and bright, too—skipped an entire year at
school. I don't know what I'll do if she wants to go.

The door bell shrilled, and my heart jumped as I pictured Fima
behind the front door.

Instead, I found Jack slouched in the door frame, his finger still pressing down on the button. He withdrew his finger and sighed with relief
when he saw me.

"My goodness, I was ready to call the police. I've been ringing for
five minutes."

Jack's a computer nut and looks like one: expensive clothes in slight
disarray, tie knotted to one side, light-brown almost blond hair touching
his glasses. He walked in and cocked his head to listen to the quiet of the
house. His eyes wandered down my body.

"Tanya's spending the night at Alice's." I removed his hands from
my hips. "I don't feel like going to the health club."

"What's wrong?"

My face may have been composed, but inside I was terrified, terrified
of Tanya's interest in Fima's expectations. And I was angry at Fima for
reappearing in my life when there's no place for him. Yet, there's an excitement, too, like a soldier before battle. I cherish every moment of my
new life and I will fight to keep it. The past is like a millstone, a shadow
wherever I turn, trailing and haunting me, holding me back.

I met Jack at work and our relationship has become a routine with a
set of rules he's agreed to. For Tanya's sake we don't overnight at each
other's house. We don't talk about marriage. We are only together
whenever and for as long as both of us feel like it. Why he agreed, I
don't know, but he did, and after three years we are comfortable with
each other.

Jack's convinced people create their own problems. However, he says,
this does not apply to me, as my "mysterious Russian soul" and "mysterious Russian past" allow for unanswered questions.

Jack sat on my embarrassingly worn, Salvation Army sofa watching
me patiently, his arms stretched along its back.

"Why so pensive? What happened between leaving work this after-noon and now?"

Jack seems indifferent to things I feel should be important to him—for example, his ex-wife of ten years, being married to a rich businessman from Minnesota, whose new last name he doesn't even know. Would he understand my childhood fears; my anxieties; my relationship with Sasha; the austere, vacant life Lonya and I led, filled with despair and hopeless-ness; no roots, no relatives, no family graves?

With a past so different, how could I expect him to understand? His mother is an American, and his father was an Argentine, with an enor-mous estancia about an hour's drive from Buenos Aires, where his family raised polo ponies, selling them to players all over the world. I find it hard to comprehend his childhood, like the horseback riding or being driven to the synagogue in a limousine. In the States, Jack refused to ride on horse trails in plain view of city traffic. He said it was a joke and he only rode when he visited Argentina. As a teenager he spent his Ameri-can summers with his grandmother who lived on the Park Avenue of Buenos Aires—Avenida de Libertad. Jack said the winter weather there was really rotten, but it never snowed. He didn't mind missing summers as he loved accompanying his grandmother everywhere, being spoiled by his aunt Lilliana, visiting the estancia, and hanging around with his cous-ins. He remains a part-owner of the estancia, along with his cousins, but he leaves the income from his share to be used for expansion.

"Well . . . I'm not sure you'll understand."

"Try me. I'll understand, and I promise I won't correct your English."

My English. Enough for work, for vacation, for shopping. It doesn't require as many corrections as it did two or three years ago, even by Jack's unyielding standards, but the vocabulary is still pitifully poor.

"I've received a letter from my ex-husband. He feels Tanya belongs in the Soviet Union. With all the reforms taking place, he sees no ob-stacles to her going back."

"If I remember correctly, you and your ex haven't kept in touch, have you?" Jack spoke in a slow, low voice. He moved forward as if to get up.

"We haven't, but this letter has opened some old wounds. My fear is that Tanya might wish to see her father. She might be kept there." I walked across the living room to the window, pushed the curtains apart and stood with my back to Jack. "I know if I tell Tanya not to go she won't. I've even thought of destroying the letter, but I can't. She has a right to know."

I watched silhouettes in the window across the street.

"Jack, one can't be twenty years old and have missed five and twelve. How does one explain two independent lives: one, like this letter, that is my past and my past revisited, and another that started ten years ago when I came to the United States?

"If Tanya was your daughter, you'd probably tell her to make her own decision and you would feel good about it. I'm not saying that's wrong, I just can't resolve it all with an either/or. Maybe because of my background, any choice comes with strings attached. I want to be fair to Tanya, but without feeling guilty about Fima. After all, I did take her away from him."

"What do you have to feel guilty about? Your ex is the one who let you emigrate—alone with a child. As far as I can see he forfeited his rights then and there. There's no deep philosophical meaning to that."

"There is no absolute right or absolute wrong." My intonation was so reminiscent of Lonya's that I shivered. "Fima didn't let me go, never would have. When I insisted on emigrating he divorced me and tried to get custody of Tanya, citing my minuscule salary. Luckily, I still got custody. I've told you all this before. What I haven't told you was that Tanya couldn't leave the Soviet Union without Fima's written permission, and there wasn't a chance in hell he would have signed the consent papers. In a common, Soviet way, Fima is a fairly decent man, and I know he loved Tanya. He loved me, too. Not passionately, perhaps, but steadily."

The sofa made a whispering sound. I felt Jack's hands on my shoulders as he turned me around to face him. "Stop right there. This does not make any sense. You're here with Tanya and you're doing beautifully. That's all that counts. Tanya may be curious about her father, but remember, she's an American kid. Don't you think she would miss getting her driver's license next year, driving my BMW, all the other things American kids do?" His voice was intimate and soothing.

Does he care or is he trying to calm me down to simplify his life? Well, he's free to go.

Jack and I headed to the kitchen. I started to make coffee for him and tea for myself. We were silent as the coffee maker brewed and the water in the kettle boiled. I put some brownies on a plate and brought them to the table. I devoured a brownie while Jack quietly sipped his coffee, wincing at its temperature. Tears were churning inside me.

"Do you want one, too?" I inquired formally, pointing to the pastry.

He shook his head and pushed his mug away, spilling some of its contents.

I surprised myself when I got up abruptly and marched out of the kitchen to my bedroom. A shoe box on the top closet shelf held our most valuable possessions: our certificates of naturalization, birth, marriage, and divorce; my university diploma; Tanya's baby pictures, and her little presents for me beginning with kindergarten. It also stored the one document that would remain even more meaningful to me than proof of the

United States citizenship—the exit visa from the Soviet Union, a strip of paper, about five-by-twelve, folded in three, so thin one could see through it, complete with a photograph of Tanya and me, with the stamps of the Soviet Interior Ministry and of the bank that doled out the one hundred dollars per person that the emigrants received from the state before departing. The small black folder hadn't prevented the folds from drying and disintegrating. Tanya and I recently connected the three parts with wide scotch tape.

With this document, the color of faded pink, in my hand, I marched back to the kitchen. Jack sat in the same position, watching the spilled coffee make slow progress toward the middle of the table.

"Here's our exit visa," I said solemnly.

He wiped his hands with a napkin, and as he took the visa gingerly, I realized that my hands shook.

"You look worn out," Jack remarked after studying the photograph. "What does the text say?"

"It says, 'Exit visa for head of family Fishman Anna Lvovna born in 1941 with her daughter Tatyana born in 1970. The purpose of the trip is permanent settlement in Israel.'"

Jack ran his hand over the cheap, faded paper. "You should keep this in the bank," he said seriously. "Surely, this will pass to future generations of your family."

I nodded. The same emotion flooded me that I had felt when the officer of the Kiev Department of Visas had handed the document to me. I couldn't speak.

"I was born in the States. It was my mother's wish that there would be no question of my citizenship. So, I guess I can't fully appreciate how you felt . . ."

"How I feel," I interrupted.

"I suppose," Jack agreed. "You don't have to talk about this if you don't want to, but you never mentioned how you managed to get your ex-husband's permission for Tanya."

"I didn't get it. I forged it. I took a draft of a technical article he had written and practiced every letter then every word, until it flowed naturally. And then, my knees shaking, my palms sweating, and my throat tight, I signed Fima's name. I remember acting confident and composed as I submitted my papers to the immigration service. Afterwards, for three months, I waited to be found out, to go to jail, to lose Tanya — everything else was a blur. Then, incredibly, we were at the station Chop, a small town on the border with Czechoslovakia, and on our way to Vienna."

After what seemed like endless silence, Jack asked if I wanted to be alone. I guess forging documents didn't sit well with him.

As we walked to the door I placed the visa on the kitchen counter.

Jack opened the door and said, "So long," but didn't move.

I looked out. The days are short now, but it's warm, and the leaves on the ground give the air a soft scent. Jack put his arms around me then covered the back of my neck with quick, light kisses.

How long is it since Sasha asked, "What do you like more, kisses on your neck or kisses on your lips?"

A car passed, its radio screaming. I knew Jack was smiling and I smiled, too. I was enjoying his warmth against my back. He pressed my breasts gently with his arms and stepped back, pulling me toward the bedroom. I pushed the front door shut.

We walked the short distance to the bedroom. I didn't feel like sex —I never do—but I wanted to recapture the warmth I felt at the door.

We kissed for a long time. Jack undid the buttons on my blouse and I slid off my suit jacket and blouse together. He only released me so we could take off the rest of our clothes. Jack likes to watch me undress. He says it's erotic.

In bed we lay quietly in each other's arms. I ran my fingers through the thick hair on his chest. Funny, with clothes on he doesn't look like the kind of man who'd have chest hair. I remember being surprised the first time I saw him without a shirt.

Jack's a considerate lover, which isn't easy since he usually finds me unresponsive. This time, the warm sensations made me feel, for a fleeting instant, that he might really care. As he entered me it brought back reality, and the truth. I tried to immerse myself in the feeling of his warm body, but the bed wasn't any more comfortable than earlier and, combined with his forceful thrusts, it made me wish I was somewhere else.

Jack slumped on top of me. When I pushed him off he rolled over, closing his eyes.

I got up and went to the sofa in the living room. I hid under the brown-and-beige Afghan Tanya made for my birthday. After a while I felt a tug on the edge of the Afghan. I peeked out to see Jack with an uncertain look on his face.

There was no way to avoid talking.

"Anna, please. I'm not saying past experiences have no meaning to your present life, but it seems like you're condemning and praising yourself at the same time. I realize you went through hell and made it. What I don't understand is why you bothered to change your life if you don't want to shake off your past."

Even under the Afghan my feet were cold.

"Frankly, if my wife did to me what you did to your ex-husband, I'd be furious. On the other hand, you were really acting against the system. Tanya justifiably was, and is, a priority. Like you always say, there's no such thing as absolute right or absolute wrong. The more scruples a person has, the tougher it is to draw the line."

Jack's discourse, and the subdued tone in which it was delivered, didn't stop him from touching me, trying to ease my mood. By his own admission, he expects everyone around him to be even-keeled; unpleasantness doesn't belong in his world. He works because he wants to, he divorced amiably because he "grew apart" from his wife, he rarely calls his mother because she continually calls him from Miami to make sure he's eaten enough vegetables and to fix him up with another "wonderful girl."

Jack's mother doesn't obviously dislike me and enjoys reminiscing about her parents' Russian background. But I don't count as a real relationship, considering my limited English, my ignorance in you-look-marvelous small talk, and my past-child-bearing age. In her eyes, I am supposed to inexpensively and safely tide her son over between wives in exchange for lessons in American life and language. She doesn't realize I'm not the golddigger she thinks I am.

Jack and I laugh every time he repeats one of his mother's descriptions of a yet another perfect woman she's found for him: "Jackele, you should have seen her picture! Absolutely gorgeous! Tall, blonde, slim. Mrs. Greenbaum says she's a natural blonde. And only thirty-two! Jackele, you absolutely must give her a call."

Thank heavens, Jack finally turned on the television to watch the basketball game.

I'll have to tell Tanya about the letter. I wish she were home so I could do it now. Waiting is hard.

We watched the nine o'clock news. A Soviet journalist was talking about past mistakes of former Soviet premiers.

I remembered how each premier after Stalin happily admitted past, but not his own, mistakes. According to those admissions, there wasn't a period for the entire sixty-eight years after the revolution when the right things were done. Every period began with the new man conceding current, temporary difficulties, and ended with the new man admitting to past mistakes.

It seems *glasnost* might actually be catching on in the Soviet Union. Gloomy, no-smile Muscovites were on the screen, spitting clichés about their new hopes for the future into the reporter's microphone.

Lucky people, they don't understand how pitiful they are. I wonder if Tanya will understand what she escaped.

"See, people are happy." Jack sank into the sofa, his fingers drumming down my spine.

"Well, things must have really changed, because these people are talking to a foreign reporter. I hope no one is keeping tabs on them."

"Why are you always so bitter and pessimistic? After all, in worse years, they let you and Tanya and others go, didn't they?"

I moved away from him, my temples throbbing. Anger and helplessness choked tears from my eyes.

"That's what you always say when the subject of life in the Soviet Union comes up. That's why I try to avoid discussing it with you. Not that you notice. You are so damn content with yourself! You have never been unhappy with so much as your lawn care. You've never been hungry —plain hungry—lonely, insulted, intimidated, or scared, with nothing ahead but more of the same, year after year, with newspapers, radio, television, your boss, and your government telling you that you're happy, strong, proud, and lucky to live the way you do.

"That represents the first thirty-five years of my life. It represents my youth and motherhood. It formed my ambitions. And you ask if my knee-jerk reaction to anything reminding me of or associated with my past will ever disappear? Well, I don't know."

I faced Jack defiantly. "I told you I was born in The Ukraine during the summer of 1941. Since, apparently, you don't understand what that means, here's a history lesson for you," I said clicking off the television.

"I was born in a freight car, on a sheet thrown over hay mixed with manure, on a train speeding away from Kiev shortly before the Nazis took the city. These trains—that's to say, the ones that made it—delivered their passengers, mostly Jewish women, children, and old people, to the safety of filth, fleas, TB, and dysentery in Middle Asia and Siberia.

"My mother's father was a dentist and had a three-room apartment, which was unusual because most people lived communally. There were eight people in the family, living in the apartment before the war: my great-grandparents and grandparents; my mother's younger, unmarried sister; my parents; and my half-brother Lonya. Lonya's father, my mother's first husband, left her when Lonya was only six months old. Everyone presumed my father was dead as he had been sent to the front prior to the invasion and had never written.

"Most of what I'm telling you I've pieced together from bits and pieces I've picked up along the way."

Jack tried to squeeze my hand, but I pulled away.

"My mother taught Russian literature at Kiev University. My aunt and my father taught history there. I vividly remember the university, a large building at the top of a hill, symbolically painted red to represent the spilling of blood during the unsuccessful revolution of 1905. Lonya had just finished a year of math studies there when the war broke out.

"My grandfather decided my mother and Lonya should leave Kiev. The older members of the family felt there was nothing to fear from the Germans, especially since no one was a party member. They remembered how polite and helpful the German officers and soldiers had been during World War I. My grandfather always said they were more respectful and cultured than the domestic Gentile swine. He was afraid that Lonya, who hadn't been drafted because of poor eyesight, would be forced into the German army. He drew the line when it came to his grandson becoming a German soldier.

"Lonya helped my grandmother hide the silver trays, candlesticks, and silverware in a trunk under her, her mother's, and my mother's wedding dresses.

"My grandmother made two small pockets of thick linen and attached them with safety pins to the inside of Lonya's underwear and my mother's blouse, so each had their documents, some money, and some jewelry. Lonya carried a suitcase and two pillows tied together with a rope. Mother had a purse and a bag, with a tea kettle, a pot, and a few utensils.

"I wasn't due to be born for another month, and Lonya counted on that month. His mother would be settled, and he could again try to join the army. He never did, something that troubled him all his life.

"I was born in the middle of the night, delivered by Lonya, who wrapped me in his soft hand-knit sweater. Trying not to wake the children, my mother cried quietly, and I know Lonya must have been crying too, scared and embarrassed. Sheltered, ignorant of sex, sensitive, and shy, he had been pampered by his mother, grandmother, great-grandmother, and aunt, as an only and fatherless child can be.

"My mother was bleeding and weak. Lonya used up all the bed linen. Fear finally forced him to wake the women sleeping nearest to them. They pushed him away and, using the drinking water they had saved from the last stop, washed my mother and me. They chided Lonya for not waking them sooner.

"Suddenly the Luftwaffe strafed the train. The locomotive was hit, stopping the train abruptly, its live load sliding forward, screaming hysterically.

"The engineers ran alongside the train shouting for everyone to get out, to run to the open fields for cover. People began pushing and shoving, rolling over each other, falling, getting up, crawling to get to the wide, heavy doors which had miraculously opened.

"'Run, Lonichka, run! Take her and run!' my mother pleaded.

"Lonya grabbed me from her arms, jumped out and ran. It's hard to visualize the Lonya I remember—tall, pale, and scrawny, with huge dark eyes, behind thick glasses resting on a large red nose—holding on to a newborn baby with his thin, venous arms. I remember his hands constantly flying around his body, clasping, unclasping, rubbing his nose and chin, gesticulating and adjusting his glasses. He reached the fields just as the second round of strafing began. Some of the cars caught on fire, then some more.

"The few souls left behind in the freight cars didn't have a chance. Some of the people in the fields were wounded or injured, but most survived. Lonya lay on his back holding me on his stomach. He never said so, but I'm sure he was crying. One of the women took her scarf off and threw it to him yelling, 'Wipe your face, wrap the baby, and get going.'

"Some of the train cars were not completely burned and Lonya wanted to go back to find his mother. One of the women asked him, 'What do you expect to find? Don't be a fool. Get going, the baby may yet live to need a doctor.'

"The younger women started walking parallel to the burning train without even a sideways glance, marching forward silently, mercilessly pulling their children behind them.

"Old people picked themselves up, calling out to their daughters to wait.

"It took three hours to walk to the next station. It was surrounded by a small village with no men between eighteen and fifty, and few young women. There was no doctor. I truly believe that's when Lonya started to hate me. He hated me for wetting on him, for whimpering, for his being a young man not in the army, and for taking away his mother.

"She was always his mother, never mine. Lonya said, 'She was only thirty-seven when she died. She was so bright, so elegant, and she danced so gracefully. You don't deserve her. Such a squealing insect, you ended her life." I always accepted his pronouncement unquestioningly. I only wish his pronouncement hadn't been repeated over and over until he died."

Seeing a stunned look on Jack's face, I stopped. Maybe I'm too blunt. I don't care. He has to know.

"In the village, an old, blue-nosed veterinarian, smelling of liquor, listened to my heart, hiccuped, and said I was big and strong and in need of food. He took Lonya in a horse-drawn cart to the closest military camp to register my birth. Lonya named me Anya, short for Anna, after his mother."

A bitter laugh escaped my lips. "Even now, I hardly ever say 'my mother.'

"We were placed in a house where a baby had been born shortly before. Its mother breast-fed me for a week, until the Germans started getting closer. She begged Lonya to leave me with her. Since she couldn't keep him, too—with his large, Jewish nose—he refused, leaving in the middle of the night on a hospital train carrying wounded soldiers from the front.

"The woman, whose name Lonya regretted not remembering, cried and made the sign of the cross over my small body before handing me to Lonya. Lonya told her, 'You did a lot for me.' She then made the sign of the cross again, this time over Lonya. He now had some food, a blanket for me, and some clothes for himself tied in a flowery shawl, but he was not happy to be alone and stuck with an infant. However, he wasn't about to give me up, not the child that killed his mother.

"It hurts so much that I was never allowed to admire or to love him. Why? We had no one else, just each other. And why couldn't he love me? He knew I lost my mother, too.

"In retrospect, that train undoubtedly saved our lives. The nurses and the wounded played with me, Lonya slept and ate. They shared what warm clothes they could spare and the cook parted with some tinned food. The head doctor gave orders to supply Lonya with linen, rags for diapers, bandages, and medicine. One of the nurses had relatives in a small Siberian town we passed through and Lonya appeared on their doorstep with a backpack and a note from the nurse.

"Dasha, the woman who took us in, was young and heavy, with swollen legs and a shrill voice. She checked Lonya's military papers carefully, making sure he wasn't a deserter. The house was crowded and it smelled unpleasant. Dasha cared for her five-year-old nephew, whose parents, both nurses, had been drafted. Her husband was also at the front.

"She told Lonya, 'I've never met a Jew before. You look like a normal person. They say Jews don't fight, they always find a way to hide out while our people are being killed.'

"Although this was something Jews had learned to swallow, Lonya strongly declared, 'I wish they would have accepted me, but look at my glasses, see how thick the lenses are.'

"Dasha sneered, but she let us stay as long as Lonya worked in the fields and kept me quiet.

"I vaguely remember her nephew, Kolya, a laughing, jumping, blue-eyed boy I chased down the street. That was, of course, much later.

"I wanted to laugh, too, but laughing was taboo—I laughed a silver-bells laugh like Lonya's mother.

"I will forever remember the words he never let me forget: 'You took everything from my mother, her face, her smile—you killed her. Do you understand what you did to me? And now you have the nerve to laugh?'

"I felt guilty, but was unable to find the words to explain I didn't do anything wrong.

"We were relegated to a damp mattress in the attic. I learned to lie at its edge, without moving in my sleep—it angered Lonya if he turned and found me in his way.

"I remember dreaming of Lonya's mother, this wonderful lady I never knew. I dreamed I took her to him saying, 'See, I didn't kill her.' For many years, I opened my eyes every morning with the hope that she would be there, alive for him, and then Lonya would love me and let me climb on his lap. It wasn't until I was eight years old that I understood his mother was my mother."

Waking from my trance, I took a deep breath, blinking, amazed Jack was still there. He was sitting so still, just gaping at me.

Slowly, I asked, "Jack, has anything I've said meant anything at all to you?

Jack fidgeted and closed his mouth. He cleared his throat and said, "A great deal. But, you know, you don't have to tell me this if it hurts so much."

"I want to," I said angrily.

I sat back taking another deep breath before continuing.

"I was almost four when we returned to Kiev. The building where Lonya lived before the war was still standing and fully occupied. I stared up at it in awe. I had never seen anything larger than the small cottages in the village where we had lived. My hand felt Lonya's hand trembling and I looked down at my worn sandals—Lonya would have been mad if I had seen him crying. Inside, the elevator door was boarded over. We climbed the stairs to the fourth floor. The staircase was cold and musty and smelled of urine and sweat.

"My legs hurt as I tried hard to keep up with Lonya and be invisible, so he wouldn't be angry.

"He knocked at the first door on the left. From inside I heard someone say, 'I'm coming.' A short woman with a blue scarf tied at the back of her head opened the door. The irritation on her face turned to disbelief. She threw up her hands and through tears screamed, 'Oh, my God! It's Lonichka! Alive!'

"A door slammed somewhere in the apartment and I heard someone sob, 'Don't hit me, please, don't hit me!'

"'That's just the Berezovskys fighting again. Come in, come in.' Then she noticed me. 'Lonichka, where's your mother?'

"'My mother is dead. She died when Anya was born.' He pulled me around from behind him to indicate I was Anya. 'Her father was most likely killed in the war.'

"The hallway was a small, dark square with three brown, wooden doors and a narrow corridor to the left. There was a light in the kitchen at the end of the corridor. The door to the right suddenly flew open and a tall, middle-aged man in an undershirt and military pants with suspenders hanging, stalked out, throwing a plate viciously to the floor.

"'You whore!" he screamed. "You fuckin' bitch! I know what you were doing while I was rotting at the front!'

"I heard a woman sobbing.

"The woman with the blue scarf picked me up. She turned to the man with the hanging suspenders. 'Listen, Berezovsky, you prick, it's my turn to clean the halls. I told you, you want to break dishes, break them in your room.'

"Stepping back, the man pulled up his suspenders. A disheveled woman appeared through the door behind him, her face streaked with tears. Her white blouse, torn at the shoulder, with buttons ripped away, exposed a white breast.

Lonya tried to look away.

"'Who are these people?' The man eyed our luggage, shoved a piece with his bare foot and looked at Lonya, sizing him up. 'What are these Jews doing here? Damned parasites, hiding out while I was rotting at the front!'

"The woman held me closer, as she stepped between the man and Lonya. 'That's not your business! You're drunk.'

"A loud argument followed, everyone shouting at the same time. I wanted to tell Lonya not to scream, but instead found myself screaming, 'Don't scream! Don't scream!'

"I woke up in a short, narrow bed. Except for my shoes, I was still dressed. I could hear teaspoons jingle and I saw Lonya and the woman with the blue scarf sitting at a round table. I could see shelves filled with dishes and figurines on the far side of the room.

"'How could you do that, Auntie Olya? It wasn't your apartment,' Lonya said looking into his glass.

"'If I didn't, someone else would have. Half of the apartments in this building were empty. I have nothing against Jews. Listen, Lonya, I know, Anya is entitled to live here because her father was killed in the war. I'll move in with my mother and you and the child can have this room. The Berezovskys, that's a different story—he's a shell-shocked veteran. By the way, he can't find a job, so he drinks and takes out his anger on his wife. They fight all the time. Don't let Anya near him.'

"That room was the room where our great-grandparents, grandparents, and parents had lived. It was the room where I grew up and got married. It was the room where Lonya died and Tanya was born.

"It was the smallest room in what used to be the family apartment. My bed faced the entrance and was identical to Lonya's along the left wall. The head- and footboards were painted white and were bare, not like Asya's that had white ruffles with shiny white bows. A dark-brown wardrobe almost touched the footboard of Lonya's bed. It had two solid squeaking doors, one of them with a mirror. It stored all our possessions, yet stood half empty. The top shelf of its left side was designated for linen, the bottom shelf to shoes, including galoshes with red flannel lining, mine shiny, Lonya's dull. New galoshes were an expense Lonya reminded me of every fall, as I never wore the same size more than one season. The shelves in between held our underclothes, scarves, winter hats, and tinned food—when we had it.

"Opposite the wardrobe was a china cabinet, or in Russian a buffet, displaying whatever Auntie Olya had left when she moved in with her mother, mostly assorted plates and dishes. In the compartment I was not allowed to open was a crystal sugar bowl and vase. Lonya never remembered them belonging to our family and insisted they must have been taken from other vanished Jews and were Auntie Olya's bribe to us for not trying to get back what was rightly ours. The bottom of the china cabinet had wooden doors behind which were documents, newspapers, books, and a chess set.

"Our table next to the china cabinet, on which I did my homework, was covered with a checkered tablecloth and was also used for meals and chess games between Sasha and Lonya.

"Before the war, Auntie Olya worked as a housekeeper for someone in the building and had done laundry for our grandmother. She had taken over the apartment after our family vanished at Babi Yar. She gave Lonya three matching silver spoons and forks, which, along with the crystal, was all that was left of our family, so she said. Lonya claimed he saw many of our family's belongings in her room, but what was the point of trying to prove it.

"The Berezovskys had two boys. They spit at me and said the Germans should have killed all the Jews. Their father beat them with his wide military belt, and when they hid behind the coat rack in the hall he'd walk around and hit the walls calling them his wife's bastards.

"Auntie Olya worked in a factory, disappearing every morning while I slept. Her mother shuffled around sighing and muttering, usually locking herself in her room to avoid the Berezovskys.

"Lonya went back to school. I wasn't allowed to leave our room while he was away. If I had to go to the bathroom I had to use an old clay flowerpot. Lonya warned me daily not to break it. I still remember the cold fear that squeezed my heart when Lonya came home and I had to carry that flowerpot to the bathroom to be emptied. It was heavy and smooth, and without handles. If the bathroom was occupied, I would stand patiently next to it, holding the flowerpot with both hands. Whoever came out looked at me reproachfully with a wrinkled nose. If it was one of the Berezovsky boys, he'd stick out his tongue and push me, then run away while I screamed, petrified of breaking the flowerpot.

"Every morning Lonya would divide our bread ration in half and then each half into three portions. I never touched mine until he came home. I would circle the food, smell it, then swallow saliva until my jaws ached. Soon I wasn't hungry anymore.

"I would sit for hours on the wide window sill looking into the courtyard. The courtyard belonged to four six-storied buildings and had no direct exit to the street. From the fourth floor it looked like a well, deep and dark. Children played at the bottom of the well until their grandmothers called them in at lunchtime and then at dusk for supper.

"I tried to fantasize a life like Lonya's had been, with a real mother. But all I could picture was Auntie Olya giving me hot farina with a lump of sugar.

"In winter, the heating stove never stayed warm, even though Lonya fed it faithfully with logs out of the pile he kept under my bed, next to the potato sack. The sack with onions was under his bed, and in the spring its revolting smell kept me awake at night. We had to stockpile logs, potatoes, and onions to eat during the winter. Dinners generally consisted of potatoes cooked in their skins, a little herring, some onions, bread, and, if we were lucky, hard-boiled eggs.

"I don't know why Lonya dropped out of school. He said he did it because of me. He said he had to take care of me instead of himself. But once I saw him fall asleep over his books, wake up a few minutes later and cough. When he wiped his mouth I saw blood.

"Lonya taught me the alphabet and I taught myself to read. He found a book of fairy tales in the trash behind the building. It was the only book I had to read. After a while I started changing the plots and endings of the stories. I created dialogues and relationships with the characters. For two years I read that book again and again, until I was sent to school.

"I don't remember Lonya ever going out or ever having anyone over, except for one time when I woke up to the sound of arguing voices. I saw a bald old man resembling Lonya angrily putting on his hat. 'You are as crazy as your father was. Someone has to take the girl from you!'

"I immediately shut my eyes tight. I knew better than to keep my eyes open when the lights were on at night. I had done so only once. I was, I think, around five. Lonya was sitting on a chair near the center of the room. He had his head thrown back and was breathing heavily, moaning softly. I watched transfixed as his hand moved up and down a big skin-colored stick, which seemed like it was attached to his body. His hand moved slowly at first, then faster. Suddenly something squirted out of the end of the stick. He sighed loudly, turned toward me and, with a fury I was too young to understand, screamed in a strange high-pitched voice, 'Turn around! Turn around!' His face contorted, his eyes protruded, but he didn't move.

"Instinctively, I knew the incident was never to be mentioned.

"Maybe not now, but then, Russian children were so different from American children. It wasn't until I was eighteen and saw a drawing in a medical book that I realized Lonya's stick had been a penis. What a relief it was to know that all men, not just Lonya, were different from women. And I was in my twenties before I understood the word 'masturbation.'

"It's sad to think Lonya might never have experienced the pleasure of a warm body under his. A neighbor who knew him before the war, a gaudily dressed, rough woman, tried introducing him to young war widows, but he rudely refused until she finally gave up.

"I remember the night when my fear of Lonya changed to sympathy. He was still working, but was losing his sight and his cough was getting worse. It was New Year's Day 1948. He was in bed, tossing and turning. From across the room I could hear his heavy wheezing. I knew he would be unable to eat and I pretended to be asleep so he wouldn't have to prepare breakfast for me. His tossing stopped and, through what I thought were sobs, I heard him whisper, 'I don't know what to do.' He repeated it over and over for what seemed a very long time.

"There were loud screams followed by a door bouncing open and a heavy thud. Berezovsky was beating his wife again. I heard her whimpering as she lay in the hallway. Lonya got up, crossed the room on his tiptoes stopping near my bed. I was lying with my back to him, trying to keep my eyelids from fluttering. Lonya tucked me in, smoothed my cheek with his bony fingers and repeated, 'I don't know what to do.'"

Abruptly I stopped talking, exhausted, like after a good cry. Half afraid of what I would see, I looked up— past images started to fade, like that of Lonya, the last time I saw him, dead on the floor, his mouth open, his sightless eyes staring at the ceiling and two months later, my new husband standing on that exact spot proposing a toast.

I had to blink twice to see Jack. He hadn't spoken for a long time. I wondered what he thought, or if he thought anything at all.

Jack cleared his throat.

I moved to the overstuffed easy chair, dragging the Afghan with me.

"I'm sorry, Jack, I . . . I didn't mean to sound so angry. I just wanted you to know."

Jack came over to the easy chair and sat on the oversized arm. He cupped my chin and looked into my eyes.

"Whatever it is, I will always be here for you. Do you understand?"

He sounded genuinely touched.

I almost wished he'd stay until I went to sleep. I wanted him to tuck me in and kiss me good night. Isn't that a silly thought?

two

I took an early lunch to avoid Jack, and reread Fima's letter four times. I needed to finalize my thoughts for my conversation with Tanya. When I arrived home Tanya greeted me enthusiastically. She had just gotten out of the shower and was wrapped in a terry robe with a peach towel around her head.

Standing in the kitchen with a cup in her hand, she went on about an incredible sale at Marshall Field's and a doctor named "Who." A Doctor Who? I can't get used to hearing this word used in such a nonchalant manner. In Russian "who" means "penis" and people write it on walls like they write "fuck" on walls here. It's even called the three-letter word. Words that sound identical in different languages but have different meanings could lead to serious misunderstandings. Once, many years ago, an acquaintance and I were severely reprimanded in a store for using obscenities in public. Bewildered, we apologized and escaped, abandoning our groceries and accompanied by disgusted stares. It turned out that the Russian "fact" pronounced like "fucked" caused the commotion, but it took a while before we solved that mystery.

I've planned it all. I'm going to hand Tanya the letter and tell her I will respect whatever decision she makes.

Tanya described the so-cool jeans that some lucky friend of hers had already purchased at Marshall Field's.

"Mom, if we don't go soon they'll only have petite sizes left!" she whined.

My stomach in knots, I listened to her carefree voice, all the time willing her father's letter to transform into a bad dream.

I dried my hands. "Tanya, would you please get my handbag from the living room. We received a letter yesterday and I would like to talk to you about it."

"Who's it from?" she asked as she handed me the handbag, then sat down pulling up another chair to put her feet on.

"It's from your father."

Her feet missed the chair entirely, hitting the floor with a thud. I made myself busy unfolding the letter.

Hesitantly, she took the letter from me. "I don't believe it. He found me! Oh, God." Happiness and proud anticipation flowed from her voice. She turned the sheet of paper over. "It's in Russian. Mom, read it to me."

In my nervousness I had forgotten that Tanya couldn't read Russian. I cleared my throat and read the letter with as little emotion as possible.

"I can't believe it," Tanya mouthed, then added sound and repeated, "I can't believe it."

All my strength focused on the effort of not crying.

"Why isn't he asking about me?" Tanya got up. The towel on her head unwrapped and slid onto her shoulders. "He doesn't even know I look like him. What am I saying, of course he does."

She threw the towel on the kitchen table. With her wet hair clinging to her head she stood waiting for my hug like a helpless child.

I wanted to cry and hug her and ask her not to go, but I didn't stir. I need to be strong to withstand what's ahead of us.

"Mom, say something. Please say something. I don't know what to say," she sniffed. "I wouldn't know what to say to him. He's not even asking about me. How does he know he'll like me when I visit?"

When I visit. . . . Not if? When.

"He's your father, Tanichka. He was a good father and he loves you very much. I don't want to influence you." I knew I sounded stuffy, but it didn't matter. Tanya wasn't listening.

"Does this mean I have a different last name now? How could he give up his name? What if I had tried to find him? I have a brother now? If I write to him, will he be able to read my letter — does he know English?"

"No, he doesn't know English, but I'm sure he'll find someone who does."

"You could translate for me."

"I'd rather not. Let's write our separate letters."

"I'd like to go there and meet him. You wouldn't mind, would you? I mean, for a short visit."

"I'd be afraid they might not let you out. You simply can not trust the Soviet Union."

"Come on, Mom, that was before." She shook her head like a puppy. Her hair was almost dry.

If I hear one more time that "before" is something illusive . . . to be discarded . . .

"Well, Tanya, why don't you write your letter?"

Tanya looked at me, surprised by the coolness.

"I love you, Mom. I'd never go there to live. It's just . . . I want to love my father too." She paused. "Why does he say he's ready to forget everything?"

"Tanichka, sit down, I need to explain some things to you. Try to understand that I never wanted our family to break up. Your father and I would never have divorced had he consented to come to the United States.

"When your father and I divorced, he tried to get custody of you, even though he knew it was a hopeless undertaking. He was worried that

I would expose you to devious anti-Soviet ideology. He couldn't actually admit this was the reason; it would have jeopardized not only my life, but attracted attention to him. He explained to the court we lived in a small room in a communal apartment and that he lived with his parents in a separate two-room apartment. He said my salary was so low that even with child support we wouldn't have enough to live on.

"I didn't want you to grow up in that country, no matter what amenities your father could have provided. He didn't see it my way then and, by his letter, still doesn't.

"I was determined to emigrate, but I needed his written permission to take you out of the country. You see, according to Soviet immigration rules, regardless of age, one must provide either written permission from their parents or their parents' death certificates.

"I begged your father to sign a release, but he wouldn't. He didn't want to lose you, and he knew his giving permission could be held against him. The government might think he condoned emigration. He could have lost his job, friends, any security he had built.

"I became desperate and forged the permission papers, including his signature. Then, after our papers were submitted, I waited daily to be arrested.

"Of course, I lost my job the minute I asked personnel for the necessary documents to complete my application. I was so frightened that I never went out during the day, fearing someone would realize I wasn't working and tell your father. Every time the door bell rang I expected it to be the militia coming to take me away.

"God must have been watching over us, because, in the end, the immigration office never verified the documents, and in three months I received our exit visa.

"I told your father we were going on vacation. He never had an inkling we were leaving for good.

"To this day I'm not certain he knows how we got out and, for the time being, it's better that way. At the time he couldn't make inquiries because it would have attracted attention to him. But I'm sure he realized I had done something in an unorthodox manner."

For the first time since I started talking, I looked at Tanya. I thought she was about to cry.

"Tanya, I'm proud of the decision I made and there is no question about it — I would do it again if it needed to be done. I would take any risk necessary for your well-being."

Tanya turned to me with tears in her eyes.

"I hate it, I just hate it." She started pacing the kitchen. "Everything was fine, just fine, everything made sense and now it's like . . . suddenly my whole life has turned upside down."

"Tanichka, you won't be upside down if you don't let yourself fall over. What I mean is, do what you feel is the right thing."

Only last night, I accused Jack of saying the same thing so nonchalantly. What else is there to say?

"But I don't know what the right thing is! You've always told me that if a person does something seriously wrong once, he'll do it again. And what you did was seriously wrong. But . . . wasn't wrong." Tanya addressed me with helpless anger. "It's easy for you say 'do what you feel is right' because you have the experience, you know how to handle . . . Oh, you know what I mean!" she appealed as she made a step in my direction.

I can't help her. If I make this decision for her it will be what I want.

"Tanichka, there's an old Ukrainian folk song in which a daughter tells her mother 'It was simple for you to choose whom to marry because you were marrying my father, but I'm marrying a stranger.'"

Tanya carried her cup to the sink, lowering it thoughtfully.

"I guess I have to think about it."

For the first time in a long time I slept the night through. When I opened my eyes I found Tanya sitting next to me reading a book. She marked her place and stretched.

"I've been thinking. I don't want to write to my father. You worked so hard when we got here—living with strangers, cleaning houses. He never cared, he never wrote to us, he even changed his name. What if I had tried to look for him! The thing is, you weren't afraid, you got us out of the Soviet Union. He never cared what happened."

Tanya doesn't understand. It's not that Fima didn't want to know about her. It's not that he arbitrarily changed his name. It's the Soviet Union. The Soviet mentality forced him to give her up. Soviet reality made him take a Gentile name. Tanya hasn't experienced the Soviet Union. How can she understand what it's like? I don't want my child to hate her father. It isn't his fault.

"Tanichka, hear him out."

"There's nothing for him to explain. He thinks he's being generous wanting me back, but he never wrote, even though he was certain we were unhappy, so unhappy we would jump at the opportunity to return. No, I'm not writing to him."

"Why don't you tell him how you feel?"

"I don't want to be rude."

"I think it would be more rude to ignore him. Besides, you'd be doing me a favor if you write to him."

Is it too much for her? She's only fifteen. Sometimes I wonder if I would have made it this far without her. She's been my friend, my sister, my support, my joy, my life. She's made all the hardships worth it. But in the end, she's still a child. Perhaps she shouldn't write. Perhaps I shouldn't write.

Tanya moved closer. "I'm not sure I want to have a father anymore. I mean . . . I imagined it differently."

She's so young. It would have been easier if her father had been here, but I don't regret he wasn't. So there it is again — no absolute right, no absolute wrong.

three

The weekend passed peacefully. Answering Fima's letter became another entry on my list of things to do.

Natasha came over Sunday afternoon to brag about her upcoming trip to Israel. Her son, Isaak, had started school there last September and his letters were full of colorful descriptions of people and places. When we first met, he had been a skimpy boy, quiet but stubborn. It was in Rome where we waited for visas to the United States. We sat in the very back seat of the bus taking us for a tour of Pompeii. Natasha unsuccessfully tried to get Isaak to greet us politely and to entertain Tanya. I tried to assure her that he should not do what he didn't want to do. The next thing I remember was the complete story of Natasha's life, beginning with her childhood passion for hide-and-seek through her accomplishments in chemical engineering and much more modest ones in marriage. Our children didn't take to each other, then or ever.

By chance, we both ended up in Chicago, a couple months apart. Proudly, I played the American when she arrived. That entailed jotting down the phone numbers from the for-rent signs, taking Natasha and Isaak to apply for Social Security numbers, to meet with landlords, and to visit garage sales. Being able to lend her three hundred dollars for winter clothes was a source of special gratification to me. Recently, in one of our many evenings reminiscing, it came to light that my total savings at the time consisted of five hundred dollars. Natasha, in a huff, demanded to know why I hadn't disclosed that fact.

"It looks like I took advantage of you," she said angrily.

She agreed eventually that the less one had, the less hesitation there was to give. Not that either of us would hesitate now.

Tanya spent the afternoon in her room with her biology book, which I suspected was continually open to the same page. While Natasha was there, Jack called asking me to come over. I heard the pleading in his voice and said yes.

"You're lucky to have a guy like that," Natasha sighed, "Bright, not bad-looking, generous. That's important."

Natasha recently broke up with her long-standing boyfriend, Oleg. They had been lovers in the Soviet Union, during and after Natasha's marriage, and they had continued their relationship along each step of their emigration—Vienna, Rome, Chicago. Somehow, Oleg was never able to find work here and had moved in with Natasha, borrowing a few dollars from her son every now and then and relying on Natasha for everything else. She was really better off without him, but as a Gentile woman without a Jewish husband as a passport to an all-Jewish Russian community, she needed someone.

She admired Jack's generosity and his stately house in Winnetka.

"I'll drive you to Jack's; he can bring you back."

As soon as we were in the car, Natasha demanded, "What's going on?" Her Leningrad Russian sounded harsh.

"Why are you asking?" I adjusted the seat belt carefully.

"Listen, Anya, it's only a fifteen-minute drive; if you like I can make it thirty minutes." Natasha swerved, making a sharp left turn.

There was no point in arguing. She knows me too well. Besides, she likes playing the mother. I don't usually mind. Oftentimes it's comforting to be liked so sincerely.

"It's not life-threatening. I'll tell you soon."

"Anything to do with Jack?"

"No."

"Tanya?"

"Yes."

"A boyfriend?"

"No, thank God."

"What is it then?"

"Nata, I don't want to talk about it. It may not even be a problem, but when I told Jack, it set me off like fireworks. Please, I don't feel like going through it again right now."

"Well, Anya, you know where to find me."

Jack opened the door dressed in a black silk robe. He took my coat and my hand, leading me directly up the oak staircase to his bedroom.

He encircled me with his arms and kissed me. "Ohhh, no bra. Let me see."

He sat on one of the wing chairs across the room, watching as I undressed. Strangely, I felt risqué as I slowly pulled my sweater over my head. I tossed it at him. I kicked my shoes off, then peeled my jeans, then my panties to the floor. I crossed the room to Jack, untied his robe, and knelt between his legs.

This was not something I was accustomed to doing, and I felt awkward. Generally, Soviet women of my age have grown up very reserved. Touching their men was not something many do willingly. That was for other women, not wives. But American women did much more than touch, and I knew Jack liked it.

"Anna . . . Anna."

Jack is so good to Tanya and me, why shouldn't I please him?

Jack pulled me up. I straddled his legs and lowered myself onto him. Suddenly, with his hands grasping my buttocks, he stood up, took several steps and tossed me onto the bed. When he bent to kiss me, I wrapped my legs around him. I tried to relax, but I couldn't, and soon Jack became aware of my tension.

Afterward he stroked my hair. "I'll wake you up one day, you'll see." Will he? Sasha awakened me, and I've belonged to him ever since. I don't want to belong to anyone else.

"You drive me crazy. I feel like a twenty-year-old," Jack murmured, kissing my shoulder as he got up to take a shower.

Jack is the only man I've seen naked. Fima had my tired nights and Sasha never fully undressed, even when we had time. I don't remember Vilen's body.

Three years ago, after several months of infrequent, uncertain, and rather reserved dating, Jack and I first made love at Jack's house. He gently undressed me, conscious of my stiffness. Naked, I stood like a mannequin at the side of the bed. When Jack took off the last of his clothes, I tried to hide my panic, shifting my eyes. If only I could have disappeared into thin air.

He came close, whispering, "What is it? Did I do something wrong?"

I couldn't look at him. I wanted to cover my body with my hands. Jack pressed me to him, his warm hands on my back. I couldn't see his body, but I felt his arousal. His eyes watched my face.

"I'm embarrassed," I said, looking down at his chest, expecting him to laugh.

"Embarrassed of what? You're beautiful. You have nothing to be embarrassed about."

When he stepped back I quickly glanced away. How could I tell him that at my age I had never seen a naked man.

Jack took my hand saying, "Let's wait until you're more comfortable." He was obviously disappointed, but he wasn't laughing and he wasn't angry.

I thought, I've got to face this, what's the difference when it happens? I like him and it's bound to happen eventually.

"I'm fine."

Jack squeezed my shoulders bringing his lips to mine.

"Are you sure? Just tell me if I do anything you don't like. Anna, this is not a one-night stand. I want to make you happy."

Chilled, I pulled a blanket up to cover myself. I lay there, listening to the water from the shower. In a minute or two Jack will come out of the bathroom, naked, dry his hair with a thick beige towel, wink, then bring me a glass of cold milk and an eclair on a black-and-white plate. He'll sit at the edge of the bed, stroke my leg, and watch me eat, all the while with smiling eyes. I'm surprised he hasn't become bored with me.

"Tanya seems preoccupied these days," said Jack casually, his eyes no longer smiling.

"It's the letter from her father. At first she was excited, even asked if she could visit him. I was petrified that if she went she wouldn't be able to come back. Thank heavens, after thinking it over she decided she doesn't want to get to know him because he didn't care about her enough to find out how she was all these years. The fact he changed his last name didn't help either. I asked her to write to him and she did. Considering her age, she proved to have a rather mature attitude, but I know she's having a hard time."

"Anna, she's a fine girl, very much like you, believe it or not. Why did your ex change his last name?"

"He has to survive. He has a son, who would be beaten up if his name was Fishman. His new wife is a Jewish woman who kept her first husband's Gentile name. I would never change my name, but others do. I understand why and can't blame them."

"Being an American, in your words, I can't envision myself succumbing to such limits on my freedom."

"Anti-Semitism is a fact of life in the Soviet Union. You learn at a very early age. If you're a Jew, you get spit on."

"Are you going to write?"

"There isn't much to say."

"That's good. Even though I can't believe you'd go back, I have to admit I was nervous. I can't picture my life without you anymore."

Not giving me a chance to answer, Jack took the plate and glass from my lap, pressed his fingers to the plate then licked the crumbs from them and chuckled.

"If my mother could only see me now!"

I found Tanya asleep on the sofa when I got home, all the lights still on.

She raised her head. "Hi, I was waiting for you. What time is it?"

Nothing compares to the feeling of the two of us being one. I wish I could hold her close all the time, feel her way for her, make her life secure and carefree. I wonder what she feels.

"I want to ask you something."

She sat up, making room for me on the sofa. I sat next to her, stretching my legs.

"Don't you want to know what I wrote to my father?"

"What you write is your decision. You must decide what your relationship will be. I only ask that you don't lie to yourself to make someone else happy. You'll only feel miserable and aggravate the problem in the long run. It's like stealing and not being caught. Maybe no one else knows, but you do."

Tanya frowned. For a moment her body sagged and she stared fixedly ahead. Then abruptly she sat up, her shoulders straight, her chin up.

"I know I should love my father because he's my father, and I thought I did. I know I shouldn't analyze him, but . . . it's not fair. I feel guilty. I mean, I don't feel that way about you." She paused and the sudden metallic quality of her voice startled me. "I told him how hard it was for us when we first came here. I told him how we lived with other people so I could get a good education and not be alone after school. I told him you scrubbed floors, did laundry, and washed dishes in people's houses. I told him I baby-sat newborn twins at night. I told him it was just you and me, that all the Russian people we knew always got letters from the Soviet Union. I told him we're proud to be Jewish and haven't hid by changing our name, and that if he lived in the United States he wouldn't have been afraid to write to his daughter. I told him you work with computers and we bought a house and a new car and I want to be a doctor. I told him we have all the friends we want and we don't need anything from him—not even his letters."

Tanya's description brought back vivid memories of cleaning and cooking and paying back with my body for living in a good neighborhood with a good school. My English was pitiful, and I didn't have any marketable skills. If we wanted to eat, I had to clean houses. For almost a year we lived with a Russian family, the Korsunskys. Then we lived with another Russian family, the Kaganovs, who were very good to us. Vilen, an engineer, spoke perfect English and made good money. He paid for Tanya to go to a private school with his son, Yuri, and in his spare time taught me English. He and his wife, Irena, helped me find clients to clean for on weekends and even drove me to their houses. I wasn't surprised when he appeared at the side of my bed to collect. I wondered why it hadn't happened sooner. I looked across the room hoping Tanya was asleep, then threw back the covers. Vilen climbed in, whispered not to worry, Irena had taken a sleeping pill. He kissed me a few times, pulled up my nightgown, and crawled on top of me. I lay there, feeling the thickness of him inside me moving back and forth. In minutes he was finished and gone. I knew he'd be back another night. As I rolled over I realized that Tanya might not have been asleep; the room was too dark to be certain. I made a mental note to get a night light—I needed to be certain Tanya was asleep when Vilen visited.

Tanya tossed her hair back like I do when I'm angry. Her trembling voice rang with tears. I hugged her as she continued in a still slightly confused manner.

"I didn't mean to be rude. Please tell him that when you write."

"You don't have to feel guilty about what you wrote. It's much better to tell the truth. Then you don't get caught."

Sighing, Tanya nodded.

November 24, 1985

Dear Fima,

Your letter was unexpected and, although I don't want to make you wait for a response, I'm afraid I'm at a loss as to what to say to you. Tanya mailed you a letter yesterday.

Nothing comes easy and I never expected the steps I took to be easy, but we have adjusted rather well. The United States is a wonderful and fair country and it is our home in every sense of the word.

When we arrived our main obstacle was my lack of English, but this is behind us now. As Tanya has grown she has helped and encouraged me. I would never have made it without her by my side. She's in the eleventh grade at a very good school. She's an excellent student, a very serious and ambitious girl, and not spoiled too much. Her dream is to become a pediatrician. She is tall and has beautiful skin and lovely eyes; her hair is much darker than when she was little.

We know, from newspapers and television, about the positive changes taking place in the Soviet Union. Even so, it is inconceivable to suggest that even the most successful outcome of the reforms could influence anyone who has tasted life in the West into going back. However, all the ex-Soviets here hope the lives of the people in the Soviet Union become permanently better.

I believe it to be unrealistic of you to think we should have or need to be in contact with you. However, I appreciate your, and your family's, readiness to sacrifice for what you believe is best for Tanya. Give my regards to your family.

Anya

four

It's the first time I've invited people to my home for a holiday.

In Kiev I always had a little party to celebrate birthdays. Starting from when I was nine, Asya, and later Asya with Myron, came every year, all dressed up, with a practical present and flowers. When Lonya was alive he would smirk sarcastically out of the corner of his mouth, "The world would not have lost anything if neither of us had been born." I always called Sasha on his birthday, but birthdays were unimportant to him.

I treasured every minute I shared with Sasha. Between work and family, he had very little time for me, but how could I ask for more than he had to give—or, did he really try to limit the sinful part of his life to so little time that it wouldn't count?

Who was I to him?

The table is set, the house is in perfect order. Tanya and Jack called from the airport to say Jack's mother's plane would be twenty minutes late. My other Thanksgiving guests, Marina and Gena and Natasha aren't due for at least another hour.

Tomorrow Nina and Izya, Bella and Felix, Irena and Vilen, with their son Yuri, and Lena are coming.

Jack's car pulled into the driveway. Tanya helped Mrs. Graff out of the car. She was wearing a blue dress with a pleated skirt, white collar and belt, and had obviously gained weight. She had perfect bluish hair, pale skin with a myriad of tiny wrinkles, and thin, coral lips. I better start smiling.

"Hello, Anna, dear, how are you? Tanya has grown sooo much, such a sweet young lady! A pretty young lady, too, isn't she, Jack? You look stunning, my dear. It's sooo nice to see you again. Let me wipe my lipstick off your cheek. Thank you, I bought this dress especially for your party. Now tell me how you've been. That's good. The house looks lovely, just lovely. Jackele, darling, try to be careful with this box. Why don't you open it, Anna. It's my housewarming present. It's entirely my pleasure, dear, I am glad you like it. Thank you. Tanya, would you be a doll and find my slippers in the brown suitcase? How many people do you expect? That's nice."

When Mrs. Graff speaks, the impression is that of a single sentence said in one breath. If your mind wanders you can always return safely into the drone.

"Now, I'm sure you're busy, don't let me keep you, dear. Don't worry about me. My Jackele can show me the house."

In other words: Get lost and leave me alone with my son.

In the kitchen Tanya gasped, "Mrs. Graff said she has a T-shirt for me. Mom, I'm so happy we're having a party!"

My hands shook as I pulled the turkey from the oven.

God, you've watched over me for forty-four years, please don't quit now. Thank you for giving me strength and patience. Thank you for inspiring me to come to this country, for making my life what it has been, for Lonya, for Sasha. I don't need much attention anymore, but please don't desert me. Tanya is still a child; please let me live to see my grandchildren.

"Mom, are you crying? Mom?" Tanya's face momentarily changed from childish joy to distress. "Are you upset Mrs. Graff came?"

Silly girl, she doesn't realize I'm happy Mrs. Graff came, that the others will come.

"I'm fine, Tanichka."

"You better dry your eyes before Jack sees you!" Tanya admonished, pushing me in the direction of my bedroom.

I stopped in mid-step when I heard Jack's voice coming from the bedroom.

"Mother, I told you not to accept Anna's invitation if your intention is to try to break us up." Jack's voice sounded uncommonly high as he continued, "I'm forty-three years old, too old for you to interfere."

"Jackele, don't get so excited. You know I'm fair. Is it a crime to want grandchildren? I like Anna, but she's not for you. You can't waste years with a woman her age, a newcomer, someone who only needs help. Our family always gives so much to charity, but that doesn't mean . . ."

"Trust me," Jack interrupted, "with what Anna has accomplished it's obvious she doesn't need help. Mother, I'm very fond of Anna. Do you understand?" Jack's tone sounded like that of an adult addressing a child. "Why don't you relax. I'll call you when the guests arrive."

"Jackele, you're a spoiled child. You forget your mother is seventy-six and has no one else in the world but you. When I'm gone, all I've got would eventually go to this woman and her daughter, complete strangers."

"This conversation makes no sense whatsoever," Jack said.

Hearing steps, I retraced my own to the kitchen in panic. Tanya looked up anxiously from the phone. I signaled her to continue.

Natasha handed Jack a large box of chocolates.

"I saw Natasha drive up and decided to play host," Jack said as I approached. He put the chocolates on the coffee table and returned to take her coat.

"Where's Tanya?" Natasha looked around. "Look at this table! It's beautiful."

"Thanks. Tanya's on the phone, of course."

The table does look festive. I wish I had a camera.

Tanya came from the kitchen to hug Natasha.

"Tanya, I brought chocolates. They're on the coffee table. Would you like to see the new pictures Isaak sent me?"

I knew Tanya didn't want to see the pictures. Isaak is a brilliant boy, but the fact that he's two inches shorter than she, has a small chin and a pushy mother make him irreversibly unattractive.

Mrs. Graff swam out to the dining room, her arms outstretched, her head to one side with a wide, hospitable smile.

"Hello, Natasha, dear, how nice to see you again. How have you been? That's good. I'm fine, thank you. You look marvelous."

As their cheeks met, Natasha rolled up her eyes at the American clichés.

"Natasha, where is your wonderful son? In Israel? How exciting! You must tell me all about it. Oh, nothing new with me, getting older, envying everyone else's grandchildren and great-grandchildren. You young people don't understand."

"Let's sit down in the living room. Irena and Gena should be here any minute." I hardly recognized my own voice.

Mrs. Graff could be trusted to continue her drone indefinitely, keeping Natasha out of my hair. She acknowledged the doorbell, slipping "someone's at the door" into whatever she was saying to Natasha.

"Hi!" Marina exclaimed cheerfully in Russian. "I'm sorry we're late." She unhooked her fox jacket. "It's still too warm for fur."

Gena moved his toothpick from one side of his mouth to the other, indicating he was going to say something.

"Hi, Anya. Big house for the money."

Marina peeked into the living room, waving to Natasha and Tanya.

"Oops, sorry for the Russian." Her dimples shone at Mrs. Graff.

Marina instantly transformed into a suave society woman in the presence of what she recognized as an American.

"Mrs. Graff, this is my friend Marina Korsunsky and her husband, Gena, I mean Gene. Marina and I went to the same university in Kiev and Gene's my dentist. Marina, Gene, this is Mrs. Graff, Jack's mother."

Natasha rose from the sofa and was quickly replaced by Marina.

Somehow, Marina managed to dampen my spirits. So smug, so at ease with people. Everything she wears has that simple look only expensive clothes have, and her big, round-faced husband is the perfect match to her fragile appearance.

Mrs. Graff laid Natasha's pictures on the coffee table and turned her attention to Marina.

"It's a pleasure to meet you. What a beautiful fur you were wearing! My furs have been in storage for years. I live in Miami, you know. I do miss my mink sometimes. I've got a sable, too. Fur makes a woman feel confident and desirable, don't you think? Gene, you're so lucky to have such a charming wife. Thank you, I'm not what I used to be. Jack remembers, I'm sure, how I danced and, oh, those wonderful parties in our home."

"All right, everyone, time to eat," I said trying to sound casual, but feeling breathless.

Almost before the words were out of my mouth, Mrs. Graff said, "Jackie, dear, please sit next to your mother."

Natasha pointed to the chair at the head of the table and I took it reluctantly, conscious of being the center of attention. Jack asked Gena something and Gena's toothpick moved up and down, touching his nose and chin as he answered. Tanya sat next to me and Mrs. Graff made certain Jack did not steal to my other side by inviting Natasha to sit next to me.

Two people between Gena and me meant he would not be able to reach my knee under the table. He realized it, too, giving me a cold stare as his toothpick jumped to the middle of his puckered lips.

Jack opened a bottle of very dry red wine and a bottle of sweet Manishewitz, bought especially for his mother.

"I would like to make the first toast," announced Mrs. Graff. With Jack's help, she rose. "Let's give thanks to our hostess and wish her luck in her new home." Her hand, with sprawling age spots and long, coral nails matching her lipstick, shook slightly. "It's so nice to see people from Russia do well here. And no one deserves it more than our strong and smart Anna. I am proud of you, my dear." She touched her glass to mine and smiled at everyone.

Jack, looking at me seriously, raised his glass.

A holiday was always just any day for Lonya and me. Most evenings passed with not a word, not a glance, the two of us sitting at our little square table with the worn-out, blue-and-white checkered tablecloth. Occasionally Sasha played chess with Lonya or helped with my homework.

Jack came around with the excuse of adding more wine to my already filled glass. He caught me on the verge of slipping into my long-past world. I wondered how he sensed that, while everyone else was peacefully gobbling up their salad.

He squeezed my shoulder with his free hand.

"You seem tired, Anna. It's tough to prepare two parties."

"That's just what I said when Anna called to invite me. You can't accomplish much when you work full-time. But Anna tells me Russian women are used to that," Mrs. Graff observed.

"Natasha, Isaak's in Israel now, isn't he?" asked Gena in English, pushing away his plate then opening a small silver box filled with toothpicks. "Alex wanted to go, I wouldn't let him."

"And how old is your son?" Mrs. Graff watched Gena work a fresh toothpick.

"We have three sons," answered Marina for her husband. "Alex is the oldest. He's twenty-one, a junior at the University of Chicago," she added proudly. "Then there are the twins. They're only nine."

"Certainly, you don't work, do you, not with a family like yours?" Mrs. Graff's eyebrows crawled up her forehead.

Marina lowered her eyes. "Just three days a week. We have to make a living, you know."

"Oh, drop it. Your outfit costs more than you make in three months," Natasha said in Russian under her breath.

"It's easy to count someone else's money," Marina shot back, also in Russian, barely moving her lips.

I motioned to Jack and we rose simultaneously. "Time for turkey."

"Anya, eat some salad," Natasha berated me in heavily accented English.

"That's why she's got a figure we all envy." Marina's dimples reappeared.

I smiled modestly as I followed Jack to the kitchen to oversee the transfer of the turkey from the oven onto the large, oval platter. We returned to the dining room and the golden bird was lowered onto the center of the table, accompanied by a choir of oohs and aahs.

"Let me carve," Gena offered magnanimously in English. He took hold of the carving knife. "After all, I am the professional."

Mrs. Graff gave a short laugh. Natasha rolled her eyes. Marina smiled brightly.

Guests passed their plates to Gena, to be filled with meat, stuffing, and gravy. As plates were returned to their owners, small talk began with compliments to the hostess and acknowledgment of their immigrant's debts to America.

The same stories every Thanksgiving, but this is the first time in my home.

"So, who's giving the next toast?" Marina prompted looking around the table, interrupting Natasha.

"Can I say something?" Tanya held up her glass filled with Pepsi and looked around.

Usually she's not very talkative, and with adults she generally prefers to listen.

"This is Thanksgiving, so, I would like to thank my mother for everything she's done. I have friends in school who are surprised I have no problems and like being at home. I also want to thank the United States for accepting us and letting us do what we want and not be afraid. And thank you for coming to our first party."

Hysterically happy, I kissed her. I laughed and blushed and talked and laughed. If only Lonya could see me now. If only he could see Tanya! He would be proud. I'm sure he would be proud, and, for once, he would show it. Tears ran down my cheeks.

Mrs. Graff turned to Gena. "I understand many Russian doctors are setting up practice in the Chicago area. Are there as many dentists?"

"No, there aren't," Gena answered.

"Do you see Americans and Russians?"

"Generally, my patients are older Russians who have never learned to speak English."

"Never learned English?" Mrs. Graff looked astonished. "My goodness, how do they get along?"

Jack winked at me and I smiled back as we both remembered that his mother had lived in Argentina for over fifteen years and managed to never learn Spanish.

"A lot of them speak Yiddish, except those from Moscow or Leningrad, who assimilated to a greater degree. They live in the East Rogers Park area, where my office is, because many older shopkeepers and residents speak Yiddish there." Gena's toothpick sat respectfully in the corner of his mouth.

"It's so nice to know you're helping your own people. Do you still have family in Russia?"

"My parents and a brother."

"I hope they'll be able to come one day," Mrs. Graff continued. "They have all this freedom now. Isn't it exciting! My parents lived through the Russian pogroms, you know. They told me . . ."

I couldn't listen to Mrs. Graff anymore.

"Natasha, let's see your pictures," I suggested, and we went into the living room.

"Look, Anya, here's Isaak on the beach with friends, here's Isaak in his lab, and here's Isaak in front of his apartment building."

Here an Isaak, there an Isaak, everywhere an Isaak. I felt like singing "ee-igh, ee-igh, oh."

"I miss you so much!" Natasha kissed one of the pictures. "You should be very proud of Tanya, Anichka. You and I are lucky to have such good children. After all we've been through, we deserve it, don't we?"

"I think it must be luck, Natasha. I never had time for Tanya. I never even thanked her when she helped me. I was always too tired to have fun."

"Anya, I wish you would tell me what's been bothering you. You were very upset at the table. Both Jack and I noticed."

Gena smiled at me suavely as he and Mrs. Graff strolled into the living room arm and arm.

"Please don't address me as 'Doctor,' Mrs. Graff," said Gena smugly with his rolled Russian R's. "It's Gene, to my friends."

Mrs. Graff looked at her watch. "Anna, dear, you will excuse me, won't you? I am very tired from the trip and I think I'll let you young people have your fun." She patted Marina's hand and shook hands with Gena. "It was a real pleasure to meet you both. Please visit me when you are in Miami."

Gena bowed; Marina's dimples deepened.

"Well, Natasha, dear, good luck to Isaak. It certainly was nice to see you again. Anna, sweetheart, I'm so happy for you. Tanya, you should be very proud of your mother." Mrs. Graff brushed her cheek with mine.

I hugged Tanya.

"Mrs. Graff, I do hope you will be able to come tomorrow," I said formally.

"Thank you so much, dear. We would love to, but we need to visit my cousins. Jack's so negligent in keeping up family relationships, I have to smooth things over with them. You know how it is."

Jack waved apologetically as I closed the door.

"Good, now we can speak Russian," chirped Marina. "Gena, I want you to see the rest of the house." She unwrapped a piece of chocolate.

I definitely am not giving Gena the tour. He may be too afraid of his wife to actually come out with what he wants, but that doesn't stop him from pinching or rubbing up against me. I'm not letting him get away with anything, regardless of the money I owe him.

"Tanichka, would you please show Gena the house? My feet are killing me."

"How is Isaak, Nata? An A student?" Marina inquired.

"A's and B's equally, as usual. It doesn't bother me."

"It should," Marina exclaimed. "Alex was always a straight A student, and he had the pick of any university he wanted. The twins better do the same."

The telephone rang.

"Hello, this is Vera. May I please talk to Tanya?"

Vera spoke quickly with a slight non-Midwestern accent. Tanya had told me that her family just moved into the area.

"Tanya, phone call for you! How are you, Verochka? Getting used to the new school?" I asked in Russian.

"Yes, thanks," she answered in English.

"I got it, Mom," Tanya's voice interrupted.

Vera is the first Russian girlfriend Tanya has ever had. Her family is from Kiev. Tanya seems more relaxed with her than with Judy, Alice, or even Grace. Childhood friendships that outlast childhood are the strongest bonds. Asya never answered my letters, but I truly believe she's there for me. I know she is. Tanya hasn't had intimate Russian friendships yet. Perhaps it's for the best. She'll miss the hurt when the bonds crack, erode, or are suddenly gone.

"There's constant war there. I would go crazy if my Alex went to Israel, even for a week," said Marina's voice.

"Marina, stop scaring Nata," Gena said. He stood by the window, moving his toothpick back and forth, his legs apart, hands in his pockets.

"She's not scaring me. It's my duty to let my son live in Israel. If not for Israel, none of us would have gotten out of the Soviet Union. Israel extended me an invitation even though I'm not Jewish. I know they did it because Isaak's father was Jewish, and I feel doubly indebted."

"Had the only direction been Israel, I wouldn't have left the Soviet Union in the first place," informed Gena.

It's no secret; neither would many others.

"I'm going to make coffee. Who wants some?" said Natasha.

"There's cake too," I offered.

Natasha motioned me to stay and left the room swaying her hips and humming the "Blue Danube."

I thought now was as good a time as any.

"Marina, I won't be able to stay with the twins while you're on vacation this year."

"Anya," Marina replied, unpleasantly surprised, "we're counting on you. Our vacation is all planned. This year Tanya can help baby-sit, and you can clean Gena's new offices after the painters finish. Naturally, it would go toward what you owe us."

Marina was my Jewish Resettlement League caseworker. Natasha and I have talked about her frequently. She seems undeniably nice, but her slanting blue eyes give an impression of coldness and detachment. An unjustified impression, perhaps, but no one is close enough to know the truth. She does the expected things, says the expected words, asks the expected questions, seems to have the same problems people around her have. Her opinions are never extreme, more observations than opinions. Her reputation is good, nothing that would feed table conversation in the Russian community. Yet . . .

"You see, Marina, I thought a visit to EPCOT Center would be a nice surprise for Tanya's sixteenth birthday. All her friends have been there."

"Anya, I am not a millionaire and I cannot ignore almost five thousand dollars," Gena said, his toothpick pointing up angrily. "Do you realize I'm not charging you interest? I wish someone did something free for me."

"Gena, I've been paying you back, and I used up all my sick days at work to stay with the boys when you were between Polish ladies. I will have paid you two thousand dollars by the end of this year."

"The agreement was you would be available when we need you until you have paid everything off."

"Gena, I hate when you talk like a lawyer," Marina spoke, her tone irate. "Let's drop the subject for now. We're good friends and we'll solve everything in a friendly manner."

Natasha returned, still humming the "Blue Danube." She announced, "Coffee's ready and there's cake on the table. Marina, you cut the cake."

It felt good to say what I wanted to say! Gena's toothpick had made vicious arches in the air. Marina had looked detached and polite, but calculating.

We're going to Florida. I won't waver. Natasha said she'd lend me the money. Another year or two and Tanya may not want to spend her free time with me.

"Tanya, are you still on the phone? Do you want cake?"

"One minute, Mom."

"Tanya didn't even try the chocolates I brought," Natasha complained. "You know, I can't stand Russian stores anymore. Today a Russian taxi-driver-type, with a hairy chest and gold chains, came into the store. He pulled up his pants, wiggled his behind, bent over the counter, and whispered in the saleswoman's ear, 'Did you put aside a couple of nice herrings for me?' Without looking at him she says, 'Go to the back room, Yevgeny is there.' I swear these people still think they're in the Soviet Union."

We spent another hour or so exchanging Russian stories. Gena looked at his watch several times, but Marina gave him "the look" and he didn't move. She's the law in their family.

Underlying currents are amusing to me. I will have to ask Jack how relationships among American friends and acquaintances are made. From what I've seen at work, there are fewer true friendships and fewer lies.

Russians are made up of generations of liars. Some lies are big, like the ones the Soviet government perpetrates on its people. Some lies are small, like kowtowing to the right official to get an apartment. Is there such a thing as a small lie?

I lie. I'm tired of talking to Natasha every day, yet I do. Gena makes me sick, yet I don't slap his face. I'm apprehensive of Marina, but I invite her to my home. Vilen makes my skin crawl, yet we're still friends.

What do they feel toward me? Why is it Asya never did anything that was not perfect? And Sasha? I could always explain and accept his actions. I felt at home with Auntie Olya in her room full of pillows, silverware, and lace napkins, all collected from the vacated apartments of Jews sent to Babi Yar—much more at home than with easy-going, ever-truthful Jack.

Have I changed and they haven't? Have we all changed and just put up with each other for the sake of not being alone? Why do I feel so uncomfortable?

Around eleven everyone started to leave. I stood at the front door, smiling, thanking them for coming.

"Mom, do you mind if Vera comes tomorrow?"

"You don't have to ask."

"Their car is in the shop and her father won't let her walk this far. Could we pick her up, please?"

Typical Tanya, conscious of asking for a favor.

"That's okay. Where do they live?"

"In Skokie, on Bronx, near the train station. Thanks, Mom. Next year I'll have my license and I won't have to ask you. Jack promised I could drive his car. The kids will die when they see me driving a BMW. I'm going to call Vera back."

I'm exhausted. Thank goodness we can sleep late tomorrow. The house doesn't need much tidying and the menu is the same.

five

I woke at seven and, without opening my eyes, guessed at the weather. The street was still asleep, void of car sounds and voices. I reached to the nightstand for *Murder on the Orient Express*. So far, I've understood almost all the words and expressions, probably because I've read it in Russian. The plan is to finish it this morning.

"Hi!" Yawning, Tanya plopped on the bed next to me. "I'm so sleepy. Who's coming today? The Kaganovs, Vilen and Felix, right? With Yuri?" As she said this, Tanya blushed. She likes Yuri Kaganov, a well-mannered, seventeen-year-old boy with his father's sly smile. "Okay. That's five. Nina and Izya. Seven. Your new coworker Lena. Eight. Vera. Nine. Eleven people counting us. Wow, we've got a lot of friends!"

Friends . . . do we have friends . . . or is Tanya just using the word as loosely as it's used by everyone in America?

We picked up Vera, a plump brunette in jeans and an unbuttoned jacket, in front of one of the four-flat rentals a block from the train station. Two of these buildings are owned by Nina and Izya.

"Good afternoon, Mrs. Fishman. Thank you for inviting me." Her round, brown eyes lit up as she smiled. I found myself smiling back.

I wish I had two children, although it was hard enough with one, sharing the kitchen and bathroom with Auntie Olya and the Berezovskys. Fima's parents had a private apartment, but they steadfastly refused to exchange it for ours. When I suggested to Sasha that we have a child, he thought I was out of my mind.

The girls sat silently in the back seat.

"Where did you live before, Vera?"

"In Boston."

Vera's Russian is better than Tanya's.

"How long have you been in the States?"

"Six years."

"Where did your parents work in Kiev?"

"I don't know," she said after a pause.

I wonder why she doesn't want to tell me.

Tanya pulled Vera out of the car as soon as I turned off the engine. They ran to the house.

I pictured them in Soviet school uniforms like the one I wore: a dark-brown wool dress with a stand-up collar and long sleeves, and a black wool apron with a pocket between its wing-like sleeves for regular days and a white linen apron with longer wings and lace for holidays. Lonya washed the dress every Sunday and sewed white undercuffs and a white undercollar to it. The white edges that were supposed to fold over the dark fabric were never even. Hiding under the stairs of our building, I redid his sewing for the first time when I was nine. The seam showed in places, but the edges around my neck and wrists were almost perfectly even. That was the day I became a pioneer scout, and I remember returning home in my red scarf with a pioneer pin on the left wing of my white apron.

"Now you are Stalin's granddaughter," Lonya observed. "Try to be worthy of this honor." He had bought a handful of sunflower seeds in the market for the occasion, a treat later only reserved for my birthday. I opened each seed and put the kernels on a saucer. When they were all opened I sat down, smoothed out my skirt, and ate the kernels one at a time. I counted them all, and when I came to the last ten I counted backwards, sucking on the last three before chewing them.

Three o'clock. All we need to do is set the table. There's plenty of time.

Before following Tanya and Vera into the house, I stood by the car, watching the old lady from the corner house approaching slowly with an open book in her hand and a spotty dog on a leash. It appears she lives alone and the bookmobile stops often at her door. She passes my house at least twice a day.

I found the front door ajar when I reached it.

"You'll meet him some other time," I heard Tanya say as I pushed the door open.

"Do you want your mother to marry him?" Vera asked.

"Maybe."

"Tanya, why did you leave the door open?" I broke in.

"I thought you were right behind us. Where did you go?"

"Nowhere, just stayed outside for a while."

Tanya and Vera were sitting in opposite corners of the sofa, shoes off, knees up. Vera sat up as I walked in. I feel so warm toward her. Is it because she's Russian, one of us? Tanya has good friends, polite, sheltered, North Shore kids, but this is the first time I know I want her to keep a friend into adulthood.

The three of us set the table in minutes.

Lena drove by uncertainly, then backed up carefully until her car lined up with the driveway. She got out carrying a large gift-wrapped box. Her limp was barely noticeable under her wide poncho. She walked slowly, looking around at the expansive bi-levels and colonials surrounding my small ranch. She had been pleased, almost honored, when I invited her.

We met when Steve Ricci, the personnel manager at Harvey Manufacturing, where I work, called me to his office and introduced us with the thoughtfulness of a donkey.

"Anna, I want you to meet Lena Gurevich. We think she will be a valuable addition to our engineering department. She starts one week from Monday and is from Russia. I'm sure you will be interested in talking to each other."

There it was again: "from Russia." Why do Americans persist in calling the Soviet Union "Russia?" Russia is only one of the fifteen states which make up the whole country, fifteen states so diverse that calling a Georgian or an Estonian a Russian could bring bodily harm. Americans call us Russians and we "Russians," having arrived here as Jews—not having been allowed to be anything else in the Soviet Union—immediately started referring to ourselves as Russians.

We greeted each other stiffly, in equally imperfect English, thanked Steve, then switched to Russian in the hallway.

"Thank you. I don't think he wanted to bother with my English. I'm scared. I've got a good job now, even though it doesn't pay very much. I hope it will be stable. I need stability."

Lena was about five feet tall, slim with dark bangs reaching to her eyebrows. She limped heavily, pressing her hand to her chest when she talked. I showed her the cafeteria, washrooms, vending machines, and the exit to the parking lot.

With rare exceptions, we lunch together every day.

"Am I the first?" Lena asked, handing me the box.

"Tanichka, come here, I want you to meet Lena."

Tanya and Vera appeared like rabbits out of a hat. I handed Tanya the box. She quickly tore through the wrapping paper and peered into it with the anticipation of a child on its birthday.

"An ice bucket! Thank you!"

Lena's face was all smiles of relief.

I remembered the day we moved in: Natasha and Isaak brought a lamp for the living room; Marina arrived with a Mixmaster and a gigantic cookbook; Jack brought us a VCR and an antique phone. Leah-Malka, our former volunteer from the JRL, invaded the house with her husband Jacob, and all seven children, on our second Sunday. I saw her look of disappointment on not finding a mezuzah on the front door or at the entrance to any of the rooms. They carried in sets of silverware, kitchen towels, potholders, spatulas, and the like "just in case you want to keep kosher." She kissed me on both cheeks, ran through the house, wagged her tongue in excitement, wished us the best, then chased her family out, screaming they should let people sleep on Sunday mornings.

The Kaganov brothers, Vilen and Felix, and their families, arrived in Vilen's gray Cadillac. As was his habit when attending Russian parties, Felix had his guitar with him.

Irena scolded Vilen for wearing the wrong tie.

"He's such a dummy, my husband. If it weren't for his wife he wouldn't know what underwear to wear."

Felix sighed.

I envy Irena's ability to be blind to how what comes out of her mouth affects the people around her. She always looks so victorious that no contradicting opinions are ever voiced, at least not in her presence. If Vilen attempts to placate her, in itself an uncommon occurrence, she'll bluntly state, "If you disagree, I'll do something to ruin everyone's mood."

We lost Yuri in the middle of touring the house and later discovered him with the girls in Tanya's room, watching television.

"I can't wait until Susan's older," Felix's wife, Bella, said.

Bella and Felix's seven-year-old daughter was a petite curly-haired creature with Felix's light eyes.

Bella turned out to be Lena's gynecologist and Lena's son, Boris, was a friend to Irena's older son, Vadim. The Russian community is a small village.

"So you're Boris's mother," Irena began. "Is your son going to find a real job, or is he just planning on drifting along? Things must be terrible for you, especially after that story about your divorce."

Swallowing hard, Lena paled.

"What kind of a major is 'business,' anyway? Boris should take computers," Irena ranted on.

Lena recoiled, lowering her eyes.

"I understand Boris is working in a hardware store?" Vilen edged in mildly, taking the sting out of the conversation.

I leaned against the wall watching my guests in their petty conversations. Why do we herd together like sheep?

Felix approached me smiling. "Tanya has grown so much. Remember how little she was in Rome?"

I looked at his rapidly graying hair.

"I have less and less patience for my sister-in-law," Felix continued. "I think she enjoys hurting people. One Gentile in our family and it has to be her." He shook his head. "I need a drink if, you don't mind," Felix inclined his head asking my permission. "Do you want one?"

"Not for me. Why don't you have some wine or cognac?" I nodded toward the bottles in the center of the table.

He poured himself some wine from an opened bottle and sipped it with relish. His long, thin fingers reminded me of the first time I saw him in Rome, holding his violin. Our families shared an apartment there. He had played first violin for the Kiev Opera Orchestra. It's a pity he had to become a programmer, but their family needed a steady source of income while Bella prepared for her medical licensing exams.

"Any boys in Tanya's life yet?" he asked.

"Anya, where's Jack?" Irena interrupted. "He'll never marry you if you give him so much freedom."

With a sour expression, Felix stepped aside.

Vilen was standing with his back to everyone and as I turned, my eyes met his for a split second. I had to control myself to keep from trembling. The look of lust on his face brought back the repulsive memory of the day he caught me in the bathroom. The children were at school, Irena shopping, and Vilen at work, or so I thought. I decided to take a quick shower. When I finished, Vilen was waiting for me. He grabbed my wrist spinning me around, pushing me against the sink. One breast was in the basin, the other squashed against it. I heard the sound of his zipper and his pants falling to the ground. He pushed my legs apart and belligerently entered me. When he was done he just zipped up and left without saying a word. I escaped back to the shower where my tears mingled with the water and the noise drowned my sobs. The next day I found my breast marred by a large black-and-blue mark.

Bella's voice restored reality. "Gena and Marina are taking the same European tour we are. I hope Europe has a sufficient supply of toothpicks."

"You should be happy," lectured Irena. "At least you'll have someone to talk to. Otherwise, it's 'How are you' and 'How nice.'"

The doorbell rang. When I opened the door, Nina and Izya stood there panting.

"We're so late. Hi, guys!" Nina flashed a glance, taking in the house, the people, and the table.

"Plumbing problem in the apartment of one of our tenants. Of course, it had to happen an hour before we were to leave. Luckily, Nina remembered I had a piece of pipe in the basement," barked Izya, proudly, addressing the men as he shook hands.

Nina kissed my cheek and stuck an envelope in my hand.

"You get something yourself. You know how busy we are."

They examined every room, knocked on the walls, and in the end Izya concluded with respectful surprise, "Not bad. I'd add a second story. With all the large homes around, it would double the value."

Izya caught up with Vilen and dove into the details of plumbing repair.

This couple is so enthusiastic, so determined, so admired by everyone. When we met in an English class at the Truman Community College, they had been in the United States for almost a year, and I had just arrived. Both engineers, they managed to also carry on as janitors. That meant a rent-free apartment which they furnished with discarded furniture found in alleys and at giveaways. Izya fixed up some of the furniture and sold it at garage sales. Every minute of their lives became occupied by a practical activity.

One glance at me told them how vulnerable I was. They crowded me into a corner during a lull, eager to share their considerable knowledge of the various perks the government offered us poor, political refugees. In awe of their enthusiasm, I felt even less capable of navigating the maze around me.

Nina and Izya began a campaign to organize my life in the most efficient manner. They arranged for a cheap garden apartment in a somewhat unsafe area near Lake Michigan where they lived. They taught me about garage sales and even drove me to some. They advised me of college stipends, food stamps, public aid, food charities at local churches, and free hot lunches at a nearby synagogue. Izya drew up what he called a financial plan for me to stick to if and when I would begin to amass a great fortune.

"Just do what we tell you," Nina insisted, "and you'll have nothing to worry about."

My decision to instead become a live-in housekeeper for the Korsunskys stunned them.

"I realize that it's not practical but I want Tanya to go to a good school," I said meekly, feeling ungrateful but resolute.

"Good school?" Nina sneered. "And you would clean someone's toilets for that? It doesn't even matter in the first grade."

Our relationship cooled somewhat, as they felt offended when people ignored their advice. But we have kept in touch. In the summer, we spend an occasional Sunday with them at the beach. Last year, I drove Izya to work for two weeks when his car was in the shop after being vandalized. We know that we can rely on each other. Now they own half a dozen rental buildings in the city.

"Our eyes and wallets are always open for undervalued property," Nina likes to joke.

They renovate their purchases themselves, spending evenings and weekends putting in new floors, plastering, painting, installing furnaces. Last year they bought the building where they have lived all this time, moved from the garden apartment to the second floor, and acquired a new bedroom set. Nina boasts happily about their future "all-set retirement" in Fort Lauderdale.

Both their children use my address to prove their independent status and receive a full college scholarship. I wonder if they would let Tanya use theirs. It doesn't matter. With Tanya's grades she'll get a partial scholarship anyway, and in two years I'll have saved enough money to pay the rest. We'll survive.

Nina and Izya squeezed in at the table and dug in. With Irena looking on imperiously, Vilen and Lena analyzed different college majors. Nina's calculating eyes followed everyone.

"Dad," Yuri's young voice broke in, "I'm going for a ride with Tanya and Vera for a half-hour."

Vilen never had a chance to answer.

"Look at this rooster!" Irena thundered. "He sees two girls and he's ready to show off. Cock-a-doodle-do! You're not going anywhere!"

Lena jumped in her chair and pressed her hand to her chest, gaping at Irena stupefied.

I should have warned her.

To keep from laughing, Nina stuffed her mouth with salad.

Bella glanced at Yuri. "You should have asked, not informed, Yurochka."

Vilen took a deep breath. His fingers drummed steadily on his knee.

"Only half an hour!" Irena said gaining steam. "And you, my dear sister-in-law, who seems always ready to protect my family from me, should try to remember you are a gynecologist, not a psychiatrist."

Looking away from the girls, who quietly followed in tandem, red-faced Yuri headed to the guest closet. Vera was pale.

Irena put her hand around Vilen's shoulders, smiling benevolently.

"Yesterday we got a letter from Vilen's cousin in Kiev. Vilen, tell the joke from Galya's letter. Thank God, there are no Americans here. Those idiots don't have any sense of humor."

Now that I'm on equal footing with everyone—and that's what I wanted, a regular life—still, a nerve is missing that would make it all work together as one, like fingers that play the piano or make a fist. What do I really want? My feelings, like leftover pieces from a jigsaw puzzle, have never found their proper places. I would be different if Fima had come with us. I would be like these women, never anxious or overworked.

The people around my table are strangers, to me and to each other. There are no real bonds here, only conscious, practical acquaintanceships of lonely adults.

In the American Russian community the contours—but not the spite and scorn that define their borders—of the traditional and distinct castes and layers of the Soviet society become blurred, as the need for community arises and the sheer numbers of each class are not there.

Each city has its own perception of its place in society: the people of Moscow and Leningrad consider their cultural level significantly higher than that of all others; Kiev philosophically shrugs off these claims, feeling those of Moscow and Leningrad have their noses in the air; everyone dislikes those from Odessa, telling horror stories of jerks and swindlers; of course, Minsk is just a big village; Baltic cities are considered almost Western Europe; and no one cares about the rest.

The Kaganov brothers are close to the elite circle of Soviet-Jewish intellectuals. Bella is of even bluer blood, being the daughter of a top Soviet scientist. Irena's brazen defiance of her out-of-place position, brought on by apprehension on the part of her husband's staunchly Jewish family, provokes allegiance to her crude, traditionally anti-Semitic roots, of which she is secretly embarrassed.

Lena belongs with the Kaganov men. If they had married someone like her, this group would naturally fall together.

Nina and Izya, both mechanical engineers, are children of "salespeople." With a strong black market and constant shortages in the Soviet Union, their parents' illicit prosperity appeared gaudy, as though flaunted against the gray lives of professionals.

Here, in the United States, material life and anti-Semitism are not the criteria used to divide Russians. Since prosperity is not illegal, it's no longer shameful. This is not to say the Russian Diaspora has achieved what the Soviet Union could not—a classless society. Old ways die hard. Although class characteristics are less discernible, boundaries are easily crossed, and mixed groups coexist, the psychological barriers remain intact and subgroups form, drawn together by old, undying instincts. Russians tend to eagerly sniff out opportunities for division.

Americans are not privy to these undercurrents. Most are naive in their belief that freedom, fairness, and equality are obvious choices for societies and individuals. They don't appear to understand any other way of life, even when confronted by newspaper accounts and television specials. Perhaps this is why I don't find many close relationships between Russians and Americans. Anyone thinking my relationship with Jack is an exception isn't looking below the surface.

I caught the tail of the requisite exchange of opinions concerning Gorbachev's politics.

"They've all lost their minds over there," Nina concluded the discussion energetically. "Gorbachev is licking the same asses as everyone before him and everyone ahead of him. Otherwise he couldn't have gotten to the point where he is. The only good thing is, unlike all the rest, he's not senile."

"When I read letters from the Soviet Union, I often wonder how much longer people there will allow themselves to be screwed by jerk after jerk after jerk," said Bella.

With a screech, a car turned into the driveway. Vilen frowned as he craned his neck to look out the window.

Faces broadened into smiles when young voices were heard coming through the front door. The teenagers appeared oblivious to the inquiring grown-up glances.

"Well, they're still alive." Irena never stopped chewing.

Tanya hung up her coat and started toward her room. Yuri helped Vera with her jacket, then, conscious of the sudden silence in the room, hastily followed the girls down the hall.

"Anya, who's the tubby girl?" asked Irena. "Is she Russian? It's getting harder and harder to tell with teenagers."

"Her name's Vera Rosen. Her family just moved here from Boston. Tanya met her at school."

"Do we know her parents?" Bella inquired immediately.

"Her mother's a teller at a downtown bank. I'm not sure about her father. Tanya thinks he works in a hospital." I shrugged. "For some reason, Vera doesn't say much about her family. All I know is that they're originally from Kiev."

"I don't know any Russian doctors by that name," Bella said, wrinkling her forehead in an effort to remember.

"I'm not sure he's a doctor."

Irena turned to Izya, asking acidly, "So, how many more buildings have you bought?"

Ignoring Irena's tone, Izya answered contentedly, "Nina decided we should look at single family homes."

"And we'll buy some, too," returned Nina sharply, openly staring at Irena with distaste.

Felix stood up, hoping to ease the tension. "Do you want me to play the guitar?"

Walking to the living room Bella touched my elbow and we fell back from the group.

"Do you know if Lena has a boyfriend?" she asked into my ear.

"I've no idea," I said, feeling guilty that I knew so little about someone I invited to my home.

"Just a thought," Bella whispered excitedly, "Felix has a friend, Ilya Kotlyar, who lost his wife to cancer recently. Do you think Lena would be receptive?"

"She should be. I think she's lonely."

The kids finally came out to eat. Felix played the songs of our youth.

No Russian party ever ends without endless hours of discussion. And even among this somewhat incompatible group, we managed to have a good time.

When Americans attend Russian parties, the conversations are shorter, drier, more like small talk. The rules seem to be: Don't offend, don't argue, don't be invasive. Long after Americans have left, Russians are still there for their much-needed dose of soul-searching, bringing them together in a more cohesive group.

These days the talk is of *glasnost*. Letters from the Soviet Union are full of lists of books, articles, and movies—a must to read or see. But beneath the surface there's nothing new. There are no practical results of the new freedoms. The letter-writers act as if the country has been transformed overnight. They don't understand the Soviet Union is the Soviet Union, now and always. Things there will get much worse before they start to get better, if they ever start to get better.

Relaxed and nostalgic after Felix's impomptu concert, my guests hugged me, complemented me generously on everything from the house to the new water glasses, appealed to each other to keep in touch regularly, and drove away happy. Even Irena said that spending time with me made her feel good. I stayed outside, smiling, my light jacket wrapped around my shoulders.

When the cool air finally forced me back into the house, the light in Tanya's room was still on. I went in quietly.

"Tanichka, you should have asked if you could go for a ride, especially in someone else's expensive car."

"You didn't mind, did you?"

"No, but . . ."

"I was going to," murmured Tanya, eyes only half open, stretching under the blanket. "I was afraid after Irena got angry. Why does she hate everyone?"

"She doesn't really hate everyone, Tanya."

She turned her head away. "I think Yuri likes Vera."

I tucked her in silently and left.

What would my mother have said to me if I told her about Sasha? Rejection by a boy in favor of your girlfriend is not simple. Not all is sweet about sixteen. I wish I could fill in the blanks for her, take away all the hurts. I love her so much.

I threw the bed covers back and undressed slowly, only now organizing the snatches of conversations that swirled around me at the dining room table.

Nina's Lana is getting married. Her fiancé is a stout young man named Slava. Irena says Nina's nineteen-year-old, Victor, still hangs out with the Russian card-playing crowd. Someone said he was dating a Mexican girl. I remember seeing him on the street once, a repulsive, acne-faced young man in a leather vest, smoking a cigarette, with his arm around a small girl with long, jet-black hair, wearing the shortest skirt I'd ever seen. There are rumors he sells drugs. It's hard to tell if his parents know what's going on; they don't talk about their children, only about acquisitions and dream houses. Nina has never invited intimacy.

Soon, all of us will have grandchildren, although I can't imagine what Victor's children will look like. I'll take mine to McDonald's, read Russian poems and fairy tales to them—I remember them all, from the book Lonya found for me when I was five. I will start a dynasty. In thirty years, when I'm as old as Jack's mother, I'll preside over family gatherings: Tanya and her husband on my right, my grandchildren and, maybe, great-grandchildren around us. I'll let them talk, laugh, joke, and sometimes not pay attention to me. They'll love me and I will wonder how they have grown.

six

My eyes registered daylight, but my brain refused to make my body work—it knows I don't want to get up. I've been good and I deserve a morning in bed. Besides, it's Saturday.

I closed my eyes and let disjointed thoughts drift through my head. Hopefully Fima won't answer our letters and my life will continue as is.

It's less than a month before our vacation. I'm not telling Tanya until a few days before; I want to surprise her. We'll still have enough time to buy new swimsuits, shorts, and T-shirts. She's grown so much this year she won't have trouble holding her swimsuit up. I suppressed a chuckle in anticipation of her joy.

I really don't want to borrow money from Natasha for the trip. I still owe her the eight hundred dollars I needed for the closing on my house. If Jack would only let me pay him back, I'd borrow the money from him to pay Gena and Natasha.

In the living room the cuckoo clock cuckooed. I counted the cuckoos: nine o'clock. I don't remember ever having stayed in bed so late.

Lonya had difficulty sleeping, his first cigarette usually lit by four in the morning. When he was in the hospital I still awakened at four, waiting for the heavy smell of smoke and the tiny light descending in half-circles between his mouth and the space near the floor where he let his arm hang. I remember long, blowing sounds interrupted by rakish, choking coughs.

After Lonya passed away, I still awakened early, listening to the darkness, acclimating myself to the absence of the smell of smoke. I always tried to remain still; if Fima sensed I was awake he would make love to me. Making love in the morning bothered me; I couldn't help listening for, and expecting, Lonya's cough.

Last night, when the Kaganovs left, Vilen, looking at me through clouded eyes, squeezed my hand. Recalling his body next to mine, I shuddered. I remembered his whisper, "This is so good." That was the day he wanted it in the living room, with Irena sitting in the small foyer just steps away, talking on the telephone. I had no choice. If I had made a sound, Irena would have come in and Tanya and I would have been in the street.

It was always the same: He would catch me doing the laundry or washing dishes, he'd kiss me a few times, push me down to the floor, into a chair, or against the wall, pull my dress up, my panties down, and enter me. The year and a half I spent in their home seemed like ten. Teeth clenched, I shuddered again.

To most Russians, especially professionals, married or divorced, having affairs is part of life. Fima might have had someone on the side, Sasha had me. I wonder if Sasha thought of me as an affair?

Who was I to him?

A couple months ago Vilen called me at work. His voice was clear, his tone confident and playful, not docile and cautious as when Irena is within earshot. So sly, so sure of himself, he has never understood the intent of my demeanor since I left his home.

"Anya, why can't we be friends? Don't be mad I haven't called. I've wanted to, but you haven't been responsive. I miss our little times together. Is it because you've got Jack?"

"Vilen, you don't understand."

"Anya, Anya, I understand. We'll have to be careful picking a time and place. Let me look at my calendar, see what I can do with my schedule. I'll call you tomorrow. You'll see how much better you'll feel afterwards," he cooed.

He called the next day with directions to a motel somewhere in the western suburbs.

"No," I said slamming the phone down so hard I cracked the plastic base.

Then, I invited them. The temptation to have everyone see my house and attend my party was so overwhelming nothing seemed more important. The parties are over and now I know I'm like everyone else. I've got a good job, a house in the suburbs, a car, my daughter goes to a good school, I even have a boyfriend. That's all I've wanted since I came to the United States, although the boyfriend is a bonus. I vowed I'd do anything to make a good life for Tanya, and I did. All in all, I'm happy. Tanya is certainly happy.

"Mom, why didn't you answer me? Jack's on the phone," Tanya said from the doorway of my bedroom.

"Sorry, Tanichka, I was lost in thought."

"Good morning! Did I wake you?" Jack said, obviously in a good mood. "My salesman called me. He thinks he has a client for my software."

"Wonderful!" I cleared my throat.

"I did wake you. I am sorry. You must be tired. How was the party? Miss me?"

"The party went well. How's your mother?"

There was a sigh and a pause.

"She dragged me to see just about every cousin we have with an average age of eighty. She told them I was a bad boy and should be married. Two more today, before I take her to the airport. I can't wait to start putting the presentation together."

I wish I had old folk from the old country, in flowery dresses with hair pulled back in tight buns, who would tell me how cute I was as a baby and stories about my parents and grandparents. I'd have all the time in the world for them.

"Who's the prospective client?"

"A manufacturing company," Jack said, his voice suddenly hurried. "My mother says good morning. Sorry, I've got to go. By the way, I miss you. See you Monday at work."

I guess I'll keep Jack, and I'll keep Lena, Bella and Felix, and Asya, and Sasha. Quality over quantity.

I heard Tanya pick up the phone in the kitchen as it rang again.

The day has begun.

I stretched, slung my legs over the side of the bed, stuck my feet into old, black slippers, and padded down the hall to the kitchen.

"Mom, can I go to the movies with Vera?"

"Sure. Do you want me to take you?"

"No, Yuri Kaganov is going to drive." Tanya finished her muffin thoughtfully, avoiding my eyes.

Does being her mother give me the right to ask questions I'm sure she doesn't want to answer?

"Actually I'm not sure I want to go. Yuri asked for Vera's telephone number yesterday and this morning he asked her to go to the movies with him and his friends. She called because she didn't want to go without me. I think Vera feels guilty. I told her Yuri was only a friend, but she still feels bad." Tanya carried her cup to the sink. "I guess I'll go," she said with a casualness that seemed forced.

"Why not? It'll be fun. Did Vera like Yuri?"

"It's hard to tell. She listens, but doesn't say much. She's sort of sad." Tanya looked sad too.

"Tanichka, Yuri has known you for a very long time. To him, you'll probably always be a friend. If you think he's a good person, you should be happy for Vera."

"I don't know." Tanya screwed up her face and sighed.

Sasha knew me from the time I was ten. Is that why he kissed Lilya in my presence when they came to tell Lonya of their engagement? Is that why he talked about women in my presence? Once he told Lonya about an affair with a nurse he couldn't marry because she wasn't Jewish. I was right there, a skimpy teen, my eyes lowered. He taught me to write compositions, helped with biology, recited poetry with me. Did he do these things because his sister had died a few months before we met? How was he to know my life consisted of dreams, dreams of him acknowledging his love in flowery metaphors of classical poetry?

I first met Sasha the night Lonya collapsed in the bathroom. Berezovsky banged at our door, yelling, "Come get your drunk Jew." It was the middle of the night and I felt small and cold calling the ambulance from the phone booth at the corner. They took me and an unconscious Lonya to the hospital. Sasha, very young, but already balding and slightly stooped from overwork, with a stethoscope around his neck, met the ambulance. He told me to sit in the waiting room, inquired where my mother was, and asked when my father had collapsed.

"She said he's her brother," the ambulance doctor interceded.

The waiting room was filled with sallow-skinned people. A skinny man with a mustache snored on the floor, his pants wet at the crotch.

Sasha held my chin. "How old are you? Who do you live with?"

Stubbornly, I said, "I'm ten."

He looked around, shaking his head, then led me into an office.

"Wait in here. Don't be afraid, just wait here for me. Don't go anywhere other than the washroom!" He turned back before leaving the office. I can still see his blue eyes, apologetic and sad. "My name is Sasha."

I sat for a long time, my legs hanging, my straight back not touching the chair. My eyes never left the wall in front of me, my hands remained glued to my knees. I memorized every inch of the picture on that wall: broad-shouldered, uniformed Stalin accepting a bouquet of wildflowers from a small girl.

Sasha finally came back, minus his white robe. His eyes pled exhaustion.

"Your brother is going to be okay. I don't think it was a heart attack, but he'll have to stay here for a few days."

"I want to be with Lonya," I said looking into Sasha's eyes.

Many years later, Sasha told me how miserable and helpless I was that night: a haggard, somber girl, about his late sister's age, wrinkled clothing, short, dark, disheveled braids, oblivious to her surroundings or the consequences to her future if anything happened to her brother. Only then, when it was long immaterial, did it occur to me—giving me a terrifying pang—that I had put my faith in a complete stranger. I remember sensing Sasha's sadness. It made us equal. It made him a natural ally to be trusted absolutely and followed to what I knew in my heart was salvation.

"Right now what Lonya needs is rest," Sasha said. "Come with me."

My hand held tightly, tighter than Lonya had ever held it, felt comfortable. The trip, in the middle of the night, down empty, unfamiliar streets, excited me with an anticipation of what I must have envisioned as happiness. It never crossed my mind to worry about Lonya's reaction to my decision, as it seemed so evident that this tall, balding, silent man, puffing on a cigarette, was there to take away pain and fear.

We turned a corner and entered a building that smelled just like ours, and the elevator clanked just like ours. On the third floor Sasha unlocked one of the four doors.

"I spoke with Lonya. He knows you're here. My mother is going to put you to bed."

We tiptoed along a narrow corridor with doors on both sides until he stopped in front of one. He unlocked the door, nudged me inside, then crossed the room and knocked at a door behind plush, maroon curtains.

"What is it, Sashenka?" asked a woman's voice from behind the curtains.

Sasha gestured reassuringly as he opened the door and disappeared. I wanted to ask why he was bothering a neighbor in the middle of the night. I couldn't imagine a family having more than one room.

When Sasha came from behind the curtains he was accompanied by a short, stout lady. She had blue eyes like Sasha. The woman's hair was red with gray roots. She looked at me as she tied her robe then lit a cigarette. Her eyes glistened with tears.

"*Oy vey iz mir!*" the lady said pressing me to her full chest.

Her voice, like Lonya's, was a smoker's voice, and she smelled of stale cigarettes.

"Let me fix a bed for you. Do you want something to eat? I have some stew and barley left."

I swallowed hard; I could almost taste the meat. They exchanged glances. His mother picked up a pot from the windowsill and tiptoed out of the room. Soon she reappeared carrying a hot plate of food. With her hands on her hips, she watched as I ate the stew with a slice of dark bread, then asked for more. I ate every drop. I wanted to lick the plate, but I knew better.

"Mama, she needs new stockings. These are torn. And look at her skirt." Sitting on his bed, Sasha lit a cigarette.

His mother dabbed at her eyes with a sparkling-white handkerchief trimmed with lace. I had never seen a handkerchief like that.

"Yes, yes, Sashenka, I know, Zena's clothes will be perfect for her. Let me put her to bed. We can worry about her clothes in the morning."

Silently they made up a bed in the front room, diagonally from Sasha's. Both beds had narrow, metal headboards and footboards. The springs made squeaking noises.

I was very sleepy after eating so much of such good food. Sasha's mother took off my stockings and shook her head over my worn blue garters. She put a white, cotton nightgown over my head. It fit perfectly. She hugged me and told me to call her Auntie Riva.

The sheets were as white as the handkerchief, the blanket was dark green and thick inside a white slipcover decorated with wide lace. There were no signs of bedbugs. I stretched, trying to imagine how I would explain all this to Lonya. But even thoughts of his anger couldn't spoil the wonderful feeling of swimming in snow-white, starched linen and the taste of whole chunks of meat.

Auntie Riva stood by the window, her face covered with her hands, her shoulders shaking.

"Zinochka, my dove! *Oy vey iz mir!*"

Sasha sat on his bed, puffing rapidly on a cigarette.

Tanya hopped into Yuri's car, and I stood on the top step watching until it disappeared around the corner. Tanya's future is so exciting it takes my breath away. I went inside thinking about getting used to her being picked up, dropped off, waiting up for her. I wish Jack would call. I dialed Natasha.

"So, how did it go yesterday? Was 'Mr. Family Man' Vilen there?"

"He was. Felix too. Everyone I invited came." Pride seeped from my voice.

"Did Irena slap anyone, figuratively speaking, I mean?"

"She may have, a coworker of mine she'd never met before."

"Oh my. Is she Russian?"

"Yes. If she wasn't, there wouldn't have been anything to worry about. Irena would have sat quiet, like a mouse, smiling all evening."

"That's true. Did Jack come by?"

"No, but I didn't really expect him. Frankly, it was easier without English."

"Isn't his mother awful? She'll eat you alive when you're married . . . Anya, Anya! Are you still there?"

"Natasha, please, stop."

Call-waiting clicked in our ears.

"Nata, I'll call you back."

Lena's quiet voice sounded even shyer than usual.

"Anya, I want to thank you for inviting me. I had a very nice evening. It was the first time in almost a year I've gone out, and I'm grateful you made me feel at home and acted like nothing happened."

"What do you mean, like nothing happened?"

"Well, I mean . . . my divorce and all the scandal around it." She hesitated, then continued hurriedly, "I'm sorry. You're probably busy. I just wanted to thank you."

"I'm not busy at all. I'm glad you came and liked the party. As far as your divorce, I don't know anything about it."

"Hard to believe; the whole world seems to know."

"All I can tell you is, I know nothing, Lena, and I don't care. I like you very much."

"Anya, I hope you're not saying this just to make me feel better," Lena's voice quivered. "This lady . . . Irena, the one that yelled at her son, she'll make a point to tell you."

"Please, Lena, don't get upset. Whatever happened in your life won't change our relationship." I was beginning to feel uncomfortable.

"I'm not used to being unhappy. My life was always as perfect as a sentimental novel. At forty-two one doesn't expect it to . . . fall apart. My mother doesn't write anymore and my father sends only short notes.

"I know it sounds childish. Millions of people get divorced every day. But not Serozha and me. We grew up together, our parents were friends. He proposed before we graduated high school. I was an only child and my parents spoiled me. Even in the worst years I had everything, the best, the freshest food from the open market, even oranges and tangerines. A seamstress sewed lace blouses for me.

"Serozha was like another father. He took a day job and went to night school, so we could get married. A month before the wedding I fell and broke my ankle. The bone never healed properly, that's why I limp. Serozha carried me into the hall for the ceremony. When Boris was born, Serozha threw a party. The first month I hardly touched the baby, I simply fed him and rested."

Lena recited her story emotionlessly, like a person who has repeated the same thing many times.

"It was Serozha who decided to emigrate. I was reluctant. Our daughter, Svetlana, was twelve, and Boris was about to be drafted when we applied and left, by a miracle, practically on the last train out in 1980. My parents were refused permission to leave. We had no choice but to leave without them. When we arrived here, Serozha found an engineering job right away. Since he's a wonderful photographer, he did weddings on the side. He objected to my working in a position higher than draftsperson because he didn't want me to be tired at the end of the day. We bought a large house in Glenview, Svetochka went to a good school, Boris started college. We hired a maid. Serozha did most of our shopping and took care of the bills and investments. We traveled and entertained."

Her voice became hoarse, and I was afraid she would cry. The silence went on for so long I thought the line had gone dead. Tears gathered in my eyes.

"Two years ago we had a New Year's Eve party at our home. This was always a tradition that mattered a lot to us. It had started the first year we arrived in the United States when we invited a few people that we went to our English class with. Like us, they knew no one, so they appreciated the invitation."

Lena paused. She didn't have to tell me that her memory transported her to that special world which we shared and treasured.

"I remember," she went on with a sigh, "we didn't even have a table then. The food, some of it in pots, sat on a borrowed coffee table and on chairs. We sat on the carpet. We enjoyed each other's company so much that we all kept in touch.

"Two years ago . . . excuse me." Lena blew her nose and started again. "At our last party, while I was in the pantry a friend of mine came into the kitchen to rinse out some glasses. Serozha walked in and I was about to call on him to help me carry the plates and napkins, when I saw him suddenly plunge toward my friend. He clawed her breasts from behind. He bared his teeth. He looked like . . . like a wolf. She tried to tear his hands away. I could see dark spots from her wet hands on her light-colored dress. Neither made a sound. I had to bite my fist in order not to cry.

"Then heels clicked in the hallway, Serozha moved back, straightened his lapels, and strolled out. He almost collided with another woman friend of mine carrying some silverware. He probably smiled at her.

"The second friend said, 'What's wrong with your dress? Serozha again? He makes me sick.'

"The first woman headed toward the powder room. Before she walked out, she said, 'I wish I could tell Lena, but she thinks this jerk is the best thing that ever walked the earth. She'll only imagine I led him on.'

"I couldn't cry, I just kept biting my fists. Eventually, I scurried to the bedroom, brushed my hair, repaired my face, and rejoined the party. I even asked my friend how she happened to ruin such an elegant dress. She muttered something unintelligible. Since then, I've often cried myself to sleep, but I didn't shed a tear that night. That night I danced a lot."

I wondered if Lena remembered whom she was talking to, or even if she was on the phone.

"Two days later I filed for divorce. I told him I'd heard rumors he took advantage of other women. He begged, cried, apologized, saying he loved me dearly, but that some women just ask for it, and that women tend to exaggerate a man's attention, making it wishful thinking on their part. He insisted other women envied us. My friends—my ex-friends—tried to convince me not to break up my family. They never even hinted at any advances made to them—after all, they had their husbands to keep.

"Serozha left. Svetochka went with him. Boris thought I was crazy and now he's hardly ever home. Serozha pays the mortgage and comes over occasionally. He's confident we'll get back together, but we won't.

"You see, if you suddenly lose a person you love, it hurts, but it's not filthy, it's not humiliating. What he did, whether he actually slept with other women or not, was disgusting. Yet these same women tell me he's a nice man. They've remained friends with him and try to convince me to take him back."

I spoke softly. "Lena, a lot of people in the Soviet Union had affairs. Mostly, it didn't mean much. No Russian would ever understand your reaction, especially considering how many years you were married, his apologies, and the children."

"So, you think I should have accepted his apologies?"

"I'm not sure I'm the right person to ask. I think you have a much better opinion of me than I deserve."

"Oh, Anya, stop! You're a warm, understanding person. I want you to tell me what you think."

Lena wanted to hear she was right. But I wasn't sure.

"I think if you really loved him, it would have been hard to stay."

"Yes, that's it!" Her voice rang with unusual energy. "It's worse than if he had died, because there's nothing good left to remember. He begs me to take him back. He doesn't understand it is his lying, not his acts, I'm unable to tolerate. My parents believe I've got another man. More than likely I'll never see them again. They'll pass away thinking I destroyed my family. If they were here . . ." Lena began to cry.

Tears slowly started rolling out onto my cheeks. Here was a life I would not have dreamed existed.

seven

I left the bank with a certified check in my purse for one thousand two hundred fifty dollars, made out to Gennady Korsunsky, D.D.S.

I thought of Lena. She met a lie and stood up to it—at a terrible cost. Would she have done the same if her children were small, if she knew no English, had no skills, no friends?

I stopped at the new Baskin-Robbins for ice cream. It had opened last summer to the delight of local residents. The owner, Nancy Li, a small, round-faced Chinese woman with short, black hair was sitting on a high round stool behind a display of cakes, reading a book. When I entered, she marked the page with a napkin and jumped off the stool.

"Miz Anna! How are you? How's Tanya?"

I had tutored Nancy's daughter, Linda, in computer programming when we lived near their old store in the East Rogers Park area of Chicago. Linda looked like her mother, only taller and thinner; she was extremely bright and didn't require much help. Because I refused compensation, for three years afterwards, Nancy presented us with an ice cream cake on Thanksgiving Day. She doesn't know my new address, so she hadn't done so this year, but I could count on a scoop of my favorite—chocolate chip ice cream—and a lively conversation any time.

The smile on Nancy's face was so wide she looked all teeth. She clasped my hand with hers.

"My Linda is getting married in June! On the twenty-eighth. You and Tanya are invited. We will mail you invitation. Give me your new address, please."

"Congratulations! Who is she marrying?"

"American! Rick! Mother Irish, father half-Polish, half-German. Thirty years old, blond, blue eyes, not tall, very nice, very nice! If my husband alive, he be very proud, very proud."

Her eyes reddened, the smile remained frozen for a moment.

"Where is the wedding going to be?"

"Rented a hall, very big hall." Nancy renewed her smile. "Lawyer, he's a lawyer. Has to invite clients, important people. He pays for hall. My brother coming from Taiwan. When I left he was a boy, he has three children now." She shook her head in amazement. "Where is your nice American gentleman? He came here three weeks ago with Tanya. Very nice, very nice. American, not lazy. Our Rick not lazy, either. You should get married, have good life, you deserve it. I give you ice cream free for wedding."

She filled a cone with a scoop of chocolate chip ice cream and ran out from behind the counter. The long yellow jacket with big buttons and wide navy-blue pants made her look even shorter. I sat at a window table while Nancy chirped on about a wedding dress adorned with pearls and "lots and lots" of flowers.

A heavy man in untied athletic shoes, laces dragging along the ground, tramped in with rosy-cheeked twin boys in tow.

"Hi, there!" he said breathing heavily. The boys unzipped their jackets, producing round tummies and dirty t-shirts. They pressed their faces and palms to the display as their father purchased cups of ice cream for them. They plopped at a table on the far side and proceeded to shovel ice cream into their mouths. Their father belched from behind a newspaper.

"Americans!" whispered Nancy in a what-else-do-you-expect tone.

Though we're the same age, Nancy makes me feel like a young girl enjoying dessert as her mother looks on. I wonder if this is how Tanya feels.

Fima used to take us for ice cream at an outside café on Kreshchatik Street. Kreshchatik Street is Kiev's main street, filled with gaudy architecture of the Stalin era. Fima was good at finding seats. Even in the most crowded restaurants he would just sneak to the front of the line.

I preferred to sit on the second floor of the café to watch the weekend or holiday crowds, with women in flowery dresses and open sandals, men in white shirts guiding their ladies by the elbow.

When I was little, Sasha sometimes treated me to ice cream. He always brought it to the house, as Lonya considered eating outside bad manners.

Feeling a sudden chill I looked out the window. The sky had darkened noticeably. Hopefully the snow won't start until Tanichka is back. Irena says Yuri is a good driver, but he is only seventeen. I wonder how he deals with Irena. His father satisfies his revenge by sleeping in other beds, right under her nose.

Irena assumes she's won because Vilen doesn't fight back. Yuri seems to be suspiciously submissive with Irena, not like his older brother Vadim. For her sake, I hope Yuri is not going to repay her as cruelly as his father has. Frankly, I'm glad Yuri isn't attracted to Tanya.

Vera's different; she's watchful and reserved. Tanya looks up to her. I wonder if she's told her about Fima's letter. I used to tell Asya about everything, except Sasha. I should meet Vera's parents.

And Lena. It's hard to believe someone could spend their life in the Soviet Union and still be so susceptible to pain. She doesn't know how to behave when she's not being adored.

Nancy has such a bubbly, clear-eyed disposition. She's got everything in the right perspective. I always thought I did too. It seems, since Fima's letter, I've gotten into the habit of picking apart every emotion, every particle of my memory. The discovery that I have not been a saint and that my life was built on imperfect circumstances seems to make me disconsolate.

"Miz Anna, want more ice cream? There's lots more chocolate chip!"

"No thanks, Nancy. Tanya went to the movies with some friends and I want to get home before she gets back."

The old lady that walks with a book was peering out of her window as I walked by. I have never seen her full face this closely before. It was long, unsmiling, and dark against her white hair. She raised her hands, fixing her hair in an instinctively feminine movement. She watched me pass by as I wondered if that's how I'll be when Tanya is gone.

I made some turkey salad, put the kettle on, checked the house, and finally settled on the sofa to finish *Murder on the Orient Express.*

Simultaneously, the cuckoo and the phone tore through the quiet. My heart jumped as I put the book down and picked up the receiver.

"It's me. We decided to have something to eat after the movie at Great Godfrey Daniel's. We just got here, and we're waiting for a table."

Sounds so funny, "we decided." Hard to get used to. She's growing up.

"Do you have enough money?"

"Don't worry, I'm not that hungry, anyway."

She doesn't have enough.

"Are you glad you went?"

"Yeah, we're having a good time. I'll be home soon."

"Drive carefully." Too late—the line was already silent. I picked up my book and stretched out on the sofa.

The light switch clicked.

"Mom?"

"What?" I responded sitting up, still half-asleep, my contentment deepened by a still distinct dream. A Chinese lady in a pink blouse with a white, round collar was handing an ice-cream cone to a man with Sasha's rounded back and dark-brown hair. The man was endlessly counting coins. The lady stared at me, pointing her finger at the man, repeating desperately, in perfect Russian, "It's Sasha! It's Sasha!" I could feel myself holding my breath, keeping my eyes on the man's head, willing him to turn and look at me. A happy warmth relaxed my muscles and flowed through my body.

Tanya sat on the floor next to the sofa eating turkey salad directly from the bowl I had made it in. After several forkfuls she put the dish in her lap, exhaled, and started chewing slower.

"Do you think my father will answer the letter I sent?"

"I don't know."

She chewed, frowning, looking vacantly in front of her.

"I had only six dollars after paying for the movie. Vera didn't have anything, so we split a sandwich. I'm so hungry," she said shoving another forkful of turkey salad into her mouth. "Yuri offered to pay for her, but she wouldn't let him. She told him she wasn't his date. I think he's a little afraid of her. She always knows what she wants."

You're jealous, my little girl, you enjoy his failure.

"Did Yuri mind that you went with them?"

"I think he did at first, especially since his friend was with a girl, but Vera knew the girl's sister and made it seem like we were just all together."

"Tanichka, you need to give me Vera's phone number."

"Okay."

"Tell me about her family."

"She won't talk about them. Isn't that weird? I've met her father a couple of times. She said he asked about us."

"What about her mother?"

"She just whispers and nods and goes into her room when I'm there. She has sad eyes. Her father's nice. He actually talks to us and I think he's really interested in what we say."

"Does she have any brothers or sisters?"

"I don't think so. She wants to be a psychiatrist. She decided a long time ago."

"Well, you decided, too, didn't you?"

"Yeah." Tanya looked up excitedly. "It would be nice to share offices. I can be the pediatrician treating the kids and she can be the psychiatrist treating the parents. It'll take ages until we're done: high school, college, medical school, internship, residency. Why does it take so long? I wish I were older."

I started laughing. "Oh no, you don't!"

eight

The Monday after Thanksgiving was a working day in name only. After four days off, everyone was still in vacation mode. I found Jack in my office, legs stretched out, the sports section of the *Chicago Tribune* in his lap. He looked tired, his eyes puffy and dark behind his glasses.

"You look like you haven't slept in days."

"Mother had a million last-minute errands. From nine until I took her to the airport I never left the car. When I finally got home I went straight to the PC and stayed glued to it until four o'clock this morning. My presentation has to be ready Friday—that is, if I want to sell my software."

He rose to give me a quick kiss. His shirt was missing a button.

"This company was to have finished screening software bids last week. When I threw in two years free maintenance, they agreed to give me until Friday to make my presentation. There's absolutely no chance of rescheduling. I have to be ready. This could be the big break I've been waiting for. The only problem is, they're in Green Bay."

We went to the coffee room in our area. We were discussing Disney World when Rose Schultz strolled in, yawning ferociously, her immense breasts roaming freely under a loose, yellow top.

"Hi, guys! God, I'm tired!"

I met Rose for the first time in the company parking lot after my interview. She stood by her car shifting from one foot to another and glancing at her watch desperately. In her red top and sea-green, wide slacks she resembled a flag.

"The battery's dead," she offered as explanation, "and my mother is waiting for me to pick her up." She gave her watch a final glance and turned to walk toward the guard's station.

"I could drive you," I said.

Rose stopped in her tracks.

"Come on, girl, you don't know where my mother lives! Thirty miles each way."

I made a simple calculation.

"As long as I'm back before six, when my daughter comes home from school."

She didn't take me up on the offer, but she hugged me, her body swallowing mine.

On my first day at work, I discovered that my coworkers had been apprised of what Rose advertised as a noble gesture toward a complete stranger.

"We weren't strangers. I knew that we would be working together," I protested, trying to put my good deed in perspective.

Everyone listened politely to my attempts to explain the Russian friendship concept, but they only thought I was overly modest. Rose became my benefactor, infinitely patient with my halting English and ignorance in American ways. She introduced me to Chinese food and the idea of doggy bags.

George, our boss, stuck his arm through the doorway, pointing to his watch. Reluctantly, we got up. Rose followed me into my office, continuing her story of her family's annual reunion. I could listen to Rose's family stories forever. We were interrupted when the phone rang.

"I'd better go," said Rose regretfully, heaving herself out of the chair.

I picked up the phone. "Good morning, Anna speaking."

"You never called me back Saturday," reproached Natasha. "You weren't home yesterday, either."

"I went shopping with Tanya, then to the library."

"What's new?"

"Nothing."

"Same here. Counting the days to when I'll see Isaak. Are you still upset?"

"Listen, Natasha, I'm not upset. I just don't think we need to talk every day and report every little thing. It takes the fun out of our friendship and makes it more like a job."

"What's happened to you, Anya? You've changed practically overnight. Why can't you tell me what's wrong? It's not a job. You and I have no one else to confide in."

Better not tell Natasha anything about Jack's presentation on Friday. What if he's not successful? I would never be able to present anything. He's so untidy. He needs a new tie.

"Natasha, I'm tired. Most of our conversations are so insignificant they remind me of a ten-year-old's diary. I hope you don't feel offended, but it's true."

"I do feel offended."

Jack definitely needs a tie. Not a shirt, he's got more than enough. Why spend the money? I should remind him to stop at the cleaner's tonight.

"I'm sorry. I have to go now. I haven't even turned on my computer. Good-bye, Natasha."

I walked through the machine-oil smell of the production area to the engineering department. Lena was diligently punching buttons on her calculator. She looked up with a quiet smile, reading my eyes.

"Lunch at eleven-thirty or twelve?" I asked.

"At twelve, if it's all right with you. I have a meeting at eleven."

Back in my office, Pat McDonald's face materialized in my doorway.

"Anna, did you change the pricing module specs? Oh, and how was your holiday?"

These people make me feel I'm part of a family, make me feel like everyone else.

Jack's closets are full of worn shirts, wrinkled suits, silk ties that look like rope, enough to make trips to the cleaners as infrequent and expensive as possible. I don't usually get involved in buying his clothes; however, when he still hadn't gone to the cleaners by Wednesday, I started to worry he'd show up for the presentation in a rumpled suit and spotted tie.

Gloom descended on him as soon as I mentioned shopping, but he didn't resist. I suspect he was pleased by my interest.

He insisted on Saks, where he took the first tie his fingers could grab off the rack. I put the tie back and proceeded to interrogate him about the suit he planned to wear on Friday. After his stubborn "I have a couple of clean suits left," I decided a tie that goes with everything would be best.

He finally gave up, standing dejectedly by the counter, as I spread out an array of what I visualized as a winning addition to whatever his remaining clean suits were.

"Jack, what do you think?"

"I sort of like the green and yellow striped one on the rack."

"What!"

"Well, maybe not. How about this gray-and-red one? I still have a clean gray suit."

"Very good, Jack. I'm very proud of you."

"Never thought I'd live to hear that," Jack chuckled.

We completed the rest of his shopping almost painlessly and picked up ribs on the way home.

"Ribs! I love ribs. Jack, you're wonderful," Tanya said the minute we opened the door. She carried the box off to the kitchen. "Boy, am I glad I didn't eat yet."

"Tanya, you say the same thing about everything we bring home. I think you just love food," Jack teased.

"Mom, Mrs. Graff called five minutes ago. She asked for you."

Jack and I looked at each other in surprise.

After the ribs were completely devoured, I called Mrs. Graff. Jack sat on the sofa pretending to read Tanya's essay, while she finished another project in our little office.

Mrs. Graff's voice, aging and throaty, answered on the second ring.

"Good evening, Anna, dear, so good of you to call me back. I wanted to thank you for asking me to your Thanksgiving party. It was lovely, just lovely. How have you been since? Very good, glad to hear it. I'm fine, too, thank you. Had to rest when I got home. Travel is not easy at my age.

"Anna, I need to chat with you for a few minutes. I appreciate you, dear, you're a doll. Hear me out, would you, darling? I'm getting older, and my son worries me more and more. You know how we mothers are. I gave him everything. Now it's time for him to start a family. We're both women, I'm certain you understand my feelings. He's so stubborn. Got divorced over nothing. I assure you, Marsha was not merely good-looking, but a glorious creature and came from a good home. The sweetest girl, she simply adored him. If my husband had been alive, it would have been different. Jack's still a young, handsome man. It's not too late."

I was quiet for so long listening to Mrs. Graff that Jack put aside the essay and raised his head with a worried expression, making him look momentarily like his mother.

"Anna, my dear, you are a smart woman, practical, too, and I'm a fair person. I would never dream of interfering between you and Jack. But if you care for him, you should let him go. Any divorced or widowed man with children would be overjoyed to have you. Maybe one of your Russian community. You deserve to be happy. As for Jack, there are many presentable women in their thirties, anxious to settle down and have children. Tanya's such a pretty, well-mannered young lady, a credit to you. Jack should have children, too. I want grandchildren. Jack feels responsible for you and Tanya, especially as you're an immigrant. I'm afraid we taught him to do good deeds without regard for his own interests.

"Anna, you know I like you. You are a most deserving woman with your daughter's best interests in mind. I can't blame you, it's only natural."

My God, will this ever end?

"Mrs. Graff," I interrupted coolly.

Jack's eyes questioned me as he paced, his hands jammed in his pockets.

I spoke in a low voice. "You're right, I also want my child to have a family. Jack and I have no plans for the future. If he meets someone worthy of his affection, I'll be happy for him."

Jack stopped in front of me, his brows drawn together.

"Unfortunately, whether you believe me or not, that doesn't change the fact that he does not see himself as a family man."

"My dear, he doesn't because you are there, in need of his help and support. As a woman you should be wise, and . . ."

"I don't know what one calls 'wise,' but I know a person cannot be forced to do what he does not want to do. Mrs. Graff, I know you won't believe that as nice as receiving support would be, I don't take money from Jack, and I have no designs on Jack. Another thing—Jack may not be happier without me."

"Anna, I'm not talking about money!" Mrs. Graff sputtered. "I'm talking about his time, his energies."

"I'm sorry, Mrs. Graff, I can't help you."

Jack reached out to grab the receiver; I pushed his arm away.

Mrs. Graff's good-bye was short and hostile.

"Jack, relax, your mother's right," I said as soon as the receiver was down. "What's the point in wasting your time with me? There's no future for us." I ignored the hurt expression on his face.

"I enjoy what we've got," Jack said earnestly. "For once I'm part of something meaningful. I wouldn't mind our living together. Tanya's a big girl. I don't think she'd object. Okay, okay," he raised his hands in response to my look. "Anyway, I'll talk to my mother and straighten her out."

"No," I said heatedly, recognizing tears in my voice. "She's right. I think I would die if Tanya told me she was never going to have any children."

nine

Marina hung her fur jacket carefully in the closet, sliding a designer scarf down one of its sleeves, then removed her wet sneakers. Her gray sweatsuit made her look rounder than she actually was.

"I picked up your favorite doughnuts on the way," she said. "I figured we, old buddies that we are, could solve everything between ourselves. I mean, you know how Gena is about money."

Yes, I know. He deducted twenty cents a day from my salary for reading, or trying to read, a day-old, used newspaper. Marina had been aware of it, but had never objected. We're not buddies, not in my book, just friends, if you use a very stretched meaning of the word.

Marina's slanted eyes looked at me questioningly as I poured coffee.

"We booked a two-week trip to Rio de Janeiro at Christmas for our silver anniversary. Had we known you wouldn't be available to stay with the twins, we would have made different plans."

"I am sorry, Marina. I didn't know it was your silver anniversary. Congratulations."

"Thank you. Our Polish lady told us she has to have Christmas off, so we're going to fire her. I swear, these people come to the United States and do as little as they can to get by. It will be impossible to find a replacement with so little time and, even if I did, I couldn't leave the boys with a new, untrained person. Of all people, Anya, you should understand." Marina's tone was reproachful, slightly indignant.

There's always a new person. Housekeepers don't stay very long in Marina's house.

"Now you understand why Gena got so upset the other day."

"Whatever his reasons, it won't change my plans."

"I don't believe it!" she stared, her tidy lips compressed.

"Marina, as disappointing as it is to you, it's still only a matter of money. You know how little I was able to give Tanichka. She was a housekeeper's daughter, remember? I don't want to miss the years she's still with me, when I can show her something of the world."

"You've always been paranoid about being with Tanya. She's old enough not to need you anymore. Don't force her; have your own fun."

I walked to the sink and looked out the window. It was still drizzling.

"Listen Anya, as soon as you pay us back, you're off the hook. But you haven't paid us back, and this Christmas you will have to spend two weeks at our house. We haven't known each other for so many years for nothing. Gena needs to relax. He works twelve hours a day, so we spend little time together. It's an art to keep a husband these days. So much envy and jealousy around. In the Soviet Union, a man would have a one-night stand every now and then, but that was it. Here, especially with Gena being a dentist and such a handsome man . . . I'm sure you understand."

"Marina, I'm driving to Florida with Tanya on the twentieth of December."

When my voice is barely audible, commanding, and almost frozen, it means my decision is irreversible, my resolve absolute. Fima knows it now. Marina will know it any minute.

"Anya, you can't. Why don't you take some time off after the holidays?"

"I used up my vacation and sick days when we moved into the house. Since my company will be closed over the holidays, it's the only time we can go. Besides, Tanya is not going to miss school for a vacation," I said with indifferent patience, watching the drizzle.

"So?"

"So, I have no days I can take other than the holidays."

"Meaning, with pay?"

"Meaning, with pay."

"What about Jack?"

"What about him?"

"He will pay for your vacation."

"Jack is not going to pay for my vacation. And I already told you, Tanya is not going to miss school for a vacation."

"Why do you make every effort to hurt me? You act like a stranger. Anya, don't try to convince me you aren't taking money from Jack. I'm not stupid."

The drizzle had turned to mist. I stared fixedly through the window into the dusk.

"Gena would kill me if he knew I was sitting here, begging you to do something, something you're required to do. We have an agreement—a signed agreement. Now I understand how smart it was of Gena to get a written agreement. Do you want me to call Jack? He's an American, he knows what a contract is."

"It's unfortunate, Marina, that our trip coincides with yours. You will have to find someone else to stay with the twins. There's a clause in our contract specifying a penalty I'm to pay if I break the agreement. I have a certified check for one thousand two hundred fifty dollars on my desk. I'll give it to you before you leave. Have Gena figure the balance, including interest and penalty. I'll start payments in January."

"What's come over you?" Marina dabbed at her heart-shaped lips with a napkin. "You've always been so . . . understanding."

Marina went on talking. I turned back to watch the drizzle outside.

". . . so predictable," I heard her voice and realized that I missed what she had been saying the last few minutes.

I had no choice but to face her. What is she still doing here?

"Who is predictable?"

"What's wrong with you lately? You weren't listening, were you?"

"Marina, you will have to leave the boys with your parents."

She spat, "They don't have cable or a yard, and the area is bad." Marina got up, opening her purse.

"Wait, let me give you the check."

"No. I don't want Gena to know I was here. And if you tell him I was," she stabbed her finger at me, "I will deny it. You are a heartless, thankless creature. To think Gena and I have been so gullible!"

Nostrils flaring, she applied lipstick with a trembling hand.

"Should my heart be full of gratitude for your taking us in, for giving my daughter educational opportunities, in spite of her mother not having any skills, not speaking a word of English, for letting me be at home with her after school? Yes, I should be grateful, and I am. But Marina, I worked for it."

When my voice dropped even lower, Marina's hand stopped in midair.

"What you did was not a *mitzvah*. Would you have done the same were I old or disabled? Would you have kept me when I became old? Did I ever get up after five-thirty in the morning? Did I ever eat without being busy with something else at the same time? Was I ever dismissed before ten at night? Did you ever wake up at night to tend the twins when they were sick? Did I ever refuse to clean the seams of your pillow cases with a toothbrush as payment for being allowed to spend time with Tanya after school? Did I not clean your parents' apartment—for free—at least once a month?

"We met many years ago, Marina, but don't play it up. We only knew each other by sight. You were gay, popular, well-dressed. I had one dress, so threadbare under the arms I had to move as little as possible, keeping my arms to my sides. No one could ever say we had been friends.

"Yes, Marina, I am grateful for your taking us in, make no mistake about it. God knows, if you hadn't, I might have spent all my life on welfare, doing cleaning on the side, never learning English, living in a lousy neighborhood with rotten schools. But you didn't do it out of friendship. I didn't, either. We had an agreement and I stuck to it, stuck to it above and beyond whatever any agreement could demand and whatever any money could pay for. I will pay Gena back for his dental work; I never intended not to. I appreciate he didn't do any work that wasn't needed, like he does with others. It's only money, Marina, the easiest thing to pay with. I'll call Gena tomorrow at the office.

"And remember, Marina, what you bought when I worked for you was housework, not friendship. How in the world could you imagine any amount reduced on my debt could be worth more than ten days with my daughter!"

Marina's face glowed with anger as she marched to the door. Her voice held angry tears.

"You pretend to be helpless and agreeable, pretend to be submissive like a slave, but instead you manipulate the people around you. People told me to be careful. They said it wasn't wise to have you under the same roof as Gena. I know you wanted him. You probably thought it would be easy to lure him away. Ha!"

"Marina, you're welcome to think what you like. It won't change things."

Flushed and sizzling, she bent to put her sneakers on, her eyes ablaze with hatred.

"Only idiots believe a housekeeper can become a person," she wrenched the front door open.

When the door slammed behind her I found my hands in tight, shaking fists. I stood motionless for some time, staring at the door. It took all my will to relax my muscles and open my hands. My neck and the left side of my back ached.

Sasha, I need you. Sasha, talk to me. Don't tell me I'm a pagan. Don't tell me to be free to feel, free to survive, but not to be obvious.

I'm not a little girl anymore. I've grown up. I'm forty-four to your fifty-eight. I have a grown daughter, a career, a boyfriend, but what I really want is a mother to comfort me at times like this—and you.

Of what use am I to Tanya? How can a mother be a mother if she doesn't know what a mother should be?

In my mind, Sasha winked at me from across the room, a large Soviet box of matches in one hand, a cigarette in the other.

On my way to work I stopped at Gena's office. A new sign over the front door read "Full-Service Medical Building." I followed an old woman with a shopping bag into the lobby. She wore a black, mid-calf, heavy wool coat whose straight cut made her look cylindrical. The coat, with its fur collar, gave it a definite Russian look, but it appeared new. Perhaps it was just well-kept, something a Russian woman of her generation would be an expert at. A faded, purple knit hat appeared out of place, where only a scarf would look natural. These scarves, symbols of Russian women, are for some reason referred to as "babushkas" in the United States. I'll never know why. Babushka translates as "grandmother," or, generally, "old woman," and scarves are worn by women of any age—but there it is. One of the cultural wonders, I guess.

A gold-lettered list on an inner door displayed four names: Gennady Korsunsky, Dentist; Maria Finkel, Pediatrician; Leonard Korotki, Internist; Leonard Pankov, Internist; Bella Kaganov, Gynecologist.

The building belonged to Gena; the other doctors rented from him. Two Slavic-looking men with paint cans were arranging drop cloths. They paid no attention to the old woman or me. A slanted arrow indicated steps leading to the lab. The ceiling and one wall were freshly painted.

The old woman hesitated, finally heading down an empty corridor. Gena's was the only office open for patients. The waiting room was spacious, as waiting rooms go. Chairs stood facing the receptionist's window. A poster showing the face of a famous actor I couldn't place, with a big smile flashing a set of flawless teeth, hung next to the window. Otherwise, the walls were bare, painted light-gray. A small table in the center of the room was covered with Russian newspapers and magazines, intermingled with old *Time* and *Chicago* issues. The Russian editions were all different formats, demonstrating the multitude of attempts to bring news and fiction to a very literate community in its native tongue. A few of these attempts have been successful, but I couldn't recall any of the names I saw, except *Novoye Russkoye Slovo*, an old newspaper published in New York that had been revived with emigration.

When I first came it was difficult to avoid reading in Russian, but I succeeded, so as to force English into my mind. Later, when English became firm enough, it turned out that I didn't find the need to ever open a Russian periodical, which seemed, at times, to vaguely disturb me.

The receptionist was tall, in her fifties.

"Good morning, Raisa," said the old woman familiarly in Russian as she arranged herself on the first chair.

"Can I help you?" Raisa addressed me attentively in English with a heavy accent, ignoring the old woman's greeting.

"Is Doctor Korsunsky in?" I returned in Russian.

Her eyes widened.

What is it? Don't I look Russian to a Russian anymore?

"He's on his way. Do you have an appointment?" she finally replied in Russian, the initial heartiness gone from her voice.

"No. I'm a friend. I need to talk to him for a minute."

"Have a seat."

The old woman smiled. Her faded eyes and sagging face told me she was probably in her early seventies and, like most Russian women, worn-out and perpetually anxious.

"I would never have known you were not an American," she confided, envy in her voice.

"I *am* an American."

"Well, you know what I mean."

I leafed through an old *Time* magazine.

"He's always late. You know, you're the first young person I've seen in this office. I wish I spoke enough English to go to an American doctor. Or Yiddish. Some old Jewish doctors speak Yiddish. I don't," she sighed. "Language is such a problem." Then came the inevitable question. "How long have you been in the States?"

"Almost ten years."

"You're one of the smart ones, leaving as early as you did! We left in 1979. If not for my grandson's draft age, we wouldn't have left. Now, no one can leave, everyone is stuck. My sister is still there. I'll probably never see her again." She nodded sadly.

The door opened and a couple about the same age as the old woman came in.

"What's all the construction?" the man asked the receptionist.

"New doctors starting in January," said Raisa primly. "Let's see, you must be Sofia and Naum Lerman. The doctor is running late. You have the first appointment."

"He's always late. Good morning." The man, holding his back, sat down frowning. Tall and stooped, he wore a Russian-made coat, too heavy for the weather.

"Watch your back, Naum," his wife said, unbuttoning her coat as she plopped down. Her black-dyed hair had an orange tinge. She glanced curiously in my direction, shifting her eyes when they met mine.

"She's Russian," the old woman assured her, lowering her voice. Sofia smiled with confidence as she reached into her shiny, black purse, fishing out a small plastic bag tied with a rubber band.

"Here is my daughter's business card. She owns a travel agency."

"Thank you," I said politely.

"I don't think I need one," the old woman said with a sense of supe- riority. "My children go on vacation every year, but they avoid Russian businesses. They went to London last year."

Sofia waddled to the receptionist's window to offer the girl a card. Her husband coughed a prolonged old-man's cough.

"I can't afford vacations," mumbled the receptionist, but took the card.

Sofia returned to her chair and addressed the old woman. "If your children have money to waste, it's not my problem."

"My children know what they're doing," said the old woman. "They speak English very well. My son is a manager. I have nothing against your daughter, but you know how some of the Russian businesses are."

The telephone rang.

"Good morning, Doctor," came the perky voice from behind the receptionist's window. "Yes, the eight o'clock is here, as is the nine-thirty. Yes, okay, I'll find out. You have a message from the pharmacy. Yes, I understand. I almost forgot, Doctor, there's a friend of yours here to see you. I don't know. One minute."

The receptionist stuck her head out.

"Excuse me," she addressed me loudly, "what's your name? Dr. Korsunsky's on the phone. He's been delayed."

"My name is Anya Fishman."

She slid back into her cubbyhole.

"Her name is Anya Fishman," she said.

Her face, when it appeared again, stared at me with annoyance.

"The Doctor is asking what the problem is."

I stood up. "I'd like to talk to him."

"She will talk to you herself. Yes, Doctor," she whispered as she pushed a red button on the telephone console. "Come this way," she motioned and led me into one of the side offices.

"What's up, Anya? Why didn't you tell me you were coming to the office?" Gena's greeting held displeasure and suspicion.

"Good morning, Gena. I decided on the spur of the moment to drop by and give you a check for part of my debt. I'll start paying the rest in January. Figure out monthly payments for two years, including interest and penalty."

"You're not serious?"

"Why not?"

"You have no money. Remember, it's fifteen percent interest compounded monthly plus half of my baby-sitting expenses, regardless of where the children stay. Maybe you should think about it again."

"Gena, please remember there's no interest on the baby-sitting," I retorted cheerfully.

The sucking sound in my ear told me a toothpick sat between his lips.

"I'm sorry I'm spoiling your silver anniversary."

"Silver anniversary? What are you talking about? My silver anniversary was last spring! Listen, Anya, I know why you're doing this. You're mad I've just teased you along. I thought we were talking the same language—after all, this is not Kiev, you know; everyone here knows everyone. We have to be careful. I'll tell you what. We'll spend a couple hours together. That should make you happy. It's nice to know an American cock isn't good enough . . . hello . . . Anya . . . are you there?"

I had turned the phone away from my mouth so he wouldn't hear me laughing.

"Yes, I'm here, Gena. You're so simple-minded and arrogant I don't even feel insulted. The way you understand people, I'm glad you're not a psychiatrist."

"Listen, Anya—"

But I interrupted him.

"Gena," I said trying to keep the laughter out of my voice, "I'm leaving an envelope containing a certified check for one thousand two hundred fifty dollars with your receptionist. And please, give my regards to Marina. Good-bye."

All conversation in the waiting room stopped as I reappeared. Grinning, I handed the envelope to the receptionist.

Curious, elderly Russian eyes followed me out of the room. Elderly Russians—the tower of strength of any Russian family, where they watched their grandchildren, waited in grocery lines, shared what kopeks they could with their children—made the ultimate sacrifice when they accompanied the younger generation to this strange, new world. Their goal now consisted of not becoming a burden to their children who busied themselves in discovering America. They lived in comfortable apartments, spent their time visiting Russian doctors, shopping at Russian stores, reading Russian newspapers, listening to Russian radio, attending Russian concerts. My heart contracted with sympathy for these people, hungry for attention, anxious to learn what crumbs they could about the life around them that they will never be fully part of. My mother would have been among them now.

A remembered Russian verse from an old song ran through my head. I sang along.

> *There is a place for everything in life.*
> *Bad lives next to good.*
> *If your bride left you for another man,*
> *Who knows which one of you is lucky?*
> *Roola-ta-roola, ta-roola, ta-roola,*
> *Roola-ta-roola, ta-roola, la-la!*

Thanks, Gena.

ten

20 December 1985

My Dear Tanichka,

I was ecstatic to receive your letter, but the part of it where you attempt to scold me as if you were an adult was disappointing. In the future, please, let your mother express her grievances herself. Write to me about your life, not hers. Also, Daughter, remember, I have to ask my stepson, Igor, to translate your letters; if you continue to write in English, try not to embarrass me. Perhaps you could write in Russian. Don't worry if it's not perfect.

It doesn't surprise me you're a good student. You were very bright as a small child. Your brother, Petya, looks like you did when you were his age, and he's also bright. It's hard to imagine you're a big girl. It hurts me that I have not been able to see you.

I'm sure your mother has been telling you a lot of negative things about the Soviet Union. Some problems still remain, but we have true freedom now. Books which were previously forbidden are being published, and average citizens are able to openly criticize the government. Life is interesting and exciting. We hope material things will gradually change for the better, too. Gorbachev is on the right track and has the support of the people.

Why have you decided to become a doctor? In practical terms, it would be better for you to get into a technical field here. In addition to not being paid well, doctors work long, hard hours. And, don't forget, you'll have to take public transportation to make your house calls. A doctor will never be able to afford a car. Engineers are not only paid better, but are needed everywhere in the Soviet Union.

Tell us your size and my wife will send you some clothes. Not having been able to do or buy anything for you for so many years, it will give me pleasure to be able to do it now.

Tanya, it saddens me you are so eager to convince me you're happy. Regular people, single mothers in particular, cannot buy houses and cars. Why not admit your difficulties? You're not responsible for them. Your mother cannot provide for you — this is understandable and nothing to be embarrassed about. We'll try to get what you need.

Tell me more about your life. I love you and I miss you very much. When you are older you will realize changing my last name was best for both you and Petya. Many Jewish people wish they had this chance.

Since Igor knows some English, he asked if he could write to you. I am enclosing a drawing Petya did especially for you. We are planning on having our family picture taken professionally and will send it to you. You must learn how to read and write Russian so your life will be simpler when you return to your motherland. It wasn't my fault we parted, and I will have you back. I am still waiting for your picture. I love you and hope to see you soon.

Your Dad

20 December 1985

Dear Anya,

Who are you fooling? It's obvious you dictated Tanya's letter, and you haven't described me to her in the most favorable terms. Otherwise, a reply from a daughter who has not seen her father for ten years would have been warmer. Perhaps you feel there's nothing wrong with dictating your daughter's letter. It appears, to you, there's nothing wrong with a lot of things. I expected you to explain how you were able to secure permission to emigrate without my consent, but I didn't find it in your letter.

Obviously, you are not the person I thought you were. How did you hide it so well? My attempt to get custody of Tanya hurt you, but there was nothing underhanded about it. I had only Tanya's interests at heart and I felt, and still feel, I was right. I would not have been capable of sneaking away with Tanya, knowing you might never see her again.

I will do everything I can to restore my proper image to my daughter's eyes, to catch up on what we missed. My wife is a very intelligent person and we are happy, but I want Tanya to understand it was never my intention to part with her, or you.

Most letters that come from the United States are upbeat and happy, but how could you expect us to believe that regular citizens, honest professionals, and single mothers, buy cars and houses?

So much is going on and our life has been very exciting. We are finding out the West is very efficient and we have a lot to learn, but this does not change the fact we are, and will remain, a socialist state. I absolutely insist Tanya come back and will not hesitate to take official steps, if necessary. As I said, you are welcome too, but decisions made about her future now must be such that there will be no regrets.

Tanichka is a growing girl; I'm sure she needs clothes. Zhanna works near a new clothing store. They occasionally have imported goods there. We just need to know Tanya's size. I also would like to suggest Tanya learn Russian. I will mail you textbooks as soon as I can get them; otherwise, she will have problems catching up when she returns home.

My family is excited about our correspondence. Times are changing. If only you could read and see the books and movies available. Nothing is forbidden anymore. There aren't enough hours in the day to digest it all. Tell me if you want me to send you any books.

I'm positive Gorbachev is moving in the right direction. It's a pity you were so impatient. You would be happy here now. We had good times together, didn't we? I will find out what is required for Tanya's return and let you know.

Fima

After hearing Fima's letters read, Tanya sat silently, her chin on her palms. Her eyes, filled with tears, gazed past me. I folded the letters and pushed them to the middle of the table.

"I told you I was rude. He must have been so embarrassed." Tears rolled down her cheeks. She swept them away with the back of her hand. "We go on vacation and enjoy ourselves and he . . ." She rubbed her forehead. "I don't know. Maybe you don't care if he's hurt, and I understand that, but I should."

I clenched my teeth.

"He's really nice. And he's right, too," she blew her nose into a napkin. "Why doesn't he believe I wrote my letter? How can I prove it? Will you let me go for a visit?"

"Tanichka, you must make your own decisions. Whatever they are, I'll support them." I felt like a stone sinking to the bottom of a lake. "You better start your homework now."

Tanya was looking away. "Could you read it again, please?"

I read Fima's letter for the second time. Tanya stood with her back pressed to the sink, not stirring until I finished.

"Tanichka, nothing can be compared to losing a child. I'm not proud of what I did to get you out. I hope you never have to make such choices. But there's no use pretending. I would do it again.

"It's true, I didn't give you a childhood you can boast about. In the Soviet Union, I would have taken you to the theater, to museums, the Black Sea. You would have had a father, and your mother would not have been a housekeeper. Here, I compromised to provide for us. But I never compromised your soul, your freedom to be a mensch, to become what you are capable of, to stand for what your heart tells you, not to be brainwashed or to have the psyche of an educated slave or to be a suspicious cynic, with nothing sacred, like those left in the Soviet Union. I believe I've accomplished this. You'll go through life with good values. I've given you a good beginning, a kind of tradition you may or may not follow, understand or admire, but I've given you a choice. I'm here, Tanichka, no matter what life has prepared for you."

I got up very slowly and stood in front of her.

"Never feel guilty unless you've caused hurt intentionally or carelessly. Never feel guilty for telling the truth or expressing your feelings. As long as your conscience is clear, you need never feel guilty if your words or deeds are misunderstood. If you do, you'll spend your life trying to prove your intentions, and no matter how hard you try, it will never be enough."

Tanya's eyes filled with tears. "I understand."

I'm not going to lose you! I screamed in my head. I'm not going to lose you! Yes, Fima is right. But I'm right, too. I left him for you.

I felt empty, like after a good cry. I hid my shaking hands in the pockets of my jeans. I couldn't wait to see Jack, to get out of the house, to sit in a dark movie theater. Tanya roamed restlessly around the kitchen and living room. I ran to open the door when the bell rang.

Jack sauntered into the kitchen. He looked pleased with something.

"What's up?" he said lightly, then he saw the Soviet envelope on the kitchen table and looked from me to Tanya and back, his brow raised.

Tanya barely acknowledged him.

"Let's go," I said anxiously. The idea that he would start a conversation with Tanya filled me with an urge to leave the house immediately.

"Anything new?" Jack inquired cautiously when the door closed behind us.

"No, more of the same," I shrugged.

As we were about to pull out of the driveway Jack turned to me.

"Anna, I want to offer you a job."

I laughed.

Jack shook his head reproachfully, pushing his glasses up his nose.

"This isn't a joke, Anna. The company in Green Bay is going to buy my software. They want their Waukegan and Aurora divisions to use it. I'd like you to be the consultant for the local divisions, doing the conversions to my system. You could also provide software maintenance on an ongoing basis. I'd take care of Green Bay and commute home on weekends. What do you say?"

"No."

Jack stared at me dully.

"What a shock!" he said with exaggerated sarcasm.

"Jack, what will I do when the conversions are done?"

"Well, thanks for the encouragement. Look, I know this is my first client, but hopefully not the last. Anna, with this experience, I guarantee you won't have any problems getting a job or consulting assignment, probably from me."

"I have a good job already, at a place where everyone is good to me. Why would I want to quit?"

"Because you're worth one hundred percent more than you're making and the technology you use isn't state-of-the-art. I don't understand why you're afraid. This job will start at a minimum of thirty dollars an hour, maybe more."

"It will? What about insurance?"

"You'll have to pay it yourself, but you'll still come out ahead. Come on, Anna, don't be afraid. This is a good chance for you."

"Jack, I have to look out for myself and Tanya. I'd rather have a smaller, sure income than something risky."

"There's no such thing as a sure income. If for some unforeseen reason you have to look for a job after the conversion, I would never let you want for anything." Seeing my face, he quickly added, "A loan, not charity, don't worry."

"The travel would take up so much of my time."

"That's true. But Tanya is old enough to handle it."

"I don't even know what your software does." I felt a surge of panic.

"The contract won't be finalized until some time in March. In the meantime I can train you after work and on Saturdays. And there's one more point on the yes side: I'm not the one who will be paying you, the client will. You won't have to accept any money from me."

I had never detected such bitterness in Jack before. His knee tensed when I touched it.

Emotions are dangerous. One is stronger without them. What I feel for Jack isn't love, it can't be, it's nothing like what I feel for Sasha. But it's okay to be grateful.

"Why the hell I should feel sorry for you is beyond me. Just look at yourself, you have everything and I have nothing. I have no one except my mother, and after she's gone, who the fuck will give a damn whether I'm dead or alive? You certainly won't; you're very careful to keep your distance."

Suddenly, he seemed to relax. He reached for my hand.

"I'm sorry," he apologized in his usual soft voice. "With all the contract negotiations I haven't had enough sleep. Anna, you don't need to fear a hardship around every corner. You know, it is possible to live without them. Of course, what do I, a dumb American, know?" Jack mocked.

"Not much," I whispered smiling at the almost maternal feeling he inspired.

"Well?"

"I'll do it," I said quickly, feeling like a child being dragged away from its sandbox.

Jack squeezed my hand as he kissed it.

"I didn't want to upset you, so I kept my mouth shut, but how the hell do you think it made me feel when you drove to Florida instead of taking a plane? How much do you think a few hundred dollars means to me? What were you trying to prove?"

"Jack, you know it's not the money."

"I know it's not the money. You did it to drive home the point that we're not a serious relationship. Listen, Anna, if all I wanted was sex, I could stop at any bar and have a girl in no time. But that's not what I want or need. Listen, Anna . . ."

This conversation is taking me somewhere I don't want to go.

"Jack, I can't accept your help as if there's no tomorrow."

Jack pushed his glasses up decisively.

"I don't want to talk about this anymore."

What happens if I let myself get in the habit of depending on him, then, when we break up . . . I know he won't always be with me. What if Sasha writes like Fima did?

January 19, 1986

Dear Dad,

Mom has agreed to translate my letters. I'm sorry if you were embarrassed or disappointed by what I said, but your distrust is also disappointing. How can I prove I'm telling the truth? Why would I lie? We're not rich. Many Russians are much better off, but Mom worked hard, went to school, and has a good job now. Soon she will have an even better job. She's going to become an independent consultant and make more money. When I'm a doctor she won't have to work.

Thank you for offering, but I don't need anything. Please don't send textbooks; I don't have time to study Russian. I have to keep my grades up if I want to get merit scholarships. I understand Russian pretty well and can hold a good conversation, but I can't read or write it. Mom said it's okay if I visit you this summer. I asked at the post office and they told me a passport isn't enough. I need to request a visa from the Soviet Embassy in Washington. So far I ordered a passport.

Mom and I spent my winter vacation at Disney World. It was fantastic. The trip was her present to me for my birthday. Dad, I don't want to move to Kiev permanently. It's not practical, and I won't leave Mom; we like being together, all my friends are here, and I already know what college I want to go to.

I had a party at our house for my sixteenth birthday. We danced until very late. This spring I'll get my driver's license. We can't afford a second car, but Mom and her boyfriend promised they'll let me drive their cars.

I know you want what's best for me. Mom does too. She's told me a lot of good things about you. When you and I talk more, we'll understand each other better. I'm sending you a postcard of Chicago's skyline. I don't have a recent picture of myself, but I'll ask Jack (Mom's boyfriend) to take one.

Igor is welcome to write. Tell me if you want jeans or anything. Everyone sends clothes to the Soviet Union. We never had anyone to send them to before.

Regards to your family, and thank Petya for his drawing.

Love, Your Daughter Tanya

A birthday card for Tanya came after she sent that letter of apology. The card looked as familiar as a toy kept from childhood: blank roses and "Happy Birthday" written in Ukrainian diagonally across the bottom of the card. Soviet cards don't have ready-made text for every occasion on them. It's an old-world touch that one actually has to express appropriate feelings in one's own words. Ten years ago I was stunned that for one dollar I could buy a card with what should have been intimate and private thoughts printed right on it. I thought it was the epitome of falsehood and laziness. Now I would be hard-pressed if I had to manage the words on my own.

14 February 1986

My Dear Daughter,

Your letter was a joy. I'm very encouraged by your first official steps toward return. I can hardly wait to see you. Don't forget to bring your school transcripts. We've heard there's quite a waiting list of people wanting to come back, and you will have to apply to the Soviet government for permission. However, you shouldn't have any problems returning; we have enough meters to meet the requirement for another person in our household. Others are not so lucky; there is a shortage of apartments here. Citizens wait many years before they are assigned a place of their own. If they have to wait longer because of mass returns of former emigrants, it's not going to be fair. Many will not be happy, especially since the majority of those wanting to return are Jewish. The alternative is not to let everyone in at once. This aspect has been discussed by the Soviet media at great length.

My hope is that in September you'll start school with Igor. He'll help you adjust. I'll hire tutors to assist you with Russian, Ukrainian, physics, and math. More Jewish children are getting admitted to good universities now, but there are still problems and you have to be ready. Let's not dwell on your future plans in our letters; we will decide everything when you are home.

I'm grateful to your mother for letting you return. This is the best and fairest way to rectify the mistake she made. I will make sure you keep in touch. And, I promise I will help her return when she's ready.

You'll like Kiev; it's a beautiful city. A few years ago it turned fifteen hundred years old, and there was a great holiday. New memorials and statues were built; the main street, Kreshchatik, was completely repaved; and magnificent shows were presented at the city stadium. Even though no additional food or goods were supplied, as many assumed there would be, it was very festive.

There remains the language problem. You should start to write to me in
Russian. You need the practice. Even with tutors, it will take some time for you
to speak fluently. Meanwhile, tell me more about your vacation, your friends,
and your school.
   Did you receive the birthday card I sent you?

                                                                      Your Dad

                                                          14 February 1986

Dear Tanichka,

   I'm your stepmother, Zhanna Borisovna. I decided to write you personally
to express my gratitude for the happiness you have given your father by writing
to him and by considering to return to the Soviet Union. I would like to send
you a gift. Please tell me what you need.
   I have relatives in the United States and, in 1978, I debated myself if I
should follow them, but my first husband refused to give Igor permission to
leave. Now I believe it was for the best. It gladdens me that we will be able to
give shelter and assistance to someone who's returning.
   Your new brother, Petya, is a very active boy and outgrows or destroys his
clothes as soon as we buy them. One of my relatives sometimes sends clothes
for him. I can't imagine how she comes by such things.
   There's nothing for me to add to what your father wrote you about our
life. Time flies, so many changes every day, there isn't enough time to absorb
everything. Keep writing to us. We will see you soon in your motherland. My
regards to your mother. I think she is a very courageous woman and a good
mother. We will all keep in close touch with her after your return.

                                                   Sincerely, Zhanna Borisovna

                                                          14 February 1986

Hello, Tanya!

   My name is Igor. I'm sixteen years old and in the ninth grade. I take En-
glish in school, but I like chemistry more, and I will probably become a chemi-
cal engineer like my mother. You can write to me in English. It will be good
practice for me to translate your letters. One of my friends, Nikolai, took sec-
ond place in a science competition last year. Tell me about your friends. What
do you do besides school? What music do you like? Western music is very
popular in the Soviet Union, but it's considered a bad influence. Western clothes
are popular, too. What brands are popular in the United States? There's a girl

in our class whose uncle lives in Detroit. She wears American jeans, T-shirts, and shoes called Reebok. Her relatives must be very rich.

Best wishes, Igor

These letters resulted in feverish consultations between Tanya, Vera, Yuri, and other Russian teens, and I consulted experienced parcel-senders like Lena and the Kaganovs. All of a sudden it didn't matter who I was buying for; I was ready to buy everything I saw in every store. Finally there are people who need me to share what I have.

"How important can Reeboks be?" Tanya asked repeatedly.

We were following sale ads, running to discount stores, chasing bargains. Tanya bought a box at the post office; it's already full with jeans, a sweatsuit for Petya, Reeboks for Igor, a sweater for Fima, a knit hat, gloves, and a bra with matching panties for Zhanna. Tanya and I were like two girlfriends walking out of the stores after each successful hunt.

I wonder if Asya has anyone to send clothes to her children? What about Sasha's girls? His older one, Nonna, might have her own children by now. She must be in her mid-twenties. She had some developmental problems, but Sasha would never discuss them. His younger girl was eight months older than Tanya. He always called her Poops, a porcelain doll in Russian, for her porcelain skin and rosy cheeks. I only saw her a few times and now I realized I didn't even remember her name.

Tanya wrote Zhanna and Igor about the parcel we sent. She wrote to Fima, too.

March 7, 1986

Dear Dad,

I've changed my mind about coming this summer. The store where I work offered me a summer job and I'm going to take it. My college fund is nothing to brag about and I have to work on it. Also, I'm afraid if I come for a visit we'll only end up arguing because you'll want me to stay. I'm sorry, but I'm not ready for that. Please believe me, this is entirely my own decision. Maybe you could try to visit me. We have plenty of room, and you said yourself there's true freedom in the Soviet Union now.

Love, Daughter

I held back tears as I translated the letter into Russian. I won, I won!

A few days ago the last three-letter batch arrived. Fima had enclosed Petya's picture in an oversized, self-made envelope of rough, light-brown paper looking like it had previously been used for wrapping. Petya looks like he is Tanya's brother. Tanya had the picture on her desk until this morning. I know she showed it to Vera and the rest of her friends.

28 March 1986

Dear Tanya,

Thank you for your letter and picture. I don't understand why your mother stopped writing to me. I'm sure you think your decisions are yours; however, I entertain my doubts.

There's no need for you to spend money on packages. I can understand a toy for Petya, but definitely not jeans or sweaters. It doesn't make sense if you have to work to help support yourself and pay for your education. You will not have to do either when you return home. We have everything.

I'm sending you Petya's picture. The quality is not good because it was not professionally done. Now I understand why it took so long to send me yours. You didn't have to go to a professional studio to have it done in color or on such good paper. You are extremely pretty and look more like your mother than you did when you were younger. Your facial expression is definitely hers, but you look like Petya, too. Without explaining where it came from, I took the picture to work and bragged.

We're planning a vacation on the Black Sea in June. When we return I will go to the immigration office to apply for permission to visit you. If I need to fly over the ocean to convince you of returning, I will.

Regards from my family,

Your Dad

Letters from Zhanna and Igor came a day later. I suspected Fima hadn't checked their contents, and I suggested Tanya not mention they wanted us to send clothes, so we wouldn't be forbidden to send anything at all. It was the only time I interfered with her correspondence.

29 March 1986

Dear Tanichka,

We received your letter. When I mentioned the problems we have getting clothes for Petya, it was not meant as a request. Thank you, but you shouldn't have sent anything; I know you can't afford it. The shortages here are worse than when Igor was small. Even your mother would be unable to imagine the degree of shortages. What was readily available before, even though it wasn't much, can now only be purchased through special connections. Sometimes stores receive imported goods, but the lines are long and the products limited.

Your change of heart concerning your return seems very abrupt. It upset your father very much. Please reconsider.

Best wishes to you and your mother.

Zhanna Borisovna

29 March 1986

Dear Tanya!

I'm sorry I mentioned clothes in my previous letter. I didn't think you'd immediately send things to us. But thank you very much!

I'm very busy now. It's the end of the school year and final exams are getting close. I have trouble with Russian grammar, and my mother is worried because this subject is part of the mandatory admission test for all universities. If I were, or looked, Jewish, she would hire a tutor; but since I picked the nationality of my father, who is Ukrainian, for my passport (to make life easier), I don't think she has to worry.

I hope you will eventually come to the Soviet Union. I would like to find out more about life in the United States. My classmate's cousin is a refusenik from the seventies; they recently reapplied to emigrate.

Bye, Igor

eleven

April is almost gone. Spring has finally arrived, and to celebrate it I spent this weekend painting the kitchen. Before I came outside, I opened all the doors and windows to let the smell of the paint evaporate and, exhausted, collapsed on the faux chaise in the backyard. Not used to manual labor anymore, my arms ached. Just a spoiled American woman.

Tanya went out on her first date today. The boy, Jeff Putnik, is a senior in her high school—a status symbol in Tanya's eyes—dark and thin, with a body not yet entirely grown into his arms and legs. His father owns a small accounting firm and his mother works there as a receptionist. Jeff complained that his parents couldn't rise above their boring occupations and trivial concerns to understand and support his aspiration to become a movie director. They assumed he, the oldest of four, would join the family business after college.

Jeff was a little late, which caused Tanya to call Vera from her room. Then she came into the kitchen and, with an artificial yawn, informed me that she didn't really want to go out and, therefore, wished to help me paint. As soon as she caught a glimpse of Jeff's large maroon Buick pulling into the driveway, she swished back into her room to advise Vera of the latest developments. I heard her begin the conversation with a squeal, "He's here!"

It was a different Tanya who came out to greet Jeff, casual and confident, and very female. I tried to keep my promise of not looking at them out of the window, but I did peek between the curtains in time to see the shiny car roll out into the street and speed away.

Children. I'm glad no one can see me here smiling so broadly to myself.

The winter passed peacefully, interrupted only by the death of Jack's aunt in Argentina.

The call from Buenos Aires came one Sunday morning in the beginning of February, just after Jack and Tanya had left for another of her many "drives around the block." It always made me nervous when she practiced using Jack's new car, especially with snow on the ground. Every time they returned, Tanya bubbled with excitement and I grew weak with relief, silently thanking God that she and Jack were still alive.

He has been forwarding his phone to my number during the week when he is in Green Bay and on weekends whenever he comes over.

When I answered that morning, a man introduced himself as Julian Graff, Jack's cousin, and apologized for the intrusion in an old-movie British-English that made me sigh with envy.

Jack left Argentina at fourteen, after his father's death in 1956. Mrs. Graff couldn't wait to return to New York, a rich woman. She decided never to venture to Argentina again, and her husband's family never tried to dissuade her. One of Jack's last memories of those days was his sumptuous bar mitzvah, with three hundred guests representing the United States, Israel, South Africa, and almost every country of South America.

After moving to New York, Jack visited Buenos Aires every American summer until 1975, when during some social upheaval there after Peron's death he became a witness to a bomb explosion, and nearly a victim of it. In his interpretation, the episode seemed more comical than dangerous. It also sounded exotic because he used Spanish names for buildings, events, food, drinks, and different kinds of cafés and restaurants.

He had been sitting with two of his cousins in a café on Florida (which he pronounced "FLOR-EDA") Street, in the center of the city, when they saw a crowd of people run past the window as if someone chased them. One of his cousins deduced, based on the realities of the time, that a bomb must have been detected nearby. They stood up, but before they had a chance to join the crowd, they saw the people turn and run, with the same intensity, in the opposite direction. They sat down again and decided to wait and see.

In another minute there was an explosion that shook the old building they were in. They thought they were safe, but suddenly pieces of the ceiling began to fall, then the lights went out. The three of them, like other patrons, found cover under the tables. The bartender, obviously more used to these things, just continued to wash glasses in the darkened room. The *moso* (which I think means waiter) calmly strolled over to ask if they'd like their coffee refreshed.

Jack made the mistake of describing the incident to his mother who forbade him, he quoted, "to set foot in that wild country ever again."

In 1978, when his paternal grandmother died, Jack went to Argentina for her funeral. The day before he was supposed to return to New York, an old family servant by the name of Nestor died on the estancia. Taking advantage of the difficulty to make an international call, Jack sent his mother a telegram letting her know that he would stay longer to attend the old man's funeral. She responded with several angry telegrams demanding his immediate departure. The telegrams reached him a week later, when he returned to Buenos Aires from the estancia.

Jack commented that he had preferred any quantity of irate telegrams to an unpleasant squabble on the phone.

Nestor and his wife, Inez, Mrs. Graff's maid, like their parents before them, had spent their entire lives at the estancia. Nestor worked in the stables. He was the one who took Jack riding when his father was away. Nestor had also taught him how to care for horses, and even had him help birth a colt. Inez had fed him what Jack remembered as the tastiest food of his life.

Later, when their son, Guillermo, Jack's childhood friend, took over his father's duties, the Graff family pensioned off Nestor and Inez. But the old man rarely missed a day at the stables where, he liked to say, the horses couldn't imagine their lives without him. When talking about that trip, Jack kept using Spanish words then translating them into English, as he described the estancia, the people working there, the wide spaces, the horses and ponies. His stories brought to mind scenes of cowboy movies, but certainly not of Russian villages.

Jack's so American it's hard to believe he lived his formative years in another culture. And, like Tanya, he has virtually no foreign accent—if you don't count the one from New York.

"What do you know, old Jul called!" Jack grinned boyishly when I told him about the call. "I haven't talked to him in ages."

Jack returned the call immediately, and, to my annoyance, he used his credit card. He switched to Spanish effortlessly, speaking, I thought, much faster than he did in English. To my untrained ear, he sounded accentless. I went to the kitchen to prepare lunch for him and Tanya. After a few minutes he came into the kitchen, his face dark.

"My Aunt Lilliana, my father's youngest sister, passed away today. She was only fifteen years older than me." He pulled a kleenex from the box on the counter and wiped his glasses. "She used to tease me by calling me *baboso* when I discovered girls. Of the three children, she's the last to go." Jack coughed in his fist, shutting his eyes. "I should be able to make it to the funeral on Wednesday. Damn it, my travel agent is on vacation!"

Jack did nothing without an agent.

"Let me call Mother." He went back to the living room to call Miami.

I rummaged in my purse and found the business card that Sofia, Gena's patient, had given me several months ago when I went to his office to pay him part of my debt. When Jack joined us in the kitchen I handed him the card, proud to be of help for once, aware that the service for an American in a Russian-owned business would be exceptional. And, apparently, it was. He picked up his ticket the next morning, impressed with the agent's efficiency.

Jack ended up being away for ten days, spending the last two days at the estancia, visiting with Inez and Guillermo, who was now the father of four. When he returned, accounting to his mother for every item in Aunt Lilliana's will was no easy task. Mrs. Graff considered it a snub she wasn't mentioned, even as a token, and thought it was unfair that her son, the favorite nephew of his childless aunt, inherited the same percentage of her estate as the others. Jack thought her expectations in bad taste as, by his own admission, both he and his mother could live more than comfortably, for the rest of their lives on what his father had left them.

He described Buenos Aires as a city somewhat like Paris, with its balconies and sidewalk cafés. He gave Tanya a picture postcard book he bought at *Librerias ABC*, his favorite book store on Florida Street. One photo showed Avenida 9 de Julio, the widest street in the world, with an enormous obelisk where it crossed Corrientes Avenue, surrounded by tropical-looking trees and Parisian-style office buildings. Just beautiful. Another picture, one of the Teatro Colón Opera House, reminded me of a picture I'd seen of La Scala. When Jack's father was alive they had had their own box. Jack confessed that when he got bored, he would sneak down to the theater museum to gaze at the ancient costumes and musical instruments.

"One of these days we should go to Buenos Aires," Jack suggested when he saw my eyes light up as I listened to him and looked at the pictures. "I'll show you around, you'll meet my relatives. They're a fun bunch. You'll like them."

"How do you know?"

"I think you like big-hearted people, and my cousins are generous in everything they do. We could go after the implementation."

I laughed.

"What's so funny?"

"Jack, college for Tanya is around the corner. On top of my mortgage, I still have other debts. It's a miracle I could afford Florida, let alone Argentina. It sounds like a fairy tale."

"I see."

When Jack's expression became unreadable I knew he resented what I said.

The telephone rang inside the house. My brain told my body to get up but my body refused to move from the chaise under the tree. Most calls are for Tanya. With boys, it's strictly about school. With girls, like any teenager, she gives a lot of advice on how to act on dates.

It's unforgivable that I haven't made an effort to meet Vera's parents. On the other hand, they don't seem anxious to find out where their daughter spends so much of her time.

I'll miss seeing Lena every day when I start my new job. Sometimes I have an urge to blurt out the story of my life to her, to experience the luxury of feeling sorry for myself, to relive my most shameful deeds and most exhilarating moments, but the fear of getting used to self-pity and becoming a whining weakling holds me back.

Lena's daughter, Svetlana, has refused to speak to her mother since Lena rejected Serozha's attempts at a reconciliation. Lately, Lena looks smaller, her girlish bangs hanging sadly. Her son, Boris, has become involved in a used-car scam, telling his mother he enjoys fooling fools. His new American girlfriend, Melanie, has moved in with them. Lena's house doesn't feel her own with so much English in it, or with a strange blonde who fills the refrigerator with beer cans. Poor Lena.

There have been persistent rumors Gorbachev will let the refuseniks of the 1970s leave the Soviet Union, and Lena's parents are getting ready to reapply for emigration. Lena sent them a phony Israeli invitation and now lives day-to-day, waiting for them to receive permission to leave.

The general opinion is that a mass exodus, like that of the late 1970s, will never happen again. The Soviet regime does not make mistakes that are good for people twice. Gorbachev reaffirmed that attitude by stating publicly to foreign journalists that whoever wished to leave his country had already done so. He then proceeded to tell them the rest are happy where they are; thus, there is no need for emigration. By definition, it would be impossible for Gorbachev to be different from his predecessors. If he was, he would not be in the position he is in.

Bella's getting ready to visit her mother and sister in Kiev. She feverishly haunts discount stores, buying up jeans, underwear, shoes, and as many sale items as humanly possible. She'll have to be shrewd to get most of it into the Soviet Union without paying a duty. She'll wear two pairs of jeans, several bras and pairs of pantyhose. She'll take the tags off the women's clothing so it looks like her own. Children's and men's clothes will have to be paid for. She'll take her new luggage in but not out. She'll only need an overnight bag to come back. After all, what could the Soviet Union have she would want to bring home, except for people she can't bring back.

Natasha and I have talked infrequently but amiably, mostly about her trip to Israel. On the surface, she took Isaak's decision to live there rather matter-of-factly, but we both knew that she suffered from loneliness. She perked up somewhat when a coworker—"a burly Irish guy, extraordinarily naïve, even for an American"—had asked her out to chat about her "fascinating Russian background."

Nina and Izya's daughter, Lana, married her long-time boyfriend, Slava. The ceremony and the reception at a Russian restaurant were well-organized, like everything involving Nina. Tanya vehemently refused to go to the wedding with us, saying, "I will not be seen with the

Russian-restaurant crowd." I, too, dislike these packed, noisy islands of Soviet attitudes and relationships, stages for displaying flashy jewelry, furs, glittery clothes, big-chested women, heavy-set, self-made men, and not-too-ambitious youth.

The custom of gift-giving has been replaced with a mandatory check in an amount more than covering what your host has spent on you; I miss the intimacy of selecting a gift that would bring a smile and memories. This new rule seemed to fit with so many fake relationships—with all the trimmings—friendships easily entered, quickly built, routinely broken with no regrets.

The checks, secreted inside congratulatory cards, found their way into a large tray on a table next to the newlyweds as the guests filed past them offering their best wishes. Nina wore a all-light-gray, full-length, silk dress with one gentle-pink sleeve and a gentle-pink brooch. The gray of her outfit matched her new son-in-law's tuxedo. Lana, her upper lip wet with perspiration, and Slava, with a little paunch and the beginning of a mustache, looked irritated. Nina's son, Victor, had bags under his slow, indifferent eyes. His girlfriend, in a sky-blue satin dress and matching sky-blue satin shoes, openly rubbed his leg with her brightly-manicured fingers. Nina and Izya had spoken with assurance about their daughter's prospects, confident that family life would transform Slava's tendency to chase shady scams. Meanwhile, Lana's salary for a clerical nine-to-five job would pay the bills.

At the reception, the high-decibel noise called music made conversation impossible and kept the dance floor crowded by young men with arrogant smiles of pushy salesmen and pink-skinned girls in sparkling dresses. Jack and I were the first to leave. I shamelessly used the excuse of Jack's boredom in being the only non-Russian-speaking person there.

The food and service at Russian restaurants have become better with years of trial and error. The entrees still appear close to midnight when no one expects them to be eaten, you still need patience and persistence to get tea or an extra spoon, and the doggy bags don't necessarily contain what you had been served; but, at least the waiters are not rude anymore. For insiders, most of the Russian restaurants remain oases of old traditions in the new, strange world with new, strange rules. On weekdays, hairy-chested men of undetermined occupations spend part of their day playing cards there. At night, primitive catchy tunes are heard alongside off-color jokes. Fights erupt outside, while inside people eat, dance, lie, boast, threaten, and generally feel good about themselves. Had this crowd been able to do the same in the Soviet Union, they would never have left.

I'm beginning to realize that mentality embraces new traditions and purges old ones like a stretchable container with a spout. I witnessed this process when serving in the role of an interpreter for an organization that delivers kosher Passover food to needy Jewish families. Six years ago Leah-Malka first asked for help and gradually, with every year, I realized that help was required less and less, until this year it was required no more.

That first time, Leah-Malka, agitated to the state of tears, with her wig off-center, appealed to me, of all people, to explain why in the last few years her century-old organization had begun to encounter shortages which would leave some of their new clients, the Russian senior citizens, lacking proper groceries for their Passover meal. She suggested that the culprit was the language barrier. Not wanting to add to her anxiety, I diplomatically skipped the fact that the majority of her new clients or those who, like me, didn't have to become her clients, would not even know, or want to know, how a Passover meal should be constructed. I offered to accompany the delivery team, which included a truck driver, students, and children of volunteers, to the subsidized buildings.

We all met at the warehouse, where volunteers loaded the packages onto the delivery truck. Tanya, who was eight, couldn't believe her luck when Warren, the truck driver, invited the two of us to ride with him. The students and children followed in a van.

In spite of rain and blustery wind, a few of the recipients attempted to see the inside of the truck from their umpteen-story windows to ascertain we wouldn't prematurely run out of groceries by giving more to some than others. The majority congregated in the lobby and stubbornly refused to return to their apartments and wait. No one minded spending hours, if necessary, in the drafty lobby, as long as they would be given a chance to personally accompany the young man who carried their package and the child who carried the bag with vegetables. That rationale had been created and solidified with many years spent in Soviet grocery lines.

The delivery began smoothly, with no particular interpreting required.

"I'm so sorry," an old lady with round, gold earrings, and in poorly-fitting dentures said as she approached me, smiling sweetly, "my neighbor had salami in her package and it's missing from mine. You are welcome to come and check if you don't trust me. Would you happen to have an extra?"

I saw, in a flash, the cause of the shortages. I also knew that no American would see it, they would instead wring their hands and call the warehouse to request two salamis be immediately delivered to compensate for the emotional distress. It didn't surprise me that Leah-Malka's organization had tried for two years to figure out what they were doing wrong.

"Only if there are leftovers after we're finished," I replied politely. "If not, I'll give you a phone number to call tomorrow and complain."

Grumbling about unfairness, the woman retreated. She was not the last to claim items missing; all received the same firm response. One of them, a petite woman in her sixties, marched up to me holding a seven-year-old boy by his hand.

"My grandson noticed that eggs were missing from my package. He's so observant," she patted the child's head fondly. "If not for him, I wouldn't have noticed."

The boy's face shone with pleasure as he stood proudly near his grandmother who was repeating the story of his accomplishments to everyone in sight.

"Give me your apartment number and wait there. You'll catch a cold here. If there are leftovers . . ."

"No," she interrupted, "I'll stay right here."

She was not about to allow anyone to cheat her out or what was rightly hers.

I looked at the boy with sympathy, as if he showed signs of disease. He watched the children who dragged the delivery bags with a sense of superiority, exhibiting no desire to join them. I felt a sharp urge to hand his grandmother a dollar so that she would buy a carton of eggs, but it would not have been professional.

For over two hours, they remained in the lobby, shivering. The grandmother kept telling those who passed by of her grandson's unusual intellect. Their sacrifice wasn't in vain. In the end, they received a carton of eggs from a package of an individual who wasn't home.

Every year, the delivery process became more and more American. The older Russians finally understood they would not be left out or cheated. Shortages stopped occurring. No one waited in the lobby anymore. Gratitude replaced arrogance. Still, very few Russians participated in the packing and delivery. If not for my friendship with Leah-Malka, I most probably would not have, either. I met one family that went to the warehouse, but only to request the package meant for their father. They were not interested in delivering for strangers. Well, that's another step, another time, another tradition.

A month ago, Jack and I attended the wedding of a distant cousin on his father's side in New York. It transpired that Jack had originally declined the invitation and hadn't given it another thought until his mother informed him she was going to attend. She had introduced the couple to each other.

Jack called me at work to explain the situation.

"Anna, we'll have to go," he concluded. "My mother was furious at me for not informing her I was not going. It just hadn't occurred to me she would be invited."

"I won't leave Tanya alone in the house overnight," I said, surprised that he would suggest it.

"It doesn't have to be overnight. The ceremony is at noon on Sunday."

"But we're so busy," I said, too tired to offer serious resistance.

"Mother's all bent out of shape," Jack continued. "This match is her big accomplishment. She insists I witness it."

"Why don't you go by yourself? She doesn't want to see me."

"You know how my mother is. I've got a sneaky suspicion that she prepared a *shidekh* for me." He chuckled. "I'm sick of being her ultimate bachelor."

"That's who you are."

Jack snorted. "Fine. You'll be bored stiff, but indulge me, please."

"I won't be bored. I like weddings."

"Well, that's a relief. It's supposed to be a small wedding, less than a hundred people, and, by the way, an orthodox one . . . of sorts."

"Of sorts?"

Orthodox rituals leave little to creativity, in any religion.

"Maybe not in Leah-Malka's view," Jack laughed, "but men and women will stay separated. And, Anna, no slacks and no body parts open for inspection, besides hands and face. I understand this is a concession to the groom's dotty grandfather who is a concentration camp survivor. He has remembered these two orthodox features from his own wedding. Other than that . . . " he paused. "Other than that, I guess, it's not an orthodox wedding."

As if responding to my mental moaning about the expense of a useless, fancy dress, shoes, and a purse, Jack said softly, "If you need something to wear, please put it on my credit card." And, as if he could see my chin stubbornly lifted at the idea of using his credit card, he added, "You'll pay it back whenever you can."

"I'll manage," I said flippantly. "Time to get something dressy anyway."

Completed in one hour, my clothes shopping spree began and ended at Lord and Taylor. It netted a no-frills, midi, dark-gray, wool, turtleneck dress. It fit perfectly, not even needing to be shortened. Four gold buttons along the left shoulder and turtleneck made it look as if could be unbuttoned. The dress went well with my charcoal, soft and practical, not-so-new pumps and a charcoal leather purse I had only used on a few occasions.

The trip to New York was enlightening and sad, but not dull.

Predictably, our morning flight at seven departed a half-hour late, bringing us to LaGuardia at ten-thirty New York time. The limousine sped down the Van Wyck expressway then made questionable progress down busy Manhattan streets.

"We'll miss the ceremony," I fretted.

"So, we'll miss the ceremony," was Jack's grouchy reply.

To me, a wedding ceremony has always represented an enchanting show where nothing exists besides the bridal party. I anticipate the climax, the appearance of the bride, with bated breath and tears in my eyes. Natasha predicts that at Tanya's wedding I'll slip into a coma.

The groom's mother, a solid woman in a brown, heavy wool, two-piece suit with a lacy collar and pocket flaps and almost-flat, brown shoes paused every few steps to overcome pain. Her long skirt couldn't hide the pillows of swelling on her feet, which overflowed the rims of her shoes. The ritual headcovering, in the form of a whitish-material doilie, sat askew on her thick, yellowish hair. As Jack and I were rushing into the room a few minutes earlier, I overheard her reprimand her son for ignoring an important relative called Saul. Now, tears were sliding down her cheeks, and her hands were trembling. What memories, what emotions caused these tears? Will I cry at Tanya's wedding?

I tasted salt on my lips. A young woman in green sitting next to me met my eyes and frowned. She bore a strong resemblance to the groom's mother.

The groom, Scott, tall and skinny like a teenager, with bushy red hair, walked slowly, looking ahead so intently that I wondered if he would notice an obstacle placed in front of him. He joined his mother who waited for him half-way to the *khupe*. Her gait became more confident as she held on to him. When they reached the first row, the mother detached herself from her son, crossed the aisle, and put her arm around the shoulders of a shriveled old man in dark glasses who leaned toward her. She kissed the top of his bald head. They remained motionless. Had the room been empty, the silence could not have been more complete. Scott touched his mother's elbow, startling her. She nodded at him and they mounted the three little steps onto the stage where the *khupe* had been erected.

The bride's parents—her grandfather was Jack's father's first cousin—tanned, short, and perky, entered smiling as if the room was a dance floor. The mother carried her head high. Her shoulder-length hair, dark with blonde highlights, and her naughty expression lifted the spirits. Her headcovering matched her dark-red, satin dress showing off her girlish figure.

Heidi made a very cute bride, dark and a little plump. Her black hair had been twisted masterfully into a high tower filled with curls. It didn't make her look taller due to the enormous skirt of her dress and train, whose edge was held up by two excited, dark-skinned, school-aged girls. She maintained a permanent smile, but her chest rose and fell rapidly. As she walked down the aisle, she winked and waved surreptitiously from under her veil to someone on the women's side.

Scott came to the edge of the stage, holding his hand out to his bride. For a second, I saw Tanya in Heidi's place, and my heart sprang into my throat. I glanced to the men's side of the room, looking for Jack, but didn't see him among the identical tuxedos. The couple stood with their backs to the guests, facing an elderly rabbi in a wrinkled suit who spoke with a German accent. They would look like a flower arrangement if the expanse of Heidi's skirt would envelop Scott, with his shoulders and head sticking out.

After the ceremony, the men and women mixed in the lounge in front of the reception area where they would again be separated. I realized that I stood out among the well-groomed women in conservative-of-sorts dresses, clutching symbolic shimmering bags the size of a dollar bill. I barely had a chance to brush my hair that morning, my make-up consisted of a smudge of lipstick applied during our elevator ride, using the polished steel wall as a mirror. That, and the unembellished dress, the standard-issue, lace-like headcovering, and a purse in which a hardcover book could easily fit, characterized me as a Cinderella before her fairy godmother took care of the details.

Mrs. Graff confirmed this impression by compressing her thin, coral lips and sighing deeply at the sight of me. Her full-length, plum-colored dress with wide, flowing, silk sleeves and a plum-and-white silk flower near the shoulder somehow gave me a glimpse of her as she must have been in her youth. That poor Lower East Side girl must have looked aristocratic, distinguished, and easily identifiable as part of a wealthy family. Her arthritic fingers gripped a properly tiny silver bag with silky fringes.

Jack kissed his mother's cheek, flicked the silk flower teasingly, and pretended to listen to the story of the happy match she had initiated. Occasionally, he waved to someone or exchanged greetings. I prudently remained a few steps away from them. People around me hugged and laughed, looked each other over, complemented the hosts and the fashions, and shared family news. I seemed to be in the way. Had I taken a tray and begun delivering drinks, no one would have thought me out of place. There didn't seem to be anyone with a magic wand in attendance.

"You look as though you came from a workday on a shipping dock." Mrs. Graff pounced on Jack after the subject of matchmaking had been exhausted. "You're going to ruin your health. Why should you get involved in a new business all of a sudden? And you, Anna," she acknowledged my presence testily, "you're falling apart. You should have stayed home and rested."

Jack winked at me and smiled.

"Hello, hello!" A melodic voice behind me made these words sound like the beginning of a song.

"Oh, damn!" Jack muttered.

"Hello, my darling girl!" Mrs. Graff's wrinkles melted with delight. "I've been looking all over for you."

"Our flight was late. We missed the ceremony," the melodic voice reported cheerfully.

An elegant, curvaceous back ensconced in teal silk cut off Mrs. Graff from my view as the cheerful lady touched the wrinkled cheek with her own glowing one. Through a string of black pearls, the teal silk continued up the tall neck, draping it loosely. The teal contrasted sensuously with the blond hair molded into a frosty haircut.

"And what are *you* doing here?" Jack stared at the blonde with an expression I couldn't quite read. Had he spoken louder, his tone could have been described as barking.

"Jack!" Mrs. Graff exclaimed. "Behave yourself!"

He stuck his hands in his pockets and narrowed his eyes at his mother.

"Attending the wedding of my husband's cousin." The blonde replied angrily. "Do you mind?"

"As a matter of fact, I do," Jack replied slowly.

"Jack!" Mrs. Graff stamped her foot encased in a wide patent leather shoe.

The blonde woman's profile was strikingly cherubic, and her figure leggy and bosomy with a very flat stomach. A diamond earring glittered, dangling delicately from her ear. An envelope-size black purse with a gold clasp and a designer label attached to the zipper hung off her shoulder. In her three-inch-heeled pointy shoes that barely covered the tips of her toes, she was almost Jack's height. Somehow, she looked familiar, even though I was certain we had never met before.

"Jack, you still act like a spoiled brat," the blonde shook her head. "After all these years, why can't we just talk normally?" she pouted.

Strangely, her voice shook as if she was holding back tears.

"And, what are you interested in nowadays that you can't wear?" Jack inquired spitefully. "Any more surprises up your sleeve, Mother?" He turned to Mrs. Graff pushing up his glasses.

Neither woman bothered to reply.

"Don't let my son's manners upset you, darling. You look magnificent as always." Mrs. Graff addressed the blonde. "I'm sorry you missed the ceremony. It was very touching." She slipped into her typical monotone. "It's disappointing that the groom's family insisted on seating men and women separately. They actually shipped his poor, blind grandfather here from a nursing home, accompanied by two nurses. And where is your husband? I'd like to say hello to him."

"He stopped to talk with his cousins. Which reminds me . . . I better join them for a minute before the reception starts, or he won't let me forget it." The blonde smiled radiantly.

"I was able to switch you to my table," Mrs. Graff assured her.

Jack's eyes traveled up the blonde's body stopping at her neck. His lips became a thin, angry line. How could a man not lust after this glorious creature?

The blonde rushed past me. Her large, green-with-gold eyes complemented perfectly the rest of her features, her coloring, her dress style. The orangish tinge of her lipstick added a single garish discord to her otherwise stunning appearance. I had seen that woman before, but where?

"See you at the table, Anna," Mrs. Graff said as she walked away following the other guests that were heading in the direction of the reception area. An old, heavy woman in a dark skirt and a shimmering top joined her, then another one in something pink.

"I apologize, Anna," I heard Jack's voice say. "My mother gets the better of me sometimes."

"Who was that blonde woman?"

Only now I noticed how drawn his face was. Maybe not as if he worked on a shipping dock but very tired. I hardly looked better.

Jack rubbed his eyes under his glasses. "That was Marsha, my ex-wife. I should have handled it with more class."

"Marsha?" I looked at him with new respect. "She's incredibly beautiful."

"Yes, I know," Jack sighed.

I could clearly see them next to each other, a remarkably fitting couple. Suddenly, it came to me why Marsha seemed familiar.

"She looks like Kim Novak!" My voice came out high-pitched.

"You know who Kim Novak is?" Jack sounded like someone who just lost his last hope.

"She appeared in some episodes of *Falcon Crest*," I explained, embarrassed by my hysterical-fan outburst.

"Wonder of wonders! You watched *Falcon Crest*!" Jack said sarcastically. "Please don't ask me how I could walk out on such a glorious creature, because I'll throw up if I hear that question one more time." Jack spoke evenly but with an underlying misery that I had never imagined him capable of experiencing. "You would think I should be used to it by now, but my mother's back-door tactics anger me every time. Listen," he glanced at his watch, "we should either go back to Chicago now, or to the reception, if you don't mind my mother's and my ex-wife's company. Those two women are dangerous." He winked, his eyes thoughtful. "Here's your seating card. If it's any consolation to you, I might end up at the same table with Marsha's husband. Well, he could use some commiseration. You go ahead. I need a few minutes to collect my thoughts."

Encouraged by the return of the familiar twinkle in Jack's eyes, I headed to the reception area, eagerly anticipating the company of Kim

Novak's look-alike, with whom Jack had fallen in love and had walked out on ten years later. Wise of me to learn not to depend on anyone.

The reception area, divided by an accordion-shaped temporary wall, must have been majestic when whole. The massive columns around the perimeter and several crystal candelabra reminded me of movie scenes in the palaces of Russian tsars. The divider had only one opening, before the far wall where the family table bridged the two areas. Tall, silvery centerpieces on each table contained a dozen red roses.

Mrs. Graff's drone, even in this crowded space, provided the directions to my table, one of six in the women's area. The location of the table near the entrance indicated, as far as I could tell, the unimportance of those seated there. Of eight chairs, six were occupied. No Marsha.

"The moment I called her, Scott's aunt realized . . ." Mrs. Graff was saying as I took the chair next to the heavy woman in the shimmering top. She interrupted her sentence to gesture toward me. "Meet Anna. She is on the bride's side, as well."

"Miriam," said my neighbor.

"Emma," said a dyed blonde in her thirties, wearing a tailored red suit.

An old woman with a hearing aid smiled, her watery eyes blinking.

"Bertha," whispered the woman in the pink blouse with a bow.

"Minnie," a woman with a meaty nose completed the roll call.

"The moment I called her, Scott's aunt who is an old friend of mine realized . . ." Mrs. Graff resumed impatiently.

"Do you live here in New York?" my neighbor inquired. She had a bloated face with dark circles under her blue eyes.

"No, I'm from Chicago." I resolved to say as little as possible to avoid errors in English.

Emma raised her perfect half-moon brows.

"You might be acquainted with Mrs. Graff's son. He also lives in the Chicago area."

I opened my mouth to reply, but not fast enough.

Mrs. Graff raised her voice, "Scott's aunt realized right away that Heidi . . ."

Our table became the center of attention the moment Marsha approached it. She smiled and looked around, showing some disappointment with the location, then settled in the chair next to me.

"Hi, I'm Marsha," she said in her melodic voice.

The roll call followed, this time including me. I had the surreal feeling of being in the presence of a movie star. It never seemed possible that real people could achieve such beauty.

Mrs. Graff put aside her story to realize full benefits of her family ties to Marsha.

"Some of you might not know that Marsha is my daughter-in-law," she announced loudly, stealing glances at two other tables in the immediate vicinity to ascertain they registered the news. As she correctly foresaw, all the eyes from these tables focused on her. "Unfortunately," she continued with a loud sigh, "officially she is my ex-daughter-in-law, but emotionally she's here." Mrs. Graff placed her age-spotted hand with coral tips on her chest.

Marsha smiled, lowering her eyes.

A stocky young waiter in a black tuxedo and a red bow tie put a dish filled with asparagus topped by a cream sauce in front of each of us.

"My son, it pains me to admit," Mrs. Graff came on-line before the waiter walked away, "showed incredible shortsightedness," she rolled her eyes to underscore the depth of Jack's mistake, "when he divorced Marsha, who is as sweet as she is beautiful, if not more. She remains the daughter to me that I never had. And he's been just drifting along ever since." Her eyes ran around the table without stopping on mine.

"*He* divorced *her?*" gasped Bertha.

"For another woman?" Miriam completed Bertha's thought.

"Rather, for other women. Instead of retiring and raising a family," Mrs. Graff stated sadly.

All heads, other than Emma's, Marsha's, and mine, shook incredulously.

Inspired by the attention, Mrs. Graff embarked on the subject of frivolous divorces.

"Did you say your name was Anna?" Marsha spoke softly to allow her ex-mother-in-law's discourse to evolve without disruptions.

When I nodded she looked at me with genuine interest. The slit in her dress, from the base of her neck to the middle of her breasts, which was invisible when she stood, opened up a crack. I wilted, jealous of her firm breasts, her flat stomach, her charming, radiant face with a cleft chin, and, most of all, her confidence.

"I've been curious to meet you, ever since Mrs. Graff told me about you. You look exactly the way she described you—shy, no makeup, and tired." The luminous eyes rested on my face that now felt on fire.

Now all eyes, at least at our table, turned to me.

"Speaking from experience," Marsha continued, "my advice to you is not to take Jack seriously. After a crazy and romantic courtship, and ten blissfully happy years, with flowers and jewelry, he waltzes in one day, packs up, and waltzes out. Boredom—how is that for an explanation?" The green eyes opened wide. "I don't know what he told you about it, but that's the honest-to-goodness truth. Jack's only insatiable," Marsha brought her mouth close to my ear, "with computers and sex, in that order."

Had Jack liked to watch Marsha undress too? I bit my lip as if it would stop me from blushing.

"If you meet someone else, don't hesitate, even for a minute." Marsha gave me a wide, encouraging smile.

"I won't," I said thinking of Sasha.

Emma glared at me then turned to whisper something to Mrs. Graff who looked at me with disapproval. From her guilty expression, I guessed that Emma was Jack's *shidekh*. He didn't tell his mother that I would be coming, and she didn't tell him about Marsha or the *shidekh*. A comedy of errors.

Marsha and I exchanged a friendly glance. She took advantage of the uncomfortable silence and retrieved a picture out of her purse.

"My son, David. He just turned five," she pointed to a round-faced, curly-haired boy on a tricycle. The photograph made the rounds and returned.

"He doesn't look like you," came the unanimous opinion.

"At least, he has her eyes. I met him last year. A very sweet little boy," stated Mrs. Graff, pretending that the whispered argument with Emma hadn't happened. "My son inherited my face but the personality, that's another story."

"Did anyone ever tell you that you look like Kim Novak?" I asked Marsha who was studying herself in a miniature mirror.

"Everyone does constantly." She seemed offended by the implication that there could have been any doubts, then laughed happily. "That's the story of my life."

"Marsha, dear, tell us about the autographs you've given out in Los Angeles," Mrs. Graff prodded.

"Autographs?" Minnie and Bertha blurted out simultaneously.

"Once," Marsha began, "on our way to Hawaii, I insisted that Jack and I stop in Los Angeles for a few days. Unbeknownst to him, I had had a gray suit made like the one Kim Novak had worn in *Vertigo*. And wouldn't you know," she paused before delivering the punchline, "tourists actually congregated around me asking for autographs!"

Rays of green light shone from Marsha's eyes. Mrs. Graff looked at her, mesmerized.

"They even asked Jack for autographs because he was with me." Marsha laughed a ringing, young-girl's laugh, then a cloud cast a shadow over her face. "Not only did he refuse, he would not even take pictures as I was signing the autographs. I wanted them so much for posterity."

Suddenly, I knew why Jack had waltzed out. But I didn't understand why it took him ten years. But then, neither did I understand what he saw in me.

The entrée arrived. For the rest of the meal, Mrs. Graff conducted an analysis of Jack's traits and completed the tale of how Heidi had met Scott. I ate nonstop.

Sasha and Asya were both at my wedding, the only guests on my side. I used two hundred rubles from Lonya's life insurance to pay for it. The rest of the money bought me a badly needed winter coat. "Wedding" is hardly the right term. I still don't understand how fifteen people wedged into my little room. Auntie Olya helped serve the food and gave me a pink nightgown as a present. Asya wore a pale yellow dress. Her husband, Myron, was in the same suit he had worn on his wedding day, and for every special occasion since. Beads of sweat covered Myron's forehead as he read a poem dedicated to Fima and me, and to the friendship I shared with Asya.

A few days before the wedding the narrow beds Lonya and I had slept in were replaced by a green folding sofa, a present from my in-laws. The night before Fima and I were married I unfolded the sofa and put new sheets on it, white with pink stripes on the edges. I puffed up the pillows and stepped back trying to visualize Fima and myself undressed, lying on the impossibly wide expanse taking up half the room.

Fima, being very proper, waited until our wedding night, deliberately limiting our physical contact to respectful kisses. I was a girl to be married, not a girl to sleep with.

Sasha and Lilya sat quietly next to Myron. Sasha never once looked at me. When we toasted he looked at Fima. Lilya smiled often and pecked me on the cheek with her thick, pale lips.

Sasha, you looked so unhappy and weary. Will you ever tell me what you were thinking? Were you feeling guilty, wondering if Fima would really be as indifferent to the fact I wasn't a virgin as he had acted when I told him. Were you chiding yourself for the times you yielded to my passion? Were you avoiding thoughts of your family, my future, my nights with Fima—my legal bed-partner? Were you trying to make a resolution to take the straight and narrow path—knowing you would not? I envy your stamina, Sasha, I envy your inner purity. I wish I could be pure the way you are. I can't. Like you said, I'm a pagan.

I wasn't unhappy at my wedding. Fima was Lonya's choice for me. They met when Lonya went to a shoe factory with a note from Sasha requesting a pair of custom-made shoes. Lonya's feet were always swollen, the bones of his toes deformed. Fima worked on the casts for Lonya's shoes and they immediately became friends.

Lonya admitted to Sasha he worried about my still being single and showing no interest in marriage. He asked Sasha, one of the very few people he ever trusted, to fix me up with a steady, serious, Jewish man. Knowing the reason for my apathy, Sasha felt guilty listening to Lonya's lamentations. Sometimes I think Lonya died so soon after Fima and I became engaged because he didn't see any purpose in life beyond his responsibility for me, entrusted to him by his mother.

When I finally married, relief was evident and justified on Sasha's part. My obvious contentment with waiting—be it a short walk in the park, a furtive kiss at the subway station, or, best of all, time together in my room when Lonya was in the hospital—to a righteous person like Sasha was more oppressive than flattering. It was unbearable for him to watch my loneliness, to come to terms with my voluntary spinsterhood. My unrestrained happiness of belonging to him was a weak consolation.

Sasha, have you come to understand this was how I wanted to live? This happiness, which came from the deepest part of my being, had a permanent quality over all other happinesses.

In May, I begin working with Jack. The immediate plus will be money for Tanya's education. Professionally, it will bring me to a point in my career which presumes the ability to make decisions, instead of following someone else's blueprint. I admire how some Americans are able to achieve the things they want in life. It's a world I want to enter—I'm tired of peeking in. My English will have to improve rapidly if I'm going to be a success.

There will also be some minuses. The time I'll spend commuting will be time away from Tanya. I know she won't get into trouble, perhaps because of the protective attitude she exhibits toward me, or the commitment to her own dreams and ambitions. We've been more like friends than mother and daughter ever since she was small. There were no adults, so I talked to her like I would talk to myself.

Jack and I decided training three evenings a week would be sufficient, and it took less time and effort than I had imagined to get used to a personal computer instead of a mainframe. I discovered a bug, an insignificant one, but nevertheless a bug, in the way one of the transactions was being processed. Jack looked at me like he'd just made a major discovery, saying, "Your mind is superb." I think I blushed.

The idea of the responsibility for installing Jack's software; making decisions; conducting meetings; writing documentation in English; earning a much, much higher paycheck brings anticipation accompanied by fear. Yet, I feel proud and heady at Jack's trust and the promise of success.

It's time to look for Sasha and Asya. Since Fima feels reasonably out of danger, they should, too. I'm reluctant to write to them directly, even though there's a good chance their addresses are still the same. I wonder how they would react, hearing from me after all this time.

I'll ask Bella to try to find them when she's in Kiev. It's possible they have telephones now. Fima hasn't mentioned Sasha or Asya in his letters. It wouldn't surprise me if they lost touch after I left. He probably thinks they were in league with me, assisting me in deceiving him. They weren't. Looking back, I realize everyone must have assumed Fima gave Tanya his permission. When I received permission to emigrate, Sasha said he would care for Lonya's grave. The short fence around it needed to be painted every so often and fallen leaves had to be cleared. Many graves in the Jewish part of the cemetery are probably unattended now and only God knows if anyone will ever cry over them again.

The phone in the house rang again. I got up and stretched. The fresh air had made me drowsy. The ringing stopped. I walked slowly toward the house wondering when Tanya would be back. She said she wouldn't be out for long, but I knew she would. The phone rang again.

twelve

"Can I talk to Anya?" asked a woman's voice in rapid Russian.

"This is Anya." I tried to recall why the voice sounded familiar.

"Anya, my birdie, good evening!"

"Cece!" There goes my evening. Her time is counted in light years, not hours. "Good evening, Cece. It's been ages!"

"You recognized me! What's new?"

"Not much."

"I didn't know you moved. Why didn't you call me? I live at the same old place. I met Irena Kaganov yesterday—isn't she ugly?—and asked about you. She gave me your number, told me you've got an American boyfriend and bought a house in Lincolnwood. You never come to Russian gatherings."

"That's true. What else is new?"

"I almost got married to a violinist from Moscow. He was crazy about me, but his mother—the bitch—wouldn't let him marry me because she discovered I know—I mean, knew—so many other guys. One needs experience, you know. One day I'll sit down and count them all, arrange them by country—sort of my own United Nations. I never wanted to get married anyway. Americans are more relaxed in bed than Russian men, don't you think?"

There's no sense attempting to answer Cece. She make-believes answers and just trots along. Who knows how she's going to relate our conversation to others. She reminds me of Mrs. Graff.

"How's your daughter, Cece?" I leaped in.

"Lyuda? She's in law school and working. Listen, sunshine, you should come to a night of Russian poetry I'm organizing the first Saturday in June. Lubov Koval is touring the States."

"They let her go on tour?"

"You are crazy, birdie. She's visiting relatives and wants to make some money. Everyone remembers her. She has grandchildren already."

"Well, poetry is not exactly . . ."

"Come on! When was the last time you attended a Russian cultural event? I can't live without Russian culture. You try very hard to have nothing to do with the Russian community." Her voice changed, a note of respect creeping in. "How's your English?"

"Much better. Far from perfect, though. I need to read more."

"There's nothing to read in America. What do they know about literature?"

"How's your English, Cece?" I knew the answer to this one.

"What do I need it for? Women that come for a manicure want me to listen, not talk; men find what they want without any directions. Listen, do you mind if I stop by your house in a few minutes? I'm at a friend's in Lincolnwood."

"Uh, sure," I stammered, not quick-witted enough to think of an excuse.

I waited outside on the sidewalk, enjoying the sight and smell of the new leaves.

Cece—no one knows her real name—fluttered out of a black Mercedes with a double-chinned, mustachioed man at the wheel. Whether she wanted to see me or not, I was sure she wanted me to pay close attention to the car she arrived in.

I yawned. "Excuse me. I just spent an entire day cleaning and I'm a bit tired."

"What's the point in having an American boyfriend if you have to do those things! Can't he hire someone for you? I'd drop him if I were you. He can't have you for nothing. You're too trusting, Anya. Alex took me shopping, I didn't have an outfit for the concert. He owns a furniture store. Big bucks."

I smiled and waved to the mustache. He raised his hand regally. He has to be from Odessa.

"That's his second Mercedes."

I glanced at the polished surface. "Come in, Cece, I'll show you the house. Have Alex come in, too."

"No, my birdie, just look at him, he has no education. Some people think I sleep with him. I wouldn't stoop so low, he has no class."

There was no question she slept with him.

She pulled down her miniskirt to cover another half inch of thigh and marched up the driveway, parading her attractive legs in expensive gray boots. Alex slid down the seat, following her legs from under half-closed lids. When our eyes met he glanced away.

"I've seen bigger houses," said Cece knowingly, after peeking into every corner of the house and fixing her hair in front of the mirror in my bedroom. "Alex's house is a mansion. Even Americans like it. Do you know a rich guy to fix Lyuda up with? She's going with someone, but he just started college, has no money, and he's blond. I don't like blond men. Imagine, she's twenty-three already," Cece sighed.

A car honked.

"This prick drives me up the wall. You and I need to have some tea and chat. I'll tell Alex to wait." Cece walked out, leaving her purse on the floor by the front door.

I put on the kettle and rummaged through the cabinets. No sweets anymore. Size-six Tanya is watching her figure along with size-twelve Vera.

The kettle whistled and the cuckoo cried. Where's Cece? She might have left; with her, one never knows.

From the dining room I saw Jack and Cece confronting each other at the front door. Cece had one leg bent, resting her foot on the rung of the chair just off the entranceway, her blue, over-mascaraed eyes too wide and too innocent.

Jack scratched the back of his head.

"You don't have to leave on my account." He looked helplessly at the round knee in his way.

"Okay, okay," Cece nodded not understanding a word. "Oh, Anya," she erupted in Russian, "I think this guy is your neighbor or something."

Jack turned to me so anxiously I couldn't help smiling.

"This is my boyfriend. His name is Jack," I explained, choking back laughter.

Cece's foot abruptly fell to the floor.

"Jack, let me introduce to you . . ."

"Ce-ce," she introduced herself in two distinct syllables offering Jack a narrow palm.

"See what? What's going on?" Jack was utterly confused.

"That's her name, 'Cece.'" Turning to her, I burst out laughing. "Your name sounds like the word 'see' in English and Jack thought you wanted him to see something."

She completely missed the pun.

"I was leaving, anyway. I told him, but he wouldn't let me. Don't worry, sunshine, if he's your boyfriend he's off-limits to me. He's sexy, you better watch him."

Cece pecked me wetly on the cheek, waved good-bye to Jack, and grabbed her purse from the floor as she scooted out the door.

"He came in a BMW! Anya, you little birdie, you are quiet, but you know what you're doing," she whispered as I closed the door behind her.

I leaned against the wall then slid to the floor engulfed in laughter. Tears streamed down my face. Jack looked down at me, his expression changing from bewilderment to amusement to happy surprise.

He pulled me up.

"I never knew you could laugh like this," he said into my ear as he kissed it.

Feeling his erection, my body trembled. Jack's hands reached for my breasts as I slid back to the floor.

"Jack, please, hurry—hurry."

He unzipped and pulled off my jeans and panties in one stroke, then peeled off his own T-shirt and jeans.

He sucked and bit my nipples as his hands moved down my body. I pulled my legs up and I reached for him. My orgasm came in short, sharp spasms, and I lay astonished and grateful for the contentment. My cheeks burned with drying tears. Jack pulled my legs up, resting them on his shoulders. His tongue brought gasps, and this time when he entered I wrapped my legs around his back and matched every thrust.

It took some time to breathe normally again.

"Well, baby, I told you I'd unfreeze you one day. You're not crying, are you?"

I couldn't speak; I just shook my head. How could I have felt what I felt with Jack, I'm not in love with him. These kinds of feelings are reserved for Sasha.

Go away, Jack. Go away.

The door squeaked, my eyelids sensed light. I touched around me to make certain I was covered.

"She's not sleeping," said Tanya.

Who is she talking to?

"Who are you talking to?" I asked in Russian.

"To Jack, of course."

"Why is Jack here? What time is it?!" I blinked when Tanya switched on the light.

"Mom, are you all right? Jack said you were suddenly sleepy. He was sleeping, too, when I got home. Well, well, you're wearing a T-shirt in bed. You don't let me go to bed in my clothes."

"Did Jack spend the night here?"

"The night? It's only a quarter past ten. Jeff and I had a very nice time. I brought some lasagna home in a doggy bag."

I felt like I had slept through the night. I had forgotten the entire world.

"I thought it was morning," I said embarrassed and relieved I didn't have to get up to go to work.

Jack appeared behind Tanya.

"May I join you, ladies? Anna, may I remind you I can only understand Tanya's part of the conversation?"

I pulled up the sheet.

Jack smiled slyly. "I'm going home now. I don't think you need me anymore, do you?"

I blushed, and Tanya saw it. Sometimes Jack is so tactless.

"One more week, Tanya, and I'm your mother's boss." Pushing up his glasses, Jack winked at me, then waved. "I'll let myself out. See you tomorrow."

"Wait," Tanya turned after him. "I need help with an essay."

I got up, ran to the door on my tiptoes and closed it tightly.

I wonder what Tanya thought. The mirror is laughing at me. A middle-aged woman, in a wrinkled T-shirt, no bra, acting like an animal with her boyfriend. I looked closer at my reflection. My breasts and stomach are still firm. Well, relatively firm.

What happened with Jack . . . can't feel even remotely close to how it felt with Sasha . . . no matter how good it made me feel afterward.

Only ten years ago, Tanya and I rode in the Jewish Resettlement League van from the Vienna train station to an apartment hotel. The young couple in front of me, from Odessa, stared out the window, exchanging excited glances. Now and again the wife put her head on her husband's shoulder, and I clutched Tanya close. A tired couple in their thirties, a heavy-set, bold man and a slim, well-kept woman, with a pouting, ten-year-old boy and both grandmothers in tow, sat in the back. The grandmothers, one tall and the other petite, argued endlessly.

At the border station Chop, we had come through Soviet customs within minutes of each other and rode on the same train. In the belief that, since the man was a dental technician (a money-making occupation in the Soviet Union), the family would be smuggling out gems, the customs officials had forced the boy's mother and the petite grandmother to undergo gynecological exams in search of the precious stones. Both women had cried all night on the train.

I slipped out painlessly, with only a thin gold chain from Asya, which I still have, a gold watch from Fima, which I lost in Vienna, and Lonya's silver spoons and forks, which I've saved for Tanya. I guess, for my station in life, I was, in the eyes of the officials, endowed just right.

Our stop in Czechoslovakia went smoothly. Everyone had brought cologne and chocolate bars with them — as suggested by those who passed before — to give the Czech police and thus avoid being searched.

I constantly visualized being arrested and sent back — cases not unheard of — and held Tanya's hand so tightly she became frightened. At the Austrian border the local police came aboard to protect us from possible terrorist attacks. We shook their hands, and the boy's mother cried, wiping her nose with her kerchief.

The worst was behind. I was on my own.

Two men met us at the train station in Vienna. The younger, in a black hat, bearded, with long curls hanging on each side of his face, asked if anyone was going to Israel. When the adults shook their heads no, without a word he turned on his heel and left. The older man took us to twin vans. We all piled into the front one. The other, containing two stocky men in civilian clothes with a dog, followed. The Jewish Resettlement League, or JRL as we came to know it, was continually on the lookout for terrorists. From the van window I watched pedestrians under black umbrellas crossing streets. The wet sidewalks reflected passing store lights.

I remember thinking: I'm thirty-five, my life is over, but if I have the chance to raise Tanya until she's eighteen, to be with her when she comes home from school, then nothing will matter afterwards.

It's been ten years, and now I'm waiting for life to start. My best friend, my grown daughter, recently suggested I take a marketing class. It makes me feel good that she doesn't see the end of the road for me. I don't, either.

thirteen

I arrived at work early, the third shift not over yet. The weather was May-perfect, an unexpected gift. In Chicago, spring does not occur every year; usually winter leaps straight into summer. The young sun brightened the commercial park, its mesh fence, the trucks parked at the docks, the one-storied structures the color of faded brick. As I walked past the guard station, the man behind the glass raised his hand in greeting without taking his eyes off his newspaper.

I headed to my boss's office for our appointment. George, with the phone in one ear, waved me in and motioned me to close the door. Short, dark-haired, with strong, black eyes, he wore his customary cowboy boots and a starched, white shirt.

"After lunch is fine," he said into the phone and hung up. "Hi, Anna. I know why you're here. Graff and I spoke last week. I must say, I'm not happy to lose you, but I understand you can't pass up this opportunity." He got up, leaned across the desk and shook my hand. "Best of luck to you! I'll break the news to the group myself. Until then, do me a favor and keep it under wraps."

I never had to say a word.

Dim lights in the aisles of the data processing department cast a mysterious shadow. This has been my second home for almost seven years. I could still stay. There's still time to change my mind.

The wide doors to the computer room flew open as a two-tiered cart burst through. Behind it walked Jack, holding terminals with one hand, pushing the cart with the other, shoulder muscles pressed tight against his shirt.

I took several quick steps forward pretending not to see him.

"Good morning, Anna! Where are you running off to?"

I stopped and turned slowly. Jack's eyes were red from lack of sleep. He's not a morning person.

"Good morning, Jack. Why are you here so early?"

"A lot of things to do these last days. And I've got two people coming in today to take over for me. Why are *you* here so early?" He slid his hand around my waist. "You look rested." His eyes smiled as he lowered his face to mine.

I hated myself for blushing.

"Jack, about last night. I don't want you to think . . ."

"Shut up, Anna," he whispered. "You made me very happy last night."

My face was hot.

Jack pulled away reluctantly.

"Anna, the next couple of days are going to be hectic. I'll have to stay late, probably won't be able to see you until the weekend."

A voice drifted in from the foyer.

"Hello, hello!" Lights snapped on. "What are you two doing here in the dark?"

Our secretary, Debbie, moved toward us and playfully smacked Jack on the shoulder.

"I don't remember anyone ever coming to work before me and I've been with this place for twelve years." She left her hand on his shoulder and Jack covered it with his affectionately. Debbie jokingly pressed her cheek to his hand and sighed loudly. "I'm sure going to miss this guy!"

The main door opened a crack, wide enough for a corduroy pant leg covering part of a dusty black loafer. That could only be Bob Kurth, our department training coordinator, a short, young man who always carried several thick binders stuffed with papers. He attempted to squeeze in sideways but couldn't. I scampered over just in time to catch one of the binders in flight.

"Whew!" Bob exhaled, finally coming through the door. He held his broken-handled briefcase under one arm and hugged two binders with the other. "Thanks, Anna! Good morning. Just put it on top of these others."

"No," I said, "you'll only drop it again. I'll put it on your desk."

"Thank you." He turned to Debbie and Jack and said, "Good morning, guys!"

Debbie and Jack waved in response.

Bob traipsed to his desk. When I got there he was already on the phone, the binders on the desk, the briefcase still under his arm.

I returned to Debbie and Jack and immediately regretted it, seeing their hands in the same position. Rose came through the door, a brown bag sticking out of her purse.

"Rose! Good morning! What's with everyone today, couldn't wait to come to work?" Debbie, using her free hand, waved to Rose.

Debbie's hand bothered me and involuntarily my stare kept return-ing to it. Jack caught my gaze and removed his hand, his eyes sparkling with mischief behind his glasses.

Rose's bosom moved like giant waves under a soft, lavender sweater. She nodded to us as she waddled by.

"Oh, boy, I'm out of breath. Better go to my desk and sit down. Had to take my cousin to the airport this morning. She's going to Europe. I wish I could have gone with her."

To escape Jack's twinkling eyes, I followed Rose into her cubicle and sat down. Rose pushed herself into her chair and locked away her purse.

"Why don't you marry that guy? I worry. Now that he'll be working out of town he might find someone else."

"Well, Rose, he hasn't proposed," I laughed.

"Not many guys like him running around nowadays. Good manners, cute, not cheap or arrogant, nice to Tanya, childless, what else could you want? I remember when he first came to work here. He sat in your office pretending to read the newspaper but really watching your legs. I had the office across from you. I saw everything."

"I remember."

"I told everyone, 'Graff's off the market.' No one believed me. Bernice from personnel asked him out, and I think they did go out once. She sent him flowers for Valentine's Day, remember? I told her not to bother, Jack was off the market. I knew."

"I'm not sure you're right."

"Oh, come on, Anna. If I'm not right, it's your own fault. I remember when he asked you out the first time. I knew he would because he wasn't reading the paper, just folding and unfolding it. Strange, for a guy who's been around, he was really nervous. And you, you refused to leave Tanya alone. He offered to hire a baby-sitter, and you asked why. I almost died. Luckily he recovered in time to suggest taking you both for brunch on Sunday instead. And what was your reply? 'I think my daughter will like that.' That was real smart."

"I wasn't trying to trick him. I truly couldn't bring myself to have fun when Tanya was alone or with a stranger."

"It was fun watching the two of you. It took him a long time before he started asking if you'd go someplace, instead of asking if you'd like to go out. You should marry him."

"Jack needs someone younger, Rose."

"Don't try to tell him what he needs."

"I'm not telling him. It's just that I'm too old to be in love."

"I don't know, I wouldn't be surprised if you were in love." She eyed me speculatively. "He is. I know. He's stuck," she said as she left.

The area filled with voices, sounds of moving chairs, drawers opening, clicking keyboards. I sat at my desk looking sadly at the familiar clutter.

I'll miss these people. They'll hardly miss me. Others have quit and have been forgotten.

I listed the tasks to finish. I knew this last week at work would be full of tension. I could feel it building already.

In my mind I was saying good-bye to each person I saw. Thanks to Jack, my resignation had been easy. In February, while he had extended his contract through April, Jack had spoken to Wayne O'Connor about me. Luring away a client's employee isn't exactly ethical, but Jack's negotiations had smoothed the way.

Wayne, now a vice president, had first hired me over two other candidates, both Americans with college degrees. What a day that was! The interview was the first in a month and only my third in the two months after finishing programming school. Everything went differently from the way the placement service had said it should. I arrived ten minutes late because I made a wrong turn along the way. In his office, I sat on the edge of a chair biting my lips, unable to concentrate. Only when Wayne switched from technical to the why-did-you-leave-the-Soviet-Union topic did I relax. It was clear that I would not be hired, so we just talked, my first real conversation with an American. His phone rang several times, but he didn't pick it up.

"This is fascinating," he said after someone knocked at his door to remind him of a meeting. "Well, Anna, our salaries are, unfortunately, a little below the market; however, would you consider an offer?"

"But I didn't answer all your questions," I said, startled.

Wayne smiled. "You got the basics from school, and one can always look up what one doesn't know. You're feisty and not afraid of challenge. That's more than enough to start with."

I didn't understand what the words feisty and challenge meant, but I understood an offer for my first real American job.

"I will work hard," I vowed.

"I'm certain you will." Wayne stood and shook my hand.

Over the years, he has reminded me frequently about that interview, and he has always added, "See, I was right, wasn't I?"

Almost seven years later, a somewhat heavier Wayne strolled into my office after his conversation with Jack and shook my hand.

"Jack Graff talked to me this morning about the opportunity he's offered you, one you cannot afford to pass up." He gave me a wide smile. "I think you both made a good decision and we all wish you the best of luck!"

His good wishes somehow brought back the self-doubt I'd been battling since I'd decided to quit.

God, please, don't let me fail! Tanya has her heart set on becoming a doctor. Please, God, keep me afloat. I'll work hard. Tanya believes in me. Jack's counting on me. Sasha would be proud of me. Asya, too.

I worked until lunch, without raising my head and probably would have missed lunch if Lena hadn't called.

"Did you hear the news?" she asked anxiously. "Sweden registered high radiation levels. They say it's coming from the Soviet Union, who, of course, denied everything."

"Lying as usual."

"All I want is for my parents to get out safely. Are you coming to lunch?"

Lena was waiting for me at the entrance to the cafeteria.

"I hope Bella won't forget to call my parents when she's in Kiev."

Little doubt of that, I thought, since Lena reminded her almost every day.

"I wouldn't worry; Bella's very reliable. I asked her to call two of my friends."

"I didn't know you had anyone left there. Do you correspond?"

"No. My girlfriend was afraid, and the other . . . well, it isn't safe. He is the head doctor of a regional hospital."

In three weeks I'll have Sasha's and Asya's addresses, maybe even letters. How my life will change! I'll have everything I could possibly dream of. If Sasha, instead of Fima, had written to me, I wouldn't be resigning today, and Jack would have been out of my life.

"Lena, I've turned in my resignation. I'm leaving in a week. George asked me not to say anything, so please don't tell anyone. I didn't want you to find out from someone else."

"You're quitting?" Lena sucked in her breath. "Are you serious? Why? Is it because Jack's quitting? Where are you going?"

"I'm going to install Jack's software for his first customer. I'll be an independent contractor."

"I've always told you he has serious intentions. It's not easy with an American. He won't understand a lot of things, but he's a good man. More money?"

"Yes, quite a bit. If I fail . . ."

"You won't fail, Anya, Jack won't let you. He wouldn't have offered you the opportunity if he didn't think you could do it. Where's his customer?"

"One division, where I start next week, is in Waukegan; the other is in Aurora. Jack will work in Green Bay at their headquarters."

"He's not going to be with you?" Lena asked incredulously.

"No," I hesitated, "but I went through a training program with him." When explained out loud, the details of the job suddenly seemed somewhat nebulous, undeveloped. I fretted, "I probably shouldn't have agreed."

"Anya, you're so bright. I hear what people say about you. Why should you sit in this backwater? I wish I had done more with my life." Lowering her voice, Lena glanced around. "It's none of my business, but keep an eye on Jack. He's a good guy, but if he works out of town . . ."

"Lena, as much time as I spend with Jack, he's still an enigma. I can't explain it. No one is closer than the people from my previous life."

"You don't know, Anya, you haven't talked to them in ten years. Jack is attached to you."

"It doesn't matter. I talked to them for more than twenty years before I left."

"It's going to be lonely here without you, Anya," Lena sighed.

"I'll miss you, too. We'll keep in touch."

It would be nice to have Lena with me at my new job, a friend and confidante. I knew no one where I was going except for Bryan Krysa, the general manager, whom Jack took me to meet about a month ago. Bryan must be Slavic; his last name means "rat" in Russian. He's a bulky, young man, with a wide wedding band and a maroon college ring on thick, hairy fingers.

Bryan's office had been crowded with familiar and unfamiliar manuals and binders. A heavy-thighed woman wheeled in a third chair, offered us coffee, then closed the door.

"Glad to finally meet you. Your partner highly recommends you."

Partner? I looked at Jack with the promise of a storm. Jack smiled back politely.

"Ms. Fishman, we need your help desperately. You'll have your hands full."

"I will be happy to help. Please call me Anna."

I sensed Jack's satisfaction with my answer. Surprisingly, I began to feel part of the team as Bryan spoke unhurriedly, using the meeting to unload his problems.

Jack let us both talk, stiffening only when Bryan sighed, "I won't, unfortunately, have much time for you, but from what I understand you won't need any assistance. In terms of getting information, you'll have a green light to get whatever you need from anyone."

I held my head arrogantly high. "I'll be fine, Bryan."

Jack relaxed. It was wise on his part not to have let me know beforehand I was his "partner."

When I returned from lunch, a note on my chair informed me of a departmental meeting in the conference room at nine o'clock the next morning. "Everyone is expected to attend."

I worked with automatic efficiency until the end of the day, the last to leave. I hadn't seen Jack since early morning. I peeked into his office, hoping he wasn't there. He wasn't. Jack's coat was squashed on a chair under a pile of computer printouts, a sleeve under the chair's wheel. His tie hung from a lamp shade. I freed the coat, but it was hopelessly wrinkled and blackened on the sleeve.

On my way out I spotted Jack from afar with a petite woman I couldn't immediately place. He held a door for her and they disappeared into the data processing area. Tired and old, too old to embark on a new career, I walked slowly across the production floor.

Paul, one of the second-shift supervisors, with a pen behind his ear and a cap pushed up his forehead, yelled to me over the noise of the machines.

"How's it going, Anna? Have a long day?"

Paul had asked me out ages ago, long before Jack's time. My English was so bad that when he asked me out for dinner, I eagerly said yes, bringing him part of Tanya's and my dinner the next day. We never did go out, but remained friends. Paul eventually got married, then divorced. He was, and still is, a little jealous of Jack.

"I heard Graff's leaving town," Paul yelled coming closer, cutting off the world with his frame.

"That's right," I said cheerfully.

"Running away?"

"Do I look like an abandoned woman, Paul? Jack found a buyer for his software."

"So that's it. Rumors get all turned around by the time they reach the second shift. How's your daughter?"

"Fine. How's yours?"

"Got herself a boyfriend. A fireman."

In Waukegan not one soul will ask me about my daughter.

I got home too late to catch the news. I had hoped to hear what had happened in the Soviet Union to cause such high radiation levels in Sweden. We'll probably never know the truth.

According to the Soviet government, natural disasters and man-made mishaps do not occur in the land of socialism. And if they do, or rather, when they are so glaringly obvious that denial is impossible, casualties are either nonexistent or negligible, no matter what the scope of the calamity. Only in capitalistic countries do planes crash, does the earth move, or does radiation leak.

Tanya wanted all the details of my resignation, but was disappointed to learn my coworkers didn't know. She considered me indispensable to the company and felt sure everyone would be devastated to see me leave.

fourteen

When I arrived late at work the next day, the data processing area was already humming. A petite blonde woman in soft, loose clothes and a young man with a red beard were just leaving Debbie's desk.

The woman I saw with Jack yesterday!

"Good morning, Anna! Sandra, Greg, wait," Debbie called after them. "Anna, this is Sandra—can't pronounce her last name—and Greg Malone. They're taking over for Jack, and he refused to allow them even a minute for introductions yesterday. The three of them spent the night here. Sandra, Greg, this is Anna Fishman."

"Not the whole night, but just about," laughed Sandra. "What a way to start a new job!" She had lots of freckles and seemed charming. "Nice to meet you, Anna."

We shook hands. I noticed she wore a wedding ring.

"Ditto," Greg said, extending his hand and flashing a big smile.

Debbie turned back to me. "Jack called, asked for you to return his call ASAP. Lena Gurevich called—no message. And, don't forget to bring a chair to the meeting," Debbie reminded as she flipped on her computer. "Hey, Anna, do you think that nuclear thing in the Soviet Union is as serious as our government says?"

"I wouldn't be surprised."

In my office, I dialed Jack's extension. His phone rang three times, and when Debbie answered I hung up without speaking.

The department converged on the conference room from all directions, each person wheeling a chair.

I looked around at the others, young college graduates, twenty or more years my junior, making at least as much, or more, money than me. Of course, they were born here.

A few minutes after nine, George and Jack appeared and stood in the doorway talking.

"Where's your chair, Jack?" complained Debbie. "I told you."

Later in the day Jack's tie will end up again hanging over the lamp shade in his office, or worse squashed between computer printouts, but now it was still in its proper place around his neck. Jack smiled and pushed up his glasses. His eyes sought mine and widened.

Looking directly at Debbie, George sat down.

"Debbie, get Graff a chair."

"I knew it," she snipped.

Sighing heavily, George dropped his note pad onto the table.

"Layoff," whispered Rose dramatically, shrinking from George's black eyes.

"There's good and bad news on our agenda today. First, Pat McDonald became a father."

The group exploded in cheers.

"Jennifer Marie, eight pounds seven ounces, nineteen inches," announced Pat, and then handed out chocolate cigars to all.

George held up his hand. "We have some additions to our department. I assume you've all met Greg Malone and Sandra Dorb . . . Dorbol . . ."

"Dobrovolski," Sandra said with a smile.

"Thanks. Welcome. Both were handpicked by Jack as his replacements. As we've known for some time, Jack is leaving us, and tomorrow is his last day. In a minute he'll present changes in tech support and security procedures to be implemented on his leaving. But before he does that, here's the bad news. Anna Fishman, one of our senior employees, has resigned, effective Friday. Rose will continue Anna's pricing project. Anna will be joining Jack; let's wish both of them good luck." He nodded at Jack. "Jack, you're up."

I heard gasps around the room. Rose's face swung from me to Jack and back, her mouth agape. All eyes seemed to be on me. I stared at the wall.

"I would like your attention, please," said Jack's soft voice. He distributed a memo, then spent the next fifteen minutes speaking in technical jargon and acronyms.

"I will be very busy today wrapping things up, but I will be available tomorrow from ten until noon, along with Sandra and Greg, to answer your questions." Jack smiled unexpectedly. "I have a lunch commitment at noon tomorrow and will not return. I want to thank everyone. It has been a pleasure to work here and I sincerely mean it."

What lunch commitment? He didn't say anything about a commitment. Good, I won't have to talk to him until Saturday when he's back from Green Bay.

"Any questions?" asked George. "Anna and Rose, I would like to see you both in my office."

The chair parade did an about-face and retreated.

Jack, Sandra, and Greg sat in George's office, as Rose and I came in. Rose appeared visibly shaken. I felt bad not telling her since we had worked so closely.

"I need a word with Anna, then I'll be out of your way," Jack told George, then motioned me to the door.

Sandra watched us curiously.

"You're worn out, Anna. I know, I know, I don't look much better."

Jack did look pale and tired.

"In case I don't get to talk to you, meet me at my car tomorrow."

"Why?"

"Why? Weren't you at the meeting? I told everyone I had a lunch date tomorrow at noon. I thought you'd understand," Jack said softly. He looked as if he might say something else, but winked instead.

I couldn't erase the Mona Lisa smile from my face as I watched him hurriedly walk away.

People dropped by all afternoon. There was no point in attempting anything resembling work. I never had a chance to return Lena's call, and I didn't have a chance to explain to Rose. I stayed late and, with surprising energy, cleared off most of my desk.

I came out of the shower to find Tanya on my bed, her head resting on her hands. She listened to the description of the day's activities with obvious pride.

"I talked to Vera and we both think you're going to be very successful. Judy's father has his own engineering consulting firm, and they take five vacations a year."

"Don't forget, Tanichka, this is Jack's company, not mine."

"That's the same thing."

"No, it is not."

"It is to Jack! Why are you smiling like that? Are you making fun of me?"

My Tanichka, sixteen going on thirty. I'm sorry she had to miss so much of her childhood.

"No. I'm smiling because I'm happy you're the way you are."

"You're the mother. That's how you made me."

I'm the mother. Fima's the father.

Tanya scrambled under the blankets and fell asleep amid dreams of a Jacuzzi in our basement. I didn't fall asleep until two and, again, was late for work.

Debbie handed me a pack of pink message slips.

"You're a popular lady, Anna."

The expression in her eyes, only recognizable by another woman, said "What does he see in you? How could someone like you keep him?"

Four calls from Lena ("Please call ASAP"), a call from Jack ("Good morning"), work-related calls from Sandra and Greg, a call from Felix ("Call me at work"). Felix? What could Felix want?

Rose sat straight-backed as I passed her office.

"Anna, we need to go over some things; I reserved the conference room for ten."

Still enough time to see Lena.

"Okay, I'll meet you there."

Lena was curled up in her chair, a damp tissue in her fist. Tissue balls filled her waste basket. The swollen eyes under her bangs reminded me of an abused puppy. For a second my heart stopped.

"Lena, what happened?"

"It's Chernobyl."

"What are you talking about?"

"A meltdown at the Chernobyl nuclear plant. The Soviet government acknowledged it—officially. Of course, hardly any injuries. Anya, my parents still haven't received their permission. I will never see them again, never, never." Lena tossed the tissue she was holding into the wastebasket and whipped out another.

"Oh, my God! They acknowledged a nuclear meltdown!?" I visualized a mushroom-looking cloud like the one I had seen in a documentary about Hiroshima. "My God, Kiev is less than seventy-five miles from Chernobyl!"

"Anya, please, I don't have anyone to talk to besides you."

"Lena, if it hadn't been for the Swedes, we would never have known. I could throw up. Nothing but a bunch of low-life scum over there! That must be why Felix called."

"Does he know anything?"

"He left a message with Debbie. I'll call him from here."

Felix put me on hold and was steaming when he returned.

"Sorry, I was talking to my dear sister-in-law, Irena. Gentile peasant! Did you hear about Chernobyl?"

"Just this minute. Do you know anything?"

"Nothing. I want Bella to come back immediately."

"Do you know what happened to Kiev?"

"I don't care. I want Bella back."

"Did you try to call there?"

"This morning. No luck, all circuits were busy. I'll try again after work. I just wanted to let you know what happened. That damn country! They're all liars and jerks! I'll call you if I hear anything."

"What did he say?" Lena stopped sobbing.

"He knows about as much as you do. I'll give you his phone number. He's going to try to call Kiev tonight. Ask him to tell Bella to call your parents again to be sure they're okay. And Lena, you should try to call on your own, too."

If she hasn't already found them, it would be too much to expect Bella to look for Sasha and Asya. What if Bella found Sasha and he had no interest in me?

I mopped Lena's face, ordered her to quiet down, and returned to my desk halfheartedly.

Sasha, please be all right. I don't think I could bear it if anything happened to you.

The telephone rang, startling me back to reality.

"I will refuse to continue your project if you keep avoiding me," said Rose's angry voice.

"I'm sorry, Rose, I'll be right there."

I walked to the conference room knowing the rest of the week was going to be tough.

"Rose, I'm sorry," I repeated, settling into a chair opposite her. "I suppose you heard there was an explosion at a nuclear plant in the Soviet Union?"

"Are you serious?" Rose's eyes grew large. "I missed the news. I've been so busy. Where was it?"

"Near Kiev, where I used to live."

"Where's that? Is it a big city?"

"It's in the Ukraine, and it's the third largest city in the Soviet Union."

"Were many people killed?"

"I don't know, I didn't listen to the news, either, but that's why I'm late for our meeting. I was in engineering, with Lena Gurevich. I suppose we'll never know the truth. That, undoubtedly, will be a state secret."

"Come on, Anna, they can't keep something like this secret!"

"And why not? They've thrived on secrets for sixty-eight years. Statistics are closely held state secrets; even inquiry about them is forbidden. I wish I could see for myself what's happening. One always thinks the worst when there's no information."

"You don't have family left there, do you?" All Rose's chins and breasts melted into her usual generous self.

"No, but I do have close friends."

"Oh my God. I am sorry, Anna."

I shook my head to clear it. "Let's get to work. The explosion is there and we're here. Before we begin, I want to apologize for not telling you about my resignation. George insisted I not tell anyone."

"It's not just that," pouted Rose. "Only yesterday you sounded like you were going to spend the rest of your life here and didn't care where Jack went. And today the two of you are together."

"Rose, I'm not marrying him. I'll be working for and paid by his client."

"Bullshit. I wasn't born yesterday," Rose said.

Eventually we managed to concentrate on the work at hand, stopping only when our stomachs screamed for food. We were friends again.

"You better hurry, it's almost noon." Rose stood and stretched her big body. "I'm going to take my sandwich and sit in the sun by the fountain."

How is it that everyone except me understood what Jack meant by a lunch commitment?

I waited by Jack's freshly washed and polished car. I wish he looked after his clothes as well. I should be with Lena now, not socializing with Jack.

At a little past twelve a side door opened and Jack materialized from behind Sandra. He ran across the parking lot, his suit jacket and tie in hand.

Jack hugged and kissed me. There were dark circles under his eyes.

"It feels like I haven't seen you in a year." He looked me over, giving an appreciative raise of his eyebrows. "Is the Skokie Inn okay? I don't have too much time."

"You have a long drive ahead of you. We can have lunch another time."

Does he know about Chernobyl? If he doesn't, what's another news story about a distant country when he has so much on his mind.

"Nervous?" Jack smiled, driving with one hand on my knee.

Is it the same to him as when he held Debbie's hand? I wondered. I suddenly missed the warmth of his body next to mine.

"You're so tense. Don't worry, you should do fine." His hand moved to my thigh, tickling me lightly. "I'll be back late Saturday night."

I leaned back closing my eyes.

Strangely, the restaurant was half empty. We followed the hostess to a booth, where I immediately became immersed in the menu.

"What is it, Anna?" Jack reached for my hand.

"A lot of things. Jack, I'm not ready for this job. Did you offer it to me because I'm your girlfriend?"

"Professionally, the answer is an emphatic no. It would be suicidal for my business, and my reputation. But, psychologically, yes, in a way. I suppose if I were hiring someone else, I would have looked for more assertiveness, better mingling skills." Jack studied the menu. "Was that the answer you wanted?"

"I suppose it doesn't matter. It's a little late to worry about it now."

He ordered a roast beef sandwich, fries, and a Pepsi. I ordered a bowl of soup.

"Why did you ask about my hiring you because you're my girlfriend?" Jack sipped his drink.

"I've received a lot of compliments since yesterday. Most of them made me, and especially Tanya, feel good. But a good deal of them were compliments on succeeding with you, and I felt uncomfortable."

"About the compliments or succeeding with me?" His sarcasm hit me in the face.

"Jack, I was just curious. I didn't anticipate a serious conversation. Let's eat."

"Anna, may I ask you something?" Jack stared at me intently.

The soup was too salty, the roll a bit stale. I was beginning to be sorry I agreed to lunch.

"I know the answer I'll get will be 'get lost if you don't agree with me,' but I'll risk it anyway." Jack paused. "Anna, why are you dating me?" As the silence became intolerable, Jack reached across the small table and gently lifted my chin, "Talk to me, Anna." His eyes looked tired.

I took his hand from my chin and held it.

"I like you and trust you." I sounded neither confident nor convincing. "I don't know why you're dating me. To tell you the truth, I'm surprised you still want to see me. Evidently you like me too."

Jack's brows crawled up his forehead.

"Like you? It's been four years, Anna. If I didn't like you I would have to be an idiot to still be seeing you. Anna, I know you care, but you sometimes have a strange way of showing it."

I finished my soup slowly, occasionally looking at Jack's drawn face. His eyes are those of a different people and I don't always understand what's behind them.

Russians know their own by the eyes. In any country, in any clothes, in any situation, we know. In the beginning we immigrants thought it had to do with being more worried, tense, or suspicious, but with time, most have become more relaxed, less distrustful. But the eyes, they retain a Russianness, something we recognize and understand in each other.

Jack glanced at his watch. "I'm going to push my luck and offer you an observation. Everything needs fuel, Anna. Nothing moves forever by itself. Please stop shutting yourself off from me."

How can I be so consumed with my problems when half the people in Kiev are dying?

"Jack, we knew from the start we wouldn't be forever."

"*We* didn't. *You* did."

"I like you a lot, Jack. What bothers me is that now, after last Sunday, you're going to expect me to act differently, and I can't."

"Okay, if that's what you want," shrugged Jack chewing. "You feel guilty for a moment of happiness. No matter what you say, Anna, you were happy on Sunday. I was happy too. But you have a constant fear of happiness."

The waitress appeared at our table. I asked for tea. Jack had coffee and asked for the check.

"Anna, I know you're uncomfortable discussing sex, but I want to make something clear," he pushed up his glasses. "I'm very attracted to you physically. However, I am not, I repeat, I am not going out with you for only that reason. That would be ludicrous." Jack leaned forward stubbornly. "While I was married, I was faithful to my wife. I don't kiss and tell, but, as a matter of fact, Marsha was quite a lay. However, in the end it didn't matter. After I was divorced, whenever I became aroused, I was always able to find a willing female to relieve me. Not once did it create a relationship."

"Marsha was quite a what?"

Jack's brows came together for a moment, then he burst out laughing, and the tension broke.

"Oh, you foreigners! Let's just say she was a very sophisticated woman." Jack squeezed my hand. "I originally wanted to go to your house for lunch," he said, his eyes smiling intimately over his cup, "but I wouldn't have been able to guarantee my performance. I've only had about eight hours sleep in the last three days."

I caught myself regretting I hadn't suggested we go to my house for lunch and maybe a short nap. I blushed.

"Good!" Jack said as he glanced at his watch. "Let's get going."

As Jack paid the bill, I walked slowly to the car.

Nothing moves forever without fuel, the fuel from within. All my fuel has been for Sasha. How much do I have left?

"You know, I'm going to miss Tanya while I'm in Wisconsin," Jack said, sounding surprised himself.

"She's counting on me being rich and successful and getting a Jacuzzi for the basement. For now, I'll just be satisfied with not letting you down."

Jack laughed, "I don't think you will." He looked over at me. "As usual, I forwarded my phone to yours. If a Dr. Fagan phones, call me right away. He's my mother's doctor. She hasn't been feeling well lately."

When Jack pulled up in front of the building, he jumped out, ran around to open my door, and with a swoop pulled me out, wrapping his arms around me.

What wouldn't I give to curl up against his warm body, close my eyes, and wait for my worries to fade away.

"Relax, Anna, just relax, it's all right to enjoy yourself. Give me a chance to make you happy, will you?"

I kissed his cheek.

"So, how was lunch?" Rose blocked the doorway to my office with her body.

"Fine, thank you."

She looked at me sympathetically. "It's going to be hard, you're so used to having Jack with you all the time."

Why does everyone assume I can't find my way home without Jack?

"Come on, Rose, he'll be back in seventy-two hours."

"I'm sorry," Rose pursed her lips as we walked to the conference room.

Work did not come easily. I had visions of war movies: burning buildings, deserted streets, people on stretchers, and in the background was Kiev.

I called home before leaving. My heart fell when I heard Tanya's anxious voice.

"I've been trying to call you for an hour. Did you know there was a bad accident in a town near Kiev?"

"Yes, I know."

"Why didn't you tell me?"

"I only found out yesterday."

"The Soviet Union tried to deny it. Everyone was talking about it at school. How could they hide something so important from their own people? Should we try to call my father?"

"He never mentioned he has a phone. Why don't you write?"

"It takes too long. I want to know now."

That's how it should be.

"You know what, Tanichka, call Felix. He's going to call Bella tonight. Give him your father's full name, Yefim Petrovich Parchomenko, and his year of birth, 1938. Perhaps Bella can find a minute to look him up through the information service. Felix won't mind."

"Isn't it awful? Is it really true they'll never tell their own people?"

"The newspapers say they have, only with no details and downplaying the seriousness. The Soviet Union would not admit anything if they thought they could get away with it."

"But then, how could anyone help them?"

Her question would never occur to anyone who had lived there. Logic has no place in the Soviet mentality. How, for instance, would Tanya respond to the only natural answer to her question: they don't give a damn if the people aren't helped, as long as their image is preserved.

"Tanichka, this is one of those times when you have to believe me when I tell you it's impossible to explain. I'm going to stop by Lena's after work. She was extremely upset. Her parents are still in Kiev and I want to cheer her up a little. I won't be too late."

Lena lives in a large corner house on a winding street in Glenview. It looks on to the world with a white double door, attached garage, and bay windows behind fancy-cut bushes. The furniture, a gift from Serozha for their last anniversary, had been selected by him personally and, from the pretentious look of it, must have come from a Russian store.

A blue, beat-up Camaro belonging to Lena's son was parked in the driveway. The open-air, yellow, rented trailer attached to it contained two mattresses, a dresser, and some boxes. I debated whether to go in. We're not in the Soviet Union where people drop by unannounced.

I almost didn't recognize Boris with his permed hair and defiant look. Carrying a television and followed by his girlfriend, Melanie, in tight jeans, he grumbled an undistinguishable acknowledgement of my presence.

"Hello!" I called out from the steps.

"Who's there?" Lena responded anxiously in English. Upon seeing me she immediately switched to Russian. "Oh, Anya, hi! I was going to call you later. Did you see Boris? They're moving to Melanie's apartment in the city. What can I do?" She shook her head, resigned. "Please, come in."

"Ma," Boris said awkwardly, returning from outside, "I'm going to take our food from the refrigerator."

He spoke quite passable Russian. Scrawny in a teenage way, with Lena's round dark eyes, he looked younger than his twenty-three years, in spite of standing a foot taller than she.

"Thank you, thank you for coming." Lena clung to my arm as we watched Boris head toward the kitchen. Melanie waited just outside the front door, brushing her hair.

Returning, Boris tossed a casual, "I'll be in touch," then brought his cheek close to his mother's lips.

Lena locked the door behind them.

"Boris is very immature; he needs someone to follow. I don't think Melanie means wrong. He thinks he would appeal to her more if he weren't Russian. He thinks if he chews gum, watches baseball, eats TV dinners, and drinks beer he's an American. Everything I do annoys him, everything is my 'old-country way.' Why can't he find a nice Russian girl, or, at least, a Jewish girl?"

The house smelled of emptiness.

"I'm going to tell Serozha he can have the house. I'll rent an apartment somewhere close to work. I don't know how you knew, but I didn't want to be alone tonight. I'm so lucky to have met you, Anya." She touched my shoulder. "Let's have something to eat."

"Only tea, thanks. Tanya's making dinner. Did you talk to Felix?"

"Yes. Thank you for suggesting I call him. I've been trying every hour to get through to Kiev, but all the lines are busy."

Lena limped around the kitchen while she talked nonstop to chase away the silence of the dark house, to drown her fears, to keep me with her a little longer. If not for Tanya I would gladly have spent the night.

"Wasn't it better in the Soviet Union, when friends would come over whenever they felt like it? Here one always has to call first. I left work at lunchtime. I couldn't concentrate. I'm sorry I didn't tell you not to wait for me."

"I had lunch with Jack."

"Good. I hope you'll marry him. Jack is so devoted to you and Tanya. What else do you want? You can't be in love like it's the first time in your life."

"But I think I should be in some kind of love, Lenochka. At this point, I only want permanent people in my life. I can't handle loss anymore. Tanya is permanent. My friends from Kiev are permanent. I don't want to set an example for Tanya of easy marriage, easy divorce."

"More tea, Anichka? Who knows what's permanent? Believe me, I thought nothing was more permanent than Serozha." Lena's eyes filled with tears.

The telephone rang and Lena rushed to the wall where it hung.

"Hello. Yes. What did she say?" Her eyes, bright and expectant, suddenly dulled. "That's unbelievable. I don't blame you. Thank you very, very much." Lena sat next to me. "Felix. He finally talked to Bella. She laughed at him, said there was an insignificant accident in Chernobyl, that there was nothing to worry about and not to make a fly into an elephant, like we used to say. She didn't talk to my parents yet, but she will."

In the dim room Lena talked about her parents, particularly her father who spoke English well and was secretly studying Hebrew; about a coworker she turned down twenty years ago when he made passes at her and who had immigrated to Philadelphia; about wanting her parents to understand why she couldn't stay with Serozha; and about Svetlana's prom dress and how shopping for it would bring them closer. She spoke in whispers. We were like two Russian girls; whatever one said the other absorbed it like a sponge. As a teenager, my conversations with Asya were much the same.

"I'm sorry, Anichka," Lena stopped, embarrassed. "You're probably tired and bored."

I didn't respond, but she knew I wasn't tired or bored.

The growing closeness with Lena made me feel like a traitor. The thought that within days Bella would find Sasha and Asya, or that perhaps she has found them already, sent a fever of anticipation through my body.

fifteen

Jack called in the morning to give me phone numbers where he could be reached.

"Anna, did you hear about a nuclear accident near Kiev?" he asked cautiously.

"Yes. It's all I've been able to think about."

"That's why you were so upset yesterday! Why didn't you say something?"

"You were busy and I didn't think you'd be interested."

"Anna. . . never mind."

"Jack, unless it's sports, you're never interested in the news."

"Generally, that's true, but this news affects you."

"And just how do you propose to help me?"

"Do you want me to come back Friday night instead of Saturday?"

"Thank you, Jack, but honestly, there's no need."

The coolness of my voice surprised me. There was no reply, just a click and the line went dead.

Arriving at work, I spied a long, computer-made banner on the wall over Debbie's desk. "Good luck, Anna!" it said. Even my earlier conversation with Jack couldn't spoil my mood now.

By the end of the day Rose and I were done and my desk was clear. Tomorrow there will be almost nothing to do. I visited some people on the second shift to say good-bye.

My last day at work turned out to be one continuous party. In fact, with the gifts I received, it reminded me of a birthday party.

Asya had transferred to my school in the second grade. The government had awarded her father, a former major in the army, a disabled veteran, and a decorated hero, a special pension and the largest room in a six-room apartment across the street from the school. Asya's sister, Rimma, took ballet classes after school at the Palace for the Pioneer Scouts. Asya confided that Rimma, a preteen, already received love notes from boys. The collars and cuffs on Rimma's and Asya's school uniforms had lace around the edges unlike my plain ones.

Asya gave a birthday party a week after she joined the class. She invited the entire second grade. Her mother made round, fluffy sponge cakes. I brought a book of children's poetry by the beloved Soviet poet Samuel Marschak.

Asya's mother, Fira Naumovna — Auntie Fira — a serious, matronly woman, picked out my gift from a pile of others and leafed through it appreciatively. "Your mother was lucky to be able to get a book like this nowadays."

"Mama, Anya is the girl who doesn't have a mother," Asya blurted out.

Auntie Fira furrowed her dark brows.

"My brother got it for me," I volunteered.

When Lonya rang at the door to pick me up, Auntie Fira took me to the kitchen and wrapped two slices of sponge cake. Asya's father, a gaunt, bald man with shiny medals on his chest and an empty sleeve pinned to his coat pocket, smoked by the window. A neighbor kneaded dough on a board with her back to us.

"Here's some cake for you and your brother. And when is your birthday?"

I wondered why an adult didn't understand I didn't have a birthday because there was no mother to give me a party.

"I don't have a birthday," I explained politely. I wanted to leave immediately. Lonya would be angry if I made him wait.

"What do you mean?"

"Can I go now?"

"Yes, but surely your brother says happy birthday to you every year?"

I stared at the floor.

"Please, do me a favor, Anichka. Ask your brother when your birthday is. Asya will come to your party. And other children will, too."

I ran out of the kitchen.

I found Lonya smoking by the elevator. "Didn't Asya tell you I was waiting?"

"Don't be angry, Lonya, it's not my fault. Her mother wanted to give me some cake to take home."

He opened the napkin. Half of one slice disappeared in his mouth, then the other half. He ate in the elevator! Well-mannered people should not eat in elevators, or in the street, or with their hands! Lonya would have slapped my hands if I had done that. He put the napkin with the remaining slice in the pocket of his jacket.

"Lonya, do I have a birthday?" I asked, after walking two blocks down Shevchenko Boulevard in silence.

"What a stupid question!" Lonya exploded, jerking my hand. "You're here in this world, aren't you? You were born on the fifteenth of July. And, at what cost!"

I didn't understand the cost part.

"Asya's mother asked me when my birthday is."

"You've got no basic human feelings. How can you think of celebrating your birthday when my mother died on that day because of you?"

I stopped walking to look up at him.

"I'd only have Asya and two other girls. We'd be quiet, I promise." I was sure his mother wouldn't mind.

"You never think of your mother, do you?"

A long pause followed Lonya's question.

"My mother?" My heart was pounding. "My mother?" I repeated.

I looked at Lonya. Tears formed in his eyes, his Adam's apple moved up and down.

The tears were contagious. "My mother?" I repeated. Is it possible Lonya's mother is my mother, too?

"Let's go," Lonya jerked my hand and moved on.

The next year, on the fifteenth of July, Asya came with a sponge cake. The other girls had gone to the country for the summer break. Asya had white bows in her braids, like the ones we wore for the October Revolution and May Day holidays.

She wore a pink, cotton dress with little blue flowers and gave me a book of short stories for children by Leo Tolstoi, a red wool sweater, and a pair of brown wool socks.

"Anya doesn't need clothes! She's got everything!" Lonya burst out angrily.

He wrapped the sweater and socks back into the newspaper Asya had brought them in. I remember distinctly thinking how proud I would be to wear the sweater to school instead of the mended and stretched one I'd had for two years. The thought was too good to hope for.

"Take the clothes back with you when you leave, and tell your parents we are not paupers."

Lonya served tea, apples, and chocolate candies. There were six pieces of candy, three for each of us. He stood by the window, smoking and coughing. The sympathy in Asya's dark eyes was unbearable.

"I do have things to wear, you know. Your mother shouldn't have."

"It was my dad. There was a long line, but because he's a veteran . . ."

"Okay, you can leave it," we heard Lonya say softly.

"Thank you," we cried out simultaneously. Asya laughed her short, cackling laugh.

Rose found me shortly before lunch in the computer room.

"Anna, there are a few things we missed yesterday. Let's go to the conference room. I've already laid out the papers.

"Said good-bye to everyone yet?" she asked on the way.

"I'm so overwhelmed, Rose. I never realized so many people cared about me."

"Anna, I think you're one of the finest people that ever worked here."

"Thank you, Rose." I wanted to hug her.

When Rose opened the door to the conference room, I was blinded by flashes of light and deafened by cheers.

"Surprise!"

Countless smiling faces surrounded me. Pat stood on a chair with a camera. Rose related excitedly how she got me there without my suspecting a thing. A huge cake sat in the center of the table, reading "Good Luck, Anna!"

I didn't see Wayne O'Connor until he offered his cheek to be kissed. I felt myself approaching a state of tears when he put his hand on my shoulder.

"Let's start!" George raised his hand to get everyone's attention. "Anna, we're sorry to see you leave and we want you to know we love you. Please come back to visit, and here's a little present to bring you good luck."

In his hands he held a black leather briefcase. The inscription near the clasp read, "To Anna Fishman from her coworkers at Harvey Manufacturing."

"It's Coach, you know," said Debbie.

I didn't, but her tone was unmistakably respectful. It must have cost a fortune.

"Thank you all," I said. My knees shaking, I sat down.

There was a matching Coach folder inside the briefcase.

"It's from Jack," Debbie said raising the folder, showing it to everyone just like the girls on *The Price is Right*.

Several people came in, shook my hand, oohed and ahhed at the briefcase and folder, wished me well and wolfed down cake dished up by Rose. Finally George handed me my last paycheck, told me my day was over, and I could leave any time I wanted.

The evening news brought Ronald Reagan into our living room, again expressing his outrage at the way the Soviet government was handling the nuclear accident. Elevated radiation levels were being reported everywhere in Europe. The May Day parades had gone on as planned in all Soviet cities.

I didn't sleep well, anxious about my new job. I simply can't fail.

Jack called Saturday morning to say he would be unable to spend the weekend in Chicago. I wasn't home; he talked to Tanya. Visibly disappointed by his call, she watched for my reaction but found only tension.

"You mean if he's too tired to drive we won't see him for weeks at a time?" She demanded an answer.

"Tanya, he's under no obligation to us."

My terse reply didn't stop her angry objection. "He is—he's your boyfriend, and he's my friend, too!"

The certainty of my approaching fiasco on the coming Monday tore at me, made me restless. After Monday, Jack will surely exit my life, disillusioned and relieved. Tanya will just have to get over this loss in her life. I knew Jack was furious that he had to find out from the media and not from me about the Chernobyl accident. But I'm so scared of allowing him to get closer, especially in anticipation of Monday, and in anticipation of Bella's news from Kiev. It seems I reject anything that doesn't have a guarantee attached to it, like my Coach briefcase. Nothing in life is guaranteed, other than merchandise; and most of the time, even that's limited.

sixteen

On Monday, I awoke at a little after five in the morning, not feeling refreshed at all. The day promised to shape up to be as tense as anticipated. My new briefcase and my breakfast waited for me on the kitchen table. Tanya looked sleepy and constantly stretched and yawned. I swallowed the bagel almost without chewing. The lump of tension made the bagel feel caught in my throat.

Traffic had not gathered steam yet, and trucks seemed the only vehicles on the road besides my little Chevy. In my mind, I accused them of trying to intimidate me. I stayed in the right lane and drove at the legal speed limit. I refused to risk an accident on the morning of a new page in my life.

I arrived at twenty minutes before eight. I was supposed to meet with Brian Krysa at eight. The company parking lot, already half-full, sported freshly marked reserved and handicapped spaces. The contemporary steel-and-glass look made the two-story building nondescript. I parked in the corner farthest from the main entrance to wait until eight so that my appearance would portray the impression of punctuality, not anxiety.

The circular massaging movements on the back of my neck that so quickly released muscle pressure when Jack's warm hands applied them didn't help much when my ice-cold hands tried to imitate his. I flipped down the sun visor to look in the small mirror but flipped it back up as soon as I saw the still eyes that stared back at me.

The clock digits marched on steadily toward that moment when my decisions, my demeanor, and my expertise would become important not only to me, but to Jack and the company that had hired us. At exactly two minutes to eight I reparked in the visitor's lot and strode down the concrete path leading to the front entrance, flanked by concrete urns with small, red flowers. People hurried in front of and behind me, dispersing from the lobby in different directions.

Brian Krysa and a dark, spic-and-span-looking man stood at the reception desk. We advanced toward each other until we met in the middle of the lobby. My left hand squeezed the handle of my briefcase as if it could prevent me from fainting; my right hand shook Brian's.

I smiled at both of them and sang out, "Good morning, Brian! Nice to see you again."

"Good morning, Anna." Brian turned to the dark man. "Let me introduce John Tondelli."

"Hello, John," I smiled even wider as I shook John's hand and listened to his greeting.

Walking between them, I participated in an exchange of opinions on weather and traffic. Words flew by without leaving a trace. My accent sounded harsh against the distinct Midwestern English of my future coworkers. As far as I could tell, I had not made any mistakes yet, but I had decided beforehand not to correct myself if I did. Finally, we entered a small meeting room to the smell of fresh coffee. The donuts looked delicious.

"Anna, John will be your main contact here. Feel free to go to him with any problems."

Brian looked to John, who picked up the conversation.

"Unfortunately, there is one problem which may make your work more difficult," John took over smoothly. "Here's the story. Our division, as I'm sure you're aware, was bought by Kent International two years ago. Since then we've grown rapidly, but, for financial reasons, we're still not computerized in a modern way. That's why Graff's software attracted us so much. It's designed for poorly organized, but successful mid-sized businesses like ours. But there's one problem it doesn't address."

I began to panic.

"The bulk of our customers are small companies. We have problems collecting from them and have a plan for a credit control system."

They again exchanged glances.

"After you've finished all the requirements here, would it be possible for you to move on to the Aurora division, then return to us? By that time we'll have brought in someone to develop a credit control system, and work with you to interface with your package."

"We're aware your contract doesn't include an interface," intervened Brian. "We thought we might persuade you to deviate from your contract. It would save us a lot of money."

What do I do now? What is a credit control system? How much additional time would it take? Does Jack know about this?

"Well . . ." I said, drawing it out to fill the pause.

I can't fail. This is Jack's first customer. I can't tell them I'm not a partner; they need a decision, or at least a hint of a decision. Wait . . . if Jack could do this credit thing instead of someone else, he'll get a second contract with them.

"Do you know who's going to work on the credit control system for you?" I looked straight at John.

"Not the foggiest. We have some bids. Both budget and time are limited because our fiscal year ends August 31. But we'll find a consulting company by the time you're back from Aurora."

What's a "bid"?

"I would like to suggest developing your credit system through our company, if you have no objections, of course." I thought I sounded professional; hopefully, they thought so, too.

Brian frowned. "From our discussions with Jack," he said, sitting back and turning his pen in his fingers, "I understood your firm specializes exclusively in marketing his software."

Oh God, what did I do?

"Generally, that's true. However, we make exceptions when our software is to be part of an integrated system." Wow, that sounded great.

Brian looked at John; they nodded to each other.

"Frankly," said Brian, "we're terribly understaffed. Just the fact that we won't have to interview, negotiate, or coordinate with another company would be a big plus. Do you think a week would be enough time for you to come up with an estimate?"

I can't do estimates. I don't know how.

I narrowed my brows, as if in deep concentration.

"We will need two weeks to collect all the necessary information," I responded decisively.

Jack will have to spend some time in Chicago to work all this out. I'm sure he can hire a consultant, like he hired me, to develop what they need.

"Two weeks it is," said Brian getting up. "Thank you for your flexibility."

They didn't even notice I didn't know what they were talking about half the time.

"I'll prepare a memo," continued Brian, "covering what we discussed and give you a copy. Now I'll leave you in John's capable hands. Good luck, Anna."

By the end of the day I'd met all the people I would need to know and had the documentation I requested, or, rather, what Jack had told me to request. I had an office with a window, a desk with a computer, printer, and telephone, and a secretary I shared with John—Mrs. McLaughlin, a sharp, slim woman in her sixties who supplied me with stationery—showed me how to use the buttons on the telephone, and complimented me on my Coach briefcase.

Almost every one inquired about Chernobyl and congratulated me on the new freedoms in my old country. It's impossible to explain that changes in the Soviet Union can only be detrimental. Logic cannot be applied to a country with evil flowing through its veins for three generations. I don't try to explain anymore. I merely smile and mumble appropriately.

My head is bursting with a zillion ideas. Today was a good day. I made a favorable impression. Of course, people's names are still slightly jumbled.

I feel vibrant, not even tired. Tomorrow I'll start interviewing future system users.

My parking space will have my name on it and be in the reserved row along the front of the building. They inquired what version would be preferable: Ms. or Mrs. If American women had to stand in line for milk and onions they would laugh at this kind of question. I picked Ms., since I knew it was expected.

Soon Bella will be back and tell us about Chernobyl, and I'll have Sasha's and Asya's addresses. I'll write long letters and send clothes. I'm sure they need clothes. Sasha has never owned a decent suit. Even as a head doctor he made peanuts, and before that he worked nights, in addition to his regular hospital job, to make ends meet. How different his life would have been had he come to the United States when I did.

When we meet—and miracles do happen, just look at my life—we'll make mad, passionate love, then we'll talk. It will be heaven.

The other night I had an erotic dream: a man's hand massaging my breasts, slowly sliding down, at the last moment moving back up. Jack does that sometimes and he's succeeded in making me used to him. Now he stubbornly wants to be the one to make me happy. I won't allow him or anyone else make me as happy as Sasha did.

With Sasha I was part of an exhilarating party. With Jack I'm the designated driver: I enjoy the company, I stay, I watch. I admit his attention makes me feel needed, and that one time on the floor was crazy and wonderful. But I'm not accustomed to so much attention. And how do I pay back? Curling up next to him with my arm across his chest is as close as I want to come to happiness. I only wish he would just lie motionless.

I've heard women talk about faking orgasms. I suppose it's possible to imitate the motions and sounds, but then you have to live with a man who doesn't know the difference and with yourself who does.

seventeen

"So how was it, Mom? Boy, that soup sure smells good!"

Tanya ate; I talked about the new project.

"Would they pay you if you did it yourself?" Tanya inquired. "I could make dinner if you have to work late."

"They would, but both projects have to be done at the same time."

"Jack will find someone," Tanya said. "When he calls, remind him he promised to find me a golf instructor."

Jack can do no wrong as far as Tanya's concerned.

I took my time washing the dishes. The cuckoo announced nine o'clock. When we first bought the clock at a garage sale, it woke me up every night; now, most of the time, I don't hear it.

I called Lena and Felix. Lena reported she had reached her parents that morning. They told her nothing more than she already knew. I pictured her alone in her large, lonely house and shivered. Felix was relieved, as Bella was coming home. She told him she had completed everyone's errands and that rampant rumors were circulating in Kiev that the accident was more serious than previously thought.

A few more days—Sasha and Asya will be mine again!

I took a shower, leaving the telephone on the bathroom floor. It rang once, for Tanya.

After the ten o'clock news I became anxious. Frankly, I was scared. I had started something that, without Jack, would be a big mess. Where is he? I kept glancing at the phone.

At eleven o'clock, Jack still hadn't called. I dialed his hotel number, but there was no answer and I was automatically transferred back to the receptionist. I left a message saying it was urgent that he return my call. Now I was doubly worried. I paced the house, clenching and unclenching my fists. Lonya used to do that.

It was almost one in the morning when the telephone finally rang.

"Hi, what's up?"

Hearing Jack's familiar voice, I collapsed onto the sofa. Thank God, he's alive.

"How did it go? Did you have to work late?"

"Not really," Jack replied indifferently.

"You sound tired," I ventured, wondering how to start my story.

"I'll manage. What was so urgent?" he said in the same indifferent tone.

I was glued to the sofa.

"Anna, what is it? I've been up since seven this morning. I want to go to bed."

My God, he's talking to me like he would to any subordinate. Why am I so flustered? I am his subordinate. Where was he tonight?

"Jack, Brian and another man, John . . . something Italian, have an additional project. They need a credit control application to interface with our system. I don't know exactly what needs to be done, but I know it can be done. They asked me if I would work in Aurora when I'm done with their requirements, giving them time to hire someone to develop the credit control application, then come back and interface the two systems. I told them we could do the development and interface. They expect our estimate in two weeks."

"What do you mean you told them? I'm not a consulting company, I'm a software vendor and they know it. Who do you think you are, making decisions for me!?" Jack sounded irritated.

"Jack, you can make a lot of money if you hire someone to develop the application. And they'll have more work in the future."

"Anna, I'm not ready to have employees. Too much overhead. Consulting is not my business. Tomorrow you tell them I can't deliver on your promise. And please, in the future, I'll make all the decisions."

"Jack, you introduced me as your partner. People talk to me as your partner. They have expectations and I have an image to maintain."

"Yeah, you're right, in a way." For the first time in the conversation there was a hint of warmth in his voice. "But that doesn't change anything. We are not a consulting company."

"Then, I'm going to tell them that I'm not your partner and that I work independently."

Understanding my very quiet and very distinct tone, Jack softened slightly.

"Anna, don't try to do this yourself. You can't."

"Don't worry. My contract with you won't suffer. I'll find someone to do the credit application."

"You can't just hire people. You need to have an accountant, an attorney. You need to have insurance. Anna, you can't do this! Why are you suddenly so keen on starting your own business?"

"I'm sorry, Jack. I thought I was doing something for you. I thought it would be easy money. You know so many people."

"Anna, why don't you just forget it? You'll be extremely busy with what's at hand. Believe me, you don't need to take on more."

"Jack, we are not Siamese twins. You do not have the right to tell me what I need." My voice, barely audible, told us both my decision had been made.

The fierceness, which I had only experienced once, during my last months in the Soviet Union, and I had thought could only happen at that unique moment in time, consumed me. It gave me power that, it seemed, could incinerate anyone standing in the way. Caught unawares by what I recognized as an unstoppable plunge into a gulf with no shores, I took a deep breath and shut my eyes.

"I do have the right," I heard Jack's voice coming from somewhere beyond the horizon, "but I won't force it on you."

That right does not exclude the right to hurt or the right to walk away.

"Are you there?"

The faraway sound fluttered without penetrating the wall that grew around me. I opened my eyes to the world already changed by my choice.

"Yes, I'm here," I said.

"Listen, I don't want you to get yourself into trouble, and that's exactly where you're heading."

"I need to do it," I stated. "I simply know that I need to do it."

"Well, so be it," Jack replied with what seemed like detachment.

Please, don't hang up!

"I met some people in college and later at work that had fought in Vietnam," Jack began thoughtfully, "who suffered flashbacks. For some, those flashbacks messed up their lives, their marriages. I have wanted to believe your memories affect you the same way and I should not let them inflict permanent damage to our relationship. I really tried to be patient."

The silence that fell became the continuation of his monologue.

"Remember how you took care of me after my car accident?"

"I didn't take care of you. The nurse did." The prospect of wading into syrupy gratitude made me acutely uncomfortable.

Two years ago, a truck rear-ended Jack's car on the Dan Ryan Expressway as we were returning from the theater. With the exception of a whiplash and a short-lived fear of driving, I was fine, but Jack fractured his right wrist and his left ankle, and for a few hours he had difficulty breathing. Both of us were released from the hospital the next morning. Jack hired a nurse, who arrived and left at precise times, helped him bathe, and cleaned his glasses, but the rest of her responsibilities remained nebulous. At home, I cried incessantly night after night, haunted by mental pictures of Lonya in a hospital room, shared by a dozen patients, as real as in a 3-D movie. Natasha deposited me on Jack's doorstep two days after our discharge from the hospital. The nurse, a heavy-set, uniformed woman about our age, put aside her *Reader's Digest* and looked up at me expectantly over her reading glasses. On crutches, disheveled, and pathetic in his hand and foot contraptions, Jack looked like an abandoned child. The kitchen greeted me with empty pizza boxes, sandwich wrappers, paper cups, and a tower of ketchup and mustard packets.

"That chicken soup you made for me with those little dough things, I can still taste it," Jack mused. "I swished it around in my mouth before swallowing to make it last longer."

"You never told me you liked it so much."

"You taught me to refrain from sappiness."

I noted to look up the word "sappiness" in the dictionary.

Not to disturb Jack's magazine-picture-of-a-kitchen, I had prepared food at home while he was laid up, brought it over, and stayed as late as I could. For a few days, Natasha, Irena, or Vilen drove me, but when my medical leave came to an end, I forced myself behind the wheel again.

"I was prepared to break my other ankle to repeat the experience."

I smiled but detected no smile on the other end of the line. Why did he have to bring this up now?

"I liked it when you put my robe on to wash the dishes—don't tell me you didn't like those evenings. After the doctors allowed me to return to work, with the casts still on, you drove me every day. I prayed that my bones would never heal. Remember how you yelled at my doctor for making me wait?"

"I don't remember yelling at your doctor," I said meekly.

Does he think he's softening me up so he can discourage me from taking on the new project?

"That was the real you. I told myself that I'd never let you go. And when we made love the last time, a week ago—you do remember that, don't you? That was the real you. But when you avoided, you consciously avoided," Jack stressed and stretched out the word "consciously," "telling me about Chernobyl, even though it must have scared you stiff . . ." he paused. "You shut me off from what's important to you—is that the real you, too? What am I . . . a filler of empty space?" he asked bitterly.

My eyes filled with tears.

"Well?" He demanded. "You've got nothing to say, do you? Anyway," he went on, "I guess I did remain a stranger. By no means, don't spill those precious feelings. Hoard them all for whatever you're hoarding them for."

The silence that followed buzzed like a radio test alert that I couldn't break off.

A filler of empty space? I rubbed my forehead as if to generate sparks.

Am I saying good-bye to Jack? I did like wearing his robe, feeding him soup and potatoes, and beet salad. I even made gefilte fish from scratch. And a week ago, when we made love on the floor, I felt reborn. But the past cannot go away; it gave me shape, it held me together, and it will hold me together—the physical distance to the other side of the bridge notwithstanding. Without it, who am I . . . empty space?

"Good night, Jack."

"Good night." Jack replied evenly. "I'll call you during the week to get your status and I'll probably drive home next weekend to review the progress of the project. One more time: Do not take on the additional work."

The click on the line did nothing to stop the buzzing silence.

I couldn't sleep; even a hot shower didn't help.

In the morning Tanya took one look at me and knew.

"Jack doesn't want to do the project I told you about."

"But you promised them. What are you going to do?"

"I have someone in mind. But remember, you promised to make dinner if I have to work late and it looks like I'll have to work late, and probably weekends, if this pans out. Only, Tanichka, I always want to know where you are when I'm not home. There's one more thing: If Jack calls and I'm not here, just take a message."

I noted Tanya's long face.

"You didn't break up, did you?"

I put my arm around her shoulder, kissed her, and scurried out.

Pat McDonald was very receptive when I called him.

"You don't have to convince me. Remember, my wife couldn't work because of her high-risk pregnancy."

I collected enough information to give me a good idea as to the scope of the project. It wasn't half as bad as I had thought. On Friday, Pat came over and I presented him with a modified copy of my contract, typed by Tanya, with both our names and blanks to fill in as to our respective shares, once they were determined. Without hesitation, Pat put down equal shares for us both. Since my contract had originally been prepared by Jack's attorney, we decided not to waste money having it looked over. I didn't want to wait two weeks to present the estimate, and Pat promised to have the proposal ready on Sunday. If it's accepted, I will have to work twelve hours a day and every weekend to meet the proposed deadline, and there will be no time to develop a prototype.

Bella returned and called, leaving a message that she had invited everyone to come by on Saturday night to hear about her trip. Jack called me at the office, twice, but I didn't have time to talk to him. He gave up, started calling the house, leaving messages with Tanya. It seemed I was too exhausted at night to do anything except eat, undress, and fall into bed. Amazingly I still looked well, fit, and purposeful. Every evening Tanya had the table set, my dinner ready. She washed the dishes and made her own cocoa.

I didn't really want this schedule to change as it let me get away with listening only to my tiredness, not my thoughts. With a great degree of frustration, I realized I wished Jack to be there, like a comfy robe.

eighteen

Lena got in touch with me by leaving a message on my answering machine, saying she had news for my ears only, and I should not hesitate to call—anytime. Disoriented and anxious, she addressed me as "Mama" and burst into tears when I woke her up at five in the morning.

"I'm sorry, Lenochka, but you did say to call anytime."

"Anya, you!" She blew her nose. "I'm so glad. And I meant anytime, don't worry. I get up at six anyway. This tension . . . I constantly expect a call from my parents. Bella brought me a letter from them, and pictures. My father has shrunk and become shorter than my mother. How could I have left them behind?" Lena blew her nose again. "How could I?"

"As harsh as it sounds, you had to do it for your children," said I, the eternal frost generator.

"I understand." Lena sighed, her voice returning to its normal quality. "Anichka, I'd like you to come over this weekend with Tanya. You pick the time. My Svetochka moved back with me."

"Congratulations!" I exclaimed, surprised how happy Lena's news made me feel. I didn't realize her misfortunes concerned me so much. I visualized her bangs bobbing with excitement, her hand pressed to her chest.

"Thank you. I was sure you'd want to know. Serozha had women staying overnight without warning her. And yesterday," Lena lowered her voice, "she discovered some lacy panties drying on the towel rack. Serozha reprimanded her for using his bathroom. They had a big fight and she called me to pick her up."

"Excellent," I said glancing at my watch. "I wonder how the panties got back to the proper *tokhes*."

It's not like me, making off-color jokes, but the temptation got the better of me.

Lena giggled. She would have giggled at anything now.

"What about a rain check, Lena? Beginning Monday, I'll be working seven days a week for some time, so Tanya and I are stuffing this weekend to capacity."

"Seven days a week? Isn't that too much, Anya?"

"I think I can handle it." I was pleased by her concern.

"I'm surprised Jack lets you work so hard."

My muscles tightened and my nostrils flared as I responded crisply, "I agreed to a separate assignment in addition to what I do for Jack." I didn't want this conversation to continue.

"Let me know if you need any help," Lena said quietly.

On the way to work I compiled a mental list of things to do this weekend. Deep inside I knew that we would only cover part of the list. On Saturday, first on the list was a visit to Bella's house to get information about Sasha, Asya, and the state of the Union—meaning the Soviet Union. Plans for the rest of the weekend included laundry, ironing, stocking up on groceries, shopping for a new sofa, taking Natasha to brunch for her birthday, and, of course, driving Tanya to and from work. If you listen to her, being a weekend, part-time receptionist for the Skokie Park District will enhance her résumé tremendously. I set aside time to stop at the library and get a book, a mystery, maybe. Something to help me unwind when I come home. One day I'll introduce myself to the old lady who lives in the corner house and ask her to recommend what to read.

My personal library in Kiev had been small and, having no choice, I left it behind. I couldn't ship anything for fear Fima would become suspicious as my belongings disappeared. I took what I could carry and Tanya carried her old rag doll. My mother had left Kiev with Lonya in much the same way.

During my first years in the United States, it seemed life would not be life without Pushkin, Paustovsky, and Chekhov. Many Russian intellectuals refuse to leave the Soviet Union without their libraries. They ship numerous boxes, filled with books to be savored by themselves and future generations. Curiously, once they're here, almost no one opens a Russian book, and almost none of their children recognize the names of the authors. Yet, I don't know of a single person who would rid themselves of these useless Russian libraries, vestiges of olden days. The children, for whom the libraries were originally packed and sent, will be the ones who eventually dispose of the books their parents breathlessly knew, but now rarely caress, by offering them to public libraries or dumping them at recycling centers. To the day he died, Lonya missed the large family library that had vanished without a trace during the war.

Jack doesn't read much, unless it's business-related.

Speaking of business, I need to call Jack with a report, as a good partner should.

The week flew by leaving the concept of time in shambles. Today, Friday, I came home earlier than usual but still found Tanya already fast asleep. Full of determination to do some chores immediately after dinner in order to free up part of Saturday, I gulped down some cold borscht—a refreshing Russian summer treat—and greedily ate some cucumber salad.

My partially full stomach significantly dented my resolve. Eating the left-over stew weakened it even further.

I bet Jack is sitting in a restaurant right now—or lying in bed—with a woman who does not have a "mysterious Russian soul" in need of understanding, but who does have the talent for fun. Good thing I kept myself at a distance.

Trying to unwind, I strolled through the house, room by room, browsing through the mail in the office, straightening up some papers, tossing unwanted flyers in the waste basket, closing the blinds, and shutting off the lights. In the dark living room, I stood in front of the window peeking out to the street, debating whether fixing the light on the post at the edge of the lawn should become an item on my weekend list. A few cars passed, and then one turned sharply into my driveway, its light crossing the house.

Jack! I would recognize his manner of driving anywhere. My mouth dry, I stepped back from the window, still able to see out, but unable to be seen.

He shut off his headlights, then he got out. Looking at his watch, he walked to the dark post at the edge of the lawn. After a minute the light was on again. He crossed the lawn to the front door and looked around.

The bell rang. I didn't move. After a pause it rang again. I finally turned on the lights and opened the door, just as Jack was about to walk away. His face was a mass of dull tiredness, even as his eyes ran down my body.

"Hi. I'm sorry, Anna, you probably were asleep. I decided I needed your report, in case there are things I have to take care of tomorrow."

"Why don't you come in?" I stepped back.

We faced each other in an awkward silence I wished he would break.

"Let's sit down, Jack," I motioned him to the living room.

We sat in opposite corners of the sofa.

He doesn't seem to have any difficulty controlling himself; apparently willing females are available everywhere

"Go ahead, I'm listening," said Jack.

I presented details of my accomplishments, then my plans for the next week, carefully avoiding any mention of the credit control system.

"Have you started working on the conversion rules? They need to be coordinated with the client's headquarters."

"I know, I've got all the data. It's only a matter of organization."

"Show me the data."

I disappeared to the office, returning with my briefcase.

"Thanks for the folder."

Jack made a wry face, waving aside my comment as he read.

"You are thorough," he said, putting my notes on the coffee table and removing his glasses to rub his eyes.

"Do you want to tell me what you've decided to do about the other system?" He closed his eyes, spreading his arms along the back of the sofa.

"There's not much to say. I've been working on it with Pat McDonald."

"Pat?" Jack perked up with surprise and interest.

"I don't write well enough in English, so he's doing the proposal. He'll also do the programming. I'll handle the requirements, design, and system testing."

"Is this an informal deal?" inquired Jack cautiously.

"No. We used my contract with you as a basis for ours. Tanya has already typed it."

"You *are* stubborn, Anna."

I could swear there was satisfaction in his voice.

"What about an online prototype? My software has the capability."

"No time."

"I could give you a hand. That is, if you'll accept it."

"I'll have to check with Pat," I responded seriously, pretending I didn't notice his sarcasm.

"I'll talk to him myself tomorrow," he smiled.

One movement, one small signal, and I would be safe and warm next to him.

"Anna, before I fall asleep, would you please make me some coffee, then I'll get out of here."

I sat in the kitchen watching the coffee brew, listening for but not hearing footsteps, expecting but not feeling Jack's hands. With a cup of hot coffee, I walked carefully through the hall and dining room to the living room.

Jack was asleep on the sofa, hair falling across his forehead, glasses on the floor. I put the coffee on the table and shook his shoulder.

"Okay, okay, just a minute," he mumbled, not moving.

If I kiss him, he'll wake up. Instead, I covered him with my afghan and set my alarm clock to ring in an hour, placing it on the floor near his glasses.

He looks young, even when he's tired.

In my dark bedroom I undressed, slipped into bed and fell asleep.

I woke up to the smell of something burning. There was no reply when I called Tanya. I threw on a robe and followed the smell to the kitchen. Burned eggs, again! The pan was already cool, but the smell remained in spite of the open windows.

"Last summer you shot baskets from way over there and you didn't get tired so fast," Tanya complained.

I peeked out the window to see two heads: Tanya and Jack were sitting in chairs, side-by-side.

"I guess I got a little older," Jack replied good-humoredly.

Why did Jack come over so early?

"Come on, Jack, you're in pretty good shape for your age," Tanya said patronizingly.

"Thanks, I think," muttered Jack.

"I'm really glad you decided to stay with us for the weekend. I wish you always did."

Decided to stay with us for the weekend? What's she talking about?

"Jack, I need to ask you something. Vera and I are going to be doctors. She wants to be a psychiatrist; I'm going to be a pediatrician. We decided we're going to set up practice together. But there are these girls at school that I'm tutoring in biology, and I really enjoy it. Lately, I've been thinking, maybe I should be a teacher. Only, I want to be a doctor, but I want to teach, too. Anyway, I'm afraid if I tell Mom she'll get upset."

"Why do you think she'll be upset?"

I was touched by the softness in Jack's voice.

"Because she wants me to be successful, and independent. Teaching doesn't pay. And, I told Mom when I'm rich she won't have to work."

I saw Jack's arm toss the basketball onto the grass. It rolled just far enough for me to see it over their heads.

"I'm sure your mother will let you decide."

"I know," sighed Tanya. "But she works so hard, and it's all for college and medical school. If I change my mind . . ."

"Frankly, Tanya, as far as education goes, your mother can give you better advice than I can. But it doesn't seem to me you've really changed your mind. You could major in one of the sciences, then either get your teaching certificate or move on to medical school. Even after medical school you could teach."

"Yeah, I suppose. I don't want to talk to Mom yet. If I decide to, you'll be there, won't you?"

Jack took a long time to answer. "Certainly."

A rabbit hopped to the ball, sniffed, then hopped off.

"Mom always thinks she's going to do something wrong. It's like everything is temporary, especially now, with Dad's letters."

"Tanya, if you need me, call me, any time, day or night. Okay?"

"Yeah, thanks. Actually, now I'm not afraid because I can work, and then you're always around. It's not the same as when I was little and it was just Mom and me. That was scary, sometimes."

"I'm happy you chose to involve me. I think your mother has taken too much on herself, and she needs our support. Please, do me a favor while I'm out of town and keep an eye on things. Together we'll help her out. Okay?"

"Okay," Tanya answered seriously. "She's tired all the time, she even lets me make my own cocoa."

"Remember," Jack said slowly, "we have an agreement. Listen, if you want lox and bagels we better go to the deli before your mother gets up and makes more eggs."

"Oh, Jack, would you please tell Mom you burned the eggs?"

I was hurrying back to my room and never heard his response. The feeling of defeat made me numb. I tossed myself on the bed and rolled onto my stomach closing my eyes.

She finds it easier to talk to Jack than to me. What does that say about me as a mother? What did I do wrong? She needs a family, but I took her from her father and now I've pushed Jack away. She comes home to one person and there is no one else. That's all I knew, too. I thought I protected her and made her comfortable, and now it turns out she's been scared. Scared of the same thing that haunted me—what would happen to her if something happened to me. What can she learn from me other than to work like a slave and be alone?

God, don't let us grow apart. Jack is a friend. Maybe it's not important that I'm not in love with him, as I am with Sasha. I will never sacrifice Tanya. I promise. Please, God, you've come this far with us, please, just a little further.

I stiffened at the sound of a knock on the door.

"Mom, are you up yet?" Tanya briskly flew through the door in her new red sweatsuit. "Mom, Jack and I bought lox and bagels. Are you crying?" She sat on the bed giving me her cheek.

"No, just a bad dream," I sighed and kissed her. "That was a great idea. We haven't had lox for a long time. You set the table, I'll wash and be out in a minute."

I made the bed, washed, and changed into my old gray sweats and a T-shirt.

"Are you decent?" I heard Jack behind the closed door.

"Yes, come in," I said, setting my brush down on the dresser.

Jack opened the door but didn't come in.

"Breakfast is ready," he said with a strained smile. "I'm sorry, Anna. I just shut off the alarm and went back to sleep. This morning, Tanya caught me coming out of the bathroom and I stayed to shoot baskets with her. I'm afraid she assumed I was invited to stay."

"It's okay."

"When do you think we can meet with Pat?"

"I don't know. Tanya and I are planning to go to Bella's at six. She returned from Kiev last week and I had asked her to look up some friends of mine."

"Do you mind if I come along?"

"I don't think anyone there will be inclined to speak English."

"That's okay. I'll call Pat after breakfast. Anna, I'll have to take the papers you went over yesterday with me."

"Don't go away, Jack." I surprised myself.

Jack stepped in closing the door behind him.

"Anna, I thought I made it clear in our last conversation that if you shut me off from what's important to you, I may as well be out of your life. I only wish I could understand what you're trying to achieve."

"I just want to be honest."

"Spell it out for me, please. I'm merely an average American guy and I don't follow." Jack pushed up his glasses and stuck his hands in his pockets.

I sat down on the edge of the bed, my hands in fists to keep them from shaking.

"Well?" Jack inclined his head as though he couldn't hear well.

"I'm trying to protect myself, and you, from any blows that might be waiting, because I don't know what's going to happen. I mean, tomorrow, in a year, in ten years."

He will say now that it doesn't make sense.

"But, Anna, I don't either." Jack shifted from one foot to the other, taking his hands out of his pockets.

A burning sensation started in my shoulder muscles and expanded up into my neck.

"Let's have breakfast. Tanya is waiting." I thought there was no life in my voice.

"I've missed you something crazy. That's bad English; don't use that phrase."

Cautiously, I searched for a smile in his eyes. I thought I detected sympathy.

Jack held out his hand.

Where was he the night I called and left a message?

"Jack, where were you when I called you the other night at the hotel?"

He wrinkled his forehead. "Ah, I see. Well . . . I was sitting in the bar wishing you were a man so I could punch you out."

Now sparks exploded deep inside his eyes.

"I'm sorry." I took his hand and got up. The muscle pain retreated somewhat.

"Anna, while I commute, let's stay together on weekends. What do you say?" Jack gave my hand a light squeeze. "But, Anna, I won't be sleeping in the living room." He smiled tentatively, watching closely for my reaction.

"I can't promise anything."

"I'm not promising anything, either. Fair?"

"Fair."

With Jack, does it mean we're almost a family? Sasha, you said it yourself: Family is sacred.

I stood staring at Jack.

Jack grinned. "If we don't leave this room immediately I'm going to lock the door and we'll spend the rest of the day right here."

That sounds like the Jack I know.

"By the way," he said with artificial nonchalance, "I tried to fry some eggs earlier and burned them. I'm sorry. I bought you a new frying pan."

I raised my eyebrows. He chuckled in return.

The kitchen table looked picturesque, dressed with white plates, blue napkins, orange juice, lox, cream cheese, cucumbers, onions, and several bagels arranged in a pyramid. No trace of burned eggs except a lingering whiff.

Tanya held the phone with her shoulder, her eyes wide in response to the audible chattering rolling from the receiver.

Jack stopped at the table, suddenly shy. "Where do you want me to sit?"

Are his weekend stays going to be elevated into a world event?

"It doesn't matter," I shrugged. "You've eaten with us before."

Jack glanced in Tanya's direction, pretending to ignore the rudeness of my remark. By the heightened color of his cheeks, I knew that he hadn't.

An apology is in order, but it will only happen again. This can't work.

I brusquely told Tanya to hang up and sit down.

Jack poured juice into all three glasses.

"Why are you upset?" Tanya grabbed a bagel and plopped down. She balanced two slices of lox on her fork almost dropping one of them before it reached her plate. "What did I do?" She challenged me with a quick questioning sideways look at Jack, the burned eggs undoubtedly on her mind. Apparently satisfied with his wink, she folded the lox in half neatly on the bagel.

Jack and I turned our undivided attention to spreading cream cheese and arranging lox, cucumber, and onions on our bagels.

"Alice's mother is going to cancel tonight's party at their house if Alice doesn't clean her closet. That's not fair. She already invited everyone. We already spent money on chips, and salsa, and stuff." Tanya chewed, drank half of her juice, and shook her head. "I don't know how Alice can deal with this."

"She'll clean her closet?" suggested Jack.

"I know. She has no choice. But can you imagine—on the day of the party! And she still has to have her hair cut."

Tanya contemplated the other half of the bagel, then bit into it. We ate in silence.

"Did Alice know she had to do it?" I asked, trying to follow Jack's example of making this breakfast feel normal.

"Yeah, she did, she just didn't have a chance yet. She wanted to do it after the party. What does it matter? We don't care, we won't look into her closet."

As I opened my mouth to offer a logical, motherly reply, the telephone rang.

"I'll get it," Tanya ran across the kitchen to the telephone. "Hello? Oh, hi, Jeff."

"Could you give me one good reason . . ." started Jack in a very low voice, not looking at me.

"I apologize. Now maybe you'll see this won't work. I can't become too attached."

"And how do you measure attachment?"

"Mom," Tanya came back, "do you mind if Jeff picks me up at Bella's?"

"That's fine." I answered absetmindedly in Russian.

Jack ate energetically, but silently. I chewed slowly, dreading I would have to answer Jack's last question.

"Mom, we have to leave in the next fifteen minutes if you don't want me to be late for work. By the way, Jeff is going to pick up some tapes for the party and bring me home from work. Jack, are you going grocery shopping with Mom?"

"I don't think so."

Jack and I hadn't looked at each other for some time, which wasn't easy around such a small table.

"Anna, before you go shopping I'd like to talk to you." Jack smiled for Tanya's benefit.

"I'll clear the table," offered Tanya.

Jack followed me to my bedroom. I'd give anything to just fade from existence until he leaves.

He closed the door. "Anna, the easiest thing would be for me to turn around and leave. And I will, if you really want me to. But I think it's a mistake, that you'd be hurting all of us more than you know."

"I'm sorry, Jack. It's simply that I've become used to being with you and it frightens me." Awkwardly, I stood in the middle of the room, rimrod straight.

"It may be simple to you, but frankly I don't understand."

"Parting with someone you've grown accustomed to is very painful. I never want to experience that hurt again."

"Only an hour ago you told me I should stay."

"I would like you to stay, but why should I go through more pain when it doesn't work out?"

"Why the hell should we part? You're contradicting yourself."

"How do you know we won't? Everyone does eventually. Jack, do what you want. I have to go now, Tanya's waiting."

"Hold it," Jack moved closer, cutting off the path to the door.

He was standing so near I could feel his breath. His hands on my hips were two warm islands.

"Anna, I won't leave. I'm in love with you."

His words filled the room. He can't be talking to me. I looked up in horror.

Jack's eyes searched mine. "Why are you so frightened?" he whispered.

I put my arms around him and buried my face in his shoulder. His fingers wandered up my back.

"Jack, don't be in love with me. I'll only hurt you. I hurt everyone."

His fingers continued their gentle movement.

I sighed, burying my face even deeper into his shoulder, grateful for his seriousness.

There was a knock at the door.

"Mom, I'm going to be late for work."

I tore myself from Jack's warmth.

All I could think about all day were Jack's words: "I'm in love with you." How can they be true? I can't believe them.

For the first time since my divorce I'm going to wake up in the morning with a man in my bed. Come to think of it, tomorrow will be the first time I'll wake up with a man in my bed. Fima wasn't a man—he was the someone who had the legal right to sleep with me. To Sasha, what we were doing didn't deserve an entire night. What did he think when Bella called him?

I don't know how not to sleep alone. Tanya didn't seem to attach any special significance to Jack's presence this morning. Is it because, like a typical American teenager, she has a healthy mind? To want sex and receive it is healthy; but honestly, I hope Tanya doesn't want or receive it for quite a while. How come with Sasha no moral issues encumbered the simple physical enjoyment?

Being loved and needed are intoxicating feelings, no matter how much I try not to let them go to my head. "I'm in love with you." I want to do something nice for Jack for merely saying these words—even if he didn't mean them—and for what he's become to Tanya.

When I came home, I saw Jack talking to my neighbors down the street. It was Peggy and her husband, whose name I didn't remember.

She and I met soon after we moved in, when her car with a boat hitched to it suffered a flat tire and blocked my driveway. We spent two hours in my kitchen drinking tea, and she discussed the best areas for fishing while we waited for the motor club. Occasionally, Peggy has brought me some fresh fish, which I immediately gave to Irena as she was the only person I knew who would still clean them. Peggy and her husband sold their business several years ago. They considered this house—with an American flag always flying over the garage—their summer residence as opposed to their winter residence located on some lake in Arkansas.

I pulled up behind Jack's car and honked. Peggy waved. Jack shook hands with her husband and headed across the lawn towards me.

Does Jack remember what he said?

He stuck his head through the open window of the car and kissed me.

"Ahhh, delicious! I didn't realize your shopping would take so long. Who did you buy all these groceries for? Are we having a party?"

We?

Jack helped carry the bags in. A man in the house does have its advantages.

"I went to my house to shower and I brought back some clothes to keep here. Pat's not home, so I left a message on his machine."

"We have an extra set of house keys. Remind me to give them to you."

Now this man is going to be able to walk into my house anytime he wants. I'm not sure this is right.

"By the way, I did some grocery shopping of my own," Jack said, handing me a box of eclairs.

I went red, realizing the connotation. Jack pressed me close, covering my neck with quick, light kisses as he tried to maneuver me toward the bedroom.

"Please, Jack, not now. We're supposed to go to Bella's soon." I felt Jack's readiness against my body. "Not now, Jack."

"I've missed you, Anna. And we're not going to Bella's for a couple of hours."

I can't, Sasha's so close. It would be like doing it with Sasha in the next room.

I slipped away from Jack.

"I told you, Jack, you'll be bored at Bella's tonight."

"I better start getting used to it." Jack followed me.

"What do you mean?"

My instant apprehension made him throw up his hands and laugh, "Whoa, you did agree to weekends."

Jack wolfed down a corned beef sandwich. I made myself toast with preserves. A slice of dark Ukrainian bread, covered with a layer of preserves, made by Sasha's mother, was my breakfast every day for many years.

"Anna, would you please give me Bella's number? If Pat doesn't call back before we're ready to go, I'll leave it on his machine. I really want to meet with him tomorrow."

I can't clean the kitchen; Jack has his papers spread out all over the table. And the laundry—his laundry will be part of our laundry. I'll be sleeping with him; I can't tell him to give his laundry to his cleaning lady.

"I'm in love with you." Forever, women have been susceptible to this line, and I'm no exception. Foolishly, I want these words to be true— even if the answer to them is no.

Jack sat back wiping his glasses with his sweatshirt. I felt his eyes watching me.

"What? Anything I missed?"

"No," he put his glasses back on. "I was just thinking."

"About what?"

"You're very efficient in the kitchen, but you shouldn't have to do housework."

"Oh, yes, I should. I want to make sure Tanya has a hot meal every day."

"Anna, you need a housekeeper; you'll be very busy in the months ahead."

"Jack, I'm not wasting money on what I can do myself, or what I can do without."

"I'm spoiled, we always had at least a cook and a housekeeper. My mother couldn't survive without a companion and a cleaning service."

"It would feel funny to have someone do the things I can do myself."

"My mother grew up in the back room of her father's bakery, sweeping the floor every night after the customers were gone. Her parents barely spoke English. And you know what, after she was married, she took like a fish to water at having a staff of servants."

"She became part of a different, and superior, world. I don't think I would be comfortable in a world to which I don't belong."

We each continued our work in silence.

Mrs. Graff met Jack's father at a resort in Miami her parents had scrimped and saved to send her to. She had no qualms about marrying into a wealthy family. Perhaps it would be all right for Tanya, but not for me. Like Mrs. Graff's parents, I know my place. My mission was to bring my child here, not build my own life. Too late for that.

"Jack, what's your mother's first name?"

"Florence. Why?"

"Is Florence a Jewish name?"

"It could be. My grandparents called her something like Fanny, but she's Florence on all her legal papers. Their English wasn't good. They spoke Yiddish at home."

"They probably called her Fanya."

"That's it!" Jack sat back.

"It's a Russian-Jewish name."

"You know, I think you should talk to my mother; there're a lot of things you'd probably find in common."

"I don't think she's looking for things in common."

Jack smiled, "Anna, when we're in New York, we'll go to my mother's apartment and look through all the old pictures."

Why would we go to New York?

Jack returned to his work. Every time the cuckoo cried he screwed up his face and looked up. He didn't like it. Well, he's free to go.

"Fooood!" bellowed Tanya from the door.

The few hours at work had done wonders for her appetite.

The expression on Jack's face caught my attention. Sasha's mother used to look at me just as Jack was looking at Tanya now; then she would give me a treat or some kopeks to secretly buy ice cream from a street vendor.

Tanya pecked me on my cheek and whisked the food to the table, pushing Jack's papers aside.

"Couldn't we eat in the dining room?" Jack pleaded.

"What!"

"Mom, we should set up a place for Jack to work in the basement," Tanya interjected.

Jack's eyes had a mischievously guilty look to them as he relinquished half of the table.

On weekends I'll have to speak English in my own house. Every weekend is going to be a test of my patience. But Tanya enjoys Jack, and most weekends I'll have to work anyway. Well, when he finishes commuting he'll move back to his house and things will return to normal.

Jack sat hunched over, writing, highlighting, and drawing charts while we cleaned the kitchen and changed. I asked him, again, not to go with us. His answer was to slide his arms through Tanya's and mine, cheerfully exclaiming, "Let's get going, girls!"

nineteen

Felix and Bella had bought their house in Wilmette when Bella was still a resident doctor. It was a small ranch they barely could afford. Now they're looking for a larger house, one with a family room spacious enough for a grand piano so Felix can rehearse with his trio.

Hopefully, Bella can give me a few minutes right away to tell me about Sasha and Asya.

As the three of us got out of the car we heard a loud conversation in Russian. I recognized Irena's voice. That means Vilen is in the vicinity. Today, even he doesn't bother me.

Three men with cigarettes, Felix among them, stood on the front walk listening to Irena with blank faces.

"And here are the Fishman women." Felix turned to us, relieved. "You brought Jack?" he asked in Russian, not hiding his surprise.

"He insisted," I answered in Russian.

"You look terrible! Are you upset?" Irena, seeing her opening, pounced. "You were right to bring Jack. If you want to keep him you shouldn't leave him alone for a second."

"I'm glad to see Jack, too, but this is not exactly his crowd. He doesn't understand Russian," Felix said in an apologetic tone.

"I can interpret for him," Tanya said defiantly in English.

"Good for you, girl, you have more sense than your mother," Irena said snidely in Russian. She tapped Tanya on her cheek and went into the house.

"I don't think you've met my friends," Felix said, switching to English. He made a gesture toward the smoking men, one tall with quick, brown eyes, the other a little shorter and gray. "This is Anya Fishman and her daughter, Tanya, whom we've known since Rome, and Anya's friend, Jack Graff, an American."

"How's it going?" I heard Jack say as he came from behind us to shake the men's hands.

The men introduced themselves, then we all went inside.

The living room was full of faces. My eyes, frantically searching for Bella, almost missed her among three well-dressed women on the sofa. Some familiar faces smiled. I must have seen them before, but I couldn't connect them to names. The guests were sitting on the teal, imitation leather sofa and the matching armchair; on the dark wood dining room chairs; and on white, metal chairs with round seats brought in from the kitchen. Two large pictures, an original stilllife in a massive frame and a splashy painting of a seaside faced each other over people's heads. The glass coffee table overflowed with plates filled with cheese and fruit.

"Anichka, I'm glad you could come. We've been waiting for you."

Bella seemed fragile and lethargic. We hugged.

"You're getting prettier and prettier, Tanichka," Bella said in her American-accented Russian, then switched easily to English. "Hello, Jack, nice to see you again."

The look she gave me did not disguise her surprise.

"Jack doesn't expect to hear English tonight," I said, answering her unasked question.

Bella laughed. "Poor Jack. If you want you can watch television in the family room, and there's plenty of appetizers everywhere. Help yourself." Turning to me, she continued, "I think we'll talk about my trip first, some of the guests can't stay long."

I interrupted her in Russian. "Bella, did you have a chance to find my friends?"

Jack vanished in the direction of the family room.

"Yes, I did. Tanichka, I have a letter for you from your father." Bella's eyes met mine. "Let's go to the bedroom," she suggested hesitantly. "The letter is in my purse. Your dad came over to see me twice, the second time with his young son. He questioned me exhaustively about you and your life. Here's the letter."

The envelope had been opened. Soviet customs officials dislike anything that could possibly smell of deception.

"Is it in Russian?" asked Tanya.

"I would think so," smiled Bella. "Please, Tanichka, leave the reading until after I've answered everyone's questions. People are anxious to start. It won't be long."

As we made our way back down the hall, Bella said, "Anya, I talked to your friend, Asya, on the phone. She was supposed to visit me, but she was busy, and, as you know, I left rather abruptly."

"What did she say?"

"Nothing, really. Her older son is a programmer. He's getting married this summer to a *shiksa*. I think she said her younger son is at Moscow University. She was very pleased you remembered her. She told me she had received your letters, but her husband and mother-in-law wouldn't let her respond. Her sister is coming to America for a visit soon, but not to Chicago. That's about it."

"And my other friend?" I tried not to appear anxious.

We stopped in the living room surrounded by faces.

"I'm sorry, Anichka, according to the Kiev Information Service, no one by that name and date of birth lives there. Asya told me she lost sight of him years ago."

My God, where could Sasha be? And, Asya was pleased I remembered her? That's it?

Unbelievable. Bella had spent an entire week in Kiev and Asya was too busy to stop by? She was pleased I remembered her . . . I would have expected her to be shocked if I didn't.

A masculine voice wrenched me back to reality, as two men offered Tanya and me their chairs. One I didn't recognize; Vilen was the other, and he remained standing behind me after we sat down, his hand on the back of my chair.

Bella sat on the sofa and addressed the faces around her.

"I debated for a long time about telling everyone the truth, but some of you are getting ready to visit the Soviet Union, and I have decided you must know the truth. The truth is that, even though I hadn't seen my mother and my sister in ten years, three days after my arrival I was already counting the minutes to my departure. I'm ashamed to have to acknowledge this, but it's the truth."

All faces mirrored the same intense, wide-eyed, pained emotions.

"Carved in my memory is that the people in Kiev don't smile. Remember when we first came, how we made fun of Americans smiling at us all the time. Well, I'll tell you something, it's frightening to see people that don't smile."

I glanced at Tanya. Her eyes, fixed on Bella, expressed both fascination and puzzlement. Fima's letter lay folded in her lap.

"Whatever difficulties or problems we have, we must continue to remind ourselves where we could be—it will keep everything in perspective. I wish our children understood more of where we came from, and why we uprooted ourselves. But we all know they won't." Bella turned to someone I didn't know. "Even those who left as teenagers like yours. Our children will become, or have already become, trusting, naïve Americans. What stunned me more than anything," she smiled suddenly, a broad, amused smile, "we have too, become such Americans. We relish our new lives, and we even love the English language more than we consciously know. We should all pray constantly and thank God that we're not there, and that our children are not there."

"Do they know the truth about Chernobyl?" asked the woman sitting next to Bella.

"Rumors persist that the consequences are of catastrophic proportions. Of course, the Jews are once again at fault, as they learned from overseas calls—before others—what is only now public knowledge. Rumors fly that those 'damned Jews' are spreading panic. Anti-Semitism is worse than ever. Families of the party apparatus were immediately evacuated from Kiev. But four days after the accident, during the May Day celebration, people were picnicking in the parks. A doctor who advised her patients to wash food thoroughly got in trouble for spreading false information causing panic. A friend told me that doctors are not permitted to document radiation-related symptoms. Now, people are being told to scrub their floors and keep their windows shut. I have no doubt if this accident had happened in a part of the country farther from Western Europe, not one soul, other than the dying families, would have ever known.

"If emigration were to resume tomorrow, which doesn't seem likely, the anti-Semitism would certainly increase—even though it's hard to imagine how it could be worse. It would be said that the damned Jews are the only ones allowed to save themselves." Bella punctuated her speech with a deep sigh.

"Do you think Gorbachev will accomplish anything?" Irena's voice cut through the prolonged silence.

"History is literally being rewritten as we speak. Previously forbidden books and movies are now available and newspapers criticize officials. But, in reality, the Soviet way of life remains the same, and, at any moment, this *perestroika* may become another mistake, like all past mistakes on the glorious path to communism.

"The system isn't really changing. People talk about change, but what good is talk without action? No one knows what to do, what to believe. Everyone is waiting for directions. The Russians have always needed a Tsar; right now it happens to be Gorbachev's turn. My family and my friends told me that since they've been handed these new freedoms, there's no difference between their lives and mine. They are drunk on *perestroika* and trying to sober them only met with anger. The gratitude for an apartment or for sugar or egg rations now competes with the gratitude for freedom."

"Did they think you'd changed?" asked the short man I'd met in front of the house.

"Not at first. At the airport my sister insisted I looked exactly the way I did when I left, except for being fashionably dressed—a reference to the wardrobe from a discount store, which I had bought so I wouldn't stand out. The changes people noticed in me later—and I'm talking about people who have known me since childhood—have nothing to do with age or clothes. They were exclusively the result of a different mentality.

"Lastly," Bella continued after a pause, "unless you have ties you can't live without, I wouldn't advise anyone to go there."

"Will you go again—to see your family?" The question came from Tanya, who turned crimson from the attention she attracted.

Bella and Felix exchanged a long glance.

"No, Tanichka, I won't," Bella said gently.

Tanya lowered her head. Faces became sadder. Bella's eyes clouded.

"Is it true, as far as food and clothes go, that it's worse there now than it was before we left?" asked a woman from an easy chair on the far side of the room.

"I understand that's true. There wasn't time for me to go shopping and, as usual, the tables at the homes I visited were full with all the best foods. However, when one knows the abundance they see is the result of weeks of bribing, standing in lines, and spending one's savings, the caviar, lox, and other delicacies do not impress, only hurt. As for clothes—well, I came back in my sister's old clothes, leaving everything behind, including my bras, panties, and slippers."

Bella's daughter, Susan, ran in, followed by a small boy carrying a toy boat. Before they could head down the hallway, Felix caught her by the arm.

"Where, young lady, are you going?"

The children went into a long, confused explanation and the somber, adult faces momentarily enlivened. The sadness returned, however, as people rose and headed to the family room.

"Mom, Bella didn't say much more than what you've always said," Tanya said, sounding disappointed.

"Nothing has changed, Tanichka, nothing has changed."

"But Gorbachev is different. He even looks like a normal person."

Vilen startled me, touching my back with his hand.

"It's funny to listen to your conversation, Tanya in English, you in Russian."

I froze; Tanya went on ahead.

Vilen eyed my body. "You look lovely today."

"Anna?"

Vilen's eyes shifted as he held out his hand to Jack. They exchanged greetings. Jack put his arm around my waist, and I instinctively leaned toward him.

The crowd thinned. About twenty people remained, armed with paper plates and drinks. They broke up into multiple islands. Jack and I became such an island near the corner occupied by a floor lamp with three umbrella-shaped lights. The lamp divided us from Tanya. Her hand rolled around her father's letter, she cocked her head to one side, a shade of surprise in her eyes. The snatches of conversation suggested identical topics under discussion swirling around Bella's visit, the Soviet Union in general, and the superiority of those who had fled and, therefore, triumphed.

Asya was pleased I remembered her—whatever that meant—and Sasha remains an elusive ghost to haunt my every waking moment. The excitement of challenge solidified inside me. Somehow, somewhere, I must find him.

I expected to find a blank expression on Jack's face, but he gazed seriously from group to group, rocking heel to toe, his eyes soft and probing, as if waiting for a chance to reply to something addressed to him.

Felix entered smiling. "Tanya, there's a young man at the door asking for you."

"That's Jeff. Thanks. Mom, I'm going now."

"Home by eleven."

"I know," she said reluctantly.

"Nice-looking Jewish boy," said Felix in English. "Why are you two just standing here? I'm sorry, Jack, there are times when only one's mother tongue will do. The Russian community's mood is not very good at the moment." Felix gave the thumbs down.

"I can well imagine," Jack responded as he pressed me closer, being unusually demonstrative in front of others. "Would you fill me in on what was said?"

I wasn't up to hearing another version of Bella's recitation.

"Jack, I can tell you everything later. We have a difficult week ahead of us. We should go."

Bella appeared, holding a drink, looking pale and even more fragile than she had earlier.

"Felix, would you please see what the children are doing in the bathroom? There's probably a flood in there by now."

The telephone rang and Felix picked up the cordless phone on the bar.

"Phone call for Anna Fishman or Jack Graff," he announced jokingly, looking around as if not seeing us.

"It must be Pat." Jack took the phone from Felix.

Bella touched my arm. "Good, I want a couple minutes with you."

We navigated to an uninhabited corner.

"Anya, I don't usually stick my nose in other people's business; however, meeting your ex-husband was an extremely disquieting experience. He harbors much bitterness and distrust. He wanted to know how a woman with a small child, no skills, and no English could become financially independent, own property, and still be respected. He could not—or would not—understand that you've done these things and are still respected. He asked questions like: What moral standards has Tanya been brought up with? Why doesn't your boyfriend marry you? Is your boyfriend rich? How many boyfriends have you had over the years? He wanted to know why, if you have such a good job, does Tanya have to work? Anya," her eyes widened, "he implied that you're a whore! It was a very difficult conversation."

I couldn't tell her, but I thought of those nights (mornings, afternoons, and whenever) that Vilen took what he thought was his right.

And, of course, there was Gena, who wanted to but didn't, for fear of Marina's wrath. Thank heavens, I only had to put up with his stares and an occasional knee rub under the table.

Jack appeared at my side. "Excuse me. Anna, the only time Pat can meet with us tomorrow is in the early morning. I told him I'd call him as soon as we wake up."

"That's fine. Jack, please excuse me for a moment, I need to finish my conversation with Bella."

"Are you okay?"

"Yes."

"Okay. I'll wait for you outside."

I turned back to Bella. "Fima's right about a lot of things, Bella. Let's just leave it at that."

Bella set her drink down. "Well, all I wanted to do is warn you. And he's planning for Tanya to return, which is crazy. He was extremely agitated and quite obnoxious at times, especially when I inquired why he let you go if he was so concerned with Tanya's well-being. Our conversation ended when I told him to get lost."

"Bella, I appreciate what you did, but, like I said, he's right about a lot of things."

"Oh, please, Anya, I've known you more than ten years—since we shared an apartment in Rome. You're one of the few people I've known whom I could rely on. And you know how much that means." Bella looked around the room at the various groups and sighed. "Anya, it appears from what Jack just said you're living together?"

"Only on weekends. During the week he's in Wisconsin. We're working on the same project . . ."

"Anichka, don't apologize. He's a decent man. He and Tanya seem to get along very well."

"If he didn't make Tanya happy he wouldn't be with us."

"I know how you feel and what you've done for her. That's why your ex-husband's attitude is so perplexing."

"Bella, I've come to understand I've done less for her than people might think." I put my purse under my arm. "I better be going. Jack's waiting."

We hugged, then I moved inconspicuously along the walls of the room, wishing I could be alone tonight.

"Why are you leaving so early?"

I jumped at the sound of Vilen's voice. He obviously had been lying in wait for me.

"Go to the devil's mother," I said quickly—the strongest Russian curse I have ever been able to utter—and walked by without looking at his face, but knowing my remark incited nothing but a smirk.

Jack drove slowly, and, with each of us absorbed in our own thoughts, not a word was said until within a few blocks of the house.

I felt a subtle unease, a twirl of anguish I recognized as a presage to something imminent about to occur for the first time. A similar sensation throbbed in my chest and throat in the months before Tanya was born, and, again, while my hand readied Fima's signature. What set it off now? Could it be the first full night with Jack? How important could it be? I haven't had many first times of anything.

In my dreams there had been hundreds of first times with Sasha. Then, when the real first time came, it was completely unexpected and Sasha was gentle, understanding, apologetic, and utterly miserable.

I was twenty-six and had never been kissed. Lonya had been taken by ambulance to the emergency room at four in the morning. I had walked back from the hospital, my eyes half-closed, and then fell asleep half-dressed. I awoke to Sasha at the door, a conical bag made of newspaper in his hand (something Russians were experts in making because stores didn't provide bags). It was filled with mouth-watering grapes. He frequently dropped off hard-to-get treats for us.

"Why aren't you at work, Anya, and where's Lonya?" he asked, his voice husky.

"Lonya was taken to the hospital during the night and I overslept."

Decisively, I crossed the room, locked the door behind Sasha, tossed the bag of grapes on the table and locked my arms around his neck.

He was motionless. "Anichka, no . . . we can't."

I looked into eyes filled with lust.

"Why not, Sasha? We both want it." I brought my hand wistfully across his cheek.

Suddenly his mouth was on mine. I choked—what did I know of open-mouthed kisses?

Sasha pulled back. "Anichka, let me go . . . I can't . . . I won't."

On tiptoes, I kissed him the way he had kissed me. An inner whisper assured me that our lips would never part, then just as I relaxed, his mouth moved down my neck pecking lightly and marking its way with quick feverish breaths.

"What do you like more, Anichka, kisses on your neck or kisses on your lips?" Sasha murmured.

I responded with an indistinct sound.

His hand squeezed my nipple through my blouse, jolting my taut body into a frenzied, bewildering urge.

We moved the few steps to the bed where he gently removed my clothing. When he started to remove his, I lay back closing my eyes. In a minute, I felt him move on top of me.

He whispered, "I'll be very careful."

Something hard and thick was pushing at me. I opened my eyes, Sasha was watching me. A sharp pain made me gasp. The hard and thick thing moved in and out several times, then abruptly withdrew.

Then Sasha's body was next to mine, his face down, shaking and groaning. I felt wetness on my leg. There was a burning feeling where the hard and thick had been. Somehow, there was an incompleteness about what had happened. I was crying and angry. Avoiding my eyes he rose, dressed quickly, then sat on the side of the bed, bringing my palms to his lips.

"I'm sorry, Anichka, it was my fault."

"It's not a fault," I cried. "We wanted it. I want it again! I love you."

"I know." Sasha wiped my eyes and my nose with a corner of the sheet. "Anichka, I will never divorce my wife, and you need a husband and a family."

"I don't need a husband."

"Anya, you will come to realize that I am right. I have to go now. Don't worry, I withdrew in time."

Withdrew in time? Like any decent girl of my generation I had no idea about intercourse and its consequences.

"I'm going to feel terrible every time I see Lonya. Oh, God."

"But I wanted you."

Sasha kissed my forehead. "Anichka, if we do it again, we'll go on doing it, again and again. That's why we won't do it again."

And we probably wouldn't have, if not for me. My life was fixed on that hard and thick feeling Sasha had given me. I couldn't sleep. I couldn't concentrate. Lonya yelled at me for not caring about him. He appealed to Sasha to explain that he, Lonya, needed special care and attention.

Sasha was attentive, but detached, and we were never alone. Several months passed before it happened again. This time it wasn't an accident. Lilya was away with their older daughter, Nonna, in Evpatoria, a Crimean city famous for its children's mental and developmental institutions. Sasha came to visit Lonya. As he was putting his coat on to leave, I looked at him, my eyes telling him he should expect me at his house. His eyes disapproved, but they did not say no. After that, as Sasha had predicted, we went on doing it, again and again, taking advantage of every infrequent opportunity.

That was nineteen years ago. Now I don't know where he is, how he remembers me, or even if he's alive. And I'm in the United States of America with my grown daughter and my almost-live-in boyfriend, who says he's in love with me.

"Anna, did you see how Vilen was looking at you?"

Jack's voice startled me, but I didn't stir.

"You did, didn't you?"

Does he have the right to ask? Probably so.

"Yes, Jack, I did."

"I didn't like it and I won't ignore it if I see it again. I'm surprised you took it so calmly."

"Don't be jealous."

"I'm not jealous—and I don't think you have any interest in Vilen—but, as a man, I know that look. He has no business looking at you that way. I don't understand—his wife wasn't more than five feet away. Anyone could have noticed."

"It wouldn't phase the other people, even if they thought there was something between us. Russians are like that."

"Like what?"

"Married people frequently have affairs."

"You've got to be kidding!"

"Jack, I don't want to talk about it."

"You mean Russians don't care if their spouses cheat on them?"

"They care—if they find out."

"How do you trust each other?"

"First of all, it doesn't happen to everyone, so, like with everything else, no one believes it will happen to them."

"So, it's possible that Bella and Felix and Vilen and Irena and all the others are having affairs?"

"Some of the affairs actually make more sense than the marriages they betray. Anything is possible; it doesn't matter to me. And, Jack, how do you know I've never had an affair?"

Jack swung into the driveway. The brakes screeched as the car came to a sharp stop.

Jack turned to me. "You wouldn't do it. You wouldn't be able to live with yourself if you did."

What does he know, this straight-as-an-arrow, broad-shouldered man who says he's in love with me?

"Jack, were you serious about what you said to me this morning?"

"Why would I say something I don't mean? I don't have to tell you I love you to get you to sleep with me." He smiled suddenly, his eyes nostalgic. "Do you remember when we were introduced?"

"Yes, I remember."

"I volunteered to help you on that project so I could get to know you. I thought, 'I'll score with this chick within a week.'" He laughed softly, putting his head back and closing his eyes. "I was only about five or six months off."

It was impossible not to smile. During those months we spent hours talking in the car. Afraid Tanya would assume we were sleeping together,

I never let Jack come inside when he brought me home. He would park in the alley behind our building and wait until I put Tanya to bed and came back out.

"Oh, God, how you drove me crazy. You'd go inside every twenty minutes to check on Tanya. You were so tense and apprehensive that I knew if I as much as touched your hand it would be the end of the relationship. I bet you never noticed that bulge between my legs."

We laughed as Jack's face came closer in the dark. His mouth was hot, his tongue firm and persistent.

"And you've been driving me mad ever since. Let's go in," he whispered into my ear.

"What time is it?"

"Almost ten."

"Tanya will be home soon."

"Not for another hour; besides, she has a key."

"I always wait up for her, and she can't come in and find us in bed!"

"She won't be looking for us."

Jack moved closer pinning me against the car door.

"I'm looking forward to a quickie in the morning." He placed my hand on his rock-hard fly.

"A what?"

He chuckled.

There's never a dictionary around when I need one. What's a quickie? I guess I'll have to wait until morning to find out. My instincts told me Jack was not planning on letting me search any dictionaries tonight.

"It's exciting to finally have a whole night together, isn't it?" Jack said as my neck received quick, light kisses.

His warm hand gently rubbing my breast made me tipsy.

"Anna, I love you so much." The words were serious and stubborn.

We kissed leisurely for a long time.

"I think the car that just pulled up to the curb is Jeff's," said Jack, looking into the rear-view mirror and moving back to his side of the car.

He caught my hand as I started to open the car door. "Don't. Give them a few minutes."

"Why aren't they getting out?"

"Venture a guess." Jack squeezed my hand.

"It's simple for you to joke about. Let me go."

"It's not a joke."

Tanya doesn't think of Jeff as her boyfriend. She says they're just friends. Why would they want to sit in the car? I pictured Tanya's hand on Jeff's fly and tried to pull my hand from Jack's grip.

"Don't panic, Anna."

"What are they doing?"

"What we were doing, necking."

"They can't do that. Tanya's only a child."

"Anna, please, give them a few minutes." Jack let go of my hand.

My hands were ice-cold, I opened and closed them to improve the circulation.

Jack looked in his rear-view mirror again.

"Tanya just got out of the car. I don't think she realizes we're here."

We got out and I closed the car door with a bang. Jack came around and stood next to me, his arm around my shoulder. Tanya approached us, brushing her hair.

"Hi, Mom, Jack," she said uncertainly. "I'm not late, am I?"

What does she know that I didn't know until I was much older? Hopefully, they were just talking.

"No. How was the party?" said Jack.

Jeff appeared at the end of the driveway.

"Good evening, Mrs. Fishman. Good evening, Sir. I'm sorry, Tanya wanted to go in right away, but I needed to check with her about something for school."

I could barely return a greeting.

Jack cleared his throat, and I had the feeling he was holding back laughter.

"Let's go in," he said. "We have an early morning meeting. Good night, Jeff."

Jack winked at Tanya as she passed the car, her eyes answered him gratefully. She walked hurriedly to the front door, unlocked it, and quickly disappeared inside.

Exhausted, I covered my face with my hands. Jack locked the car and took my hands in his.

"Tanya is a good girl. Let her act her age. Jeff is quite the gentleman." Jack chuckled. "Did you see how scared he was? By the way, may I ask why we are still outside?"

Unable to face Tanya, I escaped to my bedroom. Jack sat at the dining room table, scribbling in his notebook. Not knowing when he would come in, I was reluctant to undress. I felt helpless and stupid, like a young girl.

Tanya, in her robe, stepped in cautiously.

"Mom, I wasn't doing anything wrong."

"I know, and I love you." I smiled, swallowing my tears.

"I love you, too, Mom. Would you read Dad's letter to me?" She took the folded envelope from her pocket and sat on the bed.

30 April 1986

Dear Tanichka,

I'm extremely touched that you asked Bella Kaganov to get in touch with me in order to find out how we were after the Chernobyl accident. Rest assured, the accident wasn't significant, we are not in danger.

Thank you for the parcels, but you shouldn't spend your money on such beautiful things. When Petya wears the clothes you sent, people stop us in the street asking where we got them.

I was able to learn more about your life by talking to Bella, and I feel it's vital we meet. I have decided to come for a visit instead of waiting for you to make up your mind about coming home. Although I'm sure you would prefer I stay with you during my visit, your mother and I are not on terms that would allow this, and I will be forced to stay with my wife's distant cousins in Chicago. Please find out how complicated the process of sending me an invitation is and what kind of commitments you would have to accept by inviting me.

Please let me know what you would like me to bring you. Remember, Tanya, my goal in coming will be to spend as much time with you as possible, so we can become a real father and daughter again. You will need to arrange your schedule so this will be possible. Don't delay your response.

Regards from my family, Your Father

"He wants to come for a visit?" said Tanya, looking at me guiltily.

Fima wants to come for a visit? I reread the letter.

"Please, don't be upset. I'll tell him not to come. Maybe, next year, I could go there."

"Tanya, he's your father, we'll send him an invitation. You need to know him in order to know yourself. I'll call the JRL and find out what we need to do."

My dry, monotone delivery didn't fool her. As if on cue, we embraced with a quick, impulsive movement.

"Thanks, Mom," Tanya breathed into my shoulder.

Like me, she shied away from words as one does when observing a miracle of nature; no words would suffice but any could shatter the spell.

Again, as if on cue, our arms untied. Our faces remained close, hers carrying an expression of incredulity at the stark vision of our common nucleus, ruled by the same emotions, guided by the same instincts.

Tanya took the letter from me. She passed her hand over it.

"I'll take him to see my school," she said in a businesslike manner, "and we can show him Michigan Avenue, especially Water Tower Place. I'm sure Jack knows all kinds of neat places. I'm glad his wife has relatives in Chicago, because he can't stay here now that Jack's living with us."

Jolted by her last words, I nearly asked where she had gotten that idea, then realized Jack's presence this morning justified her assumption. Of course, by the time Fima's visit materializes, if it does, Jack won't be commuting to Green Bay and will have moved back into his own house.

"Tanichka, we have time to decide where to go and what to do. Right now I want to go to bed. Jack and I have a meeting in the morning."

I undressed watching the bedroom door, expecting Jack to come in at any moment. Nervous, I sat on the edge of the bed in my short, white, cotton nightgown, my hands pressed between my knees.

I marveled at the divergence of views different people held of me. Each of these contained sound logic, and I agreed with all of them. What was true?

Lonya couldn't forgive me for not feeling guilty enough for the death of his mother. His affection for her never ebbed; his memories never faded. Every year, on my birthday, he told me, "You don't understand the meaning of loyalty. You are too shallow to be capable of real devotion." If he was alive now and knew how much Asya and Sasha have meant to me, would he reconsider?

Sasha called me a pagan. He meant it as recognition of my resolve, but was it a compliment? Did he ever wonder whether I would have betrayed *him* had he been my husband? It was betrayal; there's no use trying to sugar-coat it. Does he wonder about me now, if he ever remembers me? And, did he ever wonder the same about himself?

What about Vilen and Gena? They formed the only opinion of me that they could. Merely the thought of their names makes me cringe, makes me feel like a whore. No, I didn't offer my body, but I didn't protect it, either.

Fima didn't hesitate to imply to Bella, a stranger, what he thought of my morals, deservedly so. I betrayed him when I ran off with Tanya. I betrayed him by marrying him without love and by loving someone else. It doesn't matter that he had no knowledge of it—I knew.

My loyalty and my stamina, Jack insists, is the bedrock of my personality. My warnings to him that my loyalty belongs to the past, like Lonya's belonged to his mother, only reinforce his overly optimistic opinion. But do these warnings relieve me of responsibility and give me justification for keeping Jack and taking his warmth? Doesn't it make me worse than what Fima thinks of me?

Where is Jack? One would assume he would hurry, especially tonight. I wish his hands weren't so warm or his body so comfortable to curl up to.

"Waiting?" Jack closed the door behind him and took off his sweatshirt. "I wanted to make sure Tanya went to bed. She mentioned her father's coming for a visit."

"Why make it forbidden fruit? I want her to know her roots."

Jack dropped his sweatshirt and jeans on the floor.

"Tanya's excited, maybe cautiously excited is a better way to put it. Did Bella find your friends?" Jack shed the rest of his clothes, putting his glasses on the nightstand.

I knew he was smiling.

"One of them."

He stepped in front of me. "I've missed you."

Jack gave me his body to do what he liked most, and it brought me satisfaction to please him. I could tell he had missed me, and there were split seconds when I almost believed his words, "I'm in love with you."

Finally, I curled up against him, my arm across his chest, my eyes closed. It was strange not being alone. Unwillingly, I listened to the darkness, reminding me of those times when Vilen forced himself on me while Tanya slept on the other side of the room. I shivered, pressing myself closer to Jack. He kissed the top of my head, hugging me sleepily.

"Jack, we should cover ourselves. Tanya may forget and run in when she gets up in the morning." I remembered our earlier conversation. "Jack, what's a quickie, and why does it have to be in the morning?"

"Good question. I'll answer it in the mor . . ." Jack mumbled, falling asleep before he finished the word.

twenty

Sasha and I are in our favorite meeting place, the Vladimir Gorka Park in Kiev. The sun is just starting to set; shadows from the trees streak across the walkways. How wonderful to be outside, in the open air, with Sasha. How I relish these times. The park is deserted, except for the occasional drunk sleeping on a bench. Small children and their grandmothers have already left, and the lovers haven't arrived yet—that is, except for Sasha and me. We stop under a tree with large, spreading branches. I lean against the trunk and, for just a moment, I close my eyes. I know Sasha is standing a few steps from me, yet I can feel his entire body, like I feel Jack's when he makes love to me. One hand is gently stroking my breast, the other slowly moving down my body and, after what seems like forever, he exerts a slight pressure. Then he stops and reluctantly moves up again.

"*Yishcho*," I whisper in Russian, as my legs involuntarily move apart.

"What?" asked Jack from somewhere far away.

Suddenly fully awake, my eyes closed, I breathed heavily, helpless and unwilling to stop the wondrous sensations. The pressure of Jack's hand increased, his fingers teased.

"What did you say?" Jack whispered in my ear.

Why isn't he inside me? I'm going to explode.

"Tell me when you're ready," he tickled my ear with his tongue.

I'm not going to tell him; it's like begging. I squirmed, my movements half-conscious. This cannot be happening to me; I will not give in to a physical urge, not again. I must be dreaming.

"Jack!" I demanded.

"Now?" he said slowly.

"Yes, yes!" I almost screamed as I pulled my legs back, impatient for the sharp, sweet spasms that bring contentment and peace.

Like the time in my front hall, my body greeted him with relief and gratitude.

"You got it, baby," he gasped as he collapsed on top of me.

The excitement and tenderness in his voice touched me. He really does care how I feel.

Jack rose, covered me with a sheet, and went to take a shower. I looked at the clock: A quarter to seven.

Was that a quickie?

Jack dressed, smiled at me with twinkling eyes, disappeared, then returned carrying a glass of milk and a plate with an eclair on it.

"Jack, it's morning. Besides, that eclair must be frozen!"

"I took the box out last night."

"You deserve someone better than me."

"Don't try to give me ideas. Eat, you need to restore your energy."

If Jack gives me an eclair every time we make love, I'll soon look like a blimp.

"You'd better get up. I called Pat, he'll be over in an hour. Here's a list of issues I'd like to discuss."

"Jack, do you remember your first time?"

"First time?" he repeated absent-mindedly. "Oh, that first time." A very male grin widened Jack's face. "I don't think you'd care to hear about it. Look at this list, will you?"

"Who was she? How old were you?"

"Anna, please. No, wait. I'll tell you if you tell me what you said in Russian when you woke up."

"It was nothing, really. I was dreaming."

Cheater. Tell him you were dreaming of another man.

"So, what did you say?"

"I can't tell you."

"Why?"

"It's embarrassing. A woman is not supposed . . ."

"Tell me."

"All right, I said 'more.'"

"Yes! Just what I thought!" Jack kicked his legs in delight.

Whether I want to or not, Jack makes me smile.

"Why is it embarrassing?" Jack stroked my leg under the sheet.

"It's like propositioning, and the man is supposed to do that."

His eyes widened with amazement. "You don't really take that garbage seriously?"

"Not entirely, but I don't think you'd like for a woman to chase you."

"Not if I wasn't interested in her."

"And if you were, you'll do the chasing."

"Telling your boyfriend or husband that you want him is not chasing, it's expected."

"Jack, tell me about your first time. You promised."

"I was in Buenos Aires for my summer break, she was my cousin, and I was sixteen."

"You were Tanya's age! How old was she?"

"Twenty-eight. When she said I was big for my age, I thought she meant my height."

"How could she do such a thing?"

"She didn't seem to have any problems."

"You know what I mean!"

"Well, what can I tell you? That's the story. She's really a very nice person."

"And afterwards, did you . . ."

"Well . . . I was in Buenos Aires for the summer."

"My goodness! Do you keep in touch?"

"Not that way. Come on, Anna, don't be so dramatic. It was nothing. I see her in Argentina at family gatherings, we chat. She says I should get married. She's a widow now, with grandchildren."

"How could it be nothing?"

"Well, I suppose, at the time it wasn't, at least physically, I mean. But that was centuries ago."

Centuries ago? How can he say that? The past is not a leaf that withers, crumbles, and blows away in the wind. It has flesh; it has roots; it has life.

Jack squeezed my hand and our eyes met. Unfortunately there wasn't enough time for another quickie.

"Anna, please look through these notes, and, for goodness' sake, get up."

Tanya was still asleep when we ate breakfast. We had just put the dishes in the dishwasher when Pat arrived, waving new baby pictures.

"She smiles a lot," he bragged as he handed me a copy of the proposal. "Take a look. If there are any changes I can redo it and you can pick it up in the morning. The earlier it's finalized the more time we'll have."

Jack intercepted the document, read it, made copious notes, then read them to us. Before I knew it, both men were involved in a discussion of what needed to be done, with Jack insisting on a limited skeleton project.

I made three trips to the kitchen and back, serving coffee. The telephone rang twice and I took messages for Tanya. When she finally wandered into the kitchen, I warmed her breakfast in the microwave. America is so good to lazy people.

It was after nine and the discussion in the living room had become an argument.

I stood in the middle of the room to get their attention.

"Gentlemen, I have been waiting for a pause to get a word in. I have already determined the scope of the project, and you, Pat, agreed. Jack, your involvement is to be limited to making the prototype, which you kindly offered to do in your spare time. Now, could I please see the proposal?"

Pat's jaw dropped.

"Jack, could I please see the proposal?"

I could have easily bent over and picked it up from the coffee table, but I wanted Jack to give it to me, and he finally did, his brows arched above the frame of his glasses.

"Anna, there are valid considerations which make me question the necessity of the extensive effort you're about to get involved in."

I hate when he talks like that. I always need time to translate everything into simple English before I can translate it into Russian so I can respond.

Jack jumped up, stuck his hands in his pockets, and started pacing.

"First and foremost, Anna, you will have to work at least twelve hours a day, six days a week, just to gather the requirements and work out a viable design. How long do you suppose you will be able to keep up that kind of pace before you get sick? Second, this company doesn't expect to get a comprehensive product. They're looking for a temporary fix. They'll be happy with a few reports. And, I think your proposed fee is too low."

Take it or leave it. I don't need anyone to pamper me.

"Jack, you had a chance to do it your way. Had you chosen to take it, I wouldn't have interfered."

Clearly uncomfortable, Pat crossed and uncrossed his legs, looked at his watch, and probably was preparing an excuse to leave.

"This project is Pat's and my responsibility. Your suggestions and your assistance are welcome, but only within the framework of what Pat and I have agreed on. I feel what I included in the proposal is absolutely necessary. The client company is growing, not going out of business. Just because they don't understand what they need doesn't mean I should cheat them."

Jack looked as if he was about to explode.

"Jack, we can do the whole thing. It's just more analysis, no great shakes. It was nice of you to volunteer to do the prototype; it will be a big help to Anna when she presents the design."

Pat's pacifying tone failed to placate Jack, who resumed pacing in front of the window. After several minutes of silence he stopped and turned to face us.

"Okay, but I have some concerns."

"I saw your notes," I replied. "There are some good points there."

"Thank you," Jack said acidly. "Pat, we'll have to work closely on the prototype."

I guess that leaves me out. Time to take a shower and then pick up Natasha. Every year we go out to lunch for each other birthdays. We don't even schedule vacations that would infringe on our outings.

I said good-bye to Pat, and Jack walked him out to his car, the two of them discussing the prototype as they went.

I called Natasha to tell her I would pick her up in forty-five minutes. Then I hurried to take a shower. I found Jack's clothes strewn about the bedroom and bathroom. A nuisance. He'll have to make sure Tanya doesn't come across his carelessly discarded shorts.

As I lathered my body, I reviewed our meeting. My concept of the system was good and Jack hadn't come up with anything earth shattering. The proposal ended up much the way Pat had put it together. I have to pick up the final draft from him tomorrow morning, on the way to work. I don't know why Jack's so angry. Did he expect me to simply fold as soon he offered his assistance? Judging from his arrogance, apparently so. First, he insists on stearing clear of the project, then, after Pat and I put in so much effort, he walks in and tries to crowd me out—and, of course, for my own good. Men!

Jack stayed outside after walking Pat out. When I started to back out of the driveway he stood in my path, his legs apart, his hands on his hips. I had to stop the car so as not to run him over.

He came to the window, his face grim.

"Anna, I didn't appreciate the way you treated me, particularly in front of Pat."

"What's wrong with the way I treated you?"

Jack reached into the car, taking a tissue from the box on the dashboard. He removed his glasses and started wiping them.

"Well, Jack, what did I do?"

"All I want is to make your life easier. I'm sure you realize that you, even with Pat's help, do not have the expertise to pull off this project. Yet, you brushed off what I tried to suggest simply out of stubbornness."

"Ignoring my presence and my opinion is called 'trying to suggest'? As far as business is concerned, I'm not 'just a woman,' I'm not 'just your girlfriend,' I'm not some charity case. I don't need preferential treatment."

"Don't you think I offered to help you because you're my girlfriend?"

"Jack, I appreciate it, I really do, but if you want to make decisions, not just do the prototype, you need to receive a percentage of the fee. Otherwise, keep out."

"You're impossible, Anna."

"I was the first to tell you that, Jack, and I meant it."

"Are you going to be back before I leave?" he asked matter-of-factly.

"When are you leaving? By the way, Jack, the floor is not the place to leave your clothing. Please pick up your stuff. Tanya has started to clean the house. If I'm not back in two hours, you shouldn't wait for me. You have a long drive and need to have enough sleep to function in the morning."

I want to speak Russian at least a few hours this week . . . I want to talk with Tanya . . . I want to be alone with her in my house. Two days ago, we thought we only had our partnership left, then Tanya assumed Jack had moved in, and—he moved in.

Jack smiled. "Two women out to brunch—you won't be back so soon."

"It's been an eventful week and an even more eventful weekend," I said so seriously that I almost sounded sad.

"Anna, I'm glad you decided to let me stay on weekends. It was a good start, wasn't it?" Jack leaned into the car and quickly kissed me.

Start of what? What could I possibly start at my age?

When Tanya was born, Sasha said, "Maybe your daughter will finally make you grow up and understand that you cannot always do what you feel in your heart, that you must do what society expects of you. Anya, you must learn to conform."

I never fully learned to conform, society still does not get all I can give it, and I still believe life can be built on feelings from the heart.

twenty-one

These days, I spend considerably more money. A full tank of gas three times a week and eating lunch out every day adds up. One big—breathtakingly big—check has arrived so far. I made a photocopy of it and hid it among Tanya's old drawings and Auntie Olya's letters. Almost forty-two hundred dollars for two weeks—before taxes and insurance—but still forty-two hundred dollars.

I feel a little guilty spending money on myself, but it's so hard to resist. Last Sunday Tanya and I went shopping. She bought a pair of seventy-dollar Reebok's (which she says she'll only wear in dry weather) and then talked me into a three-hundred-dollar trench coat for myself. Can you imagine, three hundred dollars for a trench coat and seventy dollars for gym shoes! I was making only forty dollars a day seven years ago.

It's Saturday, five o'clock, and I still have a two-hour drive ahead of me. In the last three weeks I've worked over one hundred eighty hours. It's getting harder and harder to fall asleep at night. The puny weekends aren't enough; I start every week feeling beat. This Monday I'll be late for work, as I promised Tanya I would have Fima's invitation notarized, then send it by registered mail. My only real relaxation is Sunday night after Jack leaves, when I'm alone with Tanya and can speak Russian.

I talk to Natasha every couple of weeks. We have slid from friendship into acquaintanceship, and I hope she's satisfied, because I am. She's been absorbed in a debate with Isaak—conducted long-distance—on the necessity of religion in his life. The depth of the debate and the degree of his involvement remain unknown to me. The gist of Natasha's argument is that her son was not brought up to dedicate his life to religion, that religious careers do not provide adequate opportunities, and that he will regret his choice after wasting years of his life. She couldn't hide her exasperation when I asked how Isaak explained his reasons.

"He's foolish," Natasha shouted, "there could be no other reason." Then she added spitefully, "I thought I could count on your understanding, but you can afford to analyze because your daughter is here with you."

I realized that no reason would justify her not seeing her son regularly, and in our subsequent conversations I stuck to listening. Recently, another irritant came into the picture. Since Natasha isn't Jewish—in Judaism, children are considered to be the religion of the mother—Isaak is seriously considering converting, so there'll be no question. Conversion to Judaism, Isaak says, requires a person to follow many rather complex and strict rules, one of which, for a man, is circumcision. Can you imagine undergoing a circumcision at nineteen? Natasha says she won't interfere, but the idea isn't appealing to her. We were brought up in a society where circumcision was punishable by law. Fima, whom I never liked touching, said he wasn't circumcised. I think Sasha was circumcised, because I know Jack is, and he feels similar. As for Vilen, he simply made me too sick to have any realization of his penis.

Circumcision or not, like most of the newcomers from the Soviet Union, Natasha would, in principle, prefer her son remain without religion. I can't say for sure about Irena, but Natasha is not anti-Semitic. She couldn't be if she named her son Isaak and carried her husband's last name, Shapiro. In the Soviet Union, a Jewish name guaranteed restrictions and humiliation that she could have avoided by keeping her maiden name and giving it to her son along with a generic Vladimir or Boris. But not doing it constituted a form of protest on her part, having nothing to do with religion. As a matter of fact, Judaism is not considered a religion in the Soviet Union, but a nationality, like Russian or Lithuanian. Few non-Jews were as brave as Natasha—only famous personalities, like Sakharov, for example, could afford to advertise their dissent. Actually, few Jews were as brave as she, as any chance to blend into the approved majority had great appeal. Now it devastates Natasha to hear Isaak insist that Israel is his home and Judaism his religion and way of life. She only groans when I tell her that being Jewish is as much a feeling as a religion.

When Jack left last night, I called Lena to find out how her last date with Felix's friend, Ilya Kotlyar, went. She agreed to go out with him to spite her ex-husband, yet she sounded happy to get out of her cage. When Serozha discovered Lena had gone on a date with someone, he reacted by calling her a whore. Men often tend to denigrate what they can't obtain. Perhaps it makes the loss more tolerable.

Sasha, did you have a feeling of loss when I left? If only you could know that talking to you like this keeps my feet planted firmly on the ground, closer to my fragile roots. Do you think I would have been able to handle my years of cleaning houses without your understanding eyes watching over me? I'm still working hard. Well . . . yes . . . for the money . . . but also because it makes me feel good to know what I do will be appreciated. Tanya said she feels like she's the daughter of an influential business magnate. Quite a promotion for the daughter of a housekeeper, even though she was never embarrassed by being one. What do you think, Sasha? Isn't Tanya's happiness worth my effort?

Before I had a chance to blink, Jack had installed a four-slice toaster and a new microwave, occupied a shelf in my cupboard with wine, and filled half the basement with computer equipment.

One day Tanya called me at work to tell me a landscaping truck was parked in front of the house and four men were busy trimming our bushes and doing something with the grass. Making practical use of her Spanish, she learned Mr. Graff had placed a priority order to have the work done. I called the company and learned Mr. Graff was a preferred customer and had been giving them his business for three years, and if I was not happy, Mr. Graff, or I, Mrs. Graff, as they called me, ignoring my introduction, should not hesitate to contact them.

I called Mr. Graff ready to fight. He answered the phone saying, "Anna, I know, it's your house not mine. I just wanted to do something nice for your letting me have most of the basement."

"How did you know it would be me on the phone?"

"I figured Tanya came home from school and called you."

After that, I gave up. I hardly noticed the grass and the bushes, even when I had time, and why waste my energy arguing?

One Friday I came home and was almost knocked down by a burly man in overalls backing out of the house.

"My pleasure, sir. Excuse me, ma'am," he said as he stepped aside to let me pass.

"Who was that?" I asked Jack.

"My plumber."

"What happened?"

"Tanya and I were trying to take showers at the same time. Tanya's shower was fine, but there wasn't any cold water in ours. I was nearly scalded to death."

"How much did it cost to get him here so fast?"

"Listen, Anna, there are parts of my body that are priceless, and those parts were in real danger of being rendered useless for the rest of my life."

I couldn't help laughing. I wondered what it took to impress a plumber into working after hours on a Friday night.

Last week I asked Jack if he would help Tanya prepare dinner on Friday nights, since he would be home before me. The next day a soft-spoken lady called me at the office introducing herself in broken English as Donna, Mr. Graff's housekeeper. She asked what day and time was good for me.

"Good for me to do what?" I asked bewildered.

"Mr. Graff told me to come over at night, take the key, and arrange with you what day you want me to clean your house and prepare dinner."

She spoke in passable Russian. She probably had no choice but to learn it in school. I guessed correctly that her first name was actually

Danuta, and she addressed me as *Pani* Anya, a name common to both Polish and Russian.

I was fuming. To tell Donna I didn't need her and have her lose the money she already anticipated was out of the question. I was in her position once—it hit too close to home. She's probably here on an expired tourist visa, and more than likely left her children in Poland. But I don't need her on a regular basis. Tanya and I are perfectly capable of keeping the house clean, that is, if Jack picks up after himself. Maybe a good scrubbing once a month or so?

"I don't think I need you this week. Let me write down your phone number. I'll call you."

"Maybe you know someone who needs cleaning or cooking."

She didn't believe me and her subdued tone made me feel guilty.

A few years ago I asked the same question. I even typed "cleaning woman with good references available" ads and left them in north suburban stores.

"I'll ask my neighbors," I said thinking of the old lady who walks reading a book.

Realistically, I could afford to hire a cleaning lady, and it certainly would save time.

"Wait, Donna, why don't you stop by the house on Saturday, around seven. I think I could use you every other week."

"I could only come after nine."

"That's fine."

She said good-bye, disappointed but hopeful. When Jack called later in the day, I mentioned in passing that Donna had called. He hesitated, expecting a turbulent reaction, but by that time I was looking forward to being able to help her.

Jack's car was parked in front of the house. I pulled up as close as I could to the back door, dragging myself out of the car.

Tanya was making a salad, holding the phone with her shoulder. There was a light in the basement where Jack was working.

"They're still together?" Tanya yelled into the phone. "I thought she broke up with him."

"Tanichka, I need to talk to you."

I sat down and immediately regretted it, to get up would be a major task. I felt dizzy.

Tanya hung up, giving me her cheek to kiss. She's been acting more childish since Jack's been staying with us.

She filled a bowl with the salad she had made and put it in the refrigerator.

"Jack's been in the basement for hours. I'm going with Vera to see a play at school. Jeff's on the crew. It starts at seven-thirty. Vera's dad is going to drive us."

"Tanichka, I made an appointment to interview Jack's housekeeper at nine. She cooks, too."

"Us, hire a housekeeper? Great! Jack's really messy, and I hate cleaning. And you haven't ironed in ages."

"I suppose she could clean, iron, do the laundry, maybe make dinner before she leaves. Maybe she should come once a week."

"We're going to have a housekeeper! Jack is sooo cool!"

"Tanya, stop it! She's not a toy, and we're not millionaires. And, I'm paying for her services, not Jack."

"I'm sorry, I didn't mean it that way. I promised to wait for Vera outside. Gotta go."

"Wait. Did you have dinner?"

"I'm not hungry. I had some cereal and ice cream. There's some spaghetti."

If I let Donna cook, Tanya won't skip dinner. Next year she'll have even more homework. I guess Donna is a good idea. Maybe I should let her come twice a week.

I looked down the stairs toward the light in the basement. Back to Jack, back to English.

I slipped off my shoes and wiggled my toes. It felt good. The front doorbell rang twice.

Barefoot, my feet aching, I padded through the dining room.

The lady on the steps was in her late thirties, tall, with a thin face. Her light-ash hair was gathered tightly in a bun. She wore a bright-blue top and snow-white slacks.

"*Pani* Anya? I'm Donna," she said in Polish and smiled.

I returned her greeting in Polish then continued in Russian. "Come in."

The cuckoo cuckooed nine.

Donna looked around professionally—like I used to do when I went to see a house for the first time, trying to estimate the time and effort required.

"Donna, let me show you the house, then we can talk. I'm so tired, if I sit down I don't think I'd be able to get up again."

Our last stop was the basement. I walked down the stairs slowly, still dizzy. Jack in his sweats and a T-shirt clicked away on the computer. He was unshaved and looked tired.

"Hello, Mr. Graff," said Donna.

"Hi, ladies." Jack rose and stretched, reaching his arms to the ceiling and standing on his tiptoes.

Donna collected paper cups from around the terminal and dropped them into the waste basket next to the desk. I showed her the utility room, then we returned to the kitchen.

"When do you want me to start?" Donna perched on the edge of the chair, holding her bag in her lap.

"I don't know. At first I thought maybe you could come every other week to clean and iron, but . . . Donna, make yourself comfortable. Do you want some coffee or tea, maybe a Pepsi? Why don't you put your bag on the other chair?"

I put the kettle on the stove and gave Donna a glass and a can of Pepsi from the refrigerator.

"I work late hours and only cook on Sundays. My daughter starts skipping dinner by the end of the week. I'd like to know what your schedule is. Maybe you could come on Tuesday or Wednesday to clean and cook for the rest of the week."

"I work Friday and Saturday for Mr. Graff's relative. She's old, and because she's religious she needs help on her holiday. She speaks a little Polish. It's a good job. I always leave time for Mr. Graff. I go whatever day I can. He doesn't care; as long as the house is clean he's happy. A very nice gentleman, Mr. Graff. I offered to cook for him, but he doesn't eat at home. Does your daughter like American food?"

"You can make whatever you want. I don't know how to cook American food, but we like it. Do you have any family in the States?"

"No, I stay with my girlfriend. My husband and son are in Poland."

"How old is your son?"

"Twelve."

Countless are the blessings of socialism, when women are forced to slip away to the United State, on guest and student visas, to baby-sit, clean houses, watch the elderly, so that their families can survive at home.

"What did you do in Poland?"

"I was a physical therapist. My husband is an opera singer," Donna blushed, adding hurriedly, "I'm not spoiled, it doesn't matter to me what I do. Mr. Graff told me you're recently from Russia," she added cautiously.

"Ten years."

Donna nodded. Her understanding made us closer.

"Well, Donna, here's what we'll do. Come every Monday and Thursday for the whole day. I'll call you in mornings if there is anything special to do. It won't be difficult. If it is, tell me. How much do you charge?"

"No, no," she waved her hands frantically. "Mr. Graff said I'm not to talk to you about money—not under any circumstances." She made a cutting horizontal movement with her hand that was vividly Jack's.

I wonder how he communicates his commands to her so clearly and how long his commuting is going to last, because I'm getting fed up. Automatically, I told myself that I wouldn't allow him to surround me with a staff of servants, trying to turn me into a useless princess. Not a staff, just Donna . . . until I'm done with this project.

This dizziness is making me nauseated.

"You're tired, *Pani* Anya. Do you want me to make you something to eat?"

"Do you mind?" I couldn't believe my ears. "I'm going to take a shower. And, Donna, please call me Anya."

I padded out of the kitchen to the shower and stood there letting water fall over my body while I held onto the walls with my eyes closed.

Zombie-like, I padded back into the kitchen swaying and feeling vaguely hungry. Jack was seated at the table in front of a plateful of spaghetti sauce—presumably covering spaghetti—methodically pouring parmesan cheese over it. Another plate with steaming spaghetti and a little sauce—exactly the way I like it—waited across the table. He must have told Donna.

I fell into a chair, my elbows on the table, my face between my palms.

"Where's Donna?" I looked at my plate with strange displeasure.

"Picking up my stuff in the basement. She's never idle. Eat!" Jack expertly rolled spaghetti around his fork.

I felt like throwing up.

"Jack, I'm going to bed," I said starting to get up, trying to avoid looking at the food. "I should have gone straight to bed and not bothered Donna."

Jack looked up at me, dropping his fork.

Why is he staring at me?

"I think I would like some tea," I muttered, falling back into the chair.

"Donna!" he yelled. "Come here, quick!"

I heard rapid steps. Jack materialized behind me, massaging my neck.

"Please make some strong tea, right away, then turn her bed down!"

Donna moved swiftly around the kitchen, the microwave sounded and a glass of tea with lemon appeared magically in place of the plate with spaghetti.

I stared at the glass trying to collect enough energy to pick up the spoon.

Jack rubbed my shoulders then my arms. The warmth made my eyelids heavy, I swayed in the chair.

Donna poured some of the tea into the saucer blowing on it. That's how Lonya and I used to drink our tea. Lonya never put sugar in his glass. He held a cube of sugar between his lips and it usually lasted for the entire glass. I closed my eyes, knowing if I opened them I would see Lonya right there where Donna was standing.

"What the hell is the name of your doctor?" screamed Jack.

"I don't have a doctor," I replied in Russian, then automatically translated, adding, "Don't yell."

Donna disappeared. Jack pulled me up, but I slid back into the chair.

I felt like a heavy sack being picked up, my head rolled toward Jack's shoulder as he carried me to the bedroom. He took my robe off and made me put on my nightgown. I was embarrassed Donna saw him do that, but it was too much effort to object. Donna stood by the bed and covered me when Jack finished.

Jack squatted, his face close, his lips dry.

"Anna, I'm going to call my doctor . . . "

"No, I just want to sleep."

"Damn it, I told you you'd kill yourself! Your stubbornness and your pride . . ."

Donna touched his shoulder and motioned with her head to the door. He got up obediently, turned off the light and followed her out.

I stared at the ceiling, concentrating on my exhaustion. I remember seeing Jack peek around the half-closed door.

When I woke up my completely rested body pleasantly surprised me. I searched for signs of fatigue, but found none. The sun was bright, the sky was blue, the clock said eleven forty-seven. I blinked and looked again — eleven forty-seven. It seemed impossible I had slept so many hours.

The pillow next to mine showed no signs of having been disturbed. I tried to remember what time Jack came to bed but couldn't. Stretching and tossing made me sleepy again, I closed my eyes for a minute. When I opened them again it was three-twelve. Jack sat on the dresser, between the lamp and the clock, staring at me. He was freshly shaven.

"You sure look better. You really scared me yesterday."

"I was tired. Where's Tanya?"

"Making dinner. I wanted to order in, but she insisted on cooking."

"What time did she come home last night?"

"On time."

"How do you know?"

"I waited up for her."

"Your pillow looks like you never went to bed."

"I slept on the sofa."

I sat up yawning.

"Number one, Anna, I made an appointment with my doctor for you, Monday at nine. Number two is, you can't go on working the way you have been. It's too demanding on your body, and there's no justification for it."

"I'm used to working like this. I'm fine. Really. Why are you worried?"

"If you don't understand why I'm worried . . ." Jack's face stiffened. "I don't want you to work like a horse. Not as long as I'm around."

"It has nothing to do with you, Jack. Whatever I need, I need to earn." I got up and threw on my robe.

Jack took a deep breath and jumped down.

"What's wrong?" I was stunned by the fear on his face.

"I thought you were going to fall. You really frightened me last night."

Slowly I tied my robe, suppressing an urge to throw my arms around him.

Jack caught my wrist as I moved toward the bathroom.

"Anna, Tanya was very upset. I think she feels responsible that you're working so hard so she can go to college."

Tanya talked to him? Again!?

"All I needed was to catch up on my sleep. Stop babying me. By the way, there's no need for you to pay Donna. I can afford it."

"If it wasn't for me, you wouldn't need Donna. I make most of the mess, I'll pay her."

"Okay, Jack, I guess it's not that important," I sighed. "Please let go of me. I need to use the bathroom."

When I walked into the kitchen, all four burners were on and Jack was peeling—cutting is more appropriate—potatoes. Tanya, looking gloomy and determined, was stirring something in a pot.

I put my arm around her shoulders and pressed her close.

"Are you all right?" she asked offhandedly.

Jack probably told her yesterday's fainting spell was my own fault. It was a coincidence; it had nothing to do with my extra hours at work. He doesn't realize how tough I am.

"Of course, I'm all right," I said flippantly. "I'm hungry, too. How was the show?"

"It wasn't bad. I'm making vegetable soup for dinner."

I stretched. "Wonderful. I love hot soup."

"Mom, if you call the school and tell them I'm sick, I can go to the doctor with you tomorrow."

"Come on, Tanichka. Jack raised much ado about nothing. You are not going to miss school."

"Yes, I am! I'm going with you. The worst that can happen is I'll serve detention. Or Jack can stay over and take you." Tanya fixed her grey eyes on my face. "You're not going alone."

Obviously, enjoying himself, Jack raised his sly, boyish eyes from the partially destroyed potato in his hands.

Tanya spoke very calmly, I recognized in that calm my manner of reaching a decision. It was time to acknowledge my defeat as gracefully as possible.

"I'd prefer that you don't miss school unless Jack has something urgent planned for tomorrow morning. Do you?" I addressed Jack amiably.

"As a matter of fact, tomorrow morning is relatively quiet," he replied, matching my tone.

The change in Tanya was instant. She transformed back into a child.

I arranged my face to express complete satisfaction, pretending not to notice Jack choking back laugher.

I took a short nap after eating, then did the laundry, while Tanya did her homework and Jack completed the prototype. Then I felt sleepy again and took another nap.

When I woke, the house was dark, with an indistinct sound coming from the television. The clock showed midnight. I threw on a robe and went to the living room. Jack was engrossed in a sports program. I sat on the sofa next to him, and stretched.

"Tanya in bed?" I asked.

"Yes." Jack put his arm around me and switched to CNN.

One more week and I'll make my presentation. If only it didn't have to be in English! After the presentation, Pat will take over and I'll be able to relax until the system testing begins. Life is fantastic. Too fantastic to be my life.

As we watched CNN, we discussed the presentation. Jack stretched his arm along the back of the couch a few inches from me.

"Jack, this morning Tanya asked you to stay over, didn't she?"

"She's scared. I would have stayed anyway. If not here, then at my house."

"I'm grateful she trusts you."

"It makes me feel good." He turned away. "You should be in bed, Anna. The next couple weeks are still going to be tough."

The desire to be caressed, to play with him, so overwhelmed me I couldn't believe it wasn't contagious.

Jack clicked from channel to channel, finally settling on an old Western.

"Well, Jack, I guess I'll go to bed." I stood up stiffly. "Good night!"

"Good night!"

With a look of exasperation, Jack got up and walked over to the window where he stood with his back to me, his hands on the window frame.

When he turns around, I'll just matter-of-factly say it's time to go to bed.

Damn it, will he ever turn around?

"Jack," I said too dramatically.

"What is it?" Jack asked without turning around. "What is it?" He repeated when there was no answer.

Finally he turned around. "Anna, are you all right?"

"I'm all right."

"Anna, please, promise me you'll take care of yourself." He crossed the room and put his hands on my shoulders looking down at me. "You still don't understand why I worry about you?"

"Make love to me." As the words escaped I panicked and tried to step back.

"With you, life certainly is a game of chess," Jack whispered, shaking his head.

I felt weightless as he picked me up.

We attempted to prolong our lovemaking forever. I discovered new, little tricks and motions and heard my silver-bells laughter and Jack's moans and purrs.

"Don't make fun of me. I know I acted like a young girl." I relaxed in my favorite position, my arm across his chest.

"I awakened a sex maniac," Jack grinned.

Is that all that attracts him to me now?

"Jack, what attracts you to me?"

"Well . . . you've got nice legs," Jack winked.

Somehow I didn't think that was the entire answer.

"Tanya wouldn't let me buy eclairs. She said they have too many calories. I'll bring some Friday. Let's go to sleep," Jack tickled my side.

I giggled, curling up closer.

twenty-two

I couldn't tell how the presentation went; everything had seemed to swim in front of me. In spite of numerous rehearsals, I forgot some big words and used simpler ones, and I definitely had not sounded like the document I distributed edited by Jack. My hands shook as I demonstrated the prototype, then placed transparencies on the projector, and used a shiny pointer reminding me of a car antenna. The overhead projector emitted considerable heat and I hoped my new suit didn't show dark circles under the arms. The fancy silk blouse Tanya and I picked turned out to be a mistake; it would have to go to the cleaners immediately.

The audience consisted exclusively of men in white or blue shirts and dark ties. One of them puffed so much cigarette smoke that I found it necessary to suggest a break, so that he wouldn't have to smoke during the presentation. He shrugged, but squashed his cigarette in one of the dark ashtrays carrying the company logo. I tried hard not to pay attention to those who were making notes in the margins of their handouts.

At the end of the presentation, like Jack had suggested, I asked if there were questions and rather painlessly disposed of the few that were raised. In conclusion, again following Jack's directions, I implored the white and blue shirts to get back to me with any remaining questions and comments by Friday.

Coffee and donuts waited on a table in the corner of the conference room, thanks to the invisible Mrs. McLaughlin. My dry throat longed for coffee, with a lot of sugar, and holding donuts helped steady my shaking hands. I did try to mingle, as Jack had suggested.

As soon as I returned to my office, I clapped my hands, sighed a big sigh, fell into my chair, and called home to leave a message on the answering machine that everything was "wow, cool." Then I left a message on Jack's answering machine in Green Bay to call me back. Then I giggled.

Just imagine: I had given a forty-five-minute presentation—in English—to a group of American men, complete with an overview of the prototype, and hadn't become confused. No one had laughed or yawned, but had listened intently.

Look at me now, Lonya! And, I did it all by myself. If only Sasha could have seen me with that shiny pointer, and now, with my feet on my desk.

When we were in Rome waiting for our entry visas to the United States, it surprised many young men when our English teacher, an

American, asked them to keep their feet under their desks. For us, putting one's feet on a desk, wearing a ten-gallon hat, and drawling countless "okays" had always symbolized Americans.

Mrs. McLaughlin walked in with a sheet of paper in her hands and looked at me over the top of her glasses. It appeared that she didn't approve of keeping one's feet on a desk, either. Her efficiency always made me feel I should apologize every time I left a pencil outside the holder.

"Anna, I'm in the process of typing the training schedule and the installation procedures. John told me to confirm the dates with you."

She handed me the paper, and I watched her back as she closed the door behind her.

The fact that people took me seriously and let me make decisions remained a novelty. Lonya would have said that those who took me seriously must be out of their minds.

The phone rang. I sat up kicking off my shoes.

"How did it go?" Jack asked.

"It's behind me now," I closed my eyes, suddenly void of all energy.

"I suppose that's one way of interpreting results. Anything you couldn't respond to?"

"Not really. No one questioned my approach. They mostly talked among themselves."

"That's a good sign. Anna, why don't you take the rest of the day off?" Jack said cautiously, probably expecting me to tell him not to interfere.

"I have to review the training schedule." I smiled. "But I was thinking about it myself. It would be nice to have an entire evening with Tanya. She's been almost deserted by her mother. Should I ask John or Brian?"

"Don't ask." Jack sounded pleased. "Just let someone know and make sure that you bill the hours correctly. May I offer another suggestion?"

"Shoot," I kept smiling, rocking in my chair.

"You could work fewer hours while training people. Losing some money would be well-justified by the extra sleep you desperately need. You have a three-hour session with each shift daily. If you schedule them back-to-back, beginning at one in the afternoon, you'll be done by seven in the evening."

"That's a good idea," I replied, annoyed that the idea hadn't occurred to me. "Don't forget, I have to study the documentation Aurora sent me. I'm supposed to start there right after the Fourth of July."

"Anna, please remember, your blood pressure is low, you shouldn't . . ."

"All right, Jack," I interrupted decisively, "I'll structure the training schedule the way you're suggesting. I'm looking at it right now. By any chance, do you know what time the health club opens in the morning? I'd like to start swimming again. I'm getting flabby."

"Hmm, flabby? I'll have to check that out."

My body responded favorably to his words.

What will I do when Jack disappears? Run after any man?

"Stop it, Jack. I'll review the schedule and go home. See you Friday or Saturday."

Mrs. McLaughlin accepted my revised memo without comment.

"I'm going to leave early today. Would you please let John know? If he needs anything I'll be here for another twenty minutes."

As simple as that.

"Also," I continued, "I'd like to ask you to have someone tape the rough edges of my desk. I'm tired of running my hose every day."

"Certainly," Mrs. McLaughlin agreed seriously. "I should have thought of it myself." She lowered her glasses down her nose and made a note on a yellow pad.

I sounded like a big shot. Tanya would like that.

The house was silent, clean with the smell of freshness and delicious food. I marveled at Donna's efficiency and my laziness. Maybe she could come a third day? I enjoy coming home and finding the dishes washed and put away. The only things I forbade Donna to do was make our beds or change the linens. Tanya needs to do some chores so as not to become a young brat ordering an adult around. As far as my bed, I would die of embarrassment if Donna saw any telltale signs of lovemaking.

Tonight, Tanya and I can have a long talk and I'll make cocoa for her.

I heard the answering machine click on and Cece's staccato voice leave a message.

"Anichka, sunshine, call me back, I need someone to help sell tickets for the Koval poetry concert on Saturday. Bye, birdie!"

The cuckoo clock cried once then abruptly fell silent. I hurried into the dining room. The cuckoo's colorful head hung askew in the tiny window opening. It was quiet, uncomfortably quiet. Trying not to listen to the quiet, I went into the kitchen and called Lena.

"I'm glad you called, Anya. I have some news. Ilya proposed to me last night."

"Oh." I was taken aback by the rapid acceleration of such an unlikely romance.

"You know, he's very straightforward," continued Lena. "He said at our age maybe we won't be madly in love, but since I'm lonely and he's lonely . . . Tell me what you think."

So, why not be lonely together?

"Lena, can I ask you a question? Have you made love with him?"

There was an awkward pause.

Can't I think of anything but sex these days?

"Well, no," Lena said reluctantly. "It wouldn't matter at our age anyway."

"You're right, Lena, I'm sorry."

"I know, Anya, you're saying we should live together first, like you and Jack. But Jack's an American, so everyone understands. I'm not really attracted to Ilya enough to do that, and it would only reinforce the rumors about me. Ilya's a pleasant person, educated, very attentive, we have a lot in common. I don't know . . ."

Not attracted enough to live together, but enough to be married. Then my marriage *was* typical.

"I shouldn't give advice, but since you're asking me, why don't you wait, Lena? You may still fall in love. I have to tell you, though, I'm not sure it's the best advice."

"I told Ilya I wasn't sure how I would decide. Before, when I was alone, maybe . . . but now Svetochka is back, Boris comes for dinner every Sunday . . . I don't know . . ."

She can't get used to being out of place, and I don't know how being in place feels.

Two hours until Tanya's home. In a year she'll go away to college. I'll be proud to be able to pay her tuition. In a conversation that ended my friendship with Nina and Izya, I discovered that this sentiment may not be as common as I assumed.

"Anya, you can't be serious? Spending money doesn't make anyone proud," Nina had spat into the phone.

"I *am* serious. We all say we came to the United States for our children's sake," I said more to myself than to her.

"Listen, if there isn't a way to get out of paying the tuition, we'll pay, but if there is a way, why should we? Believe me, you'll do the same when it comes time to pay Tanya's tuition."

"No, I won't."

"Anya, that's dumb." Nina stated bluntly. "What is it, have you lost your mind? Smart people claim their children are independent so they can get grants. It's like taxes: The more you hide the better. I'm sure you didn't show income when you were cleaning houses, and I know you were on public aid."

"It's true about the income; it never occurred to me. But I was never on public aid."

"You weren't?" Nina exclaimed in amazement. "Anya, I thought you were smart! You could have been on public aid, claiming Tanya, and getting all kinds of perks poor people get—like reimbursement for your energy bills, a subsidized apartment, free food. Look at how the Russian seniors live. They even buy furniture for their children."

A stupid argument.

"Nina, I was young and able to work. I just didn't want to leave Tanya alone after school, and I didn't want her to go to a public school in the city. It makes me feel like a jerk to help you avoid paying for your children's college knowing how well off you are. If you don't pay, who should?"

"Probably people like you. That's not my concern," Nina said crisply. "I won't be fooled. If you won't let me use your address anymore, I'll find someone else. Anya, you sound like an American. You'll grow up fast if Jack doesn't pay Tanya's tuition and it touches your pocketbook. And, in your case, it's going to be very expensive because Tanya is a top student and won't be happy at just any school."

Jack's presence, in many people's eyes, supersedes all my accomplishments—past, present, and future.

I never missed Nina. I never missed anyone, except Sasha and Asya. Please, Sasha, be somewhere where I can find you.

The house is too quiet. I'm going to the corner house to see the old woman who is always reading when she walks her dog. I'll ask her to recommend a list of authors. She gives the impression of someone who likes good literature.

I walked to the corner and rang the bell with an inexplicable sense of expecting to see a person long known.

The light curtain over the square glass in the door moved aside then fell back in place. When the door opened, the old woman stepped back, saying "Come in" in a coarse smoker's voice tinged with a strong Slavic accent. She exhibited no surprise at my unannounced appearance. Her dog silently sniffed my shoes then trotted back into the living room.

I could swear she has Russian eyes.

"My name is Anna Fishman. I live down the street. It's hard to miss that you're an avid reader, and I was hoping you would recommend some books for me to read. My English is getting better and I miss reading good literature."

"I know where you live. My name is Sylvia Frankel. Call me Sylvia. Come in and sit down." There was no smile, but her eyes softened and she made a gesture toward the sofa.

She lived in a large two-storied house, clean but dark. Book shelves took up most of the space in the living room. I could see the dining room from the sofa. There wasn't a table, just more books and a television shoved in the corner. I supposed the door at the far end led to the kitchen.

"I've lived in this house for almost thirty years. It's too big for me now. Coffee?"

"No, thanks. I don't have a lot of time. My daughter will be home soon."

"So, what kind of literature do you like?"

"I don't know what I should start with," I admitted.

It's embarrassing. It took me ten years to get to this point.

"My English is far from perfect."

"Your English seems fine. You're from Russia, aren't you?"

"Yes."

Sylvia took a cigarette from a pack on a bookshelf and put it between her lips without lighting it, then sat in a chair near the sofa.

"I'm not allowed to smoke since my mastectomy. My high blood pressure doesn't help either, so I just suck on a cigarette once in a while. It makes me feel better." She cleared her throat. "What city are you from?"

"Kiev."

"I grew up in Minsk."

"My parents were killed in the war. The rest of my family vanished in Babi Yar. That is, except my brother and me," I said, my eyes swelling with tears.

My family—I'm taking Lonya's family like I took his mother.

"I would have thought you were born after the war. Don't be embarrassed to cry if you want."

"I was born in July of 1941," I said, wondering why I wanted to put my head on this woman's shoulder and feel her arm on mine.

Sylvia's eyes narrowed—the date required no explanation. She chewed on the cigarette for another minute, screwed up her face, and threw it into the frog-shaped ashtray on the coffee table.

"Speak Russian if you prefer. I can't converse in it anymore, but I understand it, of course."

"How long have you been in the United States?" I asked awkwardly in English—the one question every immigrant tires of after having to answer it hundreds of times.

"Thirty-five years."

"No wonder you speak English so well and can read all these books."

I took a book from the coffee table remembering the last time I was in the Kiev library. I loved to take new books from the shelves, caress the covers, inhale the fresh smell of print. It all came back, this piece of me I thought had been hopelessly smothered.

"Saul Bellow? Is he a good writer?"

"Probably one of the best. Many don't understand him, and not necessarily because of language problems. Do you have a library card?" Sylvia picked up the dog. It stretched in her lap under her hand.

"Yes. In the beginning I didn't have time to read, then I started reading well-known mysteries. I figured I couldn't go wrong there, although I prefer books that make you think. The problem is, I don't know English well enough to be able to tell what's trash and what's not."

"Here's a tip. When you go to the library, don't check out anything that has a shiny cover with a half-nude beauty held by a handsome young man." She smiled at her attempt at humor. "You're welcome to browse through my collection and borrow what you like. I'll prepare a list for you. You can get it the next time you come. What kind of education have you had?"

"Russian literature, mostly. I worked as a proofreader for a small publishing company that produced technical booklets for seminars and conventions. Working directly with books is absolutely beyond what a Jew is allowed to do in Russia nowadays. It's considered part of the ideological front."

"I studied German literature at Minsk University. When I was young, German was the language to learn. We kept hearing about this wonderful alliance we were going to have with Hitler. Some alliance, huh? In America I picked up English—for some reason it was easy for me—and became a stenographer."

Something in Sylvia's eyes made me reluctant to leave.

"Tell me, Anna, how long have you been here?"

"Ten years now."

"So, your daughter was a little girl when you came. Whom did you come with?"

"No one. My brother passed away before I was married."

Her eyes narrowed—this time with a spark of recognition. She would understand about Fima, even Sasha, and I could talk to her about Jack. Somehow, I just knew.

"I divorced my husband in Kiev."

"He didn't understand you, did he," Sylvia stated rather than asked. "Did you leave anyone else behind?"

"I have no family that I know of. Just two friends. Very close friends."

"Oh, yes, friends. That's important." Sylvia almost smiled. "I corresponded with a university friend up until three years ago. She must have died. Her children are probably afraid to write. So now only service people and nurses keep me entertained. And books, of course."

There was no complaining, no sadness, no sarcasm, merely a statement of fact.

"My friends were afraid to write to me." My tone matched hers. "Do you have any family in the United States?"

"My husband was a Polish Jew. His whole family is in the States. We escaped to Palestine with our son after the war, then my husband's brother convinced us to come here. From my generation, I'm the only one left, the younger generation is . . . well, busy. I used to be busy, too, but now all my friends are in Florida or in nursing homes or cemeteries."

If I don't leave now, I'll not leave this house. I want to tell her everything.

"I'm sorry, Sylvia, today is the first time in two months I'm going to have time to be with my daughter when she comes home from school.

Will you please give me your telephone number? I'll call you before I visit again."

"You don't need to call. If I'm not walking the dog, I'm home."

We walked to the front door together and Sylvia shook my hand.

"I always knew you would visit me one day," she said.

On an impulse, I hugged her then stepped back embarrassed. She quietly closed the door. I heard her fumble with the lock.

Next time I'll browse through her books. What does she do alone all the time? She didn't seem bored or talkative, like so many lonely people. Where's her son? One can't simply let one's mother exist as if she's on a different planet, with no thread to connect the two.

A school bus passed as I approached the house. Tanya, with a heavy backpack and gym bag, crossed the street.

"Mom, why are you home so early? Boy, am I tired and really hungry!"

I smiled, remembering that Tanya is always hungry. I've never seen anyone eat so much yet stay so thin. Must be all that youthful energy.

Tanya dropped her bag by the door and sniffed.

"Smells good. Donna's day. Oh, I almost forgot—how was the presentation?"

"I thought it went well," I said with an air of confidence that surprised me.

"If *you* say it went well, then you passed with flying colors."

We had dinner and a dish of ice cream then discussed my presentation, the relative importance of class standings and SAT scores, whether to repair the cuckoo clock or not, an itinerary for Fima's visit to Chicago, our limited summer wardrobe, Yuri's going out with Vera's lab partner to get back at Vera for not going out with him, and my visit to the corner house.

I haven't been so relaxed in . . . well, ever.

In two days Tanya will start her summer break, she's going to be very busy, including the major event of the summer—golf lessons. Finally, I can afford a true luxury for her. She certainly has been persistent in saving money for college. Her determination has never ebbed, even with my change in income. She doesn't even talk about having a car. She's a stubborn girl, wanting to do everything for herself. Wonder where she got that from!?

Tanya was organizing her desk drawers when I brought in her cocoa.

"Thanks, Mom. I've decided to save all the college catalogs in the top drawer. I really feel bad Vera can't take honors psych with me this summer. She said she can't afford it. She's going to spend more time working at the nursing home, and she's going to keep a journal on every patient she cares for."

"Tanya, sometime this summer we should have her family over for dinner. It's about time I meet them."

"That's a good idea, maybe we could have a barbecue? I wish I knew exactly what I want to do, like Vera does."

"Don't you?"

Tanya sighed. "I suppose I'll be a doctor."

"Only, Tanichka, if it's what you really want. Not for any other reason."

She bit her lip, avoiding my eyes. She's not ready to talk to me yet. She will. Thank goodness, there's Jack.

twenty-three

I called Cece and immediately her call-waiting beeped. I spent five minutes on hold. She was breathing heavily when she returned.

"I'm sorry, Anichka, there's this guy pursuing me with one hundred million phone calls."

"Alex?"

"Oh, no! Alex is not really in my circle. It was very shrewd of you to hook up with an American guy. When Russians gossip about each other he won't understand, so it won't ruin anything between you. Smart move!"

A mouthful for Cece.

"Cece, is there gossip about me?"

"You? There would be no gossip about you, birdie. Just a little bit when you lived with the Korsunskys, because he's a dentist and rolling in money. I never believed it, don't worry. I was speaking of gossip about me. Men chase me and it makes people think I sleep with every one of them."

"Why wouldn't there be gossip about me?"

"Because, birdie, you are too serious and, sunshine, one can tell you have no experience in tempting men. As for me, I know every trick in the book."

"Okay, Cece, what's happening with the concert? Usually your girl-friends and your daughter help you sell the tickets."

"My girlfriends, ha! They sit in their big houses with their boring husbands and keep them outside my reach. They're too materialistic for my taste. I can't live without culture, and Lyudochka is working tomorrow. Our telephone bills are through the roof: The Miss-Famous-Poet-ess, Lubov Koval, has called me collect from every city she's touring. I would never dream of not accepting the calls. Lyuda and I are broke. I'm not working."

"Cece, you can't go on like this. What will happen when Lyuda gets married?"

"Don't worry, birdie, I don't need much, and I can always live with my daughter."

"Whatever you say. I'm not working this Saturday. I'll be glad to help with the tickets."

"I don't know why you're working at all. Everyone says your boy-friend is loaded. You're so naïve, my sunshine."

"Where's the concert going to be?"

"At Mather High School. It starts at six. I want you there at five sharp, and bring a box to keep the money in. I'm hoping to make a big profit. Koval is very talented, you know."

"It's not just her talent—she's our youth. It will be wonderful to see her in person. The concert should be sold out!"

When I was only a little older than Tanya, I knew Lubov Koval's poems by heart. She was a decent person, too, never participating in witch-hunts of other authors. Her official status was "disapproved of." Asya had a book of her poems. I borrowed it once and copied some of them by hand. We recited them together.

Jack would never understand. He's intelligent, but I can't remember ever seeing him read a book that wasn't computer-related. American professionals don't seem to be embarrassed by this. They usually excuse their lack of interest with "I don't have time to read the good stuff."

Friday night I found the house dark and silent when I arrived home. Tanya was at Alice's celebrating the end of the school year and had begged for permission to come home at midnight, just this one time. I agreed after hearing that, according to her calculations, she finished her junior year in the top three percent of her very competitive class.

I pushed the play button on the answering machine and sat down on the sofa without turning on the lights.

"Hi, Tanya, it's Alice. Don't forget the folding chairs. My Mom won't let us use the good ones for the party. Bye."

Kids have their own problems.

"Anichka, sunshine, Cece here. Tomorrow at five. I'll call you if I need a ride. Bye, bye."

She already knows she'll need a ride.

"Anna, I decided to work tomorrow. I'll call you later or you can call me after nine at the hotel."

Jack did not mention he needed to work tomorrow because he spent so much time designing the prototype for my project.

"Tanya, hi! It's Vera. I won't be able to go to the party. Something came up at home. Tell Jeff I won't need a ride. Thanks. Talk to you later."

I positively have to meet Vera's parents.

"Anya, this is Natasha. Isaak writes he's getting married. Call me back as soon as you come in. Bye."

That will be a difficult conversation.

"Jackele, Dr. Fagan discharged me today. My blood pressure is under control now; however, just in case, he's having a nurse check on me every day for a week. I can never catch you at home. You work too hard, you bad boy. Did you have a chance to call the lawyer-girl?"

Jack hadn't mentioned his mother was in the hospital, or the lawyer-girl, for that matter. Umm, Mrs. Graff knows his phone is forwarded to mine.

"Anya, Bella speaking. If you come home before nine call me. Otherwise try sometime tomorrow, or I'll see you at the Koval concert."

When Bella calls it's always for a reason.

"Jack, Tom. What's up, guy? You seriously disappeared. It's been almost a month. A woman's voice on your answering machine? Not married, are you? Hey, listen, good news! The lead I told you about last winter contacted me this morning. They want you to get in touch with their MIS director on Monday. His name is Bill T-a-r-a-s-i-e-v-i-c-h. Phew! I hear the guy's not easy, likes to get straight to the point, doesn't talk to salesmen. I'll be golfing in Indiana over the weekend with a broad I met the other day. Let me know on Tuesday how it went. See ya."

Must be Tom Sirota (Sirota means "orphan" in Russian), Jack's rep. Man-to-man talk.

"Anichka, this is Lena. Just wanted to say 'hi.' Are you going to Lubov Koval's concert? Everyone seems to be going. Maybe we could go together? Good-bye."

Lena can sell tickets with me. I wish I had a video camera to catch the expression on her face when she meets Cece. Speaking of extremes . . .

I turned the lights on everywhere, looking at the cuckoo's lifeless head with disdain. I warmed up dinner and put on the kettle. Returning so many calls promised to keep the evening busy. I decided to start with Bella. Felix answered and I heard Susan crying as Bella came to the phone.

"Good evening, Anya! We're going out and Susan is refusing to sleep at Irena's. Just between us, I can't really blame her. Listen, I received a letter from my mother a couple days ago. Your friend Asya came to my mother to ask for your telephone number, or for us to ask you to call her. Do you want her number?"

Do I want her number! I knew Asya missed me! I knew it!

"The time difference is seven or eight hours," Bella went on evenly after I wrote down Asya's phone number. "It takes some time to get through, but past midnight, it's usually not too much of a problem."

Past midnight! Three more hours! Oh, no!

I killed some time talking on the phone until eleven, hardly remembering what was said. No one was very excited that, for the first time in ten years, I was going to talk to my closest childhood friend. When they compare friends to family, friends mean less. All people have various friends and learn how to give each just enough, and how to take just enough.

When we were in third grade Asya brought a doll to school for me. I played with it in my lap during class, making sure I looked up at the teacher frequently. The rag doll was old and worn, with a pink porcelain head. During breaks I hugged and kissed the soft, smelly doll's body. My happiness was short-lived. The teacher discovered the distraction, confiscated the doll, and told both of us to see her after class in the teacher's room.

Asya and I were petrified and cried a duet, taking turns wiping our eyes and noses with Asya's handkerchief. The teacher wrote a note to Asya's mother and threatened to write one to Lonya. She had met Lonya many times since he attended all the quarterly parent-teacher meetings. Asya was reprimanded for the sake of propriety, and her mother began inviting me over to play more frequently. She was well aware the only acceptable activities for me, by Lonya's standards, were reading and chess. I hated chess with a passion and never mastered the game.

For about forty minutes the international operator tried unsuccessfully to connect me to Asya's number.

"All circuits are busy at this time in the country you are calling," a polite prerecorded voice patiently advised me.

And then I heard Asya's telephone ring.

"The telephone is ringing. I'll be off the line. Have a good night," said the operator. As she spoke, I knew there was another operator informing Asya of the long-distance call. That's how it works in the Soviet Union, even when one calls city-to-city.

A man's coarse voice said, "*Slushayu!*" then, "Asya, come here. Chicago's on the line. Be careful what you say."

Although it must have been Myron, I didn't recognize his voice.

A woman's voice—is this Asya?—muttered, "Get lost," and the dear, short cackle accompanying a cheerful "Good morning!" forced an attack of silver-bells from me.

"Asinka, how are you? I can't believe I'm actually talking to you. I've missed you so much."

"I'm fine. I was very pleased to hear from you. It was touching you remembered me."

I grasped the telephone tightly. "How could you say that? If only you and Sasha were here . . . remember the doll you brought to school for me when we were in third grade?"

There was a pause. "Yes . . ." Asya said, confused at the turn the conversation had taken.

I'm so silly, now is not the time for reminiscing about these things. She has different priorities.

"Asya, how are the boys? Myron? Your mother? Are you all well? Tell me what you need. What do you want me to send you?"

"You shouldn't send anything, Anya. We're fine. So much has changed from what it was in your time. We can say anything. We finally have freedom! If not for Chernobyl . . ."

"Asya!" A commanding Myron warned not to go too far.

"Asya, people that return from visiting the Soviet Union tell me the supply of food and clothes is worse now than in my time."

"Oh, yes, that part is true. In your time you could get everything as long as you were willing to stand in a line or run around, but now . . ."

"Asya!" growled Myron.

"Asya, how is your mother? I think of her often."

"She has gallstones, but she's doing fine."

"Is Dima married yet?"

"Anichka, I don't want to talk about that. Please write down my address. You know, I kept all your letters. I used to feel sorry for you."

"Sorry for me?"

"Well, it had to be hard for you. Here you didn't have to do menial work. You were lucky to meet a millionaire . . . like in a fairy tale."

"What millionaire?"

"Bella told me you make really good money and Tanya is a very bright girl, you have a house, and your boyfriend showers you with money and attention."

"That's what Bella said about my boyfriend?"

"Not in so many words, but we got the picture."

"Asinka, I'm not rich, but I'm doing all right, and I did it myself . . . well, with Tanya's help. My boyfriend had nothing to do with it. You know me better than to believe I'd be with someone just for money. Forget the fairy tales—I've worked hard for everything I have. Meanwhile, if you give me sizes, I'll send all of you some clothes."

"My sons are big men, clothes for them is especially hard to come by."

I made notes of sizes converting them mentally from centimeters to inches.

"Thanks, Anichka. Bella said you are in terrific form. You never gain weight, lucky you."

"Remember, Asya, how we would share a cupcake for sixteen kopeks, you would always take the smaller half?"

"Anya, have you ever regretted leaving? I mean, before you met your boyfriend."

"I have been happy every single minute since I crossed the border. That's God's truth, Asya. I didn't look for a boyfriend to survive, and what's more, I don't need one to survive. If you don't understand that . . ."

"Yes, I understand," murmured Asya sounding confused. "Anichka, I don't want you to run up a big telephone bill. The reason I asked you to call is that Rimma is going to visit her brother-in-law in Los Angeles. Do you remember my sister Rimma?"

"Of course. Remember how we expected her to be pregnant when we found out a boy kissed her on the cheek?" I laughed lightheartedly.

"How do you remember these little things? Anyway, I was wondering if you'd be able to have Rimma visit you while she's in the United States?"

"I'd be happy to have her. When is she leaving Kiev?"

"On the twenty-first of July. Right after your birthday."

"You remember! And I remember your birthday, too."

"Can you believe it, Anya? We are going to be forty-five. Practically old women."

"Come on, Asya, we're not old."

"Odd to hear that from you. You thought we were old when we were thirty-five. You said that you were leaving for Tanya's sake, because at your age you didn't care what happened to you anymore."

"That's how I felt at thirty-five. Now I don't think forty-five is old. Not young, but far from old."

"Well, Anichka, you have become an optimist."

Me, an optimist? Every day I expect to wake up and find my life is only a dream.

"Asinka, have you heard from Sasha?"

"Sasha? Sasha Rosenberg? I told Bella I saw him last about eight years ago, when my mother-in-law had a heart attack. He was her doctor at the hospital. He asked about you and I offered to let him read your letters. He was very subdued, even depressed. If the information service couldn't help, then he's not in Kiev."

Asya never spoke of intimate moments with Myron, and this was the reason I could never share my secret with her.

"Maybe, he moved to the Crimea? Asya, would you please, as a favor, inquire at the hospital where he used to work?"

"I will, since you feel it's so important. We live in a new suburb now and the hospital is quite a distance from us, but Myron or I will make the trip. I admire you for feeling so strongly about your friends after so many years. Anya, no matter what you say, you must need something. What can I send you?"

"Asya, you don't understand. When Rimma is here she'll see. There is nothing anyone here could possibly need from the Soviet Union, except their old friends. And one doesn't have to be a millionaire, either."

Asya chuckled, taking my words as a joke.

I heard muffled words, then Asya spoke quickly, "Anichka, Myron insists we end this conversation. It will cost you a fortune. Kiss Tanya for me. I'll be expecting a letter from you soon."

"Say hi to the boys, to everyone. One more thing, Asya. Please, when you visit your father's grave, please check Lonya's for me. Sasha promised to take care of it, but if he's not in Kiev I'd like to be sure it's tended."

"I will. I promise. Good-bye, Anichka. And thanks."

"Good-bye, Asya. I love you."

We are not old—it's what's ahead of me and what's ahead of her that makes the difference in age.

How did I come to having a maid, a house with a manicured lawn, an office, golf lessons for my daughter, and dreams of starting a dynasty? With all this, is it wrong to want the only people that made my life in the Soviet Union livable and gave me something to miss, to be within reach, to continue where we left off?

Dear God, I'll never take your kindness for granted. Am I stepping beyond what should be justly mine? Will I be punished like the old woman in Pushkin's tale, who used the gratitude of a magic goldfish, saved by her husband, to fulfill her wishes, until she wished for too much and was taken back to her old hut and broken basin? You'd give me a sign when to stop, wouldn't you? Believe me, God, I will not insist on Tanya becoming a doctor just to make money. Teaching is as noble in its purpose. She has choices. She has me behind her. She can count on Jack. She doesn't know how not to be free, and she already has immeasurably more than I've ever had. I'll share what I have and know with Asya, with whoever wasn't as lucky as I was to escape.

I slept badly, and Saturday started late. I promised myself this would be the day I would tell Jack that I'm grateful to him for all he's done and I have become used to his being around, but I do not feel these are honorable reasons to continue a relationship.

I don't believe he truly loves me—not like I love Sasha. If I had believed he loved me, I would have ended our relationship a long time ago. I've never wanted to hurt Jack. Deep inside, I'm certain breaking up with me won't be a catastrophe for him, only a minor inconvenience with no lasting effects. To be guilty of causing a minor inconvenience, after all I've been guilty of, shouldn't make any difference.

My errands were done at a leisurely pace and by the time I was finished I was famished. A boy collecting shopping carts from the Jewel parking lot helped me load my groceries into the trunk. Tanya or Jack will have to help me carry them in.

I turned the ignition key. Nothing, except a small burp, whatever that signifies. My car is less than four years old and I've changed the oil regularly. What else could it need?

I called information for the number of the gas station in Winnetka where Jack takes his car, hoping that, as usual, his name would do wonders. A young man at the station assured me Richard Chin would be happy to help Mr. Graff's friend.

The motor club's tow truck showed up in an hour. The driver tried to give the car a jump, stating expertly, "I can't start it." (I could have told him that!) He hitched up the car, told me, "Hop right in next to me," and we were off.

Richard Chin was a short, skinny Chinese man in clean, navy over-alls, who spoke so fast and abruptly that I wondered, at first, if he was speaking English. My exasperated look of noncomprehension brought him to a slower pace.

"Okay, Mr. Graff's friend. Call me Monday, nine o'clock. This car's no good. Needs new tires, too. Next car, buy Japanese."

I guess Mr. Graff's name goes only so far.

Richard called me a taxi and arranged my groceries neatly in its trunk.

I tipped the cab driver to bring the bags in. It's amazing how much I pick up from Jack. And it's amazing Tanya isn't a bit surprised at my new habits.

"Jack called twice," Tanya said excitedly. "He said not to let you out of my sight until you call him back. And he told me my first golf lesson is tomorrow at eight," she squealed. "Judy practically begged to come with us, and Jack agreed." She added this last branch to her laurels.

"What happened?" I barked once I got Jack on the phone, irritated by my lack of a car.

"It might be more appropriate to ask you that question," Jack answered, not missing my tone.

"My car broke down in the Jewel parking lot."

"Call my mechanic."

"I did. He can't work on it until Monday, it took an hour for the motor club to show up, I had to bring the groceries home in a taxi, the ice cream leaked all over the bottom of the bag . . . incidentally, Jack, don't even dream of paying for the repairs."

Jack laughed. "You got it. You know you could have left the groceries at Jewel, they would have delivered them after you got home."

He knows about a service for everything.

"Anna, you do too many things other people would be happy to do for you."

"I'm used to being one of those other people."

"You can change. Use the extra time for more important things. You can have Donna do your shopping," Jack suggested softly. "Anna, I know you're going to a Russian concert tonight. Afterwards, let's go out to eat. By the way, how are you going to get to the concert?"

"Lena will have to drive."

"I should be home around seven. Call me when the concert's over, and I'll pick you up. So, what did your Russian girlfriend say?"

"Nothing I didn't already know. Her sister Rimma will be visiting relatives in Los Angeles this summer and I invited her to spend a few days in Chicago."

"Are they all right after Chernobyl?"

"She seemed reluctant to talk about it. Maybe her sister will tell us more. Anyway, I'll call you after the concert. Jack, I don't want to stay out too late. Tanya said her first golf lesson is in the morning."

"Don't worry, Anna, I wouldn't miss it for anything. She's so excited."

"I know. She was dancing around the living room when I came home."

Lena and I picked up Cece on a busy corner. She glided into the car, her long legs brought in slowly and reluctantly from the stares on the street. She wore a white, close-fitting, calf-length, linen dress with a stand-up collar and slits on the sides reaching to the middle of her thighs.

"Hi, my birdies. One guy was supposed to pick me up and changed plans at the last second—that tells you how you can trust men." Cece powdered her nose and sat back, touching the leather cushions discreetly with her thin fingers.

"Cece, this is my friend Lena Gurevich." I noticed Lena's predictably primly folded lips.

"Good evening," said Lena coolly, keeping her eyes on the road.

"Hi, sunshine," sang out Cece. "Is Serozha Gurevich your ex-husband? What a jerk! No wonder you threw him out. One time . . ."

"Cece, where is Lubov Koval staying in Chicago?" She has to be stopped from blabbing some half-truth about Serozha's advances to her. Whereas Cece forgets what she says before the last word is out of her mouth, Lena will revert to her suffering shell for months.

"She has friends here. By the way, if you've got any used clothes, she would appreciate them. She's wonderful! There are so many people in Moscow we both used to know."

"You and Koval?" I asked astonished.

"Well, we used to stay at the same resorts." Cece shrugged casually.

"You used to know Lubov Koval socially?"

"Well, not exactly. We didn't stay at the resorts at the same time."

Lena raised her eyebrows.

"And where is your good-looking hunk of an American boyfriend?"

"He wouldn't enjoy the concert. He doesn't speak Russian."

"You just didn't want him to see me again. I've been telling everyone how smart you are . . ."

Lena glanced at me with an is-she-for-real expression as she carefully parked near the front entrance to the school. Cece was out of the car in a flash.

Inside, from behind a folding table set up with Russian books for sale, a roundish man with a ready smile rushed to greet Cece. His table was in a strategic place, between the two entrances to the hall, alongside the table set up for the ticket sellers. This man, and his books, appear as a sidebar to every Russian cultural event. Trying to sound like he's from a class of society far above actuality, he speaks in long sentences, which he never ends of his own free will, because his train of thought inevitably becomes entangled somewhere in the middle. His former occupation had something to do with moviemaking, and he, like Cece, repeatedly rolls up his eyes, avowing he could not, and would not, live without culture. His wife, who had been a music teacher in the Soviet Union, became a nurse in the United States. She works full-time at a hospital and privately tutors music students on weekends to pay the bills and college tuition for their daughter, while her husband retains his culture.

Cece handed me a roll of tickets.

"Senior citizens eight dollars, the rest ten. There will be a couple kids to check the tickets. If I don't make money today, I'm dead. A friend of mine already sold a lot of tickets in senior citizen buildings and rented school buses to bring the seniors. The money from that went for my dress and sandals. I had nothing to wear! My friend, you know, the one with the Mercedes and the moustache, paid for the auditorium—thank God."

Cece was standing in the center of the lobby, greeting, smiling, kissing, chirping, pressing hands, and asking me to give about every fourth person a free ticket. The slits of her dress turned in all directions.

Cece's dress and sandals must have cost a bundle, judging from the amount of seniors getting off the buses in front of the school. The first several walked in holding their tickets, greeted Cece, went into the auditorium where the usher tore their ticket in half, then they went back out as if to go to the washroom. They passed their already torn tickets to their ticketless friends waiting for them. At this rate, before long we'll have more people than seats—we need to graduate to a hand stamp. They're counting on the fact no one is going to throw out a bunch of old people.

Maybe Cece's dress and sandals weren't that expensive after all.

I tried to talk to Cece the next time she asked me to give a free ticket to another friend.

"Cece, you're going to be in trouble. Find the janitor, have him bring chairs and place them in the aisles and in the back. You can pay him something afterwards."

"What if a fire inspector shows up?" worried Lena.

"I don't care. Those idiots don't understand anything. They all speak English!" Cece cried out.

Lena and I exchanged glances. I sighed and left my post in search of help.

Twenty dollars brought a smile to the janitor's face and additional chairs to the theater. It was only five-thirty and the theater was already three-quarters full.

Cece never saw me return, or the chairs arrive, drunk as she was from the attention she was receiving.

Natasha came alone, sentimental and aloof. Bella and Felix came with two couples. Bella had regained most of the color she had lost on her trip. Vilen didn't miss the chance to throw me a covert look. I automatically shivered. Irena warned me that I should never let Jack out of my sight on a Saturday night, then instructed Lena to keep her eyes open for available men. Her work finished, she navigated her husband past the books to their seats.

Ilya brought his mother, a heavy woman in a dark wool dress with a clear amber broach on her massive chest. He bowed seriously to me and stopped at Lena's side while his mother talked with a group of seniors. Lena lowered her eyes, answering him in monosyllables, conscious of his mother's and my presence.

Seniors constitute a big portion of any Russian audience and, in my opinion, are the pride of the community. The majority of them are war widows. After several years of freedom, these slave-like, dark-faced creatures, fresh out of communal apartments and lines for food, worn with work, worries, and uncertainties, looking years older than their counterparts in the United States, have blossomed into confident, carefree people, looking years younger than their counterparts in the Soviet Union. Their evolution is the most eloquent and convincing illustration of the difference between the world in which they worked, sweated, and fought for in their youth and the world that accepted them, introducing dignity to the final stretch of their lives.

I enjoyed listening to the Russian comments—good Russian, with only a few English words mixed in—in the well-modulated tones of well-educated people:

"They called us traitors when we left and look who's coming to entertain us for our capitalistic dollars."

"I wonder if she's going to answer any questions. I want to ask about Chernobyl."

"In the Soviet Union, we wouldn't have been privileged to attend a Koval concert. She would never have come to Kharkov."

"I reread some of Koval's poems yesterday. They sounded so distant."

"They think they can create nostalgia by letting people like Koval come to do concerts. I'm not even sure I care anymore."

Comments about vacations, performers, and Ravinia concerts, exchanges about new houses, names, and events I didn't know, but nevertheless seemed familiar, made me feel sad and sentimental. Like

Sasha used to say in Yiddish, *"mame-loshn."* It felt good to hear everything in Russian.

I recognized several people from long-ago sightings at the JRL, the old neighborhood, and the aisles of discount and second-hand stores we used to haunt. Some I couldn't place, but I listened with interest to their news and told them mine. One lady offered to fix me up with her recently widowed brother and left me her business card in case I decided I wanted to meet him. She owned a large real-estate agency.

The air crackled with sentimentality and exuberance—in perfect Russian style. Many in the audience held books by Koval, hoping to have them autographed—probably one of the rare occasions when they disturbed their personal Russian libraries for reasons beyond dusting.

A small crowd lingered outside the auditorium waiting to greet the poetess.

The intellectual elite of the Russian community had gathered for this event, stylishly dressed, basking in the newly acquired knowledge that a brain is an asset. In the Soviet Union these engineers, doctors, and musicians were considered the dregs of society. Most of them came to the United States later than I did, about eight or nine years ago. Within a short time they deservedly reached a level, in their old or new careers, that subsequently gave them a lifestyle comparable to that enjoyed by their colleagues born here.

If Asya and Sasha were here now!

All these faces are familiar, the ones I have seen before and the ones I haven't. Even the most Americanized of us recognize the common Russian core that forever remains in our eyes, that indefinable and unnamable something I don't find in Jack's eyes. He's not one of us.

These are my people. I can't stand them, I laugh at them, I avoid them, I despise their collective Soviet traits and attitudes, but at times I miss them and even need them.

Pressing forward, the crowd in the front of the auditorium gasped. All I could see from my chair was the front door being held open. Lena breathed, "Lubov Koval!" and ran limping toward the backs of people standing on their tiptoes. Suddenly the silence became complete.

Cece's staccato voice exclaimed, "Lubochka! Finally! Welcome!"

I got up, moving sideways to the edge of the last row of tense backs. Cece was hugging a tall woman flanked by two men. One of the men carried a plastic see-through bag with a bottle of vodka in it. The woman had large, dark, still eyes, feverishly brilliant. Her long arms wrapped around Cece, but her eyes, looking straight over the heads in front of her, made it seem as if her movements were half-conscious.

"Let's start, let's start!" she said listlessly, finishing Cece's embrace with a push. The men at each side caught her elbows. Swaying, Koval looked at them surprised.

Someone screamed, "Thank you for coming to Chicago!" and applause ensued.

"She's drunk?" half-asked a whisper next to me.

Marina made her way to the woman, handed her a bouquet of flowers, and said something inaudible. The tall woman made a deep bow, like actors do from the stage.

"Let's go, Lubochka, sunshine," Cece said suavely and Lubov Koval's eyes rested on her with the same surprise they had held for the men supporting her.

Cameras flashed.

Cece burst forward as the crowd made way. Lubov followed, stepping unsteadily on high heels.

Everyone hurried to find their seats. I found Lena and we sat on folding chairs close to the exit.

Lena's hands pressed her chest, her eyes filled with tears.

"Lubov Koval! A living legend! Did you see her eyes?"

"Shush!" responded the people seated around us.

In a few minutes, Lubov Koval walked across the stage, stumbled, then came to the very edge. She bowed, letting her arms hang almost to the floor, and remained in this position for almost a full minute. The applauding audience rose as one, calling out endearments and welcomes. There was a wall of backs in front of me. Lena put so much energy into her applause it made her breathless. She looked at me, astonished I hadn't risen. A couple in the last row also remained seated through the outburst; their eyes meeting mine expressed embarrassment.

The lights dimmed, leaving the dark figure on the brightly lit stage looking unusually frail. Lubov straightened up and began chanting slowly to a crowd still settling down. The noise drowned the first minute of her recital, then the words sung out, punctuated by misplaced stresses, reinforced by sharp uncoordinated movements of her arms. A short pause, filled with light coughs from the audience, preceded the beginning of every new poem.

I used all my will to concentrate on the meaning of the sounds reaching my ears, to build the mood these sounds should have induced. The words failed to hold my attention. Even my favorite poem seemed miserably disjoined from its memory. My thoughts were irreversibly slipping into worries about the car, Rimma's visit, and how to find Cece to give her the money.

My failed effort to concentrate tired and disappointed me. I sat back, closed my eyes and let the words from the stage become background sounds addressed to someone else. During one of Lubov's short pauses I left my chair and tiptoed out to the waiting area. I found a public phone down the hall. Tanya told me Vera, Alice, and Judy had come over, and that Jack had just arrived and was in the process of dumping out the contents of his briefcase.

"Please ask him to pick me up at the front entrance."

"Is the concert over?"

"No, but I don't seem to be able to concentrate."

"Okay," said Tanya indifferently, then chanted with infinitely more enthusiasm, "Golf! Golf! Golf! I can't wait until my first golf lesson!"

For safety, I went into the bathroom and counted the box of money. I wrote the total on a piece of bathroom tissue and gave Lena the box when I returned to my seat.

"You're not leaving, are you?"

"Yes. Sorry," I whispered.

The lighted lobby of the school invoked a strangely antagonizing feeling, a sense of betrayal by what I thought I held sacred and so dear to my soul as to be eternal.

I stood so close to the glass entrance door that I almost touched it with my nose. I explained this proximity to myself as important to shorten my escape time. The moment I saw Jack's car enter the driveway I ran out of the building. Jack looked tired. Lubov Koval and Jack seemed equally foreign.

"You seem perplexed. Wrong concert?" said Jack after a quick look at me.

"Everything is wrong. I was looking forward to this concert, to meeting this poet—a symbol of my youth—and she turned out to be just words, no meaning."

We drove the rest of the way home in silence.

A shower and shave returned Jack to his boyish self after his long drive from Wisconsin. He pulled me from the sofa where I had been waiting for him and kissed my ear. Whirling the car keys around his finger, he looked at me with smiling eyes.

"Let's go, Anna, I made a reservation, for now, at Windows. You look great," Jack's hands encircled me, his lips immediately on mine.

Making love has become my body's favorite pastime. I try not to remember the time when it was a forced routine, in the worst moments, and an expression of gratitude, in all others.

It took only a few minutes to get to the restaurant.

"Jack, how much do you think it will cost to repair my car?"

"Did Richard say your car needs a new engine?"

"No."

"Well, we'll see what he says. In any case, don't rush to do anything. If it needs a new engine you're better off getting a new car."

"I have fourteen more payments on this one! I was planning to keep it at least three or four more years."

"A Chevy? It won't be worth a dime as a trade-in."

Jack ordered steak and I ordered stuffed trout.

"Anna, both our cars have been taking a beating; all our driving and your trip to Florida certainly didn't help. Normally, I keep a car for two years, but I think I'll trade mine in when I'm finished in Green Bay. You should have a European or Japanese car."

A busboy refilled Jack's water glass.

"Jack, I can't spend money on a car right now."

"You can afford it. Don't be greedy."

"Greedy? My contract is up at the end of August. Even if they give me a green light on the credit system—and I haven't heard anything since the presentation—it will only add a couple months, not even full-time. I have to start thinking about what's next."

"Don't panic. There are lots of projects going on this time of the year."

The waitress placed a salad in front of Jack and soup in front of me.

"I'm not panicking. I just want to be sure I continue to work."

"Unless you happen to become independently wealthy," Jack smiled.

"Like winning the lottery? Or getting adopted by a Rockefeller?"

"There are ways," he kissed my hand, looking at me seriously.

He was nervous. He would never dare to say I should take money from him. That subject is closed.

We danced slowly to some elevator music on a tiny dance floor along with a few other couples. Jack's hands felt warm on my back.

"You're beautiful," he said softly. His hands moved to my shoulders.

What does he see in me that I don't, that Lonya didn't, that Sasha . . .?

We sat down just as the waitress arrived with our entrees. A group at a long table in the center sang an endless out-of-tune "Happy Birthday."

I need time with other Russians, but I'm glad I left the concert. Poor Lena, she'll have to drive Cece home and listen to the never-ending stories of her conquests.

Jack is in one world, Lubov Koval in another. Today I ran away from what I know so well and what has always felt so dear, to eat, talk about car repair, and hold the firm biceps of a man.

"Anna, let's check into the hotel downstairs for a few hours," Jack said as we sat down.

"Why?" I asked automatically.

"I would swear you don't need a lengthy explanation."

"Jack, I don't want to be taken to a hotel. I have a home."

"Honey, I'm alone all week long. I miss you."

"I'm not a honey. We just can't pick up and run to hotel rooms."

I envy Jack's ability to follow his desires without being self-conscious, analytical, or guilty.

"Anna, don't look at me as if I were some unknown entity. Think about it. There isn't much we don't know about each other. For God's sake, you trust me with Tanya! I don't understand why I have to prove I respect you at every turn."

"Is everything okay?" asked the waitress with friendly interest.

"More coffee, please," Jack said without looking at her.

"Jack, you don't have to prove anything. Call me a social invalid, but I'm uncomfortable going to a hotel with a man. To me, it's humiliating."

"Would you go there with your husband?"

"If we were on vacation; otherwise it would be unnecessary."

"My God! Where did you get these moronic ideas? It's nonsense. Married couples check into hotels for privacy, or for some fun."

"This is too hypothetical for me to be concerned with, and it's too late for me to change." I looked out the window at the busy intersection. The cemetery on the opposite corner looked ominous, vast, and dark.

Sometimes I think of the feelings I've missed in life, like being a daughter, a granddaughter, a wife to someone I love. The list is shorter now: Jack taught me how to feel like a woman, Tanya has given me the pride of bringing a good person into the world, and my work gives me worthiness. It's too late for all the rest.

Jack's sigh drifted across the table.

"Okay, Anna, let's go home."

Jack signaled for the check. His hand inched up my arm to my shoulder, massaging it lightly. He never hurries, controls himself amazingly well. In spite of his deliberately relaxed movements, this time I knew he could hardly wait. His impatience was suddenly contagious.

My body took over that night, relieving my mind of everything it considered of any importance. Something had happened at the concert that miraculously had made me give up crucifying myself for not feeling exactly what I should feel for Jack. The fact that I needed a man sexually suddenly didn't seem to disturb me. We made love to the point of exhaustion. It was like trying to catch up on all the missed sensations, to make up for all the lost opportunities for relief and contentment. Until it's Sasha, it may as well be Jack.

twenty-four

After falling asleep so late, it was miraculous that Jack still had the energy to get up so early to take Tanya to her golf lesson. When I opened my eyes at a little before eight, I discovered a sheet of paper on Jack's pillow that screamed out in red marker, "Out to golf! Daughter."

I dozed for a while, then stretched before getting up. Inspecting my body in the mirror, I shook my head and gave my reflection a prescription for regular doses of the health club, fortified myself with toast covered with blackberry preserves (some prescription!), and headed to the corner house.

The rumble of lawnmowers up and down the street accompanied a heavy smell of fresh-cut grass.

Sylvia opened the door. Her long face remained immobile, only her dark eyes expressed satisfaction.

"Good morning, Sylvia, I thought you might be out walking. It's a lovely day."

"I'm not feeling well. Good morning. Come in."

We sat down in the living room and looked at each other.

Sylvia's eyes held a questioning look. "You look perplexed."

"You know, my boyfriend told me the same thing."

"He did?"

"Yes. I went to a Russian poetry reading last night."

Sylvia raised her brows.

"Have you ever heard of the poet Lubov Koval?"

"No, I haven't. I only remember those from before the war and, of course, the Russian classics."

"Her works used to be like . . . like . . ." I fumbled, at a loss for an apt comparison.

"Go on," Sylvia's mouth twitched in a semblance of a smile, "I know how it is in Russia."

"Now, not only were her poems meaningless, but the language itself seemed . . . strange. It sounded so foreign I caught myself being surprised I could understand it. I left and went out to eat with my boyfriend, and I wasn't even hungry. There must be something wrong with me."

"What was your boyfriend's reaction?" Sylvia reached for a pack of cigarettes sitting on a shelf.

"Jack's an American. He's generally not interested in literature, but he could see I was confused."

"An American?" She chewed on the cigarette reflectively. "Interesting that you're attracted to an American."

"Well," I shrugged avoiding Sylvia's eyes, "I am . . . in a way . . ."

"You are," she stated with finality.

I opened my mouth to contradict, remembered how Jack and I had made love last night, and closed my mouth.

Looking at me with curiosity and humor, Sylvia took the cigarette out of her mouth.

"I'm not surprised you find it strange," I started. "But he's done so much for me and my daughter . . ."

"I don't find it strange," she interrupted softly. "It's more unusual for an American to undertake anything so close to insurmountable." The cigarette went into the ashtray. "You must realize how hard it is for him. Russians are philosophers, you know, even if they're not Jewish."

The comment caught me off guard.

"I know, Anna, you think it's harder for you, because your English needs improvement, because he probably prefers baseball to poetry, and doesn't understand how to be afraid of the KGB."

"I've told him I'm not right for him. We don't have much in common."

"You don't? How long have you known him?" Sylvia's eyes were alive with interest.

"Four years. We work together."

"What does he do?"

"Computers."

"Is he Jewish?"

"Yes, I wouldn't date a Gentile."

"I'm sure you wouldn't, not after the anti-Semitism that permeated every pore of your life in the Soviet Union. I'm sorry for intruding in your personal life. Since your first visit, I've been thinking about what books to recommend, and my first choice is *Nineteen Eighty-Four*, by George Orwell, unless, of course, you've already read it. You might need a dictionary, but the book should prove very interesting to you."

"I know it. In the West, it was translated into Russian. All the émigrés were reading it when we were in Rome. I didn't because I vowed not to read anything in Russian until I learned English. Unfortunately, I can't say I've learned English all that well, but it seems Russian has become a foreign language to me."

"Your life experiences don't support Russian culture anymore. That's more common than you think. You won't find any Russian books in my library, and I used to recite Pushkin, Lermontov, Esenin, and more by heart. You assumed you'd respond to the poetry of your youth differently?"

"Oh, yes. And it was the first time, in a long time, that I went to a Russian cultural event."

"Why do you think that is, Anna, especially if you're so deeply attached to your past?"

"I don't know. Most of the Russian community seems so . . . so Soviet. Maybe people weren't like that in your time—you emigrated only thirty years after the Revolution."

"Two more generations from that regime makes a big difference, but ugliness doesn't need much time to spread and to saturate souls. Look how quickly Nazism took hold in Germany. It's the same thing." Sylvia's eyes focused inward, probably on her own memories. After a long silence, she asked "Do you have friends outside of the Russian community?"

"Not really," I answered in Russian. "Although I feel more comfortable with some of my coworkers than with most Russians, there's no bond. As far as my childhood friends, no one has been able to replace them."

"Yes, I know," Sylvia nodded. "Do continue to speak Russian? I've rarely heard it in twenty-three years. Not since my mother passed away."

"Last Friday, I spoke to my girlfriend in Kiev for the first time in ten years. There are so many memories, so much only she would understand. You see, my foundation is my past, the people of my past."

"Is that so?" she asked quietly.

I was stunned. How could I convince Sylvia? She needs to know about Fima, who was a good husband; about my forgery; about Lonya and his mother, who was my mother; about not being allowed to love them; and about Sasha, who understood everything and gave me all I ever needed.

"Anna, your memories will always remain with you. Why is it so important to have the people with you?" Sylvia asked as she reluctantly rose. "Will you have a cup of coffee with me?"

"No, thanks," I jumped up, suddenly feeling exposed. "I shouldn't be taking up your time."

"You aren't. Why don't you take *Nineteen Eighty-Four* from the wall unit over there. I'll be right back."

The next hour was the most gratifying I'd spent in years.

Sylvia's books were organized in alphabetical order by author. Some had been read more than others, but they had all been read. I took the titles that sounded appealing, and those by authors I recognized, off the shelves, read the descriptions, testimonials, and biographies on the jackets and a page or two at random. While I recognized most words, the ideas were sometimes hard to grasp until the second or third try. I found *Nineteen Eighty-Four* and put it aside. There were other books by Saul Bellow, in addition to the one Sylvia had been reading.

"Sorry for leaving you alone for so long. I'm slow, not what I used to be."

Caught red-handed plowing through a thick book called *Atlas Shrugged*, I slammed it shut and turned to Sylvia. She was smiling openly.

"I didn't mean to startle you. By the way, that's an excellent book. It will be on the list I promised you. But there are two others you should read before it. They'll be on the list, too."

I could hear the weariness in her voice.

"You should have asked me to help you in the kitchen."

"I appreciate that, only, in my view, keeping busy is healthy. Stay and browse if you want to."

"Maybe I'll stop by tomorrow, after work, if you don't mind. Before I got married I always spent evenings and weekends in the library. Those were wonderful hours."

"Uplifting, I know," Sylvia paused, staring past me. "How's your daughter?"

"She's in the top three percent of her class. She'll be a senior in the fall," I said switching to English.

"Does she speak Russian?"

"Her vocabulary is limited and she has an American accent, but I think she understands everything. I guess we'll find out when her father comes to visit."

"Your ex-husband is coming for a visit? Doesn't it make you wonder how he'll feel, seeing the grown daughter he let go so many years ago?"

"He didn't let her go," I said in Russian. "And I think he was a good father."

"There are no exceptions—without permission, you can't leave. He must have let her go."

"He didn't," I repeated in Russian, willing Sylvia to understand.

She looked at me intently. "Well, take your time, I don't need the book back right away." Sylvia walked outside with me. "Anna, visit me whenever you can, and please come for lunch next Sunday. I'll probably have your list finished by then. Bring your daughter if you want. I'll make blintzes. It will be nice to have company."

Contentedly, I strolled home with the book under my arm, anticipating solitude and a treat in the backyard or on the sofa.

I opened the door as the answering machine was in the process of taping a message from Lena. I picked up the phone as she was saying an exuberant good-bye.

"Good morning, Anichka. This is the second time I'm calling. Where did you disappear to so early in the morning?"

"I went to visit a neighbor. How did it go last night? I meant to call you."

"Anya, you missed so much. There can't be anything comparable to Lubov Koval in America. After the concert we all—that is, all the insiders," Lena chuckled, "about twenty people, went to a Russian restaurant. Koval was falling asleep, but after some vodka she seemed to revive. She let us take pictures with her then she autographed her books. I'll be able to send pictures to my parents and friends in Kiev!"

"I'm glad you enjoyed it."

"Everyone did. Lubov Koval is not a happy person, her special position notwithstanding. Her books are widely published now, but she distrusts everything that's going on. She said she envied us. Isn't that amazing?"

"I don't think so."

"You're different, Anya. You were the one who decided. I never would have left if not for Serozha's insistence. I'm still sort of nostalgic."

"How was driving back?"

"It only took about twenty minutes to deliver Cece to her house, even with all the traffic lights. A little more coming back; I hit the after-theater traffic from the city to the suburbs. Cece was drunk and kept talking about how many Russian celebrities were her lovers. Why did you leave?"

"I don't know. I couldn't concentrate—worried about my car."

"Do you think you'll have to buy a new one?"

"I'll know tomorrow."

"Still, Lubov Koval doesn't happen every day."

"I realize that."

"By the way, I'm planning on joining a Russian fundraising committee affiliated with the JRL. Soviet anti-Semitism is out of control; there's going to be a drive to help our people get out. Would you like to join with me?"

"I wish you luck, Lena. Russians generally don't give unless it's to help people they personally know."

"You're right, but we have to try."

"We need to change. Who else is on the committee?"

"Your friend, Marina Korsunsky, is the chairwoman. She used to be my caseworker."

"Marina Korsunsky presides over a fundraising committee? Well, well."

"Why not? She has the time. I think it's very nice of her."

Interesting—Marina, the do-gooder. Whatever the reason, it's not the burning desire to help the less fortunate. More probably, her keen sense of building up connections within the JRL guides her. Does it make a difference what reasons drive her as long as benefits result?

"Okay, who else is on the committee?"

"There are eight or ten people. Two of them are other doctors' wives. What difference does it make? They're doing a good deed. Anya, you know a Russian would, without reservation, give the last shirt off his back to a friend, but not a penny to a cause. Someone has to wake us up. Why shouldn't it be you and me? Americans give to charity. Maybe you can ask Jack for a donation."

"He's always been a big contributor to the JRL, even more since we met. Have you ever seen the donor list they publish every year?"

"No, I haven't. Well, let me know. I'm still excited. I had such a good time last night. How did you get home?"

"Jack picked me up and we went out to eat."

"Oh, so you left because you had a date with Jack!"

"Not really, we had planned to eat after the concert all along. Lena, you may not believe it, but real Russian without English words mixed in sounded foreign to me."

"Foreign! Anya, you're so funny!" Lena burst out laughing.

That's probably how Lena—soft, trusting, and naïve—laughed all the years she thought Serozha loved her.

twenty-five

The book under my arm made me restless. I wiped the picnic table and benches. So nice not to have to mow the lawn anymore.

I debated whether serious reading would be possible without a dictionary. Well, it would have to be. My small English-Russian dictionary is no longer adequate.

The dust jacket was a dull, almost dark-blue color with black words on a white strip that looked as though it was torn from the top of a page—*Nineteen Eighty-Four*. One of the testimonial quotations on the dust jacket flap said, "As timely as the label on a poison bottle."

It was a bright cold day in April and the clocks were striking thirteen. The book started in England with the description of a man going home in bad weather. It resembled the beginning of a mystery novel. I had problems with a few words, but in the context they were used their meaning was clear.

The first sentence of the next paragraph, *The hallway smelt of boiled cabbage and old rag mats*, brought back the stench of staircases, complete with urine and alcohol, in old Kiev buildings, where everyone I had ever known lived, up to the beginning of the sixties when Krushchev returned from the USA with the revolutionary idea of providing a separate apartment for each family. I remember kissing Sasha, under the stairs, in the dark, behind the elevator, in the stench — and it was delicious. There had been a poster of Stalin on the wall and most days an "out of order" sign on the elevator. Lonya suffered unbearably when he had to climb the stairs. At every landing he had to sit on a step, his huge eyes staring out from behind thick glasses.

Every sentence in the book brought another heavy weight with it. In spite of not having any particular difficulties understanding the words, I felt my shoulders bending under the growing weight.

BIG BROTHER IS WATCHING YOU.

Oh, yes, the family concept! All the adults were Stalin's children, all the children were Lenin's and Stalin's grandchildren. Stalin was the beloved patriarch. Millions looked up to him, as an icon, waiting for a sign, telling them what to feel, whom to like or to hate, how every minute detail of their lives should be . . . or else. The "or else" hardly disturbed anyone. Like good children, the masses did what they were told and pointed fingers at and demanded retribution from those who lacked sufficient fervor.

Sasha's father, a devout party member, was arrested in 1938, during one of the purges at the hospital where he was head doctor. Accused of being an enemy of the people—the formula for murdering or exiling millions, most of them faithful party members—he was arrested in the presence of his patients. His pregnant wife was forced—if she didn't want to be sent into exile leaving her son behind—to write a letter denouncing her husband. The letter was published in *Pravda*—how ironic that "pravda" means "truth." Zina, Sasha's sister, was born seven months later.

As hard as it is to believe, in 1940 when Chaim Rosenberg returned from prison—a toothless invalid with his kidneys ruined from relentless beatings—he still professed party support, affirming to his thirteen-year-old son the notion that if the party thought it was best to imprison and beat him, then it must have been right.

The day the war started in 1941, Chaim volunteered to work in a military hospital at the front—"for our motherland, for our father Stalin," he said.

"Don't cry if I die," he told his family, "be proud that I gave my life for Stalin."

He was reinstated in the party posthumously when Krushchev came to power. His wife, then Sasha, proudly kept his party ticket. There were millions like Chaim Rosenberg and his family.

Sasha had no problems understanding his father, but he could not understand me when I decided to leave.

"This is your motherland," he said reproachfully.

Poor, intelligent, faithful Sasha—and all the rest. No one is immune.

It's unfortunate that normal, logical people don't recognize the threat, and the ones that do don't take it seriously. They think they are immune because they are normal and logical. Then suddenly it's too late and the souls of entire generations are irrevocably corroded. Few realize how vulnerable normal, logical people are to lies, fear, distrust, ruthlessness, apathy, and lawlessness—how little resistance they have. They don't understand—no one is immune.

We are all invalids—all who escaped—the leaders and the followers alike, even the children. Americans don't understand, even our children don't understand—and they're all vulnerable in their naïve belief that they are immune.

If there had been a chance for me to read this book in the Soviet Union, I would have swallowed it in a day, with the satisfaction that someone else understood the ugliness and danger of my surroundings. Now, from a distance, and after tasting years of freedom, it makes my hair stand on end to read and understand what brought me to where I am, and what would have become of Tanya's life had I not left.

I closed my eyes and rubbed the back of my neck in an effort to relax, to forget. I was afraid to open my eyes to let the tears out.

I can't read this book! Why did Sylvia give it to me? She should have known better. She couldn't have forgotten her own experience. There are so many other books on her shelves.

When I opened my eyes, the book was still there, open to the half-read first page.

Inside the flat a fruity voice was reading out a list of figures which had something to do with the production of pig iron.

One of the numerous discoveries I made in the United States was the absence of constant media reports on production. I remembered the format by heart: "So many liters of milk were produced in this quarter, which is so many percent more than for the same period last year, and so many hundred percent more than for the same period in 1913." Regular gloating reports of a two-digit percent GNP growth in the flourishing USSR, compared with a two or three percent growth in the decaying USA. A common joke was "What? No milk? Just put a bottle under the radio."

How come the main character in this book has an apartment of his own? My goodness, he missed the excitement of five, six, or more unrelated families living in an apartment with one room for each family, all sharing the kitchen, bathroom, and hallway. He wouldn't understand that there were as many light bulbs in the kitchen as families living in the apartment, and the same for the bathroom and hallway. If you wanted to use any of the apartment's common rooms you first had to turn on your own private light bulb, from your own private meter.

Separate apartments, when they finally came, were small, similar to studio or one-bedroom apartments in the United States. They crowded four to six people in each, but at least these people now belonged to the same family! There was a joke about the bathrooms being so tiny one had to prepare to use them before entering.

When we arrived in the United States we were all astonished by so many new concepts, one being the perception that living in the suburbs is a measure of success, that it wasn't just the outskirts for the common herd. When Asya had been assigned an apartment in a far suburb, it had meant being cut off from civilization for a long time. Stores, post offices, kindergartens, telephones, roads were never part of new developments. It took years before any sort of organized life appeared. Only libraries, the ambassadors of the ideological front, were everywhere.

Caught by an old impulse, I turned to look behind me, in case someone was there, watching my thoughts. I'm not even finished reading the first page and it has brought back my whole life under "Big Brother."

By the end of the page my tension subsided. A comment about coarse soap brought more memories. I always bought something gentler for Tanya and Fima, but I never saw the need to spend more on myself and used cheap, long-lasting, light-brown bars, good for any purpose from heavy-duty laundry and dishwashing to bathing.

The blunt razor blades mentioned in the book brought pictures to my mind of the faces and necks of Russian men, which before the introduction of electric razors were customarily decorated with dried blood.

How could Orwell possibly know the intimate details only those fortunate enough to be born into Lenin's family would be familiar with?

I was reading now at about the rate I would be reading in Russian. The pain retreated. I became entranced, reading my own past, my own thoughts, my own vision.

There was of course no way of knowing whether you were being watched at any given moment. What could be a better answer to the eternal American question, "Why didn't you just organize and fight back!?"

And this: *You had to live—did live, from habit that became instinct . . .* My life had been filled with the happinesses of small victories in acquiring things such as buttons, shoelaces, a can of peas.

Reading hurt again. My shoulders were getting numb, but I couldn't stop.

Nothing was illegal, since there were no longer any laws.

To dissemble your feelings, to control your face, to do what everyone else was doing, was an instinctive reaction.

Yes, to dissemble feelings—a society of instinctive liars, of lies that are called life because they become second nature.

To the future or to the past, to a time when thought is free, when men are different from one another and do not live alone—to a time when truth exists and what is done cannot be undone:

The plea rang in my ears. It pierced some previously unknown compartment in my mind where these exact words had lain dormant. I whispered the entreaty slowly, making it my own.

From the age of uniformity, from the age of solitude, from the age of Big Brother, from the age of doublethink—greetings!

Tanya's cool, soft hands covered my eyes; the next second she pressed a kiss on my cheek, lowered three red roses across the book, and sat beside me.

"From Jack and me. Golf is so much fun! You should have come with us."

"Good afternoon!" Jack's smiling eyes appeared at the far side of the table. They both wore glowing tans, with Tanya looking very much like Fima, as she always does when she's happy.

"We rode in a golf cart! Know what? Jack says it's okay if I shoot more than ten times against a hole, the rest won't count. It's golf etiquette! We had brunch at the country club. Guess who we met there

—Steve Rappaport and his father. Remember Steve, the senior who asked me out before I started dating Jeff?"

"Steve's a handsome young man," inserted Jack looking at me. "And seems to be very bright."

"I don't like Russian boys. Their mothers make sandwiches for them in the morning, and their grandmothers make their beds for them. They're such babies."

Jack's eyes sparkled with keen pleasure.

"Thanks for the flowers." I got up putting them to my nose.

The stench of the staircases . . . Is this life I have — for real?

"Tanya, have you ever read *Nineteen Eighty-Four*?

"Sure, in school. Is that what you're reading?"

"Yes. Did you like it?"

"It was okay, a little confusing. It's about Russia. I'm going in to put the flowers in a vase. And I need to make some phone calls!"

"Jack, did you read *Nineteen Eighty-Four*?

"No, but I've heard people discuss it. Isn't it a fictional story about a dictatorship?"

"Believe me, it's not fiction, it's an exposé."

"I suppose the premise is life in Russia."

"What's a premise?"

"Basis."

"Jack, what's in this book could happen anywhere, and it has."

"I see." Jack leaned forward taking my hand. "I had a great time with the girls. People thought Tanya was my daughter. I guess, between the two, she was the most likely candidate, since Judy's Korean. Were you lonely here all by yourself?"

"No, I visited a lady who lives down the street. Her name's Sylvia. She lives in the corner house, the one with the picture window. I really like her. She's originally from Russia, and I find her easy to talk to. She loaned me this book."

"Anna, I'm going to have to leave soon. Don't . . . I'm a lump of putty when you look at me like that." Jack hid my hand in his warm palms.

"Like what?"

"I don't know . . . like you're suddenly seeing something you've never seen before."

I took back my hand and closed the book.

"Jack, do you really think I'm so difficult?"

From his suddenly serious face I realized my question wasn't as off-handed as I meant it to be.

"Does this have something to do with what you just read?"

"It was just a question."

"Well, you are certainly set in your ideas, and I, from your perspective, don't have any ideas . . . but there's nothing like a good challenge to keep a guy going. Why the question?"

"Just wondering."

We heard Tanya's laughter from the kitchen. By now everyone knew she had taken her first golf lesson.

"Do you think you'll need any help with the car in the morning?" Jack asked.

"I can handle it."

"Then I better get going. If the repair turns out to be expensive, instead of buying a new car you might consider leasing one. It would be a tax-deductible business expense."

"That's a good idea, but meanwhile I need a car for tomorrow. I guess I'll rent one."

"Here, let me give you a number. Ask for Dale. He'll take care of you and he'll see that the car is delivered. Have him charge it to my account—don't worry, it's tax-deductible."

"Thank you." I looked at him guiltily. "Jack, would you mind rubbing my shoulders? The tension from reading has given me a backache."

Jack kissed my neck with quick, light kisses, then his fingers started steady, firm movements. My head limply fell forward as the tension eased and Jack's fingers continued their job.

twenty-six

Early Monday morning Richard Chin called.

"Two thousand dollars for now. You need more repairs soon. Time to get new car."

I was not overly surprised by his report, and I arrived at work two hours late in a rented gray Continental. Only in America could this luxury automobile be the best bargain, and with unlimited mileage.

Raising her eyebrows as I walked past her desk, my secretary, Mrs. McLaughlin, glanced at the clock, her sign of disapproval.

"Anna, Bruce asked to see you as soon as you arrived. I advised him you had a problem with your car. He has a luncheon engagement in twenty-five minutes," she related dutifully.

I'm sure this will be the final okay for the credit system. Strange, Bruce Krysa is becoming involved himself.

The door to Bruce's office was wide open.

"Anna, come in. Have a seat. How's your car?" Bruce sipped coffee from a styrofoam cup.

"I probably need a new one. I've rented one until I decide what to do."

"My wife just blew the transmission on hers. Cost a fortune to repair. Anyway, Anna, Jim Karlson, our senior VP, informed me this morning he wanted to set up a meeting with you and Jack at two o'clock. Are you available to drive to Green Bay this afternoon?"

I froze. Here it comes. I screwed up. Hopefully, my stubbornness hasn't damaged Jack's prospects.

"That shouldn't be a problem, Bruce. I'll have something to eat and leave right away. Just give me directions on how to get there." I hoped my smile looked natural.

Oh God, I really screwed up. I wonder if Harvey Manufacturing would take me back. It was the best place for me. Everyone knew and liked me.

I drank a can of Pepsi as I dialed Jack's number.

"Jack Graff is in a meeting," an older man's voice informed me. "Would you like to leave a message?"

I didn't leave a message.

Driving to Green Bay, I rehearsed what I would say at the meeting. Hardly breathing, I pulled open the front door of a new, two-story building. I introduced myself as Ms. Fishman, expected by Mr. Karlson, to a uniformed guard in a round booth in the reception area.

"Mr. Karlson's secretary will be down momentarily to get you, ma'am."

I pressed a sticky visitor's badge to my left lapel as several people passed by, casually glancing in my direction.

"Ms. Fishman?" asked a voice behind me.

I turned to see a woman in her mid-thirties, with light hair arranged in neat waves. She smiled amiably, "I'm Mary, Mr. Karlson's secretary. Let me show you to his office."

My stomach knotted, unmistakably reminding me that every step I took brought me closer to facing Jack.

We entered a waiting room with two dark doors on opposite sides. Each had a silver name tag. Mary opened one of the doors and motioned me in.

A bulky, gray-haired man with a double chin, impressive belly, and surprisingly sharp, blue eyes easily raised himself from his chair and offered me his hand, which I shook silently, my throat in spasms.

"Jim Karlson, pleased to meet you."

The binder with my presentation took up the middle of his desk, between two stand-up framed photographs on one side and a pile of correspondence on the other.

"Anna Fishman," I said, aware of my uncommonly high voice. I felt drained, having spent all my energy on the introduction.

"Please sit down, make yourself comfortable. Would you like something to drink? Iced tea maybe?"

I hate iced tea. I nodded yes.

Jim buzzed Mary and she pushed in a cart with a pitcher and tall, frosted glasses. She filled the glasses, handing one to each of us.

"I'll send Mr. Graff in as soon as he arrives," she said closing the door firmly behind her.

Where is Jack? Why didn't he warn me?

"I have to apologize for not giving you more notice. We only finalized our decision to talk with your company Friday night." Jim downed his iced tea in one long gulp. "So, how have you liked working with us?"

Have liked working with us. Is he trying to let me down gently? Jack was right.

"I've liked it very much." I sipped the iced tea, holding it in my mouth, working up the courage to swallow it without changing my facial expression.

"You don't sound very enthusiastic."

What difference does it make now whether I liked it or not? The question is like the proverbial exchange between the doctor and his deceased patient's wife in one of Chekhov's short stories. Something like: "Did the deceased perspire before he passed away?" "Yes, he did." "That's very good."

Left with no choice, I swallowed the iced tea.

"I do mean it, Mr. Karlson, I have enjoyed the project very much."

"I'm glad to hear that. Please, call me Jim. Your performance and your attitude have earned you rave reviews."

If I earned rave reviews, what am I doing here?

"First of all, Bruce noticed that you worked more hours than you billed."

Only because some of my work had to be redone.

"But what we appreciate even more is the long-term view you took of our needs. In here," Jim tapped the binder, "are some very helpful suggestions how your system can feed our other systems." He smiled. "You went far outside the project scope, building in hooks for several enhancements, which you identified."

Only because Jack had to introduce me to the business basics of this project which included some of these suggestions.

"Both John and Bruce couldn't say enough about your attitude. Your little manual will shorten the user's learning curve."

Manual? I just collected my notes into one document and made copies for the users.

Jim looked at his watch. "Your partner had another meeting, but he should be here shortly, so we have a few minutes to spare. Tell me about yourself, Anna."

Jim poured more iced tea, took two big gulps then wiped his lips with a handkerchief.

I pretended to sip again.

He wouldn't make me drive all the way here to praise me. He must be warming up to let me go. I wish he would tell me before Jack gets here.

"When did you come to the United States?"

"About ten years ago."

"And where did you learn such good English?" Jim pushed himself back placing his hands on his stomach, lacing his fingers. His face beamed with genial compassion.

Good English! I wonder if it will make him feel bad to fire me.

"I took classes, watched television, my daughter taught me by talking to me."

"It must have been quite a challenge. We Americans take everything for granted. How old is your daughter?"

"Sixteen."

A short rap and the door opened. Jack strode in, winked at me, and shook hands with Jim. He looked pleased, not upset.

I don't know why I blushed.

"Thanks for waiting. Remember, Jim, you have to have a good reason for this meeting or Anna and I will charge this time to your project."

Smiling, Jim dismissed the remark with a wave of his hand.

"Anna's company was quite enjoyable. In fact, we were getting along just fine."

Jack's left brow rose as he spotted the glass of iced tea in my hand. He pushed up his glasses to hide the twinkle in his eyes as he took in my legs.

"Jim, before you begin, do you mind if Mary brings me a cup of coffee?"

My hand holding the iced tea began to shake. I put my glass on the edge of the desk. My temples were pounding.

Mary brought in coffee for Jack and a new pitcher of iced tea. Jack and Jim entered into a brief conversation concerning their respective weekend golf outings.

This preamble is too long.

Jim consulted his watch and raised his eyes, sizing us up.

"I called this meeting today to talk to you about what our company needs in systems development."

Jack looked up with a shrewd expression as though he already knew what Jim was going to say.

They understand each other well. American business small talk and innuendoes are beyond me. In Russia they say it's being the fifth wheel on a wagon.

The binder with my presentation on the desk didn't appear to be part of why we were here. I turned to Jack. He was busy with his coffee, his expression calculating and displeased.

Jim pressed the tips of his fingers together. "First, I would like to tell you we're satisfied with your performance, and particularly your attitude."

More compliments—why call a meeting?

"The right attitude is a rare commodity nowadays. You're quite lucky to have each other as partners."

Does he mean that Jack is lucky too? Oh, brother, he doesn't know as much as he thinks he does!

Jack threw me a quick, mischievous glance—he saw it as amusing when Jim complimented me on what Jack had given me the insight on. After fighting with me for taking on this project, he now seemed as proud as a peacock.

"This document, Anna," Jim picked up my presentation, "is amazing. You approached your task like you would have if this was your own company."

I couldn't take my eyes off the black binder in Jim's hands.

"Thank you," said Jack when it became clear that no sound was able to escape my frozen lips.

"The management's view is that we need to install your credit system." Jim returned the binder to his desk. "Thanks to you it will not just become a disposable, short-term patch as originally visualized."

Jim paused, turning his empty glass in his hands. I was beginning to thaw and couldn't resist a piercing glance at Jack.

"The reason we are meeting here today is the following."

No, tell me more about how wonderful I am!

"We would like you to give us a dollar amount and time estimate for producing a cost/benefit study to combine our order management for all divisions. The study is to include hardware, software, staff, the whole shot. However, there is one stipulation: the study must be completed before the end of the year. I trust your common sense and your expertise. If your figures are acceptable, you will be able to proceed with the study in September when your present assignment is completed. We have allocated money in next year's budget for the first phase of the project, and should we find your recommendations feasible—and I have a hunch we will—your company will manage the project from inception through installation."

The quiet made my ears buzz.

"I have to remind you, Jim," I heard Jack's cold voice, "only this morning we agreed my contract would be extended to install my software at your new Chicago division. That will bring us well into November and now you're talking about a new project for us in September."

"I'm not telling you how to approach this, but we thought since Anna will be available starting in September—unless she's already committed somewhere else . . . Jack, as long as the two of you are in charge, we don't care who does the work."

The two of us?

"Jim, what you've said is flattering, and your proposition is rather tempting, but there are other considerations that affect . . ."

"Jim," I interrupted, "do we have to give you an answer this minute?"

Jack's coiled fists fell to his knees.

"No, absolutely not. You two talk it over, think about it, and let me know, let's say, before the end of the week."

There were more pleasantries and handshaking. From Mary's desk I called Pat with the news he could start working on the programs for the credit system and left a message on the answering machine for Tanya that I'd be home late.

Jack and I never exchanged a word until we reached the parking lot.

"You don't seriously expect me to take this project," stated Jack as we stopped at the side of my car.

He didn't even notice I was unlocking a Continental!

"Didn't you hear—you personally don't have to do everything?"

"I heard. I also heard it could be you, and both of us know that you can't do it alone, and that I wrote your presentation, in addition to building the prototype."

"That's not fair, Jack. I wrote it all, my only problem was my English."

"Anna, trust me, what they envision is very different from the narrow application you've been involved in. We're talking about millions of dollars. This is no longer a matter of simple intelligence and the physical ability to put in sixty or seventy hours a week. Don't be offended, but you don't even fully understand how a company works. There is no question, you can not professionally handle a project of this magnitude."

"I know that, Jack. But I also know we could hire someone."

Jack's eyes softened as they ran down my body.

"Listen, don't feel bad about it. This is a moneymaker, a dream for any consulting company, and Jim knows it. It just fell into our lap, but I'm not a consulting company. I thought I made that clear to you. I'll admit your approach was the right one, but why should we start all this hassle, especially since I want to retire, or at least semi-retire in a few years, about the time Tanya finishes college?"

What does he have to lose? Like he said, this project is a moneymaker. Jack's wrong, he doesn't understand. His entire life has been retirement, only instead of gardening or golfing his retirement has been a paying hobby. He picks and chooses when, where, and how to do what he loves to do. He inherited his retirement.

I'll be forty-five in a couple of weeks. Retirement—I can't enjoy what I haven't earned.

Jack cupped my chin. "You look tired. Better head home and forget about all this. Wow, look at this, you rented a Continental! So, what did Chin say about your car?"

"Around two thousand dollars."

Jack whistled. "It's not worth the bother. Do you want to get something to eat?"

"I'm not hungry. Did you contact the company your salesman called you about?"

"It turned out I used to work with this guy's cousin on the East Coast. He understood that I'm in Wisconsin all week. I'll make my presentation Saturday morning."

I got into the car feeling like a popped balloon. I started the engine and lowered the window.

"Jack, I'm grateful to you for giving me this opportunity to work for myself. I love it, I simply love it. I know I only just started, but why can't I move ahead?"

One hand in his pocket, Jack leaned on the car door.

"Anna, gratitude is not the right feeling."

"Gratitude is the right feeling. No one else would have ever considered me for a job like this. I was afraid I'd let you down. But I didn't. Jack, please." I took his unresponsive hand. "I don't need a big salary. We could hire people, and I can learn from you before you retire. Jack, it's very important to me that I accomplish something significant on my own."

"You've accomplished more than enough for one life. Remember, Tanya wants you alive and well. I wouldn't mind that either, for what it's worth."

"Jack, for most of my life I heard about one achievement of mine—that my mother died on the day I was born. It seems, whatever I want can never be mine, whatever I touch interferes with someone else's plans. But this could be mine. I'll learn. It doesn't have anything to do with your retirement. I can't even see the connection."

Jack freed his hand and stepped back, thrusting it into his pocket.

"Anna, I wonder if you hurt me on purpose, or merely because you hurt."

"I hurt you now? I'm sorry. Maybe hurt is all I'm capable of giving."

"Go home, it's a long drive. I'll talk to you tomorrow."

Jeff's car pulled out of the driveway as mine pulled in. Tanya and Vera were standing in the driveway. Vera saw me first, her eyes lighting up, mine answering with a smile. Tanya turned around.

"Mom, wow, a Continental!"

I was conscious of Vera's quick, childishly jealous glance at the car.

"Hi, girls. I had to rent it. Mine needs a lot of repairs and believe it or not, this was the best deal."

"Mom, can I drive it?"

"No one under twenty-one can drive it. Did anyone call?"

"Lena and Natasha. We're waiting for Vera's Dad to pick her up. Dinner's still warm. Oh, I almost forgot. Jack called. He was worried because you weren't home yet."

"Traffic was terrible and I stopped at Wendy's for a hamburger. I'm going in to take a shower."

I expected the water to relax me, shake off the tiredness, but it didn't.

When I came out of the bathroom I found Tanya sitting cross-legged on my bed.

"Jack called again. I told him traffic was terrible and you were in the shower."

We went into the living room, settling ourselves comfortably on the sofa.

"Vera started working at a nursing home last week."

"What does she do?"

"She gets paid for helping in the kitchen and cleaning patients' rooms. Sometimes she writes letters for patients and combs their hair. One lady's family told her they'd pay her twenty-five dollars a week for helping their mother. She's going to keep a diary describing the medical problems of the patients. Her father says if we want to be doctors we need to develop a feel for what's wrong with patients."

"A doctor is not an occupation or a career, it's a calling, a mission. Do you remember what I told you about Uncle Sasha? The same goes for a teacher. Any vocation can be a mission."

Tanya tensed. "Teachers are not paid very well, and no one really respects teachers."

"If money or prestige is your top priority, then it's not a calling."

Tanya sat quietly for a moment.

"Jeff chose the University of Boston. He'll be leaving for college in a week."

"Did he decide on his major yet?"

"No."

"Tanichka, I think you should go to bed. In fact, I will too. I'm tired from the long drive. Jack was probably worried because I had to drive back from Green Bay in rush-hour traffic alone."

"You went to Green Bay? Why?"

"We had a meeting with the vice president of the company."

"Are you serious?" Tanya's admiring look was too much for me. I knew she was picturing *Dynasty*'s Alexis Colby in a business meeting.

"He just wanted to meet me and approve the next stage of the system Pat and I have been working on."

"Does he have a big office and a limo and a secretary and a window with a nice view?"

"Not really. He does have a secretary, but I'm sure he drives his own car. Go to bed, Tanichka."

"What about my cocoa?"

We were reluctant to part, we felt so cozy together.

twenty-seven

Light shone through the curtains of Sylvia's windows. Still, mindful of the late hour, I hesitated before ringing the bell. Thinking of Sylvia always makes me think of my mother. I wondered if I would have felt as comfortable talking to her as I do to Sylvia.

Dark puffy circles underscored Sylvia's eyes, making her face look old and worn. Her dog gave my shoes his usual perfunctory sniff.

"Come in, Anna." She rubbed her temple as she opened the door. "I've got a terrible headache."

"I'm sorry, Sylvia. I can come back another time. It's really too late for browsing through books."

Sylvia looked at her watch and sighed, "You're right. But don't go yet. Let's just have a cup of coffee."

We walked to the kitchen side by side. Her wrinkles appeared deeper and my heart contracted.

"Sylvia, have you talked to your doctor? Do you want me to take you to the emergency room?"

"I called my doctor earlier. I'll be all right."

I was grateful Sylvia didn't thank me for offering help, saying something like "It's so sweet of you to ask." But then she wouldn't—we're Russian and . . . somehow, not strangers.

I spooned a considerable amount of sugar into my coffee and for the first time I saw Sylvia smile.

"Sylvia, I'm almost finished with *Nineteen Eighty-Four*. Why did you give me this particular book?"

She stirred her coffee thoughtfully, answering, as was her habit, with a question.

"Why do *you* think I did?"

"You wanted me to see my life in the Soviet Union for what it was. But I already appreciate what I have now," I sputtered defensively. "I realize how lucky I am."

"I know you do." Sylvia's eyes looked stern. "Realizing the obvious is not that difficult."

The silence that followed reminded me of the silences in some of my conversations with Jack.

"The notion that I detected, and I might be mistaken," Sylvia got up after several quick sips of coffee, "is that you have designated a part of yourself to the past, forcibly keeping that part dead for all other intents. Excuse me, I'm going to get a cigarette."

She moved heavily, her dog trotting ahead.

Like Jack, she doesn't understand. If I tell her about Lonya, Fima, Sasha, and Asya, and about my mother, then she'll understand that all this can not, and should not, be forgotten.

"So, I gather you were impressed by the book. Did you need a dictionary?" Sylvia said, returning puffing on a lit cigarette and carrying the dog. "I hope my smoking doesn't bother you. It's my second one today. Feels good. I doubt abstaining helps."

Her matter-of-fact tone produced a sense of finality. Contradiction would have sounded false.

"The book was mesmerizing. With the first page, it brought back my entire life in the Soviet Union. I was too busy feeling the horror of it all to let myself be distracted over occasional unfamiliar words."

"You should do the same in your life." Sylvia sipped her coffee.

"It's interesting that you think I attach too much importance to the past. Jack says the same thing. Only, he's . . . he's so American, I don't think he understands how absolutely irreplaceable some people and relationships are. You would understand if you knew. . . ." I was overcome with a frantic urge to recapture the closeness with Sylvia I felt ebbing away.

"I'm not arguing with you," Sylvia said patiently. "I was in your place once. Under no circumstances are relationships and people replaceable—each is different, each has its own place. Don't look so defeated, Anna." She extinguished the cigarette in her cup, then patted my arm.

"Today, I was made to pass up a chance that will never present itself again." The admission came out of my mouth unexpectedly. "And I resent not only my helplessness, but Jack's refusal to help."

Sylvia's eyes expressed interest.

I found myself describing the meeting with Jim Karlson and Jack's selfishly negative response to the opportunity offered. When I was finished I rubbed my eyes, sniffling away tears. Sylvia's face looked parched.

"I'm sorry, Sylvia, this must be boring, and you're not feeling well."

"Your boyfriend cares about you, doesn't he?"

The half-question half-statement way she spoke left me with no answer.

"Anna, why is it so vital that you do this big project?"

"It's not the project," I cried out in Russian. "I need to prove to myself that I'm capable of doing something other than simply feeding or sheltering us."

"No one seems to be questioning your ability to succeed."

It was exactly what Jack would say.

"That's what Jack would say, but not you. Sylvia, please, I was not allowed to have abilities, or even feelings, for so long that I want to touch the results of my efforts. Sylvia, please . . ."

Her dark eyes narrowed as she nodded.

"I guess I don't know everything. We'll talk about it again, when I feel better."

"I shouldn't be bothering you. You need to rest," I got up regretfully. "It was too late for me to stop by."

"You're so wound up, Anna . . . Don't forget Sunday. Come at noon. I'll have blintzes ready."

Tired, but no longer sleepy, I walked through the house aimlessly. This morning I had planned to write Asya a letter. Ideas for the letter were plentiful, so many that I hadn't been able to concentrate on writing. Things were clearer now and for the first time in a long time I sat down at my desk in the office.

June 16, 1986

Dear Asya,

To hear your voice made me feel twenty-five years younger. I have found it impossible to develop the closeness I feel for the people of my youth with the people I've met later in life. I wonder if you've found this to be true.

There hasn't been a day in all the years I've been here that I haven't been sorry that my friends are not with me. Not only for my sake, but for theirs. It would have been hard at first, but hardships don't necessarily ruin happiness. Remember how we borrowed each other's children to wait in line for toilet tissue when we could only get two rolls per person? Many little episodes are cherished memories, aren't they? If—rather, when—we meet again, we'll need years to catch up.

I was heartened to learn you had received my letters. Had I been sure they were reaching you, I would have continued to write. My last letters were sent shortly after I started taking computer courses. With luck on my side, I found a job in only a couple of months. I stayed with one company for over six years until my boyfriend recently offered me a job installing his software. It's more money, which is good because we have to pay for our own college education here, and it's very expensive.

Tanya is one of the brightest students in her school. Hopefully, she'll get a scholarship. She's a wonderful girl and I'm terribly proud of her. When Rimma is here I'll give her pictures to take back.

I'm almost forty-five, but I don't agree we're old. True, our children are grown, but that only means we have more time to devote to ourselves. I'm going to interrogate Rimma mercilessly about you and your family. It's hard to imagine that your cute little boys are grown men. Is there anything I can send you?

Everyone in the West, and especially the Russian community, has been disturbed by the nuclear accident in Chernobyl.

Tanya sent Fima an invitation to come for a visit. More than likely he has already received it. You may not know that he has remarried and has a five-year-old son and a sixteen-year-old stepson. When you decide to come for a visit I'll be more than happy to send you an invitation.

The faint uneasiness brought about by Asya's remark "a millionaire like in a fairy tale" is restraining my uninhibitedness. One image I don't want to encourage is that of my bucolic existence shielded by the powers of a fairy tale millionaire overcome by fairy tale love. Of course, she's happy for me, but now, after Chernobyl, her family life must be her foremost concern, and that, on top of the expected everyday anxieties of a normal Soviet routine, is more than enough for anyone to bear. The nature of my difficulties, no matter how modestly and tactfully I try to present them, is indeed a fairy tale when compared to her existence. Can I really blame Asya if she sees me as Cinderella in the last act? I'm ready to share everything with her, but would she understand? After all, when Cinderella ends up a princess how much do her woes in the beginning count?

Not everything can be said in letters . . . and, I'm afraid my new life has become a routine to such a degree that I don't know what would interest you. Asya, please write to me. Give my regards to your family, especially your mother. I can't wait to see Rimma.

Love, Anya

There's no way to describe the last two days except as just plain dull. Even when Pat finishes his work and I have to juggle my schedule between Aurora and Waukegan, my days will never be as hectic as they once were. My thoroughness in the beginning translated into an almost flawless implementation. Jack did his homework, but I was good, too. We discovered that we worked well as a team. For the credit control system, he tried hard, but couldn't come up with a better design than mine. It took him some time to adjust to carrying out my decisions, while I simply flung myself into making them.

Taking on this project over Jack's objections has given me proof of my abilities. It also has given me a taste of professional freedom, which has resulted in an addiction—a longing for more of the same. And this addiction would have lain dormant had Jim Karlson not suggested we consider his new project. This time, Jack's refusal determined the outcome.

Engrossed in my thoughts, I've been talking with Jack, when he calls, in monosyllables. His fatherly and sympathetic manner serves as a reminder of my helplessness—and I resent that. Sometimes I have the urge to slam the receiver down, or just repeatedly bang it against the top of my desk in the middle of our conversation, but that would be irrational. It would be unfair, as well, as he should base his decisions on his best interests and not my fanciful ambitions. So, instead of rebelling, I listen, not really hearing what he says.

Strange, it feels like something is missing from my life, something that I never had. Maybe Jack's right that we don't need the hassle. Unfortunately, I'll never know. Only, I wish I could overcome this sense of loss.

At dinner Tanya proclaimed she had finished the essay for her final exam. Unexpectedly, I asked her to read it to me while I was making her cocoa. Aware of my limited English vocabulary, I normally avoided asking her to read to me. But after doing such a good job with *Nineteen Eighty-Four* I felt brave. I surprised Tanya by suggesting she redo some portions as the style was a little choppy and the tone somewhat artificial. Recognizing my old editor-turned-proofreader self I thought had perished for lack of use, I indicated places that needed to be reworked, circling them confidently with a yellow marker.

On Thursday, Jack called during the ten o'clock news, which overflowed with reports about the Soviet Union—*perestroika*, smashing reforms, and defectors.

The West actually believes this rot about *perestroika* and reforms— very frustrating. The defectors are real, of course, but no one questions the logic of defections accompanying that magic transformation from bad to good. If everything is so great, why are so many people willing to risk their lives and the lives of their families to escape? How does *perestroika* explain that Lena's parents are still denied permission to reunite with their daughter because—isn't there always a reason?—Lena left the Soviet Union for Israel and ended up, like almost everyone else, in the United States.

I listened to Jack with one ear, the news with the other. My responses to his customary what's-up-type remarks came automatically. Conversations with him just don't seem appealing anymore.

"Anna, I've done some research on the offer you were so keen about."

The words came as I thought our conversation was winding down. Caught off-guard, I sat holding the receiver tightly, unable to reply.

"Hello . . . Anna . . . are you there?"

"I'm sorry Jack, let me turn the television off." I reached for the remote control.

"I've decided we can do the cost/benefit study and see what happens."

"What made you change your mind?" I answered with distrustful attention.

"You did."

"That's impossible. I never mentioned it to you again."

"Perhaps it hasn't been a conscious attempt on your part, but I've been tamed."

"Tamed?"

"I can't function when I know you're unhappy," Jack said slowly.

"Come on, Jack."

"It's true, and I'm still not sure I'm ready for something like this." Jack paused. "Here it is. We need about two months to present our strategy and the cost/benefit document. We'll start in October; I'm sure that will be okay. You will need crash courses in the practical aspects of accounting, finance, marketing, business policies and law, and business writing. You'll have to do it part-time in July and August and full-time in September. My accountant and my attorney will do most of your training. I'll make sure you read up on computer technology and the newest software trends."

My God, is he making this up?

"Jack, I don't think I'd be able to do all that in a year, let alone three months."

Jack's tone was distant. "It's your baby, you call the shots. I'm meeting with Jim Karlson tomorrow at ten-thirty. Believe me, I'd be very happy to tell him we have other commitments and can't accept his offer."

Blood raced through my veins.

"Well, Anna, what should I tell him?" Jack questioned, clearly irritated.

I felt like I was going round and round on a carousel. I reached out and there was the brass ring in my hand.

"I'll do it, Jack!"

"Okay. Here's the plan. You and I will have to work closely on the proposal. If they accept our numbers, I'll be with you every step of the way for three to four months, and then, my darling, you are on your own. If you feel you need additional consulting, we'll budget my time in the project, and there will be no discount.

"Let's move on to the legal questions. Please listen carefully. Right now I'm not incorporated, but I've been planning on doing so. If we get this project, we will incorporate with you as vice president and equal partner. You're in charge of consulting; I'm the software vendor.

"The cost of entry is relatively low, and it limits our risk. Your share of legal and other organizational expenses is fifty percent and so is your portion of stock—contrary to my attorney's advice."

"Jack, how can we be equal partners when I have to learn everything from the ground up? I don't need to be a partner, I could . . ."

"Oh no, Anna, you can't have it both ways." Jack interrupted me sounding firm and caustic. "I won't take on this elephant just to train you along the way. If you fail, you will have learned a valuable lesson. You can't only have the part you already know how to do; it all goes together. Besides, if I remember correctly . . . *all* is what you wanted and, if we succeed, consulting will become the larger portion of the business. Personally, I want to keep away from anything outside my software and, particularly, out of the people-management aspect. Remember, this is not an exercise; this is real life, and it could become brutal out there. But, what the heck, you wanted a multi-million dollar company overnight, and, you just might get it. Only, I'm not sure it will be as glamorous as you've imagined."

"I don't need a multimillion-dollar company," I dared to say.

"Well, that's what it's going to be. This particular project is a bonanza. The strategy I envision will keep our estimates relatively low and the client happy. It will give us an excellent profit margin and grow into ongoing technical support and maintenance for years to come. The company went public about five years ago. With automated order processing they'll be an ideal candidate for takeover."

I was almost out of breath. "Jack, I have to interrupt you. I'm not sure I understood most of what you said."

"What didn't you understand?"

"Why do we need to have stock in our own company? What's 'cost of entry,' 'went public,' 'takeover,' 'incorporated'—and everything else?"

"I suspected as much. I'm warning you, Anna, if you still don't understand the practical significance of this kind of terminology after your training, we'll back out before it's too late. Just don't ever tell me I should have talked you out of this mess."

"I'll make it." Tears formed in my eyes. "Thank you, Jack. I wish I could do something for you."

"Anna, this is part of my birthday present to you. I wanted . . . I needed to give you something you couldn't give back, like you did with the pearls. Why are you crying? It's what you wanted, isn't it?" Jack sounded flustered. "Anna, why are you crying? If you've changed your mind, it's okay."

"Jack, if you're doing it because we . . . because I'm your girlfriend . . . then what if, what if . . ."

What if I find Sasha?

"Business is business. Isn't that how we Americans are supposed to act? Stop crying, dry your eyes, go to bed. I'll see you tomorrow night, we'll talk some more, maybe even celebrate a little."

"But, Jack, what if, what if . . ."

"Anna, let's take one day at a time. Besides, you can still call the whole thing off as long as it's before ten-thirty tomorrow morning."

"I won't," I said, barely audible.

"I know you won't. You're one crazy Russian lady. What you need this headache for is beyond me." Jack relaxed. "Listen, I promised my accountant we'd stop by Saturday night. It's their baby's first birthday, and it's easier to meet people in a social setting."

"My English is so bad that people will laugh at you."

"How the hell do you come up with these ideas? Your English is fine, you're educated, witty, and very attractive. But that's not the point. You're my girlfriend. As far as I'm concerned, people can think what they want." Jack was uncharacteristically abrupt.

"Do you want me to buy a present?"

"Would you?" He sounded surprised. "That would be nice. By the way, the dress code for the party is more-or-less informal."

How will I ever repay him?

"Anna, relax, take it easy. I'll call you in the morning before I leave for work. Good night, baby, I miss you. Oh, by the way, try to think up a name for our company. We can't be Graff Software anymore."

A company as part of my birthday gift. A gift with years of hard work ahead. I shouldn't get so excited; after all, we don't have the project yet.

My company. It sounds more like a fairy tale than a fairy tale.

I wonder what the other part of my gift is—probably his usual roses. The first year he sent a dozen roses and two cards, one for me and one for Tanya. Fima used to run to the open market at the crack of dawn on the morning of my birthday and by the time I woke up there were flowers on the table. Fima was a husband; it was expected. He also made a point of making love to me on my birthday. Asya had a little book in which she kept track of dates: birthdays, anniversaries, everything. I never had a lonely birthday from the time I met her until I left the Soviet Union. Sasha never remembered my birthday. Of course, he couldn't give me flowers. How would I have explained his flowers to Lonya or Fima?

I don't understand why Bella or Asya couldn't find Sasha. Where is he? I suppose Asya could look up Lilya through the information service, but I don't know Lilya's patronymic. It's conceivable Sasha died. God, no! I don't want to think about it. There has to be a way to find out. Maybe Asya could inquire at the cemeteries.

I went to the kitchen and put the kettle on the stove. I may as well finish the last few pages of the book. Sleep won't come easily.

Roses from Jack have taught me to anticipate my birthday as being a good day, with only a bitter after-taste from my years with Lonya.

I poured water into a mug and dunked a tea bag, playing with the slice of lemon floating on the surface.

The second year, Jack gave me roses and a beautiful watch, which I still wear, in addition to taking Tanya and me to dinner. Just as we were about to leave the restaurant, Natasha suddenly appeared to collect Tanya, insisting Jack and I should have some time alone. I was touched by her thoughtfulness, but extremely uncomfortable. It made it seem as though

Tanya was in my way. Jack and I went dancing. I tried to feel festive, or whatever people normally feel on their birthdays. It was impossible. I kept seeing Lonya, his eyes huge behind thick lenses, saying "My mother died on the day you were born." I would have preferred to stay home, and it showed.

A year ago, the third year, was the pearl fiasco, as Jack calls it. The pearls, a double, opera-length strand with a diamond clasp, were exquisite. Marina gasped and had trouble catching her breath when she saw them.

"I don't know what you're doing for Jack, but whatever it is, he likes it. These pearls are real; so are the diamonds. They must have cost several—and I mean several—thousand dollars. Do you want me to have them appraised for you? You'll have to have them insured. You need a safety deposit box at the bank; you can't keep them in the house."

Owning any kind of jewelry that had to be appraised and insured seemed extravagant. Several thousand dollars sounded sinfully extravagant and suggestive. It burned my fingers to touch the quiet, warm pearls in the black case and soft-scented bag tied with thin gold ribbon. It was the only time I had ever gone to Jack's house without being invited.

His smile faded when he saw the case in my hands.

"Jack, I don't want you to give me anything I will never be able to afford myself."

"Anna, I wanted to give you something I knew you would never buy. I simply wanted to make you happy. I can see I haven't succeeded." His face paled in anger.

"Jack, you're trying to make me into something I'm not. I'm not at your level and I won't pretend to be." I handed him the pearls and left.

I drove around for hours to unwind. The following day a bottle of Chanel No. 5 was delivered to the house by special courier.

So, I returned the pearls and now I've accepted a company?

Sasha, can you believe it? Me, running a company? I know, one should know one's place, and life may yet prove you right. But I have to try. Don't worry, Tanya won't be neglected. She's so busy these days, and she's almost grown. If I haven't given her what she needs by now, it's too late.

Sasha, I wish you could read *Nineteen Eighty-Four*. Then you would understand.

Slowly, but surely, in this new land of mine, I've built my foundation. There is no parallel to anything I have ever felt or wished for. But there has to be a bridge, otherwise how do you get from one part of your life to another. Is it possible, can there be a bridge from nowhere?

I finished the book and put it by the front door. At two o'clock in the morning I sat down to compile a list of questions relating to the new company. Do we need an office? Who's going to answer the phone? How do I find assignments and make estimates? Where do we get employment applications? Two full pages of questions, no pages with answers.

twenty-eight

On Friday, relieved that the post-implementation of Jack's software had gone so smoothly, I pulled into Sylvia's driveway behind a black Cadillac. Then, realizing she had company, I decided to return the book at our lunch date on Sunday.

Before I had a chance to back out of the driveway the door flew open.

"Finally," exclaimed a tanned woman with bushy, dark hair, wearing white shorts and an orange tank top. "I thought I requested . . ." The woman stopped in confusion. "You're not Maria, are you?"

I got out of the car. "I'm Anna Fishman. I live down the block. Is Sylvia home?" I asked, reaching into the car for the book, putting it under my arm as I approached the lady.

"I'm sorry. The cleaning service was supposed to send someone an hour ago. My flight is at eight o'clock and there's so much to finish. Sylvia died. I'm her daughter-in-law. Can I help you?"

My heart dropped, then suddenly reappeared in my throat. As the book fell on the steps, I pressed my hands to my cheeks. The woman observed my reaction curiously.

"When?" The words barely escaped my lips.

"Tuesday. She had a stroke. The doctor said she had the stroke Monday night, but she wasn't found until Tuesday."

Monday night . . . my God, it must have happened soon after I left. I picked up the book, standing silently, afraid I'd fall if I moved an inch.

"Who found her?"

"The cleaning service."

"Where's her dog?"

"We put the dog to sleep. Were you her friend? I wasn't aware she had any friends."

"Yes, I am, I mean, was, her friend. I borrowed this book from her. Here." The book in my hand shook as I handed it over.

"Thank you. I appreciate your returning it." A tanned hand snatched the book. "I'm wondering now what else she gave away. My husband says the only thing her books are good for is a nice write-off as a donation to some library. Did you have anything else that belonged to my mother-in-law? If this isn't Maria, I'm going to scream!" the woman looked past me.

A stout Hispanic girl in jeans had hopped out of a van.

"Where was Sylvia buried?" I asked hurriedly.

"What? I'm sorry, what did you say?" The tanned woman said impatiently.

"Where was Sylvia buried?" I repeated.

"The cemetery's not far from here. I don't know the area, I'm from California, I just remember a shopping center with a Saks in it across the street. Well, you take care now."

Sylvia had said she wasn't feeling well. I should have come back to check on her. Why did this have to happen? We had so little time.

I drove the short distance home and sat on the steps. I kicked off my shoes and stretched my legs. Tanya's working late. The house promises nothing but empty rooms.

Jack's car pulled in long after darkness fell. I impassively watched the car lights go out and the door open. He approached, unbuttoning his shirt. It seemed like watching a scene in a movie, familiar yet unfamiliar.

He stopped in front of me, his legs firmly apart.

"Waiting for someone, Miss?"

I hesitated for a minute. "Jack, you know Sylvia, the lady that lives in the corner house, the one who loaned me the book? She passed away."

"I'm sorry to hear that," he said seriously. His legs moved to the side as he sat next to me. "When did you find out?"

"A couple of hours ago."

"When is the funeral?"

"I missed the funeral. I went to return her book and her daughter-in-law was there. She told me."

"You really feel bad, don't you?"

"I felt close to her."

Jack took off his shirt tossing it to the ground and stretched. His hand landed on my shoulder. It felt heavy.

"Anna, it's so humid, let's go in. You haven't changed since work." Jack turned my head to face him and wiped away a tear with his finger. "In the last few days you have cried more frequently than in the previous three years. I never realized you could cry so easily."

"I didn't, either. Let's go inside." I avoided Jack's eyes so he wouldn't read mine telling him to go away. I wanted him to go, but I wanted him to stay too.

I took a shower and changed into shorts. Jack did the same. Neither of us were hungry. Tanya came in from work with Jeff and they disappeared into her room, arguing. I looked through the mail. Nothing from Fima. Hopefully, he lost our address.

Jack followed me into the office.

"Anna, in case you're interested, I had a long meeting with Jim Karlson today. I called you, but you were already gone. Everything went fine. We have to schedule meetings with people from different divisions. Once things start to move they're going to move quickly. Have you thought about a company name?"

"We can keep the name you have."

"You don't seem very excited."

"I can't get over the shock of Sylvia dying. She told me she wasn't feeling well, but her doctor didn't think it was serious. I offered to take her to the emergency room. She didn't want to go."

"There was nothing you could do. You can visit her grave."

"Yes," the burden lifted somewhat, "I will. She didn't have any close relatives and her son lives in California."

Jack stopped briefly behind me, his hands slid down my sides. His body pressed mine uncertainly.

"Don't sulk, life goes on, you don't realize how busy we're going to be," he said kissing me on the top of my head.

I'll tell Asya about Sylvia.

Jeff left with a polite good-bye then Tanya, Jack, and I sat in the kitchen talking about Jack's and my new company. Tanya fired countless questions at us, brushing off our warnings that the company may not materialize if our estimate isn't accepted.

My title of vice president was the most significant feature.

"I don't want to be an I-told-you-so, but I have been saying all along you should take a marketing class," reproached Tanya.

Finally she finished her cocoa, kissed me, and went to bed in a dreamy mood.

Jack flew across the kitchen, nearly colliding with the refrigerator, as he took an eclair out to defrost.

"I was supposed to visit Sylvia on Sunday. I needed to talk to her."

"What did you want to talk to her about?"

"I'm not sure."

Jack smiled and shook his head with a "woman's-logic" expression.

"Why did it have to happen to her?" I didn't expect an answer. "She was right, I didn't find *Nineteen Eighty-Four* difficult, even though it wasn't simply written. Someone at the library should be able to give me advice. I have to read, otherwise it will seem as if I only live here temporarily."

"It doesn't sound as if it was books that made your relationship important. You were both from Russia. Sometimes I wish I were, too, so that you wouldn't have an excuse to tell me I don't understand you." Jack's voice held a trace of bitterness.

Oddly, Sylvia had been on his side. I can't tell him that.

"I don't need an excuse," I shrugged.

"I see," Jack muttered sarcastically, "and I suppose there's no question that you understand yourself perfectly. Anna, it may not console you, but we all lose people we love and need. I'm no exception. There are people and places in Argentina that make my heart skip a beat when

I see them or think about them, but it's part of my past. After I moved to the States, I called Argentina at least once a week, sometimes more. As time went by, the once or twice a week became once or twice a month, and now it's a few times a year. You have to learn to leave the past in the past," he said quietly. "We take what those who are far away or those who have passed away give us and move on." Jack's voice became warm and soothing. "Anna, you've become more thoughtful and softer since you met Sylvia. Don't cry; at least you met her."

I shut my eyes tight to stop the tears.

Jack stroked my hand. "Anna, I know you're not in the mood but we need to talk about our business."

There's so much involved in breathing life into a company. I listened to Jack's words carefully. He diligently answered my two full pages of questions. On some he gave examples which made the explanations sound like exciting stories. He made up lists of people to contact and ways to market our services.

When we finished, Jack's eyes were all smiles, wandering down my body. To me, this evening marked the beginning of a new chapter in my life; to Jack it constituted foreplay, slow and subtle. As we walked to the bedroom hand-in-hand, making love with Jack seemed suddenly not only an expression of gratitude or an urge that brought contentment, but also a part of being his partner.

"We are real partners now, Jack, not just for show. It feels different."

"It does, doesn't it?" His hands became very assertive.

twenty-nine

I took out my only more-or-less informal outfit, a black, silk pant suit and laid it out on the bed. In the back of my mind I keep rehearsing how I'll act and what I'll say at Jack's accountant's party. I've rehearsed everything from acceptance and fun to complete ignorance and failure. I could always sit in the corner and say nothing, but what would that do for Jack's reputation?

Jack returned from his meeting with his prospective client looking cheerful, having arranged for a presentation. He looked at me and immediately understood.

"Anna, chin up, you'll do just fine."

On the way to the party, Jack told me about his accountant's family: Howard Smolin, age fifty-five, the only son of a wealthy accountant, lived with his mother until she passed away three years ago; his wife, Helena, escaped from Czechoslovakia with her parents and two brothers after the Soviet invasion of 1968. Helena is forty years old, a real-estate saleswoman, and converted to Judaism when she married Howard. Their daughter was more than they had ever hoped for and Jack said they were completely wrapped up in her. She already had three rooms in the house, where she reigned supreme. Her father recently bought a grand piano for her, because she stopped crying when she heard music.

The narrow street looked aristocratically old, and so did the distinguished European-style mansions.

Do people actually live in these houses?

The façade of the Smolin's mansion formed an angle with a tower that was loosely covered with ivy. The house looked like a small castle.

Jack stole a glance at me.

"Like it?"

"Very much."

Tanya will have a house like this.

Two cars ahead of us parked on the street behind a line of other cars, under "No Parking Anytime" signs. A police officer approached each car, "Mr. Smolin's party? Very good." Then he wrote down each license plate number.

"You'd like a car like that." Jack pointed to the white Mercedes in front of us.

How will I ever describe this castle to Asya?

The couple from the Mercedes caught up with us. I felt Jack's hand on my shoulder and heard him say, "How are you doing? I'd like you to meet Anna Fishman. Anna, these are friends of mine, Allen Gould and his wife Marilyn." The man and woman smiled and greeted me in unison.

"Haven't seen you around recently," Allen addressed Jack after shaking hands with me.

"Humid day," said Marilyn leading the way.

"Humidity doesn't bother me." I sounded too serious.

Jack told me I should mingle, smile, and say meaningless things. He said it would be fun.

"Did you play tennis this morning?" continued Marilyn.

She wasn't paying attention to the house!

"I don't play tennis," I answered softly.

Marilyn replied encouragingly, "That can easily be rectified. I can refer you to my daughter's instructor. He's incredible."

We stopped at the front door. Marilyn rang the bell. One more couple joined us: a woman in her thirties and a very tall, erect, older gentleman sporting a cane and an old-fashioned hat. We all exchanged society smiles. The young woman, a blonde in a red shawl with long fringe over an open, off-white dress, looked familiar.

A dark-haired woman in a navy skirt, white blouse, and a lacy token of an apron opened the door and welcomed us in. The foyer was magnificent with a marble floor and a wide, marble staircase opposite the entry An enormous urn, almost my height, stood near the foot of the stairs.

In the almost four years of dating, I have met some of Jack's friends, but always at theaters, restaurants, or at other large gatherings. By now, he has gotten used to my avoidance of intimate family events with his friends, where my participation would extend beyond initial greetings. I have always assumed their houses to be similar to Jack's, or to some of those where I had been admitted to clean. And, of course, my friends' houses, though large and comfortable, belong to the "mass production" category. Nothing had prepared me for this castle, museum, palace.

Do people really live here?

Two wide arches connected the foyer with a living room on one side and with a gigantic family room, brightly lit and inviting, on the other.

The woman took the old man's hat.

A man resembling Danny De Vito scuttled out of the family room with a drink in his hand.

"Come in, come in. Ladies, you look great. Nice to see you guys. Courtney is ready for bed, you won't be able to see her tonight. That's your punishment for being late."

Marilyn and the blonde made appropriately regretful noises.

"We have great news for you, but I want Helena to be the one to tell you. She's with Courtney. Bernadette, our nanny, has the night off. Go right ahead, make yourself comfortable. The bar near the west fireplace is tended."

The men shook hands and the young blonde steered her elderly companion by the elbow in the direction of the family room.

"My, aren't the ladies especially attractive today," smiled De Vito, sipping his drink, looking up at me.

"Anna, this is Howard Smolin, my . . . our accountant and friend."

Howard's clever eyes ran from Jack to me and back.

"I'm glad to finally meet you, Anna." He gave me his hand. "Jack says you don't like going out. That will have to change. My wife has been looking forward to meeting you. She speaks some Russian. She's Czech, you know. The stories she tells me . . . well, I don't want to keep you from meeting my other guests, we'll talk later."

I liked the little man and thought he liked me. Trying not to be stiff and tense, I joined Marilyn and moved toward the family room.

"You lucky dog, you," I heard Howard say to Jack.

"Cut the bullshit," Jack muttered amiably.

Allen laughed.

The family room was cozy in spite of its gigantic size and massive family portraits in antique frames. Several waiters circulated among the guests offering trays laden with appetizers and drinks. One of them lowered his tray in front of us as we stepped in. Marilyn and I took small plates from the waiter accompanying him, then some fruit and cheese on toothpicks. Someone called to Marilyn and she excused herself.

"Do you want me to get you a drink?" asked Jack, approaching me as he waved to someone.

My stomach tightened in panic.

"I'll come with you, I can't stand here alone."

"Listen, Anna, I'll introduce you to those I know, and you can take it from there. Don't worry, Howard is rather selective. I'm sure you won't have any problems."

A bass voice boomed from a nearby group.

"Graff? Haven't seen you in ages." The bass, who was well built with a salt-and-pepper mane, shook Jack's hand then turned to me expectantly.

"Dr. Harry Berkowitz, Anna Fishman. How are you, old man? Unload your lake property?"

"Unload, my foot! No people with money anymore. Interested?"

"No, just curious. Where's Karen?"

I took another appetizer from a tray that appeared from nowhere.

"Around. Gossiping, no doubt," Dr. Berkowitz made a general movement with his drink. "Why not, Jack? You can afford it. Stop fooling around, settle down, buy that house. It's on two acres. You've seen it. It's never too late to start a family. Look at Howard and Helena."

"You sound like my mother, Harry."

I followed Jack to the bar and we asked for drinks.

"Why is this fireplace called the west fireplace?"

"Because there are three in the room. Let me tell you who's who. The doctor we just talked to is a prominent neurologist. He's trying to sell off his real estate, retire, travel, maybe lecture a little. His wife, Karen, knows everything about everybody, drives him up the wall. There she is, in brown, talking to Marilyn. Allen owns a large real estate company in Highland Park. He's a client of Howard's. I bought my house through him. The old man that came with the blonde is Howard's cousin Marty. He had a stroke recently. The blonde is his girlfriend."

"His girlfriend? How old is he?"

"In his early seventies. A retired attorney. His wife died last spring. Why are you surprised? A man is as young as his woman makes him feel."

Jack gave me one of his let's-have-a-quickie looks, and I felt hot when his hand drummed down my spine to my waist.

"The old man's girlfriend, Cassie, used to be his secretary. They were having an affair long before he became widowed." Jack sipped his drink. "Listen, let's split and mingle."

"Cassie!" Now I knew why the blonde looked familiar. She had been one of my cleaning clients. I wonder if she recognized me.

"What's wrong?"

"I cleaned Cassie's house weekly for quite some time, and I remember seeing that man there. I thought he was her father."

An unmistakable shadow crossed Jack's face.

It shouldn't matter what kind of work I did in my lifetime. I'm only his partner and girlfriend, not a member of his family. If he doesn't like it he can find another girlfriend.

"Hello, darling." Karen Berkowitz made Jack bend down so she could kiss his cheek. She looked older than her impressive husband. "You look wonderful. And this lovely lady must be your Russian friend."

Mrs. Berkowitz snapped her fingers and a waiter scurried to her side. She gave him explicit details as to how to fix her drink.

"Did you get your ensemble at Elisa's? They had something similar. I looove that boutique." Mrs. Berkowitz rubbed the sleeve of my suit between her fingers. "Howard tells me your name is Anna. I'm Karen."

Karen took possession, presenting me proudly, like a new toy, to cluster after cluster of guests. She exhibited quite a talent for interrogation. Before I knew it, the number of rooms in my house, my origin, occupation, favorite stores, and the fact that Tanya wanted to be a doctor were common knowledge.

Cassie apparently failed to recognize me. Her boyfriend sat in an easy chair and she never left his side. They were surrounded by a group of people that, judging by the animated chatter, knew each other well.

Two men in their forties stood close behind her, their hands occasionally touching her back, waist, and arms lightly as if to add accent to the banter. Her laugh was contagious. The men smacked their lips, sure she was there for the highest bidder, and that they could give her more in bed than her feeble boyfriend.

As Karen and I approached their circle, she addressed someone in it called Suzanne with an invitation to meet me. Suzanne, a tall, very tanned brunette in a short lavender dress revealing well-shaped, muscular legs and a wrinkled neck, made a welcoming sign with her drink. An antique-looking brooch matching her earings held her dress together on her chest. She smiled and extended her hand as though she had waited for that exact moment to occur. She and some others broke away from the group, making a circle around Karen and myself. Spontaneously, a discussion started about the reforms in the Soviet Union. Anything, even this topic, was better than walking from group to group, forcing my company on others.

Jack looked around to locate a waiter and raised his hand. He placed his empty glass on the tray nodding to something the waiter said. He approached Cassie's group, shook hands with one of the men standing next to her. A drink arrived, he retrieved it not looking at the waiter, and sipped while listening to the conversation, his face expressionless. After a few minutes he spoke to Cassie, his hand parked on her waist. She turned her smiling face to him. When he turned away to talk with Howard and Dr. Berkowitz, he was intercepted by several ladies. One of them wiggled her finger at him in mocked anger. He stretched his face into a broad smile. The three men escaped into the foyer.

Jack never once looked in my direction. My back longed for his warm hands. I wondered why he was suddenly embarrassed by my being a cleaning lady in the past.

I participated in a lively political conversation, told a couple Russian anecdotes, and ended up as the center of attention for half the guests. Cassie was one of them, her boyfriend dozing in the corner.

I should have realized that with my Russian accent I wouldn't have to worry what the small talk would be about. What else but the Soviet Union?

The circle broke apart when Howard's face appeared.

"Dessert has arrived, and so has my wife. Courtney finally fell asleep."

I found myself sauntering along with everyone else, smiling like dancers do in the middle of a routine.

"If you don't mind, Anna, I'd like to talk to you before you leave," Howard said as Karen Berkowitz almost collided with us. She presented me with a penetrating glance.

"Yes, I'd like to talk to you, too."

"Excuse me, Karen," said Howard, his voice dripping with sarcasm. "I hope we're not in your way."

"That's all right," Karen said through her primly set lips. She was clearly offended at not being privy to our conversation.

A table was set next to the north fireplace, under a large painting of a woman in a white dress with ruffles around the neck. The table supported an enormous heart-shaped cake covered with chocolate cream. It read, "We love you, Courtney."

A uniformed woman was cutting the cake and placing slices on small, cream-colored plates with gold edges. A tall, fair lady with a broad, Slavic face took the plates and offered them to the guests. Her only jewelry was a small, golden Star of David around her neck and a gold wedding band. She spoke briefly to each guest in easy English, with only a slight accent. Another uniformed woman filled glasses with champagne, soda, or iced tea. I followed the tall lady's adoring eyes and realized she was looking at Howard.

"Helena, you haven't met Jack's Anna yet. They were late." Howard moved closer to his wife, the top of his head level with her chin.

"Good evening, Jack's Anna," said Helena laughing. "Let me carry out my wifely duties, then we can talk. By the way, Howard, where's Anna's Jack?"

Helena and I looked at each other like coconspirators. I erupted in a silver-bells laugh feeling completely at ease in the presence of this woman that seemed so unlike me—confident and dignified. That impulsive laugh, I noted, began visiting me recently, like when I talked to Asya and when Jack and I made love—that same laugh that Lonya had forbidden, my mother's laugh.

"Anna's Jack is right here," came Jack's voice. My laughter died. The tension I had allowed myself to forget returned.

"Well," said Helena, "here's some cake for you, a nice, large piece. It's a prize for finally bringing Anna to our home." Then she turned her gaze out toward the other guests. "I would like everyone's attention for a moment." Although Helena didn't actually raise her voice, the crowd quieted down. Howard took her hand.

"I have an announcement to make. This morning we found out, for certain, we're going to have another baby. It's due in January."

Howard's eyes glistened.

Cut off from Helena and Howard by guests offering congratulations, I retreated to the far corner where Marty sat slumped in his armchair.

He addressed me very quietly. "Would you please find Cassie for me. I need her help to get up."

"I'll help you." I placed my cake on a tray swimming by and offered him my hand.

The old man shook his head. "No, only Cassie knows how. What's all the noise about?"

"Helena and Howard are going to have another baby."

"Fools. Children . . . when they're little they want you to provide for them, and when they're grown they want you to be busy with your illnesses. Children . . ."

I found Cassie at the far end of the room listening to a stout woman in a yellow jacket.

"Just continue walking him every day until he tires. I did that with my late husband and it helped a lot." The woman spoke sincerely, intent on sharing her experience.

"Cassie, I'm sorry to interrupt. Marty would like to see you."

"Thank you," she said earnestly, covering her shoulders with her shawl.

I followed her to Marty's chair and we pushed him up and gave him his cane, which had fallen while he was dozing. He shuffled away to the bathroom.

Cassie shrugged indifferently. "Well, I think we're ready to go. Thanks for your help." She looked tired. "You know," she said, "I recognized you right away. I didn't say anything, and perhaps we shouldn't." She shrugged again, glancing at her watch. "Jack's not a bad guy. Good luck, Anna."

A waiter appeared, his head inclined toward me, his face a mask of undivided attention.

"Would you care to order a drink, ma'am?"

I shook my head and he backed away.

Cassie maneuvered expertly across the room. The needle-like heels of her red sandals made it appear as if she were running away on tiptoes.

The recently vacated easy chair warmed me as I sank into it. I only wished I could curl up and not be bothered. I don't belong with these people, with this house, with Jack. They're all out of my league.

The crowd grew smaller. Jack, with his back to me, was engrossed in conversation with Allen. Howard stood next to them eating cake.

Helena escorted her departing guests to the great arch where a uniformed man led them away. She looked around and headed straight for my hideout.

"Anna, I've been an awful hostess, I'm sorry. Courtney's teething, and she's so difficult when she hurts. Did you have problems with your Tanya?"

"For a few months, but it wasn't too bad. She had eight teeth before she was a year."

"Courtney started late. She only has six. Tanya is actually Tatyana, isn't it? I used to know Pushkin's *Eugene Onegin* by heart with his charming Tatyana Larina."

"My daughter's named after her."

"Really? I prefer Tolstoi these days. My mother used to teach Russian in Prague. I still speak a few words. You and I should have lunch together soon. Jack's so proud of you and your recent accomplishments."

"I haven't done anything extraordinary."

"Well, you came to America."

"That's not enough."

"That's more than enough, Anna. I know. I also came here from a communist country." Helena's eyes hardened, then smiled at me again. "That *is* the real accomplishment. The rest is more or less a matter of effort. We all arrive here scared and watchful. . . . Listen, fifteen years ago I wouldn't have talked to you because you were Russian. My grandfather was killed in the street by a Russian tank in 1968."

"My motherland hasn't done much good for anyone."

Howard approached us. "Sweetheart, I need to spend a few minutes with Anna. Do you mind?" he said smiling.

"Okay. Anna, we're going to have a barbecue soon. I'll call you. Thank you for coming. Next time you'll meet our Courtney."

Howard took over forcefully. The smile in his eyes was gone.

"Anna, you must realize I can't really teach you accounting in a matter of weeks. I can merely explain the accounting principles you need to know to run a company."

"I understand. And, Howard, I want to thank you. I hope my English won't be a problem."

"Don't thank me. Jack's a good client and a good friend. Here's my card, call me Monday, I'll know then what my schedule for the week will be. Forget Wednesday—I play golf on Wednesdays. Don't worry about your English, it's fine."

The waiters and the uniformed women finished folding the serving tables and carried them out. The empty room with its crystal chandeliers and the whimsical design of its hardwood floor looked as though it awaited a reception to begin. Jack paced near the west fireplace waiting for me.

Jack's car stood out like a mound on the dark, secluded street. I wish I could find a logical explanation as to why the residential streets of the exclusive, northern suburbs of Chicago are not lighted at night.

The lights on the second floor of the Smolin house, unlike the ones in the surrounding formidable castles, shone out from long rectangular windows. Six people emerged out of the side of the house. One of the women lit a cigarette. The men carried folded serving tables.

"Decent tip for a small party," said a tall man's shadow.

"The baby's ugly," yawned a woman.

"Sh-sh-sh," hissed the rest.

The group walked past us in the middle of the street.

"A three-block walk to the van. How could a van spoil the view of a street?" complained the yawning woman.

Some of the lights on the second floor went out. I tried to picture Howard and Helena in bed together, but couldn't.

"Tanya will have a house like this one day."

"I knew you'd like it. Why Tanya? Why not you?"

He seemed perfectly serious.

We leaned against the car facing the house. A police car slowly rolled to a stop, raising the darkness.

"Mr. Smolin's party, sir? Anything the matter?"

"Just enjoying the fresh air," replied Jack with lazy authority, dismissing the officer. "Thanks for checking."

"Have a good night, sir." The police car continued on.

"You know, Jack, I've driven through this area admiring the houses, but it only hit me tonight that real people actually live in them."

The long silence felt comforting.

"How did you like the party?"

"It was interesting."

"You didn't enjoy it, did you?"

"I did, Jack, I really did. Probably because I know it's something I will have to do from now on as part of what I want to do."

"That doesn't mean enjoying."

"It does."

"Okay, let's leave it at that. Why did it upset you so much that Cassie might have recognized you as her one-time cleaning lady?"

"It didn't upset me, it upset you."

"That's not true."

I sensed a movement and knew that Jack had decisively stuck his hands in his pockets.

"Yes, Jack, it is true. You personally don't care—as long as I don't do it now. You want me to be accepted as an equal by your crowd. And, unfortunately, former cleaning ladies don't really fit."

"What's wrong with being accepted by my crowd?"

"Nothing. Except, maybe, Jack, that we are worlds apart."

"Your Russian parties are the same, only you sit and talk instead of stand and talk."

"And we remember most of what was discussed."

"Anna, what are we talking about?"

"You didn't like the fact Cassie might have recognized me."

"Cassie is the last person in the world I would want to feel superior to you, or think she might have a hold on you."

"Jack, you have to understand, I don't belong with a crowd like yours. I don't have the money. The only reason they tolerate me is because of you."

The police car cruised by again and the policeman waved. He'll keep coming back until we leave.

"Jack, why is Cassie the last person, et cetera, et cetera?"

"Why? Cassie was a secretary who slept with her married boss! How much cheaper can one get?"

"Maybe she was in love with him?"

"Come on, don't give me that! Marty's a fool. She owns a penthouse on the Gold Coast, shops in Michigan Avenue stores, and drives a Jaguar."

And she would have accepted pearls . . . but it doesn't prove anything. Like Lonya used to say, there is no absolute right and no absolute wrong.

"She seems to be very devoted to Marty."

"Anna, they're both jerks. In Russia it may not be considered immoral, but it is here. He wanted a body, and she's a fortune hunter."

"And so am I."

"What?" Jack's voice rose to a shout.

"Well, wouldn't you prefer I stay home and let you take care of my bills? What do you think people take me for? Don't tell me you haven't heard the whispers. You would hear more if I drove a Jaguar . . . or wore pearls."

The thud of Jack's fist on the car made me jump.

"Damn it, Anna. Don't ever compare yourself to Cassie!"

"Maybe she plays around, but she hasn't been doing it alone. You were not above touching her. Neither were the other men entertaining her tonight."

"Let's go." Jack unlocked the car door and opened it for me. Instead of getting in, I turned to look at him. His face was tense.

"Jack, did you sleep with her?"

Looking unhappy, Jack took off his glasses.

"Yes."

Instead of being angry or indignant, I wanted to laugh at his guilty, boyish face.

"I'm sorry, Anna." Jack wiped his glasses with his handkerchief. "It was after we met, but before we went out."

I put my hands on his shoulders.

"As one crazy Russian lady, I find you not guilty."

"I am, in hindsight," Jack stood his ground. "But at the time, I didn't know we were going to have a relationship."

"Forget all that, Jack. Let's go home."

"I haven't touched anyone since we started dating, and you don't know what hell it was those first few months." Jack's eyes smiled, his warm hands on my back pressed me closer. "I'm not a saint, but I don't cheat. Whoever cheats once will do it again."

I cheated once . . .

"Why are you staring at me like that?" he covered my neck with quick, light kisses.

"Jack, Cassie recognized me. She was very tactful about it."

"Anna, please . . ." The kisses broke off.

"Let's go, Jack, the police car is coming back."

When we arrived home Tanya was sitting on the sofa watching *Saturday Night Live*. Her features looked refined and relaxed in the semi-dark room. She shot an expectant glance at Jack. He nodded in response.

"Hi. Bella and Lena called," Tanya said without a smile. "How was the party?"

"I was in the most beautiful house I have ever seen—even in the movies. Oh, Tanichka, I know someday you'll have a house like that."

"That depends on how much money I make." Tanya clicked the remote and the television blinked off. "Mom, I need to talk to you. Jack, please don't go away."

"If you want my company, the conversation will have to be in English." Jack's hands rubbed my shoulders.

Tanya has made her decision. Like Fima, she has to be sure what she does is the right and the only thing to do.

We headed for the kitchen. I put the kettle on. Jack stood leaning against the door frame, smiling nervously.

Tanya sat down at the kitchen table.

"I've decided to quit my job." For a split second she shifted her glance to Jack.

I lowered myself into a chair and met Tanya's thoughtful eyes.

"Vera and I discussed it," she continued evenly, not asking my permission, simply imforming me of her decision, "and we've come to the conclusion that I should begin volunteering at the nursing home with her. It will give me a better idea of whether I really want to be a doctor."

Tanya took a deep breath.

Have come to the conclusion . . . What is my role in this decision?

"Vera says it's very depressing at the nursing home," she said looking past me, a trace of anxiety in her voice, "but she has to be perky."

Her father had done almost the same when he was her age. Having him visit will be good for her.

Jack came closer to the table, but remained standing.

"Vera's father said that being around sick people, getting used to the unpleasant smells, listening to their complaints, and even . . ." Tanya screwed up her face and swallowed, ". . . even seeing someone die might be the best test whether we should be doctors." Tanya looked straight into my eyes, searching for my disappointment.

"Tanya, I'm only upset that you thought you had to be a doctor to please me." I said, resisting the urge to cry. "You are so much like your father, Tanichka. After high school he went to work as a laborer in a shop that manufactured custom-made shoes for handicapped people. He wanted to be sure that becoming an engineer, designing machines for these shops, was what he really wanted to do."

"I can't wait to meet Dad," said Tanya with childish sincerity. "He'll be so proud you're a vice president."

"Time for another drink," Jack said a little too loudly. He fled to the dining room.

"Mom, are you sure . . . you really, really don't mind?"

"Really, really. I'll just put you back on an allowance." Then I added in Russian, "Let me make your cocoa, and some tea for me."

"Tell me about the house you saw today," Tanya said in Russian, placing her feet on the chair next to her.

Amazingly relaxed, I launched into a Russian-English monologue covering all the details of the party, with the exception of Cassie-related material and my upcoming lessons with Howard Smolin.

"Wow!" Tanya's eyes shone. "Life is so interesting." She took her empty cocoa cup to the sink, stretched deliciously, and added in Russian, "We are going to be very busy."

I found Jack in the living room with a drink in one hand, the remote in the other.

"Did Tanya go to bed?"

"Almost," I sat next to him.

"I'm glad you weren't upset by her decision."

"Well, I still think she'd make a wonderful doctor. But it's her decision. Why should I be upset? I'm very pleased with Tanya."

I laid my head on Jack's shoulder and closed my eyes.

"Anna, please don't begin distrusting me because of Cassie. In the eight years I was divorced, before you and I met, I tried just about everything."

"You're still divorced," I murmured, too tired for discussion. Every muscle in my body relaxed, readying for sleep.

"I guess." Jack squeezed my hand. "Nothing will make sense if you don't trust me like I trust you."

Sasha and I are cheaters. Whoever cheats once will do it again.

"How do you know you can trust me?"

"I know."

Oh, well.

"Anna," Jack kissed my palm. "We need to talk. Do you think we can go on being like this forever?"

"That sounds like my line. It's funny to hear you say it. For now, I think that unless you want out, we're partners, friends, and lovers. They're all important, but especially partners. I'm going to give my all to our company."

"Me too." Jack sounded disappointed.

He doesn't really want a company.

"Anna, your birthday is soon. Let's do something special. You have a lot to celebrate this time. Why don't you call your friends and throw a party?"

"I don't want to think about my birthday. In fact, I wish everyone would forget about it."

"Then how would I have been able to give you a company?"

We laughed quietly.

Jack clicked off the television.

"Com'on, kiddo, we need some sleep."

What does "kiddo" mean?

thirty

The one day a year that is my birthday invariably begins with a blind impulse to shrink into a ball and wait for Lonya's choking voice, piercing like a rapier, "My mother died on this day," accompanied by his always present, coarse cough. On my last birthday that started with these words, I turned twenty-seven. Eighteen years have passed since then, but the pain is just as sharp. I imagine Lonya's pain when he relived those minutes as a tiny, crying creature appeared and his mother was gone. And the older I got, the more I looked like her and the greater Lonya's pain.

On my twenty-eighth birthday, the first without Lonya, I was married and three months pregnant. Fima's gift to me was a blue nightgown, with wide, crude, Soviet-made lace around the bottom and sleeves. Expecting to hear Lonya's cough and tirade at any moment, I lay in bed, frozen, in fearful anticipation of Fima's lovemaking with its usual pain. He would put his hand over my mouth so no one would hear when I cried out.

My next birthday, when Tanya was six months old, I thought, for the first time, that perhaps my birth wasn't entirely a waste. The previous year's fearful anticipation became a ritual I had learned to submit to.

My pastoral life of the last few years has done nothing to dull the pain. My birthday wouldn't be complete without it.

This birthday I awoke too early to get up for work, but too late to go back to sleep. My back would welcome Jack's massaging fingers.

Howard lectured on stocks last night. The flood of information kept me awake long after I came home. I tried to ask practical questions to limit the flood, but it seemed that everything was necessary. Howard and I have been meeting twice a week at his office in Lake Bluff. Used to Jack's six feet and broad shoulders, I felt like I should take my five-foot-three instructor to his car after each session instead of the other way around. The fact that he took me seriously made it easy to show my ignorance, and I hoped he realized my thanks were not just a figure of speech. I understood Helena's feelings for him. Sexy, witty, and sharp, Howard lacked the typical insecurity of short men. I wasn't at all surprised by his admission that he was too much of a lady's man to get married at a younger age.

I sensed movement in the room. Tanya left what I assumed was a present on my nightstand and tiptoed out. With my mind's eye, I

distinctly saw Lonya's reproachful, red eyes and my heart contracted
with familiar pain and guilt.

With extreme effort I opened my eyes. A rectangular, gift-wrapped
box sat on my nightstand, a card under the red bow. I sat up, shook the
box, and giggled. I opened the card. "I love you, Mom. Happy Birthday,
you're the best." I touched it with my lips and placed it carefully on the
pillow. Under the wrapping paper was a Coach purse.

The door squeaked, opened a crack then widened, and Tanya, still in
her nightgown, slipped into the bed.

"Do you like it, Mom? It's the same color as your briefcase. It's very
professional. And Coach never goes out of style and almost never wears
out." She smiled shyly. "Will you take it to work today?"

"I love it, and I will use it today."

"The minute I saw it, I knew it was you. Are you going to keep
my card?"

Every year she asks the same question, and every year she watches
me put her card into a box with all the other cards and drawings she has
given me over the years.

She stretched under the sheet. I enjoy it when she crawls into my
bed. On weekends when Jack's here she can't. On Sunday mornings,
when she was little, she used to dive between Fima and me, then
fall asleep.

When I finished my shower, Tanya was still in my bed, now with a
textbook, looking too absorbed and too demure. Something's up for sure.

"Jack called, he'll call back." Her eyes never left the book.

What is this mystery?

Jack called again while I was eating breakfast.

"Happy birthday, Anna."

"Thank you."

"Anna, do me a favor. Take a taxi to work. I'll pick you up."

"Come on, Jack, you're not going to drive for hours just to say happy
birthday in person, and then have to drive right back. It's not worth it.
Besides, it will cost a small fortune to take a taxi to Aurora."

"I'm coming, and that's that. I'll be there at six. We'll celebrate and
I'll stay over, and, hopefully, 'I'm coming' will be a true statement. What
do you say?"

I blushed.

"Anna, don't be so stubborn. It's your birthday."

"Well . . . if you put it that way . . . okay, I'll be waiting for you."

I feel uncomfortable and annoyed with myself for becoming depen-
dent on Jack to satisfy me physically. I still think he'll tire of me and toss
me aside. By Friday of each week, waiting for Jack to come home from
Green Bay is almost unbearable and I become irritable and absent-minded.

One time, fifteen minutes after he arrived, I angrily reprimanded him for dropping his briefcase by the front door. He gave me a funny look, walked over, ran his hands over my body, and whispered into my ear, "Want to make love, baby?"

My recent Aurora implementation had given me a good taste of what having full control was really like. At first it both startled and discouraged me that management would come to me with problems that should be directed to others. Jack warned me not to assume—under any circumstances—responsibilities that were not mentioned in my contract or might be construed as affecting client policies, even if these policies were obviously wrong. What Jack didn't tell me was how to discern what was in or out of the scope of my contract. I understood my contract, but everything interacts, and production management continually bombarded me with problems needing resolution. My stomach was constantly in knots, and my hand itched to grab my briefcase and run.

In its final days of family atmosphere, this small company, pushed blindly into the state-of-the-art world, rewarded me every morning with a warm sense of coming home. It hadn't yet graduated to cubicle seating. Several people occupied each office, using the same desks and chairs for years. They shared one telephone, family news, cookies, and jokes. Baby, vacation, and office-party pictures decorated the walls.

One of my office mates was on maternity leave and the other, a round-faced woman in a checked shirt, jeans, and tennis shoes greeted me with homemade cupcakes on my first morning.

"Hope," she said. Seeing my bewildered expression, she threw her head back in a luscious chuckle. "My name is Hope. There is always a Hope in our family. My mother refused to make an exception in spite of our last name, Pope."

We both rolled with laughter. I told her that before the Russian revolution, when families were large, parents commonly named their first daughter Vera, which meant "faith," the second Nadejda, which meant "hope," and the third Lubov, which meant "love."

It transpired that Hope had joined the company as a teenager on the day I was born—forging almost a blood connection between us. I often gave Hope a ride home. We sometimes sat in the car swapping family stories or stopped at McDonald's for a milk shake. The quality of my English never seemed to matter.

Although my schedule was flexible, I usually got to work early to give myself additional time at home in the evening. Occasionally I went in late, like the time I visited Sylvia's grave. If not for the standard, colorless marker with the name of the deceased and date of burial, Sylvia's grave would not be distinguishable from the uninhabited lots around it.

The flowers I brought did nothing to help it compete with the cared-for graves nearby.

I thought of Lonya's grave, with a cheap flat stone among tall proud stones around it and cried a little from the helplessness to explain to him I wasn't so bad that he couldn't love me and that I missed him. The bribes needed to install his simple stone had cost as much as the stone itself.

Sylvia's name on the marker seemed disengaged from reality. It didn't offer a connection to the fact that she was gone, just as my failure to locate Sasha hadn't proven he was beyond my reach. I could not convince myself that this grave should touch my life to the degree that the person in it had. I wondered if Sylvia had finished the list of books for me.

Today, as a gift to myself, I decided to stop at the library before going to work. The solid two-storied building shared its parking lot with the Village Hall in downtown Skokie. Recently, Skokie had erected a Holocaust monument in front of the library. It depicted a young man with a bandolier but without a weapon, his hands protectively spread over an older man, with a small boy hugging his legs and a kneeling woman in a kerchief holding a baby in her lap. The inscription said: *In memory of the six million Jews and all other victims who perished at the hands of the Nazis.*

The dedication had attracted a large crowd, politicians, media, and, within a few days, some anonymous swastika-painters. Crammed in on all sides, Tanya and I had stood behind several rows of chairs set up for the dignitaries, the Holocaust monument committee, and the donors, listening to the speeches delivered from the podium installed near the library entrance. Many in the crowd were teary-eyed, some held old photographs, some cried desperately as those burying their families do.

Focused on the single purpose to keep my tears inside, I clenched my teeth and stared straight ahead, letting the sun dry my eyes. I didn't have photographs or memories, only Lonya's reddened, angry, accusing gaze.

"You should tell everyone about your family too," Tanya whispered in my ear as we applauded an older man who had just delivered his speech about his family wiped out at Babi Yar. I didn't feel I could face her without erupting in desperate wailing, so I simply squeezed her arm.

In front of us, a blond boy of about seven fidgeted, made faces at Tanya, and tugged at his grandmother's skirt every few minutes with the same question: "Is it over yet?" When the ceremony ended, the reporters with video cameras on their shoulders rushed to extract human-interest stories from the crying people. The little boy, finally freed, dragged his grandmother from reporter to reporter, addressing each of them politely, "What channel are you from? Put me in a movie, please." They smiled and assured the flustered grandmother that the little boy was no bother at all.

I found myself next to one of the reporters, a young woman in a conspicuously bright dress holding a conspicuously new video camera. During the ceremony she had kept her camera steadily aimed at the podium; now she was trying to wiggle out of the crowd.

"What channel are you from?" The blond boy placed himself in the path of the young woman reporter. She stared down at him as if wondering whether she should step on him and soil her spiked heels. The boy, suddenly speechless and open-mouthed, backed away into his grandmother's skirt.

"I represent the Soviet Union." The reporter's words in clear, accented English fell out like boulders, her expression defiant. Some curious faces turned to stare at her. The grandmother caught her breath then pulled the boy closer. I pulled Tanya closer. The bright dress swirled as the Soviet reporter marched proudly across the parking lot.

"Why is she so angry?" Tanya asked, taken aback. "He just asked a simple question."

The memory of that episode has accompanied my every visit to the library. Today, I headed straight for the information desk, preparing a grammatically correct question in my mind. It would be embarrassing to ask for good literature in broken English.

"How can I help you?" A young man with a long ponytail interrupted my mental grammar exercise before it was quite finished. In a Soviet library there would be an elderly, refined female bibliographer in his place.

"I need your advice," I began slowly. "I've been in the United States for ten yeas and I've read a lot of mysteries and *Nineteen Eighty-Four*. What should I read next? I like good literature but my English is still not great."

"Let's see." The man stuck a pencil behind his ear and wrinkled his forehead. "Well, I think you could probably read anything. Did you enjoy Orwell?"

"Yes, very much, but I'm not sure my English is good enough to read 'anything.'"

"If you liked *Nineteen Eighty-Four* you might like *We the Living* by Ayn Rand. Somehow, even though they're by different authors, they seem like companion books. It's small and not difficult to read."

I checked out *We the Living*. As I walked back to the car scanning the pages, I knew it would have been on Sylvia's list. I dropped the book at the house and called a taxi.

At six sharp Jack appeared at the front door of my office, roses in hand. Evidently he had been standing to the side for some time watching me work. When he finally knocked, caught unawares, I looked up and blushed. Whenever I blush Jack tries to pretend he doesn't notice, but the sly "gotcha" expression in his eyes gives him away. I think he even knows when we're on the phone.

Fima never made me blush, neither did other men who tried to court me, and Sasha's role in our relationship was making me happy by succumbing to temptation, not inducing it.

"Happy birthday, Anna," Jack approached, handing me the roses.

Lonya's face among the petals, the color of dark blood, smirked bitterly.

"You're going to have fun tonight," Jack smiled as he cupped my chin and kissed me. "Let's go, traffic is terrible."

"Where're we going?"

"It's a surprise."

Speaking Russian and being with Tanya on my birthday would be more natural. As on every birthday in the last few years, it doesn't seem right to be with Jack.

Jack drove, whistling, one hand on my knee.

What is he so elated about?

The car turned into Lena's street, and Jack honked twice.

"Is Lena coming with us?"

"Yep."

I expected her to be waiting outside, but the house was lifeless. The aroma of grilled food filled the air. Jack was a few steps behind as I stopped at the half-opened front door. I knocked and peeked in. The foyer was dark and silent.

"Lena?" I called out. Concerned at not receiving a response, I turned to Jack. "The door's open and Lena's not home. Something must be wrong."

"Let's go in and see." Jack said pushing the door open further.

We stepped inside, and Jack closed the door behind us.

Like lightning, the lights went on and familiar faces were everywhere yelling "Surprise!" I blinked. Tanya was clapping, jumping, and laughing as she threw her arms around me. I hugged her and squeezed Jack's hand. I moved forward, my hands shaking.

"Look how surprised Anya is! She didn't suspect a thing!" Lena, her bangs cut short and her hand on her chest, was laughing and pointing at me.

People came into view face by face. Ilya, at Lena's side, looked at me seriously. Natasha smiled broadly. She was with a large, bearded, American-looking man. Vera whispered, in English, "Happy birthday, Mrs. Fishman." Irena kissed me on my cheek then wiped off a trace of lipstick and ordered the crowd to go to the backyard and eat before the food got cold. Leah-Malka, in a blue head scarf, nodded cheerfully. Bella hugged me. Felix removed a cigarette from his mouth, kissed me on my cheek and winked. Gena Korsunsky's toothpick drew circles. Suddenly, I burst out laughing. Vilen's clouded eyes looked directly at my chest and his lips parted as he leaned toward my laughing mouth. Nausea rolled up my stomach to my throat and I turned my face catching his wet kiss on my cheek and earlobe. Jack and I followed the crowd to the backyard.

Donna was at the grill, in her quiet efficient manner adding to the pile of appetizing-looking chicken and beef.

What does she feel serving those who came from a country that destroyed her own, that keeps her away from her son?

"*Wszystkiego najlepszego z okazji urodzin, Pani* Anya," she said softly in Polish. Then, switching to English, she added, "Good evening, Mr. Graff."

In response, Jack made a circle with his thumb and index finger.

"*Dziekuje bardzo, Pani* Danuta." I matched her respectful tone and accepted a chicken leg. "I'll help you clean up," I continued in Russian.

Donna's eyes shot past me to Jack. "*Pani* Anya, you can't do anything. Mr. Graff told me you should be a princess today," she begged in a combination of Polish and Russian.

I wonder how much Jack pays her.

"A princess? Look who's a princess," muttered Irena sarcastically.

So what, she must have been a princess to Vilen, once. Why couldn't I be a princess, even temporarily? Maybe I'm not worth it, but if Jack believes that I am, why would I want to disillusion him?

"If you're a princess to someone, why can't I be?" I sounded indifferent, as if asking about the weather.

Does Jack really think I'm a princess?

Lena took a deep breath, looking from Irena to me and back again. Tennis anyone?

I started to move away to a table laden with food.

"I'm a princess to my own husband. I don't have to earn the honor from some American prick, who probably slept with the whole world, and shake in my shoes that he'll leave me. How long do you think a pretty face and a nice ass will work for you?"

"Why, Irena, thank you for the compliment," I laughed, genuinely pleased, while Irena snarled aggressively.

Pretty face and nice ass. Not bad, coming from Irena.

"Somehow, Irena, I'm not envious of your marriage," intervened Natasha.

The men never knew of the war within our civilized circle. They were getting their food, talking about cars and Soviet politics. I wondered if Jack was curious about what was being said.

The bearded man, who evidently didn't understand a word of Russian, applied himself to the mountain of salad and meat on his plate.

"Vilen," yelled Irena, "interrupt your conversation and take care of your wife! Get me some Sprite!"

"One second, Irochka," we heard Vilen's soft voice say.

Natasha and I looked at each other and laughed.

"Anna, I would like you to meet my friend, Joe," Natasha addressed me in English.

The bearded giant gave me his hand. "Nice to meet you. Naty, I mean, Natasha, talks a lot about you." He released my hand to place his on Natasha's shoulder; she lowered her eyes appropriately.

"Nice to meet you, Joe. I've heard a lot about you too." I stopped, realizing that all I had heard was that his erection lasted forever.

I do enjoy seeing everyone here. Not all of them like me, but they came. I would go to their parties, even though I don't like all of them. Divorce from your own people is not easy. To Irena, the fact she's married constitutes the meaning of life. She may be one of the luckiest. Not many could boast of capturing the meaning of their lives. Vilen has no qualms about meeting me in public. Look who's moralizing! After all, I had no qualms about meeting Sasha's wife in public.

Jack and the Kaganov men were sitting at a picnic table engrossed in cutting their steaks. Gena was laughing loudly, his head bent toward Ilya. It looks like Gena's here without Marina. How does he manage to never lose his toothpick? I don't see Nina or Izya, either.

Stories of immigrants' inexplicable friendships and animosities abound. How will I ever be able to explain all this to Asya? She probably thinks we all stick together in a strange land. I guess in some ways we do. Each of these people, with perhaps the exception of Gena, can be counted on in an emergency for assistance and favors for which most Americans wouldn't even be considered.

"Natasha tells me you operate your own computer consulting company," said Joe, wiping his lips with a napkin.

I do?

"Yes," I replied, glancing in Jack's direction.

"You may not be interested in a small job, but my company has been interviewing consultants for a few short-term coding positions."

"What company are you with?"

"Reynolds-Smith in Elmhurst. Here's my card."

Natasha looked at Joe proudly.

"I'm sorry. I don't have any cards with me," I sighed dramatically. "You know, my daughter says I should never go anywhere without them. I guess she's right. When do you need someone to start?"

I'm probably not asking the right questions. Jack will be angry.

"Within six weeks. Do you have someone in mind?"

"Tell me exactly what you need."

I accepted the pen that Joe unclipped from his breast pocket and made notes on a napkin before he drifted away with Natasha on his arm.

Lena took my hands. Her fluffy bangs made her look young today.

"I'm glad Irena didn't upset you. I want only peace in my house. She's not really a bad person, and she does like you in her own way. She just doesn't understand what tact is. You know, she volunteered to go grocery shopping with Tanya for the party?"

I smiled at Lena's breathless effort to maintain peace.

"I'm not surprised. Irena would always help. But afterward she can viciously bite your head off and destroy everything."

Lena relaxed, changing the subject.

"Anya, Tanya is absolutely wonderful. She organized everything. At first we were going to have it at your house, but we decided it would be too difficult to hide."

"Thank you, Lenochka, for giving your house. Whose idea was it to have a surprise party?"

"Jack's, I think. He wanted to do something different. Tanya told me he was planning a surprise cruise. But she knew you wouldn't go without her and convinced him to have a party instead. Anya, he's a fine man, but I don't know how you handle speaking English all the time."

I'd prefer Russian myself.

"Anichka, my parents called last night. They've been encouraged to go to Moscow to seek a waiver for my father's security clearance. This is their third attempt and each time I think the outcome will be quick and positive, but, of course, it hasn't been. At least now some hope has been extended."

"When are they going to Moscow?"

"Soon. A cousin promised to accompany them. Luckily, I just recently sent my parents some money via my next door neighbor who went to Kiev to visit her brother. My father needs to buy some bottles of good cognac for bribes. Considering that he has not worked for nearly twenty years and, of course, the new, liberal times, the waiver sounds like a formality."

Lena's round eyes searched mine.

"I don't believe they would direct him to get a waiver unless they knew he could get it," I said confidently, hoping my reasoning reflected the new Soviet reality that appeared not to have distanced itself from the old Soviet reality.

"They're in their eighties. I count every day." Lena held up her hands with crossed fingers. "How do you like Natasha's boyfriend? He's Irish."

"An Irish boyfriend and an Orthodox Jewish son."

"At least she's not anti-Semitic like Irena."

Bella appeared from around the corner of the house.

"Let me tell you something, Anichka, I hope my Susan grows up to be like Tanya."

"Thank you," I faked matter-of-factness. "She takes after her father. He's a very thoughtful person."

"I don't know about that." Bella screwed up her face. "My mother has applied to come for a visit. When she gets here I'm going to try to convince her to stay."

Leah-Malka joined us. "I'm sorry Jacob couldn't make it. Tanya, *kineahora*, is a fine girl. To give such a party for her mother," she clicked her tongue and shook her head. "We should start thinking about a suitable young man for her."

Leah-Malka's singing Yiddish intonation always reminds me of Jewish grandmothers baby-sitting their grandchildren in the parks of Kiev.

"Leah, I'm sorry, I don't think we have any kosher food." I kissed her kind, round cheeks. "Tanya's too young for marriage."

"Who's getting married?" inquired Irena, placing herself between Bella and Leah-Malka.

"Not yet, but soon," Leah-Malka insisted, "after she gets out of high school. Watch it, Anna, she'll bring a *goy* home from college. Then what?"

"My husband's family hates my guts and Anna will hate her son-in-law. What else?" Irena's loud admonition was not missed by anyone.

Bella shrugged, rolling her eyes. She moved away as Felix approached, lighting a cigarette, blowing the smoke sideways.

"Irena, you're a bitch!" Felix said in Russian under his breath.

Leah-Malka stared from me to Irena and back, utterly confused. More tennis. She obviously never realized Irena's not Jewish. Most Americans can't tell that many Russian immigrants are not Jewish, and the fact is not advertised by mixed families. Sponsoring Jewish organizations existing on private donations would not be thrilled.

Lena turned on the outside lights. The backyard looked so festive that I threw back my head expecting to see fireworks. Tanya, Vera, and Donna were arranging sweets on trays. A huge, masterfully cut watermelon occupied a large tray on one of the tables. I kissed Tanya on the back of her neck.

"How do you like the party so far, Mom?"

"It's a very happy day for me, Tanichka."

"I invited everyone you would have invited yourself. Nina couldn't make it, she's working overtime. Marina had a headache. I'm so upset, I forgot Leah-Malka keeps kosher. I feel bad there's nothing she can eat."

"Don't worry, Tanya, I saw her eating some fruit. She understands."

Tanya feels the birthday girl today. She should. If not for her, I would have to agree with Lonya that the world would not have been worse off without me. I'm happy.

"Mom, Vera, Yuri, and I want to go for ice cream later. I hope it's okay. I took your car. I hope that's okay, too." Tanya looked at me with "pleeease" in her eyes.

"Yes, Tanichka. Everything's okay."

"Attention, everyone!" Lena called out in English, standing next to Jack in the middle of the yard. He was holding a gift-wrapped box. "Before dessert let's give Anna her present. It's from all of us."

Conscious of being the center of attention, I went to where Lena and Jack were standing. I smiled stupidly as everyone sang "Happy Birthday."

I like getting presents.

Lena and I hugged. Jack kissed me, saying, "You're beautiful" in my ear. He carried the box to a table. I blushed, smiling and blinking to chase away the tears. Impatiently, I tore off the wrapping paper, opened the box, and peeked in.

My dream glasses! The Baccarat wine and champagne glasses I've always wanted.

I met Natasha's eyes. She was the only one who knew. I can't believe she remembered.

"Thank you," I whispered.

"Now we expect to be invited to use them," said Vilen, turning the silence into lively noise.

If Irena called me pretty, then maybe Jack does think I'm beautiful, and, contrary to Natasha's theory, not a touch to the ugly side.

"Mom, stop crying. You need to wash your face," Tanya said softly, setting a tray of sweets down near me.

With a lightness I hadn't known before, I circulated around the yard. I even smiled to Gena, interrupting his conversation with Jack to inquire about Marina and the boys and to express my regrets they couldn't share this happy occasion with me. Leah-Malka left, promising to find a nice Jewish boy for Tanya.

Natasha touched my arm. "We're going to leave."

"Natasha, I'm so touched you remembered the glasses."

"Joe, do you mind if Anna and I talk for a minute?"

Joe kissed my hand and went ahead.

"Jack drove Lena and me crazy. He wanted something that would make you divinely happy. Let me tell you, it was a tall order, until I remembered those glasses."

"It made me divinely happy."

Natasha powdered her face and clicked her purse shut. "I saw, and I'm glad. How do you like Joe?"

In the semi-darkness her attractive, somewhat rigid features impressed me with the character and will that during the day were toned down by her turned-up nose and quick, curious, gray eyes.

"How's Isaak?"

"You didn't answer my question."

"Okay, I like Joe. How's Isaak?"

"Fine. He has decided to stay in Israel." She spat out the words like bullets. "Well, I'm glad you like Joe. I had a good time tonight."

"Natasha, why are you so upset? As long as it's not the Soviet Union, it doesn't matter where he lives."

"What would you do if Tanya decided to live in another country?"

"Probably move to that country."

"I can't move to Israel!"

"Why not?"

"I'm not Jewish."

"Your son's there."

"I wonder. My son is excited because he's now circumcised and can pray or do something with the Torah. Anya, he's so talented. One can't compare the opportunities in Israel with those in the United States. He's ruining his future."

"He feels Jewish, and apparently he feels the need to live in Israel."

"Isaak doesn't even remember his father, who, by the way, didn't feel Jewish. How can one feel Jewish? That's nonsense."

"It's not nonsense, but at least you know how one doesn't feel Jewish."

"Don't be cruel. You didn't think I was being anti-Semitic, did you?"

"No, Natasha. You're just . . . not Jewish. I'd better return to my guests. Good luck with Joe."

"Joe is strictly for sex. We've had sex everywhere, even on a desk in his office and in the shower."

"In the shower?"

"Yes, have you tried it?" Natasha's face briefly lit then faded. "I can't talk to him. Well, I shouldn't have to tell *you* that; we're in the same boat. My advice to you is to get rid of Jack and marry a Russian. That's what I'm going to do. We're not getting any younger. Even if Jack were the marriageable type, can you picture yourself speaking English twenty-four hours a day and constantly explaining to his friends why you didn't escape from the Soviet Union sooner? I couldn't stand it."

"I'll call you, Natasha. I need to go inside and wash the tears from my face. And although everyone's probably talking politics and has completely forgotten about me, I should be with the guests."

The bathroom off the stairway on the second floor was spacious, decorated in shades of gray, with a wall-sized mirror and a charcoal sink, toilet, and bathtub. Spotless, with bottles and jars in a line in front of the mirror and thick gray towels hanging on a wide silvery rack, it appeared to have never been used.

The evening is happy and exciting. Jack has stayed in the background letting me mingle in my Russian way. Lena is pleased to be useful. It's a good evening for everyone.

I thought I heard a noise and looked out the open door into the empty hallway. It must have been my imagination. I turned back to the mirror and there, again, was the noise, only more distinct.

I started to turn back to the door as a body came through it, pinning me against the wall. Shivers ran up my back as I recognized Vilen. I felt nausea in the pit of my stomach.

"Don't be afraid. Everyone's busy talking."

Vilen rubbed his stomach against my body as I ducked his mouth. The towel bar on the wall hurt my chest as I whirled around.

"Good, I like it better from behind." Vilen's hands were pulling up my skirt.

The nausea was unbearable. I thought of Tanya and doubled my energy to stop his hands and avoid his face getting close to mine.

"What's wrong, Anya? Why are you suddenly resisting?" came Vilen's rasp. "You always liked it."

I felt his arousal now. Thrusting against me, he croaked some endearments sounding like curses. He had my skirt up and my panties down, but I kept his hands from unzipping his pants. With each thrust the towel bar rammed unmercifully into my chest. I wrenched away, losing my grip on his hands, and found myself half-sprawled across the sink, his large, wet mouth over mine. I heard his pants unzip, he pushed my leg back across the sink, covering it with his as he inched forward.

"What the fuck!!" Jack's voice raged as he ripped Vilen from atop me.

A loud crash and the sound of breaking glass accompanied my release. For a few seconds my hands continued their wild, defensive movements. When I straightened up, quite disoriented, I saw a hole with ragged edges in the shower door. Vilen had careened through the door into the bathtub, where he lay, pieces of glass strewn over him, his head supported by the tub, his legs hanging over its edge like a rag doll's. Blood dripped from his mouth to a quickly growing stain on his shirt, his slacks were torn from the hip down. His one fully opened eye blinked rapidly. Jack stepped toward him with clenched fists.

"Don't!" I touched Jack's arm, swallowing to suppress nausea, trying to put myself back together, and looking around for a place to sit down. "Where's Tanya?"

"What the fuck is going on? Why the fuck didn't you scream for help?"

"You . . . you, whore!" stammered Vilen in Russian. More blood appeared through his lips.

Jack didn't understand the language, but the meaning was unmistakable. He half-picked up Vilen by his shirt with one hand forming his other into a fist. Vilen looked pathetic with his head rolling and his fly open.

"Don't, please!" I stretched my hand over Vilen and swayed.

Jack opened his hand, dropped Vilen, and stepped toward me. He splashed cold water on my face, drying it clumsily with a towel. From the bathtub Vilen stared at Jack wondrously, his hand cupping his jaw.

"Come on, baby, don't pass out on me." Jack was pale and breathing heavily. He sat me down on the toilet.

"I've been watching you, you fucking son of a bitch." Jack shoved Vilen's hanging leg into the bathtub. "Touch her again and I'll kill you!"

Jack supported me down the stairs. The fresh air made me dizzy.

"Where's Tanya?"

"She was looking for you, but the house was dark, thank God, so she didn't go in. She wants to go for ice cream with her friends."

"Here you are, we've been looking for you." Lena's voice, in carefree English, immediately changed to concerned Russian when she saw me at closer range, "What's wrong, Anya? What happened to your clothes?"

"Where's Tanya?"

"I'm here, Mom, but I'm leaving with Vera and Yuri. Mom, what happened, are you sick?"

"Your mother isn't feeling well. We're going home." Jack let me hide behind him.

Tanya, flanked by Vera and bored, absent-minded Yuri, stood for a minute silently. "Do you want me to come with you?"

"No, Tanichka, I'll be all right. You go ahead, just don't be late."

Tanya looked at Jack and he nodded.

The children hurried past us. I exhaled with relief.

"Jack, we can't leave him there."

"We can and we will."

"Leave who?" asked Lena.

"Lena, I'm sorry. Vilen and Jack had . . . had some words. Vilen . . . he's in your bathtub."

Jack sighed listening to our Russian, then took a few steps toward the yard and gestured to Gena to come closer.

"In my bathtub . . . some words . . .?" The understanding of what had possibly occurred gradually transformed Lena's bafflement to horror. "Oh, no. Vilen's such a refined person. Why should things like this always happen in my house?" she whined, covering her mouth hastily, her other hand flying to her chest. Her eyes under her short bangs stood out like two giant, helpless buttons.

"Lena, Jack will send someone to replace the shower doors. Don't worry, we'll pay for the damage."

"The damage? Oh, my God . . . oh, my God. I think I have to sit down."

"Gene, don't make a fuss," Jack said in a low voice as Gena approached, "but you have a patient waiting in the upstairs bathtub.

Keep it quiet, will you? Send me the bill, and call me if there are any problems."

Jack pushed the hair from my forehead gently, his look both questioning and concerned.

Gena's toothpick, pointing at Jack, moved up and down. His small, dark eyes took in my destroyed skirt and sickly face. He slowly nodded with sneaky satisfaction—I had refused him, and this was his just reward.

"You can count on me," Gena said, man to man. "I'll do all I can."

"We're leaving now, Lena. I'm sorry. Please apologize to the guests for us," Jack patted her hand, then took two one-hundred-dollar bills and a twenty from his wallet. "Do me a favor, give this to Donna and call a taxi for her when she's done."

Will anyone believe I didn't lead Vilen on? Irena certainly won't and I can't expect her to take this silently. Lena understood, probably remembering her own experience. She won't say anything. If this episode becomes known within the Russian community, the lingering no-smoke-without-fire will remain forever, affecting Tanya and her relationships with her Russian friends and even her own reputation.

"The first time I actually felt you were happy, and that asshole had to ruin everything." Jack unlocked the car door and helped me in. His lips were a straight, tight line.

"I am happy, Jack. Aside from what happened, of course."

"I hope so," Jack remarked skeptically. "Why didn't you call for help?"

And shatter Tanya's little family world, wreck her trust, all I've been building and protecting? I wouldn't have called for help even if Vilen, God forbid, had again succeeded.

I took the roses off the dashboard and laid them across my lap closing my eyes. I wasn't as eager to talk as Jack.

"Anna, for God's sake, he was trying to rape you. Could you please tell me why, in Heaven's name, you didn't scream for help?"

"He didn't succeed, and I couldn't have Tanya see it all. And what about Yuri?"

"Was the alternative more appealing?" Jack's voice was strangely high.

The alternative . . . I shuddered. That time, years ago, in Vilen's bathroom, the sound of his pants hitting the floor, my breast squashed in the sink, the feel of him inside me . . . The nausea returned. The only good side to what had happened was that I would never again have to deal with Vilen.

"The louse! Did he ever try anything like that before?"

He didn't have to try; it was another function, like eating. If not, Tanya and I would have been in the street.

"What the fuck is going on here? He hasn't tried since we met, has he? Anna, would you please talk to me?"

He doesn't understand. Where would I be if not for this particular man having taught me English? Certainly not in the position of Jack's girlfriend.

"Okay, but I'm warning you, if I ever come up against that bastard again, you won't be able to stop me."

"Jack, I left my purse and my gift at Lena's."

"We're not going back." The car picked up speed.

"My driver's license is in my purse."

"Call me if you get caught. I'll come bond you out. I'm not going back to those people."

"Jack, I'm part of those people!" My defiance came naturally.

"Yeah, so then why were you cringing under Vilen's hands, trying to fight him off, if you like everything about those people so much?"

The pointed "under Vilen's hands" made me feel humiliated.

As much as Vilen and Gena make me sick, as much as Irena irritates me, as much as Natasha induces an eternal Jewish distrust, as much as chance, not chosen, acquaintances are merely floating by, not leaving traces, they are my roots, the continuity of what started forty-five years ago.

For the remainder of the ride I sat rigidly, holding the roses, staring ahead, ready to jump to defend my own ugly corner of the world.

At home I went through the motions of putting the flowers into a vase, taking off my clothes, throwing them in a garbage bag—knowing I'd never wear them again—taking a shower, and getting into my night-gown. I was shaken and still didn't feel clean. I started making tea, then poured it into the sink, fleeing to the bedroom, leaving Jack to gloomily pace the living room. The sight of a book waiting for me on the night table brought back some measure of equilibrium, but I couldn't concentrate on someone else's life.

Tanya ran in breaking the tense stillness.

"Mom, are you all right? You're really pale."

"I'm all right. Did you have a good time with Yuri and Vera?"

"Yeah, I had a chocolate two-scooper. Nancy asked me to say 'Hi' to you."

"Thanks. Everyone told me how hard you worked putting the party together. I'm very proud of you."

"It wasn't hard, but I felt funny buying stuff and not saying anything to you. I was afraid it would rain or people would forget or you'd discover everything." Tanya yawned, gave me her cheek, and walked out gratified.

The stillness returned, broken only by a knock on the door.

"Anna, I'm going home." Jack stood rigidly in the half-open doorway. "I have to get up early and you need a good night's sleep. It's probably a good idea for you to take the day off tomorrow."

"Jack, you know who you remind me of? The Count of Monte Cristo."

"How's that?" Jack replied without enthusiasm.

"You're always there for me. But in return, you want me to start my life at the point where I met you. Even if it were possible, I wouldn't want to do that." I paused and took a deep breath. "Jack, we don't fit."

"Exactly. I won't overstay my welcome." Jack's tone remained flat.

My eyes prickled with approaching tears. "Come here," I said unexpectedly.

Jack sat on the edge of the bed looking away from me.

"Let me tell you something before you leave." I wanted to hug him with the same emotion I hug Tanya. "Jack, you mean a lot to me."

"Do I really," he said, his monotone taking the inquiry out of the question.

"No one besides you ever needed me to be happy. There are a few who don't want me to be unhappy, and those are the closest people, and will always be, but it's not the same thing."

I sat next to Jack, wrapping my arms around him. His shoulders were tight, his body wooden.

"I know you don't like the word gratitude, but I don't know how else to call what I feel toward you. You mean a lot to me."

Jack rubbed his eye under his glasses.

"Thanks to you, I was a princess tonight." I tried to meet his eyes. "Vilen can't take that away. I didn't invite his attention. Why should I feel guilty?"

"You've got it all wrong, Anna," Jack's shoulders slumped forward. "What makes me angry is that I walk on eggshells, watching my every word, and you'll think nothing of seeing Vilen and his family after what he's done. The docile way in which you take this crap is disgusting. It's bizarre."

"Jack, try to understand: Vilen was the one who convinced me to go to school and who taught me enough English to go; he helped me with my homework; he and Irena found me an apartment; they took Tanya on vacation with them, giving me time to study for finals." I took his lifeless fingers. "I didn't have anyone. What would have happened to Tanya if something had happened to me? Where would we be if we had lived where we could afford to live? Not that it would have bothered me to remain a cleaning lady for the rest of my life, but Tanya needed a chance for a good education and nice friends. I did what I did, for better or for worse."

Jack's hand in mine stiffened.

"I'm not justifying what Vilen did. You just need to know that . . . the Russian community is my community. We don't know how to trust, we're always on guard, we don't know how to relax, we adhere to a rather loose definition of what a lie is—the list goes on and on. What do you want me to do? Pretend I'm not one of these people, or different? I can't. And what's more, I don't want to. It would be like not knowing my name anymore."

"I don't know, Anna. I don't know," Jack sighed, "Your face tonight, with Vilen . . . it follows me everywhere. It's hell." Jack got up. "It's always the same story. We talk and I see everything your way. Well . . . I'm too tired to drive now. I'll get a sheet and sleep on the sofa." Without looking at me, Jack turned off the light and left the room, closing the door behind him.

I woke up at close to three in the morning, tossing and turning to relieve the stiffness of my aching muscles. My mind was suddenly alert. I tiptoed barefoot into the living room, looked at the motionless mound on the sofa, and knew Jack wasn't asleep.

"Jack, Natasha's boyfriend told me that his company is interviewing consultants."

"I know. I told him to talk to you."

We both sounded as if we were continuing a conversation started earlier. My laughter rang out in the darkness.

"What's so funny?" Jack asked, faking roughness in his voice.

"It's hilarious! I knew you weren't sleeping, and you weren't surprised I woke up."

"I was sleeping. You woke me up."

"I did not! You weren't sleeping."

Jack didn't reply.

"Why did you tell Joe to talk to me?"

"Because you're in charge of consulting."

I wanted to kiss him!

"I wrote down the qualifications they're looking for. We could place an ad in the *Chicago Tribune*."

"Offering what? Are you looking for an independent contractor?" he sounded irate.

"I guess we'll have to. We don't have any benefits to offer."

"I'll call a couple people. Wait with the ad. Did you think of a name for the company?"

I sat down on the floor by the sofa and let my hand run down Jack's neck and shoulders. He turned to face me. The semi-darkness muted his features.

"Jack, let's keep the name 'Graff Software.' My name doesn't mean anything to anyone."

"But the company really means more to you than to me. What about 'Fishman-Graff Software and Consulting'?"

"Your name has to be first. I insist."

"'Graff and Anna?'" Jack was now grinning.

For a while we tossed around several other suggestions, finally settling on "Graff and Fishman Management Services."

Sitting up, Jack sighed. "Anna, I need a cup of coffee, then I'll hit the road before I get sleepy again."

In a half-hour he stood by the door, a big boy, uneasy and serious, with his hair still wet from his shower.

"Thank you for the party, and for the flowers, and for the glasses, and for everything. Drive carefully, partner."

He smiled briefly, shaking his head in a naughty-girl, what-am-I-going-to-do-with-you movement.

"You make me so angry sometimes, Anna, but I wish I didn't have to leave you alone now. Who knows what your crazy Russians will think of doing?"

I wanted to ask him about making love in the shower, but decided against it. After all, he had a long drive ahead.

"That blush certainly lets me know what you were thinking." His eyes still anxious, Jack smiled with familiar intimacy. "Hold that thought. So long, partner."

His hands touched my body teasingly, then the door closed behind him.

Business partner. Sex partner. Love would only be in the way. Thank God, I'm immune. Sasha knew my daughter would make me grow up to learn that life could not be built on feelings.

thirty-one

Dear Tanichka,

I thank you and your mother for sending me an invitation so quickly. Please excuse me for not answering the short letter that came with it as I was busy collecting all the papers necessary to apply for a visa. They have been ready for a week, but I had to wait for our party organization head to return from his vacation to make sure that there wouldn't be any problems with my applying. As I expected, he confirmed that these things are no longer getting people into trouble. He even asked me to bring him back a T-shirt. It makes me very proud of my country that we are experiencing more freedom every day. I will turn my papers in tomorrow. On the average it takes five to six months to get a visa.

Tanichka, there are no words to express how much I want to see you. Don't forget, you will need to arrange your schedule so we can spend the maximum amount of time together.

Now, let me tell you about what seems to be worrying everyone in the West most—Chernobyl. Exactly two months have passed since the accident occurred on Saturday, the twenty-sixth of April. Like most people, we found out about it on Monday when we arrived at work. No one imagined this accident presented any danger to Kiev. And, in the beginning, the danger was negligible, but when the wind started blowing toward Kiev, radiation increased significantly. We were not aware what the levels were, only that it increased. Like everyone else, we spent the May First holiday in the park with Petya and Igor, and we devoted a day to cleaning the graves of our parents. On the fifth of May a statement was broadcast urging us not to go outside for long periods of time, to keep our windows closed, and some other rules.

Summer recess at the schools started unusually early, and many people with small children took vacations. All children aged seven through fourteen were sent to summer camps throughout the Soviet Union for forty-five days. This time has since been extended for an additional forty-five days. Our government has been very noble. I applaud them for taking such good care of our children, even though it has been difficult for us to endure. Can you imagine a large city like Kiev without children? Can you imagine walking through a city and not seeing or hearing children playing or laughing? Can you imagine the heartbreak of parents being separated from their children for so long? If you can imagine all this, then you know how these parents felt, and how I feel without you.

The government has begun giving away vacation packages to far away resorts to mothers with toddlers. Not to everyone at once, but gradually. My wife didn't want to wait her turn and went with Petya and Igor to Kishinev. She's staying with some relatives. I miss them very much.

Psychologically, there is great uncertainty among the people here. You see, radiation has no color, smell, or any other noticeable features. Even chemists, like Zhanna, or doctors don't know how much of a threat it really is. Nor, obviously, did the people that worked at Chernobyl. They all tried to save what could be saved and all became victims of the radiation. The consequences are not good, but our government has told us they are not as bad as our capitalistic enemies report. A lot of work will have to be done in order to isolate the destruction to a small region. We can't rest until the reactor is buried. The government has been trying to prevent panic. Doctors and members of the government committee are regularly interviewed on television and radio. They make every effort to give our people an objective picture.

There are more and more tourists coming to us now. Mostly they come from the European socialist countries, or from Cuba, a few come from the West and the United States. No one knows what is going to happen next. Thank you for offering your help. The most significant help we have received so far is from an American doctor who arrived with a medical team and from Armand Hammer in the form of money, even though we don't need it.

I'm planning on spending part of my vacation with the boys in Kishinev when my wife's vacation is over. See you very, very soon. Tell me what you want me to bring you.

Your Father

26 June 1986

Anya,

I hope you realize your responsibility for organizing Tanya's time, aside from school, in such a way that she spends the majority of it with me.

Don't plan anything special, I'm not a guest. All I want is to be involved in Tanya's life for the entire time of my visit, so that after I leave we have a close and meaningful relationship, a relationship I always wanted and you obviously didn't consider important.

Fima

July 24, 1986

Dear Dad,

Your letter arrived yesterday and I was very happy to know you are really coming. Mom and I sat up late, and she told me how you played and read to me, and it was you who taught me gymnastics. I will spend all my out-of-class time with you. I'm on the basketball team at school and I'm sure you'll want to come to one of the games. Jack, Mom's boyfriend, has promised to take you to some sporting events.

I quit my job so I could volunteer at a nursing home. I help out the patients, like taking them for walks, writing letters, or just listening to them talk. It's very depressing. Sometimes it's scary, especially when they don't feel well, but when I think of how they wait for me, I realize I must go back the next day. One old man always waits outside his room and kisses my hand. My girlfriend works there too. She wants to be a doctor.

Actually, I'm not sure what I want to be, a teacher or a doctor. I hope working with these weak and sick people will help me make a decision, so that I don't waste time changing majors in college. I also take some biology and chemistry classes at a community college that will give me a head start in college.

Every Sunday morning Jack plays golf while I take golf lessons. If you come in good weather you'll be able to watch me play. Mom says I take to sports just like you did. Something else very exciting has happened—Mom joined Jack's company as a vice president! It's a computer consulting firm, and they're trying to place someone with a client, and soon they'll start working on a really big project. I don't know exactly how it all works, and Mom is nervous, but she's very happy. They're terribly busy, and Mom says they might need office space and a receptionist. Now that she makes more money, I can't expect a big scholarship, so I'll use my savings to pay for textbooks.

I guess you're lucky that Petya and Igor had a chance to leave Kiev and wait out the effects of Chernobyl in another city. Everyone here is convinced these effects will be forever.

Dad, I don't need anything. Just don't forget to bring my baby pictures with you. Mom left the family album behind.

Love, Your daughter Tanya.

P.S. I forgot to tell you: Mom's car broke down and she rented a new Continental. Jack insists when she starts getting money for the big project we should buy a European or Japanese car. Mom's leaning toward a Volvo. She says it's a safe car. I prefer BMWs, and I absolutely love driving!

All Tanya's letters have been a real lesson in sociology. To keep from changing this last letter was a struggle.

It took an enire page to present the concept of consulting as an enterprise. The same applied to the terms: volunteer, changing majors, community college, scholarship—and how do I explain office space to someone with no concept of private property? Or scholarship—when education is free?

"Volunteer" means the same in Russian as it means in English, but the common connotation in Russian is "someone who's forced to do something useless and that no one else wants to do." I added an assurance that Tanya alone had made her decision to volunteer, not unusual in the States.

"Changing majors"—Fima will be bewildered that a specialty can be changed.

"Community college" has no translation to any of the educational institutions in the Soviet Union, neither does "credit," with the Soviet system using a grade-for-class system.

"Golf"—this is a real lesson in sociology. The translation of the word isn't a problem, but, in the Soviet Union, golf is a symbol of capitalism at its worst, an award to blood-thirsty exploiters, a sign of decadence in Western societies. It will reflect negatively on me, another proof of my getting to the top by shameful means, abandoning my daughter to the mercy of rotten, immoral imperialists who constantly hatch insidious schemes aimed at destroying the haven of the working people—socialism.

The brand names of cars mean nothing to the average Russian. Only Rolls-Royce would make a splash, being a symbol of wealth in all anti-West books.

To forty-eight-year-old Fima, who will never have a car, bragging by his sixteen-year-old daughter will be an irritant, a sign of bad manners attributed to smug boasting, encouraged or instructed by me. The frequent mentioning of Jack is inconsiderate, even from a child, and he won't believe the rest.

Oh, well. That's what Tanya wrote, that's what Fima gets.

I was dozing when Jack kissed my forehead and crawled out of bed. I vaguely heard him leave the room. Somewhere, in the back of my mind, I thought I heard a telephone ring.

"Anna, it's the Soviet Union!"

Sasha! I was suddenly awake. I flew to the phone, wrapping myself in the bed sheet.

"Hello! Good morning!" I heard my clear and breathless voice.

"Anichka, good afternoon and happy birthday! When a man answered I thought it was a wrong number again."

A twinge of disappointment was immediately replaced by joy as I recognized Asya's cackle.

"You remembered! Thank you!"

"You silly, sure I remembered, it's still written down in my famous notebook. I called on the fifteenth, but it was a wrong number. A woman's voice answered in English, and she just kept talking and talking."

"That was Tanya's voice on our answering machine. If you had left a message I would have called you back." I automatically used the English word "message" in the all-Russian sentence.

"Left what?"

I explained what a message was.

"I couldn't do that. The voice wouldn't stop talking and then there was a beep and it was too late."

"Asinka, let's not waste time. Tell me what's new. Did you get my letter?"

"Not yet. Rimma's leaving for the States the day after tomorrow. She'll call you from Los Angeles. Oy, we're so agitated . . . with the information that's available now . . . Rimma will tell you everything."

"Everything" was firmly stressed, meaning it could only be discussed in person.

"Asya, give her your pictures. Did you find Sasha?"

"Not yet. We're very busy with Rimma. After she leaves and everything quiets down, I'll try going to the hospital where he used to work. Anichka, who was the man who answered the phone? I heard the operator talk to him."

"My boyfriend." I wished there was a one-word equivalent in Russian for boyfriend. The closest translation has the meaning "lover." So, I used a more vague "a man I've been seeing."

"I see."

A shocked pause.

"I didn't know you lived with a man. Where's Tanya?" she said in one breath.

Her incredulity opened a gulf between us. I wasn't the Anya she remembered.

"We don't live together. He's only here on weekends. Tanya's still asleep. Do you want to talk to her?" I grasped at straws trying to revive the conversation.

"Don't wake her, Anya. Some other time."

"How's your family?"

"Fine. Where are you going on vacation?"

"I won't have a vacation this summer. Are you going anywhere?"

"Yes, to some clean place."

"A clean place?"

"Somewhere with no radiation," explained Asya with surprise.

"I see." I felt guilty for not understanding right away and for not living with radiation. "Asinka, tell Rimma I'm looking forward to seeing her. Say hi to your family."

"Thanks. Say hi to Tanya."

The line clicked.

"Bad news?" Jack looked down at me.

I hung up the receiver. Asya's "I didn't know you lived with a man. Where's Tanya?" rang in my ears.

"What?" I looked at Jack and I realized he had been standing next to me the entire time.

"Bad news from Kiev?"

"Why?" I closed my eyes and rubbed my face to bring myself back to reality. The sheet fell. I looked down at it, then rapidly picked it up as I scurried to the bedroom.

"What's wrong?"

Why did Jack have to follow me?

"That was my friend Asya on the phone."

"The one that's going to visit us?"

Us? I fought down resentment.

"It's her sister that's going to visit. Is it that difficult to remember? Jack, have I changed since we first met?"

"In some ways. But, then, of course, you've had some highly skilled help."

The joke failed to diminish my anxiety. "I need to know—have I changed?"

"You're not half bad."

"Asya and I have known each other for thirty-seven years, yet, for some reason, we had a hard time communicating today. I could tell she felt I'd changed, somehow becoming worse than I used to be."

"In what respect?" He grew serious.

"I don't know. But I do know, I don't want to lose her. She's very important to me." Goose bumps prickled down my spine as I remembered Asya's inference.

"Would you tell me what she said?"

Tanya, disheveled, her brows raised to keep her eyelids from drooping, appeared in the doorway.

"Did the telephone ring or was I dreaming? Hi, Jack. What time is my golf lesson?"

"Tanichka, Auntie Asya called."

"Who? Oh, your girlfriend from Russia. She's coming to the States, right?"

"What's wrong with everyone's memory? It's her sister who's coming."

"I'm sorry." Tanya stretched, screwing up her eyes like a kitten. "So, Jack, when's my lesson?"

"At eleven. The instructor couldn't make it earlier." Jack sounded strangely cool.

Asya's right. Tanya shouldn't live under the same roof with my boyfriend, walk in my bedroom half-dressed, see my bed all messed up, and Jack wearing nothing but a loosely tied robe. What does it teach her?

She ignored Jack's cool tone. "I'm not going back to bed. Jack, do you want to shoot baskets with me?" Tanya's eyes looked more awake.

"Okay, but I want to talk to your mother first."

"Anna, what did your girlfriend say?" Jack closed the door behind Tanya.

"She didn't say anything."

"She must have said something to upset you so much."

"I'm not upset. I just wish I had answered the phone, not you."

Jack spoke slowly and patiently. "Honey, if what she didn't approve of has anything to do with morals, then I advise you to stick to non-Russian standards."

"Let me remind you, my friend," my voice dropped dangerously low, "that these are the standards that made me the person with whom, as you claimed once, you fell in love. You're free to go at any time." I paused to catch my breath.

I'd never seen Jack so pale. He threw his robe on the floor. I watched the muscles on his back and arms flex as he pulled out a drawer to get a pair of shorts and a shirt. He dressed and left the room slamming the door behind him.

I deflated into a small ball on the bed pressing my face into the pillow. The tension of the argument made me wish the telephone would ring, or the doorbell sound, or even the cuckoo cuckoo.

I've always known the "Era of Jack" would pass. Now, when it's about to happen, I can't ignore what this will do to Tanya. Four out of sixteen years are not easy to erase. Without Jack she'll be back to just me, in an organized, silent house. I'm sorry, Tanya.

Fortunately, after Sasha appeared, I never had to go back to just Lonya. Had I, it would have killed the little that Sasha managed, consciously or not, to salvage.

I must have dozed off. When I came out of the bedroom and called Tanya's name, silence answered. The note on the refrigerator said "Out to golf! Daughter." I nibbled on a piece of toast, washed the breakfast dishes piled in the sink, and dusted a few things. Donna kept the house in immaculate order.

Lena and Ilya had invited me, along with Bella and Felix Kaganov, to a picnic at Ravinia this afternoon, before the evening concert. I had accepted, sans Jack. I didn't think he was ready to spend more time with an all-Russian crowd. I never told him my plans; now it doesn't matter. As far as I'm concerned, business is business, and if that doesn't work, I'll find a job. I did it before, I can do it again. As for sex, I'll find that, too, if and when I need it.

I should have kept my mouth shut after Asya's call. To think that I've become so American that Asya's incredulity with my lifestyle shocked me! In her place I would also have taken it as a relinquishing of maternal duties. But I resented being made to feel I was not a good mother. Sasha wouldn't approve, either, but he would understand I've been waiting for him, whatever else I've been doing. In the Soviet Union, my affair, whether the man was married or not, would have been perfectly acceptable according to Russian standards, as long as it stayed a secret from Tanya. Asya would have been the first to help. According to the same standards, living with a boyfriend is taboo. What are the Russian standards?

I dressed and called Lena, leaving a message for her to pick me up on her way to Ravinia. Leaving my slippers next to Jack's by the front door—bad habits are contagious—I slipped on a pair of loafers, went out, and automatically headed toward Sylvia's house. Still unoccupied with no "for sale" sign, it looked exactly as it had in her lifetime. Even the lawn was freshly mowed, the door knob newly polished, the curtains drawn aside, the yellow lamp shade in the center of the window—only her non-smiling face with inquisitive eyes was missing.

An elderly couple in a large sedan stopped and asked for directions to the expressway. A white poodle eyed me suspiciously from the back seat.

Nancy's ice-cream parlor wasn't open yet, but I saw her head bob from behind the counter. I knocked at the door. She glanced up, and immediately her small feet in wide, flat shoes moved quickly toward the door.

"Miz Anna! Come in, come in. Haven't seen you since wedding." Nancy smiled broadly.

"Good morning, Nancy. How are you?"

"Not bad, not bad," she nodded contently. "Let me get scoop of ice cream for you."

"No thanks, I only wanted to say hello. How are your newlyweds?"

"Just fine." Nancy's face exploded into an even bigger smile. "Looking for a house. What's happened, Miz Anna? Everything okay? You look sad." Nancy took me by my hand and sat me at one of the tables.

"I'm not sad."

Nancy nodded sympathetically.

"I'm not sad," I repeated stubbornly and smiled.

Nancy continued nodding, ignoring my words. She took off her faded blue apron and sat across from me.

"I shouldn't keep you, Nancy, you have things to do."

"You my friend, Miz Anna. We not Americans who just say how are you. You tell me what's wrong."

"Nothing's wrong."

"Tanya says you in business with your American friend. Very nice, very nice. You should get married. I give you ice cream free for wedding."

"Thanks, Nancy."

"Tanya says she volunteers for nursing home. Very good girl, very good. I will never be in nursing home." Nancy pressed her palms together and rolled up her eyes. "My daughter wouldn't do that to me. We not Americans."

"One doesn't want to be a burden, though."

"In our culture, mother is never a burden. Tanya says her father is coming to visit."

"He applied for a visa."

"You don't like that, yes, Miz Anna?"

"Actually, I think Tanya should see her father again."

"Don't worry, Miz Anna. He come, he go. You have your American life. My brother wants me to visit old country. Maybe I go in winter, maybe. We so lucky to be in America. Everything else . . . who cares?" Nancy waved her hand dismissing the everying else. "Just one scoop, Miz Anna, please, one scoop?"

"Okay."

Nancy put her apron back on and hurried behind the counter. She threw a handful of nuts on a very generous scoop of chocolate-chip ice cream. I sat in the corner licking slowly, watching her clean and wash, and nod at me approvingly.

Life gets brighter in the presence of a motherly woman.

Tanya had not yet returned from her golf lesson when Lena and Ilya picked me up to go to Ravinia. I placed a note over Tanya's: "Tanichka, I went to Ravinia with Lena. Dinner's in the oven. Love, Mom."

Our group of eleven—five couples and me—consisted of familiar faces, and conversation flowed easily. Always among the audience of classical concerts, many newly arrived immigrants from the Soviet Union requested opera and symphony schedules in the same breath as asking for help in searching for their first jobs and apartments. Before the concert started, Bella asked me to accompany her to the washroom. On our way, we passed several knots of chatting Russians. As if by a prearranged signal, we went silent, so the others could neither eavesdrop on us nor know we could do the same. A silly instinct—after all, if we could tell they were Russian, they certainly could tell we were Russian.

Many English words now punctuate our Russian: appointment, message, come on, shut up, take care, insurance, accident, real estate, apartment, and many more, which either do not have a Russian equivalent or are just more conveniently said in English. My meetings with Howard and with Jack's attorney, and the intensive reading of the last month have added even more of these words. When terminology is involved, I don't have to translate anymore before I understand or reply. But informal chatter in English still doesn't come naturally.

"Tanya still taking golf lessons?" Bella asked when we were on a more-or-less Russianless path.

"Yes. Hard to believe a Russian would play golf."

"Well, our children don't consider it strange. How's Jack?"

"I'm glad he's not with us. It spoils everything to be obliged to interpret for him. Sometimes I just don't feel like doing it."

"That's understandable," Bella sighed. "Listen, Anya, Irena's really angry with you. This time I think she has a point. You never called to inquire about Vilen after his nasty fall—by the way, I still can't understand how it could result in a black eye, broken jaw, and the loss of two teeth. On top of it, it happened at your birthday party."

"That's my luck."

"Every time we talk, she lists what she and Vilen have done for you. Her conclusion—you don't need them now, since you have Jack to take care of you."

"Come on, Bella."

"I know, but what do you have to lose by calling?"

"I won't."

"Did Irena say or do something more outrageous than usual? I've told Vilen he should try to keep her from wrecking their relationships. He's more sensitive than she is."

The nausea normally associated with Vilen rolled in my stomach.

"Anichka, I don't want to complicate our lives. Irena insists she won't come to our house if you're invited, which is fine with me, but Felix adores his older brother."

"Bella, there's no question, Vilen and Irena must have priority."

"Why won't you call them?"

"I can't. I remember what they've done and I appreciate it, but I can't."

"I'm surprised at you, Anya. I always thought you were above petty Russian fights and messes."

It's a rare occasion to see Bella openly irritated.

"You're mistaken, Bella, I'm not above anything," I said indifferently and proceeded to change the subject.

Throughout the evening Bella's eyes returned to me with persistent questioning. They held the same look as Jack's.

thirty-two

I walked into the kitchen as Tanya slurped up the last of her cereal. She's grown in the last months and her hair seems to have darkened, taking on a chestnut color. Like millions of mothers, I'm struck by the disbelief that this is the same wrinkled baby whose buttocks fit in my hand only a short time ago.

"Hi, Mom! How was Ravinia? I think Jack is going to buy me a set of golf clubs next summer! Don't get mad, I didn't ask for them. We were talking about it and he said I don't need equipment this year and we'll look at some next year—that means he's going to buy me a set of clubs."

I sat down slowly.

"Mom, do you want some tea?" Tanya addressed me in Russian. "You know what?" She paused significantly and continued in English, "Jeff's going to write me from college!"

I couldn't help laughing at the victory in her voice. "That's expected if you're friends. Yes, I'd like some tea." Every chance I had I spoke Russian with her.

Tanya got up and walked to the stove to pour hot water into my mug. Her face went pink. "You know, I think he likes me more than just as a friend. I mean," she stammered, "different than a friend."

She avoided the word love.

"I'm sort of glad he's going away," Tanya said.

She brought the mug and tea bag to the table and sat down again.

"You are?" I smiled. "You'll see, you'll miss him."

"Maybe. But I want to meet other guys. Besides, Jeff isn't taller than me anymore."

"You can still be friends."

"I guess," Tanya agreed absent-mindedly. "You know, Jack was upset yesterday—even angry. He had a terrible golf game and he just dropped me off on the corner and left."

"I see." I tried to fill the pause remembering the argument with Jack after Asya's call.

I hurt him with my blind, instinctive reaction to protect the sacred space he invaded with his straightforward definitions of right and wrong. Our arguments, though infrequent, seem to get more hostile. The remnants of my pain, fear, and distrust surface in a tide of concentrated venom that floods me into surrender. But the intervals between the arguments seem to get warmer and more relaxed. How much patience does Jack have left?

Somehow, my conversation with Asya yesterday morning left me hurt and helpless. I need her and Sasha to understand, to respect me, to approve of me, and be as close as we've always been—so close that understanding, respect, and approval is a natural reflex.

"There're some messages for you." Tanya picked up a note pad from the table and started reading: "Helena Smolin is having a barbecue party three weeks from today. Call her. She said I should come too. Please, can I go? I want to see her house. Gena Korsunsky asked for Jack to call him. He said it was important. I gave him Jack's number in Green Bay, but he didn't want to make a long-distance call. Pat McDonald asked for you to call him in the morning before you leave for work. Joe Conley called from Natasha's house. He expects you to call him at eight tomorrow morning. His boss selected one of the people you sent to get a second interview."

Goosebumps prickled my back and arms.

Oh my, it's really happening. A second interview usually means a favorable decision. I'm going to be someone's boss, pay salaries and taxes, provide benefits, send invoices. Asya won't believe it. I almost don't believe it.

I will have to call Jack. My stomach tensed at the thought. Well, business is business.

Why did Helena invite me separately from Jack? Could he have already told her we're not going together anymore? It would be awkward, but I would like Tanya to see her house.

What does Gena want with Jack? It was important, but not enough to make a long-distance call—that's Gena all right. Someone told me Marina ordered a new ten-thousand-dollar designer fur coat. It would be interesting to know how much unnecessary root canal work Gena did, and how thick he had to pad his patients' insurance claims to pay for it.

This Soviet-made-Russian-American community is mine. It still lives by those Russian standards, so repulsive to Jack, that presume a stretchable definition of honesty, selective decency, and a deliberately sedated conscience. This sense of belonging is a reflex not present in my relationship with Jack.

I climbed into bed and opened my book. In a few minutes Tanya joined me, and for a while we just read.

I no longer count the pages I read; I simply read. Unfamiliar words do not stop me from understanding the plot and even from admiring or critiquing the style.

Tanya sighed, closed her book, and got up. I looked at the dent in the pillow where her head had been and, to my embarrassment, pictured Jack lustily smiling at me. There had been no desire for an eclair yesterday. My book went on the night table.

"Mom," Tanya's voice broke my concentration, "since I don't have a full course load my senior year, would you mind if I play golf on Wednesday mornings. I'd leave very early and only skip first period. I want to see how good I can get."

"How are you going to get to the golf course and back? We're not going to buy a second car."

"Jack's planning on playing, and in a month he'll be finished in Wisconsin and be with us all the time."

"What do you mean with us all the time?"

"I mean here, home. What else would I mean?"

"We'll see, Tanya."

"Thanks, Mom."

Jack answered the phone on the first ring.

"I hope I didn't wake you. I need to talk to you," I said quickly in response to a reserved hello.

"Well, what do you know? I thought decent women aren't allowed to call men."

I ignored the sarcasm. "Jack, Joe left a message that one of our people has been selected to come for a second interview. I'm supposed to call him in the morning."

"Did he say who it was?" I recognized the crisp, businesslike Jack.

"No, but I'll find out. There's also an urgent message for you from Gena Korsunsky."

"Why didn't you give him the phone number here?" Jack was irritated.

"Tanya spoke to him. He apparently doesn't make long-distance calls."

"Interesting. It's probably the normal Russian beginning of a potentially top-dollar real estate deal he offered me at your birthday party."

"What deal?"

"Anna, I'll handle it," Jack said, openly hostile.

"Don't enter into any deals with Gena!" I pleaded.

"I beg your pardon?" he inquired acidly.

"You don't have to talk to me like that. I apologize for what I said yesterday. It's unforgivable, and . . ." My voice trembled no matter how hard I tried to control it. "I know we're through."

"That's a fair picture. I'm ready to call it quits." Oddly, Jack's intonation had lost its sharp edge.

"Jack, Gena's a jerk. He commits fraud every day and he's proud of it."

"If that's true, isn't it commendable by Russian standards?"

"Unfortunately, it's perfectly acceptable, and it's done pretty much in the open. Listen, I need to talk to you about Tanya, but only if you could, for a moment, forget you hate me."

"I'm listening," he said after a long silence.

"Tanya is under the assumption you're going to live with us after you finish your project. In fact, she's looking forward to it. I don't know what to do."

"Anna, you know that has been my wish for a long time, but never my assumption."

I was grateful for the concerned, measured tone.

"I'm not saying you gave her the idea. I'm saying I haven't succeeded in making a home for her."

"You have nothing to blame yourself for," Jack sounded exasperated.

"Jack, I'm the only family she has, and she is happier with you than with me."

"Don't try to compare. Tanya admires you."

"I'm scared, Jack."

"You must be if you're discussing it with me."

"Tanya's attached to you."

"I know," Jack said quietly, "and it's mutual. Anna, don't cry. Crying won't help. Do you want me to talk to her?"

"I want her to be happy."

"I wonder if you want that more than you want to bring your past back. You snapped at me when your ex-husband wrote to you, you snapped at me yesterday when your girlfriend called. You snap at me every time something from your past comes up. I'm tired, Anna. Every time I wonder what's next."

"Nothing is more important to me than Tanya."

"Get out of your dream world and make your decisions."

"What do you want me to say, that we should live together for her sake?"

"Not at our expense," Jack responded.

"Well, at present, it isn't intolerable."

"That's all it is, not intolerable? Anna, do us both a favor. Don't try to make me a temporary father. I'm not father material. Tanya can always count on me, but as far as you and I are concerned, there can be only one reason for a commitment."

Commitment?

"Jack, I remember neither of us wanted a commitment. That's what made our relationship possible in the first place. There's a business commitment, but that's different."

"It's true that no one wants a commitment when a relationship first begins. In time, though . . . Listen, Anna, I don't know what you expect to feel, but don't tell me that your only emotions towards me have to do with Tanya and business. I might not be well-versed in vibes, but I sleep with you, and there are definitely some things you do not fake."

What are "vibes"?

I blushed. A long pause followed. I started wondering if Jack was still there.

"This conversation had to happen; a decision has to be made," his voice said unexpectedly. "I never imagined that after my return we would simply go back to sneaking around like we did before."

"Making love is not everything."

"Okay, Anna. Tell me one thing: would you want to live without it?"

"No." The reply escaped my lips before Jack had even finished the sentence. I could almost see his boyish grin. "All right, Jack, I enjoy making love with you, and I want to be in business with you. I just . . ."

"Anna, here's what we can do," he interrupted decisively. "I will move in, and we'll take it one day at a time, but not indefinitely."

"Well . . . as long as it's not indefinitely."

"Oh, God, I'm such a schmuck," he said with conviction.

The following week I showed up at home, limp from exhaustion every day, finding Tanya already in bed and my dinner, diligently warmed by her, lukewarm on the stove. By the time my mind and muscles unwound enough to let me feel hunger, but not nearly enough to force me to reheat the food, I compromised on a cold dinner washed down with hot tea.

Tanya and I spoke on the phone every day and left notes for each other on the refrigerator. Only once, on Tuesday, she waited up for me, sitting in the kitchen in her nightgown, her shoulders bent forward, her hands pressed between her knees. The delicious steam rising from the pot on the stove hit my nostrils and awakened my stomach, but my heart jumped to my throat as I caught the mournful expression on Tanya's face.

"Mom," she looked up and sniffed, "you know what happened?"

I sat down fighting the lump in my throat.

Tanya sniffed again. "The old man at the nursing home, Mr. Rifkin, the one that always kisses my hand—he died last night." She looked at me, swallowing her tears, waiting for a sign that his death could be reversed.

The image of Lonya on the floor of our room, staring up lifelessly, his glasses askew on his face, hovered so close I could almost touch it, then it floated away across my field of vision replaced by Tanya's terrified face. I pulled up my chair and took her hands in mine. Her face scrunched up in an effort to choke away the tears.

"You don't understand, Mom, I just saw him yesterday. He sang me a song that his mother used to sing to him, and he tapped his foot. I even thought how good his memory must be if he could remember that song."

"It's hard," I said hoping it was what she expected to hear. "It's going to hurt for a while."

"Yeah, it hurts. It's not fair. I just saw him yesterday."

"Did he have any family?"

Tanya retrieved her hands to blow her nose into a napkin.

"His son lives in Indiana. I met him today; I recognized him from the pictures Mr. Rifkin had shown me. He has . . . had . . . tons of pictures in his room. Vera says that the hardest is to visit a new patient in the same room where someone you knew died. We're going to the funeral tomorrow."

"Do you want to take a break from the nursing home for a couple weeks?" I suggested.

"Oh no." Tanya stared at me with astonishment. "I can't show the old people that I'm scared. They must always be scared. Somebody is always dying around them."

Helena Smolin was sincerely glad to hear I accepted her invitation. It turned out she assumed I, the lady of the house, would bring Jack. Ha! The lady of the house!

To Jack's amazement, Smith-Reynolds, Joe's company, hired our consultant.

Pat discovered a problem in my system design which made me work late into the night two days in a row, making changes that would enable him to proceed with programming.

I, and sometimes Tanya, kept Jack up-to-date. Jack's and my exchanges remained short and to the point, the way he liked it and the way I have come to like it. Neither of us mentioned our conversation of last Sunday.

On Thursday afternoon, I traveled to Green Bay to meet with the division heads. I could only hope that my firm gait and confident smile looked genuine. After the meeting I looked for Jack, but couldn't find him. I drove to his hotel, parked in the parking lot, and got out of the car right away, afraid I would lose my nerve if I let myself contemplate my next step.

In the Soviet Union for a lone woman to visit someone in a hotel would be practically admitting to prostitution. Nervously, I looked myself over in the ladies' room mirror, as if preparing for a date.

I could hear the television in Jack's room from the hallway. His door was slightly ajar, but he didn't answer when I knocked. I shrank at the sight of a couple exiting a room three doors down. What will they think of me? I knocked louder.

"Come in!" Jack yelled over the sound of the television.

I pushed the door open. Jack sat on the bed, making notes on a computer printout, a drink on the nightstand.

"Just put the tray on the table. I'll be with you in a second," he said without looking up.

The only table was a small round one to my left covered with more printouts.

"Good evening," I said flippantly, frozen inside. "There is no room on the table."

Jack's head bobbed up, and when the concentration cleared, his eyes twinkled with pleasure. I giggled.

"Anna!" Jack jumped up, knocking the drink to the carpet in his haste. "Why didn't you call to say you were coming?"

"I just came from a meeting with the division heads."

Jack's stare slowly drifted down my body, then he walked around me to lock the door.

"I thought you would want to know what we discussed."

Our eyes met. My sixth sense told me he was more nervous than me.

"Jack, have you ever done it in the shower?" For the first time I succeeded in willing myself not to blush.

For an instant there was total incomprehension, changing to surprise as his warm hands magically found their place around my shoulders.

"I don't care if you think I'm a pushover," he whispered in my ear then bit it lightly and covered my neck with quick, light kisses.

August 1, 1986

Dear Asya,

Just a note to tell you how touched I was that you went to the trouble of calling me to say happy birthday. Like the saying goes, one old friend is better than two new ones. Your call and the surprise party Tanichka, with the help of my boyfriend, Jack, threw for me made my birthday very special this year. I was so proud of Tanya. Remember my birthdays when we were in school? You were the only guest until I got married. Nothing will ever put a dent in the tie between us.

I know you were unpleasantly surprised about Jack living with us. Asinka, you will have to trust me that Tanya does not suffer from this arrangement. You know me, I would never to anything that would hurt her. Jack and I met four years ago. He's great friends with Tanya, and he's a wonderful person, but the differences between Russians and Americans on a personal level are insurmountable. He's divorced, and neither of us wants to get married again. What for? Too late for love. This way he doesn't have to worry I'm after his freedom or his money, and I don't have to worry about losing my freedom or suppressing my idiosyncrasies. Understandably, freedom is the common denominator. I hope Tanya follows old-fashioned relationships with men, but it's her decision to make.

She has volunteered, of her own accord, to work for a Jewish nursing home this summer. She's trying to decide if she wants to be a doctor or a teacher and feels the experience will help with her decision.

Asinka, I wish you were here. One of the most exciting weeks of my life just ended and I know that there are more to come. We placed our first consultant with a client. In a month we'll start working on a bid for a very large project. I'm sure that you are happy for me, even if you don't understand.

Rimma hasn't called yet. I can't wait to see her, to have her meet Tanya and Jack and the few acquaintances I've acquired over the years. She'll tell you all about my life when she returns.

Fima applied for permission to come for a visit. I know you don't like him, but he was a good father, and I'm glad he's coming. Tanya's waiting impatiently—she wants to have a father.

You know, Asinka, I'm beginning to believe we will see each other again. Life has so much more meaning with old, trusted, irreplaceable friends in my life.

Best wishes to your family.

Love, Anya

thirty-three

I took a half-day off work to make sure Rimma didn't miss her flight to New York, where she would change planes and continue on to Moscow, where a relative would meet her and put her on a train to Kiev. The traffic on the way to O'Hare Airport was so light I wondered if the airport hadn't gone out of business. After we checked her luggage, received her boarding pass, and found the correct gate, we still had more than an hour to spare.

"So, if the rumors are true and immediate family members are allowed to emigrate, you'll help my son Shura if he doesn't find a job in Los Angeles?"

"Yes, Rimma, I told you many times."

"But you said you can't guarantee."

"How can I guarantee? First of all, I don't know what experience he has."

"He's a very good programmer. He was an A student in school."

"I'm sure, but there are many sides to programming."

"Still, you have your own company."

"Rimma, if I can place him with a client, I'll be happy to. If not, Jack and I will give him some leads and show him how to search for a position."

"A client will take Shura if you tell them he's your friend, or maybe a nephew."

"No one is going to pay him if his skills can't be used. We compete with other companies to place every consultant. This is not the Soviet Union. If his skills are marketable, I will make an exception and hire him and then try to place him, but I don't think he would want to be paid and not do any work."

"Does it matter, Anichka? We're almost family."

"I hope it matters to him. Don't worry, Rimma. A young man with good English and a computer science education will find a job."

"Is there a guarantee?"

"There are no guarantees in the United States."

"See, and you tell me not to worry."

This dialogue, with minor variations, has been the main theme of Rimma's two-week-plus visit. Thank God, soon she will board a plane and fly out of my life. The day after tomorrow she will be in Kiev.

I found a water fountain and swallowed two extra-strength Tylenols before returning to her.

"So, in your opinion, my daughter-in-law should learn programming and not even dream of remaining a math teacher when she comes here?"

"Rimma, what makes you think if you ask the same question fifty times, and get the same answer fifty times, on the fifty-first try the answer will be different?"

That wasn't necessary. I've been patient for so long, what would another hour matter?

"Why can't you answer a simple question?" Rimma pursed her furry upper lip.

"I believe it would be prudent for your daughter-in-law to learn programming," I repeated for the fifty-first time.

"To think we could have left when my brother-in-law did! We didn't even consider it. My husband was the head of his department, I was a project leader, and I knew we couldn't get positions like those here. My father-in-law was a tailor and the tips for comleting clothes on time were more than my husband and I made combined. We had a car, we could even afford to buy tangerines on the open market. My brother-in-law and his wife were simple engineers and not on good terms with my father-in-law, so, they had nothing to lose by emigrating. Now these paupers have a house and two luxury cars and we have to struggle for food poisoned by radiation. Do you know how that makes me feel?"

"No."

"Angry, very angry," Rimma stated meanly.

"Project leader, a car . . . the Soviet system is still the Soviet system. Be happy for your relatives."

"Easy for you to say, Anya. You had nothing to lose, either."

"I had plenty to lose. My daughter's father to begin with. You're mistaken, Rimma, it's not your material welfare that kept you from emigrating—you were satisfied with the system. Admit it, you still are. Look at Asya; she had nothing to lose, but she stayed."

"Yeah. Anyway, I liked the climate in Los Angeles better than Chicago or Philadelphia, but if Shura doesn't find a job in Los Angeles . . ."

"Rimma, what are you talking about! No one even knows if emigration is going to resume."

"Shura will pay you back if you spend anything on him," Rimma assumed a dignified expression.

I peeked at my watch. Fifty more minutes.

The bag on the floor was stretched to the limit. Rimma sat protecting it with a leg on each side. Any and everything one could imagine was inside that bag: shoes, cosmetics, a leather jacket for her daughter-in-law, several calculators—the most tempting items, in Rimma's view, for the Russian customs officers to confiscate. She, too, wore a new leather coat in spite of the hot weather, fearing to pack it in one of the five large suitcases filled with clothes we had checked. I had paid a small fortune for the extra weight. Rimma had tearfully watched them disappear down a moving black belt. One could reasonably assume that by the time she claimed them in Moscow, not all of them would be returned, and those that were would probably not contain all their original contents.

The Russian community envied me my modest guest: Rimma never refused to accept used clothing, so I had less to buy. At my insistence, she went through the closets in my house picking out what she thought looked like received-in-a-parcel-from-abroad. Clothes carrying the received-from-the-West look marked a person as a breed apart. We made a trip to Jack's to do the same. Rimma's eyes sparkled at the sight of Jack's house. God knows what she'll say when she returns to Kiev. Her eyes shifted in all directions at once with a wild urge to take everything.

A large part of the contents of the suitcases were new, like the suitcases themselves: endless jeans, tennis shoes, T-shirts, sweaters, and an assortment of underwear.

The one evening I was not with Rimma I had shopped for Asya's family. My most expensive gifts were for Auntie Fira, Asya's mother. Not that I could put a price on her sponge cakes, warm pajamas, stockings, and scarves which Asya presented me with on my birthdays, but I wanted her to feel I remembered.

"Public aid is pretty good in Los Angeles." Rimma applied fresh lipstick, rubbing it even with her lips. "My husband and I would have enough to live on without depending on Shura."

"If emigration starts soon, you may still be able to find a job when you come here. You're only fifty."

"I worked hard to reach my position, especially with my 'disability.'" Rimma used the common euphemism for being Jewish. "Nothing similar is waiting for me in the United States. Why should I bother to look for a job?"

"Truthfully, the main thing is to get out of the Soviet Union, but Rimma, it won't feel right to become a user of the country taking you in."

"Anya, you talk like you're making a speech from a podium. My brother-in-law explained that with the status of political refugee, one is entitled to," Rimma ticked off each item with a finger, "public aid, food stamps, a subsidized apartment, stipends at city colleges, energy cost reimbursements, and . . . something else, I forgot."

Patience. Whatever she says, she deserves sympathy—she's going back to the Soviet Union.

"Rimma, he told you about American life. He wasn't giving you ideas on how to avoid working and to cheat the system. We all pay taxes to provide for those in need, not for those who can still be productive."

Rimma returned a blank stare.

"I'm not an idiot," she burst out, "I will not do menial work or accept a position beneath me. Not with my education."

"You have to start somewhere. And remember, Rimma, I'm one of the many idiots who did menial work."

"Of course, because you had a useless master's degree in literature and no husband."

I bit my lip.

"Easy for you, Anya, your future's all set. You look ten years younger than your age, you're clad in beautiful clothes, own a big house, get invited to parties by Americans, have a millionaire boyfriend. You have everything, so does everyone else, and neither my relatives nor any other person has been willing to explain how to achieve this level of comfort."

"I don't mind telling you. By hard work."

"Everyone gives me this standard, vague answer."

I started mentally counting the people beginning to congregate in the waiting area.

"Under the best of circumstances, we won't ever have as much as we have in Kiev." Rimma couldn't hide her irritation. "My daughter-in-law and her parents won't listen to me. They're refuseniks, dead set on emigrating. What can I do? I have only one son and one grandson. My daughter-in-law said I would never see them again if I didn't sign the consent papers for them to leave."

Consent papers—regardless of the child's age—nothing has changed.

Soviet problems. Soviet ugliness. Soviet hopelessness.

"Rimma, I'm sorry I didn't have more time to spend with you. I'm getting ready to begin a very large project. I've been so busy with work and helping Tanya apply for college, I sometimes feel my brain has turned to mush."

"What can I say, Anichka? In Los Angeles, my brother-in-law was unwilling to keep me longer than a week. He sent me off to a distant cousin in Philadelphia. My husband did so much for his younger brother, and that's his gratitude. You've been kinder to me than I ever expected. It was important I see different parts of the United States—to compare the climates. If my former coworker was not on vacation, I would stay in New York for a couple days instead of going straight to the Soviet Union," sighed Rimma. "They say, in New York one doesn't need to speak English, which would suit my husband well, and that it's possible to get good stuff cheap. I have no boots. I don't know what I'm going to wear this winter."

"I'll send you a pair."

"You shouldn't, Anichka."

I looked at my watch openly. Forty more minutes.

"Anichka, I want to ask you . . . your watch is not new . . . can you give it to me? You can buy yourself another one. My brother-in-law got one for my husband, but I need one too."

"We could still go to one of the shops here at the airport and get you one similar to mine."

I had to raise the credit limit on both my Visa and MasterCard during Rimma's visit.

"Absolutely not. You've spent too much on me already. It doesn't have to be a new watch."

"Rimma, this watch was a birthday present from Jack."

"In that case, forget I asked. You need to be careful and not displease him."

"Or what, he'll spank me?" I laughed.

Rimma's brown eyes, under neatly penciled brows, expressed shock.

"How can you be so flippant? Living together is no guarantee. You have to maneuver with extreme delicacy."

"Why?"

Her eyes held pity. "Anichka," she chided. "You can't be picky at your age, and with a child. Jack always has a wad of bills in his wallet. Money is number one in America."

"In America? Rimma, you told me you never considered leaving the Soviet Union because you had the money to buy tangerines! At least Americans place more value on freedom than fruit."

"I didn't mean to insult your Americans," Rimma patted my leg, smiling condescendingly. "You're just upset because Jack hasn't married you. It's so typical of men—they become disinterested in a woman after they sleep with her. The universal truth is, the more you give in to a man, the less likely he'll be serious about you."

"In what way did I give in to Jack?"

"You live with him, don't you, with no guarantees? He could drop you at any moment. Now, don't jump to conclusions, I'm not blaming you. Like any man he wants his pleasures when he wants them, but, Anya, Tanya sees it. If that isn't making the supreme sacrifice, I don't know what is."

She's right.

"I assure you, Rimma, Tanya's not in the room when we have sex."

"Anya!" Rimma's hands sprung convulsively to her cheeks. "Don't you think Tanya understands why you and Jack sleep in the same room?" she said, lowering her eyes. "Tanya shouldn't be exposed to . . . these things . . . unless, of course, Jack is to become your husband."

"Tanya wouldn't understand a relationship without sex, and, Rimma, she's not exposed to anything negative." I tried to sound pacifying.

"My God, you talk so nonchalantly! I warn you, she'll do the same, you'll see," Rimma stated in prophetic tones.

It's none of your business! Go back to the Soviet Union!

"Don't look at me like that, Anya. I wish you only the best, but a Russian man in his fifties would be better for you, if you ask me."

You're right, but I'm not asking you. A certain Russian man of fifty-nine, by the name of Sasha Rosenberg, would be just perfect.

"Tell me, does it bother you that Jack isn't educated?"

"Formally, you mean? No, not really. When he was growing up there wasn't as much emphasis on university training. He's very knowledgeable in his field, and he's a natural businessman, extremely hard-working."

"I'm not trying to discourage you. It's just . . . Anya, he didn't even know *Cherry Orchard* was written by Chekhov!"

"Rimma, I'm sure there are equally well-received pieces of American literature you don't know. Have you heard of Saul Bellow?"

"Okay, Anya, you don't have to fight with me. I'm not trying to take you away from your America."

"No one ever will."

"I'm not trying to take you away from your Jack, either."

A British accent announced boarding had begun for Rimma's flight to New York.

"Tanya's practical, not like you. She's already started playing golf so she'll meet the right crowd."

That's it. No more.

"Rimma, I'm sorry, I have to go now. It's the end of the day and I have to make some calls. We don't have a secretary. With my payments on the house and car, along with everything else, I can't afford one."

"You're paying for the house!?" Rimma boomed.

"Of course I'm paying for the house. I explained to you about the mortgage."

"You live with a man, an American man, a millionaire American man," Rimma screeched, "and you're paying for your house!?"

Leave. Leave. Leave.

I got up. "Rimma, I think you should board the plane."

Rimma, still flushed from the shock that Jack lived with me rent-free, picked herself up from the uncomfortable chair.

"Once again, Anichka, thank you very much, and good luck in whatever you're doing and however you're doing it."

"Good luck, Rimma. Kiss your mother, Asya, and the boys for me. And, Rimma, if you're happy with your life, don't emigrate—there's more than climate to consider."

"Hopefully, the decision won't have to be made. Our country is very different since Gorbachev came to power. He's an unusual person for his position."

"Rimma, Gorbachev is part of the old system and will never turn against it. How long and how many times do people have to be fooled, cheated, and beaten before they seek the roots of their problems? He told foreign reporters everyone was so happy in his country now that they don't want to emigrate."

"Don't be so hasty, Anya. It makes more sense than you think. There are better times ahead for us."

"Rimma, if there's any chance, any chance at all, people should take advantage of it and run, run as fast as they can. It doesn't matter where. What are you free of? Are you free of anti-Semitism? Are you free to be what you want to be?"

Tears streamed from Rimma's eyes as she threw her arms around me. "Anichka, I realize there's no future for young people in the Soviet Union. But it's so scary."

We kissed.

Rimma placed her leather coat between the handles of her bag. From the boarding ramp, she looked back twice, uncertainly.

I have to admit, when Rimma arrived I would have never recognized her if there had been other Russian women on her flight. The worried look and worn-out features gave her away. They couldn't have belonged to anyone but a Russian woman. She knew me immediately in spite of the ten-year separation.

"She looks so Russian," a disappointed Tanya had whispered in English, as Rimma waddled towards us, her smile displaying dark teeth.

Suddenly I found myself in Rimma's arms, squashed and drowning in the thick, forgotten smell of perspiration.

"You haven't changed." Rimma pulled back to inspect me as she shook her head, smiling broadly. "In shorts! A real American!"

She was only five years older than I, but the age difference seemed significant, and I felt inappropriately young.

Jack suggested I buy deodorant for Rimma then, except for one outing, firmly removed himself from any contact with her. He disliked her subservience and nosiness.

Our one outing all together had been for dinner at a seafood restaurant where Jack had arranged for Rimma to sample every appetizer and several entrees. She exhibited a remarkable appetite, telling Jack, in her slow but passable English, that she never thought Americans were so generous, and she would tell everyone in Kiev she had eaten shrimp. The grateful after-dinner kiss Rimma plopped on Jack's cheek was the last straw. She had grabbed his arm, leaned over, with her large breasts resting in the crook of his other arm, and laid a big wet kiss on his cheek. Jack extricated himself, motioned to the waiter, threw some bills on the table, and with a curt "Let's get the hell out of here!" moved toward the exit.

At the Smolin's barbecue, Rimma's Soviet guest status propelled her to the center of attention. She impressed everyone—besides us—with her English, her admiration for the United States, and her martyrdom of living in the Soviet Union.

Americans!

Cassie had now become dear old Marty's lawful wife. He spent the entire barbecue in an armchair dozing. She looked like his gentle grand-daughter. Diplomatically, Jack followed "Miss Manner's Rules of Etiquette" when in her company.

For the duration of Rimma's stay, assorted "petitioners" invaded my house, pleading with her to take various letters, pictures, medications, toys, clothes, and verbal messages back to Kiev for their relatives and friends. Although every story behind every request sounded different, they were also the same: stories of broken, bleeding ties, of longing to transmit and share the seductive feeling of freedom. I ran interference for Rimma as much as possible; she couldn't physically take or remember everything. I never yielded in my refusal to accept clothes and toys, as sending them through the mail was fairly reliable and affordable. A lady with a Leningrad accent berated me for not accepting a down coat for her sick sister, and with an eye on an unsuspecting Jack crossing the room, she accused me of trying to kiss up to an American by becoming as heartless as they are.

Irena, chin in the air, arrived with Bella.

"I'm not here to see you, I'm here to see your visitor," she announced producing a small package.

Bella shook her head, and I never interrogated Irena about the pack-age which, as Bella explained, contained two pairs of panties, a bra, and a purse for Irena's mother and niece. If only for the fact of my not having to see Vilen again, I allowed the package. I made another exception for Bella, who sent shoes for her mother and a shaving brush for her brother-in-law.

Out of her savings, Tanya bought a blue jeans suit and a matching cap for Petya. She wrote a short note to Fima: "Dear Dad, I'm sending a small present for Petya. Let me know as soon as you get permission. Love, Daughter."

"Is your friend Asya very much like her sister?" Jack asked after all the bags were packed and Rimma had disappeared in the bathroom for her last bubble bath.

"No, not at all. Their parents considered Rimma prettier and brighter, and that made her a little pushy. Asya is warm and considerate," I said wistfully.

"I hope so," said Jack. "Good night." He turned on his side, with his back to me.

We made love only once while Rimma stayed with us, on the night she arrived. The moment we finished, a knock on the door startled us.

Rimma's voice apologized in English, expressing hope she hadn't awakened us. She inquired how to turn on the shower.

"You know, I have this gnawing feeling she was eavesdropping," muttered Jack when I returned to bed.

After that, Jack made one or two futile attempts at lovemaking, then began turning away, sleeping at the edge of the bed. In the dark I felt surrounded by Asya, Sasha, Lonya, school dances, Sasha's first kiss, an elderly admirer at work who left poetry on my desk, Asya's wedding, Auntie Olya, and the Berezovsky boys. Slipping back into familiar apathy toward Jack came easily and naturally. Only my work brought reality.

As I watched Rimma walk away, down the ramp to the airplane that would take her back to a life she cherished, a life I thought worse than hell, my resentment dissipated. I had expected Rimma to bring my past—alive and bleeding—filling my present with roots, meaning, and a sense of continuity. I felt only sorrow.

Sasha, will you envy me like Rimma does, will you be angry like she is? Please, don't. Understand, freedom and opportunity come at prices matching their value. Foolish of me to expect to build my new life cleanly. Lies came along, lies of choice. Lonya always knew I was a bad lot.

For God's sake, Sasha, where are you?

"How did it go at the airport?" Tanya greeted me at the front door.

"Fine. I'm whipped."

"Cece called earlier and Jack just called."

"What did they want?" All I want is to be alone.

"Jack said he had to work late. Cece said to call her back. Something about a concert. Her Russian's too fast for me."

First a shower, then a few pages of my book to unwind. The day is almost over. The warm water streaming down my breasts to my thighs tickled, reminding me of the time when Jack and I made love in the shower. I turned up the hot water. The teasing subsided.

I wonder if Tanya ever thinks of Jack and me as lovers, or are we as sexless as natural parents or older adults are to a child? Her distress at any sign of tension between us is obvious, but she doesn't seem to be interested in how the tension is resolved, as long as it's replaced by what she perceives as harmony.

Tanya was in her room, half asleep, reading. I took my book and sat on the sofa in the living room to wait for Jack. Without him the house seemed empty. Concentration escaped me as I sat listening to the quiet. The ringing telephone was a welcome sound.

"Anya, birdie! Good news! Why didn't you call me back? Guess what?" Cece managed to make four sentences sound like one word.

"Good evening, Cece. What's the news?"

Car lights lit the living room.

"Aron Lerner will be giving a concert in Chicago!" The pause she made was calculated to hear the explosion this news would cause.

My heart contracted. "*The* Aron Lerner?"

Comedian Aron Lerner, the pride of Soviet Jewry, had never been allowed to tour in the West. His shows had always been strictly censored. Rumors ascribed stereotypical Jewish sins to him, like smuggling gold from Israel and God knows what else. Lerner is an institution, a tradition, a symbol. He's eternal.

"Speechless, aren't you?" Cece enjoyed the effect of her news.

Jack appeared in the living room carrying roses.

"How did you find out?" my incredulity made Cece laugh smugly.

"Find out? If it weren't for me, he wouldn't even be coming!"

Jack sat beside me. The roses in my lap emitted an intoxicating smell. My attention was on Cece.

"Who's on the phone?" whispered Jack.

My face answered, "Never mind."

"I convinced one gorgeous guy from New York to pay for his ticket. This guy used to be madly in love with me back in Moscow. He's a former movie producer from Moscow. You wouldn't believe it, he banged me everywhere. His wife hated me . . . ."

I hope Jack never learns Russian.

"Who are you talking to?" Jack's fingers were slowly tapping my arm. "Another guest coming from Russia?" he added sarcastically.

I shook my head, squirming to avoid his hands.

"Thank God. One more old bat and I'll be impotent forever."

"Cece, we're talking about Aron Lerner, not your former boyfriend."

Jack covered my neck with quick, light kisses, his hand crawled up my thigh.

"I'm trying to tell you, Anya, but you're not paying attention. My former boyfriend used to know Lerner's cousin, and she called him, and he called me. Are you talking to someone else?"

"My boyfriend just came in," I said, fighting a losing battle with Jack's hands.

"Hang up," Jack muttered from my chest.

I managed to move away for a moment.

"How old is Lerner?" I asked, trying to keep Cece on a subject other than men.

"Very old. He had a stroke, and his left side's no good. I bet we could price tickets as high as twenty dollars. Lerner will be happy with a couple hundred."

Jack closed my mouth with his. The phone fell to the floor chattering nonstop.

"I think I'm cured," Jack murmured, his hand way up my thigh.

Hot and tipsy from the kiss, the scent of roses, and Jack's hand, I picked up the receiver.

"Don't be long, I'll get an eclair," Jack said, disappearing into the kitchen.

". . . and I didn't even care about that man," Cece continued breathlessly, oblivious to the fact I hadn't responded for several minutes.

"Cece, what if Lerner has another stroke?"

"As long as it doesn't happen the night he's in Chicago. To visit the United States has been his lifelong dream. You and Lena can sell tickets."

"No. Frankly, I'd rather remember Lerner the way he was."

"Anya, birdie, you're too romantic. To take a picture with Lerner himself, isn't that worth anything to you? I thought you were a cultured person," came Cece's indignant voice.

"I guess I'm not that cultured."

"It's your American boyfriend's fault. You probably spend all your time in the sack. Americans are nuts about sex."

"Slow down, Cece. Lena might be willing to help sell the tickets. Got to go. Don't want to make my American boyfriend wait."

thirty-four

16 October 1986

Dear Anichka,

Thank you for the hospitality you showed Rimma and for the gifts you sent. You still have excellent taste.

You know from Rimma about our lives—nothing exciting. Rimma's machetunim are in the process of adding her son's and grandson's names to an old invitation received before their daughter was married and are planning to reapply for emigration.

They went through hell after they were refused six years ago. You've probably heard how these people were treated. For three years they couldn't find work. They sold their furniture and slept on the floor until quite recently, but they never lost faith. I would never be able to handle such a situation.

Life was actually never as bad as the dissidents portray it. Who needs all this freedom? It only brings all kinds of crooks to the surface. Of course, Chernobyl has changed things a lot. We don't know what we breathe, eat or drink anymore. But the worst was Kiev this summer, without children. They were evacuated to areas not affected by radiation. Even I would rather leave the country than live through another summer in a city with no children.

Rimma doesn't seem to be as upset at the prospect of emigrating as she was before her trip. She found the United States fascinating and can't stop talking about the abundance, the service, and the fact that people don't yell at each other in stores. Her husband wrote his brother in Los Angeles asking him to send them an invitation so they can apply as soon as possible. We know people who recently applied and were not fired from their jobs. Times have changed. Rimma and I are not very close, but the thought of never seeing her again is depressing.

From your letter and from what Rimma told me, I know your personal life has not been exactly the way you would like it to be. I'm not blaming you for taking a risk with Jack. After all, he has turned out to be a rather stable man, even if he doesn't want to marry you. Rimma and I decided not to tell anyone you're living with him. Maybe it's a good idea to try and hide it from Fima when he visits you. It would be best if Fima does not know, since he thinks the world of his daughter. Just to think he let her go—no wonder I always disliked him.

Fima spent two hours at Rimma's house when he came to pick up his gifts. He was extremely inquisitive about Tanya. Rimma was impressed with Tanya and with your professional success. Your pictures are beautiful. We can't get over how young and attractive you are. Rimma says you're a real American lady, that you wear shorts! Good for you! I remember how tense and down-trodden you were before. I'm very happy for you.

The information service gave the same answer: no Sasha Rosenberg. Myron made a special trip to the hospital where Sasha used to work, but the personnel office refused any information, telling him the usual thing about going to Israel if he doesn't like the Soviet Union. Those hateful anti-Semites! He asked some doctors in the hallways, but no one remembered Sasha.

We went to Lonya's grave. It's in perfect order: clean, with flowers and a little birch tree. The fence was freshly painted. I don't know what to tell you except that Lonya probably does have some relatives.

My mother asked me to send you a special kiss. She said she knew nature blessed you with many gifts; there simply was no love to make you blossom. She doesn't know about Rimma's plans yet. It will break her heart.

Regards from everyone.

Best wishes, Asya

20 October 1986

Dear Tanichka,

No answer from the immigration officials, but I expect to know about my trip before the end of the year. Thank you for the gifts.

Rimma, like everyone else who returns from a visit to the United States, gathered all her friends and relatives at her house and gave a "press conference." Her stories sounded like fairy tales. She praised you a lot, making me very proud. Thank you for the pictures. I put them out for everyone to see. Times have changed, I don't have to be afraid anymore. You look like a combination of your mother and my mother.

Rumors fly that refuseniks and immediate family members of emigrants should quietly apply for permission to leave. The process under way is not liberalization, but glasnost. Changes are not drastic; still, your mother wouldn't believe the things that are said openly now. Sometimes I wonder if it isn't too much. We'll see.

The government tells us the reactors in Chernobyl are practically buried, but our streets are constantly washed to decrease radiation. Much depends on the direction of the wind. Falling leaves contribute to increases in radiation. So they're loaded on trucks and buried in special landfills. This is not an easy job, considering Kiev is the greenest city in Europe. Professionals are being released from work to help collect leaves in the parks and streets. School-age children are forbidden to be used for this task, as no masks or gloves are available.

The number one problem is food. Not in terms of supply, we're not hungry, but in terms of radiation. Right after the Chernobyl accident groceries were delivered to Kiev from other parts of the country. Then we were told our own supplies were clean and we didn't need outside help anymore. But if the leaves are bad . . . People that own cars and have relatives in other regions are in a better position, at least as far as fruits and vegetables are concerned. I don't have either.

We live in an exciting time. Gorbachev has started programs against alcoholism, corruption, and irresponsibility. For success, he needs to breathe enthusiasm into those who've lost it. If he succeeds, a new generation will grow up as an entirely different people.

A Jewish theater opened in Moscow, and, for the first time in the history of Soviet television, a Jewish show was broadcast. It was a holiday for all Jews here. Hopefully, Jews will be allowed to prove themselves to the party and other organizations.

Recently there was an announcement that small, private service companies will be allowed. Writers and moviemakers are telling the whole shocking truth about the past. Tell your mother to read to you, or perhaps you could try to do it yourself, the latest issues of Soviet newspapers and magazines. You will be excited and impressed. Gorbachev is admired by everyone. If those who emigrated were here now, they would have an easier time, as the majority of them were honest and responsible. They're needed here. We'll talk about it when we meet.

See you soon, Your Dad

November 27, 1986

Dear Asya,

I reread your letter many times. Lonya's grave being tended is good news. He's all the family I've ever known and he sacrificed a lot for me. You always thought he was too harsh and overbearing, but I needed a strict hand. I wish he were with me now. Sasha was the only person who ever looked after the grave and its condition tells me he's alive, well, and in Kiev—perhaps under a different name. Hard to believe, but it is conceivable that Sasha, like Fima, found a way to change his name. Tanya's planning on interrogating her father about his name-changing. To her, it's not entirely aboveboard. Well, we know that it is and it isn't, but Tanya's an American kid believing in freedom or death.

I'm sorry for not writing right away. The last two months have been so busy that, except for business associates and their families, I've lost touch with almost everyone. I even had to relinquish grocery shopping to my housekeeper. About the only time Tanya and I relax and talk is on Saturday afternoons just before our company status meeting. I'm not complaining. I enjoy being in business, in spite of all the risks, responsibilities, and difficulties stemming from my lack of knowledge and experience. It's hard work, but I love it. My former coworker, Pat, agreed to join our company , even though our benefits aren't as good as he had. But he said my enthusiasm was contagious and he thought our company would go places.

My English is better, much more fluent. I try to read as much as possible, even if it's only a few minutes at a time. So, as you see, I haven't really changed that much.

Today is Thanksgiving, and it's the most meaningful holiday for newcomers to the United States. Tanya and I had dinner together and reminisced about our early Thanksgivings here. Jack went to Florida to have a traditional turkey dinner with his mother, and he's already called to say he missed us.

His mother hasn't been well lately. He always spends the long Thanksgiving weekend with her. (Thanksgiving is always on a Thursday, and he leaves on Wednesday and returns on Sunday evening.) Last year I had a housewarming party on Thanksgiving and his mother came to Chicago. It was the first party I had given in ten years.

Jack's mother dislikes me and constantly asks Jack to break up with me and marry a younger woman who can have children. I agree with her wholeheartedly, and she knows it, but that doesn't prevent her from considering me a golddigger. I don't dislike her. To me, mothers seem to hold a special fascination. At my age it would be ridiculous to suppose they induce a daughter's longing.

Like most American Jews, Jack's maternal grandparents came to America in the early part of the century from a shtetl in the Ukraine, I think it was Skvira, where your father was from. They spoke mostly Yiddish. His grandfather owned a bakery in New York where the entire family worked. It's a typical story. Jack's father was a wealthy Jewish businessman from Argentina. He died when Jack was fourteen. It's interesting, Asya, every family in the United States of America comes originally from somewhere else and has a reason to give thanks to this country.

Asinka, I'm touched you're concerned about my reputation, but believe me, there's nothing shameful about my living with Jack, and it would be demeaning to cover it up while Fima is visiting. It's my new life and he'll have to take it or leave it. Jack's not someone whose friendship Tanya or I should be embarrassed about. It would be a poor way of repaying him for what he's become to Tanya. She wouldn't understand the benefits of your suggestion. I do realize there's merit to it, only these years outside the Soviet Union have made me a lousy liar. As far as my reputation is concerned, to you I'm the same Anya you've known for thirty-seven years.

Tanichka has started her last year in high school and is still volunteering time at a nursing home. I don't know where she got all the patience and compassion from. She was dating a boy from her school for a few months, but he graduated and left for college in another state. It doesn't seem like a serious relationship, on her side anyway, thank God. I'm not in a hurry. I hope, someday, she has a big family. I want her to be happy.

Asinka, don't worry about Rimma, she won't be alone here. The important thing is to get out if the opportunity presents itself.

Doesn't it feel good to talk again, like in the old days? Many kisses to you and your family, especially your mother, and happy new year to all of you.

Love, Anya

November 27, 1986

Dear Dad,

I was disappointed that you haven't received permission yet. Why is it so difficult, and why do you need permission to visit your daughter? Hopefully, you will come next year before I start college, when I will have time to take you to all the places I've been planning to show you.

Today is a holiday called Thanksgiving. It's an American, not a religious holiday. Everyone celebrates it since the first pilgrims reached America and gave thanks to the land they found. It's always on the fourth Thursday in November.

For immigrants this holiday is very special. Mom gets really sentimental and always reminds me that in America everyone came from somewhere else and we should never forget how fortunate we are, we should never take anything for granted. I know what she means, especially after reading your letters and hearing so much about Russia on TV, and from listening to Mom's stories of her life in Russia.

I don't understand how you can say your life is exciting if your government makes you collect radioactive leaves with bare hands. Now that you have all these freedoms you should protest.

Mom and Jack's business is doing very well. They've placed eight people, and after the New Year they're starting a big project. Jack says Mom is hard as nails. Right now our house is the company office. They work and argue and have big meetings. Mom started looking for office space and interviewing more people. She's really busy and always tired. She hardly has any time to read, but she loves what she's doing and she's always in a good mood.

I'm still volunteering for the nursing home, but I spend fewer hours there because of my homework. I really like some of the patients. I'll introduce you to them. You'll meet everyone I know. Many of the patients came from Russia a long time ago and can still speak Russian.

Tomorrow, Mom and I are going shopping for a car. I can't wait. She's worried about spending the money, but I think she should buy a good car, because she's an executive. When I have my own money, I'm going to buy a convertible. Before I thought my money would go for all kinds of school expenses, or I'd just give it to Mom so she wouldn't have to work.

I'm looking forward to seeing you.

Love, Daughter

8 January 1987

My Dear Tanichka,

This morning the permission to visit you was finally in my hands. Next to the day you were born, this is the happiest day of my life. Thanks to my wife's foresight and connections, a month ago my name was placed on Aeroflot's waiting list. My boss told me that I could only take my regular thirty-day vacation if I travel now, but if my trip is delayed until after March when my project is due, I could have six weeks! As eager as we are to see each other as soon as possible, I hope you'll agree that two additional weeks together are worth the wait. My wife will write her cousins, Roman and Valentina Bloom, where I'm going to stay, and they will get in touch with you. I will take the night train from Kiev to Moscow on April 8. My airplane ticket will be for travel on April 9, from Moscow to New York. From there, as I know from others, you will have to either meet me or have someone else meet me with tickets to Chicago.

I wish I could buy something beautiful for you, but for the last two years the variety, quality, and quantity of goods hasn't improved. On the contrary, the supply of some goods is scarce and some items are more expensive. People like myself who live honestly on their salary haven't really lost much, but thanks to Gorbachev, the crooks and machinators are now threatened.

It has to be understood, however, that whatever the democratic reforms are going to be, socialism must and will remain socialism and not transform into capitalism. Gorbachev didn't get smart overnight. Everyone on the top knew what was going on, but no one wanted to change the familiar order or cause trouble and risk their privileges. They would do anything to keep their privileges.

It's incredible, but true, that in exchange for American grain, they let hundreds of thousands of Jews emigrate, the majority of whom, like your mother, were not anti-Soviet, merely honest professionals that Gorbachev needs so badly now. If these people hadn't felt useless, and if it had been possible to survive on the peanuts they were paid, I am positive they would never have left their motherland. Never.

Those who remained true to our land will support perestroika. If the principles of perestroika succeed, the principle of social justice, cherished by Marx, Engels, and Lenin, and fought for by our fathers and grandfathers, will win. Only social justice can guarantee, for our children and grandchildren, life in accordance with their abilities and ambitions. Gorbachev deserves respect for what he's done. For him, there's no way back now. He has stood up against the very institutions people have been afraid to even mention.

It won't be easy to throw out the old apparatus and replace it with decent people. Positive results will take time. In fifteen or twenty years a whole new generation will have grown up as decent people. There are many now who understand freedom as a license to rob and cheat, to form Nazi-like organizations such as Pamyat, which accuses Jews of any and everything. For them the *old song that your mother must remember hasn't changed: "If there is no water coming from your faucet, it can only mean the Jews drank it all."*

I will bring some newly published books with me, books that tell the truth about the past. Please, let me know what else you want. Soon, very soon, my little girl, we'll be able to sit down next to each other and talk. That's what my visit to you is all about.

Love, Dad

12 January 1987

Dear Anichka,

Your letter arrived December 28, the day Myron's mother was rushed to the hospital. She died the next morning. She was a very active seventy-one-year old woman who died due to an erroneous diagnosis and plain laziness on the part of the hospital doctors. They don't even try to hide the fact that Soviet medicine is thirty to forty years behind times.

Myron is devastated. His confidence is gone. He even said you were right eleven years ago when you saw things which are only now being exposed. I'm afraid we have no choice. Few people have applied to emigrate, as we all believe the Soviet government will not repeat the same mistake of allowing large numbers to leave the country. Only those proving they have immediate family abroad, dissidents, refuseniks, and crooks may be able to leave. Those who have not been active in anti-Soviet campaigns in the West are welcome to visit us. The Soviet government is desperate for hard currency. Perestroika is good, but we do envy you in a friendly way.

Rimma's son, Shura, has collected almost all the paperwork necessary to submit to the immigration office. Rimma and her husband have already signed their consent. My older son, Dima, spends a lot of time with Shura and it makes me anxious. Rimma has become moody, still talking about her visit. She constantly compares her everyday life to that in the United States, and the comparison is not to our advantage. Sometimes I think it would be better if she hadn't taken that trip. Their income isn't bad and she was always satisfied before.

All we do is work, stand in food lines, and read, read, read. It's impossible to catch up with all the news and previously forbidden fiction. You should read some of it, you'd be impressed. Anichka, please write to me regularly. Your letters light up our dull existence with a touch of fairy tale fantasy.

Anichka, I'd like to ask a favor. Myron's doctor refuses to take money in payment for her visits. She's afraid of being caught, besides there's not much one can buy. She wants something from the West. Since she's a very fashionable lady, we thought maybe you could send some fabric for her. I know fabric is considered raw material and is not allowed into our country, so if you would sew it together, fold it on top and make a simple hem, it could be called a skirt on your postal declaration and easily sent. Don't forget to attach a tag to it, so they can see it's a new item. Any tag will do, the customs people don't know the difference. If we don't thank her, Myron will have to go to his official, regional doctor, and although he's free, he's a jerk and doesn't know a man from a woman.

It sounds from your letter you've become quite an American business-woman. It's hard for me to understand your relationship with your boyfriend. Don't show him you're in love; he'll only take advantage of you. Be careful. If Tanya sees him drop you, it could be even worse than knowing you live together.

Kiss Tanya for me.

Love, Asya

January 28, 1987

Dear Dad,

I danced around the house with your letter. Mom cried and said I'm fortunate to know both parents. We already have a list of places to take you. I don't need anything. It's too bad you don't have a telephone. Maybe you could call us from someone else's house when you get your ticket. Don't worry, we'll find a way to fly you from New York to Chicago. Learn some English.

See you soon.

Daughter

January 28, 1987

Dear Asya,

Your letter came today along with a letter from Fima telling us he received permission to come for a visit. All of a sudden the whole world seems to have lost its luster. On one hand, I realize how fortunate Tanichka is to know and be loved by both parents. On the other hand, just the thought of seeing Fima again brings nothing but distress and anxiety. You should read his letters. His praising of Gorbachev sounds like a broken record made from an official Soviet newspaper. But then, that's also how he sounded when he was praising Brezhnev. I wish his visit were over.

We are starting a very big long-term project in a few days and we're moving into our new offices on February fifteenth. Jack had both our accountant and lawyer provide me with some invaluable training, but I'm still somewhat awkward and insecure in many business situations.

I regularly work ten-hour days, go to the health club once a week, and on Sundays visit the library to read magazines and browse. Soon, due to our housekeeper, Donna, I'll probably forget how to wash even a cup. It's annoying *sometimes. If my business fails, I'll find myself a good-for-nothing, spoiled, middle-aged woman.*

Asya, why did you come to the conclusion I'm in love with Jack? Thankfully, I'm not. There's nothing I wouldn't do for him; after all, he's done wonders with Tanya. She used to be ten going on thirty, now she's simply a teenager. Being serious and responsible is her nature, but now she's a normal, carefree . . . well, almost carefree, teen. I'm very grateful to Jack and I enjoy having him as a partner. Anyway, love it is not, but, nevertheless, while it lasts it's a good relationship.

Tanya is radiant. She called all her girlfriends to tell them her father is coming. Seeing her so happy is a consolation. Let's hope she won't be disappointed.

Fima will stay at his wife's cousin's home. I expect they'll call us soon. Frankly, I'm not interested in seeing new Russian faces.

Say hi to all your family.

Love, Anya

P.S. I've become involved with a fund-raising campaign for the JRL and am enjoying it. Generally, Russians don't donate to causes, but we have to start learning to.

This turned out to be my last letter to Asya before Fima's visit. The postscript referred to my spending evenings on the phone soliciting donations from Russians. How I fit it into my schedule I'll never know, but I did. Lena had been canvassing Soviet immigrants for funds for quite a while, muttering complaints, sighing, and threatening to never talk to Russians again.

The fair-share concept has always been hotly debated in our community. It leans toward the opinion that people who only have a few years to enjoy success are entitled to liberal treatment and shouldn't be held accountable to the same standards as Americans, who have the same income but were born here.

It's a rather common notion of "We suffered enough; now we're due for compensation." After a job—education for children, a house in the suburbs, furniture, a car, good vacations, fur coats, subscriptions to the symphony and opera are considered integral parts of our lives. Then a bigger house in a better suburb and a better car. And on it goes.

Donations in any form have not made it onto the list of priorities. Some lament they simply can't afford it. Some suggest whoever helped us should have enough money to help others. Fair-share remains a loose concept formalized as "Why should I give? I'm not on my feet yet myself." The society of bathrooms shared by many families, of common property, and of universal equality of paupers has given birth to the most "give me" group of people imaginable.

What neither Lena nor Leah-Malka were ever able to convince me to do, a Russian colleague of theirs from the fund-raising committee did with one phone call.

After verifying my name and address this lady spoke in a tone allowing no argument.

"You donated five hundred dollars last year and your pledge for this year is one thousand dollars."

I conceded these were the facts.

"Would you increase your pledge? JRL needs the money to help Russian Jews get out of the Soviet Union," reproached the lady.

"Well, the year has just started and my daughter is beginning college in the fall . . . I will send more if I can."

"Bear in mind, we have information about everyone's income, and we not only know how much you give, but how much you can afford to give."

"I thought incomes are confidential information."

"We have our sources," retorted the lady menacingly.

"Well, in that case, I am definitely not increasing my pledge!" I fumed.

After listening to my repetition of the conversation, Jack laughed heartily.

"That's one way of scaring potential donors. Listen, what she said is bullshit, pardon my French." He grew serious. "I'll call the JRL. Did you get her name?"

"Jack, the point is, it's time for non-Russian concepts to rub off on us. We can't use the very methods we ran away from. There are times when I wish I could hide the fact that I'm Russian."

"The JRL needs better training for their volunteers. Don't worry; they have no income information."

"I wouldn't be worried if they did. That's not the point. Don't call the JRL. I'll call myself."

When I told her, Lena moaned and groaned over the blunder and pleaded with me not to mention it to their American fundraising supervisor, but eventually she released her name and phone number.

The supervisor, a pleasant, very suburban, American lady tried to placate me with platitudes like: "nice of you," "isn't that awful," "let me assure you," "we are grateful for every dollar," "will meet with my volunteers again," and "I do appreciate." Americans always try to make one feel comfortable, whether they plan to do anything about the situation or not.

Needless to say, her efforts can do nothing to change my people. We have a long way to go, and it's high time some of us started and, if I was one of the first to come here, why shouldn't I start?

My fundraising activities met with limited success and brought aggravation galore, but then there were those who understood and who promised to talk to their friends, and who actually thanked me. When the campaign folded in the spring I had the feeling of having grown. I now distinguished more shades in the world around me.

thirty-five

Fima's relatives appeared on my doorstep one Sunday morning two weeks before Fima's arrival. Tanya was shooting baskets in the yard and Jack had gone to get lox and bagels. Working in the office, I faintly heard the doorbell and walked to the door wondering why Jack hadn't come around to the open back door as usual.

The couple smiling at me were obviously Russian: a stocky, blond man, with pinkish cheeks and a stomach overflowing his jeans, and a heavy, blonde woman with a fresh perm, deep-green eye shadow, and purple lipstick. The man wore a red V-neck sweater with dark glasses hanging from the vee. Two thick, gold chains hung around his neck and graying tufts of hair protruded around the neckline of his sweater. The woman's black sweater with white metallic leaves shimmered as she moved. Her black pants appeared one size too small. They greeted me in such familiar Russian that I panicked for a moment thinking they were expected.

"Sorry for not making an appointment," said the woman coarsely. She smelled of nicotine. "We're not Americans with their stupid appointments."

"Are you sure you're at the right address?" I asked politely.

"Aren't you Anya Fishman?" the man broke in.

"Yes, I'm Anya Fishman. How can I help you?"

"You look exactly the way Fima described you in his letter." The man hooked his fingers behind his belt, barely seen under his stomach and looked me over with approval. "I'm Roman Bloom and this is my wife Valentina. I'm Zhanna's cousin. She's married to your first husband. We were in the neighborhood and decided to meet our new relatives." He spoke too loudly.

Following my hospitable gesture, the pair advanced into the house.

"Excuse me, may I come in?" Jack magically materialized behind the couple with two large brown bags.

My guests let him pass. Jack's brows flew up questioningly.

"Take care of your delivery," said Valentina benevolently, sizing up the rooms.

"It's not a delivery. My boyfriend bought breakfast. Would you care to join us?"

Valentina's hand stabbed her husband's thigh meaningfully. Roman's eyes critiqued Jack's stretched and faded sweat pants.

"Thanks, we already had breakfast," she said primly.

"Then, perhaps, some tea or coffee?"

They followed me to the kitchen.

"An American!" I heard a coarse whisper from behind.

"Sh-sh-sh," replied another whisper.

Tanya turned from the sink, her hands dripping soap suds. Jack was unwrapping the food. The kettle began to whistle.

"This is my daughter, Tanya, and this is my boyfriend, Jack," I said in English.

Tanya dried her hands with a paper towel. Roman retrieved one hand from behind the invisible belt and shook hands with Tanya and Jack. Although clearly disapproving, Valentina did the same.

"Nice to meet you," muttered Jack.

"Tanichka, these are your father's relatives. He's going to stay with them while he's in Chicago," I said formally in English.

As the couple sat down, Roman said, "It's easier for me to speak Russian. We didn't know you have . . . that you are . . ." he cleared his throat into his fist ". . . busy. We only wanted to meet you, to give you our telephone number and decide who will meet Fima at the airport. We think you should, since some friends of ours will meet him in New York. You'll have to pay for his ticket to Chicago and back to New York . . . he's really coming to see you . . . and . . . you know." Roman glanced sideways at his wife for support. "We wanted to tell you . . . I mean, we don't make enough to feed a grown man for six weeks. We are not rich like our Soviet relatives think, and as Zhanna met Fima after we left . . ."

Tanya went crimson. "We'll pay for his ticket and we'll buy the groceries," she cried out in English looking at me.

Jack raised his eyes from the sandwich he was preparing.

"I understand perfectly." I hoped I sounded casual. "It's not a problem. You'll have everything you need."

Tanya nodded gratefully at me.

"Maybe you can give us a call when you can talk freely." Roman stressed "freely" then, glancing at Jack, added in heavy-accented Russian-English, "I wish you good appetite," a verbatim translation of a Russian idiom.

His eyes full of laughter, Jack thanked him.

"I can talk freely now." I wanted to get this visit over with and see as little of these people as possible in the future.

Valentina took a striped pink candy from the bowl in the center of the table.

"I'm a frank person and let me tell you, one never knows what Americans think. They're pay-nas." Valentina's sense of superiority came through clearly.

"What's 'pay-nas'? I don't remember any such word in Russian."

"It's not a Russian word. It's what Americans always say."

"They do?"

Judging from Jack and Tanya's indifference, they hadn't recognized the word, either.

"Yes," confirmed Valentina, "you hear them all the time when they don't like something—'pay-nas, pay-nas.'"

"Valya, I keep telling you." Roman got up and motioned his wife to do the same. "It's not 'pay-nas,' it's 'pain-in-ass.'" The words, with long pauses between them, were pronounced in a loud, patronizing tone.

Tanya opened her eyes wide. Amazement appeared on Jack's face. I bit my lip.

"That's what I said, didn't I? My husband thinks he's a professor. Anyway, write down our number and call us. Let's go, Roma." Valentina nudged her husband with her shoulder then addressed Jack primly in English. "Good-bye, nice meeting you."

Jack rose and bowed.

The computer display informed us Fima's plane had already arrived at the same gate Rimma's had departed from last September.

"We're late," whined Tanya in despair, holding back tears.

"Quick!" I ran ahead without looking at her.

During the trip to the airport we hadn't said a word, even while sitting in the parking lot commonly called a traffic jam. I felt an irrational fear of spilling out emotions and energy accumulated in anticipation of our meeting Fima. For a week, ever since Valentina called with his flight information and a warning that Soviet guests eat like they've never seen food before, we have been robot-like.

Tanya had put together an enormous grocery list. The Blooms would certainly not lack food. Tanya continually apologized for the expensive and unusual items she had on the list.

Last night, while Jack was working in the basement, Tanya came into my bed and snuggled next to me. After a while she said, "What if it turns out I don't love my father?"

I didn't know what to say, so we just lay there motionless until Tanya rolled out of the bed and quietly said good night.

Tanya, up at five in the morning, waited for me in the kitchen, her thick hair combed, cereal eaten, face solemn. We didn't have to leave until noon. To ask why she got up so early was unnecessary. Again, I had nothing to say. The butterflies in my stomach made me choke on my food.

Jack strode in as I finished my tasteless tea and toast, glanced at us and pushed up his glasses.

"Good morning, ladies!"

"Jack, what if it turns out I don't love my father?" asked Tanya playing with the spoon in her empty bowl.

Jack stopped in his tracks. I looked past him through the window.

Jack straddled a chair. "Your father loves you."

"How do you know? He hasn't seen me in eleven years. It wasn't his fault, but still . . . he could have written. What if *glasnost* hadn't happened?"

"He loves you, Tanya," said Jack slowly. "Trust me."

Tanya raised her eyes. "But what if I don't love him?" she demanded. "I don't want to lie to him."

"Be fair, keep an open mind. It might be best to just play it by ear."

"I don't want to hurt him."

"Tanya," Jack rested his chin on the top of the chair's back, "you can't expect to love him as if you've known him since you were a baby. But remember, adults develop all kinds of bonds that are very rewarding, whether they call them bonds or not," he threw a glance at me. "I'd better go and shave."

The gate, of course, was the farthest. My calves ached from running in heels.

"Tanichka?" said a man's voice.

A middle-aged man in a long, dark, wool coat stood awkwardly amid the chairs in the almost empty waiting area. Tanya and I stared at him, unsure the voice belonged to him.

Tears swelled slowly in his eyes. "Tanichka!" the tears slowly rolled over his lashes, hesitated then continued down his cheeks. Through his tears he smiled.

"Fima!" I yelped, immediately covering my mouth with my hand.

He didn't seem to hear me.

Tanya stepped back, closer to me, crying.

"Tanichka, I'm your father," Fima said quietly, his arms hanging limp. His voice seemed unfamiliar, but his face as familiar as an old portrait.

"I'm sorry, Fima, I'm sorry." My words were not loud enough to reach him.

In Russian the meaning of the expression used as "sorry" is "forgive me," and this was not the time to explain I only meant sorry, sorry I had to hurt him and that forgiveness was not possible—was, indeed, irrelevant.

Tanya approached Fima stiffly, her eyes glistening. He hugged her firmly, his face haggard. My stomach tensed to the point of nausea. Fima took Tanya's face between his hands studying her features.

Without the smile, the family resemblance was not nearly as strong as I always believed.

"You're a beautiful girl." Fima spoke with more ease, his hands relinquishing her face.

Tanya sniffed, looking from Fima to me, wiping her eyes with the back of her hand. She apparently sensed, with a child's unmistakable intuitiveness, we had our adult business to attend to.

"Let's get your luggage." Her English sounded out of place and she repeated herself in incorrect, American-accented Russian.

"She should learn Russian," Fima reproached me, our eyes meeting for the first time.

I felt nothing.

"How are you, Anya?"

This man gave me Tanya. I took her away.

"I'm sorry, Fima."

Tanya lowered her head, her cheeks red.

"How could you do this to me?" There was no anger in his voice, merely incomprehension.

"I had to. You'll see why."

He looked at my hair and every feature of my face separately, as if reacquainting himself, then moved his lips to say something, but didn't.

Tanya led the way to the lower level to retrieve a bulging brown suitcase, then to the parking lot.

"Who do all these cars belong to?" Fima gazed around at the endless rows of bumpers.

"To people that come to the airport," Tanya said in a brash, teenage, what-a-stupid-question tone, accompanying her reply with a shrug.

Fima took off his coat, folding it neatly.

"Why don't you put your coat in the trunk," suggested Tanya.

She hasn't said "Dad" yet.

"What? This is a good coat, we built it just before I left," Fima sounded offended.

"Built?" Tanya looked at me helplessly.

"I needed a coat for the trip. It's still cool outside."

With no further objections, the coat was placed respectfully on the back seat.

The forgotten expression "built" referred to the making of fundamental clothes like suits and coats, to the struggle of getting the fabric, lining, buttons, padding. I guess perestroika, which means "rebuilding," hadn't yet touched this particular construction site.

Tanya, in the back seat, leaned forward and Fima, sitting in front, turned sideways to face her, not always following her finger as it pointed to the sights we passed. His voice gradually became more familiar, but the eerie sensation that I was dreaming seemed stronger than the physical awareness of the three of us driving home together in the United States of America.

My participation in the conversation was limited to the translation of English words and phrases Tanya didn't know in Russian and to the explanation of phenomena and actions Tanya didn't realize required explanation. The need to keep my eyes on the road gave me a good reason not to look at Fima as I spoke.

Fima's comment "a one-storied America," a quote from the Russian poet Mayakowsky, who visited the United States soon after the Bolshevik revolution, was the same I had made eleven years ago. Unexpectedly, I turned to Fima and smiled with understanding, an understanding which naturally escaped Tanya. Fima's eyes sprung alive. He diligently explained to Tanya that practically everyone in Soviet cities lived in big buildings where the state allotted each family an apartment.

"It's like the projects, right, Mom?" She drew a parallel quickly, anxious to assure Fima she understood.

Now he was lost and Tanya, in twisted Russian, presented to her die-hard communist father the capitalistic system of public aid, justifiably reminding her of the socialistic system.

True to the preplanned arrangement, I drove by Tanya's school. Classes had just ended and a line of yellow school buses and student cars merged with oncoming traffic, slowing us down.

She still hasn't called Fima "Dad."

"Whose cars are these?" Fima inquired.

"What cars?"

"The cars coming out of your school."

"The students'." Tanya had the same incredulous inflection in her voice.

I'll have to make sure she doesn't use this tone again.

"School children have cars?"

"The majority of juniors and seniors do. I don't," Tanya sighed. "Don't worry, though, we rented a car for Mom so I can drive you around in hers."

"Thank you, Daughter. What are all these yellow buses?"

"School buses. They bring kids back and forth to school."

When we made the last turn Tanya said all in one breath, "This is our street. This is the house where Mom's friend used to live; she passed away. And this our house."

Fima got out, carefully retrieving his coat from the back seat. In the bright daylight his skin had a sallow tinge.

"Why an American flag—is that an official building?" Fima pointed to Peggy's house down the street.

Tanya laughed. "No, it's our neighbor's house. They just wanted a flag over their garage door."

"Who gave them the flag?"

"Gave? They bought it."

"Tanichka, a flag is sacred and someone has to control whose hands it falls into."

Tanya's eyes begged for help. When Rimma, in a Russian food store, asked us not to mention she was here on a visit so that she would not be recruited by the CIA, Tanya had called all her friends, laughing over the story. She couldn't laugh now; Fima was her father.

"Let's go into the house, Fima. We have some time before Roman picks you up."

"Wait, we need to get my suitcase. I've got presents for you."

I unlocked the door and walked in, trying to see my house with Fima's eyes and Fima's mind.

"So this is where you live." Fima put his suitcase down near the sofa. "A lot of space."

"Tanya, show your father around. I'll make something to eat."

On the way to the kitchen I heard Tanya reciting the features of the house like a real-estate broker.

She still hasn't called Fima "Dad."

Fima and Tanya came into the kitchen holding hands. We really weren't hungry. Fima only ate a salad, unable to fathom fresh vegetables in April.

"Anya, my wife has a distant relative in Chicago who's a doctor. His name is Korotki. Have you heard of him? She wrote asking him to see me. I'm having some stomach problems." He didn't even skip a beat. "You will pay for it, won't you?"

"I haven't heard of him. Would you like to see my doctor?"

"Does he speak Russian?"

"No. But Tanya or I can go with you."

"I think I would feel more comfortable with one of our own. Why don't you use a Russian doctor? They say Russian doctors here are rolling in money."

"Maybe. Some also have a feeling of invincibility and power over their patients, who generally don't speak English."

"Do you think Dr. Korotki would be too expensive?"

"If you need a check-up, who the doctor is doesn't matter." I was curt.

"Anya, if I'm not angry with you, why should you be angry with me?"

"I'm sorry."

Tanya finished her food silently. I left most of mine on the plate.

"Fima, you look tired. Why don't you lie down on the sofa in the living room?"

"I'm fine. Let's go to the living room. I would like to show you the presents I brought."

Fima took off his suit jacket, knelt on the floor, and opened his suitcase. Tanya knelt next to him. I remained standing unable to relax. The smell of perspiration made Tanya screw up her nose. Fima removed a used plastic bag from his suitcase. Plastic bags are of great value in the

Soviet Union and ensuring their longevity is an art. The first gift was a white blouse with wide sleeves adorned with needlepoint, part of a Ukrainian folk costume and rarely worn offstage.

"This is for you, Tanichka. Why don't you try it on?"

"Thanks." Tanya held the blouse to herself, perplexed. "I'll try it on later."

"Okay. This is also for you." With the gesture of a magician perform-ing his star trick, Fima unfolded a thin, white, wool Orenburg scarf, named after the city in Siberia where most of them were originally woven. The scarf was soft and beautiful, but I couldn't imagine Tanya wearing it.

"Wow, this is pretty, thank you." Tanya folded the scarf in half and threw it around her neck.

"You should wear it on your head." Fima took the scarf, folded it diagonally, and placed it on Tanya's head like what an American would call a babushka. "It's very becoming." His eyes were shining gently.

My heart jumped.

Tanya ran away to look at herself in the mirror.

"And this is for you, Anya." Out came a long strand of golden amber and a matching brooch in the shape of a bug.

"You shouldn't have." I stepped back with my hands behind my back.

Fima swallowed. "You will never understand what you did to me. I still can't believe it." He lowered the amber to the sofa. "Was this big house worth it?"

"Thank you very, very much, it's fantastic." Tanya ran back, carrying the scarf over her arm. "What's that?" she picked up the brooch.

"That's for your mother," said Fima brusquely.

"Mom, try it on! It's perfect to wear with your new black dress."

"I will, later."

Tanya looked at us with alarm.

"And this is . . ." Fima bent over his suitcase. When he straightened up there was a chocolate-colored teddy bear with black eyes and a thin, pink bow in his hands. ". . . for you, Tanichka."

The morbid feeling associated with his words made me shudder. Tanya took the bear uncertainly.

"This is the teddy bear I had with me when I went to visit you and found your mother's letter . . . when I found out you and your mother had left the country. Here is the letter." Fima took a folded sheet of paper out of his breast pocket and handed it to me. "I don't want it back."

"I'm sorry, Dad," Tanya whispered. Her lips trembling, she threw her arms around Fima; the bear in her hand hung down his back.

She called him "Dad."

I tiptoed around the sofa and through the hall to my bedroom. I shut the door to my bedroom.

God, please don't make me pay with Tanya for what I've done to this man. I've done the worst thing one person can do to another, but I didn't do it for myself, not for this house, not for anything that could be measured. I wouldn't wish my worst enemy to have to go through what he must have gone through when he found this letter.

Dear Fima,

I realized you would never agree to emigrate with us or allow me to take Tanya away. At my age it's too late to want anything for myself, but I cannot let my daughter live the only way it is possible to live in the Soviet Union. By the time you read this letter we will be in Vienna—free. While I'm alive, Tanichka will always be taken care of. She will always get the best, no matter what it takes. She will grow up a free person. I will tell her what a good father you were. I know you can never forgive me for doing this, but you left me no choice.

Anya

"Mom," Tanya peeked into the bedroom, "please . . . I told Dad how you were able to get me out of Russia, you know, the forgery. Mom, you have to talk to him," she pleaded tearfully.

Fima sat on the sofa rubbing his forehead, his lips pasted together. Tanya stood next to me.

"Fima, I won't ask you to forgive me."

Tanya disappeared. I sat on the sofa.

"You don't understand, Anya. I was close to committing suicide. Life didn't seem to make any sense. I loved you, I loved Tanya, and I lost both of you. I always wondered how you managed it, and now it turns out it was forgery. I hadn't expected that."

I took his hand. He wore a thick wedding band, too tight for his finger. Our wedding bands had been narrow and pale. I had left mine behind.

"Fima, I would do it all again. You'll see why after you spend some time in the United States. You'll be happy for Tanya."

"Anichka, I'm forty-nine, but I feel like eighty. Zhanna's a nice woman, a good mother, but it's not the same. I can't get you out of my mind. Sometimes I love you, sometimes I hate you. You look so different," Fima took my hands in his, "so rested, so confident. Do you ever think of our life together?"

"I do."

"Are you in love with your boyfriend?"

"He's a good person. You'll meet him. He and Tanya are close friends, she trusts him. What else do I need?"

"You've done a fine job with Tanya. I realize it wasn't easy."

I didn't dare take my hands away.

The telephone rang.

"Mom, Jack's on the phone." Tanya came in with plates and a bowl of peaches and grapes. Her eyes were drawn to my hands in Fima's.

I went to the phone in the kitchen.

"So, how's it going, Anna? Tanya assures me peace reigns."

"That's true. Fima's tired, but otherwise we're doing fine."

"I'll be home by seven unless you want me to be there earlier so I can meet him today."

"It doesn't have to be today. Fima needs some rest after such a long trip and Roman should be here by six at the latest."

"You sound like you need some rest yourself. I'll see you later."

I returned to find Tanya and Fima discussing *perestroika*, Vera, the nursing home, Petya, Igor, rules for getting permission for visits, golf, basketball, college, a convertible, and EPCOT Center.

To Roman, when he showed up in a shirt open halfway to his waist and displaying the familiar gold chains, sunglasses, and chest hair, we appeared one happy, reunited family.

The next day started unremarkably. Jack decided to get together with the electrical and painting contractors before paying the next installments for our office expansion and to do some negotiating with an office equipment wholesaler. In the afternoon, Tanya brought Fima to the office to meet Jack, and, I suspected, to show off. I spent most of the day with our mama-client, as Jack called Jim Karlson's mammoth project, which would unfold full strength in the summer. In the evening, Jack's plan had called for a get-to-know-each-other conversation with Fima over a meal.

Electricians and carpenters had already finished their work for the day when I arrived a few minutes after four. Bev, our receptionist, raised her curly head and waived with a napkin. Fima held his slice of pizza awkwardly with both hands, not used to eating standing up or without silverware. Tanya and Jack chewed happily, holding their slices on paper napkins, blind to Fima's discomfort. Slim and tanned, Bev puffed her cheeks and patted her flat stomach to indicate gross overeating on her part. Fima's coat, neatly folded, its lining out, like Lonya taught me to fold my clothes, found sanctuary on one of the two available chairs pushed into the corner, farthest from the pizza.

We're in the process of expanding our small office down the hall and around the corner. Eventually, our area will consist of five offices, a reception area with two workstations, an interview room, a decent-sized conference room furnished with a solid, oval table with twelve chairs, and a private lounge between the offices earmarked for Jack and myself. The lounge will contain a black leather sofa; a kitchenette with a refrigerator, coffeemaker, and microwave; and a washroom with a shower. It had increased our rent and our insurance costs, but Jack insisted that our success directly depended on its existence. I gave in.

I also have my heart set on a suite of three offices across the hall, which is expected to be vacated in October, and which would serve as a training facility for our employees and clients. Jack rolled his eyes and reminded me of our age, that, in his words, lent itself to retirement and not to expansion.

Today, Fima looked not much changed for eleven years. Did I actually sleep with this man?

"You mean personal computers aren't common in Russia?" Jack, half-sitting sideways on the edge of Bev's desk, was being his genial American self.

Tanya translated.

"You see, now is a period of changing directions," Fima lectured, insulted by Jack's breezy attitude toward the turmoil in the Soviet Union. "As soon as Gorbachev points us to the next step . . ."

"Hello!" I interrupted, smiling to everyone and placing my briefcase on the floor.

Fima nodded as he returned his half-eaten pizza to the box.

Jack hopped off the desk and strolled toward me.

"Hi there. You must be famished."

"I am." I said, suddenly realizing how hungry I was.

Jack handed me a slice of pizza which I immediately bit into greedily and proceeded to get tomato sauce on my lips and cheeks.

Tanya laughed. Fima watched somberly as Jack wiped my mouth with a napkin. I apologized to Fima for our messy eating habits. The anger in his gray eyes brought back the nights I had spent with him, making me long for Jack's warm body.

"We have paper plates in the credenza," I said in English, then continued in Russian, "Tanya, didn't you notice your father needed a plate?"

Bev jumped up. "I'll get the plates."

I frowned at my daughter who was acting spoiled. She bit her lip, knowing she should have gotten the plates.

"I know, Fima," I said amiably, remembering my own first awkward experience eating pizza, "it's awkward without a plate. You should have just asked Tanya."

"It wasn't awkward," Fima shrugged. "I simply don't like pizza."

He had never seen pizza before, but he wouldn't admit it.

"You don't?" Tanya made an incredulous "O" with her mouth.

"Translation, please," Jack laughed. "It looks like you forgot that I only speak English and Spanish. No Russian yet."

"It turns out that Dad doesn't like pizza." Tanya offered her interpretation of what was said in Russian. "Okay, Mom, I'm going to take Dad home with me. Jack says you two still need to work. I'll feed Dad and we'll wait for you. Jack wants to have a drink with him tonight."

Tanya's apparent acceptance of Fima created a cloud on my horizon. I always wanted her to know fatherly love. Rotten creature that I was, I wished Fima would provide this experience from the other side of the world.

Nothing seemed appropriate, except a generic American smile. I couldn't think of anything to say, so I nodded and disappeared into my office.

"It's terrifying you don't see your environment for what it is!" Fima screamed, shaking his finger at Tanya.

"Dad, what did Mom do? Why are you yelling?" Tanya's slow Russian sentences made me feel sorry for her.

They hadn't heard us come in. "What's going on?" My eyes were fixed on the familiar, deep, vertical creases between Fima's brows.

"Mom!" bellowed Tanya with relief.

"What's going on here?" Jack asked.

"What is he saying? What right does he have to ruin my daughter's life?" Fima's voice rose to such a high pitch he had to stand on his tiptoes to support the sound.

"Tanya, what in the hell is going on here?" repeated Jack with determination.

"I don't know," cried Tanya in English, trembling. "We were looking at my baby pictures and talking. Then suddenly he started yelling and screaming that I've grown up with all the wrong values."

"What are you saying?" Fima jerked Tanya's arm.

She translated as Jack took a step forward surveying the scene.

"That's not what you really said! I could tell. You know very well what I'm angry about!" screamed Fima.

"Fima, would you please let go of Tanya's arm and keep your voice down." I was impressed how measured and low my tone was, while my insides were frozen, my hands in a cold sweat.

I felt Jack's hand on my shoulder and my body thawed a bit.

"I know everything! Everything!" shrieked Fima. "You thought you could fool me!"

Fima released Tanya and she took two quick steps closer to us.

"Anna, do you have any idea . . ." started Jack, gathering steam.

"I don't, and translating for you won't help." I shook off Jack's hand and continued in Russian, staring into Fima's eyes. "Neither Tanya, nor I understand the cause of this commotion," I said quietly.

"I can't stand it when you lower your voice!" Fima barked, shaking his fists in the air. "You have not only destroyed my life, you have taught my daughter there is nothing sacred in the world."

"Fima, spare me general statements."

"General?" he shrieked again. "You didn't get this castle of a house, a fleet of cars, an office with a personal secretary, and all this new confidence by working. It's not possible. Your lovers, like this one," Fima stabbed his finger at Jack, "gave you what you've got. It doesn't even bother you that you sleep with them under the same roof as my daughter."

"Dad, how can you say that!" Tanya blushed, looking quickly at Jack as if he understood Russian. "There was never anyone but Jack. He's not a lover. He's like . . . like . . . family." Tanya planted herself firmly in front of Jack.

Jack stood, his hands deep in his pockets, his eyes threatening behind his glasses.

"I'm not going to stand by idly and watch my daughter's mind destroyed. You flaunt your lovers in front of her shamelessly. Tanya told me everything!"

"What did I say?" Tanya looked at me helplessly. "I just said Jack and I usually shoot baskets on Sunday mornings before you get up, and I said Jack waits up for me when you're too tired. Suddenly Dad flew into a rage and called you 'immoral,'" she whined in her very flawed Russian.

"Not immoral, a whore . . . a whore!"

Tanya didn't understand *blyad*, a common word on any Russian street, but I could tell she understood the meaning in context.

"You're smart, my quiet wife, you picked the right ones, those with money. Someone like me wouldn't be good enough anymore," he added bitterly.

Is he jealous?

"Fima," I held my hand up, "evidently you have determined Tanya is mature enough to listen to you, obscenities and all. And she is. Understand that she and I know the truth, and that is the only thing that matters."

"She's my daughter!" Fima screeched.

"Everyone who came from the Soviet Union received letters from those left behind. You never wrote. You even changed your name. What if I had wanted to find you?" Tanya blurted out.

How many times had Tanya asked me this very question?

"I did it for my son," Fima stated emphatically, his throat tight with emotion. "There was no other way."

"And I did it for my daughter. There was no other way," I broke in. "Now let's resolve our relationship for the duration of your visit, so we can remain civil to each other." My voice was low, crisp, commanding, and cold. "You came here to see your daughter, and you will have as much time with her as she can give you without compromising her grades. I will pay for your medical check-up. I believe it would be wise for you and I to limit our contact. Good night, Fima. Tanichka, please take your father home, and don't be late. You have school tomorrow."

I turned on my heel and marched past Tanya and Jack, who watched me intently. In the kitchen, I dropped into a chair, put my head in my arms on the table and cried softly.

"Whatever you said, I wouldn't have wanted to be the recipient," Jack massaged my neck. "Will you tell me what happened, why my name was mentioned?"

"He's right. I destroyed his life."

"Anna, not again," Jack murmured soothingly.

Fima's right. Vilen was allowed into my bed, ten feet from where Tanya slept. Gena pinched and tried to feel me at every turn. Jack's charged with assisting me in bringing up Tanya and developing my business skills. Only Sasha is truly for himself.

Lies, lies, always lies. Fima's right. I didn't want Jack here under the same roof with Tanya. I don't even know why I let it happen, or why I didn't resist. But it's Jack, Tanya's friend. And, he did say he was in love with me.

Jack's fingers continued their neck therapy for some time then moved to my shoulders. I stopped crying. Drowsy, I concentrated on the feeling from Jack's fingers.

Tanya returned almost immediately. I had the feeling she and her father hadn't exchanged a word in the car.

"Mom, Jack, I'm sorry. I was sure Dad liked Jack." Tanya sounded tired, resigned, old. "I don't understand his problem. We don't have anything against his family." She sighed. "I'll make some tea for you. Coffee, Jack? I think I'll have some cocoa then go to bed. I'm really beat."

In my sleep I tried to chase away my dreams, but they stubbornly slipped back, leaving me exhausted in the morning. I resisted one of them until it forced me to capitulate and live through it: Fima, waiting in bed, rolls on top of me before my head reaches the pillow—one night Tanya is conceived—a night like any other.

The only way to escape is to wake up. Only then do the ghosts grudgingly fade away. I lay quietly, then tiptoed into Tanya's room and listened. I heard her even breathing. How is it that a child loved so much was born from an act with no emotion?

Was Fima able to sleep? I wish I could do something to ease his pain.

I returned to bed, trying not to wake Jack.

"Anna, I know it's none of my business, but would you tell me what upset Fima last night?" Jack's voice startled me.

"Jack, I can't explain, but I understand where he's coming from. Go to sleep."

"Do I come into play in any way?"

"In his mind, yes."

"He can't be jealous. He's remarried and has a son."

"Fima feels that you and I living together is a bad influence on Tanya's values. He sees this as being the same as if I were bringing a different man home every night."

"That's crazy!"

"I would think the same in his place."

The silence was deafening.

"Anna, do you still have feelings for Fima?"

"Come on, Jack, I didn't have feelings for him when I was married to him. I liked him . . . sort of."

Silence again. I wish he'd get mad, shake me, scream—anything but silence.

"Jack, touch me, shake me, do something."

Jack turned toward me.

"Anna, these last months have made me happier than I have ever been. What I should do is take you away, far away where no one from that strange land of yours can find you." Jack stretched out his arm and I put my head on his shoulder, my arm across his chest.

His warmth made the silence bearable.

"I understand Fima and Asya and Rimma." I whispered. "It doesn't mean I condone or prefer their reasoning, but I understand it because it's mine too. It's in my blood."

I'm sure Fima isn't sleeping now, tossing and turning, picturing Jack and me making love, aggravating his wounds.

Jack's lips touched my neck with quick, light kisses.

"Jack, please, don't. It's almost time to get up."

"Shut up," he murmured in my ear.

We overslept by so much we had to change our morning schedule.

"Dad said he wasn't too interested in shopping, but I need to go to both Jewel and Venture so I'll take him with me anyway," Tanya reported in Russian over cereal. "He's probably sorry about yesterday."

"Tanichka, you grew up here, you think differently. Please be patient with your father. Let him have warm memories of his visit."

Tanya smiled hopefully, called Fima, told him to wait for her outside at three, then left for school.

"Is Fima coming over today?" inquired Jack casually, fussing with his tie in front of the hallway mirror.

"No. Tanya's going shopping and taking him with her."

"Should I still plan to take him golfing?"

"We'll see," I said quietly.

Our eyes crossed in the mirror. "Jack, hurry or you won't have time to set up your presentation."

"Baby, you were fantastic this morning."

I blushed.

"Bye, Anna. I'll call you after the presentation. We'll have lunch. A date? "

"A date."

Silly, foolish, forty-five-year-old woman.

"Mom, I'm sorry I'm late, but I spent the entire time with Dad in Jewel and then at Venture. He went crazy—worse than Rimma. At least she came to Chicago after a couple weeks in Los Angeles. He wants you to call him. And he wants to go back to Venture tomorrow."

"Do you know why he wants me to call him?"

"No, but he was upset."

"Tanya, tomorrow is your nursing home day."

"I know. I suggested he come along, but he wouldn't listen. I couldn't get him out of the housewares department at Venture. We bought some kitchen stuff for his wife."

"Are you hungry? Donna made your favorite quiche."

"I'm really not hungry. I'll just have a small piece. Dad had a terrible stomach ache, he had to have something to eat so we went to Baker's Square. His stomach got better after we ate. I only had fourteen dollars left, but it was enough for soup and sandwiches. He was shocked that the waitress was polite. Can you believe it? She's a waitress, she's got to be polite! Aren't they polite in Russia?"

"They're very rude. Tanichka, try not to act surprised by the things your father tells you. You would think the same way had you stayed in the Soviet Union."

"But we were never like that."

"Oh, yes, we were. We knew even less, and there was no one to show us around."

"I guess. You know he didn't trust me when I told him plastic bags are free. He actually went and took a whole bunch at Jewel just to see if anyone would stop him. Then he accused me of having arranged the whole thing with the store manager, just to put on a show for him. How could I do that?"

"Tanichka, don't try to be logical. When Western delegations are shown stores in a Soviet city, the customers are asked to leave and are replaced by KGB agents and goods are placed on normally half-empty shelves for the foreign guests to see. When the foreigners leave, the goods leave."

Tanya was eating quickly, shaking her head, overwhelmed by the glimpse of the world her father had brought with him. Hopefully she doesn't think him as alien as that world.

"Is Jack in the basement?" Tanya washed and dried her plate. "I'm going downstairs to say hi. I hardly see you guys anymore. Dad was supposed to do some things with us, but he doesn't want to. He acts like we owe him something."

My debt to him can never be repaid.

"If I went to Kiev," Tanya continued, opening the basement door, "I would spend most of the time with his family."

"If you went to Kiev, you would bring your world with you. Your father brought his world with him. It's not his fault."

"Mom, please don't forget to call Dad. He probably wants to apologize for yesterday."

I dialed the Bloom's number as Tanya went downstairs with her familiar, "Hi, Jack."

Valentina picked up the phone after several rings.

"This is Anya. I'm sorry to call so late, but Fima asked me to call him."

"Anya, Fima's wife? How are you? Fima saw an American store for the first time today. He's delirious!" She coughed a deep smoker's cough. "Why did your daughter take him to such an upscale store? Russian visitors should only be taken to discount stores."

"As far as I know, Tanya took him to Jewel and to Venture."

"That's all? Aren't these Soviets pay-nas?" Valentina interjected her favorite sampling of English into an otherwise entirely Russian conversation. "All our relatives want to visit us now. They'd kill for a pair of jeans. Is Fima your first guest?"

"Yes."

"I've had two already. I'll tell you how to act with them." Valentina sounded as if she was speaking from a podium.

"I'm sure it would be extremely informative, but it's getting late and I would like to talk to Fima, if he hasn't gone to bed." My tone was formal.

"He hasn't. They're watching television. Fima!" she yelled without moving the phone away.

I almost dropped the receiver.

"Your former wife's on the phone!"

I would prefer a title not including the word "wife."

"Fima! Roma, is Fima with you?"

I was holding the receiver several inches from my ear.

"His former wife is on the phone! The one that lives with the American!"

What a distinction. I wonder how Fima feels hearing that.

"*Slushayu,*" Fima's voice came on the line.

"Good evening, Fima. Tanya told me you asked to talk to me."

Tanya appeared at the top of the basement stairs yawning.

"It's too late. I can't disturb my hosts," he said, deliberately rude.

"When do you want me to call back?" I felt only pity.

"In the morning." It sounded like an order.

"I have a meeting from eight to nine. Will nine o'clock suffice?"

"Yes. Good night."

"Good night, Fima," I said, hanging up the telephone.

"Did Dad apologize?"

The intensity in Tanya's eyes told me how much she had hoped he would.

"No. But, it's all right, Tanichka. He might not have chosen the best way to express his opinion, but he does have legitimate reasons for the way he feels. In the Soviet Union it's inconceivable for a man and woman to live together without being married and I myself am convinced that dating then marriage is the only proper avenue."

"That's in the Soviet Union!" Tanya said in a slightly haughty way. "He had no right to say what he did. Vera told me what that word means. It was nasty, especially since he knew that you and Jack are, like married, and that I want you to be together."

"How did he know that?"

"I told him. Dad will apologize. I'll make him."

"Let me make you some cocoa." I kissed Tanya on her cheek. "Five more months and you'll be making cocoa for yourself in your college dormitory."

"Not on weekends," she wrinkled her nose teasingly. "On weekends my laundry and my cocoa are coming right here."

I need to have a talk with Tanya about Jack remaining a friend, but not necessarily being part of my life until the day I die. It will be easier for her to accept when she's in college, busy studying, and meeting new people. She's becoming too set in her expectations. Or maybe I should let it go so she doesn't worry like she used to that I'm lonely without her—which is true, but not for her to know.

The meeting in my office ended close to eleven. It was an intense brainstorming session with all Green Bay department heads and our senior consultant, Fred Kangles. When Fred invited the clients for lunch I made a wish-I-could-come-with-you face and excused myself.

When I move into my new office I'll have a sofa and a microwave to accompany my breaks. For now, I closed the door tightly, kicked off my shoes, threw a piece of hard candy into my mouth, flipped through my messages, then dialed Fima.

"If you think by delaying the moment of truth you'll avoid it, you're very much mistaken," Fima's voice elevated the moment he recognized mine. "You were supposed to call at nine."

"I apologize. My meeting took longer than expected. How can I help you?" Fima's agitation produced only boredom and distance. I wiggled my toes.

"What kind of a question is that?"

"I'm sure you didn't ask me to call you simply to chat. That's why I'm asking what can I do for you."

"Don't worry, you'll do plenty for me," Fima gloated. "You certainly owe me! I never believed the stories people told about American stores when they returned from visiting their relatives. Zhanna believed them, I didn't. How could everyone be a millionaire? Now I know."

Oh, God, please let this visit be over soon.

"Fima, please come to the point."

"Of course, you're a big shot, you're busy," sneered Fima, "a decoration for your boyfriend's company, always there when he needs you." He was drowning in scorn and jealousy. "Is this American's prick better than mine?"

"As a matter of fact, Fima, yes," I said seriously, translating one of Jack's phrases into Russian.

Fima gasped.

Gena Korsunsky had asked me the same question once. Vilen had hinted he was curious. Fools! It's how I react that makes the difference. It's what I want to give in return.

Had someone listened to that exchange they would have laughed. But the sad irony of Fima's effort to bolster the guilty feeling in me by humiliation only served to free me from remorse similar to the humiliation at the Soviet border-crossing that invariably cured any lingering doubts and nostalgia.

"Fima, if that was all you wanted to know . . ."

"I know all about what kind of a person you are!" he shrieked. "I also know what you've been teaching my daughter."

"By the way, Fima, Tanya inquired what *blyad* meant. She didn't appreciate your calling me a whore." I took advantage of an awkward pause. "Tanya needs to carry out her usual responsibilities while you're visiting. She expected to show you the nursing home where she volunteers, but instead you insisted she not go there today. She will not be allowed to miss it again."

"Is that what you want, for me to sit here day after day doing nothing, so you don't have to spend any money?"

Why am I wasting my time on this conversation?

"I don't want anything at all. It's you who insisted shopping didn't interest you and you'd spend time with Tanya when she was available."

Bev's head appeared around the door.

"Excuse me, Fima." I covered the phone with my hand. "Yes, Bev?"

"Tom Sirota, line two, for Jack, about some contract. He's calling from a customer's office."

"Thanks. Fima, I will have to put you on hold. Don't hang up."

Fima objected. I didn't listen. Tom, a natural salesman, knew how to talk, but he also knew how to be brief when a deal approached closing, which was the case now. Jack will be happy to hear the news.

My mood showed a marked improvement when I returned to Fima.

"What happened? I thought you hung up on me," Fima sputtered.

He's become neurotic, loud, and suspicious, not at all the Fima I remembered.

"I had another call. Again, Fima, how can I help you?"

"Why is it you never wrote when you discovered what a rich country the United States was? You've been shopping in stores like the ones Tanya took me to, and the restaurant . . . I don't know how regular people could afford such luxury and service!"

"Fima, these places are the cheapest around. Besides, what would have changed had I written?"

"I would have joined you. The emigration continued until 1980."

Did I understand correctly?

"Fima, this doesn't make sense."

"Why? Because you didn't need me anymore? There were plenty of others?"

"I find it difficult to believe material considerations could have in-fluenced you. Only recently you wanted Tanya back. Just a minute ago you said you never believed the stories of people who visited the United States. You wouldn't have believed me, either."

"I would have, and we would now be a family. I pictured you among the people they showed on Soviet television, eating at a charity kitchen, huddling by a sewer grating for warmth in winter. I almost lost my mind with worry, and all the time you were laughing at me in your big house with your American men."

"Fima, you are not the kind of person that would have dropped ev-erything and emigrated because of a letter describing an American store. At least, I don't recall your being that way. And how could you have expected a healthy relationship if the incentive for you to join us was a store full of goods. Even had I remained in Kiev, we could never have resumed our relationship after you refused to leave with us."

"You say it now to justify your actions."

"There is no need to justify *my* actions. I think your rage indicates you regret *your* actions."

"That's nonsense!" he shrieked.

"I'm curious, Fima, would you have come if I had written that the stores weren't full, and life wasn't much better than in the Soviet Union?"

"I would have insisted you return. The point is, you found out salaries were high, stores were full, and service was good, and you didn't tell me!"

"I wrote regularly to Asya."

"The humiliation of being betrayed by my wife wasn't enough? You expected me to be friends with the people who assisted you in deceiving me?"

"No one assisted me, no one knew until the last moment, and not one soul realized you hadn't given your consent. What I find curious is you pictured us homeless, but never cared to read my letters to find out how we were actually doing."

"Don't take my words out of context!"

His shriek no longer surprised me. I remained as bored and distant as in the beginning of the conversation, angry for wasting time.

"Fima, this conversation is going nowhere. Starting tomorrow, Tanya will always have some cash and a credit card with her. You can buy whatever you need for yourself and for your family."

"Yes, you will pay, you will pay dearly for everything I could have owned and don't because of you."

"What I have and you haven't owned for eleven years, one can't buy."

He didn't understand.

"I'll buy clothes, I'll go to the doctor, I'll call Kiev every day. You think if I don't have a telephone at home I won't be able to? We have a neighbor on the sixth floor who promised to let us use her telephone while I'm here."

"My punishment, I guess. A real moment of truth, isn't it?"

"In just a couple of days here I've learned more about you than during the six years of our marriage. You're selfish and greedy, Anya."

"Why go on talking to such a person?" I inquired, impatient to finish the conversation.

"Anya, wait!" Fima's former, more familiar voice caught me off guard. Bev brought in the mail.

"Anya, for Tanya's sake, you shouldn't have a boyfriend living with you."

He had the right to an explanation.

"Fima, in the United States it is not considered extraordinary to live with one's boyfriend. Jack means a lot to Tanya."

For a brief moment we were man and wife, united by a child. The moment passed.

"I'll never believe that. You merely want an easier life for yourself." Fima's hostility returned.

"Yes, I do." This simple admission spurred my energy. "Fima, I've got to go. When she's available, Tanya will take you shopping as much as you want. Good-bye."

And Tanya took Fima shopping. At first her father's indifference to her school, basketball games, Nancy's ice-cream parlor, her patients at the nursing home, and, especially, her golf lessons embarrassed her. It hurt her that he called her plans to show him the places and people she had boasted to him about "childish." Gradually, she limited her mission to accompanying him to stores, translating labels, presenting her credit card, and taking him home.

Roman and Valentina refused to store Fima's purchases at their house and our little home office began to look more and more like a discount store. Tanya became disappointed, but remained dutiful. She had waited too long for her father to rebel now.

Her stories were both funny and sad. I understood Fima's neurotic attempt not to miss anything his family may possibly need in the foreseeable future.

"When I took Dad to Jewel, he asked if the meat was wrapped because it was spoiled and picked up some packages and sniffed them. He said, 'If it's not spoiled, why isn't anyone buying it?' I was so embarrassed.

"After Jewel, I was terrified to take him to K-Mart, but I needed film and it's cheaper there. He walked around, not saying a word. Then he saw some sale stuff in a bin, and he pushed and shoved people out of the way, shaking his fists at them. He kept muttering in Russian, 'She never told me, she never told me.' Whatever that meant. When I took his arm to try and steer him away, he shook me off so violently I nearly fell over. I wanted to cry, but there were too many people. And I'd like to know, what is he going to do with seven identical purses?

"I can't take this much longer. He doesn't care about me, he only wants to shop. Shop, shop, shop. He asked me to take him to Marshall Field's. He said it was a better class of store and he was tired of being taken to bargain stores. God, he went crazy."

Fima's choice of punishment only proved how much we have changed or, perhaps, how much we haven't changed. Essentially, it simplified my life. Luckily, he came this year instead of last year. I wouldn't have been able to afford much in terms of presents, Tanya wouldn't have had a car at her disposal to chauffeur him around, and calling Kiev every day would have been out of the question.

His punishment left me to fend off an obstinate buying machine, not a heartbroken father interested in his daughter's every movement as I had envisioned.

An old Russian adage, "The mother is not the one who gave birth to the baby; the mother is the one who brought it up," might sadly prove to be correct if applied to Fima and Tanya. He loves his little, red-haired girl with white bows and thoughtful eyes, sitting on his lap, learning her alphabet. The tall, young woman with thick, fashionably cut hair, in torn jeans, who speaks his language both poorly and with an American accent, knows how to drive a car and uses a credit card, has nothing in common with his little girl.

The past eleven years haven't passed unnoticed for any of us. Fima used to be a non-materialistic, soft-spoken person, happy with very little—like Sasha and me. He was proud to be a Soviet citizen, somewhat of a demagogue, perhaps, but genuinely driven by ideals. Different ideals than mine, but still, ideals—not jeans and athletic shoes.

I used to be quiet and taciturn, absent-minded, subservient, and stubborn. Well, I'm still stubborn.

"You sold out, Anya," said Fima one evening helping Tanya carry more bags into the house. "This American air about you is disgusting. It's like you don't want people to think you were ever a Russian."

What a fool Fima is. I'm no American. I wish I could speak Russian all the time. My life would be miserable without meaningless conversations with Lena and Bella, occasional gossip with Cece, endless reminiscing with practically every Russian person who ever crosses my path. Because I'm not downtrodden, scared, distrustful, and don't smell of perspiration, it doesn't mean I'm not Russian. Or does it?

thirty-six

Gena Korsunsky's medical building has changed significantly since the fall of 1985 when I last saw it. Now it has a decidedly dilapidated look and smell. The directory on the wall has press-in, white letters and boasts eight Russian doctors and dentists in random order, including Bella Kaganov, who has a part-time practice here. I remembered the paper arrow pointing to the basement for the lab. The pharmacy to the left, behind a glass wall, is new. Half a dozen older Russian women, none of them in kerchiefs, stood in line at the counter chatting. The pharmacy wall informed in silver letters: "Pharmacist Jerry Rappaport; Pharmacist Jerry Eydel." The Jerry on duty had a fat nose, situated between Brezhnev-type eyebrows and a thick, jet-black mustache. He resembled a Halloween mask. I stopped to watch the people in line. They were younger than my mother would be.

Some of the press-in letters on the directory were missing. The "Den is" next to Gena's name was too tempting to ignore. I took a quick look down the empty corridor leading to the doctors' offices, at the line in the pharmacy where everyone had their backs to me, and at the closed front door. Holding my breath, I slid the two surviving parts of Gena's title together, plucked out the "D," exchanged it with the "P" from "Pediatrician" below, stepped back, and giggled as I surveyed my handiwork. The sign now read, "Gennady Korsunsky, Penis, Suite 101." How appropriate. Not that many turn to this directory for information or know English well enough to appreciate my prank, but telling Lena and Bella—and Cece, to be sure—will undoubtedly generate gossip. And, besides, it made me feel good.

Fima's doctor is Leonard Korotki, "Internist, Suite 105."

Why didn't I warn Fima that I might not be able to—or would not want to—pay for his treatment? Amazing—he simply called at the office to inform me that the doctor would meet with me today at six o'clock to discuss tests that needed to be done, and here I was, at six o'clock on the dot. My feelings of guilt have turned me into a slave. Once a slave, always a slave. Why did I ever answer Fima's first letter?

Suite 105 was next to the men's room, and I almost collided with a very tall, imposing gentleman as he came out of it pushing his shirt into his pants. He looked around forty-five. His sports coat had suede elbow patches. The crease on his dark-brown pants looked as sharp as though they had jumped off the ironing board only minutes before. The man followed me into the suite. He carried his full head of brown hair with an aura of assurance. The empty chairs and the closed receptionist window in the waiting room made me think that Fima had given me the wrong time or the doctor had forgotten about my appointment.

"Are you here to pick someone up?" the man asked impatiently. "Some patients are still being examined. Our last appointment was scheduled for half and hour ago."

"I was supposed to meet Dr. Korotki at six to . . . "

"I'm Dr. Korotki," he interrupted.

I smiled to myself—"korotki" meant "short" in Russian.

"In another minute you would have missed me. I need to go to the hospital for an emergency." He shot a glance at a clock over a brightly illuminated fishbowl gurgling with playful air bubbles and motioned me to a chair.

His Russian had a comfortable English lilt to it.

"When I talked to your husband today . . ." he began.

"My former husband," I interjected, unnecessarily brusque.

"Former husband," Dr. Korotki repeated with a gesture that implied that the distinction had no relevance. "He didn't know whether you had insurance coverage or how much you would be willing to spend." His green eyes appraised my silk blouse and Coach purse. "I presume you have insurance?"

"Yes, I do, but it only covers myself and my daughter," I said. "Anything seriously wrong with his health?"

"Sounds like gastritis, but it's hard to tell without tests. I asked Dr. Rosen to give you recommendations and maybe some sample medications. He's with a patient right now. He was my mentor in Kiev. You can trust him as you trust me."

Why is he so certain I trust him?

"How much would the tests cost?"

Dr. Korotki gave me a speculative look and rubbed his chin.

"A couple thousand, I would think," he said slowly. "I could run them under your insurance . . ." his voice trailed off to give me a chance to express my gratitude.

"This is not a large amount," I said, pretending that I didn't hear the part about the insurance. I also pretended not to notice his quick glance at the clock. "My former husband is here on a short visit. He'll go back in a little over a month. How much time would the tests take?"

"I suppose we could fit the X-rays into this time frame, but we won't be able to follow up on his treatment. Frankly, based on the symptoms, I don't see any reason to hurry and undergo tests now, especially since all these procedures will be covered by Medicaid when he immigrates."

That last word had the effect of putting my finger into an electric socket.

"Immigrates?" I heard my voice say.

"Yes. If he applies right after his return to Kiev, as he intends, it shouldn't take more than a few months—unless the political situation changes."

Hypnotized by this casual mention of Fima and immigration in the same breath, I stared glassy-eyed at Dr. Korotki.

"I'm inclined to think he may just need a better diet. When he's here as a refugee . . . "

"As a refugee?" I repeated like a parrot.

"How else?" Dr. Korotki looked at his dark-faced watch. "Again, that will take some time . . ."

"What will take some time?"

Obviously, my swiftness did not impress him.

"I'm sorry, I have to go now. My receptionist has left for the day, but the building is open until seven. You can wait in the office over there. Here's my card." His hand shook mine.

Dr. Korotki must have confused Fima with someone else. He couldn't have meant Fima wanted to emigrate. That's ridiculous. The passionate monologues on the merits of *glasnost* he delivers daily to Tanya are undoubtedly sincere.

A short, gray-haired nurse in soft, white shoes opened the second door on the left. Over the head of the nurse I saw a doctor in a blue lab coat, his back to the door, holding a stethoscope to the chest of a middle-aged man with a double chin. The sight of the doctor's back made my heart jump. His shoulders reminded me of Sasha.

Suddenly, I felt warm—the news about Fima, no doubt. My confidence dissipated into tiredness.

No sounds, even with the door ajar. I fixed my eyes on the blood pressure machine attached to the wall across from me.

A man started talking in the hallway.

"I don't think you need a higher dosage, but I'll speak to Dr. Korotki."

Sasha? Sasha? My God, I'm losing my mind. The blood pressure machine and the wall began to swim slowly to the right. I've got to leave. I can call for another appointment.

A young, perky-looking girl in a nurse's uniform peeked in.

"You're here about Dr. Korotki's relative, right?"

Brought back to reality by her Midwestern accent, I nodded.

"Do you speak English?" she asked slowly.

I nodded again.

"Okay, Dr. Rosen will be with you shortly."

"Do you think you'll need me for the lady in room six?" the girl asked from behind the door.

"Dr. Korotki's relative? Not likely. I'm really tired. Maybe Dr. Karas will talk to her. Where's the chart?"

Sasha? No, impossible, this man is speaking English, correct English with a heavy Russian accent, heavier than mine—but he sounds like Sasha, except that Sasha doesn't speak English.

"Dr. Rosen? Are you okay? Do you want me to get Dr. Karas?"

"No, I'm all right. Go home, Cindy, it's after six. I'll see you next week."

A hand pushed the door fully open and I looked up to see Sasha, in a blue lab coat with a stethoscope around his neck. I stumbled to my feet as he came closer. His hand was on my elbow. There were deep lines in his forehead.

It *is* Sasha! It has to be. There are no other hands in the world like his. I would know his hands.

"Sasha, what are you doing here?" I sat down unbuttoning the collar of my blouse.

"Working," his eyes followed my trembling fingers. He put the chart and stethoscope on the examining table then moved his hand slowly over his balding head.

No smile, no joy on his face, not even surprise after eleven years. Who was I to him?

"When did you come to Chicago?"

"In February of 1985," his voice was as patient as I always remembered it.

"Two years ago!"

He never contacted me in two years! How did he manage to emigrate in 1985? No one was allowed to emigrate then. He couldn't have gotten a medical license in two years. Did he try to find me?

"Yes, two years," Sasha whispered.

"Is your name Rosen now?" I wanted to touch his face.

"Rosen seemed more American than Rosenberg. And like every Alexander, I am Alex." He smiled his familiar smile.

Sasha's here. Here to answer all my questions. I reached out to touch his cheek. He didn't move to meet my hand as he used to.

Who was I to him?

"You've got some gray hair," he said after a pause.

Eleven years ago he said, "What you're doing is wrong, but I wish you the best of luck."

I got up. My palms were cold and wet. Is this how my dream is to come true?

"Sasha, I don't understand . . . you're not surprised, or glad, to see me." I jerked the strap of my purse over my shoulder.

"We could have met on numerous occasions."

"And how could that miracle have happened?" My attempt at sarcasm failed.

Sasha's fingers circled my wrist as I tried to get out the door. He led me back. His hand generated all the old familiar electricity.

"Anichka, I called you many times, but only during the day when I knew you would be at work. I thought, if you were interested you'd find a way to let me know." His hand was still holding my wrist firmly.

"Sasha, I dream about you all the time. Somehow, I've felt you knew everything about me, and that thought has sustained me for years. Recently, Asya tried to find you in Kiev."

He looked at me in astonishment.

"If I didn't know you, Anya, I'd think you were lying."

I took back my hand to rub my temple. The room continued to swim slowly to the right.

"Sit down. Let me take your blood pressure. You're very pale."

I took off my suit coat, rolled up my sleeve. Sasha wasn't looking at me. The blood pressure cuff squeezed my arm as the silver column of mercury slid upward.

"Eighty-five over sixty-five. This can't be your usual blood pressure?"

"Well . . ."

"Who's your doctor?"

"Dr. Shuster."

"American?"

"Yes."

"I bet you don't see him regularly."

Now I'll ask him who I was to him.

"Silly little girl!" Sasha shook his head in a painfully familiar gesture. "You need to have some lab work done right away."

"Sasha, do you remember . . . ?"

He removed the cuff from my arm.

"I remember everything." He kissed my palm then held it to his chest.

A familiar sense of safety brought me back to the ten-year-old girl whose hand he took in his, thirty-five years ago.

"Take care of me, Sasha." I said the words that that ten-year-old girl had longed to say.

"I can't," he sighed. "I don't have a medical license."

That wasn't what I meant—what did I mean?

Sasha smiled, his eyes sad.

"I could get into trouble as it is. Dr. Korotki used to work for me in Kiev. Now, once a week, he lets me consult on some of his cases—in the official capacity of an assistant." He smiled bitterly. "That's why I moved to Chicago. I couldn't live without practicing medicine."

"Moved to Chicago?" I removed my hand from under Sasha's and it immediately felt cold. "One doesn't call immigrating moving."

"But, you know I lived in Boston for six years before I came to Chicago. We immigrated in 1979."

"You did?" I raised my voice. "How was I supposed to know?"

"My daughter told you, I know."

"Your daughter?"

"Anya, what's going on?" Sasha looked genuinely bewildered. "She told me all about you and Tanya. She loves Tanya. I've always wondered if you had asked her about us."

"How does she know Tanya?"

We stared at each other dumbfounded.

The ghost of an old memory—a bundled up toddler with dark eyes and rosy cheeks—surfaced like a movie.

It all came together in a flash.

"Of course! Vera! You used to call her 'Poops.'"

"I still do." Now he smiled his real smile, warm and patient.

"When I last saw her in Kiev, she was only four. When Tanya introduced us I felt I knew her smile. I didn't recognize her. But you knew where I was . . . you knew all this time!"

He bit his lip.

"And you thought I knew?"

Sasha nodded.

"How would I know? Vera doesn't talk about her family, even when asked. Tanya has only referred to you as Vera's father. You don't know how many times I've said I need to meet Vera's parents, and then postponed it ."

Sasha stood dejectedly clutching his stethoscope.

"And, Sasha, don't forget, Vera's last name is Rosen, not Rosenberg!" I got up and grabbed my purse hanging over the back of the chair. "So, were you glad the silly little girl from Kiev didn't come running to you like she used to? Well, here I am, again! You didn't hide very well."

I made a dash to the door.

"Don't go," he said hoarsely.

Sasha's blue eyes were begging. They told me what I've wanted to know from him all my life.

"Anichka, my little girl, what do you need me for now? I know you've been involved with someone else, very happily involved. I saw you several times from a distance. You look younger than eleven years ago. You must be in love."

My hands shook, my knees shook, I couldn't breathe. I felt overwhelmed with an urge to talk, to spill out all my questions and little speeches addressed to him that had given me the strength to survive and had rewarded me with a thread to my past, my safety net.

"Sasha, you don't understand. All these years I've been waiting for you."

I had to stop speaking because my lips trembled. I bit them as painfully as I could until they steadied. Sasha watched me with an odd, nostalgic expression.

"In the beginning, the memories of you, the hope to hear from you kept me going."

I had to stop again, to force back my tears.

I took a deep breath and continued. "Then, the hope diminished but the memories stayed so alive that I always felt you next to me. I talked to you, I asked you for advice, I explained my actions to you."

The blue eyes fixed on my face transported me back to my little room in Kiev. It surrounded us now, all one hundred and fifty square feet of it, with the heavy wardrobe, the china cabinet with the crystal sugar bowl and vase, the oval table covered with the blue-and-white checkered tablecloth where Sasha used to play chess with Lonya. Does he see what I see?

"Asya's husband had forbidden her to correspond with me, but recently we finally talked and I asked her to find you. She couldn't. I didn't want to think you had died. When she visited Lonya's grave and found it in perfect order—I didn't know what to think."

"My friend, Mark Yampolsky, has been caring for it since I left," Sasha said. "A high-security clearance will never allow him to emigrate."

I went on, hearing but not fully registering his words.

"I knew that only you would care for Lonya's grave. And I was happy that you were alive, even if it meant I would never find you." A sheet of tears flowed down my cheeks. "Sasha, who else would remember Lonya besides you and I?"

"Anichka," Sasha said placing his hands on my shoulders.

Sobbing threatened to choke me. I couldn't swallow my tears fast enough to catch my breath.

Sasha gripped my shoulders painfully, making me cry out. His grip eased as my breathing became more stable.

"Anichka, I don't dare come back into your life. I can't offer you anything."

Without taking his tense eyes off me, Sasha reached to the shelf over the sink and pulled a tissue out of a flat, blue box. He pressed it to my nose, to my cheeks, to my chin, tenderly, as if touching a raw wound.

These eyes gave me back the world I had belonged to and had been waiting for—they *were* the world I had been waiting for.

Suddenly, completely calm, I said, "Tanya once said that I act like everything is temporary." I didn't volunteer the fact that she had said it to Jack. "I had to keep everything temporary, so that I could be yours again, when we met." My throat tightened to meet approaching tears. "A half-hour once in a while, a phone call whenever you had a minute—as long as we had each other, nothing else would be important. I never wanted anyone else."

Why am I crying again?

Before I had a chance to move away, Sasha's lips touched my neck. My body swelled with anticipation as I inhaled his familiar scent.

Now he will cup my left breast and squeeze my nipple.

Sasha cupped my left breast and gently squeezed my nipple. Abruptly, he drew back. "I'm sorry, Anichka. I'm acting like a teenager. Do you think we could see each other sometime soon? It's probably too much to ask, but my shift doesn't start until noon tomorrow . . ." His eyes begged.

I can not say no to Sasha.

A knock at the door startled us. The gray-haired nurse poked her head in.

"Doctor, the patient in room two is frazzled."

"Thank you, I'll be right there."

"Come in the morning, around nine," I said quickly, not looking at him. "We'll have breakfast."

I combed my hair, adjusted my clothes and washed my face in the examining room, then called home from the receptionist's desk. The answering machine took my cheerful message.

Twenty years ago I would have waited until Sasha left, just to see him again. It would be pathetic at my age.

I backed up my car almost to the corner of the block and shut off the engine. Just fifteen minutes, then I'll leave. A short woman in a dark sari and sandals waiting at the bus stop watched me suspiciously. Some Orthodox Jews in long black coats, *peyes*, and hats walked by, their arms flying as they talked.

In a few minutes Sasha appeared and crossed the street with a bouncy, young step. At that moment it hit me that we never spoke about Fima's health or about Lilya and his older daughter, Nonna. Nonna must be married, maybe in another city. Tanya never mentioned Vera had a sister. Sasha unlocked the door of a big, white car, looked around then got in. I tried to guess his expression. He turned on his headlights, I turned on mine. I wondered if he noticed.

I wish I could wander around until morning. In Kiev, before I was married, I used to sneak out at night and spend hours walking and dreaming. Those were the sweetest hours. I don't do that anymore. Walking is restricted to the treadmill. And dreaming . . . well, one of my dreams just came true. My Tanya lives her dreams, talks her dreams, has them all on a list of things to do.

The dark, quiet house greeted me with the clean smell of lemons.

Relieved for the first time ever not to find Tanya at home, I switched on all the lights. A note awaited me on the refrigerator door: "Mom, salad and stew in the refrigerator. I had some of both. Going shopping with Dad. Love, Daughter."

I put on the tea kettle, then took the salad, covered with plastic, from the refrigerator and transferred half of it to a plate. Waiting for the water to boil, I walked to the bedroom. The mirror returned an image of a slim, pale woman in a gray suit and purple blouse with an unbuttoned collar, and short, jet-black hair. Definitely not old looking, but with light circles under the eyes. I need more rest. Not too bad.

I changed into my robe and hung my suit in the closet next to Jack's navy slacks. My heart jumped as they reminded me of him. If Jack doesn't leave early tomorrow, I'll have to introduce him to Sasha. If Jack didn't live with us, breaking up with him would be easier. What explanation can I offer Tanya to justify her loss? She must not ever suspect the truth. Hopefully, she'll trust my decision. Jack and I will still work together. I hope that won't change. Soon Tanya will start college and live in the dormitory. Weekends will be hers, the rest of the days will belong to waiting for Sasha's call—that's all I want, these two people.

I checked the answering machine. From Jack: "Hello, girls. Six o'clock now. Be home soon." I wish I knew his schedule for tomorrow. From Vera: "Tanya, it's me. Call me back, I need your bio notes." Dear, sad Vera with her father's smile. And my own, left from the doctor's office: "Hi, Tanya, Jack. Coming home soon."

The kettle whistled and I ran to the kitchen. I actually ran. Tanya would never believe that.

When Tanya came in, she found me in the kitchen. I sat at the table smiling, dangling my feet, sipping tea, and munching on a cheese Danish. The remnants of my dinner, a plate of half-eaten salad and a plate with some stew that I hadn't touched, stood in the middle of the table. She greeted me with a curt "Hi" and splashed milk over some cereal—her first line of defense against hunger.

"I have to tell you something," she said angrily after half the cereal was gone. "You have to talk to Dad. It's crazy, all this shopping. We don't have the time and we can't spend all this money. I can understand jeans and makeup, but do you know where he insisted on going today? To electronic stores! Do you know what he wants? A VCR, a television, a stereo. I almost died when I heard.

"I thought when he came we'd talk and eat out and go to Wisconsin to see the golf course Jack knows, and visit my school and go to basketball practice. There is never time for anything. He's in such a hurry—like the stupid stuff is going to disappear from the shelves. What's the rush? We could always send him whatever he wants. You know what made me mad? I told him we can't afford all this stuff, and you know what he said? 'I'm disappointed that you, like all Americans, convert everything into dollars.'"

"What's all the noise about?" Jack's voice surprised us.

"Hi, Jack," Tanya finished her cereal and sighed.

Jack looked at us with smiling eyes, spinning his key ring on his finger. I returned my attention to the Danish.

"Anna, tomorrow is six months since we hired Pat." He brought the salad bowl to the table, whipped off the plastic and dug in.

"Aren't you going to share that?" Tanya playfully tugged at the dish.

"Oh, I guess." Jack regretfully released the large bowl to Tanya.

Jack's tie pulled down to the middle of his wrinkled shirt annoyed me. Why are his shirts constantly wrinkled as soon as he touches them? At times his presence and mandatory English are taxing.

"So, Mom, will you talk to Dad?"

"Yes. We aren't buying a VCR or a TV," I answered in Russian as I usually do with Tanya.

Jack caught the English acronyms. "What about a VCR or TV?"

"Oh, Jack, it's so embarrassing," Tanya whined. "My father comes for a visit after more than eleven years and all he wants is money and a chauffeur to take him shopping. I don't even like driving anymore."

"What does that have to do with a VCR?"

"He wants a VCR, a television, a stereo, a Walkman. His wife dictated a list over the phone. I saw it." Tanya stood by the back door pointing an accusing finger at Jack. "There are stores on the list where he's supposed to shop at—like Neiman Marcus! He said his wife talked with a lot of people who had traveled to the United States, specifically to arm him with useful information. Useful information! One can't buy a pair of slippers at Neiman Marcus for less than a hundred bucks. Oh yes, let's not forget, he came here to convince me to go back to the Soviet Union with him," she snorted.

"You're not saying your father is one of those guests the Russian community calls vacuum cleaners, are you?" Amused, Jack stretched, smiling contentedly.

Tanya snorted again. "And he says that we, Americans, think only about money." Tanya pouted, but her anger had died down. She appreciated Jack's sense of humor.

"Look at it this way, Tanya." I put my arm around her shoulders and spoke English for Jack's benefit. "It could have been you in his place. Don't you feel sorry for people that come and have to go back?"

"He's taking advantage."

"Well, what your mother says is true. They don't have this stuff in Russia. What's the big deal?" Jack shrugged. "Let your father make his family happy. Tell me if you want me to chip in."

"No thanks, that would be too much," Tanya snapped. "I have to study. Anyone call?"

"Vera left a message to call her back."

Tanya marched out.

Jack made coffee in silence.

"You look tired," he observed, returning to the table.

"You said something about Pat's six-month anniversary." I sipped my tea, looking past Jack.

"Yeah. We promised him a review and a raise. He deserves it, too. Take him to lunch tomorrow, tell him about the three percent, like we discussed. See how he reacts. Play it by ear. Be diplomatic. We don't want to lose him."

"Jack, I don't feel like doing it tomorrow."

Jack narrowed his eyes watching me.

"Is it Fima?" he asked slowly.

"Don't you ever get angry?" I exploded. "Why aren't you angry with me now? You don't care enough about anything."

"I won't answer that," Jack said evenly, "but damn it, do you ever care about anything but your own feelings?"

Sasha's here, nothing else matters.

"No," came my hostile reply, "because no one else ever has."

"I have, and I'm not going to pay for what someone else has done. You're not ready to talk—fine. One thing, though—I am not a roommate and your problems cannot be none of my business forever." Jack got up pulling his tie off. "I know you won't hesitate to tell me if I'm in the way."

Last night Jack kissed me hungrily, tickled me mercilessly. His warm body on mine made me feel young and desirable. Today, it doesn't seem real.

"Let's go to bed," I sighed. "I'm very sleepy." I made it clear there'd be no tickling tonight.

"Gotcha," Jack remarked sarcastically. "It's not even ten o'clock. You go ahead, I'm going to work for a while."

I avoided his searching eyes.

Who is he to me? It doesn't matter now. Starting tomorrow, everything and everyone will be in their proper place.

I spent the rest of the evening in the shower, examining every part of my body, shaving and scrubbing, attempting to see myself through Sasha's eyes. Then came the hunt through my closet: Shall I wear a robe with nothing underneath? No, Sasha is very conservative. Jeans or a sweat suit? What if Sasha's dressed up? Something professional? Sasha may be intimidated, he's somewhat reserved. Shorts and a top? No, it might seem like I'm trying to look younger, and Sasha has always been sensitive to the difference in our ages. Sexy, black-lace panties and bra? No, Jack bought them for me. Shoes? Something easy to kick off?

I felt both exhausted and hyped up when I finally turned off the closet light without making a decision. Tanya sat at her desk with her head resting on her hand when I brought her cup of hot cocoa. I wandered through the house, then watched the news. When I finally came back to the bedroom I found Jack stretched the length of the bed, pretending to be asleep. I pretended to believe him.

There is no use preparing conversation. With Sasha it can't be planned.

My life has completed its circle.

The memory of my physical desire for Sasha was so intense I could almost taste his mouth, feel his fingers caressing my nipples. I had to bite my lips to keep from uttering a long, low moan. If I don't calm down, I'll be tired and pale in the morning.

Midnight. If the cuckoo clock were working, it would cuckoo now. I can't bear the quiet.

Jack tossed in his sleep. I moved closer to the edge of the bed.

What is Sasha doing now? What if Lilya is in a romantic mood . . . he can't refuse. And why should he? I remember he once said Lilya's mother told her she should keep track of how often her husband made love to her. If it was less than twice a week she should be on guard against another woman.

Sasha had dated Lilya for two years before he married her. I met her when I was fifteen. She was tall, big-boned, with mousy-brown hair and clear, friendly, brown eyes. At first I liked her, but after I saw Sasha's hand on her waist I wasn't able to sleep an entire night. Sasha didn't belong to Lonya and me anymore.

I remember lying hot and uncomfortable on my narrow spring bed, embracing my pillow, imagining Sasha declaring his love to me. When morning came I had felt guilty for my thoughts and frightened of the pleasure it had given me to rub my breasts against the pillow.

Sasha and Lilya visited regularly. Sasha played chess with Lonya; Lilya taught me to knit. When Lonya dozed off over the chessboard, the three of us talked politics and literature. I convinced myself that Sasha didn't love Lilya—that he loved me. I felt sorry for Lilya.

Then one evening they arrived with a bottle of champagne. I drank some sweet wine that Auntie Riva, Sasha's mother, had made herself from tart cherries. Lonya toasted Sasha and Lilya wishing them a happy life together. They kissed. I sat through the evening without saying a word, my eyes lowered. I thought, vengefully, that Lilya had big feet.

"Hey, Anya," Sasha took my chin with the tips of his fingers, "cheer up. Wish us happiness."

When our eyes met, I saw surprise, then a spark of understanding. He stepped back, abruptly changing the subject.

Sasha continued to see Lonya professionally and to bring hard-to-find groceries—chicken, eggs, even tangerines once—that his patients helped him get, but chess games were not very frequent anymore. Lilya was too tired to go out at night, even before Nonna was born.

I wonder if Sasha remembers.

Then there was my school graduation. Lonya stayed home recovering from the flu and, I suspect, petrified at the idea of a crowded, brightly lit hall. Sasha offered to accompany me. Lilya couldn't come, she had no one to stay with Nonna. Auntie Riva, ill with cancer, couldn't come either, but had made my dress. It was beautiful—white, with a soft belt of the same fabric.

I walked into the hall, my hand holding Sasha's arm tightly, my head proudly in the air. I introduced Sasha to the principal, teachers, and to some girls and their families, as my friend. The girls, whispering behind our backs, looked at me with new respect and envy. Teachers raised their brows. The principal, a war veteran with a ceramic hand in a black glove, boomed, "Sorry your brother couldn't be here today. You take care of our Anichka, young man, she's a good girl." Sasha shifted uncomfortably from one foot to the other. He danced with Asya, with me, and with a few girls who worked up the courage to ask him. His hand on my back made me breathless. Every time his leg touched mine on the dance floor I tensed, wetting my lips with the tip of my tongue.

"You shouldn't look at me like that," Sasha said into my ear.

"Like what?"

"I'm only human," he replied.

I didn't understand what he meant.

Lonya, who was leery of the boys I might meet, forbade me to participate in the traditional graduation night walk to the picturesque hills over the Dnieper River.

We missed the last streetcar and had to walk home. Sasha was silent, his hands in his pockets. I chirped all the way, laughed, jumped on one foot and yelled, "Wait for me," when he was too far ahead. We were almost home when I plopped onto a bench by the statue of Lenin on Shevchenko Boulevard. Exhausted, I threw back my head looking into the starry sky, reciting Pushkin.

"Let's go, let's go," Sasha prompted, pointing at his watch. "Lonya will be worried."

"I want to stay here until morning. Let's dance. There are no people around. Why are you so serious?"

He was serious. I had never seen him so serious before. I jumped up and put my hands on his shoulders. He remained still.

"Kiss me," I demanded.

"Anya, I cherish my relationship with you and Lonya and I don't want any filth in it. You're like my little sister."

"Filth? How can you use that word? So what if you are family and if you are married? Why can't you kiss me, once?"

"Anichka, you aren't making this any easier. I don't think you realize what you're doing. Even my self-control has limits. Let's go. I'm due at work in a couple of hours." Sasha tried to gently tear my hands from his shoulders. His fingers were cold.

I moved and something hard touched me. At first I thought it was his leg, but the feeling was different. I looked down then quickly up again, alarmed. Two deep creases appeared on Sasha's forehead. He stood motionless for some time, his eyes half-closed, his lips in a tight line. Fear made me quiet and motionless too. Sasha finally exhaled, rubbing his face with his hands.

"I wish I'd noticed before how much you've grown. Let's go."

Again, I didn't understand, but went obediently this time, full of love and devotion, overwhelmed with the unspoken secret that bound us, with the sweet fear of urges stronger than reason, with the inexplicable need to give my body and soul to this man who called me his little sister.

My first sex educator was Asya, who reported to our little group with an air of superiority when we were about fourteen, "Boys have a thing between their legs that they use to pee. They stick it inside a girl and pee, and the girl gets pregnant."

More knowledge came the year following graduation. I had enough points on my entrance exams to the university, but as expected I wasn't accepted. The number of points wasn't enforced as rigidly and eagerly as the quota for Jews, and I was only above average, not brilliant. Sasha said Jews should be grateful that they were allowed to live in the country and shouldn't complain.

While awaiting the next exams, I worked at a clothing factory, a shelter for unskilled females, mostly war widows and newcomers from villages who enjoyed priorities over city people, particularly Jews, in getting jobs, higher education, and apartments.

My ironing career failed miserably. A short, sturdy, young woman with muscular arms, who looked at me as if I were an insect and said that the damned Jews were not capable of anything except exploiting others, replaced me. I transferred to a less physically demanding position in quality control. My new responsibilities still required me to sit in a room smelling of machine oil, perspiration, and cheap cigarettes with old, noisy machinery and chattering, arguing, laughing women.

Jews and sex were the main topics of conversation. With Jews it was simple—clearly, the permanent hard times were their fault. Some identified anyone they didn't like as a Jew. It had become a curse. Sex seemed simple too. Men needed it to have fun, like the technicians with dark circles under their arms, who pinched our buttocks and laughed heartily with open mouths. Men needed to "come," which in turn brought about abortions, infections, and babies. Sex and penises were evils worse than drinking and were referred to as "it." "He could take a whore to have 'it.' I'm a decent woman, I don't need this nonsense every night." Or "I have two children and as far as I'm concerned he can cut 'it' off." Dead tired, in the same room as their children and parents or in-laws, with other families behind thin walls or behind furniture or curtains dividing the room, how could these women inconspicuously welcome or fight off their husbands' advances?

In my heart of hearts I hoped "it" did not exist. Tolstoi, Turgenev, Chekhov made no mention of "it." Although their characters fell in love, got married, and had children, the physical part was the lowest priority, a means of completing and perfecting, not the source or purpose.

With my brain unoccupied and the surroundings repulsive, I thought of Sasha constantly, doing what became the meaning of my whole life, until yesterday—waiting for him to understand he needed me.

An ambulance siren tore through the night outside. Jack turned to face me, placing his hand on my chest. He was sound asleep. I crawled out from under his arm and walked through the house.

Too much space just for me and Tanya! No wonder Fima mistakes me for a woman being kept by a millionaire.

Sasha will like my house. No potato or onion sacks under the bed, that's for sure.

What wouldn't I give for one night with Sasha! We never had a full night.

He certainly won't have more time now. Run in, run out, hiding from the children. God forbid that Vera or Tanya discover us.

The light blinded me, sending my heart racing as if I were already caught. Jack appeared in the opening to the living room looking at me angrily. I stood in the middle of the room blinking.

"May I ask, what you are doing? Not sleepwalking, I hope?"

My usual impulse to shrug him off stirred.

"Listen, Anna, I remember you acting like this when Fima's first letter arrived. What is it? Is he still insisting on taking Tanya back?"

Jack's face, dear and familiar, looked at me with an impenetrable expression—I suddenly couldn't remember a time in my life when I didn't know it, I couldn't remember how I ever slept alone. Strange that roots sprout between people where one would think there's nothing to make them grow.

"What? Why are you staring? Do you know what time it is? Almost four in the morning," Jack said sternly. "You'll fall asleep driving to work and have an accident. Come to bed. Now, Anna."

He let me pass, turned off the light and followed me down the hall.

Jack's no longer a stranger. How did that happen? When did I cross that bridge?

After some tossing, I drifted to sleep and, immediately, it seemed, I felt Jack's hand shake my shoulder. My eyelids were glued in the down position. I rolled away from him.

"Anna, someone's here to see you. Time to get up, anyway."

Disoriented, I expected electric lights. The sun shining through the windows seemed part of a dream. It felt like I had only slept a few minutes. My eyes hurt, and I shut them again.

"Anna, baby, wake up, someone's here to see you."

Jack, in gray shorts and undershirt, one cheek covered with shaving foam sat on the bed. A dollop of foam fell on the sheet. My lids refused to stay up.

"To see me? Who?"

"I don't know. An older gentleman. He wouldn't come in."

"Why can't you handle it?" I grouched, walking to the front door, tying my robe like a zombie.

Sasha in a polyester, navy suit stood stiffly on the front porch. The dark circles under his eyes stood out against his sallow skin.

"Oh my God, what time is it?" I exclaimed in English, brushing my hair with my fingers.

I must look awful.

"About nine. I didn't realize . . ." Sasha spoke Russian.

"Come in. Jack is leaving soon."

Sasha is not an older gentleman. Jack and his American descriptions! Sasha's trim and agile. Balding, but not gray, and his lips on my neck yesterday were as young as twenty years ago. Nothing has changed.

I left Sasha in the living room.

Jack was dressing.

"Who is he?"

"Sasha, 'Alex' in English, a dear friend of mine from many years ago. We ran into each other at the doctor's office yesterday and I invited him for breakfast."

"You had to go to the doctor?" Jack frowned.

"For Fima. He has stomach problems and needs some tests."

"Who's going to pay?"

"Any other questions?"

"Yes, as a matter of fact. Does breakfast on a working day make a lot of sense?"

"It does to us. It won't take long."

"Are you going to change into something more than a nightgown and robe? Why didn't you mention this last night?"

"Jack, stop it. You sound like a husband."

"Okay, okay, introduce us, then I'm out of here."

The two men shook hands, Jack hurriedly, Sasha nervously.

"I hope I didn't get you in trouble," Sasha said when Jack left, adding wistfully, "Your boyfriend is a young man."

The refrigerator contained not one thing that could be served for breakfast.

Sasha leaned against the wall.

"Sorry, Sasha, I planned a hero's welcome, but I didn't fall asleep until after four."

"I couldn't sleep, either."

I started wiping the sink to hide my shaking hands.

"Do you work shifts?"

"Yes, I'm an EKG technician at Highland Park Hospital."

Sasha—an EKG technician. That's unfair.

"When we emigrated, I had a minor heart attack in Rome. Lilya thought the licensing exams and completing a residency would be too taxing."

Sasha's mother used to say, "My husband was a doctor by God's will and Sasha is a doctor by God's will."

I continued to wipe the sink.

"You look so young, Anichka. I wrote to you from Kiev before we left. Asya gave me your address, but both letters came back. In Boston I couldn't find a job for a long time and I thought, what was the point in looking for you? I would have just added my problems to yours.

"When we moved to Chicago we didn't know anyone except Dr. Korotki and he didn't know you. Then Vera came home from school one day saying she'd met a Russian girl named Tanya Fishman. I thought it was a coincidence, until I saw her. Through Vera, I learned about your new career and that Tanya wants you to marry Jack, and that he's well off."

"How's Lilya? And Nonna? Where is Nonna? Tanya mentioned she met Lilya, but she's under the impression that Vera is an only child."

"I'll tell you, but not now." His face darkened.

A key turned in the back door lock and Jack appeared with a bag from Dunkin' Donuts. He raised his eyebrows at the sight of my nightgown and robe.

"You will have to excuse us. The lady of the house is not very hospitable." Jack put the bag on the table. "I was having coffee and decided to bring you two something to eat."

"Do you want to stay for a cup of coffee?" I asked dutifully.

"I've got mine in the car. Don't forget to call Pat. Talk to you later. Pleasure meeting you, Alex."

The silence that replaced the sound of Jack's car pulling away charged the air with tension so palpable that my breath became short and rapid.

I motioned Sasha to sit down but he made a step toward me and remained standing, his lips dry, his arms hanging awkwardly.

He and I will be happy, starting right now, the way I saw it in my dreams.

I took a deep breath and said, "I'll change and we'll go to a hotel." My decisive tone resonated harshly like a music track attached to the wrong movie scene.

"To a hotel?" Sasha stiffened. "Why?"

"Why not?"

"It doesn't seem the right place for someone like you."

For someone like me?

"I don't want to do it here, Sasha."

I stepped back as he walked toward me. He pressed me close with the confidence of ownership. The touch, the scent that had haunted my dreams, made me dizzy. I locked my fingers behind his neck. His hands untied my robe and pushed it aside. He kissed my lips, my eyes, my neck, my breasts with quick, light kisses.

"We will never lose each other again, Anichka, I promise," whispered Sasha between kisses.

I felt his hand unzipping his fly.

No, not again fully clothed, looking at his watch!

"No!" My voice sounded loud and desperate. I pushed him away. Sasha looked stunned. He looked old.

My legs felt as though they were made of cotton. I led him into the living room and began by unbuttoning his shirt. For the first time I saw him undressed. We lay on the sofa. Sasha's cool, impatient hands and body demanded response. I slid down and kissed him with quick, light kisses. I saw disbelief on his face. His Anya has learned a few things in the United States. The familiar, strong feeling of him inside me ushered in a brief, sharp, convulsing spasm that ended in breathless and complete release. Plastered to the sofa, I found myself surprised at the finality of that release as Sasha made love to me with a crudeness and energy I hadn't known in him. My eyes, wide open, watched his face with two deep creases along each cheek. If I hadn't seen his face, I would have thought it was Fima. Sasha's thrusts became furious and he finished groaning and crying.

We stretched next to each other, my head on his shoulder. The way my arm lazily rested across Sasha's chest reminded me of Jack, and I quickly removed it.

"Now, Anichka, I finally believe I'm not dreaming. You don't know how much I've missed you."

No, I don't.

"I guess it wasn't how much time we had, it was how much we condensed into the little time we did have, and how much it meant to have each other." Sasha paused to smile at me. "The truth hit me shortly after you left. The realization that I would never see you again made me moody and absent-minded.

"When I called Fima to get news about you, he gave me your address, but he also screamed at the top of his lungs some nonsense that I had assisted you behind his back and that he had had to ask Asya for your address." Sasha kissed my forehead. "The other day, when I ran into him at the clinic, he was barely civil. He told me he's visiting Tanya. Obviously he never told you he saw me."

Now that Sasha had relaxed, I marveled at how young he looked. I would like to watch him dress just like Jack watches me. How many times have I dreamt this meeting, this explosion contained for so many years. Now he's here to claim his little girl.

"We will never lose each other again," murmured Sasha. "You will always be my little girl."

I laughed my silver-bells laugh.

Sasha pressed me closer. "I need to make a phone call." He crawled over me, kissing me on the way.

Sasha picked up his clothes and went to the other side of the room to dress and make his call.

This is not what I had seen in my dreams. In my dreams after an explosion an unearthly tranquility reigned forever.

Our time is up. Nothing new in that.

Sasha dialed, waited, then spoke softly in English.

Fully dressed, he came back, sat on the sofa, his fingers combing through my hair thoughtfully.

"I spent the whole night preparing to talk to you today, picturing you shy and apprehensive."

Ah, I was supposed to have been shy and apprehensive.

"I was so nervous," he smiled apologetically.

I can't tear this man away—why even think of tearing him away.

"Remember, Sasha, how you called me a pagan."

"I remember. You expected to build your life on your feelings, with complete disregard for the norm. Unlike most girls, you never thought of marriage. You didn't even want to be courted. Frankly, if I hadn't known you as I did, I would have thought you . . ."

"Loose?"

"Well," Sasha laughed. "I wouldn't go that far. At any rate, you're not a pagan now. You're simply a confident American woman."

Yes, as a matter of fact, like Jack says, I, Anya Fishman, am a confident American woman.

He got up stealing a glance at his watch.

"Why did you want to go to a hotel?" he asked.

I got up and stretched. Sasha's eyes covered my body with an admiring look.

"You see, Sasha," I said, wary of causing him pain, "I have discovered that Jack is not a stranger."

"Discovered?" Sasha asked, surprised but not visibly upset.

"Yes, I know, it sounds odd. I'm beginning to think my mind's light bulb only lights up when a crisis strikes. After I met you yesterday, I discovered I want to protect Jack from being hurt."

"You never felt like that with Fima, and he was your husband."

In those days sleeping with Fima made me feel unfaithful to Sasha.

"I'm not indifferent to Jack."

"He won't find out."

No, he won't. But I'll know.

"Sashenka, I'll give you my office phone number. Call me when you have time."

We went into the bedroom. Sasha sat on the bed, waiting while I took a shower, then watched as I dressed for work. He glanced around observing the signs of Jack's presence: a shirt over the back of a chair, a tie, a pair of jeans on the bed.

He's jealous. Sasha's jealous! This is beyond my wildest dreams.

"You have a big house."

"Yes. A big, old house. Too much for two, I mean three. Remember my room in Kiev?"

We smiled and fell silent, engrossed in the same memories.

"I'm going to tell Tanya about meeting you." I said, examining my business image in the mirror. "Did you say anything to Lilya or Vera yet? I would like to see Lilya."

"No, I didn't, but you're right, we should. I wanted to check with you first."

"Why not do it tonight? Let's go back to the kitchen. I'm famished. Would you like some coffee?" I asked.

The doughnuts Jack had brought were my favorite, chocolate and Boston cream.

"I don't drink coffee, but I would have some tea." Sasha watched my hands put the sweets on a plate. "Your hands are so soft."

"I prefer tea myself. I noticed you don't smoke anymore." Turning my hands in front of me, I added unexpectedly, "Jack talked me into hiring a housekeeper."

Silently, Sasha stirred his tea.

"I'm sorry, Sasha."

I felt his pain, but I couldn't lie to him.

"Sasha, our families have always been a part of our relationship. We've never been lovers in the standard sense of the word. Don't forget—if Lonya had consented, your mother would have adopted me. In a lot of ways we *are* family."

"You don't have to apologize, Anichka. I'm happy for you," Sasha said earnestly. "Divorce is not an option I've ever had. At this point, even if I could divorce, what could I offer you? You're used to a different life now."

"No, no, you mustn't divorce," I said hastily, immediately wishing I could take the unfeeling words back. Softly, I added, "There is no comparison between you and anyone else in the world. You are the dearest person."

Sasha pressed my hand to his chest. "You're mine, my silly little girl."

I walked him to the front door and kissed his cheek.

Sasha and I will never make love again. I don't know how I'm going to look into Jack's eyes.

I staggered into the kitchen, slid into a chair, covered my face with my hands, and wailed as though at a funeral. I mourned the little girl who had scooped up a few sunrays with a butterfly net and erected a shrine to keep them unscathed. I mourned the life dedicated to the shrine from which the sunrays had long ago escaped, the shrine that had become a cage from which the little girl refused to flee. I wept for the little girl that yearned for forgiveness. I wept for the years filled with guilt, distrust, helplessness, and fear that had kept away the sun and rejected kindness and affection. I wept for the man who replaced the little girl in the cage, as if it were still a shrine illuminated by those long-ago precious sunrays and for the inescapable moment when his eyes open to see it is truly a cage. My body shook violently. I couldn't stop for a long time.

My tears left an emptiness, a sense of conclusion over which I had no control. Strangely detached, relieved, and collected, I picked up my nightgown and robe from the living room floor, looked at the dark wet spot where Sasha and I had been, threw the clothes down the laundry chute, washed my face with cold water, brushed my hair, and called Pat to arrange a lunch meeting to discuss his evaluation and raise.

The computer and printer were already hooked up and the furniture was in place in my new office. The blinds on the wall-sized window were raised and I could see a sun-filled street with people and traffic.

"I wanted to have everything finished before you came in. So, how do you like it?"

The sound of Jack's voice struck like lightning. I became glued to the carpet with my back to him.

"How did it go?"

"Fine." Facing Jack was out of the question.

"I didn't expect it to be so fast. Was he happy?"

"We were both happy." I turned and looked Jack straight in the eyes, expecting a slap.

"Good. You wouldn't want to lose him now."

"Good? That's all you're going to say?"

Jack raised his brows. "What else do you want me to say?" He looked at me searchingly. "Anna, are you all right?"

"I certainly am!" I snapped.

He doesn't care. I knew he wasn't in love with me. I suppose it's for the best.

"Okay," Jack said cautiously, "I'm glad there were no complications."

"Jack, is it that unimportant?" I asked in a small voice, still unable to move.

Jack hesitated then spoke. "It's important, but we wouldn't die if Pat quit. Those things happen, you know."

"Pat? You were talking about Pat?" I cried out hysterically.

"Anna, calm down! Who were *you* talking about?" Jack said slowly. "Didn't you just come from lunch with Pat?"

"Yes, I did." Avoiding his eyes, I hugged him, putting my head on his shoulder in spite of the open door. "I gave him the three percent raise we talked about and a promotion to staff manager."

His warm hands on my back would have made me cry if there had been any tears left.

"I wasn't aware we had a range of positions available."

"I invented it to make Pat feel good in spite of the small increase. I thought a title would induce him to stay, and it did."

Jack patted my back.

Petrified of meeting his eyes, I looked up and saw a strange, almost knowing look mixed with understanding. I wondered what he understood.

"Anna, do you want to go home early today?"

"Why?" I said, quickly looking away. "There are too many things to do. I'll talk to you later." I headed to my desk and picked up a pile of pink message slips.

"Okay, see you later," Jack said leaving my office, whistling.

I forced myself to call Lilya the day after Sasha's visit, and my sympathy for him grew into a yearning to bring light into his life, like he had brought light into my dreary existence thirty-five years ago.

Vera reluctantly called her mother to the phone.

"Good evening, Lilya," I said as cheerfully as I could. "I wonder if you recognize my voice. This is Anya."

"Yes, yes," her voice was as low as a man's. "Sasha told me," she breathed heavily into the phone saying nothing.

"How are you? I didn't know you had left the Soviet Union. A friend of mine recently tried to locate you in Kiev."

"We should have stayed in Kiev. It was all my fault. Everyone said in America they can cure anything. I made Sasha leave."

I listened to her breathe until it became clear that her reply had ended.

"What did you have to cure?"

"Nonna. But they couldn't cure her. She got worse. They can't cure anything in America. I have nothing to live for."

I wondered if she'd notice if I hung up.

"Don't say that, Lilya. Vera's a charming girl and I'm very happy she's friends with my Tanya."

"Vera, yes." A long pause. "She's Sasha's girl. Nonna's my girl and she's sick."

She burst into a sound that gave me goose bumps, that of a wounded animal, somewhere between a cry and a laugh.

"Mommy, stop, I'll call Daddy!" I heard Vera scream.

"I hate Sasha. He keeps Nonna locked up, away from me. No one knows about Nonna, but you're an old friend. Come over, I'll tell you about my girl."

"Of course, Lilya, I will. I'm a little busy right now."

"Never mind, no one ever visits us. I've met your girl . . . Tanya. Serious girl, like Vera. I remember your husband. He divorced you. You were a quiet girl, Anya, I remember."

My heart contracted with sympathy for Sasha.

"Well, Lilya, give me a call some time, we'll have lunch." I said casually as if nothing in our conversation was out of the ordinary.

"Sasha won't let me out of the house because I got fired from my job for cutting my wrists. None of their business. I worked hard. I have to listen to Sasha or he won't take me to see Nonna . . ."

I heard sounds of a struggle and Vera came on the phone. "I'm sorry, Mrs. Fishman, my mother is tired. She has to go now."

I sat on the sofa shivering until Tanya came home and turned on the light. We exchanged a few sentences, she pressed her lips to my cheek and, terror-stricken, I squeezed her so hard she looked at me in surprise.

On an impulse, I called Sasha at work the next day. By the time he answered his page I regretted calling.

"Anichka, good evening! You don't know how happy I am you called."

Sasha is declaring his love to me—like in my teenage dreams. Why does it take so long to sink in? Why don't I feel exuberant, ecstatic, care-free? I never feel what I'm supposed to.

"Sasha, I called your house and talked to Lilya."

The macabre silence that followed made me shiver.

"I'm sorry, Sasha. You didn't tell me about Lilya. What happened? She was such a content, friendly person. Where's Nonna?"

"Anya, I don't want anyone else besides you to know," Sasha said finally. "It's hereditary. I want Vera to have friends, boyfriends."

That's why Lilya goes to her room when Vera's friends visit.

"You don't have to tell me."

"Lilya's mother jumped from a window to her death when she was fifty-one. Nonna has always had problems and now she's beyond help mentally.

"I wish I could have afforded to send Vera to a boarding school. What kind of life is this for a young girl, to watch over her mother so she won't commit suicide? Anya, please don't think I don't trust you. It's just so painful. Thank God, my mother didn't live to see this."

"I understand."

"When are we going to see each other again? Your boyfriend wasn't suspicious, was he?"

"No, he wasn't."

"I want to see you. How about Monday after work? We could just sit in the car and talk."

"Call me Monday morning at the office."

On Monday and two other occasions something came up at work and I cancelled my dates with Sasha at the last minute. Sasha began stopping in at the house when he picked up Vera. I was home only once, and our conversation never ventured past casual greetings.

Evenings became torture. Jack spent them working in the basement, then watching a game on TV or going straight to bed. No matter how I tried to kill time with long hours at the office or visits to the health club, I found myself restless and fidgety and unable to sleep. I paced through the house or hid away in the bedroom where I immersed myself in a mystery, into a long conversation with Lena, or a shorter one with Natasha. Absorbed by endless shopping misadventures with her father, Tanya had become withdrawn. Even the fact that her girlfriend's father turned out to be my close friend, whom she had met as a child and whose name she had heard all her life, wasn't able to penetrate her preoccupation.

Nights brought a new torment. The perpetual fear of Jack touching me and causing revelations of Sasha to fall from my lips forced me to the edge of the bed. I tossed in my sleep, haunted by the same fear, and awoke wound up and more tired than when I went to bed.

But the worst anguish awaited me on weekend mornings. Jack would scoop me up from the edge of the bed and roll me into his arms, petting me gently, until my body thawed and my dirty deed surfaced to the tip of my tongue. But at that moment, as if he could sense it, Jack would re-member something that required his immediate attention. He would peck me lightly on my cheek and vanish until breakfast, where the topics around the table were of interest only to him and Tanya.

This lull in our lovemaking came at the most convenient time, as I felt delaying my inevitable confession until Fima left would simplify things.

What reason will I give Tanya when her perfect world falls apart? I wish I weren't the rotten person I am.

Too late.

thirty-seven

The steady flow of people carrying letters, medications, pictures, all for hand delivery in Kiev, grew as Fima's visit came to a close.

Sasha declined to take advantage of this opportunity for Fima to take a package to the Yampolsky family, who have been caring for his family's and Lonya's graves. Lena gave Fima thirty dollars as an incentive to take shoes and slippers for her mother's arthritic feet. Bella took Fima on a couple of shopping excursions and asked him to take adult diapers for her aunt and a phony invitation from Israel, made by some Russian entrepreneurs in New York, which would enable her mother and sister to apply for emigration.

The new wave of immigration is beginning to show signs of life. To many, the reason behind the decision is Chernobyl. To even more, the reason is envy of, and the desire to catch up with, their American relatives. The Russian community is slowly awakening from its comfortable nap to the possibility of newcomers.

Saturday—four days until Fima leaves. I'll say good-bye to him today. Monday I have to be in Green Bay and tomorrow we have a meeting with Howard Smolin to discuss next year's tax strategy, then a meeting with our attorney to check a contract for our first full-time marketing representative.

Immediately after breakfast Tanya left for the nursing home with balloons and streamers. She and Vera had prepared a surprise eightieth birthday party for one of the patients. Jack hurried to the basement, where he refused to be disturbed.

I called Fima and learned from Roman that he had been taken out by my girlfriend, the doctor, to breakfast and then to shop.

"I used to be the manager of a hardware store in Kiev," Roman paused significantly, "and that tells you we were fairly well-to-do." He added a pinch of proper modesty to his tone. "But I never expected anyone like Fima. He thinks money grows on trees! What does your American boyfriend think of all this?"

"Not much."

Most Russians, regardless of how many years they've lived in the United States, invariably add the clarifying adjective American when referring to someone born here. If one doesn't, it's assumed the person in question is Russian.

"Roman, I would like to come over to say good-bye to Fima. I won't have any other time. Do you know when he's going to be back?"

"Who knows? He bought another suitcase. Fima will squeeze the last dollar out of you. You're lucky to have an American," Roman laughed, proud of his sense of humor.

My plan for getting out of the house hadn't worked. Time passed slowly. Taking a shower and folding the laundry brought me to almost noon. Maybe now is as good a time as any to talk to Jack. I've known all along if I found Sasha, Jack would have to leave. Sasha is not only back— he wants me, he needs me.

"Let's go out for lunch!" Jack caught me around my waist as I folded the last sheet. He pressed me close.

"Jack," I mumbled into his shoulder.

The doorbell rang.

Fima's flushed face, in combination with several full shopping bags, spoke of success. Smiling her refined, tolerant smile, Bella held a box sporting a picture of a toaster.

"Good morning. Sorry for barging in on you." Unable to hide her relief, Bella handed the box to Jack. "We decided to drop these off and I need to call Felix. He's going to kill me for leaving him with Susan for the entire day," she said in English.

"Good morning!" Fima barked, heading straight to the little office, barely acknowledging Jack's presence.

Bella went into the kitchen to make her call.

"I assume that was good morning," Jack winked at me. "And what am I supposed to do with this toaster?"

"I'll take it. Why don't you entertain Bella for a few minutes? I need to say good-bye to Fima. I won't be long."

Fima had transferred my papers to Tanya's desk and was using mine to smooth out beach towels embroidered with Disney designs.

"Four dollars each on sale!" he said excitedly. "I got a pair of Adidas athletic shoes too! Adidas is the most popular brand in the Soviet Union! We're going to a store now that sells from catalogs!"

"Perhaps you should wait for Tanya. I don't think Bella has time to take you shopping again."

"Tanya's too young and impatient. I like going with Bella. She gives good advice. She promised to get me catalogs from different stores and sale flyers to take home." He sat down, stretching his legs.

"By the way, Fima, Tanya is counting on you to watch her play golf tomorrow. This is your last weekend."

"I can't. Marshall Field's is having a huge sale." Fima had learned the names of all the stores and used the English word "sale" freely now. "My time is valuable. I only have so many days. You know, everyone saved plastic bags for me from all kinds of stores. I'll have a whole pile!" He smiled Tanya's smile.

I placed the toaster on the towels.

"Well, Fima, we should say good-bye. I'll be busy tomorrow and then out of town for three days. I bought some things for you to take back for me."

I stood on my tiptoes to reach a bag from the top of the bookshelves.

"Let me," Fima said softly.

He pulled down the bag, put it on a chair and took my hand. I flinched, prepared to take it away if he tried to kiss it.

"Anya, I wish our marriage hadn't fallen apart," he said. He stood a few inches away from me. "I think my constant talk about Tanya and you makes my wife jealous."

His warm tone and sad demeanor set off some old, guilty ramblings inside me, keeping me from increasing the distance between us. Surely, he expected me to say something nostalgic, but I didn't know what to say besides repeating I was sorry.

I finally mustered a reply. "Your wife shouldn't be jealous."

"You acted so cruelly. And why? You couldn't predict that Tanya's future would be better outside her motherland."

I cringed at the hypocritical Soviet cliché used only in jest, or to prove party loyalty, or by those few who, like Fima, actually believed it.

"I knew it couldn't be worse."

"It wasn't that bad, was it?"

His nostrils twitched. I tried to free my hand.

Suddenly his arms encircled me tightly.

"Anichka, for old time's sake, give me a kiss."

I studied his dry lips. "Please, Fima, let me go," I said in a monotone, not angry, only mildly surprised.

"Just one kiss."

His open mouth hanging over my face reminded me of Vilen.

Did I ever sleep with this man? And of my own free will?

"Fima, don't make things even worse."

Whatever my expression was, it caused Fima to unlock his arms, his eyes hostile. I stepped back so quickly I bumped into the desk.

"You used to like it," he said through gritted teeth. "You were always ready for me."

"I never liked it," I said indifferently, as if we were discussing the weather. It felt good to say what I thought. "You don't know what ready is. You scarcely gave me time to get in bed before you attacked me."

"What did you need time for?" Fima shrieked, raising his fists. "You were my wife. Supposedly, you loved me. If you were into tricks, you shouldn't have gotten married."

"Fima, bringing this up now is ridiculous. What difference does it make?" I shrugged.

"You're lying! You did like it. I know you did! Tell me you did!"

These shrieks were definitely something I was not going to miss.

"Fima, Bella's waiting for you."

"Anichka, every night I picture you and Jack together. Who is Jack, if not just one of many men? I was your husband, the father of your child." Fima directed my hand to his zipper. "I'm entitled to the same treatment." His face moved closer.

This man did not seem a man at all—he didn't even sicken me, he was just a nuisance.

"You're not trying to have sex with me this very minute, are you?" I inquired politely.

"You have an icicle instead of a heart." Fima pushed me away and ran his fingers through his hair. "Without any misgivings you destroyed our family. You don't know how to have a family." Foam began to collect in the corners of his mouth. "You don't care about Tanya. You just don't want to lose your benefactor."

He had used a more neutral word than "pimp," but his disgusted expression underscored the implication. I felt Fima had intended his last words to give him a reason to void what he considered the dishonor of being deserted.

"You're right, Fima," I replied with sympathy for him and grief over our past lives. "Sensitivity is not my strong suit, and I don't know how to have a family. You're Tanya's father and she needs you and her new brothers. Let's salvage the memories of our marriage and remain on good terms for the children's sake."

Closing his eyes, Fima ran his fingers through his hair again. He appeared shrunken and thoroughly defeated.

"We shouldn't make Bella wait." I sounded as moved as I was.

Fima remained silent, his eyes were lifeless.

"Before we go, I'd like to ask you a favor." I said quietly. "There is a family in Kiev that takes care of Lonya's grave. I only learned about them recently and I would like to send them some clothes. Would you take them, so they won't have to pay a customs fee?"

"Ever so practical." Fima straightened up and stared at me with scorn. "But I'm practical, too. I already have too much to take back. If you have money to burn, spend it on me and my children, not on strangers."

"Lonya was my brother. For what it's worth, he introduced us."

"Not worth much to you," he sneered. "At first I didn't understand why you acted so meek with him, why he constantly worried about you. You were always on his mind."

"I was?"

Does he mean that Lonya loved me and not merely followed his exaggerated sense of duty?

"When you admitted, after I proposed, to not being a virgin, I knew immediately the nature of your relationship with Lonya. I was so infatuated with you, it made me feel good to play the role of your prince, your savior. What an idiot I was!" Fima's laugh sounded unnatural.

I shivered. "What are you talking about, Fima? Lonya was my brother." My voice dropped dangerously low.

"You never realized I knew, did you? A brilliant mathematician and chess player, he had no life outside of you. He was absolutely immersed in you. Only one reason that . . ."

"Lonya was my brother! Lonya was my brother and I loved him!"

"I bet you did!—He started you off!" Fima grew into a dragon with fire coming from his all-knowing smile.

"Lonya was my brother!"

From the corner of my eye I saw the door open and Jack walk in with Tanya and Bella behind him.

"Lonya was my brother!" My fist shook.

"What is it, Anna?" Jack asked tentatively.

"Lonya was my brother, do you hear me!?" I shrugged Jack's hand off my shoulder. "You filthy-minded worm! Lonya was the most noble, sacrificing, gentle person in the world. You would never understand that! I'm proud to have had him as a brother!" I was ready to pounce at Fima.

"Tanya, what is your mother saying?" Jack demanded.

"Don't, Tanya! This is between your father and me," I commanded without looking at her. "Lonya was my brother, Fima! You're not going to take that from me!"

Fima, foam now bubbling out of the corners of his mouth, shrieked, "If not Lonya, you had other adventures before me!"

"Yes, Fima, yes, I had adventures before you." The relief was so complete it made me sway. "But Lonya was my brother."

Jack turned. "Bella, please tell me what's happening before I do something rash!"

"No!" I said.

Bella hesitated.

"Bella, whatever it is, I have the right to know," Jack insisted.

I had no energy to object.

Bella translated.

Jack observed Fima curiously.

"What's going on?" Tanya's unfriendly eyes watched her father.

She didn't understand Russian well enough to follow the nuances of our argument.

Automatically, Bella translated Tanya's English for Fima.

"It's nothing, Tanichka," I pulled her to me.

Tanya looked up at Jack, his face impenetrable.

"Dad, I'm going to take you shopping. Bella has to go home," she spoke without enthusiasm.

"Okay," replied Fima, "let's go."

"We're going to the golf course tomorrow," Tanya said first in Russian then English, looking at Jack. He nodded.

"I can't," Fima said sternly. "I told you, Marshall Field's has a very big sale."

"Dad, you're leaving in a couple of days and you haven't seen anything. We can always send you stuff."

"You are too young to understand, Tanya. I must bring back enough to sell."

"Why?" Tanya rounded her eyes.

"Because this trip was a big expense. I need to make it worthwhile."

"Didn't you come to see me!?"

"Daughter, one doesn't exclude the other."

Tanya straightened up and said quietly, "Going shopping all the time is fine, but then don't say you came to see me." Her jaw tightened.

Bella sighed and reluctantly translated the entire exchange for Jack. It took considerable effort for her to maintain an emotionless expression.

Jack narrowed his eyes at Fima.

"I'm not going to talk to you, if my every word is to be repeated in English to your mother's lover." Fima turned to the door.

"Dad, it's embarrassing that we may not ever see each other again and all you care about are the things you'll take back."

"We'll see each other again. I already ordered an invitation from Israel."

Bella, Tanya, and I stared dumbfounded.

"Dr. Korotki told me, but I thought he made a mistake," I said, still not believing Fima's emigration was under discussion.

Bella translated. Jack whistled, leaned against the wall, and stuck his hands in his pockets.

"Why didn't you tell me? Why did we have to run around from store to store?" Tanya blinked rapidly, too shocked to cry.

"Would you still be buying me all I need if you knew? When I'm here for good, Tanichka, we'll have a lot of time to talk and to do things together."

In the background I heard Bella translate to Jack.

"It wasn't right. And tell me, did you ever apologize for what you said to Mom the day you arrived?" interrogated Tanya.

"No," replied Fima defiantly.

"You promised me you would. For once would you tell the truth?" Tanya spoke as if it made her ill to address her father.

Bella translated loudly, pleased to be justified in her dislike of Fima.

"You can't talk in that tone to your father!" reprimanded Fima, pointedly ignoring the rest of us.

"So many Russians are slime and have no morals," Tanya exploded. "They cheat even when there's no reason. They think people that don't cheat are beneath them. You're like that. I was waiting for you—I didn't even go to the prom so I wouldn't have to take time from you to shop for a dress—and you lied to me. You changed your name too! How would I have been able to find you? Buy your stupid stuff yourself!" Tanya had made her angry speech in English oblivious to the fact that Fima couldn't understand a word.

Bella conscientiously translated for him.

Fima jerked Tanya's arm so hard she stumbled forward, almost losing her balance.

"How do you dare talk to your father like this? Apologize at once!" he shrieked.

"Let her go!"

Through blurred eyes, in almost slow motion, I saw Jack advance toward Fima.

"This is none of his business!" Fima addressed Bella, pointing at Jack. "Tanya is my daughter! This is my family! Tell him that! Tell him that!"

Bella translated and stepped in front of Jack who moved her aside without, it seemed, being conscious of his action. He now stood with his back to me, facing Fima.

"Wrong, pal! It *was* your family. It's *mine* now."

I froze. A brief impulse to stop Jack faded.

Bella translated in a quick, uncomfortable whisper, glancing at me with concern.

Fima dropped Tanya's arm. Looking scared, she instinctively moved closer to Jack.

"Who are you to antagonize my daughter against me! When I come here to live, I will bring order to Tanya's life."

Jack waited for Bella to finish translating.

"When you come here to live, you and Tanya will decide your relationship." Jack spoke quietly and evenly, controlling himself with difficulty. "I will either get you a job or set you up in business. I will give you enough money to get started. Only, you are not to set foot in my house again—not ever again. I warn you to remember what I just said. Remember—this is *my* home and *my* family."

Fima stared thunderstruck as he listened to Bella's translation.

"Your lover is in command of my daughter's life!" he recovered finally with a shriek. "You're not protecting her. Tell him he has no right. I'm Tanya's father! He bought you!" Short, abrupt words flew from Fima's mouth followed by his taunting sneer. "All his might is behind his zipper and in his wallet. He'll regret this!"

Tanya gasped, clapping her hand to her mouth. Jack put his arm around her shoulders.

"Bella!" prodded Jack. She blushed but translated verbatim.

"Don't you dare, Fima," I heard myself speak slowly, stretching every word. "Don't you dare."

Jack turned to me.

I took a deep breath. Oh God, I can't lose Jack. Please, God, I don't want to lose Jack.

When the words finally came out I couldn't stop.

"Tanya may be your daughter, but we are not your family. You don't belong with us." I felt as though I had been awakened from a dream. "You lost your rights by not emigrating with us. For years I felt guilty for having taken Tanya from you. At times I wished as punishment I wouldn't succeed. I was ready to let Tanya visit you in Kiev, even if there was a chance she would decide to stay. That's how guilty I felt. Well, Fima, I don't feel guilty anymore. Tanya must decide for herself, but, emigration or not, I personally never want her to be like you or to even know you, for that matter. I wish I'd never answered your first letter. Jack has made a family out of two scared women. He has been a father to Tanya. Remember well what he told you. Don't you dare refer to Jack ever again in the manner you have. I love this man. Go away, Fima. Go away." My hands were cold and shaking. I felt nothing but relief.

Bella translated. Fima swallowed and opened his mouth to say something.

"Bella, repeat it," Jack interrupted in a husky voice.

Bella's soft recital in English and Jack's warm hands on my shoulders made me weak.

"Anna, did you really say that?"

"What?"

"You've destroyed my life and don't think you won't be punished," spat Fima.

"Bella, did she really say that?" repeated Jack.

"What exactly do you mean? I translated word for word." Bella rubbed her face tiredly. "Anichka," she said in Russian, "I'm going home. I'm sorry for being in the middle of a family quarrel. Jack," she switched back to English, "take it easy. The past has a way of catching up with people."

"Tanya's my daughter. You can't just ignore me," Fima squeaked.

"Thank you, Bella," Jack shook hands with her, his other hand on my waist. "I owe you one."

"Tanya, take me home. Bring all my bags to Roman's. I'm not coming to your mother's house again." Fima assumed a busy, indifferent expression, organizing a multitude of boxes and rustling bags, his hands shaking.

Distraught, Tanya, picked up some of the bags and looked at Jack. He nodded in return and she left with Bella.

Jack and I stood silently watching Fima fold the beach towels, then carry out his treasures. He wasn't in a hurry. He moved around as if he were alone in the room, making many trips to the car, paying close attention to not leaving anything behind.

"Anna, did you really say that?" repeated Jack as soon as Fima was gone.

Jack followed me into the living room.

I sank to the sofa and closed my eyes.

"Say what?"

"I want you to say it again, only this time to me. God knows, I was beginning to lose hope of ever hearing you say it."

"Jack, I want to forget everything I said and everything Fima said. Most of all, I wish Tanya had not been present."

"Everything?"

"Come on, Jack, what do you want? Give me some time to relax."

"Unless Bella exhibited some creativity of her own, you said . . . think, Anna. I want *you* to say it to me."

What did I say? What could be so important to Jack?

He sat next to me, holding my hands, solemn and quiet, as if prepared for a momentous event.

"In short, I said to Fima he had no right to Tanya and he couldn't speak rudely of you."

"What else?" Jack insisted looking into my eyes.

"Nothing."

"Unless, of course, you didn't mean it."

"Didn't mean what?"

An attack of panic suddenly made me retreat to the corner of the sofa.

"I want you to say it to me. And we don't need a translator." Jack's smiling eyes searched my face.

"I can't say it."

"But you did."

His American eyes will never become Russian. He will never understand my Russian aches and pains. I don't care, I love him. And that is what I said. When did it happen? I was waiting for Sasha, dreaming of Sasha. How did this happen?

"Don't cry, darling. Just say it." Jack kissed my palms.

"Don't make me."

"Say it."

I looked up at Jack. There was no sign of pity.

"I love you, Jack."

The sound of the words terrified me for a moment, then the dam broke. I heard my silver-bells laugh and repeated, "I love you, I love you, I love you," listening to the sound of the words.

Jack swooped me up and whirled me around, finally tossing me back on the sofa and tickling me until I slid to the floor sending a pillow flying across the room almost knocking over a lamp.

Exhausted, we ended up side by side on the sofa, gasping for breath, still laughing.

"Anna, there's something I've wanted to ask you for a very long time." Jack was suddenly serious.

I stopped laughing and put my head on his shoulder, blissfully thoughtless.

"Anna, will you marry me?"

My body stiffened, the happiness of the last minutes evaporated.

We can't be married. We can't even keep what we've got. I cheated on him with Sasha and I'm not going to lie to him.

"We can't be married, Jack."

"Why? Your divorce papers are in order, aren't they?"

"They are. Only, you don't want to marry me."

"When a man asks a woman to marry him," he took my face in his hands, "it is generally assumed he wants to marry her."

I forced a smile. "Jack, I haven't been completely honest with you."

"You have," Jack said quietly.

"I haven't, and I'm not talking about the past."

"Yes, you are."

"No, Jack, you don't know everything."

"No, Anna, you don't know everything. I want very much to marry you. Will you marry me?"

How did he find out? It doesn't matter; it's in the past.

"Yes, I will marry you."

"No more tears. It's the one condition I'm going to impose on my wife," Jack said, pulling me close.

I rubbed my wet face on Jack's sweatshirt.

"There's so much I've never done or felt. At almost forty-six I'm like a child discovering the world. It sounds crazy, Jack, but I don't think I was ever a wife before."

"It doesn't sound crazy, not after today's scene with Fima."

"I'm not sure I know how to be a wife."

"Just stay the way you are, Anna. Let's get married right away."

"Wait, what about your mother?"

"I'll tell her," Jack shrugged, "eventually."

"She's your mother. You have to tell her now."

"Sweetheart, first things first. I'll call a couple of jewelers and you'll pick out a ring.

"Jack, she's your mother."

"Well?"

"What do you mean, 'Well?' Don't you want to tell her?"

"To be frank, not really."

"It doesn't make any difference whether she likes me or not, she's your mother and she will be my mother-in-law."

"Anna, I don't understand why you're so adamant about this."

"She's your mother, Jack. If you don't tell her now, I will."

We heard Tanya unlocking the front door. I moved away from Jack.

"I took Dad home," Tanya reported with a sour face. "Anyone call?" She was in no mood to talk.

"No." I looked at Jack for support.

"Tanya, come over here." Jack got up, pulling me with him. "I realize you're upset, but your Mom has some news for you that I'm sure you'll like."

How can he be sure?

Tanya came into the room and looked at me expectantly.

"Tanichka, Jack asked me to marry him."

Her lips curled up and her eyes filled with childish delight.

"Oh, Mom, I'm so happy! Jack, what took you so long?" She hugged and kissed both of us. "My mother always wanted to marry you," Tanya lectured, one adult to another.

Jack glanced at me slyly and we laughed.

"Are you making fun of me?" inquired Tanya with mocking suspicion. "Let's go out and celebrate."

"Absolutely," I turned to Jack, "as soon as Jack calls his mother."

"Mom, can I help you pick out your ring?"

"Definitely. I need a woman's advice."

"We have to tell everyone." Tanya became thoughtful. "I'll see Dad before he leaves, but I don't know if I want to tell him. Wasn't it bizarre the way he acted?" she sighed. "Can I tell my friends about you and Jack? You know, Vera's father told her you used to be really close friends. Do you want to tell him yourself?"

My stomach tightened. I hesitated, trying feverishly to guess what Jack felt and thought.

"You can tell your friends, Tanichka, Vera included. She can tell her father, and I'll talk to him myself in a day or so."

Tanya ran to the telephone.

Jack's fingers rubbed my neck. I worked up the courage to meet his eyes.

"I love you, Jack." It came easy now.

"Don't you think I've known all along?" he questioned seriously. "Let's go to the kitchen. I need a cup of coffee. I'll call my mother as soon as Tanya's off the phone."

Jack didn't have to worry; teenager Tanya was on the phone.

thirty-eight

I called Asya at seven in the morning Kiev time to tell her about my engagement. I intended it as a quick girl-to-girl conversation that just couldn't be put off. In the beginning, she kept asking, "Jack and you, what?" and I laughed my silver-bells laugh when it dawned on me that in my excitement I used the word "engaged" without bothering to translate it into Russian.

With the misunderstanding cleared up, Asya cackled and giggled and congratulated me profusely, then we giggled together, until we heard Myron.

"Asya, are you crazy? What are you doing talking on the phone when you're supposed to be at work in fifteen minutes?"

"Myron, get lost! It's Anya calling! Her American boyfriend is going to marry her!" Asya dealt with her husband then returned to me. "I cannot tell you how happy I am for you!" she sobbed. "You must write me about every tiny detail! I have to run to work now. Bye."

I hung up the phone and sobbed a little too.

25 May 1987

Dear Tanichka,

I'm writing to let you know I arrived home yesterday and my family shares in my desire to apply for emigration. We will start collecting our papers immediately. One of my suitcases disappeared at the Moscow airport. I consider myself lucky only one was lost.

Soon I will take my rightful place in your life, and my foremost concern will be to expose you to the right values and bring order to your life.

Do not send more parcels as we will be together in less than a year and we will never part again.

Love, Dad

"Why didn't you tell me the truth about my father?" Tanya said as she sat down in a chair at the patio table, looking away from me.

"What do you mean?"

The Soviet envelope in Tanya's hands appeared out of place.

"You never told me he was so rude, so loud, so . . . and he doesn't really care about me." Tanya looked up and I realized, with a mix of relief and pain, she wasn't suffering, only disappointed.

"Tanya, I told you the truth about your father, the truth as I knew it."

"A person can't change that much," she stated with teenage confidence. "You taught me not to lie, but I can't write to him like I'm a real daughter." Her face held contempt.

"Tanya, no one is perfect. There are things I've done I'm not proud of."

"But you had to leave Russia, even if my father didn't want to. It wasn't wrong."

Unable to talk, I closed my eyes. She'll never know how I've waited for her words to exonerate me.

"It wasn't. I know that now." I said finally. "Nothing is absolutely right or absolutely wrong. But, think about it. How would you feel in your father's place?"

"I'd probably feel a lot of hate," whispered Tanya after a pause, ready to cry.

"Write to him, Tanichka. He does care. Please, write to him."

June 16, 1987

Dear Dad,

I'm sorry we didn't say a nice good-bye to each other. In all your letters you told me the only reason for your visit was to learn as much as possible about my life and to spend time with me. I'm disappointed it didn't happen that way. I understood you needed to do some shopping, but why so much? After all, we were sending you stuff. You still don't know much about my life. When you come here for good I'll be in college and won't have much time. Mom says I should take into account your shock at the difference in life between the United States and the Soviet Union. She says every Russian is shocked when he sees Western stores for the first time.

The reason I'm writing is to tell you that Mom and Jack have decided to get married. The wedding is set for October twenty-third. I can't tell you how happy I am! Mom is very happy too. You didn't get to know Jack well, but you could see, I'm sure, that he's a very nice person and the best friend we ever had, and he loves Mom and me. I would like you to be happy for us.

Mom doesn't want a big wedding. She thinks she's too old, but Jack wants to make it a very special day. Mother won, sort of. The wedding will be medium-sized. We don't have any family, only a few friends. Jack has his mother, some friends, and distant cousins in the States, and he says some of his relatives from Argentina will come. People connected with their business are on the list too. Planning the wedding is exciting.

We're going to continue to live in our house, even though Jack's house is much bigger. There's enough room here. Mom and Jack can't leave their business for a long time, so they haven't made any plans for their honeymoon yet.

Regards to your family.

Love, Daughter

Asya called in the middle of the night on July fifteenth to say happy birthday. She startled me with a dramatic, "In the name of our past friendship, please sponsor my son. He will pay you back." Her older son, Dima, had married Ella, the Gentile girl Asya had been against. They were waiting, along with Asya's sister, Rimma, and her family, for permission to leave. Rimma's brother-in-law in Los Angeles had refused to pay the sponsorship fee, an extra of fifteen hundred dollars per person, for Dima. Asya was frantic. I tried to explain to her that there was no sponsorship fee in Chicago and it would be my pleasure to sponsor her son, whatever the cost, but she didn't listen, just cried.

After the call I couldn't fall asleep. If Dima was coming, Asya wouldn't be far behind. I imagined our future reunion as mature women, having arrived at the same physical point after following such different paths.

The next day Jack decided on a trip to Kiev for our honeymoon and as a present to Tanya.

I longed to visit Lonya's grave, Tanya was curious, and Jack . . . well, I think he just knew it was time for me to go back.

18 July 1987

Dear Tanichka,

We received your letter some time ago, and I expected to tell you in my response that we had applied to leave. Sadly, this is not the case. Igor's father has refused to sign the consent form needed for his son to emigrate. They are not close and only see each other a couple times a year, but he insists that people should not betray a motherland which has given them so much. He must be blind. I don't know what we're going to do. My wife is going to talk to him again, but she doesn't think there's any hope, and she absolutely refuses to leave Igor behind. Understandably, I would not leave without Petya. We either go as a family or not at all.

Give my belated happy birthday to your mother and my congratulations on her engagement. Jack staying in your house, in God knows what capacity, was disturbing. I don't want you to think this mode of life is acceptable.

Tanichka, I feel bad that my time was so disproportionately spent on shopping. Your mother was right. The shock of seeing abundance for the first time in my life was too much and, combined with the frustration and pain of my family not being able to get even basic things as easily as you do—well, I just couldn't control myself. I don't know when we're going to meet again, but if we do it will be different.

My family was pleased with the things I bought for them. Some of the clothes, the VCR, and the hand-held calculators I sold, making enough to cover all my expenses from the trip. Your mother's girlfriend, Asya, came over soon after my return to hear the latest news about you. Her older son, Dima, and her sister, Rimma, recently applied to emigrate. Lucky family, they don't have to put up with a stubborn, short-sighted individual ruining their lives.

I love you, Tanichka.

Dad

August 15, 1987

Dear Dad,

Mom and Jack have decided to spend their honeymoon in Kiev and I'm going with them—they wouldn't go without me. So, we will be able to see each other again. Mom wants to go to Uncle Lonya's grave, show us the building where we used to live, the university she went to, the Bessarabka open market where she used to buy fruits for me when I was sick, the Dnieper River, and a lot of other places. We'll only have a few days there.

We'll stay at a hotel. I'll visit you and meet Petya and Igor. The trip is Jack's idea. He wants to see how we lived before we came to the United States. He tries very hard to understand Mom's past and why she thinks about it so much.

Dad, I don't like the way you talk about Jack. He has never been "in a God-knows-what capacity." I don't know how to explain it, because I have never known any family besides Mom, but he has been almost like an uncle to me since I was twelve. I was always afraid if something happened to Mom I would be left alone, but now I know he will always be there too. He has helped me with my homework, let me use his expensive car, takes me to basketball games and golf competitions, and shoots baskets with me. He even found someone to teach me golf. I can always count on him no matter what I need, or even if I just want to talk. I really care about him and I hope we never lose him.

Mom bought her wedding dress in Los Angeles at her friend Helena's favorite store. I went with them to help pick it out. We'll have to go again for a fitting. It's absolutely gorgeous. We'll bring pictures. My dress is really neat. We got it in Chicago. Jack ordered so many flowers for the wedding Mom says there won't be room for people.

I'm sorry Igor's father won't let him leave. Maybe he'll change his mind. But you shouldn't be upset. You said yourself, Gorbachev is on the right track and life will get better eventually.

College starts at the end of September. It's going to be tough, but I can't wait.

Regards to your family.

Love, Daughter

When a phone call woke me up in the middle of the morning and Asya's voice said, "Good evening," I thought for a second that one of us was hallucinating. I was taking a nap after the red-eye flight from Los

Angeles where I had gone for the fitting of my wedding dress. I suddenly realized it was evening in Kiev and laughed, completely awake and happy.

"Why are you laughing?" Asya sounded upset.

I explained but didn't improve her mood.

"Fima just called. Anya, I'm very disappointed. You're going to honeymoon in Kiev and you're planning on staying at a hotel," Asya spit out.

"I know, Asinka," I said guiltily. "I would have told you next week when I called to say happy birthday."

"I'm very disappointed." Asya's voice showed signs of approaching tears. "To stay at a hotel in a city where I live! I never expected that from you!"

Cold with fear that my breach of Russian friendship ethics would fracture our new-found relationship, I frantically groped in my mind for a solution.

"Listen, Asinka, Jack doesn't speak Russian. It would be awkward," I said soothingly.

"Why should it be awkward? You can translate."

"He would never agree. He doesn't like to disrupt someone else's life if he doesn't have to. Besides, there are three of us and three of you . . ."

"So what?" Asya interrupted heatedly. "Tanya could sleep on the little sofa in my mother's room. Myron and I would sleep in the living room, and you would have our room to yourself. And, you know, our bathroom with the tub and sink, and the toilet room, are separate, so that two people could use the facilities at the same time."

Horrified by the vision of that arrangement, I remembered Lonya's and my room, and the kitchen and bathroom shared with the Berezovskys, Auntie Olya, and, for a while, her mother. How quickly one forgets!

"Tell her I still remember some English from high school," Myron chimed in.

"Myron still remembers some English from high school," Asya introduced a new argument in her favor.

"Asinka, we will have to stay at a hotel," I said with such conviction that Asya fell silent.

"I promise to spend an entire day with you, it will be even better without interruptions and translation—just the two of us."

"I guess you should do what your fiancé wants you to," she said finally. "I mean, under the circumstances, it appears you have no choice."

"I knew you'd understand," I replied, filled with warmth for the kind, generous Asya that had come back into my life. "And now, hang up. Let me call you back, it's too expensive for you."

I finally got connected on the fourth try.

"Fima irritates me," Asya said as soon we were connected. "He yelled at me as though I were his wife, that he, and only he, will show Tanya and Jack the city. All of a sudden, he's become a devoted father. Allow me not to believe that," she continued, dripping venom. "There are fathers that leave their children behind, but a father that let his child go . . . unheard of."

"Let's not rehash the past," I said. "I'm not really interested in sightseeing. Fima knows the city well, and he wants to spend time with Tanya. Let him."

"I guess. Kiev has become so beautiful you won't want to go back. The St. Andrew's Cathedral, St. Sophia's Cathedral, St. Vladimir's Cathedral, the Golden Gate, the hills over the Dnieper river, the Vladimir Gorka, the Opera House, the Lavra Monastery, the Victory Monument, Kreshchatik Street, the University, the Pechersk area."

I realized that Kiev had stopped being a city to me. It had become my past. "I'll just visit people, dead and alive, and places dear to me. I'm not a tourist."

Asya sighed. I could see her nodding seriously.

"When you talk to Fima," I went on, "ask him to take Tanya to some stores, to a hospital, maybe to someone's place of work. Especially, a hospital. As a future doctor, she will find it interesting."

"I will tell him. Anichka, I can't wait to see you. I know I won't recognize Tanya. Rimma thought that she was a pleasant girl, and that your fiancé was not really good-looking, but manly, and that you had transformed into a princess, like Cinderella."

"You'll be disappointed," I chuckled. "Self-service doesn't work as well as a magic wand."

21 September 1987

Dear Tanichka,

I hope this letter will arrive before you leave on your trip. Since I don't have a telephone, would you please ask your mother to call Asya with your flight information. I want to meet you in Moscow.

There's a lot of crime in the Soviet Union, especially aimed at foreigners, with taxi drivers often robbing their passengers. I'll make arrangements with a Moscovite I know and we'll pick you up with his car and show you the city before your flight to Kiev.

Tanichka, don't bring us anything. I'm very happy you'll be able to meet my family and see your motherland. You can come to us for dinner and we'll go sightseeing.

There's no change in our status. I can't sleep at night for trying to think of a way to convince Igor's father to let him leave. This man just doesn't want to listen.

I'm glad you and Jack have a good relationship. I didn't mean to be so negative toward him. I never realized the United States would be so different from the Soviet Union.

See you soon, Your Dad

21 September 1987

Anya,

I would like to apologize to you and Jack for my rudeness. Even with the little time we had in Chicago, I realized, like never before, how happy we could have been. My sincere congratulations on your upcoming marriage and best wishes for a long and happy life.

I hope to see both of you, with Tanya, at my home when you are in Kiev. I would have never dreamed that people like you and me would have more than one marriage. At times I have difficulty believing it has really happened.

Fima

thirty-nine

The preparation for our honeymoon took very little time, thanks to our experiences with Rimma and Fima. Tanya insisted on personally getting toys for Petya leaving to me the rest of, in her words, "stuff-buying." A five-hour raid on the popular discount store, TJ Maxx, where I loaded two shopping carts to overflowing status, would satisfy, I thought, Asya's and Fima's clothing needs for the forseeable future, both to wear and to resell. I followed it up with a quick stop at Sears to purchase two large suitcases, one for Asya and one for Fima. Donna volunteered to cut off the price tags and refold all the items, except Petya's, in a way that would make them appear used. We knew that we could not avoid paying a customs fee for children's clothes, since we could not claim them as ours.

The honeymoon nature of my trip to Kiev kept petitioners away, which, for some reason, made me feel abandoned. I had to argue with Lena and Bella that visiting their families in Kiev would not rob my honeymoon of its meaning or distract us from sightseeing. Eventually, Lena relented and gave me her parents' phone number and warm gloves for her mother.

Bella stood firm. But a few days before our departure she called.

"Anya, it looks like I do have to ask you for a favor in Kiev," she said, sounding guilty.

"Wonderful!" I exhaled.

"I will understand if you refuse," she continued as if she hadn't heard me.

"Why would I refuse?"

I listened to the sound of Susan practicing on the piano as a pause ensued.

Finally, Bella took a deep breath. "Anya, Irena just received the fake Israeli invitation she ordered from New York for her mother and niece. A collegue of mine had agreed to take it with her to Kiev when she visits there next week, but her husband is ill and she has cancelled her trip."

It took me a minute to convince myself I had heard correctly.

Bella read my silence for what it was.

"I know," she said in the same guilty tone, "it's hard to believe that Irena's mother, the former head of human resources for a research institute, would even consider emigration."

Feared and despised, the human resources departments in the Soviet Union enforced the hiring quotas and watched for subversive activity, which meant, with the exception of some backwater industries, not hiring those with even one Jewish parent. Work for this department presumed anti-Semitism and reeked of the party apparatus.

"She wouldn't have allowed anyone to hire you or me, or her son-in-law, for that matter."

"Her son-in-law was rejected when he applied. That's a fact," Bella sighed.

"Do you remember Irena saying that she embarrassed her family by becoming part of a Jewish family?"

"I remember. That was not the worst she has said over the years. Felix suggested I burn the invitation. Listen, if this errand makes you sick you can refuse."

"It makes me sick."

"You know," Bella mused, "in spite of Irena's nastiness I feel sorry for her. Ever since her younger sister died from leukemia two years ago, she pretty much supports her mother and niece who is only eighteen and not terribly bright. She works hard, she is ready to help anyone with anything, and, of course, she's a loyal wife."

I shivered at the thought of Vilen.

"I'll deliver the invitation," I said, wanting to cut the conversation short.

"Thanks, Anichka." Bella sounded brighter. "I knew you would."

I shut my eyes tight to keep away the memory of Vilen's contorted face in Lena's bathroom.

"In a way, it's not fair," Bella continued thoughtfully, "that Vilen running around getting medications for his mother-in-law, who treated him as her worst enemy, only confirms his decency, but whenever Irena does anything positive it shocks people. Sometimes I think that her good heart is not connected to any other part of her personality."

Nothing is absolutely right or absolutely wrong.

"I won't visit them," I said firmly. "I'll leave the invitation at my girlfriend's house."

"Irena is still angry at you for not even inquiring about Vilen's condition after his accident at Lena's house, and frankly I can't argue with her." Bella paused long enough for me to offer an explanation for the irrational behavior I knew she was always curious about. She sighed when, again, it was not forthcoming. "She won't accept a favor from you, so I'll let her think that my colleague will leave it at her friend's house."

I added Irena's mother's phone number to my list.

When I emigrated, only foreign numbers and addresses were permitted in the emigrants' phone books; the local ones had to be memorized or hidden. In official eyes, that policy limited the influence of the departing black sheep of Soviet citizenry on the flock staying put. That rule did not present any difficulties for me, as Asya's and Auntie

Olya's addresses were ingrained in my brain, and Sasha was afraid to correspond. Recent visitors assured me that *perestroika* had gone so far as to eliminate the scrutiny of people's phone books during customs inspections.

The visit to Kiev took me outside time and reality. I discovered the link between my memories and what I experienced in Kiev to be nonexistent. The bridge was shattered; there was no retreat. I understood why the Sasha of my youth was not the Sasha of Chicago. Asya, when we finally met, was merely a face I had known for many years. Fima, in spite of our quite recent contact, was also only another familiar face. It struck me, on our return flight, that Jack, Tanya, and I had exchanged very few words during our five-day stay in Kiev, and that I had never explained to them the reasons for most of my sightseeing choices.

We left Chicago immediately after our wedding reception, flying Chicago-New York-Moscow-Kiev and back in ten days. In New York, Tanya stayed with Jack's childhood friend and his wife for a day and a night, giving Jack and me a little time for ourselves.

As soon as Tanya disappeared, I was overcome with jitters appropriate for a girl half my age, not a mature woman whose husband had been living with her for some time before their marriage. A limousine deposited us at Jack's mother's Manhattan apartment.

It was pleasantly warm in the spacious Fifty-Seventh Street apartment on the seventy-fifth floor overlooking the Hudson River. A bottle of champagne peeked out of an ice bucket on a marble coffee table next to a dozen roses in a tall vase, a tray with two crystal flutes, and a plate with fresh petite eclairs.

Jack uncorked the champagne and filled the glasses. My hand shook, spilling some on the white carpet.

"You don't ever have to be nervous again, my darling—you are my wife," Jack came close with his glass. It was shaking slightly. "See, you made me nervous too." He touched my glass with his. "To us. I love you, Anna."

We drank, then put the glasses on the table. I glanced at the eclairs.

"Not yet." Jack covered my neck with quick, light kisses.

I blushed, burying my face in his chest.

"When I think of it now," I pressed closer to him, "it seems foolish of me to have been so scared for so long, for absolutely no reason."

"There were reasons." He played with my hair.

"I love you, Jack."

We drank more champagne. A long, slow kiss left me pleasantly tipsy.

Jack turned off the light and picked me up.

"So far, I love being married." I heard my silver-bells laugh as I was carried rapidly across the living room and through a short hall and double doors.

Fima met us at the Moscow airport with his Muscovite friend and a car. He demanded to know if any of our luggage had disappeared.

"Nothing lost, um?"

He narrowed his eyes at me suspiciously. I refrained from mentioning that if one or both of the suitcases with presents disappeared I could always send parcels from Chicago. To minimize the risk, each of us only had a carry-on bag and Tanya managed to bring the bag with toys onto the plane. I was astounded at the change in Fima. His movements were jerky and he smiled by pulling up the corner of his mouth.

"Don't ask me how I'm doing!" he shouted at Tanya. "We have no hope of emigrating. Don't you understand what that means?"

We were told the connecting flight to Kiev hadn't materialized, as often happens in Moscow, and we paid a hundred and fifty American dollars to spend the night at a hotel for foreigners. Jack, with his straightforward American logic, unsuccessfully attempted to find out why a Soviet citizen, who accompanied his daughter, could not get a room at the same hotel, even if paid for in hard currency. Fima's friend felt insulted when Jack offered him money to let Fima stay with him and his family in their two-room apartment.

And, after discovering that a hundred and fifty dollars paid only for an ill-kept, roadside-motel-type room with three narrow beds and a leaky faucet, Jack, again unsuccessfully, protested we could not possibly all stay in one room. In the morning he demanded orange juice with his breakfast instead of warm Pepsi, but no one could understand why he didn't want the warm Pepsi. Having traveled all over the world, Jack said he had never encountered anything like the hotel we were in.

The next evening all of us, including Fima, boarded a plane to Kiev. In Kiev, we were again, compliments of Fima, spared taking a taxi. We had a suite of two rooms at Intourist—it's name meaning "Foreign Tourist," the local hotel for foreigners—and Jack, this time successfully, demanded the twin beds in our room be pushed together. The laborers, in battered nylon jackets, smelling of sour perspiration, unaware Tanya and I understood Russian, made lewd comments about oversexed Americans who couldn't handle a week without getting "it." Tanya, crimson, pretended she hadn't heard. I couldn't bring myself to interfere in Jack's misadventures. I only watched and chuckled.

"How do they expect tourism to grow if they don't provide good service and decent food? Why are you laughing, Anna? I am right."

In the Soviet Union questions like these would never enter one's mind, let alone be asked.

"Jack, you're right, but no one cares whether tourism grows. Foreign-ers get so much more than average citizens that it's hard for Russians to understand why anyone wouldn't be happy. You are a naïve American." I kissed him, then took a shower in the semi-clean bathroom, and fell into bed, still not used to the time change.

We left the hotel after a late breakfast and walked to the building where I had lived. Were the streets always so bleak? Were there as many military uniforms among the crowds? Were the store fronts as drab? Had everyone always looked so troubled?

The city smelled of gas and rotten food. People smelled of perspira-tion. There were no smiles. Even the children, faces pale, had no smiles.

The elevator was out of order. We almost choked in the lobby from the mix of smells: alcohol, urine, and dampness.

"Don't they have a janitor?" Tanya held her nose with her fingers.

Another American—thank you, God.

I peeked under the stairs behind the elevator where Sasha and I used to kiss. The stench was unbearable, the walls filthy, and empty alcohol bottles peered out of brown bags. Was it always this smelly and slimy?

We reached the door on the fourth floor, my door for over thirty years.

"This is where I was born?" Tanya failed to disguise her disappointment.

"Yes, and from here our family was taken to Babi Yar."

"It's spooky." She moved closer to Jack.

I rang the bell several times. The door opened a crack and a woman's voice asked who we were.

"I'm sorry to bother you. I used to live in this apartment. My name is Anya Fishman. I'm looking for Auntie Olya, I mean Olga Pavlenko or the Berezovsky family."

The door opened wider and a disheveled, pregnant woman in her late thirties appeared, wearing a soiled, short robe displaying thin, white thighs.

"Are you the one that went to America?"

"Yes. I've come for a visit and want to show my daughter where we lived."

"Come in. I'm Sveta Berezovsky, Tolya's third wife. Tolya mentions Olga Pavlenko sometimes; she had died before he and I married."

The apartment looked different. It had four rooms now, a large kitchen, a toilet room—a powder room minus a sink—and a bathroom—a room with a bathtub and sink—where our room had been. Jack and Tanya followed me through the apartment without saying a word.

"I remember Tolya was the younger son. Are his parents still alive?" I stood in the middle of the bathroom staring at the gas water heater attached to the wall over the tub. The tub had replaced Lonya's bed.

"No. His father died from cirrhosis of the liver while Tolya was still married to his second wife. His mother died last year. Vitaly, Tolya's older brother, isn't working anymore. He has cirrhosis, too. From drinking, you know."

"How many people live here now?"

"Let's see." Sveta brought us into the largest room and motioned us to sit down around a table covered with a white tablecloth. "Tolya and myself, and my daughter from my first marriage, and Tolya's son from his second marriage, because his mother is a prostitute," Sveta counted matter-of-factly, "and Vitaly and his wife and their two children, Kostya and Inna, and Inna's boy, Vova. She's divorced, but her husband spends the night here sometimes. It's not bad, at least we live in the center of the city, not in the suburbs. There's so much crime there now, and the stores are emptier there. Tolya doesn't drink, except for paydays. He tries to watch it, but they say drinking helps ward off radiation," she added with satisfaction. "I'll tell him you stopped by. Do you really live in America?" Sveta's blue eyes suddenly came alive.

"Yes. This is my husband, Jack, he's an American, and this is my daughter, Tanya. She was five when we left."

"You know, they always told us Americans were poor and planned to attack us, and Jews like you—excuse me, I don't mean anything bad—who left, would want to come back—and now . . ." Sveta ran her eyes over our clothes, "it turns out Americans have everything in their stores, every day, and everyone has a car. Is that true?"

"Just about. Sveta, thanks. I don't want to keep you. Is the elevator broken as frequently as it used to be?"

"It's not actually broken. A new neighbor is moving in on the fifth floor. The building manager turned the elevator off so they wouldn't break it."

Tanya looked as though she wasn't sure she understood.

I took a pack of Marlboros and a pair of pantyhose out of my purse and handed them to Sveta. Her jaw dropped. She was too overwhelmed to thank me. Tanya and Jack exchanged incredulous glances.

We returned to the street, visited stores with naked shelves, watched worn out, emotionless women waiting in lines, their dull expressions changing only when someone tried to cut in or when it became known there wasn't enough of whatever product they were in line for, meaning many would go home empty-handed. Then passions exploded and accusations of fraud on the part of the government, the store manager, the people in front of them, and life in general started flying. One line led to an empty counter, thanks to a rumor that imported detergent was going to be sold sometime during the day.

I translated, explaining as though giving a lecture. No pain, no sympathy, no memories. I felt as alive as a brick wall.

"I don't understand. If there's no private enterprise and no unemployment how come so many working-aged people are standing in lines on a workday morning?" Jack inquired, dumbfounded, but not really expecting an answer.

The Bessarabka open market smelled of food. Its medieval entrance arch was smaller than I remembered and reminded me of a scene from a period movie. The prices and abundance of goods were strikingly different from that of the government stores. We bought tangerines and walnuts—as treats for our next-day dinner at Fima's house—from a stereotypical Georgian, replete with mustache and a flat, round cap, who recognized us as foreigners because we didn't have anything to put our purchase in. He borrowed a newspaper for us, and I took some pages and made, to the Georgian's astonishment, some conical bags. I used swift, expert movements, once learned never forgotten.

On a tall, round pedestal across from the market sat the familiar statue of Lenin, residing at the foot of Schevchenko Boulevard, the street leading to my former university, lined with poplar trees.

We took pictures by my alma mater, a heavy, red-columned building and by the statue of Schevchenko, the Ukrainian poet and an unofficial symbol of the Ukrainian soul: free, in spite of attempts by its eternal enemies—Russians, Jews, and Communists—to strangle it.

Jack and Tanya listened to my explanations and comments and to the description of my joy when I was finally admitted to the university. They nodded, looked around seriously, and, as expected, didn't understand. I felt like a tour guide. I couldn't quite recapture what was missing.

After dropping off the Bessarabka treats at the hotel, we took the trolley to the Vladimir Gorka, an old, much-loved park overlooking the Dnieper River. I translated Gorka for Jack as a small hill, but it didn't even come close to the tenderness that word carried for a Kiev citizen. Sasha had referred to this park as the heart of Kiev, as opposed to the body of Kiev that encompassed the many other impressive sights. The statue of the Grand Prince Vladimir, credited with christening the local pagans, whether they wished to be or not, stood on the tallest point, cross in hand, blessing the river and the city below. Deserted, as expected, on a late-fall, Friday afternoon, the park looked as intimate and gentle as I remembered it, full of history, tradition, memories of rare actual dates with Sasha. A drunk sleeping on a bench added the final touch to my memories. A large chunk of the hill to the left of the entrance, across from the quaint, old Philharmonic, had been flattened to give way to a new Lenin Museum, a low, contemporary, white building, destined to remain empty except for the schoolchildren groups on their mandatory field trips. The underground part of this building, I heard, contained a bomb shelter for the privileged.

Jack suggested we should see the Victory Monument he saw in the tour book he bought at the hotel store. The monument depicted a lady of Teutonic build, holding up a shield with the USSR State Emblem in one hand and a sword with the other. I replied brusquely that Fima would probably take them there, that I had my own agenda, and, considering we had all begun yawning fairly regularly, we should return to the hotel, eat, and go to bed. Tanya embraced my suggestion with enthusiasm. Sensing my anxiety, Jack put his hand on my shoulder, which almost made me cry.

Next morning, again, started late. My instinct of not volunteering the fact that we were Jewish kicked in, alive and well, making me apprehensive to ask the hotel staff about the Babi Yar memorial, installed after I left the country. Many people had fought for its creation in the many years they gathered at the site on the anniversary of the massacre, when doing so had been grounds for arrest.

My memory retained perfect directions. When we reached the Babi Yar—the word Yar means "ravine"—Tanya's and Jack's solemn faces showed not their typical open-mouthed, detached curiosity, but sincere interest. No path led to the small memorial, which sat in the middle of the wide ravine. I imagined my grandparents walking—where I was standing—forty-six years ago.

The figure of a man in a military coat, a Ukrainian woman with a child, and some interwoven bodies meant nothing. The structure appeared insignificant compared to the event that had taken place in September 1941, and unrelated to it. Jack's tour book mentioned that one hundred thousand Soviet citizens perished in this ravine, including members of the anti-Nazi underground and prisoners of war. There was no mention of the overwhelming majority of the victims being killed simply because they were Jewish. I remembered the first words of Yevgeny Yevtushenko's poem *Babi Yar*, *No monument stands over Babi Yar*. I recited parts of it that I could still recall, knowing that Tanya didn't understand, and that any translation would trash the real meaning. Only when she, sad and red-eyed, hugged me and stood sniffling into my shoulder, did I realize that tears were streaming down my cheeks. Jack's eyes glistened.

Silently, we went back to the hotel to change and pick up the presents and the treats, then headed to Fima's house for dinner. Jack carried the suitcase with presents, and Tanya the bag full of toys for Petya, and I hugged the conical bags from Bessarabka.

We took a crowded trolley where leaky, smelly bags were pushed against or dragged past our legs. The sharp smell of perspiration gave us all headaches.

Fima waited for us at the trolley stop, on edge as he had been at the airport. He muttered, "You shouldn't have," looking at the suitcase in Jack's hand.

"The table is set. We've been waiting for you." Fima half-ran ahead of us toward a nine-storied building with a grocery store on the first floor, lit but empty. People never enter uncrowded stores. When there are no goods, there are no people.

Zhanna, Igor, and Petya stood anxiously in the entranceway of their apartment, awaiting our arrival. The minute we stepped off the elevator on the fifth floor, Zhanna pecked each of us on the cheek and took my bags. She distinctly smelled of perfume mixed with perspiration. Jack rubbed his forehead; I knew he needed the aspirin I had in my purse.

Petya ran out into the hallway, straight to Tanya. He let her pick him up and carry him back into the apartment. He said seriously, "You are my American sister, you have red hair like mine, and you speak English." Tanya laughed, said *da*, and put him down. He poked his head inside her bag, let out a yelp, then, in a flash, swished it away to his room. The suitcase Jack had carried remained tactfully by the door.

"Fima! Look! Tangerines!" cried out Zhanna. "And walnuts. Thank you, thank you very much, you shouldn't have."

She was tall, a bit taller than Fima, with black hair and intelligent, brown eyes. She reminded me of Asya's mother. Igor, a wiry, thin-featured Slavic boy, had nothing in common with her. Petya's hair was a brighter red than Tanya's had ever been.

The table was set in the small living room. Doors to the left and to the right led to two smaller rooms. Petya came flying through the door on the right holding a small, bright-red, toy fire engine.

"Daddy, look what Tanya brought me!"

"That's where you would have lived," said Fima to Tanya pointing to the door Petya had just exited. "It's Petya's room now, but at his age he really doesn't need his own room."

The center of the table contained cold cuts, canned fish, and salads, in addition to a bowl filled with black caviar mixed with chunks of butter.

"Caviar." Zhanna looked at us with pride.

"I'm going to throw up," murmured Tanya. Jack just rubbed his forehead again.

"Speak Russian, Tanichka. Your father tells me your Russian is very good." Zhanna smiled and moved some chairs so when we were ready we could easily slip in. Her large hands showed the usual dark lines on the tips of her fingers from peeling vegetables.

I looked around with a knowing smile at a phenomenon which can never be explained, and is a source of many Russian jokes—there is nothing in the stores and everything on the table.

The doorbell rang.

"Must be my uncle. Igor, open the door." Zhanna seated us at the head of the table where we had no chance of escape, except to the balcony.

"I understand you have a neighbor that allows you to use her telephone," I addressed Zhanna, rummaging in my purse for some aspirin I knew Jack would need any second, and the list with the telephone numbers of people I needed to contact. "Would it be possible for me to make a couple calls before the rest of the guests arrive?"

She knew as I did I could not make telephone calls from the hotel. It was standard practice for the phones to be bugged. I had warned Jack and Tanya not to call anyone locally from the hotel, not to mention names, phone numbers, or addresses in any conversations in our rooms, and not to expect anyone to visit. *Big Brother* needed to retain the monopoly on the information Soviet citizens received.

"Definitely," Zhanna replied eagerly. "Fima! Anya needs to use the telephone. Please take her to Lusya's apartment." She made it sound urgent as if I needed to use the bathroom.

I handed Jack the aspirin, and heard him sigh, and as I made my way out of the room, I heard Tanya translating the conversation to him.

In the entranceway, we found the older couple that Igor had just let in. The husband, stout and gray, wore a navy, felt hat and a raincoat. He kissed Igor's cheek, nodded to Fima, then stared at me when I smiled my American smile. The wife whose dyed, brown hair had an orange tinge, wore a light-colored coat making her look completely round.

"Is that her?" I heard the old man ask before the front door closed behind Fima and me.

Fima ran up the stairs to the next floor. When I caught up with him, he was ringing the doorbell of an apartment directly in line with his. An elderly, bleached blonde with neat curls answered the door. She wore a red robe and white slippers. Her face contained a smug look, as if she needn't be complimented on her young look because she already knew.

Fima made introductions.

I turned on my American smile.

"Lusya." The blonde, offered me her stiff hand. "Please come in." I felt I was being photographed by her strong, blue eyes.

Her apartment boasted a living room full of shiny, dark furniture. A dining table, surrounded with tall, pompous chairs, reflected a crystal dish filled with chocolate candy. A wall unit stuffed with crystal vases and glasses, stretched along an entire wall. In combination with the crystal chandelier, this furniture removed any doubts of Lusya's financial superiority over Fima. Neither did I have any doubts that she worked as a store salesperson, and, therefore, could sell whatever the store offered from under-the-counter.

Lusya's eyes followed mine around the room.

"It's a Romanian-made set," she said with fake modesty.

"I can tell." I gushed.

Fima smirked, whether at Lusya's taste or my compliment I couldn't tell.

Through the partially open door to the room that in Fima's household was Petya's, I caught a glimpse of a beach towel with a Disney scene that could only have been a gift from Fima after his visit to the United States.

"How was your flight?" Smiling, Lusya continued our small talk as she pulled up a chair to the telephone hanging on the wall near a television set.

"It was long, we're still somewhat tired," I replied, unfolding my list with telephone numbers.

"I'll be in the kitchen with Fima. Take your time." Lusya floated out of the room, the open heels of her slippers flapping against her feet.

To get the most unpleasant call over with with, I dialed Irena's mother's telephone number. The line rang for a long time. I panicked, realizing I wasn't equipped to deal with the absence of answering machines or call-waiting. Then, a breathless voice, resembling Irena's, answered.

"Good evening. Svetlana Pavlovna?" For the first time in eleven years I was addressing someone using both first name and patronymic.

"Yes. And who are you?" Irena's mother evidently liked to get straight to the point.

"My name is Anya. I brought you a present from your daughter Irena." How naturally I reverted to the camouflaged talk of my past.

Governed by the same instinct, Svetlana Pavlovna lowered her voice. "My granddaughter will come to pick it up, just give me the address."

"My girlfriend, Asya, will call you within a day or two."

She grunted, "If that suits you better," then added with somewhat less displeasure, "Have you seen Irena and her boys recently?"

"Not recently, but I as far as I know they are fine," I replied politely. "Good-bye."

The call to Sonya, the sister of Mark Yampolsky, Sasha's friend who had been taking care of Lonya's grave and who didn't have a telephone at home, was, Sasha had insisted, not necessary, but I was determined to make it.

"Good evening. My name is Anya. I'm Sasha Rosenberg's friend," I said when a man picked up the phone. "May I speak to Sonya?"

Before he had a chance to respond, the sounds of sneezing and cough-ing in the background told me that my call came at an inopportune time.

"Sonya is not feeling well," the man said, "but since you're Sasha's friend perhaps you would like to speak to Mark? He's here now." His Russian was that of a very educated person.

"Mark speaking. Good evening. Is Sasha all right?" The man that took over spoke the same quality Russian but in a softer and older voice.

"Yes, he is," I said slowly, not sure how much he knew about Sasha's family life.

"Thank God. Are you his friend . . . from here?" He phrased his question avoiding the word emigration.

Another attack of cough in the background gave me a chance to catch my breath before speaking.

"From everywhere," I replied evenly, then immediately changed the subject. "I'm here on a short visit and I wanted to personally thank you for keeping my brother's grave in perfect order all these years. You don't know how much it means to me." I cleared my throat.

"And your brother is . . . ?" Mark asked in the same careful tone. "Sorry, but I do it for several friends."

"Leonid Shermer. Lonya." I said.

"Lonya," he echoed. "I see."

Did I detect a deeper meaning in his tone or was I unreasonably sensitive?

"Sasha and I go back some time but, unfortunately, we met after your brother's demise." Mark continued. "Sasha had always spoken very highly of him. He thought that Lonya's chess-playing talent would have brought him great success had his life not been disrupted so severely by the war."

And my birth.

"Sasha always spoke very highly, and very warmly, of you too," Mark sighed. "As far as the reason for your call, it's touching, but my effort doesn't warrant any special consideration. My parents-in-law are buried at the Kurenevsky cemetery near Sasha's mother, and my mother is bur-ied near Lonya, at the Berkovtsy cemetery. Caring for family graves is the least I could do for my faraway friends who have faithfully supplied my children and my grandson with jeans."

"These graves are our connection to the past," my voice shook.

"I wish I were geographically far away from my family's graves and able to have someone care for them," Mark said wistfully.

How easily I forget how lucky I have been.

One more call left, to Lena's parents. I consulted my list for the cor-rect names and patronymics. Impatiently, I dialed several times before the line finally became free. A woman's clear voice interrupted the ring-ing of the telephone with the standard *"Slushayu."*

"Good evening. My name is Anya," I began for the third time in the last fifteen minutes. "Is this Maria Borisovna?"

"Yes," the voice said. "Good evening. What did you say your name was?"

"Anya. I'm Lena's friend."

I heard a gasp, then quiet, then whispers, then quiet, then a man's voice.

"I'm sorry, my wife asked me to continue. I'm Aron Mikhailovich, Lena's father."

He sounded older than his wife, and more decisive.

"My name is Anya. I'm a friend of Lena's and I'm in Kiev on a short visit," I said. "I'd like to stop by to meet you. I have a little present to you from Lena."

"Yes, yes, of course," he said, at the same time listening to a whisper from, I assumed, his wife. "You're so kind, but could I just pick up the package? You don't have to waste time coming over." He spoke in spurts, trying to simultaneously pay attention to the continuing whisper.

"If you don't mind," I sprinkled some metal into my voice, "I'd like to stop by. Lena and I are close, and I wouldn't want to go back without meeting you. How does Monday afternoon sound?"

I suspected that I got my way only because Lena's parents didn't want to be rude.

I found Fima and Lusya in the kitchen facing each other over a small, square table covered with an orange tablecloth displaying a paisley design. Homemade cookies on a white plate looked inviting. I realized I was famished. Fima glared at me, then at his watch, then rose. Lusya directed my attention to the cookies.

"Thank you, but we have to go back downstairs. I appreciate your letting me use your telephone. It was nice meeting you." I smiled and added as a bonus to Lusya, "Your furnishings are very elegant."

Lusya's cheekbones blushed.

"Thank you," she responded with a wide smile as she straightened the lapels of her robe.

In the hallway, Fima traipsed down the stairs, ahead of me.

While we were away, a dozen people had gathered at Fima's dining table. Zhanna's, Jack's, and Tanya's faces expressed disapproval of my long absence. In the next half-hour another dozen appeared, crowding themselves into the already crowded room. Jack was referred to as "The American" and waited on hand and foot. The bowl of caviar was gingerly passed around once then returned respectfully to us.

"Butter keeps caviar fresh. When I found out you were coming, I gave one of the sweaters you sent to a saleswoman who put some caviar

'under the counter' for me," Zhanna said loudly and immediately became the center of attention.

Behind every item on the table there was a spellbinding story of how
it was procured, and we were made privy to all of them—nothing in the
stores and everything on the table.

I was interrogated on my purchases of the tangerines and walnuts. I
responded so naturally as though I had never emigrated. Tanya blinked,
trying hard to comprehend the significance of such stories exciting
everyone so much. Jack listened to her translations with a
blank expression.

The small talk orbited back to the unavoidable topic of emigration.
Half of those present had either applied to leave or were ready to do so.
They spoke of their American relatives' wealth, demonstrated by
obligatory houses, cars, and vacations. Someone even included a
hundred-thousand-dollar mortgage in their list. They discussed various
theories on what to say to the American authorities in Rome in order to
prove one's political, not economical, reasons qualifying for a U.S. entry
visa. Typical for governmental organizations, the individual representa-
tives of the United States Immigration Service in Rome interpreted the
entry criteria according to their mood and personality. As a result, families could not predict their fates even in similar circumstances;
sometimes families were split up when, in their infinite wisdom, the bu-
reaucrats considered the parents less of a risk than their adult children.
Hunger strikes ensued. Almost the only alternative to the United States
was Israel with its inevitable wars and mandatory draft. The only other
possibility was Germany, which had taken a few Jews each year. Whatever the destination, no one argued for remaining in the Soviet Union.

With a little time, the smells, amplified by the heat, became familiar.
Fima and Zhanna were endlessly serving food. Jack tried the Armenian
whiskey, but refused straight vodka, causing a murmur among the men
and the loss of some of their respect. The older women asked Tanya repeatedly if she had a boyfriend and winked at Igor. Someone was surprised to find out she didn't keep a gun under her pillow, because they
knew for sure that everyone in America had a gun.

I met Fima's tense eyes. He smiled bitterly, probably comparing his
surroundings with mine.

Zhanna looked worn out. To set a table like this took her several
weeks of hunting and bribing. I felt guilty to be the reason for this needless commotion, to be a rested observer of the life that would have been
Fima's and mine had I not forged his signature.

"Igor, did you talk to your father again?" asked one of the guests.

"I did, I did!" the boy shouted tearfully. "I ask him all the time! I've
begged for his signature! He's just not going to give his consent!"

"That damned *goy*! Zhanna, you should do something. You're going to be stuck here and Igor will be drafted into the Army." The old man I had met at the door, a medal on his suit jacket, aimed his fork at her.

"What do you want me to do!? How many times must I repeat—my children and I go together or stay together," Zhanna's voice cracked as she sat down. "If Fima wants to go, let him. Who's holding him?"

"What kind of talk is this?" Fima slammed his fist on the table. "I'm not going anywhere without Petya. We'll all stay and that's that!"

Fima and Zhanna avoided each other's eyes.

I briefly wondered what their relationship was like, when Zhanna knew Fima stayed because of Petya and not her.

Damn this life, damn this country! Thank you, God, thank you for showing me the way out!

Jack excused himself and retreated to the balcony. I felt lost without him.

"He looks like an intelligent man," the relative with the medal slid closer to me. His breath and red face bespoke alcohol.

"And built very well," his wife with orange hair added. "My grand-daughter is visiting her cousin in Detroit. We're hoping she'll meet a boy there and stay. I've heard that American men love Russian women. And here's the proof." She glanced toward the balcony.

Fima stood behind her, a hurt expression on his face.

"Fima, you're a schmuck for letting Anya go," Zhanna's bemedaled relative yawned.

The bowl in Fima's hands shook.

I joined Jack on the balcony.

"Let's get going," he said. "This is hardly an intimate family dinner. Even Tanya is having a difficult time."

The street below was empty. Few cars went by, only trolleys and buses.

"Yes, let's get going. Do you regret the trip?"

"No," his fingers automatically drummed down my back. "I needed to see what it was that kept you under its spell. Still does, somewhat. You're different here, not like you are in your office, not like you are with me."

"So, you finally understand?"

"I don't know, Anna. Is that what it was? The lines, the stuffy apart-ments, the smells, noisy people reporting to each other how they bought salami?"

"That was my life."

"As a matter of fact, you blended right in," Jack commented not look-ing at me.

"They say, one cannot unlearn to ride a bike."

"My father used to say a horse doesn't unlearn the path to its watering hole."

"Don't forget I escaped this life by forging a document."

"Are you sorry? Do you still feel guilty?"

"No and no," I replied with a firmness that surprised me. "Only don't make the mistake of considering these people fools for not doing the same."

"I know." Jack hugged me. "I'm very lucky and proud of what you did."

We stood looking down at a woman carrying two bags, stopping every few steps to take a breath.

"That's how I used to come home from work," I related. The experience seemed far away, but the numbness in my fingers caused by the rough handles of the meshed, cotton bags called "*avoska*" felt real. Their name came from the word *avos* that meant "somehow" or "just in case." Because they could fit in a pocket or a purse, these bags remained the favorite mode of transporting groceries, even when shopping bags began making their way in parcels from the West. They also reflected the social side of Soviet shopping: constant preparedness to join a line to a store counter as soon as it formed whether one needed the goods offered at that moment or not.

The woman picked up her *avoskas* again.

"When I came home carrying bags like this woman, after wandering from store to store, standing in lines, then standing in the trolleys and buses, my fingers were blue. I had to pump my fists to restart my circulation."

I pumped my fists, feeling the long-ago sensation of reviving circulation.

"And, if I was lucky enough to fill the bags, the adrenaline made the twenty or more pounds in each hand feel like feathers."

"You carried forty pounds?" Jack responded with incredulity.

"I've told you how strong I am. You just didn't believe me."

He shook his head, his eyes following the woman below who stopped again on the corner waiting to cross the street.

Fima appeared on the balcony.

"Excuse me for interrupting, but we're going to have dessert now." His eyes focused on Jack's hand caressing my shoulder, and he smiled his one-sided smile.

I translated and Jack said, "Thanks, we've had enough to eat."

I translated for Fima.

"Zhanna baked everything herself," insisted Fima.

We nodded and obediently followed him inside. Several people were leaving, but not before shaking our hands and reminding us we were related and should keep in touch.

Most of these people had come not because they were relatives, but because we were Americans. They wanted confirmation that they should consider emigration. They were trying to prepare by extracting every little detail they could. They still didn't understand they should leave the Soviet Union; the destination was not important.

Petya, led by his mother, said good night and invited us to visit again. He looked up at Zhanna for approval of his performance, with exactly the same expression as when Tanya sought approval from Jack.

After dessert, the remaining guests departed. Igor turned on the television to watch a midnight comedy program with Tanya, Jack, and Fima. Igor and Fima laughed at a joke that I didn't get because it referred to a local event, Tanya didn't understand the language nuances, and Jack, of course, didn't understand the language. Displeased, Fima looked at Tanya sideways. I think he thought he could bring order to her life and improve her Russian if only he could get to America. Igor tried to explain the gist of the joke, which Tanya diligently translated to Jack, but their faces remained staid.

I joined Zhanna in the kitchen. She washed the dishes and I dried them with a long, white towel.

"You are truly a beautiful family," said Zhanna, "and so calm. That's what I envy, the calm, nothing else. I'm eight years younger than you and look at me. I'm an old woman compared to you. Everyone who comes to visit from the West or from Israel is like that, calm and young." Her tone was wistful. "They tell us of unemployment, expensive medicine, crime, the wars in Israel, yet they're calm. How can we be calm?" The dishes in the sink made angry noises. "The stores are empty, the radiation is so high children aren't allowed to sit on the grass. What's going to happen to us?" She pretended to clear her throat when her voice broke.

My mind groped for a reply. All I could think of was, it could have been me in her place.

Zhanna continued in an almost formal tone.

"It means a lot to Fima that Tanya accompanied you on your honeymoon and was able to visit him. Of course," she added softer, with a quick glance at me, "not everyone in your position would insist on it like you did . . . and it was decent of your husband to agree." She violently applied a yellow piece of soap to the back of a greasy bowl. "You are nice people."

No dishwashing liquid in the Soviet Union.

"Thank you," I responded meekly.

If not for Jack, I'm not certain I would have taken Tanya . . . but, then, I'm certain that Kiev, wisely or not, would not have been my honeymoon destination.

"Coming to Kiev and bringing Tanya was Jack's idea. He arranged the entire trip," I added, knowing Zhanna would not believe me.

"I guess Fima's concern that there wasn't a good relationship with Tanya during his trip was groundless. He has been so restless since his return, and so angry." Zhanna handed me the bowl and pushed a limp strand of hair away from her face. "I was looking forward to meeting you."

She didn't like the silence.

"I was looking forward to meeting you too," I finally responded.

Zhanna watched me, her lower lip wrinkled under her teeth.

"Anya, it bothers me that you spent so much money on Fima—the overseas calls, the clothes, the doctor—if we could pay you back . . ."

"Don't worry about it," I interrupted searching for a smooth way to change the subject. "Fima is Tanya's father. It was only natural that I would try to help . . ."

"That's what he told me when he called from Chicago. He said you'd get the best for him." Zhanna's intelligent eyes never left my face. "Anya, the goods he brought back have been a big help. He didn't ask for them, did he?" Her voice rose anxiously as she turned off the faucet.

"Definitely not!" I exclaimed as if appalled at the suggestion, marveling at my acting ability.

"All he really wanted was to see Tanya. It must be annoying to you that I talk about Fima all the time?"

"Not at all," I said sincerely. "I just think how sad it is that he and Tanya didn't get to know each other well and that Petya and Tanya will not be close. I wish they could be, I really do. I was brought up by my half-brother."

Why am I telling her about Lonya?

"I know your brother was very devoted to you. Fima told me about your family," she said thoughtfully. "For many years he felt betrayed that you left and took Tanya—you know how loyal he is. Now he's infuriated with my first husband's refusal to consent to Igor's emigration. He hurts." Her words fell into silence.

She loves Fima. I hope he understands that.

"Fima's whole existence since his return has been concentrated on the idea of emigrating. Who could have expected such a reaction from him?" She handed me a plate to dry. "Sometimes I wish he hadn't gone on that trip in the first place. I mean . . . not because I was against him seeing Tanya," Zhanna hastened to add, then regarded me steadily for a moment. "He wanted to see you, too."

"Zhanna, don't overestimate that part of his reason for the trip."

"I don't overestimate anything." The dishes clanked in the sink. "Anyway, what I meant to say is that my entire family suffers because of me. I'm cruel . . ."

"You're not cruel, Zhanna, but I was."

"Fima told me how you got permission to leave." Zhanna said, slowly raising her eyes to look at me. "I'm glad he finally found out. He has always been obsessed with knowing. Anya, you did the right thing, you are a very brave woman. I can't do it."

I wondered who was brave, she or I. A Russian saying came to mind, "Cowards leave and brave people stay."

"Igor begs me to let him visit our relatives in the United States," said Zhanna finally as if continuing an old argument.

"Zhanna, perhaps Igor could come for a visit then ask for political asylum. People do it all the time, no one has been turned down. He can stay with us until you emigrate. It's the only way out for you, and it, too, may not be viable forever."

"No, no," sobbed Zhanna, "I might not ever see Igor again. I can't take the chance. No, no."

Let Igor go, silly woman! Even if the rest of you are stuck . . . won't his good fortune be a consolation . . . don't you realize you suffer the most from hopelessness?

Jack appeared in the doorway to the kitchen, tapping his watch with his finger.

"You should go," Zhanna wiped her eyes with the edge of her towel. "This is your honeymoon. You should have fun, not talk about emigration."

On that optimistic note, we parted.

The next day, Sunday, Fima accompanied us to Asya's house. Asya stared at Jack and kissed Tanya and me wetly. She accepted the suitcase containing presents with sighs of gratitude and resignation. Unless my knowledge of the Soviet middle-class dress code was hopelessly outdated, Asya's black pumps and a navy, knit dress with white stripes along the edges of the collar and the sleeves represented her best outfit. She had gained considerable weight and appeared shorter than I remembered. Myron, in bed with a kidney stone attack, related a long story of suffering, bribing doctors and nurses, and the collapse of the Soviet medical system.

I wouldn't have recognized Auntie Fira had I met her anywhere other than at Asya's house. She had changed from a grande dame into a large woman with swollen legs in thick, loose stockings, constantly arguing with everyone. Her robe, black and brown squiggles on white flannel, had a hole where the lower button used to be, and reached almost to her wide slippers of undeterminable color. She examined each of us closely with sad, blinking, light-brown eyes as though we were exhibits in a museum. She was only seventy-five, eight years younger than my mother.

"I won't ever forget your sponge cakes, Auntie Fira," I said, smiling nostalgically.

"I wanted to bake something for you, but Myron got sick again. My children never appreciated what I did." The old woman pouted like a child. "Tanya looks like her father, poor girl." Auntie Fira shook her head, disregarding Fima's heavy breathing, Tanya's raised brows, and Asya's widened eyes. "Anya's so pretty," she addressed Asya. "I've always told you she was. No one saw it because no one loved her. Her brother was a brute."

"Mama, think before you speak," Asya begged.

"Anya is not a stranger. I can say what I want." Auntie Fira pulled me close and kissed my cheeks like she used to when I was a child. "You," her sausage-like finger stopped an inch from Jack's nose, "got yourself a good wife."

"Mama," Asya pleaded, flustered, "Anya's husband only speaks English."

"English, shminglish," Auntie Fira mumbled, heading to her room.

Amused by the scene that didn't require translation, Jack winked at me before leaving with Tanya for a day of Fima-guided sightseeing.

Asya's younger son, Senya, was away at school in Moscow. Her older son, Dima, stopped by for a few minutes with his new wife, a pretty, soft-spoken girl. A loud argument between Asya and her son erupted for no reason whatsoever as far as I could see. Asya looked like a witch with her half-gray, thick hair, fists on her hips, and pointy nose. Fists were something new for the delicate, feminine Asya I remembered.

My all-out effort to feel closeness proved unproductive, but it pleased me that Asya seemed to have rekindled her sense of closeness. Faces, mannerisms, voices, food were familiar—familiar, but nothing else. Asya hugged and kissed me easily. She produced a bundle wrapped in newspaper from the bottom of a drawer. It contained all my letters to her.

Under the continual harangue of Asya's mother, the family was in the process of collecting the papers needed to apply for emigration. Their irritating and petty arguments vented their fears of parting with Dima, who had already applied, and of their future. I tired quickly and longed for Jack's warmth.

In the late afternoon, Asya pulled me into the kitchen while she made dinner. She carefully closed the door behind us and put on a flowery, cotton apron made from an old dress.

"Jack is an American, so Rimma says he wants sex all the time. You were never into sex before. At least, I never thought you were . . . you would have told me. How do you handle it? You're blushing!" she blurted out, producing her familiar cackle. "Tell me how Americans do it. Tell me everything. Is it very different?"

Fima's house had been noisier, but there had been no need to prove intimacy.

"Different from what?"

"From Fima. You only knew Fima."

"The entire relationship is different," I busied myself peeling a carrot.

"Forget the carrot!" Asya took away the knife. "Sit down, Anichka, tell me. They say Americans love oral sex. You would never do that, would you? Wow! You did! I can tell by your eyes! Wow! I could never bring myself to try, and Myron finally stopped asking. He's sick most of the time, anyway. Besides, I have so much on my mind and my legs hurt so much by the end of the day. I'm afraid I'm going to have my mother's legs. Do you like it, or does Jack force you?"

"Jack doesn't force me to do anything." I looked straight at Asya without any embarrassment.

"You're so different, Anichka, you look radiant." Asya blinked. She shook her head. "I guess you still feel something physically."

Still? My God, I just started.

"I love Jack."

"Of course, you love him. With his money, who wouldn't? If he wanted you, you would have to be insane to turn him down. I love Myron, too, but then sex for women depends on age."

"If it does, I'm a teenager," I laughed happily and caught myself. My laugh didn't sound appropriate in this house.

"You're joking," smiled Asya tiredly. "What does he do to turn you on? Is he big?"

Where is the past I put Jack through hell for?

"Asya, I was never really alive until I immigrated to the United States, and, except for Tanya, I never knew how to be happy until I met Jack."

She squinted at me, her expression changing from curiosity to misery. Her round face was the little Asya's face of my childhood.

"I'm sorry, Anichka, I shouldn't badger you, I just wanted some fun like we used to have. After Gorbachev came to power everything became much better, then everyone started talking about leaving, especially the young people. Dima and Ella both work. She's pregnant. Her parents and Myron and I help them out from our savings. They have nothing to complain about. Why should they want to leave? For you, it was different. You had nothing to lose, no money, no apartment. I wouldn't be happy if I had to clean someone else's toilets. What am I going to accomplish in America?"

"Nothing spectacular, but, Asya, your life here is pitiful, don't you see?" I took Asya's plump hand, with the tips of her fingers sporting dark lines from peeling vegetables. "Don't you want your children and grandchildren to have a better life?"

"That's all I hear from Myron and my mother. What can I do? I can't fight everyone."

"Asya, don't worry, I'll help you as much as I can."

"Anichka, you've turned out to be a true friend."

"And you, Asya? Remember the doll you brought to school for me in third grade?"

"Com'on, Anya, that's nothing. You know, Rimma told me you had transformed into a tough, confident, purposeful woman, and you have, but, to me, you are also the same quiet and sad girl you used to be. Tell me, did Jack object to your taking Tanya on your honeymoon?"

"He organized the entire trip. He tries very hard to understand my past. It's difficult to tell whether this visit will clarify anything for him."

"Anichka, you had no family, almost no friends, a low-paying job, and Fima for a husband—there isn't much to understand."

For dinner, everyone had spruced themselves up. Myron's black suit looked identical to the suit he had worn at both his wedding and mine, but considering his significantly padded waist, it could not be the same suit. His shirt buttons, pressed into thin slivers, bore witness that laundry service technology had not progressed to the level where buttons didn't have to be replaced after almost each wash. Auntie Fira, her gray hair neatly brushed, made an entrance, wearing the same slippers, light stockings, and a deep-green dress with a belt of the same material, and with a lacy, off-white collar. I recognized the dress I had sent back with Rimma.

Asya finally took off her apron, and we sat down around the living room table set in all the splendor of the familiar Czech-made china set. Asya's concerned eyes and sighs followed Myron as he hurried out of the room every few minutes, which apparently had to to with his kidney stones. Without a murmur, I let Auntie Fira stuff me with the familiar dishes, planned and executed especially for me. The family argued among themselves for reasons they immediately forgot, complained of Asya's reluctance to emigrate, warned me to pay more attention to my appearance so younger women wouldn't tempt Jack, explained to me the intricacies of American life, critiqued Gorbachev's strategy, encouraged me to teach Jack some Russian, carped at Auntie Fira for ruining their lives, criticized the younger generation's lack of respect, demanded to know how come I claimed to be busy if no time was spent in grocery lines, and suggested that Tanya should wear good quality wool slacks, and not frayed jeans.

I felt a child again, savoring the unconditional acceptance that I had missed so much for so many years. When Fima returned with Tanya and Jack to pick me up and deliver us back to the hotel, I was tempted to stay where I was. Asya's offer to accommodate us for the duration of our visit didn't seem, at that moment, so outrageous anymore.

Outside, Tanya pounced on Fima, evidently continuing an earlier argument.

"No matter what you say, eight people in a maternity room is inexcusable!" Agitated, she slipped into a mix of English and Russian. "And wilted bouquets on the floor of the bathroom!" She turned to me chattering in English, "Dad took us to see the company where he works and then Zhanna's girlfriend, who's a pediatrician, snuck us into a maternity ward. Let me tell you—it was a sight!" she concluded, fuming.

It took some effort to tear myself away from the emotions I had been immersed in at Asya's dinner table.

"I don't know how typical this hospital was," Jack chimed in, "but the conditions were appalling. I wish we hadn't gone."

"Exactly!" Tanya spat at Fima in English, then apologized and translated Jack's words into Russian.

Fima, exhausted after a day as a tour guide for foreigners, frowned.

"I thought you would be interested. It wasn't easy to arrange. We needed to get the lab coats and make sure that no one saw you."

"I appreciate it," Tanya said, having lost most of her steam. "I was really interested, but what I don't understand is you gave me that lecture about the wonders of free medicine."

"By the way, you and Igor and Petya were born at similar hospitals and grew up without any problems. At least women stay in the hospital for a week, not a day like in your America," Fima shot back.

I sympathized with Fima, who appeared too tired to argue.

"Dad!" Tanya's face, as she appealed to her father, acquired the look of an old woman. "Why did you insist that I should return to Kiev for good? Why?" Her Russian sounded rather good, for once.

"The trolley is coming," Fima said sternly. "Please be quiet. This subject is not suitable for public discussion, especially with your accent."

Tanya took a deep breath, letting it out noisily.

I hastened to translate to Jack before we got on the trolley where we obediently remained silent. Fima accompanied us to within a block of the hotel, instructed Tanya and Jack to wait for him at that spot at ten o'clock tomorrow morning, said good night without looking at any of us, and started to walk away.

"Dad!" Tanya called in English and ran after him.

Fima stopped but didn't turn back.

Tanya threw her hands around his neck.

"I'm sorry. I get upset that you just think what someone tells you to think." She placed a quick kiss on her father's cheek.

Fima ran his fingers through her hair, nodded, and continued walking. The three of us stood silently, trying to unwind, enjoying the pleasantly cool evening.

"Tanichka, I have come to understand that the Soviet population evolved into a very sturdy group of people. It had no choice. Were American women forced to give birth in Soviet hospitals, half of them would die." I spoke in English, but slower than usual after spending the day at Asya's house. "Before you were born, your father found a good doctor and paid her for the delivery. Otherwise, it would have been too risky, especially if injections were needed. The problem was not so much the reusable syringes, but that nurses often didn't sterilize them properly." I remembered the smell of the unwashed women in my room. "There were ten women in the room where I was after your delivery. No shower, just a little wipe every evening. A gown was only changed if a stay longer than a week was necessary due to complications. A mother stayed for as long as the baby did. Most of us came down with a breast infection. Some babies also developed infections requiring antibiotics."

Jack put his arm around Tanya's shoulders. I looked past them seeing that hospital room: a twin bed, a nightstand, a twin bed, a nightstand, a twin bed, a nightstand.

"No personal belongings were allowed, not even watches, for fear of introducing outside germs, but cockroaches visited our nightstands unencumbered."

Tanya's and Jack's eyes stared at me, not blinking. My whole body felt wooden.

"You never told me that before," Tanya said in Russian for some reason.

"I never thought about it. It was just another part of normal life," I responded also in Russian. "Your father just wanted you back into his normal life. How do you know that I wouldn't have reacted similarly had he been the one to take you away?" I said having switched back to English.

Jack pulled me close. My eyes filled with tears as his fingers began their massaging movements.

Fima took off work Monday to complete his sightseeing program and to spend the rest of the day and evening with Tanya. Jack opted to spend a quiet evening at the hotel. I had left the hotel early in the morning after swallowing a soggy sandwich and a glass of tepid tea at the hotel restaurant. Although tepid, I enjoyed drinking the tea from a glass after so many years in the States using a cup. The trip to the Kurenevsky cemetery took over an hour. The young woman at the office, engrossed in a book, never saw me enter. Her china-doll complexion, shiny brown hair, tight jeans, and black boots with spike heels didn't belong so close to a cemetery.

"Excuse me," I said meekly, as a Soviet person usually would in any office or store.

The what-do-you-want-from-me expression in the lively blue eyes didn't surprise me. I would not have known what to do had the response been different.

"I'd like some help with directions. I haven't visited this cemetery for a while."

"Do you have the exact name?" The rough voice didn't match the young woman's appearance.

"I know the section, the row, and the lot, but I don't remember how to get there."

"I'm not a tour guide." She began to get annoyed. "And we are open today only until noon." By the time she finished the sentence her eyes had returned to her book.

Jack would have argued but I knew better.

I thanked her, not expecting and not getting a response and walked out. An unpaved, winding path led into the small, old-world cemetery on the top of a little hill which had been closed to new burials for many years. I climbed the path slowly, my feet leading me past the old stones, some well-kept, some fallen down or tipped sideways. I could taste the stew with whole chunks of meat and the barley and the dark bread that Auntie Riva fed me that night thirty-six years ago when I put my faith in her and Sasha. Had the plate stood in front of me now, I would have wanted to lick it as I wanted to that night. I saw her blue eyes glistening with tears, her cigarette, her red hair with gray roots. I saw a skinny, haggard, somber girl in wrinkled clothing, in torn stockings, with short, dark, disheveled braids. I saw the plush, maroon curtains on the door to her room. The vision of the snow-white handkerchief trimmed with lace and the starched sheets with no signs of bedbugs, the cotton nightgown, and the thick, green blanket inside a white slipcover decorated with lace made my eyes prickle with tears. I felt the happiness of belonging that she uncovered for me.

My feet stopped by a short, black fence. Startled, I looked up. Seeing Auntie Riva's young, smiling face on the faded black-and-white photograph covered with glass in the center of the gray, narrow stone had the effect of a needle piercing through my chest. I swayed and had to hold on to the fence for support.

"Hello, Auntie Riva," I said through my tears. "I miss you. I miss you so much." Although, according to the old Jewish tradition, I only needed a stone, I picked up a handful of pebbles to put on the grave. I opened the miniature gate, stepped inside, and formed the letter "A" with the pebbles. "I still need you. Sasha needs you. You have a wonderful granddaughter. It feels like she's part of our family." My fingers caressed the glass over the photograph. "I remember the dress you made me for my high school graduation. And, I still eat toast with preserves almost every morning. You said it was good for me. You used to make wonderful preserves." I backed out of the gate and closed it tightly.

It took a few minutes to find a tissue in my purse to dry my eyes.

"You couldn't save your daughter's life," I whispered, "but that stew and barley and dark bread probably saved mine."

Walking back down the hilly path took a long time. I noticed a heavy lock hung on the cemetery office door.

I had to transfer to three different trolleys and buses and take the metro to get to Lena's parents' home. The part of the city they lived in was the poorest after the war. It was called "Stalinka." Later it became famous for the huge permanent exhibition center demonstrating Soviet technical and agricultural accomplishments. Beginning with Krushchev's time, buildings, similar to where Fima lived, quickly grew. I had never been to this area. Lena's father had said he would wait for me at the bus stop, so that I wouldn't have to navigate the maze of identical streets and buildings by myself.

From the description he had given me over the phone, I recognized him right away. I would have probably recognized him without the description, as Lena looked exactly like him. Our eyes met, and he stepped away quickly from the small crowd waiting for the bus.

"I'm Aron Mikhailovich," he said extending his hand.

"I'm Anya," I said as we shook hands.

Looking young for his age and muscular, he was one of those people who would never become frail. His round, black eyes gave the impression of intense concentration.

"How is your visit going?" Aron Mikhailovich began walking briskly across the street. "Kiev has changed to the best. There is so much to see."

"Yes, the city is beautiful," I replied. "My husband and my daughter are doing some very extensive sightseeing."

"What about you?" He threw me a curious glance.

"I haven't forgotten enough. My objective is to see the people I know and visit some graves at the cemeteries."

"Was your daughter born here?"

"Yes, but she was five when we left."

"Doesn't your husband have places to visit?"

I didn't have a chance to reply because he stopped by a door covered with chipped, brown paint and motioned me to open it.

The staircase, more dilapidated than in Fima's or Asya's buildings, smelled of borscht. All the doors on each landing, like those in other buildings, were upholstered similarly to a leather sofa in a waiting room.

"Maria!" Aron Mikhailovich called out as he unlocked the door to our left on the third floor.

I was surprised that he didn't address his wife as Masha or Musya, common Russian variations used at home.

"I'm in the kitchen," a voice replied.

In the United States, this apartment would have been called a studio. It consisted of one large room, an entranceway with a closet, a kitchen, and a bathroom. Maria Borisovna, a spatula in one hand and a pot lid in another, stood by the stove which emitted delicious smells. Her red apron had her name on it in English; it must have been sent by Lena. Aron Mikhailovich helped me take off my jacket and disappeared. His wife, whose face wore unmistakable traces of recent tears, looked at me anxiously, reminding me of Lena. Her wide hips, disproportionate with her slim shoulders, made her look squat.

"Good afternoon. I'm Anya," I said smiling, wondering how our conversation would evolve.

"I'm Maria Borisovna as you've probably guessed," she replied. "I'm almost ready. You must be hungry."

"You know, I actually am hungry," I said surprising myself with the admission. "I need to wash my hands as I visited a cemetery this morning."

Another Jewish tradition is to wash your hands after returning from a cemetery. Amazing how traditions become part of one's blood.

The bathroom contained a bathtub, a sink, and a toilet which told me that the building belonged to the first batches built during the Krushchev era.

Lena's parents waited for me just outside the bathroom. A round table near the balcony door was covered with a yellow, cotton tablecloth and loaded with food. Persian-like rugs covered the walls over two sofas facing each other. They reminded me of those at every house in Kiev. Lena's family's pictures covered the wall on both sides of the china cabinet. Some of the shelves in the china cabinet were half-empty, the dishes and glasses needed to serve the guest from America.

Aron Mikhailovich pulled a chair out for me. His wife, more traces of tears on her face, sat down and immediately began filling my plate with stewed eggplant, a dish called "eggplant caviar."

"I didn't know that you are in Kiev with your family. You should have come with them," Maria Borisovna said, deep in her thoughts, but playing the proper host.

I ate, not noticing right away that the couple was not touching their food. When I noticed and reprimanded them jokingly, they placed some food on their plates and pretended to eat.

"I have a present for you from Lena," I said.

"Hopefully, this time we'll get our permission. She didn't have to burden you with errands," Aron Mikhailovich said.

"It's not a burden. I really wanted to meet you." I put my fork on the plate and pushed it away. "Lena is my friend."

"It's nice to know she has good friends. Hard to picture her life now—maybe we better not picture it," Maria Borisovna said so softly I could barely hear her. "If not for my husband, I never would have agreed to emigrate. I can't forgive Lena her behavior."

"What behavior?" I asked looking straight into her reddened eyes.

Aron Mikhailovich cleared his throat. He got up decisively and went to the display of photographs on the wall.

"Here." He held a large color picture in front of me.

The picture taken relatively recently in Lena's backyard showed her, the children, and a big-faced, burly man around a picnic table.

"She destroyed this family with her own two hands," Aron Mikhailovich stated as if pronouncing a verdict.

"Stop it," I raised my voice, then repeated quietly, "Stop it, please."

I got up and walked to the balcony door. With my back to my hosts, I stood like a statue seeing nothing except Auntie Riva's face on her stone. I was unable to move. Sniffling broke the silence behind me. I turned around. Maria Borisovna, her hands in her lap, cried without a sound, sniffling, her tears dropping off her chin onto her blouse. Her husband still held the photograph in his hands. His eyes stood out feverishly under his dark brows.

"I didn't understand why I wanted to meet you so much," I said, realizing that only a second ago I didn't know what to say. "And now I know."

The couple faced me motionlessly.

"I envy Lena so much that she has her parents. I envy everyone who has a mother." I clenched my teeth, waiting until the urge to cry passed. "As soon as you get your permission, please do not delay. Lena has been waiting for you. She needs you so badly."

The photograph fluttered down on the floor from Aron Mikhailovich's shaking hands as he sat down, suddenly looking very much his age. Maria Borisovna wiped her nose with a napkin.

"Believe me, you can trust your daughter's judgement. But even if you don't, what does it matter?" I stepped back to the table and sat down. "Do not deprive your daughter from being a daughter; do not deprive your grandchildren from having grandparents. If you feel she has made a mistake, that only means she needs you even more."

I reached for the dish with chopped liver and put some on my plate.

"I'm still hungry," I said. "Lena has told me many times how good your chopped liver is."

"Yes, please, help yourself," whispered Maria Borisovna.

"Tell me," Aron Mikhailovich said in a hoarse voice, "did she leave Serozha for another man?"

"What does it matter? You can't hire or fire your child."

"So, she did." He lowered his head.

"Why can't you consider that Serozha left her?" I said as I finished the chopped liver and took some more from the dish.

"Because she admitted that she applied for the divorce. Serozha worshipped her, he would have never done anything to hurt her little finger." He raised his little finger to illustrate his point.

"Nothing is absolutely right or absolutely wrong," I said, startling myself.

Lena's parents exchanged a look that only people that had known each other so well they became one could understand. Jack and I sometimes exchanged a look like that.

"How does she manage now?" Aron Mikhailovich asked, finally a father concerned for his little girl. "Her salary, I understand, is not very large. When we get to America, we'll live together so that Lena can add our pension, or whatever it's called in America, to her budget."

"She's fine. Her children are fine. All she needs is you."

"For so many years, we waited for a child." Maria Borisovna blew her nose into her napkin again with the same movement Lena had made when she found out about Chernobyl. "We did everything for Lenochka to become a perfect human being."

"And she has," I said, suddenly cheerful. "Let me give you the gloves she got for you."

I took the bag with the fluffy, gray gloves out of my purse and handed them to Maria Borisovna.

"Aron, this is perfect for my new gray coat," she smiled at her husband then at me. "I built myself a coat last year, so, in case we get permission, I'll have a nice coat to wear in the United States."

"That was very smart," I concluded. "You will definitely need a coat in Chicago."

"Aron, I forgot the jellied meat in the refrigerator!" she cried out in horror.

Aron jumped up and trotted out.

"Jellied meat." I closed my eyes in anticipation of a treat that I hadn't had for many years. "I love jellied meat."

I ate an incredible amount of the jellied meat, and more chopped liver, and cheese-with-garlic salad, and the eggplant caviar, and then a stew with rice that was good but couldn't compare with Auntie Riva's, and then some apple strudel and sponge cake that did compare with Auntie Fira's. Lena's parents ate almost nothing, but they showed me pictures of Lena; her almost-straight-A report cards; wedding pictures, where Serozha carried her in for the ceremony; and their grandchildren-made presents.

"Please don't tell Lenochka how much food I ate at your house. It's embarrassing," I said as I was putting on my jacket.

"And you," Maria Borisovna began, her hand on her chest, "please, don't tell her that I cried. Tell her that we are in good health and that we can't wait to see her. My husband tries to read books in English, but the words are so hard to remember. I'm just trying to memorize some simple words and phrases. We don't want to be completely helpless."

It was already dark when Aron Mikhailovich walked me to the bus stop. I carried a paper bag containing treats for Jack and Tanya.

"We took Lenochka's divorce very hard," he said quietly. "First, my wife absolutely refused to emigrate because of it, but," he shrugged, "I told her just what you said, that we need to see for ourselves. And, then, we don't want to be buried here where we don't have anyone anymore."

We saw the light of the bus approaching.

"I'm glad we met," I said and shook his hand. "I'll see you soon in America."

"See you in America."

Lonya's grave had yellow leaves across it; the fence and little bench were freshly painted. There were few visitors to the Jewish part of the expansive cemetery on this windy work day.

Lonya's name stared at me from the gravestone as I walked quickly through the gate of the little fence. Tanya and Jack followed at a distance, stopping at the gate.

"Lonya," I whispered, "don't be angry."

I could not remember a day during our life together when that phrase had not been uttered.

"Lonya, I miss you, I really do." I sat on the edge of the small bench pressing my hands between my knees. "Don't be angry, Lonya. I want you to meet my family, my almost-grown daughter, and my husband. I wish you had lived to see Tanya. She's very talented and takes after your mother's side of the family. You would be pleased."

Lonya listened suspiciously.

"I hurt Fima badly, but you must see what would have become of Tanya and me had I stayed. True, Tanya's first years in America weren't great. Perhaps I could have done things differently, but I didn't know how. In a way, Jack has done more for her than anyone. Please, don't be angry, Lonya." I shivered under my thin jacket. "The past won't be forgotten. The people from my past will always be able to count on me."

I sat silently, my eyes closed.

"Tanya's children will have grandparents. Jack will spoil them, like he spoils us. It's a pity we won't have children." I smiled and started crying noiselessly.

"I loved you, Lonya. I would have loved your mother, our mother, as much as you did. I never wanted her to die." I wiped my tears with the back of my hand. "I celebrate my birthdays now, and I do laugh—I know our mother would have wanted me to. There is so much to celebrate. You're not angry, Lonya, are you?"

His stare softened.

"I'm glad I came to visit you. Oh, Lonya, I love Jack. Please, wish us happiness." The tears made me choke. A long time must have passed.

"Mom, let's go. It's getting chilly." I felt Tanya sit down next to me. "Don't cry," she said in Russian. "Jack says we can rebury Uncle Lonya in Chicago."

Our shoulders met.

"Uncle Lonya belongs here, Tanichka. I can come and visit again." We went through the gate.

I looked back. Lonya's stare was no longer angry. I couldn't envision it smiling, but I knew it wasn't angry.

Jack was waiting nearby, his cheeks and nose red, the collar of his jacket turned up. He put his arm around me. Tanya walked ahead, anxious to leave.

I kept looking back at the freshly painted fence. My eyes hurt from the wind.

All the fences seemed to melt together.

Fall 1987

epilogue
August 1991

Between 1988 and 1990, any Soviet Jew who had a sponsor was allowed to enter the United States, and it seemed that almost everyone was sponsoring someone. The complaints about newcomers and the quarrels never stopped, but the sponsoring, advising, and aid continued unreservedly. The immigrants of my time now found themselves in the role of Americans, or as the new immigrants referred to us—worse than Americans. We were amused to learn that, according to bona fide sources, we had encountered no hardships upon our arrival—apartments, jobs, and English had been ours for the taking. Therefore, it was only logical that they, following in our footsteps, should receive the same benefits.

In 1990, the United States modified immigration rules and only accepted those Soviet citizens with immediate family already here. For the rest, the options still open remained staying home, going to Germany or, out of desperation, to Israel.

The Russian white-collar community generally enjoyed an excellent reputation. Our clients were very happy with our five Russian employees. They didn't mingle well—neither do I, in spite of Jack's coaching—but their professionalism was beyond reproach. It was hard to explain and useless to fight with the undue weight most American companies placed on American experience. Jack couldn't hide his apprehension when I placed Asya's older son, Dima, who had little experience in the Soviet Union, no experience in the United States, and only a hint of English, with our biggest client in Green Bay. The young man represented a typical Russian professional. Hardworking, efficient, loyal, unassuming, he became our live advertisement.

Unlike a dozen years ago, the Soviet Union now had well-educated programmers, and most of those who emigrated between 1988 and 1990 landed jobs within months of arrival. A portion of the latest arrivals were refuseniks (those turned down in 1980 and 1981). The children who had been old enough to understand the agony their families had gone through were now the driving forces behind their emigration. The parents, usually in their mid- to late fifties, and, therefore, often unemployable—with due respect to America's anti-age discrimination laws—had retired to the public aid ranks, some defiantly, some with embarrassment, some perfectly satisfied.

The Soviet way of survival—dodging, shifting, and turning on one's own axis—certainly came in handy for these new arrivals. The collective feeling of this new mass was that they had all the information about life in the United States necessary to take advantage of everything to the fullest, and without delay. The collective feeling of my group was that the newcomers expected results without suffering the road to them. Our past and present letters about receiving help from the JRL, public aid, the importance of real estate for easing taxes, and the like, were thrown in our faces with remarks such as "It was easy for you. In your time, the JRL took you by the hand and got you your first job" or "I didn't come to the United States to work. I worked enough in the Soviet Union." Our warnings that prematurely obtained home mortgages would result in working only for the sake of paying a mortgage and put them in danger of losing their houses were met with cold, blank stares and statements like "Rent is a waste; you said so yourself. You have a house. Why shouldn't I?"

Most of those who left when I did, did so to leave the Soviet Union. Many who left now, did so to come to America. This made all the difference in the world.

About three years ago, Lena and I started assisting new arrivals with résumé writing, general advice, translating, and running various errands. We also actively solicited donations of household goods and had scouts reporting and securing in their homes anything usable which had been discarded in the alleys of the East and West Rogers Park areas. Gradually, more and more volunteers joined us. Our acquaintances sent the first clients to us in the fall of 1988.

Bella's older sister, Masha, spent an entire afternoon with me in a conversation that turned out to be indicative of many others and reminded me of conversations with Rimma, Asya's sister, a few years ago.

"In your opinion, Anya, should I take a programming class?"

"There is a better chance for a programmer to find a job than an engineer."

"But it's hard."

"True, but that's not a valid reason to forego the training."

My reply, offered in many variations, was always left unanswered.

Masha told Bella I was stuck-up and didn't understand real problems. She went on public aid and by registering at a city college to take— and retake continually—English and other classes, such as History of Music and Russian Literature, accepted a popular and legal dividend: a cash stipend from the city government.

We subleased a room from a Russian travel agency owned by the daughter of one of Gena Korsunsky's patients. We advertised through word of mouth and JRL social workers that we made calls, wrote résumés and letters, distributed clothes, simply listened, and gave conversational English classes—the advanced level conducted by Jack or by Howard

Smolin. Officially, we did it twice a week, plus weekends. In reality, we were on call twenty-four hours a day, as there could be no schedule for translating in a medical emergency, calling a towing service, or clarifying a message left by a prospective employer on an answering machine.

There were many frustrating times when we tactfully tried to undo the work of some JRL caseworkers, who advised people over forty-five not to waste time looking for jobs, just to rely on welfare benefits and subsidized apartments. They intimated to the newcomers, whose sponsors, themselves on public assistance, had taken out bank loans for them, arranged by the JRL, that paying the bank back would be unnecessary because in America poor people didn't have to pay back.

On weekends, we haunted garage sales and alleys and transported chairs, mattresses, bookshelves, televisions, and the like on the tops of our cars, and clothes and kitchenware in trunks and back seats. Jack instinctively understood and never offered money to our clients, or suggested hiring movers. I had a hunch our visit to Kiev and the stories of my first years in America had finally started making sense to him—their abstract sentimentalities becoming real life with its pain and fear, and everyday losses and victories. In spite of that visit, the realization of how little most people needed to feel comfortable in their first American homes overwhelmed him.

Jack kept a low profile when we delivered our loot; he was one of us, occasionally not even recognized as an American, unless he had to speak. The recipients, animated and high-spirited, would surround our cars, drool over the goods, describe how easily everything could be fixed and beautified to become useful for years to come. Entire families participated in carrying and arranging the bounty in their rooms and cabinets. Their appreciation, their wishes of luck, their insistence on sharing their meals filled me with such joy and gratification that I wished I didn't have to do anything else—ever.

Jack declined our clients' invitations to stay after completion of the deliveries so as not to force anyone to speak English, but I sometimes accepted—just to chat, to hear one more life story, or, when the family had an older woman in it, just for a cup of tea. One such old woman, called Anna, refused to let Jack leave. She and her husband, Maxim, both former teachers, had called several times asking for a desk—"any desk in any condition." Finally, one of our scouts located a small wooden desk with two sets of drawers and three-and-a-half legs. Anna and Maxim did what Jack called "a ritual dance" around his car looking with what could only be described as lust at the desk tied to the top. When I pulled up behind Jack and opened my trunk, the couple, in their late seventies, couldn't catch their collective breath for a long time when they saw an almost complete set of dishes; three pots, two pans with one lid; and a box with tablecloths, a new shower curtain, pot holders, serving spoons, and water glasses.

Anna, a short slim woman in glasses, wore a straight, black skirt; a light-blue blouse with a bow; and laced, thick-heeled, black shoes. Her gray hair was cut short in a style called *à la boy*, a loose translation from Russian. I had no trouble visualizing her in a classroom. Maxim, also in glasses, was tall, rosy-cheeked, gray-whiskered, in a green jacket that looked as if it came from a garage sale. I could easily visualize him in a Santa Claus costume. He spread his arms indicating that no words could adequately express his emotions.

"You better go and help!" Anna pushed her husband toward Jack who by that time had untied the desk and pulled it onto his shoulders. "The poor man can't carry it by himself."

I convinced Maxim that it would be better if he took the drawers and let the poor man handle the desk. He dove eagerly into Jack's trunk while Anna marched ahead of Jack with the key to their apartment, held like a gun. I knew by Jack's smile that he liked these people too.

In their third-floor, one-bedroom apartment, Anna had gestured as if she was directing the operation of a crane when Jack lowered the desk into the corner of the living room she had indicated. By the time we returned from the second trip with the rest of their things, folded flyers had made a perfect temporary half-leg and a newspaper and a telephone gave the desk a cheerful look.

"You're probably surprised that at our age we need a desk." Anna's quick, blue eyes addressed both of us. She hadn't realized yet that Jack did not speak Russian. "We have always had a desk, a large desk," she added nostalgically. "A home is just not a home without a desk."

Suddenly, she pounced, catching Jack in the act of turning the front door knob to leave unobtrusively as he usually did.

"And where do you think you are going, young man?" Anna demanded to know.

Jack froze with a guilty look on his face. I could swear he had understood what she said.

"It will be easier when my wife doesn't have to interpret," he said smiling.

I translated.

Maxim stood thunderstruck, but Anna didn't seem impressed. She pointed to the kitchen and ordered, "You two are not leaving without having some of my borscht. Who do you think I made it for this morning? And from fresh beets too! Not those stupid American cans!"

Trying not to laugh, I translated for Jack.

"Another Anna to boss me around," he muttered pushing up his glasses, which meant he, like me, was having a hard time trying not to laugh.

Our hosts corralled us into the kitchen where we sat in the only two chairs they owned. The tiny rectangular table covered with a snow-white runner looked suspiciously like a serving tray. Standing with their backs to the cabinets they beamed as we ate the borscht—with sour cream, for me, like any good Russian. In spite of Anna's stern warning that one could not have borscht without sour cream, Jack won the round.

Jack made a sign not to translate for him; he preferred uninterrupted conversation. Anna told me, with Maxim interjecting his comments cautiously, how their students had loved them, corresponded with them, and those that had immigrated to Chicago even offered to have them tutor their children. Even the neighbors from their communal apartment wrote to them.

"Do you know how rarely that happens?" Anna asked us rhetorically and, after seeing Jack smile and nod, added confidently, "He understands Russian."

Their grandson, thirty years old, a math wiz, *kineahora*, enrolled in a Ph.D. program and had started dating a girl named Maureen. They called her "Marina" because it sounded more normal. They tried to teach Marina some Russian, but their accomplishments so far included only a few words because they didn't see her often enough.

"She will have to learn fast," Anna frowned. "We are not that young and we have to communicate somehow."

Their widowed daughter, an electrical engineer, couldn't find a job in her field and was thinking of becoming a manicurist. Her former classmate and admirer, who now lived in Boston, visited her, so, maybe. . . . At that point, Maxim looked at his wife with disapproval and she then spoke of their progress in English and their extensive correspondence.

"Now that we have a desk, our lives will become completely stabilized," concluded Anna.

Jack thanked Anna for the borscht, clicked his heels, and kissed her hand.

"You should learn Russian . . . or better Russian," she instructed him, completely won over. "Translating back and forth only wastes time."

"Sometimes I think that I could like some of your Russians," Jack said to me when we walked out of the building still smiling. "Make a note that these people need a kitchen table and chairs."

I stretched without opening my eyes.

Sleep doesn't come naturally following thoughts of my community. Tanya is probably still asleep, her palms tidily under her cheek. Only God knows how late she came home last night. We don't wait up for her anymore . . . actually, I only pretend not to. On the evenings she's out I read to an unusually late hour. Still, last night I fell asleep before she got home. My fear of waking up from a dream and finding emptiness still lurks just below the surface. The relief of looking around and finding reality often makes me weak with happy tears. Jack hugs me, massages my shoulders, and says, "I'm here, sweetheart, and I'm not going anywhere!"

Change is not easy for me. Every little change has taken years, and it's never entirely complete.

I have problems believing that I'm a wife. This is partially Jack's fault. He has never learned to act like a husband. He still takes me out on dates, calls from his office—which is directly across the hall from mine—in the middle of the day to say hello, brings me little gifts, makes love spontaneously and as lovingly and hungrily as he always has.

Not surprisingly, my relationship with Jack's mother was rocky. To put it simply, she hated me. Some of it was Jack's fault as he fueled her resentment by kissing me in front of her and bringing me flowers.

Mrs. Graff—the late Mrs. Graff—had vehemently opposed our marriage. Finally, realizing Jack was determined to marry me, she demanded he have me sign a prenuptial agreement. He refused. She never would have believed I had offered to sign such an agreement before she ever mentioned it. I think she later regretted her words and deeds, the transformation being entirely Tanya's doing, whether Mrs. Graff realized it or not.

At first, Mrs. Graff refused to attend our wedding and only agreed to make the trip when Jack suggested we could get married in Miami for her convenience. She didn't congratulate her son, ignored me, snubbed her Argentine relatives, and was the first to leave the ceremony, heading directly to the airport. Had there been any hope she would have listened I would have begged her to stay for the reception.

I shuddered at the idea of a wedding reception without a mother. Lonya's angry eyes glared at me from the bottom of a pit. I tried to catch my mother's face behind his, but became cognizant only of Jack's concerned look and Tanya's excited smile. Jack had picked his favorite tango for our first dance and had given me tango lessons for weeks. I held my new husband's arm as we walked to the dance floor. My hand shook so much that he covered it, making a show of kneeling and kissing it. Everyone clapped. Lonya's eyes stalked me, smiling faces forced into the background.

A split second before tears broke through all my defenses, Nancy came into view in a shapeless pink dress and flat, brown shoes. She looked all teeth as she applauded us from the table she shared with her daughter, Linda, very pregnant in an elegant black maternity outfit, and her son-in-law Rick. I remembered her first description of him—"American! Rick! Mother Irish, father half-Polish half-German. Thirty years old, blond, blue eyes, not tall, very nice, very nice!"—and suddenly I threw my head back and laughed my silver-bells laugh. Lonya's eyes retreated.

"You didn't forget the steps, did you?" Jack looked at me seriously. He led me firmly, his hand barely touching my back. "Very good," he said, his brows rising in surprise. "See, I've taught you to tango too." Jack smiled at my silver bells.

A few months later Mrs. Graff had a mild stroke, leaving her with some memory loss and a slightly weaker left arm and leg, but no speech impairment. I received a phone call from her doctor and tried to reach Jack who was in Denver making a presentation. I succeeded only in leaving a message for him that his mother was sick and that I was flying to Miami.

She was in intensive care, scared and confused, but conscious.

"Marsha would have come with Jack," she spoke curtly. She kept asking when Jackele was coming, and why Jackele hadn't called and accused me of keeping Jackele away from her.

Shaken and grouchy, Jack reached me at the hotel, and upon learning his mother was out of danger, instructed me to hire some nurses and do whatever else had to be done and come home, since, except for a grave emergency, he could not leave Denver.

By the time Mrs. Graff was transferred to a regular room two days later, I had hired a private nurse and a nurse's aid. Mrs. Graff dispatched the nurse's aid to her apartment with a list of items required for a comfortable hospital stay, among them a blue terrycloth robe and matching slippers with feather-like pompons, a cosmetic bag, and her phone book. Instructed by Mrs. Graff, the nurse called many numbers which appeared in the book, one of them Marsha's, to advise them of Mrs. Graff's illness.

"Well, Anna, it was nice of you, but you can't win me over by playing up to me," the thin-lipped Mrs. Graff greeted me testily when I stopped at the hospital on my way to the airport.

"Mrs. Graff," I leaned toward her, fighting an urge to kiss the tiny wrinkles on her cheek, "I love your son. You're his mother, that's almost the same as my own mother. You know, I never knew my mother."

For a fleeting second I detected an expression of softness.

"Don't try that with me. You got my son, that's enough."

"Mrs. Graff, when you're better, we'll bring you to Chicago and you'll live with us. My daughter is away at college, you can have her room. When she comes home on weekends she can sleep in our little office."

"You're trying to control me."

"It's Jack who wants you to stay with us, if you don't mind, of course. You see him so infrequently."

"He feels guilty, foolish boy. He knows what he did to me when he divorced Marsha and then married you. They would have had such beautiful children," she sighed wistfully. "Why would you agree that I stay with you?" She gave me a knowing look. "For your information, I don't have to leave my money to Jack, and I won't."

"I agreed because I also would like you to stay with us. You're my husband's mother."

"I won't live in your hut. I'm not used to such places. My son has a decent place of his own."

"I'm sorry, Mrs. Graff, it's our home and there is enough room in it for my family—all my family. My mother would have stayed with us."

Mrs. Graff turned away, dismissing me with a faint good-bye.

"You don't know how difficult my mother can be," Jack exploded when I informed him of my decision to move his mother into our house.

"She's your mother" was my only reply.

He finally gave up and immediately started making plans to buy an apartment for her, hire nurses, cooks, and a chauffeur.

"Your mother is sick and scared. She needs a family, not a crew of servants—she's staying with us. The house is big enough. Donna will drive her everywhere. Your mother is staying with us, and, as far as she's concerned, it was your initiative."

"You are the most obstinate person I've ever known. I don't want to have anything to do with this," barked Jack. He fled to the health club.

True to his word, he pretended not to notice the transfer of Tanya's futon to the bedroom we used as an office; her desk, book shelves, and dresser to the basement; the remodeling of Tanya's room, and its subsequent furnishings: a walnut sleigh bed and a matching dresser from Plunkett, two small landscapes in light, wooden frames, and soft, cream curtains.

When shopping to decorate my mother-in-law's room while she was in a rehabilitation center in Miami, I made believe that I was doing it for my mother. I wondered how different my life, and Lonya's too, would have turned out had she survived the war. For the first time, a brief thought of my father, of whom I knew nothing besides his name, Lev Isaakovich Vozinsky, which had given me my patronymic "Lvovna," also entered my mind. We would probably have lived in the same room as the one Lonya and I had lived in. Another bed would have fit if the table, where Lonya had played chess with Sasha, stood not by the wall but in the middle of the room. Of course, then we would have had to move around sideways, but how happy my childhood would have been, how complete a person I would have become. If Lonya had to be taken to the hospital he would have had a mother to stay with him, so that Sasha would not have come into my life. I had to admit, however, that I would not have cherished my mother as deeply had she survived to bring me up, and that she would live now, like almost all mothers, in a subsidized building, going to Russian concerts, and seeing me once a week.

Mrs. Graff's opinion of my house as a hut notwithstanding, I couldn't see Jack's with its *Architectural Digest* layout and furnishings as a home. I suppose my background only prepared me to relate positively to hardships and simple living and to distrust elaborate comfort, pouring cold water over my feelings.

Tanya, too busy to accompany me to the stores, helped me plan the purchases over the phone. Drawing on her experience at the nursing home, she insisted on a warm, light-blue paint for the walls and warned me that the dresser must be low, not very deep, and not have drawer knobs but handles easy for weakened hands to pull. Jack did visit his mother twice—each time leaving Saturday morning and returning Sunday night—but I was convinced he did it because he realized Tanya and I expected him to. On his second visit, which fell during Tanya's school break, she went with him, but not before soliciting advice from Vera, her main authority on senior psychology.

"What is important for your mother to have around her? I mean, furniture, a lamp, books, anything?" Tanya interrogated Jack when I was driving them to the airport.

"Listen, we're not moving her furniture, only her clothes, and if she wants a lamp or something, it shouldn't be a problem. The rest stays behind in Miami, for now." Then he added with a trace of irritation, "I already told her that, and she said she didn't want anything besides her jewelry and photo albums."

"You did?" Tanya sighed like a mother at the antics of her child. "I knew I should have talked to you about it sooner. Now she probably feels like she's being transferred from one prison to another."

"Com'on, Tanya," Jack replied lazily, "you're making it more complex than it is."

"Unfortunately, it is complex," Tanya coached him from the back seat. "In order for your mother to feel at home in our house, she must have her favorite things here. Our goal is to carefully extract the information from her about what these things are."

"Good luck," Jack muttered.

"I know she may not be receptive to my inquiries. That's why you should try it."

"You know what," Jack smiled, "why don't you just tag everything in my mother's apartment that seems like it's worth shipping to Chicago? No furniture, though. Our house is already crowded."

"You don't understand," Tanya whispered.

Jack turned to look at Tanya, his eyebrows raised.

Surprisingly, Tanya's mission succeeded. The next day, I saw her run along the ramp from the plane, weaving between other passengers, and far ahead of Jack, who strolled out a few minutes later, smiling and shaking his head.

"It's the rug!" Tanya exclaimed as soon as she spotted me in the crowd. She kissed my cheek and repeated, "It's the rug in her bedroom! It's an antique Persian one! Turns out Jack's father gave it to her and she brought it from Argentina and she loves it!"

"How did you find out?" I chuckled.

"Maybe, she should be a psychiatrist instead of a pediatrician." Jack kissed my other cheek and put his hand around my shoulders. We headed to the airport garage.

"We stopped at the apartment before going to the rehab center and I made some mental notes about what items to mention. Mrs. Graff wasn't really thrilled that Jack showed up with me, but he just stuck his nose in a newspaper so she had no choice but to listen to me." Tanya skipped impatiently, probably annoyed that we were not running. "And I started telling her that she had a talent for interior decorating and how much I liked what she had in her house. She liked the compliments, so she told me where she shopped, the prices, and so on. But then, when it came to the rug . . . she didn't want to talk about it. She became very quiet." Tanya caught her breath. "Jack told me the history of the rug later. I don't understand why he didn't think of it before."

"Well, my mother has other things that my father bought her, like silverware, dishes, fur."

Jack seemed mystified by the secrets of a female mind.

"But she didn't become quiet when I mentioned them," Tanya pointed out when we boarded the elevator. She rolled her eyes, not finding appropriate words to express disappointment with Jack's lack of understanding. "Also," she continued decisively, "Donna can do some physical therapy for Mrs. Graff, and we have to get a subscription to the *Miami Herald* and the *Forward*."

Tanya walked ahead resolutely, as if the publishers of those newspapers waited for her in the garage.

"She is so much like you. I'm not sure if I can handle two Annas," Jack said in my ear, his hand squeezing my shoulder.

As long as life doesn't present her with my choices, I thought.

Six weeks later, Jack and Tanya flew back to Miami to bring Mrs. Graff to her new home. Tanya charged Jack with the task of dissuading his mother from going to her apartment, prior to heading to the airport, where she would discover the absence of the rug. Mrs. Graff's luggage had arrived a week earlier. The Persian rug was one of the few things we had unpacked, the rest waited for their owner in boxes, and several issues of the *Miami Herald* and the *Forward* waited on the night stand. After not having to cook for such a long while, I personally made an old-fashioned stew that my mother-in-law had once said she liked.

"You don't think I'm going to be seen riding in this car!"

These were the first words uttered by Mrs. Graff when she arrived at our house as she glared at Jack, pointing to Donna's six-year-old, white Ford Escort.

"Mother!" Jack growled, avoiding Tanya's eyes. "You'll ride in whatever is available."

Mrs. Graff, pale, her gray eyes faded, her left hand shaking rapidly, refused to take her son's arm. Not looking at anyone, she followed him to her room very slowly, stopping every few steps. He opened the door and motioned her in, but she placed her hand on the door frame for support and stood silently.

"Thank you, Jackele." Her trembling voice, in stark contrast to her remark only a few minutes before, made Tanya move closer to her. "I really wanted my rug," she said softly.

"Tanya thought you would," Jack said.

"You don't have to act generous." Mrs. Graff finally entered her room. "No one else would understand but you."

Mrs. Graff found fault with everything. She criticized me to Jack, compared me unfavorably to Marsha, kept her own grocery and long-distance telephone accounts—to the penny—and shut herself in her room as soon as I came home from work.

"These unlicensed exercises will only bring me closer to paralysis," she said of the regular sessions with Donna that visibly strengthened her arm and made her walk more confidently.

Only Tanya seemed to elicit any sort of civil conversation from the angry, old woman. She didn't actually make it her goal, it just happened. It began when Tanya suggested to us that Mrs. Graff should decide what car she would want to be seen riding in and should get it. The process of choosing the car and haggling with the dealer somehow proved therapeutic. She referred to the white Cadillac DeVille as her car, kept the key in her possession at all times, allowed Donna to take her shopping in it only as a special treat, and waited patiently for Tanya's weekend visits, when she tagged along on some of Tanya's errands. Tanya read the papers to her, asked her about her parents and about Jack's father's courtship, and took her to the nursing home to meet some of the residents she still visited on occasion. Somehow these trips got longer and longer as they magically coincided with Mrs. Graff's appointments at the beauty salon, where Tanya was referred to as her granddaughter. One day, with great secrecy, they disappeared in the morning and didn't return until the late afternoon. Jack and I were sick with worry, ready to call the police and hospitals.

"You're silly," shrugged Mrs. Graff. "Tanya wasn't just wandering about on her own. She was with me!" Their eyes were bright, and Tanya carried a heavy doggy bag from a restaurant.

On weekends when Tanya stayed in the dormitory to study she always informed Mrs. Graff personally why she could not come home. And Mrs. Graff proved to be exceptionally crabby when it became necessary for me to drive her to her hair appointment. Tanya called her Gram instead of the formal Mrs. Graff that I became relegated to.

It gave me, oddly enough, great pleasure to listen to Mrs. Graff scold me for being too lenient with my only daughter and criticize Donna's way of making soup, frying potatoes, drying dishes, or cutting vegetables. My house was a real home with a mother in it. The nineteen months she lived with us were difficult, but they were probably more difficult for her than us.

Mrs. Graff passed away in her sleep. As hard as Jack and I took her death, Tanya suffered even more. She lashed out at Jack for not paying enough attention to his mother and for a month stayed at the dormitory, calling me at the office only occasionally.

I found Marsha's phone number in Mrs. Graff's telephone book and called her.

"I'm so sorry," Marsha sang out. "She was over eighty, wasn't she? She called me only a few days ago."

Marsha's sing-song drawl expressed no particular interest. I didn't volunteer the time and place of the funeral service, and she—the former daughter-in-law Mrs. Graff liked to call "the daughter I never had"—didn't inquire.

As expected, Jack went to the synagogue every morning for the first thirty days. I tried to go with him, but I was restless, finding no relevance between the prayers and the sense of loss the prayers would never alleviate. My preference was to visit Mrs. Graff's grave, and to do it alone. Somehow, this act had a connection to my emotions and filled the emptiness with acceptance of the inevitable.

There are two graves at this American cemetery of two people I wish had not passed away so soon. I stop there almost every Sunday for a few minutes. Sylvia's grave is covered with grass and there still is no stone, only a marker. If she could only know of the books I've read, if she could only see my library. And it all started with *Nineteen Eighty-Four*, the book she loaned me.

Mrs. Graff left a small part of her estate to the JRL, specifically to the Russian Fund, and to other Jewish charities, including an orphanage in Israel her late husband and his family had supported for many years. With tact I didn't suspect of her, Mrs. Graff left a note asking me to give Donna two thousand dollars and to thank her for her golden hands and infinite patience. Marsha received a ten-thousand-dollar savings bond. The majority of her estate, including the Persian rug, went to Tanya, referred to in her will as "Tanya Fishman, my granddaughter," to be kept in trust until she was thirty years old and ready to start private practice or pursue research projects. When Tanya discovered the enormity of her inheritance she was astounded. She danced around the room, bobbing about—building her own hospital and having her own research center. Well, I thought, maybe not all that . . . but let her dream.

Tanya admitted that she, at Mrs. Graff's request, had taken her to our attorney to finalize her will and had known of Mrs. Graff's intentions, but not of the amounts. That's what their secret outing had been. They had spent the day at the attorney's office and then celebrated at a restaurant. Mrs. Graff left Jack her father's pocket watch and her Manhattan and Miami apartments. She knew that financially her gesture would not affect him, as he had almost no need to touch what he had received from his father. But, as she had probably anticipated, Jack was somewhat discomfited by the symbolism of his mother's will. I guess he never realized how much he had hurt her over the years. I was mentioned as "Anna Graff, my son's wife and friend, and my daughter-in-law," and received Mrs. Graff's jewelry and family photo albums.

Except for a small, diamond Star of David set in platinum with a white gold chain, the jewelry remained where it was, in a safety deposit box at the bank. The five thick, battered, originally green albums held an endless and undying fascination for me. They moved to our library where before going to bed I sometimes became engrossed in the turn-of-the-century pictures of Jews from Russian shtetls, frozen-faced men in hats and women with dark hair parted in the middle under a kerchief; Jack's baby pictures; his parents' wedding and vacation pictures. When I saw his father I knew where the broad shoulders and smiling eyes came from. I marveled at his Argentine grandparents, aunts, uncles, and a horde of cousins in summer hats, sipping tea on a wide veranda. At my request, Jack pointed out the cousin who introduced him so successfully to sex. The only picture of Lonya I ever saw was on his passport, and it had to be turned in to the Kiev city hall when he died. And then there were Jack's and Marsha's wedding pictures. On one of them, Mrs. Graff was kissing Marsha, who looked stunning. I added our wedding pictures and the few pictures of Tanya as a baby that had accompanied me to the United States, her graduation pictures from high school, and some newly taken college photos. My family has grown roots; there are five generations of us in the albums.

On Mrs. Graff's last birthday we took her to brunch at Windows. She wasn't feeling well and sat quietly, not bothering to argue with Jack. A tiny old woman with a walker and a young couple approached our table.

"Is this you, Fanya?" asked the tiny woman speaking loudly, like people who don't hear well.

The Fanya sounded so Russian I looked up curiously.

"Basya!" Mrs. Graff dropped her fork, pressing her palms together. "I mean, Bessy. It's been years! I didn't know you lived in Chicago."

The womens' cheeks touched. The young man accompanying Bessy took her walker, and Jack rose to help her sit down. The look in Mrs. Graff's and Bessy's eyes as they spoke of years gone by and good times made the sudden change in Mrs. Graff outstanding.

"This is my grandson, Jonathan, the apple of my eye. He's Miriam's son. This is his wife, Gail. He's an accountant. She's an accountant too," Basya added casually. "What are you doing in Chicago?"

"I had a mild stroke and my son insisted I come to live with him." Pride in Mrs. Graff's voice.

"Such a *mensch*. Most kids are so selfish nowadays. Thank God, Florence, you're not looking bad. I've got terrible arthritis. Is this your Jackele? It seems like only yesterday he was that high." Basya held her hand about a foot from the floor. "And this is your daughter-in-law. Very nice. And your granddaughter. Are you going to school, young lady? You know, she looks a little like you when you were young."

I held my breath.

"She does, doesn't she? She attends the University of Chicago. She's going to be a doctor!" responded Mrs. Graff, pink and alive.

She definitely scored against Basya's accountant grandson.

Apparently, Basya felt so, too, because she pinched her lips together and rose with the help of her grandson.

"The kids take me out for brunch once a month and Miriam takes me out shopping sometimes. It's so lonely in the apartment. To hire a companion is too expensive, even if she doesn't speak English. But then, you wouldn't know how that is."

"Call me. We have a lot of catching up to do," Mrs. Graff nodded sympathetically, "Jackele, give Basya our phone number." They hugged and parted.

The rest of the day found Mrs. Graff in a thoughtful and nostalgic mood.

"Bessy and I grew up on the same street on New York's Lower East Side," Mrs. Graff said when she came into the kitchen that evening for her tea. "Her family was poor, even poorer than mine. Bessy married a car salesman. They never had money. I told her not to marry him. She was such a pretty girl, what was the rush? When my future husband came to my parents he was in a good car, in a good suit, and carried a walking stick. Our whole block watched. Bessy was so jealous. Well, I was patient. I had told her there must be fine, rich, Jewish boys.

"My Eduardo was a good man," Mrs. Graff's eyes stared at the wall, seeing what only she could see. "He bought a small house for my parents. My father had bad veins. He couldn't handle the bakery anymore. Eduardo sent my parents a check every month and for Passover something extra.

I never had to ask." Tears rolled out of her faded eyes. "He loved me. He did. He brought me flowers and jewelry, I had servants. His family thought I was a golddigger. Oh, my God, why did he have to die so young?" Mrs. Graff stretched out her arms to God. "They said he had a bad heart. Basya wanted me to marry her brother when his wife died. He liked me, but what did I need another husband for? He would only have made me miss my Eduardo even more. Jackele, let him live long," she said in Yiddish, "looks like me, but he's like his father. I see that now." Mrs. Graff nodded seriously and added dryly, "You take good care of my Jackele. He needs to eat more vegetables." She shuffled out of the kitchen sighing and shaking her head, forgetting her tea.

That was the closest she ever came to accepting me and acknowledging my presence in her son's life.

When I think of the shock which made me finally desert my home and move to Jack's house I get goose bumps, and I'm convinced that, along with our marriage, that shock shortened Jack's mother's life.

One night I was besieged by a dream . . . a dream like a scene in a war documentary. There were airplanes over a field releasing bombs, smoldering freight cars, and smells of smoke. Lonya held my shoulder tightly and a woman in a kerchief, with Mrs. Graff's face, stood on the steps of one of the cars, screaming, "Fire! Fire! Run, Lonichka, run!" "Mama!" I cried out in Russian, trying to tear myself from Lonya's bony grip. The woman, not noticing me, screamed, "Run, Lonichka, run!" Then she vanished behind a veil of smoke.

"Anna, honey." I awoke to bright light and Jack's hand shaking my shoulder. "Don't be alarmed. My mother accidentally started a fire in the kitchen. The fire department is on the way. Let's get out of the house."

I threw on my robe, trembling from the visions of my dream, following Jack's orders blindly. The smell of smoke, the lights of the fire truck, the police cars, and the ambulance appeared as a continuation of my dream. Only the airplanes were missing. I kept looking up to the sky.

Mrs. Graff was ready to be taken away to the hospital. Her right arm burned, she looked small and miserable packed on the stretcher, her face screwed up in pain. Her frightened eyes longingly followed Jack as he ran toward the house.

"Mrs. Graff, Jack will change and go with you to the hospital." I walked, swaying, alongside the stretcher, patting her shaking hand.

She ordered in a surprisingly strong voice, "Don't let him leave you alone. Look at you, you're going to faint!"

I stayed with our neighbor Peggy until morning when Jack came back from the hospital, upset and exhausted. I was still in my pajamas and robe, the dream still haunting me.

"Why didn't you go home? The house is fine except for the kitchen, dining room, and part of the hallway," Jack chided me as we walked home across the lawn.

He unlocked the front door.

"I don't want to go in, Jack."

"Why?" he was irritated. "You need to change. We'll grab some clothes and check into a hotel."

"You don't understand. I can't go into this house. I don't want to live in this house anymore. I don't want to see it burnt." Unable to stop, I sounded hysterical. "Before you woke me, I was dreaming of my mother. Her freight car was burning." I was talking into Jack's chest. "Let's go to your house. This is not a home anymore."

Holding me close, Jack touched my forehead with his lips.

"My God," he said softly, "I thought all that was over. I thought you were happy."

"I am happy, Jack." I looked up at him. "I can't tell you how happy you've made me. Only, there's always some baggage. I didn't start the day we met. I didn't even start when I was born. No one does."

He smiled, but his eyes were anxious. "I love you, darling."

It never sounds meaningless coming from him.

"I love you, sweetheart," I whispered.

We left a note for Donna, and that was the last time I saw my house.

My fears aren't as sharp anymore, or as deep, or as lasting. The fear that Tanya would not turn out to be the person I wanted her to be has been replaced by the fear that something may happen to her, or she won't meet the right man, or she won't have children. She has good friends; young men call for dates, but she rarely accepts. Involved in her own young pursuits, Tanya is so different since Jack took me from her charge.

She accompanied him to Buenos Aires and the estancia two years ago for a cousin's wedding. With my busy schedule, I had thought the ten days would fly. But I missed them. I missed Jack's quick, light kisses and the warmth of his body, among other things; and, of course, I missed Tanya, continually worrying about her, even though I knew she was in good hands. I was relieved when they returned.

The first night they were back, we all sat down in the kitchen, where I fixed tea, coffee, and cocoa. Tanya was bubbling over with her impressions of her first riding lesson with Jack. Tanya, who had never ridden a horse before, had difficulty mounting the horse, in spite of Jack's assistance. Finally, Jack led the horse to the corral fence and she climbed onto a rail and mounted the horse with a loud sigh of relief. She was in awe watching Jack ride at a full gallop, racing with his old friend Guillermo and two other estancia workers.

Jack and Tanya visited Guillermo and his family at their house on the estancia, where Jack introduced Tanya to Guillermo's mother, Inez, and to his wife, Maria Elizabeth. Inez, who lately had given over the cooking chores to Maria Elizabeth, quietly started making dough for empanadas, as soon as she saw Jack. Tanya had said that Jack had eaten more than she had ever seen him eat and had kissed Inez' cheek, saying "*Gracias, mi amor.*" For once, Tanya felt the tables were turned as Jack had to translate for her.

Jack told me his relatives fell in love with Tanya and that some of the younger cousins had argued over who would take her sightseeing. One in particular Osvaldo, a young neurologist, evidently argued better than all the rest. At the wedding, which took place at the estancia, Osvaldo never left her side, and she tripped all over him trying to follow his tango instructions.

In Buenos Aires, they stayed at Jack's Aunt Lilliana's apartment, which now belonged to the family. Tanya thought it was a bit old-fashioned, but quaint in its own way, and, at least Osvaldo, who had followed them from the estancia, was at his own apartment.

Tanya went on for a week, telling me little things she had forgotten to mention, until the beginning of the school year brought her back down to earth.

Osvaldo followed up his very brief courtship with a letter, and then, impatiently, with a phone call.

Thank God, Tanya wasn't interested.

That incident gave rise to the horror that someday she might not live in the same city or country as us. Jack countered by saying that we could retire and move to wherever she lives.

The fear of my not deserving love had gradually ebbed, and Helena Smolin deserved full credit. We had spent considerable time together looking for my wedding dress. If someone were to ask me how it happened that Helena, Tanya, and I flew to Los Angeles—more specifically, Rodeo Drive, Beverly Hills—twice, to buy my dress and have fittings, I would never be able to answer. My dress—cream-colored, one-of-a-kind, ankle length, deceivingly simple, and incredibly elegant—fit like a glove. It required rigorous workouts. Tanya sucked in her breath at the European-sounding name of the designer, which informed me—as had the absence of a price tag—that the price exceeded any comprehensible range.

"Don't show the dress to Jack before the wedding," warned Helena on our return flight, presuming exactly what I intended to do immediately upon arrival.

"Helena, this dress costs a fortune, not to mention the trips to Los Angeles." I already regretted my temporary loss of will.

"Don't forget to include the jewels this dress absolutely screams for," Helena commented in a mock professional tone. "Jack can afford it, believe me. My husband is his accountant." She winked. "You'll get used to it. Trust a simple Prague girl."

"It's not just the money, Helena. I'm not eighteen years old and I don't need anything nearly as extravagant. Jack should know how much I've spent," I said, cold with guilt.

"I would be very surprised, and extremely disappointed, if he wanted to," Helena smiled confidently. "Relax. Jack is crazy about you. He's not doing you a favor, just as Howard wasn't doing me a favor. We give our men something money can't buy."

As she predicted, when I raised the subject of the cost of my dress, Jack placed a finger over my lips. "Honey, buy what you like."

Helena helped make the months before the wedding almost stress-free. She gave me a beautiful bridal shower under an enormous tent in her back yard. I tried to refuse, but she wouldn't hear of it.

Lena gave me a small, intimate shower at her home on a Sunday afternoon. Everyone invited had been present at Helena's shower, but here we could simply sit and talk.

Leah-Malka, amazingly, recalled many funny episodes from the time when we met, just a few days after our arrival, when her synagogue assigned her to assist us.

"Remember, you told me you were sick of me instead of saying you worried about me?"

Leah-Malka laughed so deliciously, rocking from side to side in her chair, that even I, though embarrassed, laughed with everyone.

"How did you know what my mother meant?" Tanya asked, choking with laughter. She sat on the carpet hugging her knees and wiggling her toes in white socks with delight.

"Oh, I just looked into her eyes." Leah-Malka made a movement with her hands as if chasing away a fly. "I'm a bit of a psychologist. Why do you think I volunteered to work with you newcomers?"

Helena, comfortable on the sofa with her legs folded under her, told us how her family escaped from Czechoslovakia in 1968 "after Soviet tanks had liberated it."

"Even Howard still doesn't know every detail," she said swallowing hard.

We pretended not to see the tears in her eyes.

She added, "There are things. . . I know I'll cry if I talk about them."

Then we spent a long time in silence, picking on the grapes and raspberries and tiny, fancy pastries.

When the non-Russian-speaking guests left, Natasha, Lena, Bella, and I reminisced about going through customs as we left the Soviet Union—we all knew these stories by heart but invariably listened with undivided attention each time they were repeated. Lena announced she had accepted Ilya's marriage proposal, proving charitable work hadn't done much to alleviate her loneliness and boredom. Bella who had recently purchased some land in Barrington, related some extraordinary tales of their builder's arrogance. Natasha showed photographs taken on her trip to Israel a month earlier. She had finally met her daughter-in-law and new grandson, named Shmuel, after his maternal great-grandfather. The baby had inherited Natasha's turned-up nose which she sarcastically referred to as his *goy* nose. With Joe out of the picture, she had begun a serious hunt for a Russian husband.

Only when Jack and Felix called, within minutes of each other, to find out when the shower would end, did we realize it was after eleven in the evening.

Outside, Natasha asked, "What did you do to get Jack to propose?" She refused to believe that he had proposed in spite of what I had done, or that marriage had never been my goal. The rift between us did not seem deep and we had no reasons for distrust, but nevertheless we silently acknowledged both the rift and the distrust.

Sasha knew from Vera of my upcoming marriage, and when I called him he warmly wished me the best. I detected no jealousy or emotion in his voice as the chain of events in my life took the course expected by society. To Sasha, nothing would affect my always being there for him, like he would be there for me. For some inexplicable reason, my repeated admissions that I cared for Jack had never impressed Sasha as being relevant to our relationship. I wished I had the courage to tell him once and for all that, sadly, his friend remained, but his silly little girl had faded into the past, Jack or no Jack. I didn't have the courage and only asked him not to call me anymore. I promised to call him, which I did, about once a month. A few times we stopped for hot chocolate at McDonald's where Sasha thought we wouldn't encounter a familiar face. Every time he asked if we could meet more privately my answer consisted of vague complaints about my schedule.

"Don't get upset, Anichka. I understand. I don't blame Jack for watching you. We don't want him to suspect anything. We're used to waiting."

Jack knew of my every call and of the hot chocolate outings, and of Lilya and Nonna, and that I couldn't cut Sasha off—neither of us ever violated the unspoken understanding not to discuss Sasha and our past relationship.

What was I waiting for all those years of waiting for Sasha?

I raised one eyelid slightly, aiming my vision at the clock. It was eight. Jack must still be jogging. Hopefully, Tanya would knock on the door and drag me out of bed. But the knock on the door came from Yadviga. She surprised me, as Sunday was her day off.

We hired Yadviga, our live-in housekeeper and Donna's acquaintance, when Donna returned to Poland two years ago. She spoke very good English and had been a professional cook in Poland, then a house-keeper for many years for some real estate mogul in Chicago. She was in her early sixties, an American citizen, and had no family. She performed her duties and managed the cleaning lady and gardener admirably. She disapproved of being forbidden to serve us food and drinks, screen our calls, answer the front door, or announce our guests. I did finally learn to put up with her use of our surnames. When Jack was home alone, she had a field day waiting on him hand and foot, which he hardly noticed, and he thus earned her deep respect. She evidently considered our marriage a misalliance. Her face expressed contempt every time she saw Jack serve himself. Once she attempted to take a plate out of his hands to carry it to the sink. That's when I put my foot down and told her in an icy tone, "Yadviga, as much as I appreciate your effort, I do not expect you to work after six, unless it has been specifically requested beforehand. We want our privacy." She turned on her heel and left the kitchen without a word, whereupon Jack burst out laughing.

Yadviga stuck her head in. "Mrs. Graff, I am very sorry, but there is a call for you from a Sasha. He said it was an emergency. He declined to give his last name. Do you want me to plug in your telephone?"

My heart jumped. "Yes, please."

Instantly awake, I sat up and swung my legs to the floor, looking for my slippers. Yadviga hurried to my nightstand and plugged in the telephone, then placed my slippers, heel to toe, in front of my feet.

"Thank you, Yadviga. Sasha, what's wrong?"

"Anichka, I'm sorry if I scared you." He paused. "Lilya's in the hospital."

My stomach contracted aware of what was about to follow.

"She's not expected to live through the day."

"Oh, my God, what happened?"

"I can't tell you," Sasha said firmly, "it's too gruesome. Anya, please, I need a favor. Vera is spending the weekend with a friend in Milwaukee. She needs to be told, but not over the phone. I must stay with Lilya. She's conscious now and keeps asking for me."

"I'll leave right away. Give me the address."

"Please, Anichka, I didn't mean . . . I thought . . . maybe you know someone. I don't know anyone I could ask."

"Sasha, give me the address!"

I put the kettle on the stove and climbed the spiral stairs to Yadviga's apartment. She was dusting her already immaculate sitting room, singing in Polish.

"Yadviga, Tanya and I have to leave on an urgent errand. Would you mind making breakfast for us right away, and for Mr. Graff when he returns from jogging?"

Tanya was sound asleep. I hesitated before waking her. Well, she won't be happy if I leave her behind.

"Tanichka." I sat on the bed playing with her hair. She growled, trying to shake off my hand. "Tanichka, you have to get up. We have to go and get Vera."

"Vera's in Milwaukee." Tanya's eyes blinked open then closed again. "I'm so sleepy. Tell Jack I don't want to work out today."

Tanya didn't know about Vera's mother's condition and this was not the time to tell her.

"Tanichka, Vera's mother is very ill. Her father just called."

Tanya's eyes popped open.

"Please get up. Yadviga's making breakfast. We have to go to get Vera."

"What happened? Is it serious?" asked Tanya, her eyes wide with fear.

"Very."

We showered, changed, and appeared in the breakfast room at almost the same time.

"Ms. Fishman, there was no rye bread for your toast. I used white. Mrs. Graff, Mr. Graff is in the downstairs shower. I told him you were leaving." Yadviga poured juice for Tanya.

"Good. I was going to write him a note." I chewed quickly, stirring my tea.

Tanya ate silently, choking on her food.

Jack's cheerful greeting failed to produce smiles.

"Where are my girls off to?"

"Sasha called. His wife is dying," I looked straight into his eyes. "Vera's in Milwaukee. She doesn't know yet and we're going to get her."

Yadviga placed a plate of food in front of Jack.

"Do you want me to come with you?" He squeezed my hand.

"No. You need to call the Smolins. We might not be able to attend the concert at Ravinia tonight. Yadviga will make you lunch after she's returned from church."

"Anna, sweetheart, and you, too, Tanya, take it easy. There's nothing you can accomplish by falling apart."

Jack's patent consolation—"There's nothing you can do." For the first time in the four years of our marriage I was annoyed with him.

By the time we arrived at the address in Milwaukee I felt nauseated. Tanya was tense and pale. She got out of the car and moved decisively toward the front door. I stood by the car holding my breath. The door opened before Tanya knocked. A girl with long, straight hair appeared followed by Vera, both carrying tennis rackets. Vera's face radiated her special smile, until she spotted us.

"My mother," she stated unemotionally.

Tanya nodded.

"This is your mother?" the girl next to her asked amiably.

"Tracy, I have to go. My mother has passed away." She handed her racket to the girl.

Tracy gasped. Vera disappeared into the house.

"I'm sorry," said Tracy. "Why don't you come in? I didn't know Vera's mother was sick."

Vera appeared with a backpack slung over her shoulder.

"Tracy, please say good-bye to your mom for me." She smiled then walked to the car.

"Thanks for coming for me, Mrs. Graff. How's my father?" Her voice held no tears.

She doesn't make it easy to feel sorry for her.

"Verochka, your mother is in serious condition. She hasn't died. Your father called around eight." I tried to maintain a conversational tone.

"He wouldn't have called if there was any hope," Vera stated without emotion.

The girls packed themselves into the back seat of the car. Tanya's face was distraught, Vera's composed.

After a while, Vera repeated her question. "How's my father?"

"He sounded okay on the phone."

"Vera, what was wrong with your mother?" Tanya said softly.

"She didn't want to live."

The matter-of-fact reply sent a ripple though my body. Tanya was stunned.

"We have a lady who watches her, but she has weekends off. My father works such long hours, he's always tired. He probably fell asleep. I shouldn't have gone away, but he insisted." Vera's voice remained level.

"Don't blame yourself, Verochka." I must have sounded stupid. There was really nothing to say.

"I'm not," answered Vera. "We knew we couldn't prevent it."

All of a sudden I realized Vera wasn't composed, she was numb. She had to be.

"Would you mind coming to visit my father?" continued Vera. "He told me he used to know you when you were a little girl. Mr. Graff won't have any problems; my father's English is very good."

Will we visit Sasha? We must. But we won't. I don't want to visit him.

Tanya's round eyes met mine pleadingly in the rearview mirror.

"Of course, Verochka, we'll keep in touch."

Vera watched me thoughtfully.

The drive back became so quiet I wanted to scream. We finally exited the expressway and headed west to the hospital.

"Mrs. Graff," said Vera anxiously, "our landlord just raised our rent by seventy-five dollars a month and this month we had to borrow from a friend to pay it. There's going to be a lot of expenses now. Would it be possible for you to lend me some money? Only, I don't want my father to find out. He doesn't know what my savings are from my school and summer jobs, and I'll let him think it came from that. I'll pay you back any way you want, with interest, or whatever." She leaned over resting her arms on top of the front seat, her intense face next to mine. "If he borrows from someone himself, he'll keep working two shifts to repay the loan, and I don't want him to do that."

I fought back tears. "Tell me how much you need, Verochka, and don't worry about paying it back. You can't work more than you already do."

"But I'm only starting medical school. I can't ask you to wait."

"Verochka, you can borrow the money from me under two conditions: no interest ever and no repayment until you have a real job."

"Thank you very much. I will pay you back. Only, I never want my father to know," she added again.

Tanya's eyes blinked at me in the mirror. "Why was the rent raised so much?" she asked.

"The owners are Russians. I met them once at your house. Their name is Schwartz."

"Nina and Izya?" I asked.

"Yes. They own some buildings on our block and maintain them themselves. My father tried to talk to them, but they are rehabbing a big building they just bought. Their son got caught with drugs, so they had to pay lawyers, and their daughter and son-in-law couldn't find jobs after college, so they claim they need the money."

"All right, Verochka, whatever you need, let me know. And remember, you are always welcome in our home."

"Thank you, Mrs. Graff," she whispered.

Sasha was waiting at the front entrance to the hospital, his face in gray stubble, his eyes red. I remembered the description Jack used when they first met—an older gentleman. Vera jumped out as soon as I stopped the car. They didn't hug, only looked at each other. Sasha bit his lip and nodded. Vera lowered her head.

"I'm sorry, Sasha," I said, angry at myself for not putting my arms around him.

"I'm sorry, Mr. Rosen," echoed Tanya behind me.

"Can I see her?" Vera's face held the same composed expression. Not a tear.

"Yes. Why don't you wait for me in the lobby?"

Tanya put her arm around Vera and they went inside.

"Is there anything I can do for you?" I said in Russian—Jack's very American formula. A Russian friend does not ask, he does.

"Not really, Anichka. I appreciate what you've already done. You didn't have a problem with Jack, did you?"

"No, he understands."

"I wish you had waited," Sasha raised his voice suddenly, "but I suppose it wasn't meant to be."

He was as numb as Vera. Any feelings for Lilya had died long ago.

"I did wait. I'm sorry, Sasha."

Now he knew.

His red eyes moved dully over my hair, my face, down my body.

"Well, Anya, I'm happy you're happy. I mean it."

"I know." There was nothing to say. "Call us when Tanya is ready to be picked up."

"We will."

"Let me know about the funeral."

"Of course."

I drove home as if someone chased me, staring ahead fixedly, my teeth clenched, wishing I could curl up into a ball and stop time. I choked up as I thought that just a few years ago Jack had had to face the brunt of my pain, my fears, and my anger. A police car flashed its lights behind me. My foot hit the brakes. The police car screeched, pulled around me, and continued winding down the street, its siren screaming. Amazing, it wasn't for me. I continued at a slower pace, and when I reached the corner of our block I turned and pulled over. Explosive sounds and lights of the police car followed me. I leaned back and closed my eyes, my neck muscles wooden, hands cotton. Gradually, the sounds and lights faded.

Well, Anya Fishman, Anna Graff, what are you running from? Is this how you repay the special people in your life when they need you most—with detachment and indifference? But what Sasha and Asya meant to me could not be measured; what they did for me could not be repaid—certainly not by pretending to feel close.

Time to face the truth, Anichka!

The truth is, Sasha will remain special for as long as I live—special but far away. He now understands why we have found ourselves on the opposite sides of the bridge. The truth is, Asya is not special at all—sometimes I wonder why this woman looks familiar. Still, the memory of closeness throbs like the memory of a limb aching and throbbing long after it's been amputated. The truth is, my obstinate effort to put my life on hold to give my past a chance to catch up with me was a misguided, foolish waste. We build memories as we live, like a tree builds year rings. But year rings merely point to springs and summers gone by, they don't signify life. Only fresh leaves and blossoms of today signify life. The past cannot become a cause for survival; it only serves as a foundation, a link, a bridge.

The truth is, my craving to speak Russian, to assist the Russians, to hold on to my Russian foundation is exactly that, a craving to rub shoulders with what surrounded my first thirty-five years. Would this craving remain as strong had I to give up a particle of my new life to satisfy it? The truth is, it would not. Asya took the easiest route, attributing my obvious alienation to quantifiable incidentals—my big house, my Mercedes, my domestic help. Numerous others drew the same short-sighted conclusions about their American families and friends. Becoming poor would not bring Asya and me, or Bella and her sister closer, but how can I prove it? The truth is, I have no desire to prove anything.

If this is a sign of betrayal, of callousness, of inability to recognize and safeguard true bonds, of selling out for marble stairs and two fireplaces, so be it.

Dear God, I know I promised to handle my life on my own now because there are so many people that need your helping hand more. But I'm asking you once again for something. If you would just let me make Jack happy. If you would just grant Jack and me a long, happy life together, and make Tanya's dreams come true, and, please, make sure that we have grandchildren, that will be all—I promise.

I drove into our garage, passing a red convertible decorating our driveway. John Singer, the architect who remodeled our house, a playboy well into his sixties, must have arrived early for his one o'clock appointment. At Jack's insistence, we had a swimming pool built at the right edge of the back lawn. The pool had ruined the expansive view of the foliage and lake, and after consulting with John we decided to put in a terrace and plant a small grove around the pool. John was here for us to sign the contract.

Jack, in his swimming trunks, with a towel over his shoulder, sat with John Singer and two other people at a patio table under a large umbrella. John had his portfolio propped against his chair.

Jack loves weekends. He doesn't enjoy the responsibility of running a company. On the other hand, I start every week full of energy and ideas. He, like any self-respecting man, wouldn't retire while I'm still working. A month ago, a large software corporation approached us with a lucrative buyout offer. They expect our official response in two weeks. Big dollar amounts sound as meaningless to me as the numbers of the federal deficit, but if we accept the offer we could stay on as consultants, do charity work, go to shows, travel. I don't know . . .

Drinks in tall glasses and a tray with munchies told me that Yadviga had done her part.

John, a formerly good-looking man, tall, with long, gray hair tied back in a ponytail, wearing a green golf top and fashionably baggy, cotton slacks, leapt up as I appeared on the patio. The other two looked like recent Russian arrivals. The man rose slowly. In his fifties, he was small-boned and bald, with a cautious smile, piercing, black eyes, and a short, black beard. His wife, with large eyes and an aquiline nose, must have been attractive once. She held her drink in a stiff hand, smiling artificially, sweating in her tight, black, leather pants and angora sweater.

Mutual dislike, instantaneously.

"Anna, beautiful Anna." John took the tips of my fingers in his.

He adopted a different greeting for every woman. This happened to be mine.

"Cut it out, John," muttered Jack, aware the Russian couple would not understand. "How was your trip, Anna? You must be exhausted. Where's Tanya?"

"The trip was fine." I reported peacefully. "Tanya's going to stay with Vera today, or possibly overnight. Shouldn't you have changed?" I frowned at his trunks.

"I was in the pool when John arrived."

"I apologize, I should have called to say I was coming early," John raised his hands in surrender. "Anna," he pointed to the couple, "let me introduce my new friends, Eugene and Tamara Kaplan. From Kiev!"

I assembled my face into an expression of delight and reinforced it with a greeting in Russian. My reaction visibly deflated John's excitement. He obviously had anticipated less controlled emotions.

"They immigrated less than a year ago. Eugene's an architect," John went on smoothly.

"Welcome to America," I addressed the couple in Russian. "I'm Anya Graff. Tamara, you don't have to hold your drink all the time. I did that, too, in the beginning."

Tamara hastened to put her glass on the table then discreetly wiped her hand on her pants.

I smiled remembering the iced-tea at my first meeting with Jim Karlson. Jack caught the meaning of this scene; his eyes twinkled as he evidently recalled my countless snafus.

"We met in an art supply store," John cut in. "Eugene restores furniture. I saw a sample of his work. Outstanding, simply outstanding! His English is quite good, as well," he added as an afterthought.

I disregarded the last statement. Americans are generous with their compliments. For all practical purposes, this couple did not speak English.

We sat down. I put several cubes of cheese and a cracker on a plate.

"Anna, I'm going to let Yadviga throw together a light meal for everyone," Jack said.

"Thanks." I smiled at him, knowing he had invented an excuse to leave the patio. "Have you begun looking for a job yet?" I asked Eugene in English.

His beard twitched as he concentrated on a reply.

"Yes, I look," he answered finally, glancing sideways at John.

"John, do you mind if we speak Russian?" I took another cracker, wishing I could make myself a substantial sandwich and take a nap.

"Go right ahead. I brought them here because I knew you would want to help your former compatriots, and you had mentioned that Jack wanted a piece of antique furniture restored." John obviously was enjoying his good deed.

I switched to Russian.

"My husband is planning on restoring an antique chest. He'll show it to you after lunch. Where did you live in Kiev?"

"On the Rusanovka. We had a three-room apartment near the well-known Slavutich food store," Tamara said with the self-importance many Russians assume when they describe apartments and furniture left behind.

"Oh, yes, I remember that store." I added the tinge of respect they expected.

Not a nerve reacted to the sound of the familiar names.

"Kiev has become even more beautiful now than it used to be. Have you visited recently?" Eugene's beard moved as he spoke.

"About four years ago, and it was beautiful. How is your job search progressing?"

"It's practically impossible to find a job as an architect. I need a license, but even with a license . . . at my age . . ."

"I know," I said. "Maybe you could find a position as a draftsman. And furniture restoration could become quite a lucrative business with time. I would be glad to refer clients to you."

"Thank you. I guess I will have to try," Eugene looked humble, "although that's not what I expected with my experience."

"What did you expect?" I inquired, already aware how the conversation would shape up.

"First of all, I didn't realize speaking English would be so vital. Also, I brought some designs with me to sell, but John said there is no market for these particular types of designs."

"John would know."

Eugene glanced briefly at John who sat back in his chair, eyes closed, a straw from his drink in his mouth.

"John doesn't understand, but . . . maybe, you would know if there is any way of selling my designs to a builder. I won't forget your effort," he added the familiar euphemism meaning a kickback or bribe.

"It doesn't work that way."

"You don't have to be afraid of me. John told us you help Russians and donate money to JRL. If only I knew the right JRL person . . ." Eugene coughed into his fist ". . . to thank for introducing me to the right builder, you wouldn't even have to be personally involved."

I longed to cancel the meal.

"When you immigrated, the JRL found everyone jobs and provided business connections. It was so much easier for you than it is for us," continued Eugene, throwing a handful of cheese cubes into the opening in his beard.

"And what's your occupation, Tamara?" This seemed to be the only other subject open.

"I'm an economist." Tamara turned her attention to Jack who approached us, fully dressed.

"Lunch is being served in the breakfast room. Let's go inside, shall we?" he said formally.

I translated.

We led our guests through the house to the breakfast room off the kitchen where Yadviga, happily in charge, had set the table with the same attention she gave black-tie dinners.

"Yadviga, would you please show our guests where they can freshen up?" I added in Russian, "Yadviga understands some Russian, in case you need any help."

My tone, that of a genial hostess, moderately friendly, moderately respectful—when did I acquire it?

Eugene and Tamara smirked imperceptibly and, with John, followed Yadviga. To them, I'm a shameless showoff. Oh, well.

"I'm sorry, Anna," Jack placed a piece of fish on his plate. "I've already told John not to bring strangers again without asking for permission in advance. What are you going to have?"

I washed my hands in the kitchen sink and returned to the table.

"Fish is fine. I'm famished. Jack, let's make this lunch short. Have you looked through John's contract? Did he make the changes we asked for?"

"Listen, they caught me with my pants down, so to speak. I didn't have a chance."

"Did you call Howard?"

"I left a message with one of the nannies, but she wasn't sure if Helena and Howard would be home before Ravinia."

"Good. I think we'll go to Ravinia, after all. It's supposed to be a great concert, mostly Tchaikovsky. Lena has also planned to attend. I'm glad because I haven't seen her in a while."

"Are you sure you want to go?"

"Positive."

Jack narrowed his eyes questioningly.

John and his victims took their seats. The presence of the silent and efficient Yadviga intimidated the Kaplans. I understood only too well—I'm still not entirely comfortable being served.

"Please help yourself," I looked around the table, "and ask Yadviga for anything you need," I said in Russian and then in English. "So, Tamara, you used to be an economist? What are your plans here?" I continued the small talk in Russian leaving Jack and John to their own devices. "As you probably know, the Soviet definition of an economist—part book-keeper, part accountant—doesn't exist here."

"I'm forty-eight. At my age," sighed Tamara, "I'm not even going to look for a job. Our caseworker is of the same opinion. I'm taking some classes now to become a home attendant."

"Do they have a placement service?"

"Oh no, I wouldn't take care of strangers. The government will pay me for taking care of my mother as if she were my patient."

"Is your mother sick?" On that subject, I didn't have to feign interest.

"She's still pretty independent. She doesn't really need anyone."

"Would you be willing to baby-sit?" I changed the topic before my anger got the best of me.

"Baby-sitting would come in handy, if it's not far from home and with a school-aged child, preferably a boy."

"There's not always a choice," I said listening to my sympathetic tone with approval. "When your English improves, you might find something clerical."

Tamara's English will never improve and she will never work.

"We can only work for cash. We can't risk losing our welfare benefits."

Like most of the immigrants of my time, I accepted their reasoning with hostility, even as I acknowledged its common sense. I guess there is no absolute right or absolute wrong.

"Well, let me know if I can help."

"Actually," Eugene finished his Seven-Up and patted his beard where his mouth must have been, "I wonder if you would call our grandson's school to tell them that he can't pay his tuition."

"What do you mean?"

"Our grandson goes to a Jewish school. The public schools in the Rogers Park area are terrible. The school didn't award him a full scholar-ship because his parents earn good salaries. So, they have to pay one hundred dollars a month. That's not fair!"

"Why?"

"Why?" Eugene wrinkled his forehead.

"Yes, why isn't it fair, if his parents have good salaries?"

There was something in my voice that made Jack look up.

"But they only came to this country recently. Our children have to save for a house. They're already paying off two new cars, and they're paying for the boy's violin and chess lessons."

"Perhaps they should have bought used cars?"

"Why?"

"So they could afford the tuition."

"They could afford it, but they need a house."

"Aren't you pleased your children can afford to pay what I know to be a very modest amount?"

"Anya," Tamara sounded annoyed, "they can't really afford it. They need to move to the suburbs as soon as possible, so their son can go to a good public school. The last thing we need is for our only grandson to become religious." An expression of horror appeared on Tamara's face. "God forbid."

"Let me make sure I understand," I said in my best professional manner. "This religious school should provide free education for your grandson so that he can move to the suburbs and go to a public school?"

Eugene and Tamara nodded, somewhat more enthusiastic. They obviously found nothing wrong with this logic.

"I don't think it's fair to award full scholarship to your grandson," I concluded.

Eugene cleared his throat warning his wife to be quiet.

Yes, the immigrants of my time are worse than Americans. Americans are always concerned with making people feel happy.

"More dessert anyone?" I smiled hospitably pointing to tiny raisin cupcakes.

It was a relief to return to English.

Jack took his cue and turned the conversation to the contract. To Tamara's disappointment, we went back outside. The Kaplans sat morosely on the far side of the table. John retrieved the drawings and we walked to the site of the future terrace and grove so he could show us the exact spot of each tree and bench. On the way back, I pressed my shoulder to Jack gratefully.

As we approached the Kaplans who sat with their backs to us we heard sounds of an argument.

"What did we have to lose by coming?" Tamara was on the defensive.

"I don't enjoy being lectured by this arrogant, spoiled cold fish."

"At least we got to see this house," countered Tamara.

"The gall she's got to advise us to work! She thinks everything is so simple!" Eugene was breathing fire. "She just crawled under this bull. *That* was her work."

"Americans are such idiots. I bet he believes she is a young chick. I'm sure she's not much younger than me." Tamara seemed to feel her revenge was complete.

"Thank you, Tamara, that's quite a compliment. Actually, I'm older than you," I came from behind her chair, smiling.

She sat transfixed, eyes wide. Eugene's beard twitched angrily.

"Aren't they sweet?" John piped in, misled by my smile.

"Most definitely," I assured him.

We signed the contract and instructed Yadviga to let John and his crew in beginning on the coming Tuesday.

"Now, Anna," John spread out a sheet of drawing paper, "remember, Tanya once commented that this house lacks a gazebo, and you wanted some ideas? Take a look."

The Kaplans craned their necks toward the drawing.

The picture presented a toy-like, souvenir-looking structure.

"This isn't a gazebo, this is a toy," I said. Suddenly, a gazebo became a dire necessity. "Jack, what do you think?"

Jack shrugged.

"John," I spoke earnestly, "the gazebo has to be very simple, Russian style, the type Russian squires used to have in Turgenev's time."

"A very romantic project for a very romantic lady."

"Spare me, John," Jack said curtly, pushing up his glasses. "Listen to what Anna wants, and we'll wrap it up for today."

"You could enlist Eugene's help," I suggested.

I translated into Russian.

Tamara wiped her face with a napkin. Eugene rubbed his beard thoughtfully.

"Will he pay cash?" Eugene asked avoiding my eyes.

"I don't think so," I replied.

"Will he agree to make the check out to my daughter's name?"

"Eugene, John's firm has been in business for thirty years. This job is small, but it could lead to more in the future."

"At fifty-two, I can't risk to be taken off welfare. He can't guarantee other projects, and I have to think long-term." Eugene was nervous but firm.

"Well, there are no guarantees in America. You make your own decisions and take your own risks."

"In this sense, it was better in the Soviet Union," whispered Eugene miserably, his eyes on the drawing.

"In this sense, it was," I agreed. "John, Eugene won't be able to assist you, but you have your resources. There's no hurry."

We showed Eugene the chest needing restoration, for cash, then watched our visitors stuff themselves into John's tiny red convertible.

Where in the world did Tamara get those leather pants?

Jack locked the door slowly, not looking at me. He acted uncharacteristically irritable. It usually took much more than uninvited guests to affect his mood.

"How's Vera's mother?"

We were climbing the stairs to the bedroom.

"She died. You know, Jack, Vera's had a very difficult life. She'll never completely recover." I took a deep breath then slowly let out the air. "Let's go swimming."

"Maybe Tanya should ask her to stay over for a few days?"

"She won't leave her father. I understand, I wouldn't have left Lonya. I promised to lend her some money. Other than that, you were right, there's nothing I can do."

"I'm always right, you just don't listen," Jack said lightly, although I sensed it wasn't a joke.

Under Jack's watchful eyes I changed into my swimsuit. Jack changed into his swim trunks.

As I adjusted my suit in the mirror I watched Jack pacing.

"What's wrong?" I said to the mirror.

"Anna, since we've been married, I generally haven't complained about your moods, but when you returned from your trip today, you looked as if you don't have a care in the world." Jack's words contradicted his accusing expression.

"Are you disappointed?" I couldn't hide my bewilderment.

"Baffled."

"Why?"

"I've come to admire your loyalty to the special people in your life. I realize Sasha was special to you, so anxiety today would be natural."

"What is it you don't believe, that I'm happy or that I'm loyal?"

"Sweetheart, this is not a question of trust." The face in the mirror was impenetrable.

"That's what you were implying." It was easier to reply to the mirror than to the live, unsmiling eyes.

"I'm not implying anything. I'm puzzled."

He's never been jealous, not even when he punched out Vilen.

"I'm not very good at explanations, Jack."

"I'm not demanding an explanation." Jack pushed up his glasses and pursed his lips, reminding me of his mother. "Let's go down to the pool while the sun is still up."

The images in the mirror stood their ground.

"Jack, I won't keep up appearances for Sasha. It would be wrong."

Jack rubbed his eyes under his glasses.

"You've kept in touch with him all this time because you felt sorry for a dear, old friend. What happened today, Anna? Why today, when his wife died, would it be keeping up appearances?"

"I don't know. Maybe, because," I smiled and wondered, very inappropriately, how young my smile looked, "today was the day. There was the day I knew I'd take Tanya away. There was the day I knew I was in love with you. It takes quite a while for each day to arrive. My timing, as you've noticed, isn't always the best, but I always know when the day is at hand and then appearances and opinions are unimportant. I guess I am a pagan, as I was once called."

Jack's hand appeared around my shoulders in the mirror. What an attractive couple we are! I may not look like Kim Novak, or any movie star for that matter, but like Jack says, I'm not half bad.

"And I thought, by now, I knew you. Who called you a pagan?"

"Sasha. Listen, Jack, Sasha is a closed chapter." Our eyes met in the mirror. "He's simply a very decent man who tried to live righteously by devoting his life to the care of his sick wife and older daughter who's confined to a mental institution. And, of course, to Vera, who's too numb to feel anything." I pressed my cheek to Jack's shoulder. "There are just the two of them now, like Tanya and I were before you came along. I don't feel sorry for Sasha; he made his choices. But Vera worries me. For her sake, we need to stay in touch with them."

"My God, you used to be ready to toss me aside for any crumb from your past." In the mirror Jack appeared tired with graying temples and chest, but still looking younger than his age.

"I wouldn't change anything in my past, but when I look back now . . . I wasted so much time. You know, all day I've been thinking about us, how late we started, how perfect your body is, and," I smiled mischievously, "what a handsome couple we are."

"That's an awful lot of thinking." Jack turned me to face him and the world came back in place at the sight of his boyish eyes. "It's not too late. If you exercise regularly and stop working so hard, we have at least another thirty years. Don't laugh! We do! And how many couples do you know that have thirty years, nowadays?"

"Jack, I don't mind your being jealous."

"I'm not jealous." He pushed me away slightly, his indignant tone proving his remark false.

Does he think I'd cheat on him with Sasha, now that Lilya is gone? Well, I did, once.

"I'm sorry, Anna. You always yearned for your past as though it would be your only salvation. When I saw such peace of mind today, I became afraid you'd just pack your suitcase and leave. No tears, darling, please, no tears," he cupped my chin and raised my face. "I'm sorry. You scared me. What did you expect from a dumb American?"

When we returned from Ravinia we found Tanya sitting in the back yard with her feet up on the patio table, listening to a talk radio program.

These shows, with their rowdy phone calls and jokes, will forever remain beyond my grasp of American life. Tanya turned off the radio and kissed the cheek Jack proffered. I patted her shoulder.

"What a day!" Tanya ran her fingers through her hair. "I just got home a few minutes ago. Now I understand why Vera wants to be a psychiatrist."

This grown woman is my daughter, the same tiny Tanichka with a white bow in her hair who held tight to my skirt in the Soviet customs office over fifteen years ago.

Jack and I sat at the table.

"Jack, it was terrible. Mom probably told you already," Tanya shivered. "The worst part was that Vera acted like it was a normal day. I don't believe she didn't care about her mother. I think she's scared."

"You should take her out or bring her over as much as you can," Jack said, his voice telling me he wanted to hug Tanya.

"You don't know how hard it is," Tanya whined, detecting an adult's weakness with the unmistakable instinct of a child. "She doesn't let anyone get close. I offered her everything I could and she only smiled and repeated she was fine because she was always ready for anything." She paused. "In a way, I know what she means, at least I think I do."

"You can't possibly know what she means." Jack got up and stuck his hands in his pockets. "You've always had a home where everything revolved around you."

"But I do know, Jack." Tanya looked up with the old woman's expression I hadn't seen for such a long time, "Don't you remember, I told you I was always scared something would happen to Mom and I'd have to stay with strangers, cleaning for them and not going to school? Of course, you appeared from nowhere," she smiled, "and that changed everything."

"I remember what you told me, Tanya, but don't forget you had loving parents when you were little, and I'm glad that long before your mother and I married, I was part of the family. At least I made every effort to be. It's not fair to compare your circumstances to Vera's," Jack said slowly and stubbornly.

"Oh, I'm not comparing, I've always had both of you—and Vera has only had her father."

Jack inhaled sharply and coughed.

Is that what he needed to hear?

"Vera's father is such an interesting person." Tanya's tone enlivened. "He told us about his years at medical school in Kiev, about different patients and rare diseases he treated. It was fascinating. He also told us about Uncle Lonya and you, Mom, how you were devoted to each other. At the end he told us some funny stories. I didn't want to leave, but they were tired. I think you should visit Vera's father," she concluded patronizingly.

With that, Jack said, "Well, girls, I'm going to watch the news then the game I recorded yesterday. Don't stay up too late." He waved as he strolled back to the house.

I put my feet on the chair next to me. "Who brought you home?"

"Vera. She's so worried that her father will be lonely. She's even considering delaying medical school until next year."

"She shouldn't do that."

"That's what I told her. She understands." Tanya paused. "Her father must have been a good doctor."

"One of the best."

We sat silently for a long time in the fresh air.

"Next weekend I'm going away. We, I mean my usual crowd, except, probably, Vera, reserved rooms at a hotel in St. Charles, Michigan. We're just going to hang out, you know, sort of say good-bye to summer."

I looked at Tanya. Did I have a choice other than to agree?

"Don't worry," she laughed, "it's only a couple hours drive and you know all the people I'm going to be with. Actually, there is one new guy," she added casually . . . too casually.

My heart sank. "Who is he?"

"Vladimir Slobodsky. Volodya, in Russian." Tanya threw a quick glance in my direction. "He came here from Moscow to visit his aunt a year ago and defected. Don't look at me like that. He's just a friend. He's not handsome or anything and he wears glasses. He plays chess. You know, the Russian-Jewish academic type. I'm going to drive to Michigan with him."

"You said you'd never date a Russian."

"I'm not going out with him, he's just a friend. We met a couple times at Alice's house. He's friends with Vera too."

"Is he working? How old is he?"

"He's twenty-eight. He works part-time at Radio Shack. In September he starts post-grad work in physics at the University of Chicago and he'll work as a teacher's assistant there. His English is perfect. Of course, his Russian education . . ." Tanya smiled gently. "We all feel so stupid when we compare ourselves to those who came recently."

My hands turned cold. "Well, Tanichka, I'll be happy to meet him when he picks you up."

Her eyes became large with terror. "He can't pick me up here!"

"Why not?"

"He lives with his aunt in East Rogers Park. She's only been here for two years. I can't show him this house and the cars and the other houses on our street. Do you know how it'll make him feel? Some other time. He can park at the train station and we'll take my car from there. He hates when we use my car, but his is falling apart."

Is she going to have her own room in that hotel or share one with one of the girls—or with this Volodya, the academic type?

"I'm sleepy," Tanya yawned, stretching. "Are you still going to read?"

"Yes, I have a new book I want to start tonight."

"We absolutely have to buy dresses for Asya's fiftieth surprise birthday party. Did you decide on a present?"

"Yes, a family membership at the health club."

"That's perfect. They need to lose weight. Hopefully, she doesn't suspect her sons are making a party. Where are Rimma and her husband going to stay? Don't forget, they're coming from LA the day before the party. I've never understood why Russians feel insulted if they're put up at a hotel. It's crazy."

"I know, Tanichka. She's probably going to want to stay here, she can't stay at either of her nephews' homes because Asya drops by every day."

"For some reason Jack doesn't like Rimma, but I think he could handle her for one day. He's pretty easy these days. You know, Mom, we could get away with murder," Tanya wrinkled her nose and giggled very much the way I do.

"I don't really like Rimma that much myself, so it will have to be a hotel. Let her feel insulted."

"Okay, your call."

We went into the house, closing and locking the giant patio doors. At the door to the library Tanya pecked me on my cheek then continued down the hall to the stairs.

Looking at the cover of a book, anticipating the magic after it's opened, is something I love almost as much as reading it. A ritual accompanies the beginning of each new book. I place it on the desk in the library, turn it over and run my fingers across the cover. The excitement is akin to the first touch or glance of a lover. Never losing sight of the book, I take out my glasses, a new feature, and put them on slowly. I lie down on the black leather chaise and move the soft pillow under my head. Impatience builds. I look at the clock on the coffee table in front of the chaise and screw up my face in disappointment as it's usually late and Jack will soon appear, turn off the light and lead me out, covering my neck with quick, light kisses. I run my hand across the cover again and sigh deeply. My mind shuts off every connection to my body, to the room, to the house, to the universe. Regardless of how a particular book affects me afterward, the emotion of opening it for the first time always remains sharp, new, and welcome.

Today, Saul Bellow's *Something to Remember Me By* awaited me. A book by Bellow is always a special treat, a journey into a sophisticated mind.

Jack, his hair wet, a towel around his waist, materialized in the doorway as I started reading. My eyes strayed to the towel. I blushed, turning away from his sly, smiling eyes.

"I want to talk to you." I tried not to look at the towel. "Tanya's going away with some friends next weekend and there's going to be someone named Vladimir there. I think she likes him." I sat up.

"That's hardly a bombshell," Jack's eyes tensed. "Do you disapprove of him?"

I was grateful for his serious tone.

"Not from what I've heard so far. He's from Moscow. He came for a visit a year ago and defected. Tanya doesn't want to bring him here because of the difference in lifestyles."

"I understand that, to a point. What about dinner for the four of us some time during the week?"

"Thanks, Jack."

"Don't thank me. I want to meet him as much as you do."

"Jack, he's twenty-eight."

"Well?"

"He's a man. Tanya is still a child."

"Honey, she's perfectly capable of taking care of herself. Where are they going to stay?"

"At a hotel. Jack, she really likes him, I could tell."

"Calm down, sweetheart. What did you tell her?"

"Nothing. What can I tell her? She's an adult."

"Right." Jack grinned at my female logic. "I don't have any problems trusting Tanya's judgment. Do you?"

"No," I whispered.

"Well, then, for now, let's take one day at a time."

"I guess there's no choice."

Jack smiled. "Anna, I know you want to read, but I just heard on CNN that there's been a coup in Moscow. Something about Gorbachev being sick and someone else taking over for him. It hasn't been confirmed yet."

"Are you serious?" I felt a stab of curiosity.

"It may turn out not to be true." Jack watched me closely. "Don't get upset."

"There goes *perestroika*. Tomorrow the Soviet newspapers will have an official statement that to meet the wishes of the working people the old order has been restored and *perestroika* was only a slight diversion from the shining path to communism."

"Do you think that's it?"

"What do you mean?" I glanced at the towel.

"No more freedom again?" Jack was clearly impressed by the news.

I searched and found nothing inside me except my original curiosity.

"Jack, there never was freedom, you should understand that by now. And I will never be surprised at anything negative that happens in the Soviet Union. I'm merely curious at how events are going to unfold." My eyes returned to the towel.

"What about the Jews who applied to emigrate? Will they be persecuted?"

"Yes, and frankly, I have no sympathy with most who are still there. They calculate what they have and what they may not get somewhere else, then remain where they are. There's nothing wrong in trying to live better economically—there is everything wrong considering it more important than being a slave. Adults pay for the decisions they make. Unfortunately, their children pay along with them."

"You Russians are so harsh sometimes. I feel sorry for them. And what's going to happen to Gorbachev?"

"What an American question. Who cares?" My hands wanted to tear the towel from his body.

"People who came recently, like Asya, will probably be more upset than you when they find out. There could be a war over there, for all you know," Jack closed and locked the door, and the towel moved closer.

"There won't be a war, Jack. No one believes in anything anymore. Let's go upstairs and watch CNN."

The news Jack brought should have suppressed everything else, but it didn't. If anything, I felt a selfish relief at being far away, in every sense, from that ugly country.

"Are you sure?" Jack's voice was husky.

"Sure of what?"

"That there won't be a war?" the towel was now directly in front of me.

"Pretty sure." I attempted to get up and felt Jack's hands on my shoulders.

"You seem to have this irresistible fascination for my towel."

I blushed, looked up into his smiling eyes, and burst out laughing.

"Jack, we can't act like teenagers all our lives."

"Luckily, darling, that's how we feel." Jack put a knee on the chaise. A slight tug and the towel was on the floor.

Tanya spent Monday evening notifying friends of Lilya's funeral on Tuesday.

I called Asya.

"It must have been a heart attack," she stated. "How's Sasha holding up?"

"Apparently, not bad."

"Are you going to stay with him tomorrow?"

"No, why?" I couldn't hide my surprise at the question.

"You were so anxious to find him when you thought he was in Kiev. We made all these trips—to the hospital where he used to work, to his old building, even to the cemetery."

"I know, Asya, he's an old friend. I haven't forgotten. But his daughter is home, and they probably would prefer to be left alone. I'm not family."

"Anichka, this is not like you. I mean, you've done so much for us and other Russians, but you yourself remain far away, like you belong to a different class."

"Asya, what do you think would change if you lived next to me and drove a Mercedes? And tell me something: you've been in the United States for over two years. Could you imagine living in the Soviet Union again?"

"That's impossible! We think differently now," Asya cried out as though I was trying to convince her to go back.

"Doesn't that answer your questions about me?"

Asya sighed. "Still," she said after a pause, "you're too American- ized. I think that's why human bonds are secondary to you. You're not like you were before."

"Secondary to what?" I was losing my patience. "What are my bonds with Tanya secondary to?"

"I'm not talking about Tanya."

"Americans know as much about bonds as we do," I said brusquely, in my mind defending Jack. "If you mean our bonds . . ."

Had she not brought that rag doll with a ceramic head to class for me when we were in third grade, I would have never owned a doll.

"Asya, I will never forget the doll you brought to class for me when we were in third grade. I will never forget your mother's sponge cakes." For a moment, tears clogged my throat. "How I wish you had emigrated when I did! We both know it's not the same now." I changed the subject to prevent her from responding. "Is your car still in the shop? Do you need a lift to the funeral tomorrow?"

"Myron fixed the car himself. We don't need a lift," she said with pride.

Tanya and Jack were already eating when I entered the dining room.

"You look distraught," remarked Jack.

"I was talking to Asya."

"I see." Jack shook his head. "Oh, I forgot, Lena called the office this morning while you were on a conference call. The JRL has organized an urgent fundraising breakfast for Russians this coming Sunday. I think we should go. Apparently the Jewish exodus from Russia needs help."

"We just mailed a check to the JRL, a very nice donation I might add." I visualized a Russian crowd and sighed, "I never feel like doing it, but you're right, I guess we should go."

"Tanya just told me she's going out of town," Jack said, without raising his head. "Your mother mentioned it to me yesterday, Tanya. I understand you're going to be driving with a new friend of yours."

"Yeah . . . why?"

"We would feel more comfortable if we met him before you go. What
do you think of the four of us having dinner?" Jack stated, rather
than asked.

"Jack, I'm not a child, I'll be twenty-two soon. Vladimir is a very nice
person, a gentleman."

"I don't doubt that," his eyes smiled, "but we've met all of your friends
and we should meet him, too."

"Com'on, he lives with his aunt and her family in a two-bedroom
apartment. He sleeps on a mattress in the dining room. If I bring him
here, he'll think I'm a showoff."

"You can't show off; this is not your house. This is your parents' house,"
Jack countered.

"I know, but I don't want to make him feel bad," Tanya pleaded. "You
know how men are."

"Yes, I have an inkling of how men are," replied Jack slowly, not
taking the bait.

I laughed. Tanya smiled.

"I suggest we go out for pizza on Wednesday. We can go to Edwardo's.
You like their pizza, and it's not a fancy place." There was something in
his quiet voice that made the invitation an order.

"I don't understand," Tanya pushed away her plate. "Why don't you
trust me all of sudden?"

"Your mother and I will be worried if we don't meet Vladimir. Listen,
we're not telling you what to do or not to do, all we ask for is to be
introduced to someone you plan to spend a weekend with. I'm surprised
you are so upset, Tanya." Jack took her wrist as she prepared to leave the
table. "We're old-fashioned parents. Do us this favor and be gracious
about it."

Tanya, deflated, lowered her eyes.

"Okay. Seven o'clock. Who's going to make the reservation?"

"Let it be my treat." Jack got up, putting his arm around Tanya. "You
know how men are."

This week has been a mini-series entitled "The Coup" with intermis-
sions for work, Lilya's funeral, and pizza with Tanya's new friend Vladimir.
Jack stayed riveted to the television in the lounge adjacent to his office
and inundated me with logical American questions about the coup and
its consequences.

Most of my predictions turned out to be wrong. The Soviet Union is
apparently very different from what I remembered, even from our short

visit four years ago. This realization added to my sense of complete disassociation. The sudden illness that allegedly struck Gorbachev was a familiar feature to every change of Soviet hierarchy. The inefficiency of the coup leaders was unusual, even for Russian party bosses. Their appearance, however, was not unusual: arrogant, crude, dull, alcoholic. The gallery of faces appropriately reminded Tanya of "most wanted" posters.

This cabinet had been hand-picked by the "great reformer" Gorbachev. I wondered, who, besides the West, ever credited him with breaking the machine that produced him. He must be dizzy from the chaos in his country. All he had wanted was to announce to his people that they were free. The rest was supposed to proceed in the old, orderly fashion. It wasn't his fault the tired, half-strangled country took his announcement literally, even if it didn't know exactly what freedom was. Perhaps freedom is an instinct, like a baby's to grab and to suck?

It was a different country and a different people that starred in the mini-series, "The Coup." Only the faces and language were familiar. The surly, impetuous, slippery Yeltsin on a tank—a folk hero of sorts (I'd watch my back with this quasi-democratic statesman), Moscovites fraternizing with the army, flowers on the tanks, open broadcasts from the center of events, criticism of the coup by Soviet journalists assigned to Western countries . . . Ironically, the mini-series did not come across as a drama, but more as a social comedy. The country and the people were not mine; they only stirred a superficial curiosity of someone who watches a story of a place once visited a long time ago or people once met many years before.

To my amazement, the recent immigrants were not curious at all. They were angry, claiming they had always predicted nothing good would come out of *perestroika*. One question worried those with families left behind: how will all this affect emigration? To old-timers, even with families left behind, this question became more academic. They accepted the logical American there's-nothing-we-can-do as a justification and explanation for their complete absorption in their new life routines, problems, and joys. If the mere notion of freedom changed the country we had escaped from into what we saw on television, no wonder that freedom changed us so deeply, so irreversibly.

The funeral home was cool and officially sad. Two boxes, one with black *yarmulkes* for men, the other with lacy, black headpieces with bobby pins for women, were placed by the door. Next to them stood Sasha and Vera. Sasha, still unshaven, according to Jewish tradition, in a dark suit, shook everyone's hand in his usual reserved manner. Vera, in a black dress, appeared uncomfortable. Two dozen or so people had gathered, mostly Vera's friends. I knew all of them, which meant Vladimir was not among them. The young people were trying hard to look gloomy, but at their age the idea of death was so abstract that they only managed to look tense and self-conscious. Asya, as someone who had known Sasha for many years, placed herself behind him and periodically sighed, touching his and Vera's shoulders or hands, until Tanya stepped between Asya and Vera. Myron smoked outside.

Jack and I arrived immediately after Gena Korsunsky and parked our Mercedes next to his. Gena's toothpick pointed spitefully at my car, the toothpick's owner acknowledging me with a sour nod and Jack with a hearty handshake. Two more Mercedes followed containing Dr. Korotki, who failed to recognize me, and a female doctor I remembered from the medical building.

Sasha's expression remained frozen when he saw me. Vera's eyes lit up briefly when I kissed her cheek.

I glanced at Jack. He looked genuinely sympathetic.

"Why is the coffin closed? What did she really die of?" Asya sat next to me after Sasha and Vera were seated in the first row and her duties as an old friend were temporarily interrupted.

"I don't know," I said truthfully.

"Terrible, terrible. She was only fifty-eight. Sasha's devastated. He said Nonna couldn't come. That's very strange."

A stocky, generously bearded rabbi took the podium. Lilya was described as a devoted mother, a good friend, and a faithful wife. It was all true. I looked at Sasha's and Vera's straight and immobile backs thinking that perhaps it's not too late for Vera to break into life. Tanya's serious profile made her look older.

Asya, with Myron and Vera's friends, went to the cemetery. The rest—every last one in a Mercedes—did not.

Vladimir was the last to arrive. His car had stalled on the way and getting it going again had taken some time. He looked old for his age and much older than Tanya. I thought he was quite handsome. His dark eyes behind round glasses were large and serious, like Lonya's had been. He was very tall and slim; sitting down he looked as if he had folded in half. His clothes, dark slacks and a blue shirt, looked as though they had come directly from a store shelf.

Out of the corner of her eye, Tanya sought our impression. Her introduction was short and somewhat curt. "My friend Vladimir, my parents."

The conversation was unexpectedly dominated by Jack, asking all the questions I would have hesitated to bring up. Vladimir expressed little emotion, answering respectfully in excellent British English. He covered Tanya's hand with his as she tried to object to Jack's direct inquiry of how much a teacher's assistant made at the University of Chicago.

Vladimir's gesture wasn't meant to be intimate, only that of an older adult. Tanya bit her lip and turned away. His hand remained firmly on hers until she calmed down and needed it to get a slice of pizza.

"It's only a part-time job. I'm promised about seven thousand dollars for the school year, plus access to labs and libraries, and no tuition. My expenses are minimal, and my aunt provides room and board for me. I will be able to save quite a bit by the time my parents get their permission."

Vladimir's parents were very much on his mind, especially his father, a violin player, age fifty-seven, who had little chance of finding a job in the United States. He hoped his mother, a kindergarten teacher, would baby-sit, adding extra cash to their welfare benefits.

"I've been preparing my parents for the fact that they will not be able to work here. I don't think they realize how final it is. They will be very unhappy without their work."

Jack didn't eat much. I wondered if he liked Vladimir. I was afraid to like him.

"What do you think of the coup in Moscow?" Jack's first nonpersonal question in over half-hour.

"Not much. As long as my parents get out, I don't care what happens there. The Soviet Union needs centuries to join civilization."

Tanya became fidgety. The Russian theme was unable to hold her attention.

Vladimir looked down at her then addressed me.

"Tanya doesn't understand how lucky she is that you brought her here when you did. My mother wanted to leave in 1978, but my father was afraid. Now he regrets it."

"On one hand, she's lucky she doesn't understand, on the other hand, I wish she did," I said in English knowing in Russian I could have said more.

Isn't Vladimir bored with Tanya? What do they have in common?

Tanya glanced at her watch.

"We're going to the movies with Julie and Slava. They'll be waiting for us, so we should go."

"Well, it was a pleasure meeting you, Vladimir," Jack sounded stern. "Tanya tells us you'll be driving together on Saturday."

Tanya and Vladimir got up.

"Yes, sir, in her car. Mine is not suited for a long trip. I bought it for four hundred fifty dollars." Vladimir smiled for the first time. It made him look shy. "I'm told everyone starts with an old car."

"I understand. Have a good time," Jack replied warmly.

"It was nice meeting you," I chimed in.

"Don't worry about Tanya." Vladimir looked at me briefly, then straight into Jack's eyes.

"I'm sure we won't have to." Jack and Vladimir shook hands and something, man-to-man, passed between them.

"Let's go." Tanya pulled Vladimir's arm.

We watched silently as they approached the door. Tanya turned, sent us a kiss and waved cheerfully. Vladimir opened the door and they left, his hand on her waist.

"Did you like him?" my voice quivered.

"Fortunately for Tanya, yes," Jack finished his beer.

"Umm."

"If I didn't, I would have opposed Tanya seeing him. Shit, when I think of the girls her age that I . . . Let's just say I look at things very differently now."

"What if they . . . ?" My stomach was in knots.

"Not yet, but eventually they will, and they should. Be reasonable, honey."

"How do you know not yet?"

"Well, men have their ways of communicating." Jack's hand touched my shoulder. "Let's go home. We're both nervous wrecks. The Jacuzzi will do us a ton of good."

Although we arrived at the fundraising breakfast early, half the JRL parking lot was already full. The people walking from the cars were undoubtedly Russian—Russians having immigrated when I did. The new ones, working or not, were of the mind to let the Americans pay.

A sense of belonging overpowered me. The fact that we were born and grew up in the same land was apparently enough. It had nothing to do with relationships, traits, or personalities.

Lena, flushed and excited, sat at a table just inside the entrance issuing pledge cards.

"Over one hundred fifty people already," she said excitedly, "and we only have two hundred chairs! Some Americans came too. They thought there wouldn't be enough Russians to fill the hall. Ilya's saving two seats for you."

More folding chairs arrived through a side door and were propped against the wall. A few guests volunteered to deliver them to the tables making eight people per table into ten. Deep into various discussions, no one seemed to mind.

Ilya, as the husband of a member of the organizing committee, had the privilege of sitting at one of the tables in front of the podium. I noticed that the seating at these tables remained eight. He and Lena had gotten married two years ago, and she had moved to his house in Buffalo Grove. She appeared content. Had we met now I would have assumed theirs was a first marriage. Ilya and Jack share season tickets to the Bulls games with four others. They have great seats and get to go to every third game.

The Korsunskys sat at the table next to ours. Marina, having lost weight, looked elegant and confident. Her slanting eyes flickered as her gaze met mine. I smiled politely, then chose a chair that let me sit with my back to them. Jack, awaiting opportunities to mingle, remained standing. Gena joined him, relating loudly, for my benefit I'm sure, the tale of an umpteen-square-foot addition to their house.

Ilya introduced me to a couple sitting at our table, Sima and Boris, both stout and smiling, like many in the audience. Sima had a giant white bow in her hair and wore a plaid dress.

"You don't recognize us, do you?" asked Sima. "We must have changed."

I looked closer. Their faces looked as familiar as any other Russian faces.

"About ten years ago we lived in the same building on Farwell. You had the basement apartment; we lived on the third floor."

The woman's light-gray eyes and round cheeks slowly came back to me.

"Of course, I remember you. You gave my daughter some of your daughter's clothes," I mumbled guiltily, trying to recall their last name.

"How are you doing? Where do you live now? How's Tanya? See, I remember your daughter's name."

"I'm doing fine. Tanya graduated from high school and from college early. She starts medical school this fall."

"My goodness, how time flies! Are you working? I remember you had just found your first programming job with some big company."

"Yes, I'm working. How are you doing?" I smiled broadly at the forgotten faces from my first hard years.

"We are heat and air-conditioning engineers. Boris was laid off last month, but I'm working. Our Emma is a beautician, her husband is an accountant. A nice boy from Gomel. They've been married for five years and have a four-year-old son. They live in Niles. Thank God, everything is all right. Can you imagine being in the Soviet Union now?" Sima shuddered.

Jack finally sat down and Sima introduced herself and her husband in Russian. Russian greetings and—thanks to Ilya—profanity have by now become familiar to Jack.

"Jack Graff," he said, shaking hands. "How are you?"

"Your friend is an American?" Sima's eyes sparkled with interest.

"He's my husband," I admitted.

Sima automatically glanced at our left hands.

"I'm sorry, I didn't notice. Why didn't you say something right away? Is he a real American or a Russian that came here a long time ago?"

"A real American."

"You mean you have to speak English all the time?" Sima wrinkled her forehead with sympathy. "How long have you been married? What does he do for a living?"

"Four years. He's also in computers. We work together."

"Talking about me?" Jack chuckled good-naturedly. "I know when you say '*Americanyetz*' it's about me, right?"

"I apologize," said Sima, returning to English. "We knew your wife many years ago. We used to watch her in awe: a full-time job, cleaning jobs on weekends. She wanted to keep her clients in case her job didn't last. Sometimes, she even took Tanya with her to help." Suddenly, Sima stopped and pressed her hands to her cheeks. She appeared flustered. "I'm sorry, Anichka," she said in Russian. "Your husband probably doesn't know that . . ." Sima looked at her husband imploring him to come to her rescue but Boris only shook his head with disapproval.

"My husband knows everything about me," I assured her. "In the beginning, almost everyone had a little side income. I remember that you baby-sat for a family in our building before you found a job."

"I did," Sima nodded enthusiastically, relieved that she hadn't caused my marriage any harm, "but it's different . . ." She glanced at Jack who smiled in response. He rarely expressed curiosity when conversations took a Russian turn.

"Why?"

Sima shrugged. "Oh, I don't know. Maybe, it's not." She switched to English as she addressed Jack, "You know, Russian women are very hardworking, like horses, but I never met anyone who worked harder than Anya."

"She still does," said Jack with feeling, "and don't ask me why."

"They say American men love Russian women." Sima's interest became piqued.

"This American man loves this Russian woman." Jack's fingers drummed down my back.

"No wonder your wife hasn't changed in ten years. They say love keeps a woman young."

"Sima, enough." Boris attempted meekly to change the topic.

"I don't think I look young, but I'm in love all right." I restrained my smile as much as I could.

Jack's fingers moved dangerously forward under my arm.

It is so easy to say I'm in love. I wish I could repeat it to every person I meet, to every tree on the street, to every car passing by. Jack hears it from me all too often. So far, he's not bored.

"How is he with Tanya?" Sima switched back to Russian.

"All I could wish for." My eyes prickled with tears and I turned around to look at the audience.

Quite a number of nameless but familiar faces smiled and greeted me by name. I smiled back, genuinely pleased to be recognized. It felt good to see Asya's son, Dima, in the crowd. Lena, who apparently had finished her duties as a pledge-card-issuer, motioned to us from a distance, pointing to the line of people in the back of the hall.

"Let's go and get some food," Sima suggested in English.

Taciturn and shy, Ilya and Boris remained at the table. I would have preferred to do the same, but I was hungry.

A line of smiling, relaxed people moved slowly past the breakfast buffet—not at all like a line for food at a Soviet store.

Lena took two plates. "They have blintzes from Golda's Bakery!" she reported to us, then her happy expression abruptly altered into horror.

I followed her stare only to meet Vilen's cold eyes. He and Irena walked toward us as they headed to the end of the line. The sight of Vilen made me cringe. For a split second, everyone else faded into the background. I had to swallow hard to repress my nausea.

"Look, the rich people came!" exclaimed Irena.

Vilen forced a smile. With great satisfaction, I noted that the coloring of two of his front teeth differed from the others. Did Jack notice that? Did Gena do the dental work for Vilen? I was surprised how quickly these thoughts revived me.

Lena gave Jack a frightened look. I glanced at him sideways, cognizant of his narrowed eyes, compressed lips, and the bulge on his cheek when he clenched his jaw.

"You're holding up the line, girls," Sima said behind us as she craned her neck to see the food. "The lox sure looks fresh."

"I guess we don't even deserve a greeting anymore!" Irena said loudly as she and Vilen passed us.

"Good morning," mumbled Lena.

"Good morning, Irena." I had difficulty believing that the dispassioned words came from me.

She didn't reply, but I saw her shrug.

"Are you okay?" Jack finally looked at me. His frozen face told me how much effort it took to control himself.

"Yes, of course," I said lightly. The active movements of Sima's white bow as she watched our little scene unfold proved she was beginning to pay close attention. "Why don't you take some French toast? It's your favorite for breakfast."

Jack went ahead of Lena and placed a piece of French toast and some sliced strawberries on his plate, then poured some coffee into a tall, white mug from the dispenser with a tag saying "regular." As he strolled back to the table I turned to Lena. Her round eyes stood out under her dark bangs. The plates in her hands shook slightly, and I realized that my hands shook too.

"I think you're right. The lox looks scrumptious," I smiled at Sima.

The white bow fluttered as she nodded in agreement.

Bella and Felix joined us in line for a minute, asking us to say hi to Jack and Ilya, and reminding Lena and me of Susan's *bat mitzvah* in two weeks. Vilen would, of course, attend, and it should give me pleasure to see those two discolored teeth again. It was the same day as Asya's surprise birthday party and it promised to be a busy day. Poor Jack, an entire day with Russians.

An active, obviously American woman in loose clothes stood next to Jack gesticulating as she talked when I returned to the table.

"You must, it will help us so much. Mr. Graff, we are so honored to have you here." She sounded extremely agitated.

"Well," muttered Jack, "I'm just one of many. The audience seems to be rather responsive without being spoken to. I'm not good at making speeches. Here's my wife, Anna." He pointed to me, relieved.

The woman turned to me sharply.

"Mrs. Graff, I'm Karen Feldman, Chair of the Jewish Resettlement League's Russian Committee. It's very nice to meet you. We had a speaker, the executive director of the JRL, but his son broke his leg about two hours ago. When I saw your name on the list—and thank you very much for your generous support—I realized how uplifting it would be to have your husband give a short talk on the importance of becoming part of the Jewish community. We want him to speak just before we start the fundraising, but he's refusing."

"It's up to him." I placed my plate on the table, aware Jack expected me to save him and was disappointed with my answer.

"Mrs. Graff!" Karen exclaimed bringing her palms together. "You're Russian yourself! Your own example could be a tremendous selling point. Would you?"

I chuckled. "To save my husband, I will say a few words, but only in Russian and only a few words."

I met Jack's astonished but grateful look, raised my head high, and followed Karen to the microphone.

"I'll come with you to translate for the Americans," I heard Lena's nervous voice at my side.

Karen thanked the still chattering audience, explained why the JRL needed more funds, talked of worsening conditions in the Soviet Union and concluded with: "We are not going to have long speeches today, but we have asked Mrs. Anna Graff, Vice President of Graff and Fishman Management Services, and a great friend of the JRL, to say a few words."

I stepped up to the microphone, holding it tight, waiting for quiet. Faces turned in my direction, followed by whispers, then silence. Jack eyed me intently.

"I'm not going to bore you with my life story. You know it, like I know yours. No matter how different they are, they are the same. No matter where or what we came from, we all have become—or are about to become—the stupid, naïve Americans we felt so superior to, whom we envied so much, and whom we thought we'd never catch up to or understand. But we have. Those who came recently, and call us worse than Americans, have helped us realize the ultimate truth."

Faces smiled. Jack leaned over to Ilya for translation. Sima turned to the people sitting at the next table whispering to them.

"I often try to identify the moment when I felt 'American.' I don't mean the time when I applied for citizenship, and I don't mean the ceremony when I received my certificate—as inspirational and moving as that was. There was no one moment; it was an arduous road."

Sima patted her eyes with a napkin. I cleared my throat.

"Somewhere along the way this country became part of me, part of my blood, part of my thoughts and concerns, part of my family. When I place my hand on my heart while listening to the American anthem or the Pledge of Allegiance, tears come to my eyes. It won't ever become routine, like my daughter and my husband won't be taken for granted."

Jack took off his glasses and started wiping them with his handkerchief as Ilya spoke into his ear.

"I'm not capable of delivering a fiery diatribe, but I will say that it is a privilege and a joy to be part of this country that is my home and my family."

I paused to catch my breath. Lena, her hands pressed to her chest, stared at me round-eyed.

I didn't mean this to be so long, I thought, taking another breath and continuing.

"As if it isn't enough to be Jewish, we are also Russian. No matter how much we avoid each other, no matter how distrustful we are of each other, we are one people."

Faces nodded in thoughtful agreement.

"We are one people, whether we came fifteen years ago, or two years ago, or just applied to leave the Soviet Union. Even though I don't know most of you personally, and don't like some I do know, you are my people. Many gave so we could come. If you are not certain how much to give, one percent of what you would give not to find yourself in the Soviet Union now seems a fair measure. If we don't help our own, who will?"

I returned the microphone to Karen and fled the stage. Applause ensued. Jack rose to receive me with a bear hug and a quick kiss. Still shaking, but reinforced by his warmth, my stomach tense, I finally sat down wishing I could hide. Suddenly, I was very hungry. Over the noise, Karen thanked me, then called upon Lena to translate my words to the non-Russian guests and start announcing the pledges.

Lena and Karen took turns calling out names, repeating amounts, expressing appreciation.

"Why didn't you tell us you're a vice president?" Sima demanded, all flushed. Jack would say that she was tickled pink. "And you said it so well! Sometimes I hate Russians, but what can I do? I'm one, too," Sima continued addressing everyone who wanted to listen.

"Dr. Korsunsky: one thousand dollars! Thank you very much," squeaked Lena. "Dr. Korsunsky is very generous."

Well, the generous Dr. Korsunsky, who has milked insurance companies for years, belongs to my people too. It takes every kind.

Sima jumped up as she heard her name.

"My husband just lost his job, so I cannot afford to give more than two hundred dollars."

Jack filled out our pledge card and showed it to me for approval. He doesn't know how to give little, but this amount did not even come close to the one percent of what I should give for not finding Tanya and myself in the Soviet Union.

Jack got up but I took the card from him and walked quickly onto the stage. I stood in a queue of four more people with pledge cards. A tall, sun-tanned woman in her fifties, in a long, mustard-colored dress turned to me, her brown eyes intense. She pointed to her card.

"I can't really afford to donate anything, but you said it so well about the one percent that I would feel guilty not giving my share."

We both had tears in our eyes.

Her turn came to hand her card to Lena.

"It's not much," she said.

"It doesn't matter," Lena interrupted with a smile. "Thank you."

Lena took my card and hugged me. I requested that she not announce our names.

"I'll announce you as anonymous donors." For some reason, the idea excited her, her eyes lit up mischievously.

The woman in the mustard-colored dress waited for me by the stage steps.

"My father immigrated last week." She brought her face close to make sure that I heard her. "Twelve years ago, I had to fight with him to get his written permission. Eventually, I won. Meanwhile, my mother died. But, at least, he's here now."

"Fifteen years ago, I had to fight with my ex-husband to get his written permission for my daughter. Eventually, I won." I had to control myself not to blurt out my life's story.

We smiled and parted, probably never to see each other again. But if we should, it would not be as strangers.

I sat through the next hour, entranced, listening to Lena and Karen. By the time the event came to an end, their voices had become hoarse. On average, the pledges went from a hundred to a thousand dollars with a few less and a few of many thousand dollars, from the Americans. Many people went to the payphones in the lobby and returned with pledges from their relatives and friends.

Finally, Karen and Lena announced the totals. Almost two hundred fifty thousand dollars! My Russians came through! Considering the transformation they had to accomplish, perhaps it didn't really take them all that long.

"Very good," Jack said with satisfaction. "I'm glad we came. Are you?"

"Yes, I am. I need my Russians so badly—occasionally."

We got up and I found myself surrounded by people. As a group we inched toward the exit. Jack walked ahead talking to Gena; Marina followed me flanked by two blonde women, all of them looking good in mini-skirts. The Kaganovs strolled in front of us, Irena holding Vilen's arm tightly.

Asya's son, Dima, appeared at my side from nowhere. He shook my hand, addressing me like he did outside of work.

"Auntie Anya, thank you for all you've done. My mother keeps saying that we couldn't have survived without you, and that we're in your debt forever."

"She does?" I tried to sound jovial, but after being called Auntie Anya I was ready to melt. "I hope she means it figuratively."

How will I ever repay her for the doll she brought to class for me when we were in third grade?

"I'll see you at work," Dima smiled with his mother's eyes, laughed his mother's short cackle, and rushed ahead.

My God, how happy, how lucky I am!

I saw Jack standing by our car shaking Gena's hand.

Marina caught up with me in the parking lot. The two blondes walked away, their mini-skirts swaying rhythmically.

"Well, Anya, Miss Bigshot, Miss Mercedes Benz!"

"Marina, please, don't start," I said quietly.

"Oh, Miss Nose-Up-In-The-Air, I guess it's too much to be bothered by us little people anymore. Now that you've tricked Jack into marrying poor, helpless you, and into giving you all the money you want, and a Mercedes to replace the Chevy you deserve, we're not good enough for you." Marina took a deep breath. "You don't invite us over, you don't even call us. And after all we did for you!"

"Marina . . ."

"You think you can assuage your conscience by volunteering and donating big bucks . . . well, you can't!"

"Marina, you're creating a scene."

I saw Jack look at us over the top of the car as Gena marched toward us.

"You used us, then threw us aside. We worked so hard to become free while you worked on Jack. Now you spit in our faces!"

"Free? Free? Marina, you don't know the meaning of the word! If I were to give you my Mercedes you would feel more free because you would have two and I would have none."

Gena stood next to Marina, his hand on her shoulder, a toothpick aiming at me.

I walked past them but then returned.

"You will never be free. Simply emigrating does not make one free. Getting a naturalization certificate doesn't make one an American. Freedom can only come from within. It's like crossing a bridge. When you get to the other side you can't see the place where you started from. You remember it, but it's not a real place anymore. There are no lines to stand in, no food to grab for, no reason to gloat over having three times as much as someone who has nothing. Freedom does not have a price tag.

"I've come across that bridge. You are still on the other side."

I turned on my heel, waved to Jack, ran the rest of the way to my Mercedes, unlocked the door, and got in.

glossary

To simplify reading, the following is a short list (alphabetically) of names and foreign phrases used in this book.

Anichka	Russian—Gentle, diminutive for Anna
Anya	Russian—Short, informal for Anna
Asinka	Russian—Gentle, diminutive for Asya
Baboso	Spanish—Skirt-chaser
Bar mitzvah	In Jewish tradition, a ceremony that recognizes a Thirteen-year-old boy as an adult
Bat mitzvah	In Jewish tradition, a ceremony that recognizes a Twelve-year-old girl as an adult
Borisovich	Russian—Male version of patronymic from Boris (patronymic is a part of full, official name; derivative of one's father's name)
Borisovna	Russian—Female version of patronymic from Boris (patronymic is a part of full, official name, a derivative of one's father's name)
Boruch Hashem	Hebrew—Thank God!
Da	Russian—Yes
Dima	Russian—Short, informal for Dmitry
Dziekuje bardzo	Polish—Thank you very much
Fima	Russian—Short, informal for Yefim
Gena	Russian—Short, informal for Gennady
Goy	Yiddish—Gentile (usually with a negative connotation)
Irochka	Russian—Gentle diminutive for Irena
Isaakovich	Russian—Male version of patronymic from Isaak (patronymic is a part of full, official name, derivative of one's father's name)
Jackele	Yiddish—Gentle, diminutive for Jack
Khupe	Hebrew—Wedding canopy
Kineahora	Yiddish—Phrase to protect a loved one, to ward off an evil eye
Lana	Russian—Short, informal for Svetlana
Lena	Russian—Short, informal for Yelena
Lenochka	Russian—Gentle, diminutive for Yelena
Lonichka	Russian—Gentle, diminutive for Leonid
Lonya	Russian—Short, informal for Leonid

Lvovna	Russian—Female version of patronymic from Lev (patronymic is a part of full, official name, derivative of one's father's name)
Lyuba	Russian—Short, informal for Lvovna
Lyubochka	Russian—Gentle, diminutive for Lubov
Lyuda	Russian—Short, informal for Lyudmila
Machetunim	Yiddish—The in-laws of one's child
Mame-loshn	Yiddish—Mother tongue
Mensch	Yiddish—A "real" human being
Mikhailovich	Russian—Male version of patronymic from Mikhail (patronymic is a part of full, official name; derivative of one's father's name)
Mitzvah	Hebrew—Good deed
Naumovna	Russian—Female version of patronymic from Naum (patronymic is a part of full, official name, a derivative of one's father's name)
Nata	Russian—Short, informal for Natalia
Oy yey iz mir!	Yiddish—Oh, woe is me!
Natasha	Russian—Short, informal for Natalia
Pani	Polish—Equivalent of Ms. or Mrs.
Pavlovna	Russian—Female version of patronymic from Pavel (patronymic is a part of full, official name; derivative of one's father's name)
Petrovich	Russian—Male version of patronymic from Pyotr (patronymic is a part of full, official name; derivative of one's father's name)
Petya	Russian—Short, informal for Pyotr
Peyes	Yiddish—Earlocks worn by some Orthodox Jews
Roma	Russian—Short, informal for Roman
Sasha	Russian—Short, informal for Alexander
Sashenka	Russian—Gentle, diminutive for Alexander
Senya	Russian—Short, informal for Semyon
Sha, sha	Yiddish—Be quiet
Shidekh	Hebrew—Marriage match
Shiksa	Yiddish—Female, generally young, Gentile (usually with a negative connotation)
Shtetl	Yiddish—A small Eastern European Jewish community of former times
Shura	Russian—Short, informal for Alexander
Slushayu	Russian—I'm listening (used instead of "Hello" for answering the telephone)
Sveta	Russian—Short, informal for Svetlana
Svetochka	Russian—Gentle, diminutive for Svetlana
Tanichka	Russian—Gentle, diminutive for Tatyana

Tanya	Russian—Short, informal for Tatyana
Tokhes	Yiddish—Buttocks
Valya	Russian—Short, informal for Valentina
Verochka	Russian—Gentle, diminutive for Vera
Wszystkiego najlepszego z okazji urodzin	Polish—Best wishes for your birthday
Yarmulke	Yiddish—The traditional male head covering
Yishcho	Russian—More
Yurochka	Russian—Gentle, diminutive for Yuri
Zinochka	Russian—Gentle, diminutive for Zina

A Note About Russian Names

Russian names are famous for the multitude of their suffixes and variations. These forms help express an entire range of emotions from crude to subtle. In addition, they may reveal the nature or nuances of relationships. Russian names are a means of communication, enriching the language as much as any other language tool.

Throughout this book, you will find some characters being addressed or referred to by what appear to be different names. These variations reflect the normal speech patterns of native Russian speakers and serve to retain the unique flavor of the story.